BL...
O...
INFINITY WAR

BY

STEPHANIE HUDSON

Blood of the Infinity War
The Afterlife Saga #10
Copyright © 2020 Stephanie Hudson
Published by Hudson Indie Ink
www.hudsonindieink.com

This book is licensed for your personal enjoyment only.
This book may not be re-sold or given away to other people. If you would like to share this book with another person, please purchase an additional copy for each recipient. If you're reading this book and did not purchase it, or it wasn't purchased for your use only, then please return to your favourite book retailer and purchase your own copy. Thank you for respecting the hard work of this author.
All rights reserved.
This is a work of fiction. Names, characters, places, brands, media, and incidents are either the product of the authors imagination or are used fictitiously. The author acknowledges the trademark status and trademark owners of various products referred to in this work of fiction, which have been used without permission. The publication/use of these trademarks is not authorised, associated with, or sponsored by the trademark owners.
Blood of the Infinity War/Stephanie Hudson – 2nd ed.
ISBN-13 - 978-1-913769-27-7

This last book is dedicated to the ones who deserve it the most…

You, my Fans.

Without you guys supporting me through this incredible journey then I would still just be a waitress with a dream. And although I believe that it is a powerful thing, dreaming big and aiming high…you guys are what made it all possible. It had been a long road ahead when I started this saga and I feel that many of you have walked it with me. Strange that given the significance of the number seven in this saga, that it was in fact, seven years in the making.

It's been an emotional rollercoaster and it seems as though my own life was at a standstill before I took the brave leap and got on it. But it has been the ride of my life and I thank the Gods (Of Afterlife) that I took a chance at something great. Now, I thank you guys for keeping me on that ride and standing by me, giving me the motivation to carry on, through showing me your love for a world I created.

This poem is dedicated to you all as this is the last book and it comes from the very heart of me.

Sharing My World

I fall into a world of the likes of no other,
I hold it to my chest and cherish it, like a mother,
It starts off as my little secret sin,
And wraps its way around my heart, blossoming within.

The story unfolds like opening a door,
And I venture in the dark, searching for more,
I reach out and grab the words, holding them to my chest,
I write them down before I forget, the start, the middle and the rest.

One day I might let the world in, and let them see,
The treasures I hold in my heart and trust them to be free,
To set sail into the world and hope they are met by love,
To find a passionate response from those reading above.

Because this journey needs to be told and shared with love and laughter,
Tears of joy and frowns of hate, but feelings, here, there and after,
Because a story isn't told unless it read by one and held in a heart forever,
And keeping it to myself would be to condemn to a land of happy ever after... never.

So, I thank you all for sharing with me in this time together,
We walked as one through the storm and into calmer weather,
The rocky road, the smooth paths ahead and all in between we gain,
A friendship that will last the ages, of Author, to fan, to friend.

All my Love

Always
Stephanie x

WARNING

This book contains explicit sexual content, some graphic language and a highly addictive Alpha Male.

This book has been written by a UK Author with a mad sense of humour. Which means the following story contains a mixture of Northern English slang, dialect, regional colloquialisms and other quirky spellings that have been intentionally included to make the story and dialogue more realistic for modern-day characters.

Please note that for your convenience language translations have been added to optimise the readers enjoyment throughout the story.

Also meaning…

No Googling is required ;)

Also, please remember that this part of a 12 book saga, which means you are in for a long and rocky ride. So, put the kettle on, brew a cup, grab a stash of snacks and enjoy!

Thanks for reading x

CHAPTER ONE

INTIMIDATING INTERROGATION

I opened my eyes to see I was being blinded by the sun and I blinked back the dark spots in my eyes a few times before things started to become clear.

"Wakey, wakey, sunshine."

"Pip…is that you?" I asked in a groggy voice that grated on the back of my throat as if I was trying to swallow sandpaper.

"The one and only," she said in her usual happy tone.

"Where am I?" I asked trying to sit up but finding it too difficult to accomplish.

"Well, you're not in Kansas anymore," she said and my eyes widened.

"We're home!? We finally made it back…back in time!?" I shouted no matter how painful it felt to the back of my throat.

"Uh, well about that…" she started to say as I lifted myself up to look for myself where we were. The first thing I saw was the desert sand outside of the stone arched window and my heart started to sink.

We were still in Persia.

But this wasn't the worst part I now faced. Not when I saw the tall looming figure of Draven standing at the bottom of the bed with his arms folded.

Pip looked back over her shoulder and said,

"We have some explaining to do," then gave me an 'oh shit' face that I was no doubt mirroring.

"Leave us, Imp!" The sound of Draven's stern order sounded like it verged on deadly. I swallowed hard, for once welcoming the burn it caused. For there he stood in all his battle won glory as he may have been about to lose against the God, but against the Romans, it was easily classed as a victory. Which had me wondering, what must he have thought when seeing me that way? I can very easily say it was probably the first time he had seen a human woman go up against such odds…but then again, after that, could I ever really class myself as just human?

"Righty O…laters chickyd…"

"NOW!" Draven snapped interrupting her and making me frown up at him. Pip flinched and gave me a small smile before saying,

"Outta here!" Then she ran from the room as he snarled at her when she passed. This managed to do only one thing and that was morph my fear into anger.

"Don't speak to her like that!" I snapped and he gave me a look that said this was the very last thing he expected me to say…something he clearly wasn't happy about.

"I can speak to the Lesser Demon however I please…I am her King," he stated arrogantly and I laughed once without humour.

"Yes, well I wouldn't let her husband hear you say that, if you value your life that is!" I told him whipping back the covers and shifting off the bed, soon realising that thankfully I was dressed. I took a second to see that I was wearing a long red and gold kaftan dress that was pulled in at the waist thanks to the long crimson sash I had tied to one side.

"And here I was, thinking you finally knew the depths of the position I hold and with it the immeasurable power, for a threat like that has little effect on a King of my kind," he told me firmly and I rolled my eyes thinking for once he had no clue. Well, this was certainly a turnaround of events I thought wryly. Back in my world I was usually the one without a clue in a world that held only endless questions for me to ask but now, it seemed I was nearly 2000 years ahead of him.

"And where do you think you are going?!" he said blocking my path. I had to say that if I thought he was intimidating before, then crossing his arms across his still bloody breastplate and now in all his battle worn gear, it definitely had me taking a cautious step back.

"To…to make sure you haven't hurt her feelings," I told him with less of the attitude this time, but it just made him laugh cruelly and for once it wasn't a nice sound.

"A Lesser Demon is…" On hearing this for the second time, I verbally lashed out at him.

"Don't you dare finish that sentence or so help me, I will slap you!" I shouted at him and before I could think about his stunned features, I continued with my rant, telling him what for.

"And just so you know, that Lesser Demon, that you seem to think so little of, well that Imp, is one of the greatest beings to ever have graced the Earth with her soul! She has saved my life more times than I can count and is someone that I care about enough that I would *die for her!*" I told him, ending with the last three words a vow spoken in a voice that I barely even recognised.

"Easy Little Lamb, remember that you still speak this way to a King," he warned me, his voice turning cold and this was when all logic flew through the stone archway, along with the last of my cool.

"No, actually I don't…" I told him walking past him but he grabbed my arm and swung me around to face him, which is when I threw the truth at him in the worst way possible,

"…I speak this way to my husband!" Then I used his utter shock to yank myself from his hold and storm my way through his bedchamber until getting as far as the sunken living space. Then I felt bands of steel encase me from behind as he held me locked to his hard frame, one that I could feel was still shaking from what I gathered was his rage.

"I fear you are not sound of mind if you think I have taken you as my wife without my knowledge!" he told me with an underlining growl I could feel rising from his chest. This was when it hit me, he didn't yet know or realise I was from the future. So yeah, I guess in that case I did sound like a crazy person. But hey, silver lining was that at least he would haven't me put to death now he knew I was his Electus. No matter how much I said sod it to royal etiquette. I mean, Hell, it wasn't like I was any good at it any way.

"I…well I…um…" Okay, so this one had me stumped! Do I tell him everything or keep this teensy tiny…okay so, who was I kidding, more like massive, huge and crazy unbelievable fact from him?

He spun me once more and raised an eyebrow at me in question, as if waiting to hear what I would say next. His hold on the top of my arms told me he wasn't letting me go anytime soon and this, combined with his sexy, 'I am on the demonic edge' look, and I knew I was on thin ice. Okay, so this was definitely an 'oh shit' moment as I had let my mouth run away with me without engaging that oh so important 'thinking' filter.

So, in the end I blurted out the only thing right now that I thought could save me. Even said in whisper it sounded more like a confession than the declaration of love it was meant to be.

"I'm your Electus." On hearing this, something shifted deep with him and his eyes finally seeped to the purple fire I was so used to seeing and it brought me so much joy to watch, I nearly wept. It was like breaking the damn as he was showing me his true self and it felt like acceptance of the best kind.

"Yes…*yes you are."* He said this on a growl, this time one of pleasure before he pulled me to him and I literally fell into his dominating kiss. It felt as though he was trying to brand the knowledge across my tender skin for all to see. It felt as if he was tasting me for the first time, as if this new knowledge now let loose something like…well like the *demon in him*.

He could finally be himself and with it came a kind of domination that even for me, I wasn't used to. The Draven from my time was of course dominating yes, but he at least had years of restraint built up through both culture and modern-day principles, but this one? Well, this Draven was more like a Barbarian King who took whatever he wanted, whenever he wanted and with little of the consequences to care for. I knew this when he spoke,

"By the Gods girl, you are mine! Do you understand? Tell me you understand what this means?!" he demanded, finally letting me take a breath. The intensity of his stare told me he was battling emotions that he had never experienced before. I bit my lip and nodded slowly. His eyes homed into the sight and this time the rumbling in his chest made me jump.

"I told you once before Little Lamb, that lip no longer belongs to you, for it is now mine to torture," he told me and then was once again kissing me, taking possession of my bottom lip in between his teeth. I moaned as I felt myself sinking into the keeper of my heart and soul. It was as though we had been reconnected after battling the storm to get to one another.

However, this time it was I that broke away first, making him growl down at me.

"Your sister! Sop…I mean Saphira, how is she?" I asked letting all that had happened flood back to me. The look he gave me was hard to read but I guess the questioning hint I saw in his eyes was understandable, considering she had spent most of my time with him openly hating my guts and trying to kill me.

"I confess I don't know what I find more in question, the fact that you ask this of me or that my own sister asked after your wellbeing also, when waking." Ah…yeah, so that would seem odd upon reflection but then I realised what just happened to us all, so replied,

"I guess being kidnapped together is enough to form any type of friendship between the most unlikely of people," I told him, but when he scoffed I didn't take it as a great sign that he had believed me.

"Why? Did she say something different?" I enquired, trying to sound blasé about the whole thing. Of course, my appalling acting skills weren't fooling anyone and his look said it all when he folded his arms across his plated chest once more.

"Ah, Little Lamb of mine, I think what interests me more is what *you think she told me?*" he said nodding to me and once more I bit my lip, easily giving away my poker tell.

"That same thing I said?" I asked timidly trying once again not to slip up. But then he simply shook his head and said a firm,

"No." Then it was at this point that Draven started to use his greatest weapon from his jam-packed arsenal…*sexual intimidation.* He started to walk me backwards and just as I looked back and down at the floor, so as not to trip, it was too late. I was about to fall backwards into his sunken seating area when he grabbed me. So instead of hurting myself he landed with me, lowering me down to the seat, with his hand hitting out against the raised stone back next to my face to hold himself above me.

"Now, do you want to try again with the truth this time, or continue to spin me your little web of lies?" he said in a tone that told me he had hit his limit.

"I…I…can explain," I told him and I could almost feel my conscious mind nudge part of my subconscious with a shit load of sass and say 'Oh yeah, this should be good'. Because in truth what exactly I thought I was going to try and explain I had no clue.

"I sure hope so my Nāzanin, because you will not be leaving this room until you do!" he promised me and it was nothing short of a threat. He was at the edge and his intense purple gaze told me that much, if not the way the stone cracked under the strain of his punishing hold.

"You won't like it," I warned him and at this he frowned.

"I have no doubt of that, but trust my words Electus, for I like *not knowing* far less." Well okay, so I could understand that considering how much important stuff he had kept from me in the past. But this was the problem when arguing against a man who had not yet committed his own lies against me. I had nothing to throw back his way that would stick, because the devastating truth was that this time it was me…all me. I was the one keeping important choices of our life from him and it made me hate myself for it. Had this been what Draven had gone through when he made the heart-breaking decision to cut himself out of my life? To hide the truth behind the prophecy and to keep the Oracle's fated words from me. Simply put we were both as bad as each other but in this time then…

I was the only liar in the room.

I also couldn't help but wonder about my own time. Would he listen to my reasons, being the same as his own and therefore understand why, if I ever made it home, of course? Would he find it in him to forgive me, the way I eventually forgave him?

Oh god, and what if he found out all this on our wedding day? I don't think I could bare to witness the pain in his eyes, one I would have put there myself. Well, all I could hope for now was that it wasn't all in vain, which it was quickly heading down that route if the pissed off Demon above me was anything to go by. After all, it wasn't exactly the position I was hoping for, even if he was half on top of me!

"I don't know where to start," I told him honestly and finally this was when he took pity on me and granted me some much-needed space. He sighed and sat next to me, so the space he gave me ended up being as minimal as possible. Then he took my hand in his and positioned it in his lap, so that his fingers could rest over the inside of my wrist. I raised an eyebrow at him in question.

"I may not be able to read you, but your fluttering pulse will tell me when you lie," he told me completely unashamed as if this was his right and well, I guess right now it kind of was.

"Now you will answer my questions and be warned Little Lamb, you will continue to answer them until I am satisfied," he told me sternly, momentarily tightening his hold on my wrist in warning. After this I really wanted to point over his shoulder and shout 'Fire!' and then leg it, but I doubted first, he wouldn't fall for it and second, he would catch me in a heartbeat, so what was the point.

"When you first set foot in my palace, you knew what I was…yes or no?" Okay, so I wanted to point out that technically I was carried by Ranka, so did this count as lying if I said no? Oh, who was I kidding!

"Yes," I told him and at least he looked pleased that I had answered his first question truthfully.

"And did you also know what you were to me when you did step into my domain?" he asked next and I feigned being a dumb blonde, stalling for time.

"What I meant to you?" I asked shaking my head a little and pressing my luck, something he knew I was doing as he tightened his hold on my wrist again.

"Play fair Electus, for I know of your intelligence and that you are far from being a half-witted fool." I released a sigh in return, letting him know that okay, so it was a long shot. But then I decided to mentally slap myself and put some of that intelligence to good use...*finally.* So, I reached out my mind to the only one who would know what to do.

"Sophia help me! Your brother has his interrogating boots on and he's stomping all over my willpower! What the Hell do I say?!" I spoke to her in my mind, hoping...no, scratch that, actually praying for some Demon backup here. Of course, Draven noticed something was going on as he first looked down at my wrist as if he could feel my pulse going wild and then back up at me.

"What are you up to, Nāzanin?" he questioned and I laughed once nervously and said,

"Nothing, just...um...I'm sorry could you...you repeat the question?" I said stumbling on my words thanks to the dark look he was giving me.

"Come on guys! Anyone listening out there!? He is getting impatient and also royally cranky." I said trying again, but once again Draven looked down at my traitorous pulse as if it was acting like damn Morse code or something! Then he raised his gaze to mine and his eyes said it all, I had lost his trust.

"Now who might you be talking to, I wonder?" he asked

tilting his head ever so slightly and his tone was suddenly laced with a lethal edge that matched the demonic flash in his eyes.

"Talk...talking to?" I asked nervously and then suddenly he was on me. His hand circled the column of my throat and he tapped his fingers against my pulse point that was beating wildly.

"You won't hurt me." I challenged, surprised when my voice didn't waver, no matter how quietly I said it. He seemed amused by my statement and somewhat happy, so I had to say his reaction confused me. He smoothed his thumb up and down by my ear, watching his own actions before he raised his eyes back to mine where he smirked before he spoke,

"No, *never*. But don't forget, my sweet one... *I still have your chains,*" he warned seductively with that velvet voice of his, sending a shiver through my body at the obvious threat. Because if there was one thing I could be sure of about Draven, it didn't matter what time he lived in, if I was in it, then he knew my weakness. After all, there was only one...*and it was him.*

"Now, answer my question," he snapped, in a clipped hard tone that told me this was my last chance.

"I...well okay, so the thing is...um..." I was just about to cave when he growled my name in warning, only it wasn't the right one.

"Now, Nāzanin." It was at this very moment that my mouth opened ready to give him what he asked when in the end I didn't have to. The door opened behind us and Draven snarled at the interruption like a wild beast being disrupted in the middle of devouring his kill. It was my saviour Sophia, who stood there now in all her kick ass female glory, obviously not about to take any shit from her brother.

"That is not her name," she stated and I frowned as my

mouth dropped open. I was about to speak, about to say anything to cover my own ass, when she just walked right in and added the last thing I ever expected her to say...

"Her name is Keira."

CHAPTER TWO

A KING OBSESSED

I suddenly wanted to scream out 'What the Hell!?' but thought better of it, so decided to quietly seethe whilst I sat there looking at Sophia. Finally, Draven removed his hand from his primal restraint around my neck. Then he looked at me as if remembering that I had mentioned this to him before I had passed out on the battlefield.

"Keira." He uttered my name as if testing it out for himself and it sounded both foreign and sexy the way he said it. I bit my lip and struggled through the mixed emotions hearing him say it for the first time, suddenly catapulting me back to my own point in history and when I first heard it being said by a very different Draven.

Of course, the first time he had said my name I had cruelly been led to believe it was just a dream, when he had commanded me to sleep after meeting me for the first time in the woods. Well, thanks to Sophia, it had been more like a little jungle oasis or some reincarnation of the Garden of Eden, something I suppose she had seen as quite fitting at the time. Which brought me back to the present and once more I had my little interfering cupid to thank for the mess she was currently getting me into.

"Ah yes, I remember now, this was the name you gave me," he said as if playing it back for himself. Granted it was unusual for Draven to forget something like this but I think considering the circumstances and just finding out that not only was I still alive but also his Chosen One, then who could really blame him.

"Which begs the question, how you know this, Saphira?" he asked now turning his attention to his sister and the cause of my new nightmare. She simply shrugged her shoulders and said,

"We were imprisoned together and she thought she would never see you again. So, she confessed everything to me, in hopes that I might escape and relay the message to you. She wanted to die with the knowledge that you knew her real name and who she really was to you," Sophia said with such ease, as if this was something she had spent the morning rehearsing with Pip! I could almost picture her clapping once in a little mad director's chair (one possibly created by Tim Burton) and saying, 'Excellent, now once more with feeling!'.

"Is that so, Little Lamb of mine?" He turned his questioning back to me and I briefly managed to see Sophia giving me wide eyes and telling me silently to nod my bloody head and say yes before shit got worse. So, hoping that she had an end game in all this and knew what she was doing, I nodded slowly. Then, as if he didn't fully believe me, his hand snapped out again and he shifted closer to me. Once more he was feeling my pulse as he demanded,

"Words little one, I want your words." Damn demanding men, I thought with a grinding of my teeth. So, I took a deep breath and just hoped that my pounding heart didn't give me away again.

"Yes." One simple word said yet it left my lips like it was being ripped and dragged out of there. He raised an eyebrow to me and I couldn't tell with his look whether he believed me or not. I looked to Sophia and for a brief moment she looked worried, then something dawned on her, so she added something quickly,

"It's all right Keira, they can't hurt you again." I frowned at her but thankfully this was overlooked by Draven who was now shooting his sister a deadly look.

"They hurt her!?" He demanded to know on a growl, one that made him tense his hold on me before realising what he was doing. He felt me go stiff next to him before trying to pull away, something he of course, wouldn't allow.

"Ssshh my skittish little Lamb, nothing can hurt you now," he cooed bring me closer and into his protective hold. Then he started caressing my neck as if to rid the memory of his actions only seconds ago.

"Unfortunately, brother, I am afraid so…they, well should we say, they *toyed with her,*" Sophia said, leaning forward slightly, whispering this last part. Then she simply straightened and waited for it and as usual with Draven's temper, she didn't have to wait long. He stood and erupted into his other form, bellowing,

"TOYED WITH HER!" I flinched back but he was lost to his murderous thoughts enough to snap,

"Saphira, a word!" he said motioning his head towards the door.

"But of course, Brother," she replied calmly and now I knew that this had been her plan all along. Draven started to follow her when he suddenly stopped before walking through the door. Then with what sounded like a foreign spoken swear word, he stormed back over to me and for a moment I feared he would verbally take out his anger on me but if anything, what I received was the complete opposite.

He stood directly behind where I was sat and he ran a gentle hand down my cheek before gripping my chin and turning it to the side so that I could look up at him.

"You are not to leave…*understand?*" I bit my lip at the hidden severity in that demand and I nodded quickly, obviously making him happy with my acceptance.

"I will return to you shortly and take my heed little beauty, we will be continuing where we left off…" he told me and then bent at the waist getting close enough so that I wouldn't miss the whispered promise,

"…for I will know you, Electus of mine." And then he was gone and I was left shivering from his words. The last thing I heard was his harsh issued demands to the guards who no doubt stood like an impenetrable force outside the room.

"No one enters this room but I, and under no means is she to leave, understood?!"

"Yes, My King." This reply was heard from at least four different men and my shoulders slumped as I realised a new vital flaw in my plan…

I was now Draven's prisoner.

"Yo, Tootie Trotter, you awake or what?" Hearing this my head suddenly snapped up and thankfully my eyes weren't deceiving me as I saw Pip climbing through a window. I ran over to help her but as she swung her little legs over like a gymnast on a wooden horse, it became obvious that I wasn't needed.

"Jeez, what were you in another life, a cat burglar?" I asked on a laugh.

"You know, I never get that…why cats? Why not dogs, or chickens…I mean them little peckers are faster than a pair of wet knickers dropping at the sight of a big pecker!" I burst out laughing and shook my head, wondering where she came up with half of this shit. I gave her a hug and said,

"I am sorry Draven was being an ass." I told her making her bat her hand and say,

"Yeah but he's a barbarian hottie, so whatya gonna do? Besides, he's King so it kinda comes with dick status privileges." Well yes, I had to agree with her there.

"Anyway, we don't have long, I mean mushy dates on a cracker girl, that guy has got it bad for you! I thought Adam was jacked up on the possessive juice but cheesy biscuits that guy is bathing in the stuff!" she said making me frown and, if I was honest, giving me a bit of a headache trying to decipher what the heck she was going on about.

"What are you talking about, Pip?"

"What am I talking about, seriously girlfriend and booby bitch of mine, I am talking about the King with his breastplate in a twist!" Needless to say, after this I had to rub my forehead just to ease the pain before saying in a dry tone,

"Words I understand, Squeak."

"Caveman has the whole kingdom on lockdown just in case you manage to get away from him again." At this my head snapped up and my mouth dropped.

"You're shitting me!"

"I shit on you never, my friend. He has taken his obsession to new heights of insanity and thanks to now knowing you are his Electus, well let's just say he isn't taking any chances. He has even forbidden you to be seen without him by your side." Okay if I was shocked before then now I thought I would collapse to the floor. So instead I backed up a few steps and held myself up resting a hand to the wall.

"That's…that…"

"Insane, OTT, madness, stalker on a whole new level.," she

offered and I had to nod to all four. Right, well if I thought Draven could be overbearing in my own time then this took that to a whole new crazy level. Jesus, I knew that Draven could be a little protective and had a jealous streak that could murder on sight but this…

"This is insanity." I finished my thoughts out loud.

"No, this is simply a King terrified," she informed me softly, touching my arm and getting me to look at her. Her beautiful forest green eyes were sparkling under the hot Persian sun and I suddenly wished that her husband was here so that he could see the beauty staring back at me now for himself.

"You understand this don't you?" I asked, remembering all those times when Adam had burst into a room with nothing short of panic written across his features at the thought that his wife had been taken from him. And that was normally after she was only gone for an hour or two.

"I do. It's not easy for our big hunky men to love but when they do, it's not only forever, its *forevermore* and when I say more, I mean it in an 'I will destroy the Earth to get my woman back' type of way," she said nodding. I suddenly thought back to the story she had told me back when imprisoned about Adam destroying a whole island in his rage to get Pip back.

"So, what you're saying is…"

"Since he found out you're his Electus, that yep, we are royally screwed," she finished for me.

"There must be another way?" I asked knowing without her needing to explain what she meant. Since he found out about who I really was to him, that when the time came to leave the city, he had just made it so it was now firmly labelled 'Mission Impossible' in my mind. She shrugged her little shoulders and said,

"We will think of something, after all we usually do, plus we are awesome!" I gave her a little smile.

"But Toots, this is why we can't let him know you're from the future," she told me in all seriousness, one that for Pip was a big enough warning in itself.

"Why?"

"Because all we can hope for here is that he starts to relax, enough for you to see the light of day again. But think about it with your mushy pink brain, if he knew your main goal here was to get back home, *to your own time*, what do you think he would do?"

"Build me a pretty gold tower and keep me there?" I answered knowing it wasn't exactly an exaggeration, not when I briefly looked to the door, knowing there were four guards out there for a reason.

"Yep, pretty much a bingo moment. The only thing we can hope for is that he lets Tittanian see her Boobateers, otherwise I see myself climbing through that window as my new hobby." I had to laugh at that.

"So, tell me, what is the story here, because no offence to your awesome 'Sad, sad, merchant's daughter gets sold as a sex slave story' I don't think that is going to fly now." I told her after a sigh wondering when... *seriously, when* did the life of a Scouser get so damn complicated…? Oh wait, after I took my first step into Afterlife, that's when!

"Okay so you have a point, one we little girly scamps already thought about, so step closer chicken little, this is your new savvy story." Pip said pulling me closer and telling me exactly what new story I was going to tell the King, one I might add, would quickly make him realise how much I had lied the first time. And well, for someone who sucked big time at the unconventional art of lying, then this wasn't going to be easy. Especially not with Draven's new technique at playing big city cop! That being able to read my reactions via the damn blood pumping in my veins…I mean how unfair was that?

"Look Tootie cake, you wanna know the best way to beat a lie detector?" she said just as she had one leg over the wall of the window. I crossed my arms over my chest and said,

"And what's that?"

"It's simply Genie'tastic...*just believe what you say is real,*" she told me and I wanted to roll my eyes but instead found myself asking,

"And how would you know this?" This was when she winked at me and said,

"Oh, my little Tootie Lamb, you really, really don't wanna know...now get your lying ass in gear because here comes King Goat Herder now!" she said nodding to the door and then when I looked back to the window she was gone, leaving me inwardly laughing at her calling Draven a royal goat herder. Well, with the amount of times he called me 'his little lamb' then I couldn't say it was a bad nickname for him. Which had me wondering if it meant something greater here, like the way Ragnar and Sigurd always called me 'their little apple'? I couldn't say I was best pleased about everyone adding the word 'little' in their nicknames for me...I mean who was I, Thumbelina for Christ sake!

"Anything I should be aware of, General?" The sound of Draven's authoritative voice drew my attention to the door as I could hear him checking up on me.

"All quiet, my Lord." I heard his reply and knew this was my time to try and do something that was quickly becoming foreign to me around Draven...acting cool and not hot-headed. No, I needed to go back to the Keira before Draven and I ever became an item. The shy and quiet waitress I was before I became Draven's equal. Because the reality of my situation was simple, here in this time, I didn't think I would ever get to that status before I had to leave. It was too different and I had to remember what Pip had told me after reeling off my new story.

BLOOD OF THE INFINITY WAR

She reminded me that I wasn't only dealing with a volatile king of the supernatural, I was also dealing with a younger one. He hadn't had the years to adapt to the human mortal world, one where he didn't rule over them as well as his own kind. He had never felt love for those other girls in his Harem, so never got to experience the long list of sentiments that unfortunately walks hand in hand with finding a fresh new love. There were emotions like jealousy, irrational thoughts, doubts, fears, self-consciousness (okay, so granted, that one was mainly me) but also the main one...*trust*.

Now out of them all this was the biggest and most important one and it almost broke my heart that it was the one thing I couldn't give Draven, as, how could I? I had lied from the beginning and now I would simply have to continue, knowing that soon I would be leaving his world for another. So, in the end, any trust he gave me would be done before a lessoned learned and a love lost.

"They look like heavy thoughts indeed," he told me as if he had just witnessed a whole montage of thoughts playing across my face for himself. I took a deep breath as I usually did when faced with such raw, masculine beauty. He looked huge, with his muscular, bare arms on show that were still dirty from battle and strapped with leather bands across spiked metal gauntlets.

He also wore loose pants, that too were strapped with leather and other sheaths for daggers and an array of weapons, ones he was yet to remove. It became obvious that he must have just come off the battlefield with me in his arms and then not moved from my sight until now.

Thick leather belts of different designs hung off to one side from his waist, brandishing different metal seals where they joined. A thick crimson sash underneath could be seen in between all the hammered metal and stamped or carved leather.

This was all finished off with metal plates that too were

strapped to his boots and covered the knees, rising up into wicked points. He looked more like a deadly warrior general, than the mighty king he was. I mean, once I had learned about Draven and what he was, I knew that his battling days were long behind him, or so I had hoped. But seeing him like this was more like looking at him in a painting of the past, than in real life.

He stood by the door and I noticed he was letting me take in my fill of him, an action that made me blush and bite my lip. Then, before my eyes could fully witness his movements, he was right in front of me in a flash, moving so quickly that I yelped in shock.

"I think I warned you about that before, my blushing Little Lamb," he told me before gently pulling my bottom lip from the confines of my teeth. I couldn't look at him, so instead focused on the forged design on his breastplate. I reached out, slowly at first, half expecting him to grab my hand or step back but he didn't. No, instead he remained still, with only the slight lifting of his armour with his heavy breathing. I started to run my finger around the design of a winged Demon on one side, over his left pec and on the right side, what looked like an avenging Angel.

Both were on horseback and even the horses looked as musclebound as the men. Each was dressed like Draven was, a warrior from another world.

"It's...it's beautiful and very fitting," I said having first to clear my throat before I spoke. I realised now that at some point when speaking to Sophia he must have poured water over himself as some droplets still clung to his hair but mainly because his tarnished gold coloured breastplate was now minus the blood splatter from his enemies.

"I am pleased you think so, for after watching my own warrior woman fighting, I am thinking of getting you one made," he said and I looked up at him to see that he was teasing me. His soft dark eyes made me take a breath and roll my lips so that I wouldn't bite them.

"I don't think that's a good idea," I said on a little laugh and he inquired,

"No, and why is that?"

"I think it would give people the wrong impression of me as I think you would find that I could barely lift your sword," I said touching the golden handle of the massive weapon he kept hung at his side.

"Then a dagger is what you need," he told me in such a provocative way that it made me shiver. I swallowed hard when I felt the back of his fingers caress down my open neckline. Then I decided to continue my exploration of his armour.

He dropped his hand and remained still, silently watching me as I continued to trace the raised figures until I got to the one at his chest, over his heart. It was an upturned V shape entwined with a broken O shape that branched out and back on itself before it met at the bottom. I felt him suck in a sharp breath as my fingertip traced over the symbol as if he could feel my touch branding his skin.

"What is this?" I asked him, knowing just how many times I had seen it in my life, even before Draven entered it. I still had no idea why I had never received answers to any of my questions before, but it was something Draven always seemed to put off telling me.

Of course, the first time I had ever seen it was on one of my baby pictures of me watching TV. I had baby wispy hair at the time and must have only been six months old. A strange birthmark to have but one that would forever be hidden from the world as soon as my hair started to grow thicker.

But then came a front door to a hidden world and when I stepped through it, the very first thing I had touched had been that same symbol I myself had been marked with since birth. At the time, I confess I hadn't even thought about it and in fact, it was only when trying to enter into the deepest depths of Afterlife had I thought about it. The Dravens' family crest. My birthmark. And branded key into the Temple. They were one and the same.

After my question, he remained silent for a what seemed like long moments. To the point where I didn't think he would answer me, but then his voice sliced through the moment like the blade at his side. He sounded as though the answer he was about to give was a test. A test of the Gods, of the Fates, even of the very prophecy itself. And for some reason, right now in this time asking him of it, well strangely it seemed like my own test.

Which I guess it was after I finally received his answer.

An answer that was the very last thing I ever expected to hear…

"It means you, Electus."

CHAPTER THREE

CHASING LOVE

"I...I...don't understand, what do you mean?" I asked quietly still trying to process what he just told me.

"I will explain but not now," he told me making my heart drop. When I heard him laughing I frowned back at him, knowing it was a sound generated from the look of disappointment on my face.

"Upon my word, sweet girl, but that look makes me feel as though an arrow just pierced my chest...tell me Goddess, *is this all part of your magic?"* he asked leaning down and trying to catch my eyes. I couldn't help but smirk at his words and couldn't refrain myself from teasing him back when saying,

"No, I usually just turn unfortunate teasing Kings into frogs for their sins." At this he threw his head back and burst out laughing, making me momentarily fixate on his corded neck that was the colour of honey. Jesus, but how was it possible to find someone's neck sexy!?

"Is that so? Well I am to remember that one, for I must warn you, around you, *I plan to sin a lot."* He finished this sentence whispered in my ear making me shudder.

"Now it's time to come with me," he said and it was my only warning before I was suddenly hoisted up into his arms, making me cry out.

"What are you…?"

"Hush now…it is simply time to do your womanly task for your King," he told me and I gulped, thinking this wasn't exactly how I pictured our first time together.

"Umm…well, I think…uh couldn't we just, you know…?" I stumbled to find my reasons to hold this off. I didn't know why but it didn't feel right this way. I felt the rumbling in his chest and when I looked up at his face he was smirking down at me, as if what I had said had amused him greatly. Then he obviously couldn't help himself when he asked,

"Couldn't we…?"

"You know…like, talk first?" I said feeling like smacking myself on the head considering that was also the last thing I wanted to do right now, if the type of 'chatting' he preferred was anything to go by. If anything, shouldn't I be thanking my lucky stars that he didn't want to talk, or should I say, *interrogate?* Yep once again this had him laughing as if he was having the time of his life.

"I believe you were singing a sweeter tune when you were finding your release in my mouth," he told me shamelessly and I gasped at his brazen comment. Again, something he just laughed at. This was when I realised that he wasn't walking us both to his bed, but past the room and into a small tunnel.

"Where are we going?" I asked, forgetting all about his embarrassing teasing and swapping it for outright curiosity. Besides, could this lead to a way out when the time came?

"You shall soon see," he answered me grinning, which told me I was at least doing something right as he certainly seemed to be in a good mood. This then had me wondering what Sophia had told him.

We continued down the tunnel that descended ever so slightly and when I peered back over his shoulder, where we entered not only seemed now quite small but also level with his shoulders. He looked down at me to see what I was doing but didn't comment on my actions, just simply watched me. It felt like it had all that time ago when working at Afterlife and finding Draven watching me and my every move.

Of course, it became even more obvious after we first slept together. I remember telling Libby once that the only flaw I found in Draven was the fact that he stared at me too much. Okay, so when she told me about Frank's cheesy feet, then I really didn't think I had much to complain about. But then again, with that intense gaze of his, looking at me in such a way that he had every right to, it felt more like I was a species being studied. As though he was silently mapping my every move. Every sound. Every gesture I made just so that he could file it away and make sense of it later.

So, when this Draven told me that he '*Wanted to know me*' what he actually meant was, know me in a way that no other would. Body, mind and soul. Of course, that meant one thing to Draven…watch everything I did with a penetrating gaze that felt like it was powerful enough to undress me. Take now for example, at this very moment, I knew he was trying desperately to know what I was thinking. What my expression could mean. Was it thoughts about him? For someone like Draven, all of these things must have been utterly frustrating to have to ask himself with no answers found. Someone who could simply access the mind of others with little thought put into the act. But with me, someone he no doubt wanted very much to control, then that must have been infuriating indeed. No wonder when he had first seen me he had been intrigued.

"We are here," he told me, swiftly bringing me out of my thoughts.

"Oh…it's a bathroom," I said seeing that the Draven in this time also had a thing for sunken baths…or had Draven had his bath designed that way because it reminded of a home from his past. Well, that was interesting I thought with a hidden smile.

"I find you quite endearing, Electus of mine," he told me as he let go of my legs, so that they swung down before he lowered my feet to the floor.

"You do?" He nodded, looking down at me as he ran his thumb down my cheek before gripping my chin and issuing his next command.

"Now strip bare for me." I could tell the way he still held my face up that he had been counting on enjoying my response to this, as my mouth dropped open on a 'O' and I felt the heat rushing to my cheeks. The look he gave me back told me I hadn't disappointed him with my shocked and shy reaction. His bad boy grin was firmly set, framed by his dark beard. He finally let go of my chin and gave me the space I needed to freak out without his eagle eyes watching me.

The room he had walked us into was huge and much bigger than it needed to be for just one person's use. I half expected to see other people walking in and out but all I could see was one other door and it was firmly locked from this side. Which hopefully meant a possible exit for me in the future.

"Come here," he ordered looking back at me, as it was clear he was currently ridding himself of his battle gear, placing it down on a table at one side of the room. He was frowning at me and I wondered if he had been guessing my thoughts when looking at that door. I sure hoped not but it was a cold reminder to try and act a little more inconspicuous from now on when planning my escape.

I slowly started to walk around the massive pool of water

which took up most of the large round room. The bath was framed by eight massive arches and the space was big enough for Draven's commanding voice to echo. It was mostly bare, with sandstone block walls and highly polished pale marble floors that were dotted with gold six pointed stars. The pillars were also cut from the same pale marble but each of the arches was painted gold, matching the floor with their six-pointed stars cut from the centres.

The room was stunning and reflected on the dark water that was only lit by the numerous flaming torches that hung around the room on heavy iron hooks.

Draven cleared his throat and I realised I had stopped to take in the rest of the room. I looked back at him and he was giving me an inquisitive look that silently told me he wanted to know what I was thinking. I took a breath and continued towards him.

"Do you like this room?" he asked me the second I reached him.

"Well I…um, I…its nice," I said sounding stupid as I couldn't think of what to say. It wasn't like I could say, well I have never seen anything like it before because that wasn't strictly true but a worse answer would have been; 'Oh yeah, I remember something like this when I was kidnapped by Lucius in the 21st century, when I got attacked by some life sucking mud and he had to wash it off me in his own ancient bath…I remember it because the mud made me think I was having sex with him at the time.'…Um, no I didn't think this would have gone down well.

"You seem fixated," he told me, picking up on my exact reaction to it. In the end, I just went with a silent shrug of my shoulders, thinking it was safer than talking. Of course, seeing what he did next, I couldn't have spoken even if I had wanted to. Not at the sight of him pulling off the pieces of his armour and revealing one hot, hard male beneath. Jesus, it was suddenly hot in here!

I jumped after he had released the ties at the side of his breastplate and dropped it onto the marble bench. He gave me a look over his shoulder and raised an eyebrow in question but didn't say anything. Instead he continued to shed his clothes and suddenly I could barely breathe.

I tried to take in all his muscles, starting with the ones on his back as he pulled off a tunic style top. Then he arched over, placing a boot against the rim of the bench and started pulling at the ties that held the metal leg guards in place. I had to fist my hands to stop myself from running my fingertips along something that looked just as hard as his breastplate had done, but a sight definitely more inviting.

Once finished with getting his legs bare, he then turned back to me and presented me with the inside of his leather-bound arms. I didn't know what he wanted from me so I gave him unsure, wide eyes and lent forward and after placing my hands in his open palms I said,

"Is this what you...?" I never finished as he stared down at our entwined hands as if testing the feel of having someone hold them. My fingertips slowly curled slightly by his thick wrists and I hooked them into the thin leather straps, holding on. Then something snapped in him and he suddenly gripped tight and yanked me forward into him. I stumbled a step but thankfully managed to stay upright, thanks to the combined hold we had on each other.

"No, but this is better," he told me cryptically, then he raised both my hands up and he kissed each one on the back, never taking his eyes from mine. A shuddered breath left me before I could stop it. Not surprising, he took note of it and smiled before slowly lowering my hands back down.

"Now you can grant me your fingers," he said making me

frown and I could actually feel my nose wrinkling in confusion, this time making him chuckle. Then he tapped me on my nose and said,

"As adorable as I find that look on you, I will finally take pity on you and answer your silent question. Can you aid me in removing my bracers," he asked nodding down at the leather and I blushed scarlet. That was what he had wanted all along.

"Oh…yeah, okay, so I knew that," I said lamely making him throw his head back and laugh again, something that made me want to groan for two reasons and one of them was down to my libido, the other my shame. I quickly removed my other locked hand from his and started to untie the leather straps as quickly as I could without looking up at him. I don't know why but I couldn't stop my hands from shaking and I didn't understand it. I had already been naked with this warrior. I had spent the night in his arms and I had let him taste me in the most intimate way anyone could. So why was I now acting like a virgin on prom night?

"Easy," he cooed, placing a hand over mine to stop me from yanking when I started pulling at one bit that I couldn't get through the metal clasp. Then he lifted my hand up and pulled it himself, and it snapped as easily as if it had been made from paper, not the tough animal hide it was.

I dropped my hands to my side as he no longer needed my help and took a step back making him growl with displeasure. I looked up to him in surprise at hearing this and whilst frowning down at me, he nodded back in front of him to tell me silently to resume my previous position. I gulped back the sudden urge to run and braved taking a step closer to him. The sight of his huge chest breathing heavy and his tense muscles, as if holding himself back from doing something to me, was enough to make anyone want to run away from this beast of a man. Of course, it was also enough to make someone like myself want to throw myself on top of him and ride him like some X rated fairground ride.

"You look like some wide eyed, frightened fawn insight of the arrow heading her way," he told me, his voice thick and heavy with restraint. I didn't know what he expected me to say to this but the last thing I expected him to say next was what he did,

"Bare yourself to me." I couldn't help it but my bottom lip automatically found itself in between my teeth and he growled again, reminding me off that offense. I let it go and swallow hard when he crossed his massive arms across his chest causing them to grow in size, making his biceps looked as if they could crush skulls with little effort.

"Answer me this Little Lamb, do you like making me wait or do you just enjoy defying a King by keeping a body that belongs to him from gaining his pleasure in seeing it bare?" he asked me in a hard tone and I didn't know whether he was just having too much fun watching me squirm or he was being serious.

"No!" I blurted out without thinking.

"No?" he repeated, tilting his head so as to catch my eyes.

"I meant no, as in… I'm not being mean or anything." I said on a rush and it soon looked as if he was fighting a grin.

"Mean? Surely not indeed, for my Electus could never be classed as…*Mean?*" he mocked and I think this was his way of finally taking pity on me again.

"So, if you are not callous enough to deny me what is mine by right, then why do you make me wait?" he asked, more gently this time.

"I am shy, okay." I said finally giving him what he wanted to hear. He feigned surprise and raised his eyebrows at me.

"Is that so?" I nodded and hugged my arms around myself, hating that my brave, brazen behaviour had left me.

"I must say I am surprised."

"Why?" I asked quietly.

"Because I do recall *in great detail*, how you granted me sight of your delectable body the first time," he reminded me and I blushed again. Okay so he was right, the first time I had decided to turn the tables on the situation at the time and took back some small shred of power I had. Then I had pulled my torn tunic from my body and walked up to him as though I had all the confidence in the world.

"I know…!" I said suddenly surprising him as he jerked his body back slightly. However, I ignored this and carried on,

"…why don't you get in the bath first and I will join you after…like minutes later not like hours or anything, 'cause it will probably be cold then…is it warm in there because, wow its warm in here. I think I will just skip the bath." I rambled on in my nervous way making him look at me once more as if he was seeing me for the first time. It was almost as if he didn't know what to do with me and had never encountered such strange behaviour before. I decided to take his silence as acceptance that I didn't need to bathe anymore so I nodded my head and turned around quickly. I started to walk away…but in true Draven style, I didn't get far.

I yelped when I was suddenly grabbed from behind and then lifted into his arms once more. Then, laughing heartily, he walked us both into the water and only let go of my legs once I was in up to my neck.

"I…you…" I started to complain but he just looked as though he was having too much fun.

"I must confess, I have not had this much enjoyment with a female in all of my many years upon this world. You are so different, I find you utterly fascinating," he told me holding on to my shoulders so that I wouldn't move. I couldn't say that I particularly *enjoyed* hearing about his time with other females but at least in what he had said, it meant I was possibly his favourite so far.

"Now hold still," he said and I was just about to ask why when he suddenly gripped my long kaftan and whipped it up over my head, taking my arms up with it. As soon as it was out of sight and discarded over the edge with a wet, echoing slap on the marble, I ducked down lower, hiding myself under the water.

"Hiding what's mine, once again I see," he said after tutting and shaking his head.

"I told you that I was shy," I repeated moving backwards now that he didn't have hold of me. However, I soon realised the flaw in my plan as the depth of the pool was more fitting for someone of Draven's height, as too soon I couldn't feel the bottom with my feet. From the look of things, he knew it too and one side of his mouth rose into a bad boy grin.

"Umm…My Lord…?" I said stopping myself from calling him by the only name I wanted to say aloud.

"Time to play." This turned out to be my only warning as he started to lower himself down slowly into the dark water. Watching me with those all-consuming eyes of his that matched the colour of the liquid that was quickly covering up his face… *Then he was gone.*

The game began and I quickly started to move, treading water and slowly moving to the other side where I would hopefully be able to stand. I laughed nervously looking all around me for any signs of him.

I would have liked to have said it reminded me of our playful chase back when I sneaked into the swimming pool in the hotel in Milan. The one where Draven surprised me by turning up and jumping in, quickly going in for the attack by dragging me under. It felt like an age ago and I couldn't help but bite my lip, this time to stop from it trembling. *I missed my husband.*

Now though, it felt more like I was being hunted and stalked by someone who didn't need to breathe as often as I did…which meant he could take his time.

"Ah!" I shouted feeling a hand run up my leg and then disappear. I spun round and then once more I screamed out, when feeling a gentle touch against the base of my spine. It was maddening in a sexual way to feel him touching me and not knowing when or where it would strike next. A feel of my foot, a little pull of my hand, a soft graze just below my right bum cheek and the one that made me scream the most, fingertips sliding across the junction of my thighs.

"OH!" I yelled again turning fast from the hand that just caressed my breast. I decided to try and play him at his own game so I dived under the dark water and spun around, trying to see a body but there was nothing. My heart was pounding wildly in my chest from the thrill of the chase when suddenly I saw him. Two purple eyes glowing from the dark depths across from me, as though he was calmly sitting in wait for the right moment to strike.

And strike he did.

I saw him coming so I quickly pulled myself up to the surface and took a breath. Then I made one last dash to get to the other side when he finally grabbed me. I screamed before I burst out laughing, this time being the one to throw my head back and let it all out. I felt him lifting me up by the waist, which was making me laugh as it was tickling me. Finally, I stopped to see him looking down at me with a startled look. At first, I didn't know what to make of it but then I realised…this was the first time he had seen me *really* laugh and the look he gave me, was one of wonder.

Thinking about it now, I doubted that such a serious

character and important royal figure had much opportunity to make people laugh. But here I was, giggling away like a crazy person three seconds away from snorting in his arms. Had he ever experienced such a thing? Well, judging by his expression I would have guessed that he hadn't and boy didn't the idea of being his first just fill me with utter joy.

"Okay, okay you win!" I said holding up my hands in surrender.

"You can't be real," he stunned me by saying, making me freeze in his hold. I looked up at him and saw that intense purple gaze once more as if it was trying to search for my very soul. As if one single sight of it would have given him all the answers he looked for.

"My Lord?" I asked tentatively, knowing that what I was seeing was a man experiencing emotions like this for the first time and someone with great power on the edge because of it. I knew this, especially when his arm banded tightly around my torso and his other hand circled my throat, a gesture I was quickly getting used to. I really wanted to know why he did this, as it was something even my Draven did occasionally. Granted, not as much as this Draven but still, it was something I never understood. Was it a primal need to keep me compliant or submissive? A being they owned and felt they could control at will, for the power of something like that must have been heady indeed for a dominant.

He didn't hurt me, but still managed to apply enough pressure for me to know to keep still as he wished.

"You feel real, with your heart beating wildly in your chest, I can feel the life beneath my fingertips," he told me, tapping my pulse point to prove his point.

"But when I feel you in my arms, when I see the near blinding beauty in your smile and hear the warmth of your soul in merely a laugh, then I fear you are just a dream, one I never want to wake from, so I ask of you again…are you real to me?" At this I couldn't help my reaction as a single tear formed and he seemed transfixed as he watched it fall from my lashes, down my cheek and soon lost forever into the water below…or so I thought.

Instead the hand holding my neck left me and snapped out catching the tear in the palm of his hand. Then he lifted it to his lips, and tasted the salty drop. The second he did his eyes lost themselves to a deeper flame. Then he leaned closer and told me,

"You can't taste the tears of a Goddess in your dreams, so you must be real and therefore…" he paused to take a deep breath before whispering the last of his declaration across my lips…

"…This must be what love feels like."

CHAPTER FOUR

TAMING THE DEMON

I quickly realised this was the first time I had heard him say he loved me in this time and to say that it didn't make my heart soar would have been a lie. I sucked in a sharp breath and the purple in his eyes intensified because of it.

"You…you love me?" I asked him quietly and he pulled me that little bit closer because of it.

"How could I not? I fear every being with a heart would fall under the spell of loving you," he told me making me frown.

"Hearing this displeases you why?" he asked me, looking amazed by my reaction.

"You think that I have tricked you?" I asked trying to push myself out of his hold, feeling offended by his statement. However, he didn't look too worried by my reaction, no instead he even seemed pleased with it.

"This idea upsets you?" This time I didn't just frown, I got angry and he knew it.

"Of course, it does! Let me go, this bath has suddenly given me a chill," I told him now doubling my efforts to get away from him. But his arms hardened further becoming a cage of flesh, bone and muscle.

"Be still little bird and listen to my words," he hummed against my hairline as he pulled my face closer to his.

"NO, let me go now!" I snapped but his hand whipped out and quickly covered my mouth.

"You will listen to me!" He warned first in a hard tone that brooked no argument, even if I was free to speak.

"Upon the Gods woman, you fire my blood like no other! I know not of where you came from but your viper tongue lashing at me like that only makes me want you more. It makes me want to punish your beautiful body in ways that have never graced my thoughts before…" He gripped on to me, digging his fingers into my flesh and making me whimper behind his hand as the small bite of pain did confusing things to my insides. Then he continued and I nearly came undone.

"…I want to chain to you my body, so that you will never leave my side. I wanted to bury myself inside you and sleep with my cock nestled in your warm, tight sheath, keeping you locked to me even in the solace of slumber you find. I want to demand you dream only of me and when you wake, you do so remembering who it is you belong to.," he finished on a growl and I bit my lip under his hand, which seemed to be too much for him to take. He tore his hand away, gripped the back of my head and yanked me hard into his kiss…one I wanted as desperately as my next breath.

I opened up to him on a moan and he took control of both my body and my mind. I was lost to the feel of this man, taking me to ancient new heights. I was no longer trying to get away from him, but instead trying to get as close as possible. I held onto him by his neck, running one hand up the back of his head and running my fingers through his hair. I felt the rumbling in his chest rise and I smiled over his lips.

"You play a dangerous game with me, Little Lamb," he warned on a throaty growl and I knew in that moment there was nothing more in this world I wanted to do *other* than let him play with me, the only way he knew how…*beast and prey.*

So, I played the game and submitted. Without saying a word, I simply pulled back slightly and closed my eyes as I bent my head to one side, baring my neck to him. This time he didn't just growl, no…

His Demon roared.

Then the strike came making me cry out in both shock and pleasure. He sunk his fangs into me and at the first pull of my blood, I unravelled. I came so hard I thought I would pass out from it, as it looked like a flash bomb had erupted behind my eyelids. I felt him holding me too tightly, giving me barely enough space to breathe. I felt imprisoned. I felt treasured. *I felt fucking adored.*

And then I started to fall.

The second he felt it, he quickly released his beautiful and brutal hold on my tender flesh and licked at the wound he had inflicted. Even the way he slowly dragged his tongue up over the punctured flesh had me shuddering against him. I felt drunk and I wondered why it felt different this time, until he spoke.

"Goddess blood, you taste like the sweetest honey, the light of the sun and the forbidden fruit of Heaven," he told me licking his lips as if her could still taste me there.

"I think I have just found my first addiction," he added making me smile before having to rest my head against his shoulder. I suddenly felt as though my limbs had turned into over-cooked noodles.

"But I took too much. I will need to be more careful with you in future," he told me and he had no idea the true meaning behind the little laugh I let escape. If only he knew I thought, thinking of my Draven in the future and how careful he was when drinking from me. Which was why I uttered a whispered,

"You will in time."

After this I must have passed out for a few moments for when I finally opened my eyes again I was no longer clinging onto him.

"What happened?" I asked, still feeling drowsy. I looked around and realised we were still in the pool so I couldn't have been asleep for long. Draven was positioned behind me and had me in his arms, with my back flush with his chest. And what was that I felt...he was washing me?

"I am sorry, for I took too much from you and it seems an important lesson learned," he said cryptically and I tried to move so that I could look at him but his arm banded across my chest, keeping me where I was.

"Be still now and let me care for you," he said making me do as I was told thanks to the gentle way in which he said it. Then he continued to run a cloth over me that was soaped with an oily substance that smelled a lot like the roses I used to love smelling in my Grandmother's garden. It was soft against my skin and not at all like the soap I had been used to using back in my own time. Or even what had been used on me in his harem, which had me wondering...was this something only reserved for royalty?

In the end, this wasn't the question I asked, as what he had said was also still lingering in my mind.

"What do you mean lesson learned? I like it when you bite me." I told him without thinking. I could practically hear his thoughts as one eyebrow rose at this, which was confirmed when he said, "Oh, you do, do you? I must confess to find it odd that you speak of such things, as if I have tasted you before."

Okay so in hindsight my reaction to this shouldn't have been to tense up the way I did. For a single, damning second, I thought that he knew but then he softly whispered,

"Easy little lamb, for I jest. I simply mean that I will have to learn the art of restraint around you, for it is now clear you are capable of rendering me without thought of little else than what I desire to take from you."

"You mean because you think I am a witch?" I snapped before I could stop myself.

"A witch? I know not of this word which you speak with such venom," he said shifting me around in his hold no doubt to look at my face so that he could judge my reactions. I thought for a moment and then tried a word that he might know instead.

"A sorceress," I told him and I knew he finally understood when he grinned.

"Ah, upon my word, you do hold me to my words little one."

"And should I not?" I asked him, frowning and placing a fist to my hip, an action he seemed to find amusing as it was hidden under the water.

"Not when my words are taken from the destination in which they were intended." Wow and just when I thought that cryptic Draven couldn't get any more confusing, then enter Draven from the past and yep, I was stumped once more. He laughed because I think I must have made my thoughts known without speaking them.

"You twisted my words Sweetness and cast them into the shadows of something I did not mean. As for the sorcery of which I speak of, it is only of the heart you have stolen from me with an unknowing power you hold over it. I meant no offense, as I know no such trickery was involved in me falling in love with you, for I believe I did so the very first moment I saw you," he told me sweetly and he ran a thumb across my blushing cheeks. Then I decided to tease him back by saying,

"You mean when you held your blade to my neck and terrified me?" I told him, letting him know with my eyes that I was being playful with him.

"Ah, there is that punishing grudge you hold over me once again," he commented wryly and I laughed.

"But of course, it is part of my sorcery after all." This witty comeback was well worth it as now I had him laughing too.

"That I can be sure of, for no doubt you have many tricks up your sleeve, even when pleasingly, they are not concealed by the annoyance of fabric," he said lifting my naked arm up and pretending to find something there. I giggled and from his expression he liked the sound.

"I am sorry however, that I frightened you that day, for it was unavoidable, I am afraid," he said, surprising me with the sound of obvious guilt on his part.

"I confess, I was scared of you but then you started to be nice to me and well, putting down your blade helped," I teased nudging him with this last part.

"Nice?" he questioned nudging me back as if the idea of him being called 'Nice' was utterly foreign to him.

"Kind," I said changing my word.

"By the Gods woman you have no idea what restraint it took not to simply throw you over my shoulder, release my wings and fly off with you to the highest point of my kingdom…but alas, even Kings have their part to play." I blushed wondering how different the events would have turned out if this scenario had happened.

"I remember silently seething at Ranka's interference." Now this confession shocked me.

"But why?! She saved me from…" he never let me finish.

"From what, from me having you taken to my chambers so that I might question you myself...*alone?"* The word 'alone' was said with enough sexual promise that even the Pope would have known what he meant.

"Oh."

"Yes, 'oh' indeed. But of course, after Ranka stepped forward I knew I had little choice in my decision," he told me frowning as if remembering it and finding no pleasure in reliving the past.

"So, the harem it was then," I muttered making him raise an eyebrow my way before he gripped my chin in a firm grasp and said sternly,

"Yes, one you tried to escape from." Oh dear, that was definitely not a happy moment for him.

"Well, could you blame me? I mean do you really think that because you have a hall full of the most beautiful women in the world, that they will act like innocent, happy little virgins waiting to be plucked by their King and sit there behaving like Mother Teresa?" I said getting way, way, way too carried away with myself...yet again. Draven grabbed my wrists as they were being flung up and down in my rant. He looked to be fighting a grin and said,

"Happy little virgins? Upon my word young soul of mine, you seem almost jealous," he said seemingly more pleased with this idea than he should.

"And would you not be, if I had a room full of handsome suiters all ready to…" He suddenly growled and stopped me by covering my mouth with his hand, giving me a warning,

"I would not finish that sentence if I were you, little one." Well yes, okay so when he acted this way I couldn't say it didn't light that little smug spark in me. He gave me a pointed look as if he waited for something and it only disappeared when I nodded, to which he then removed his hand from my mouth.

"I think I made my point," I said and he the look he gave me was almost laughable. It was as though he begrudgingly agreed but hated the fact that I was right.

"And I think I will make my point when I say that a hall full of beauties holds no appeal to me when there is only one beauty that I wish to gaze upon for the rest of my days, as for the last thing…" He paused as he seemed to want a moment to enjoy the sight of my blush, by pushing my hair back with both hands and caressing my cheek with his thumb. Then he said,

"I know not of this Mother of which you speak." I laughed once knowing that he had no idea who Mother Teresa was and wouldn't for quite some time yet, so I told him,

"Think of the kindest person you know and triple it." This made him laugh for some unknown reason.

"Then that would be a holy spirit indeed for the kindest person I know is you and I find it hard to believe that someone could possess kindness greater than that," he said making me bite my lip at how lovely a compliment that was. I did want to point out that he hadn't known me long enough but my face must have given me away again. Which was secretly beginning to worry me on how quickly he was learning to read me.

"You don't believe I think this way? Do you not think I have been presented with enough proof…for I know you do not, as I can sense it in those expressive eyes of yours" He informed and then began to shift me around further so that I was straddling him. Thankfully he still had his pants on otherwise, I think that homing missile it felt he had stuffed in his pants would have made impact with its target without much thought needed.

"A young beauty, that even though scorned and threatened by one of her own sex, still refused to give her up and cast blame, even if it's just to escape my wrath. But a girl who was only willing to inflict pain on such a vile creature when she felt that another was threatened by the blade she carried."

"Well, she was trying to kill *you* this time and I couldn't allow that," I added making him smile before nodding respectfully and then saying,

"Ah, but I haven't finished my list, for there is also a beauty who enlisted the help of a servant to aid in her escape but then worried about the implications that such an action could cause her. And not forgetting the deadly actions which you put yourself in when you stood between me and that of a demonic god ready to kill me…No, I think you will find my Love, that it would be difficult indeed to find a purer soul than yours, *that* you can believe in." Okay so now I was blushing scarlet and I looked down at his chest and said quietly,

"But of course, I did…I would do *anything for the man I love."* As soon as the words were out I felt his hand snap out and hold my neck once more in his grasp. Then he slowly shifted his hold to position his thumb under my chin to be able to apply enough pressure to get me to look up at him.

"Say it again," he demanded, moving his hand back round putting his palm against the front of my throat. When I didn't say it quickly enough, his arm bent at the elbow, pulling me closer to his face with his firm hold. Then his Demon spoke to me,

"I want to feel the words coming from you." I quivered in his hold and that other side of him smiled, as it enjoyed what it could do to me. I swallowed hard, making his dark eyes bleed into purple fire.

"I…I love you," I told him softly and I could feel the small vibrations in his palm, as if it was connecting to him somehow. He closed his eyes and rasped out,

"Again." It was as if he *needed this*, so I gave him *this part of me*.

"I love you, Arsaces, *King of my Heart,*" I told him, saying his name for only the third time and the first time was said when I thought he was going to kill me, so I wasn't sure that counted.

Either way, the significance of what I had said didn't go unnoticed but more like…*consumed.* He seemed to devour my very words and he momentarily tightened his hold on me before his control shattered. I knew this when he growled low in his throat in a predatory manner and for a second I thought I had gone too far, too quickly. His eyes snapped open and the blaze I saw there I thought would swallow me whole. In fact, it was what made me try and put space between us, suddenly fearful of what he would do next.

"Do not fear me, I will control it but *do not* run from me… do you understand?" I decided to take his threat serious enough that my whole body froze. I nodded and decided that he was right. Running from the demonic beast held back on a single thread of control was just begging him to pull hard enough and break it. So instead I decided to try something different, I decided to try and *tame it.*

I bit my lip and knew it wasn't a great start when he began growling at me, so I let it go and shifted a bit closer to him, slowly at first. He looked shocked by my slow-moving actions and it was enough for him to cease his growling displeasure. Even his hand that still shackled my throat eased its pressure and I decided to reach out with my hand, raising it to his face. It felt a lot like stroking a wild snarling beast, in hopes that one wrong move wouldn't end up with a limb being torn from your body.

As I reached out, I also moved even closer to him, so that he had no choice but to let go of my neck. He released a rumbling sound, almost as if his Demon was speaking directly to me. As if telling me it liked my touch and I calmed him with it as I pushed his wet hair back from his face.

Draven remained so still, I didn't know if this was for my benefit or just the utter shock of my actions. So, I took it as a good sign either way and shifted even closer, feeling the evidence of his arousal as I did. This was something I loved about Draven. No matter what happened between us, he was never ashamed to show this side of himself to me. No trying to hide the power I had over him or the effects at having me close by did. Thinking back on how many times I had looked down and seen his lust there for myself in the form of one big, heavy and hard manhood standing to attention. And even given almost 2000 years between them it didn't matter for now was no different.

But right now, this wasn't about sex or trying to get him to break that iron will of his. It was the opposite. I wanted to be the one who controlled this side of him. I wanted to be able to not only calm his temper, but also his supernatural side...*both of them*.

So, with one last try, I wrapped both my arms around him and snuggled into him, resting my head at his shoulder. Then I placed my lips to his neck, where I kissed, licked and sucked at his flesh, playfully nipping at him. Soon the growls turned into groans of pleasure and he wrapped his arms around me to keep me to him in an unbreakable hold.

"If your actions are such in order to render me under *your* control, then I must confess, you easily accomplish such a task when placing your trust in my Demon in such a manner as this," he informed me once he had regained control...or should I say, *I had regained control for him.* I raised my head to look up at him and said,

"I am glad to hear it, My Lord."

"No." I frowned at him, trying to retrace my steps and find where I had gone wrong, when he quickly told me.

"I am, first and foremost, a man who owns your heart, not a king who demands it. You will therefore call me by my name, you will call me Arsaces," he told me and I raised my hand to his cheek and ran my thumb across his lips, smiling when this seemed to tickle him. Something that I found fascinating considering I had found no ticklish spots on Draven from my own time. I would have to remember this.

"And does this mean you will also call me by my own name, *Arsaces?*" I asked thinking I knew the answer, that was of course, until he gave me the last one I was ever expecting and it started with a question…and an awkward one at that.

"That depends, has this name of yours ever been spoken to you by another lover?" This question wasn't said in a happy, 'I think I know the answer, aren't I smug', kind of way. Oh no, it was said in a 'watch very carefully what you say next' type of way.

"I don't think that is something I wish to speak of and I certainly know it is not something that you would wish to hear," I told him being as honest as I could. Because the truth of the matter was that Draven was in fact the very first 'lover' to speak my name in such a way.

Even my first real boyfriend used to call me Kaz. But what could I tell him, because either answer I gave, each in their own right, would have been a lie. But even the vague answer I had given him wasn't enough to keep the anger from his face. Or from his possessive actions. He quickly took hold of each side of my face and pulled me closer to him, so that the threat he issued was said intimately over my lips.

"If you ever see him again, I *will* kill him….do you understand me, *my Nāzanin?*" The way he growled my given name and the way he said *'My'* was nothing short of a branding.

We both knew who he was referring too and there was only one of us who knew the truth. I had to wonder what he would say right now if I told him that *he* was in fact, the other man.

"I can ease your mind with a simple truth," I told him granting me a questioning look. Then he released my face on one side and let his hand slip down to my neck once more so that he could feel my pulse and detect my lie. Then he nodded for me to proceed. So, I quickly put him out of his misery, as I knew he didn't have the patience for such things and I told him,

"I can promise you, that the man whose name you already know, will never be seen again in this lifetime." I told him, knowing that the words he heard were not the ones spoken. Because it was the only way I could speak the truth, a truth he could easily read. This was when he finally relaxed because his assumption was exactly what I had made it sound like…*My Draven*, the one he heard me speak of…he thought was dead. For what else was there for him to think?

"I am glad to hear it, *Nāzanin*," he said, making sure I didn't miss the way he said my given name, one that meant more to him than the name I had been given at my birth. Because it meant it was *his* name. It belonged to him as did I. And more importantly to him, he would then be the only one to ever speak it as he entered me.

It would sound barbaric and irrational to most but for me, for someone who knew how Draven's mind worked, then I also knew how difficult it was going to be for him in discovering these new emotions. And jealously was going to be the hardest one of all for an Alpha like Draven.

"Now turn around and lean back so I may continue to tend to you," he told me now that he was relaxed once again and the storm that was Draven battling his Demon had passed. I had won…for now.

"Tend to me? I think you already did that My L… Arsaces,"

I said in a cheeky tone as I lifted my hand to my neck where he had bitten me and very kindly granted me a very powerful orgasm. He seemed to enjoy my teasing and grinned at me mischievously. Of course, I had been about to call him 'my Lord', but one look from him told me not to forget what he had asked of me. I think this was his way of showing me how important I was to him and I couldn't say I had an issue with that.

"And I will never forget it my sweet girl. Now do as you're told, I wish to care for you and hold you close before…" he paused as he turned me around and settled me back against him with his manhood still standing to attention in a way you couldn't ignore.

"Before?" I asked looking back at him over my shoulder and when he answered me, I couldn't help but shiver, even as his hands caressed softly down my arms. Because I knew my time of honesty was nearly at an end and I knew this when his last word spoken was whispered in my ear as a promise…

"Before it is time for you to tell me…*Everything.*"

CHAPTER FIVE

THE FUNNY SIDE OF SERIOUS

After he dropped this 'Oh shit' moment on me I remained silent as he continued to 'tend' to me, as he called it. This consisted of him washing every inch of my body with a tender care that blew me away. It was the actions of a warrior king who seemed to be the polar opposite to the very image of the man. Of course, I knew Draven's tender side more than anyone else in the world, but the man at my back was a very different Draven. So, it was only natural that his actions surprised me.

Like when he started washing my hair, being so gentle as though he was handling a priceless gift from the Gods, and I guess in a way, he considered this to be very much the way of things, seeing as I was his Electus. So, this reflected on the soft gentle treatment he bestowed on me. Like the way he would soap up his large hands before embedding his fingers into my hair and massaging my scalp. I couldn't help the shameful moans that kept slipping out.

"Does my touch feel good, heart of mine?" he asked and I

could only find myself nodding in his hold. After he was finished and his exploring had been more than a little thorough, he shifted me off him so that we could get out of the bath, but this was when I decided to be brave.

I placed a hand on his arm, restraining him before he could leave the pool. He looked down at my hold and then back up at me as if surprised once more. I mean jeez…did no one touch him without having his permission or something?! Well thinking about it, I guess restraining him or holding him back was something that would be utterly foreign to not only any King but one having such great power. Ok, so thinking about it like that, then yeah, no wonder he was looking at me in utter shock.

I quickly removed my hand as if his look had burned me and this was when his eyes got soft, telling me I had done no wrong.

"You look at me as though I wound you with my gaze, when this should not be the case. Only you and no other is always permitted to touch me, as is your right to do so…do you understand?" I rolled my bottom lip to stop from biting it and nodded quickly.

"Now enlighten me to what you were going to tell me, sweet one," he told me and all of a sudden, I felt a little shy in doing so.

"I…well…I just wanted to…you know…" Oh jeez, find words Keira, for God's sake! His lips quirked as if he wanted to laugh before he said,

"I am afraid I don't and am at a loss. However, I do find myself looking forward to *knowing,* greatly." I seriously had to stop myself from groaning aloud when he said this. I mean was there anything this man said that didn't have my stomach in sexual knots!?

"I just wanted to…to return the favour and…well…that," I

said not so articulately and instead nodding to the cloth he had been using to clean me with. He turned his gaze to the discarded piece of fabric and then back to me with wide eyes,

"You wish to wash me?" he asked astonished and I felt my face grow hot. Maybe this wasn't something that was done in his time, or was like some great offense. So, I quickly started to make my excuses and back track.

"Umm…well, no."

"No?" he repeated and I just ended up feeling like an idiot. Could I have been any more confusing right now? So, in true Keira fashion I let my mouth start to run away with me, leaving him even more astounded than before.

"Yes, oh I don't know, either answer that doesn't offend you. I didn't know if it was like an insult or something, so I panicked because you seemed so shocked and I just wanted to touch you…no! No, no, not touch you, I didn't mean…well, yes there would be touching, mainly from my side, but I didn't mean that in a sexual way, just like to wash you as you…" Finally, I stopped when unexpectedly, he threw his head back and started laughing and I mean really laughing, like the type you find hard to control. His whole body shook from it and I found myself frozen by the sight. *He was stunning.*

"By the Gods woman, you are entertaining!" he told me once he calmed enough to speak through his laughter. It was at this point where shame started to sink in and my embarrassment morphed into annoyance.

"Look, let's just forget I said anything," I told him sternly and then shifted to step out of the pool without looking at him. The next thing I knew he was grabbing me from behind, chuckling as if this was the most fun he'd had in years.

"Oh, but that would be difficult indeed, as it is not something I am likely to ever forget or even allow to happen as it felt gifted from the Heavens, for I don't remember a time I have ever laughed so hard." I had to admit hearing this did have my confidence doing a little happy dance in my head and giving my inner vixen a high five, taking one for the team. Then Draven pulled me tighter to him and pushed all my hair back from my forehead so that he could look at me from the side.

"You are such light in the darkness, that even the most mundane of things seems like a reason for waking with the rising sun," he said as he walked me back into the pool, with his arms still around me. Well after saying all that then how could I ever find myself mad with him for laughing. He had such a way with words that I would find myself lucky to have any bottom lip left by the end of my time here.

"But in answer to your very generous request, then the pleasure would be all mine to allow such." he told me, resuming his earlier position, and handing me a different cloth this time, as I understood he wouldn't want to smell of roses, like I did. No, this cloth smelled all male, a mixture of cloves, wood, citrus and even a hint of mint.

"Umm, alright, but could I ask for another request to be granted?" I asked, swallowing hard at the sight of all those delicious looking muscles that I would soon get to touch, although something I didn't think I could do if he didn't grant me my next wish.

"It seems I am incapable of denying you anything Little Lamb, so I can see this time to be no different…ask of me what you desire," he said and then nodded for me to do so.

"Can you close your eyes?" I asked making him do the very opposite. He gave me a puzzled look and it was almost as if he thought I was tricking him. What did he think I would do, wait for him to close his eyes and then leg it?!

"You do not wish for me to look at you?" he asked as this was an utterly foreign concept for him. So, I decided to be honest and told him.

"You make me nervous." Oh, and boy did he like this reply, so much so it wasn't just his purple eyes that told me, he voiced it as well.

"Good, for hearing such pleases me greatly."

"Why?" I asked, shocked by his bold statement, one that should have sounded more like a confession if you asked me.

"Because it is not simply the taste in which the flavours of your body gift me, in both your blood or in your sweet release that I am addicted too…" Oh God, if he didn't stop soon he would be 'Gifted' with that release again! But of course, he didn't stop.

"…No, but it is also in watching you and discovering all the hidden treasures that you grant me without knowing, most of which occur thanks to 'me making you nervous'. For I relish the sight of each blush like the blooming of a flower across your delicate pale skin. A sight that after today, will forevermore make me want to bite you and taste for myself the very lifeforce of where such an addiction stems, one the likes of no other." After this I couldn't help my reaction as I threw away all caution by jumping on him. Then I buried my head in his chest and let out a groan, wondering what on earth was I going to do with this man!

His body froze under what must have seemed like a strange reaction and he whispered my name in unsure tones.

"Nāzanin? Are you well?" I actually laughed and then grumbled into his chest a muffled,

"No." Then I raised my face to his, no longer caring about punishing my bottom lip and said,

"You will make my cheeks melt from the bone and my heart burst if you keep saying things to me as sweet and beautiful as that," I told him honestly and the smile he gave me was unlike any other. He looked so touched by my reaction to his words that he looked close to biting his own lip.

"Then I will continue to do so, for I want your heart full of the love I wish to bestow on you." At this I let my head fall to his chest and mumbled a,

"You did it again!" This time making him laugh and my whole body shook because of it.

"So, does this mean I get my wish?" I asked still not looking up at him, but instead pulling back a little and running my fingertip in between his pecks, before grazing it lightly over his dark, small nipple. The little rumble I heard made me smile before I looked up at him, giving him what I hoped was 'Puppy dog eyes'. This time it made him groan.

"It is a hard wish to grant, for I am selfish and usually take what I want, but on this occasion, then yes, for the pleasure I receive with your touch will make up for the loss," he said, taking hold of my chin and giving it a playful shake before he eased back for me to start. I watched him rest his head against the stone lip surrounding the pool and he closed his eyes as I had asked of him. Then he stretched out his arms along the sides and I had to lick my lips at the sight. I even saw him smirk a little when I released a sigh at the image he created. He looked like a borrowed toy I wanted to play with and never give back.

"I await you touch, little one," he reminded me after a moment of just basking in the sight of his God like body. *He was perfection.*

So, taking his impatience into account I shifted over, placing each knee next to his thigh, once again straddling him. Then, not liking the idea of him being uncomfortable, I made the decision to do something about it first. I placed a hand on his shoulder to steady myself and reached over to where I could see folded fabrics waiting for our use for drying no doubt. I grabbed the top one and pulled back to see he had his eyes open, staring down at where one of my breasts was level with his lips. I cleared my throat and said,

"Tut, tut, Arsaces, you're not playing by my rules," I teased and he laughed once and said,

"No, but I find I am enjoying the game greatly, along with the bountiful view." I laughed once and then I lowered myself down slightly, so that it no longer looked as though I was silently begging him to take my nipple into his mouth and 'play with me' in the best way possible. No, instead of teasing him with my feminine body parts, I reached around to his neck and applied a little pressure, making him open his eyes.

"For your head," I told him softly and once again it seemed as if I had surprised him. Seriously, had no one ever tried to take care for him before?

"You worry for my comfort, sweetest one?" he asked, this time calling me the very meaning of the name he had gifted me.

"But of course, now do as your told. Lift your head, close your eyes and let me tend *to you this time."* I told him ending my demands on a whisper. From the looks of things, I doubted very much that he had ever taken orders from a woman before…or anyone for that matter. Which was why he raised a single eyebrow at me now, one I laughed at and then added a hopefully seductive,

"Please" to it, in hopes it would help ease his mighty royal ego. However, he seemed to be teasing me with his actions as he simply answered,

"I live only to serve you, *my demanding little lamb."* Thankfully he missed the blush of this statement, because he did as he was told and closed his eyes. And so, the joy of my chosen task began, and it felt heavenly. Although from the sounds of things I wasn't the only one who relished in the feel of what I was doing. Every now and then he would make a little rumbling noise, especially as I shifted my weight across a certain 'hard' area of his. But my favourite part about it was not only did I get to touch him freely and explore his body from an ancient time. But I also got to look upon him without that intense gaze staring back at me.

I could simply take in every hard line of muscle as I ran the wet cloth over each part of his solid torso. One that no doubt had been worked hard fighting in battle and didn't he just have the body for such things…my, oh my. I felt like whistling as I quickly became fascinated with washing his rock-hard abs. In fact, I must have been getting carried away with this area because the next thing I knew he was clearing his throat and my head snapped up to see that it seemed as if he had been watching me for some time longer than I hoped.

"You cheated," I told him making him shrug his shoulders and then he grabbed me to him, so that he could speak next to my ear in a rumbling voice, thick with need,

"I never spoke of playing fair." Then he locked a fist in my hair and silently demanded a kiss from me, one I was oh so ready to give him.

After this mind consuming kiss of his, he decided enough was enough and he guided me out of the pool so that he could first dry me before drying himself. I was half tempted to ask him why he still had his trousers on but my look must have given my silent question a voice.

"It is safer to trap temptation than to tempt it and with you naked in my arms, then I feared that temptation to be too much to leave in the hands of chance and rightly so, all things considered."

"What do you mean?" I asked timidly, as I clutched the long strip of fabric to my bare body.

"What I mean, my beauty, is that my cock has been as hard as my blade since first getting a mere glimpse of that silky pale skin of yours and the first time I take you and brand myself to your soul, well…it won't be in a place where I wash away the death I brought forth this day or any other," he said casting an arm out to the pool of water we just shared our time in. And regarding what he just said, well…okay, what does a girl say to that I wondered? I mean Jesus, just hearing Draven saying the word 'cock' had me near begging for it, bath or no bath, battle or no battle!

"But I must say, keep looking at me in that lustful way, sweet girl and I fear my restraint will take my reasons and swiftly put an end to such sentiments or gentle notions." Right, well now I completely understood the 'bathing in trousers' thing and I had to say, that even now, it didn't look that 'trapped' as it was, so maybe not pushing him too much was a wiser decision. He cleared his throat once again to gain my attention as I had shamefully been staring at his erection. My head snapped up as if attached to a coil of wire and the look he gave me turned me crimson in a heartbeat.

"Umm…I guess that includes not looking at…um… *it* …I will just, turn this way and give you some privacy," I told him in a high-pitched voice turning around, this action once again, caused a raucous laughter from him.

"Upon my mighty Gods, give me the strength that is needed not to take her right here and now!" I heard him say and I looked back over my shoulder to see him with his head up, looking at the domed ceiling. I couldn't help but love the idea that he was finding it so much of a challenge trying *not* to have sex with me. Well if this was the case then my mission would be over before I knew it. Of course, then came the really hard part and that would be trying to escape my new lover…who also just happened to be my husband but just didn't know it.

Seriously though, I think if I ever sat down with a shrink and talked about my current issues, they would probably be the ones to find themselves needing therapy. Either that or I would find myself in a loony bin quicker than I could say Jiminy Cricket! Well, at least if that ever happened I knew a pretty scary bunch of people who could bust me out of the joint.

That was if Draven ever forgave me for all of this when I got home. I had to admit, it was a depressing thought if he didn't, not considering it seemed my fate had been sealed, starting with a considerably shorter life span. Of course, during all this mental turmoil, I had noticed that two things had happened. The first being that Draven had already dried and dressed, in the loosest sense of the word, as it was simply a loose pair of trousers that tied at one side. The second was that he was now watching me and he looked to be trying to see if it was possible to break into my mind and steal away my thoughts for himself.

"I… don't have anything to wear?" I told him, hopefully letting him know this was the only thing on my mind. Okay, so with the look he gave me it didn't look likely, but a girl could hope.

"Then I am blessed indeed, come," he said walking past me and left me still stood there clutching the material in front of me as if this would help.

"Dr…" I stopped myself instantly from shouting the wrong name aloud but it had already been enough as he quickly came to a standstill. So, I continued out in a rush,

"Don't…don't you think I might catch my death without clothes to cover my cold body?" I asked hoping this was enough to mask the mistake I nearly made…one I had already made once before. In the end, I realised that neither of these were the right thing to say, as I forgot another fundamental rule around Draven, and that was any mention or hint at my death…*ever.*

"Catch your death! Do you really think I would allow such a thing!" he snapped and I reached out to him and said,

"Arsaces, I didn't mean…"

"Never speak to me of your death again, even in jest…do you understand?!" he interrupted angrily and I dropped my outstretched arm with exasperation. I suddenly wanted to cry, I was so tired of carrying such emotions around with me, knowing how close to the mark my comment about death really would be. And the worst of it was that I was about to trick him into giving me that *very death*.

It felt like the most heinous act that a person in love could commit to the keeper of her heart but what other choice was there for me. I did all of this not only to save those that I loved. My family. My friends. And most of all, the man that I loved. The very man who stood opposite me now, demanding that I never die…not to mention a little thing called the entire human race!

So, with nothing else to do in this lonely, ancient land, I walked over to where he had discarded my long, wet tunic and picked it up. Then I wrung it out with my hands and pulled it over my body, to the sound of Draven's displeasure. Then I stormed back over to where he stood, silently fuming at my actions and I walked past him, without a word. I was surprised that he didn't make a move to stop me. I think I even reached the end of the tunnel before I heard the roar of anger, one that made me jump.

"Damn demanding men!" I growled as I stormed through the bedroom and was just walking past the bed when suddenly I was taken off my feet and tackled to the bed.

"Get off me!" I screamed trying to fight them off as my hair had fallen in front of my face as I shook my head.

"Calm yourself woman!" Draven growled at me and as soon as I heard his voice I stilled.

"Arsaces?" Of course, saying his name like this was too late as the door burst open and in ran four soldiers coming to my aid. Oops and in the articulate words of one funny green haired Imp…*my bad.*

Draven was currently on top of me and had me pinned to the bed by shackling my wrists. His head snapped to the men and he snarled looking like a lion about to strike.

"LEAVE OR DIE!" He bellowed at the men and they took the threat as serious as a heart attack. I wasn't sure if one of them hadn't soiled himself whilst running for the door. It was only when Draven heard the door slamming that he stopped growling. And that's when things got too much for me and all this craziness warped into one giant mess and came out of me not as expected. So, instead of bursting into uncontrollable tears, I burst into uncontrollable laughter.

I just couldn't help it. The sight of those poor men's faces when finding their King trying to wrestle with a wet soggy woman on his bed and god only knows what terrible things they thought. But I doubt that any thought was how the King's new concubine had been having a hissy fit over not being given dry clothes to wear. For starters, I doubt a man like Draven, being King and handsome would have had to have forced anyone into his bed!

"Nāzanin?" Draven said my name, no doubt in question to my sanity.

"I am sorry, just…just give me…me a minute." I told him in between laughing and finding it difficult to try and form words.

"You find this funny?" he asked incredulously. This question managed to sober me somewhat, enough to at least try and keep a straight face and say,

"Umm…no?" I said questioning it and hoping at any minute he too would break out into at least a smile.

"This is not funny," he told me sternly and I rolled my lips and shook my head, trying to be serious as well, telling him I agreed. He didn't look convinced at my attempt. Finally, I could see he was close to breaking his steely reserve and any minute I would get my way…I would get a smile.

"Nāzanin," he said my name as a warning but there was little strength behind it, so I decided to test my theory by raising myself up a little so that I could whisper over his lips,

"It was a little funny." Then I made my own little growly noise and playfully licked his nose. Well seriously anyone would have believed I had done something as shocking as paint his face as a fairy princess in his sleep. He shifted back as if I had stung him and the smile I gave him was in reaction to the priceless look he was giving me. He was stunned. Then he did something that was so out of character I was the one left speechless.

"You want to see something funny, my little captive?"

He leaned down close and whispered my only warning…

"I will show you something funny."

CHAPTER SIX

ARSACES

GIFT FROM THE GODS

By the Gods above and below, I felt as though I would soon burst like the turbulent sandstorms that cut across my land, with too many emotions to handle all at once. For she was the very meaning of heavenly perfection and I found myself questioning how the Gods could have known where my true tastes in women lay?

For the last place they were to be found was in my harem, or what my sweet one had named, 'a hall full of beauties'. Although I must confess, my favourite yet spoken from her lips... 'Happy little virgins waiting to be plucked by their King'. I had very nearly found a fist in my mouth just to stop myself from laughing at her. She was the funniest person I had ever encountered and I found myself captivated by her unusual behaviour at such things. And looking down at the beauty in my grasp, it was proven that now was no different.

I must have looked as though I had lost my senses when she had playfully challenged me, adding to this a cute little growl and a naughty lick of my nose, like some unruly pet of mine. Mmm, my Demon certainly liked the idea of that and I had to agree to the appeal of it myself. Now if I could only get away with placing a gold collar around her neck with a chain attached, one that would forever be wrapped firmly around my fist. Even for me, that was a barbaric thought indeed, but one it seemed wouldn't leave me, and the heavy weight of my cock was testament to that.

So, with the hard task of putting these fantasies aside for now, I contented myself with the delicious sight in front of me, just begging to be tortured and I knew just how to accomplish such a mission. But like any good King, I gave her a warning, one she could be ready for.

"You want to see something funny, my little captive?" I told her, leaning down close, to whisper the rest of my sentence…

"I will show you something funny." And as I thought it would be, it was worth every word spoken, for the reaction she granted me was another unveiling of a piece of her soul. Her beautiful eyes widened in surprise reminding me of staring into that of a blue moon on nights spent in solitude upon my private roof terrace. No one was permitted to enter that space and unless you had the wings of my kind, then a mortal would have to be out of their wits to try and climb it. Of course, my own kind would not dare try as their fear of my wrath outweighed that of their curiosity. But now, with this sweet soul captured in my hands, then I must confess to finding myself eager to share it with her, as I had with no other.

But not yet, for I needed to be satisfied that my little lamb was telling me the truth of how she came to be in my grasp. For even though I did not doubt her feelings for me, as she gave so much of herself away freely, that my annoyance at not being able to read her mind rarely vexed me. But this wasn't my main concern. What was, however, was why she would feel the need to lie in the first place about where she came from?

I must confess my main fear in all these mysteries, was that whatever it maybe, it would only result in her trying to leave. For this I had naturally taken the necessary precautions and in doing so, she would find it a rare occurrence not being by my side for the foreseeable future. I tried to tell myself that this was my only reason for such possessive behaviour but in truth, I found the thought of being without her a cruel and painful notion. One I could not bear thinking about unless I had need to call forth my Demon's rage. A Demon that was living both close to the edge and biting at my vessel's surface since our little lamb had stepped into my blade.

At first, I battled these feelings like no other could claim. I knew what was right by my people but I was ready to damn it all to Hell just to have her and make her mine, Fates be sacrificed. But when I then found her to be my Electus, something I'd suspected all along but with little understanding as to why, I knew the true meaning of this. I knew of the rare gift bestowed and it was one such that I would not be foolish enough to let slip through my fingers and out of my sight.

Which was why my rash and impulsive actions had contradicted my past decisions when it came to the women in my harem. But this little lamb was different and had been from the start. I almost smirked thinking back to our first meeting and how she had handled the experience.

I knew from the very first moment I saw her that she was not as the rest. The way she tried to look nervously down at my blade, her hands trembling at her sides and large eyes looking at me as though she knew me. Yet despite all her fears, she still held her head high as though in that single moment in time, she knew that if she were to find death that day, then she would welcome it by my hand.

I believe my fascination with her stemmed solely from that point alone and quickly grew out of control, as though each branch was wrapping around my heart and pulling me under her spell. I confess, it even crossed my mind that sorcery was involved and had me questioning my sanity as to how this could have happened so fast. Which is one of my reasons for teasing her as such, another reaction I enjoyed greatly.

But then she spoke my name and I knew I was lost, in both her eyes and her luring voice. After that my blade had simply remained at her throat, no longer a threat to her life, but only as a means at keeping her still and from running from me. Pushing back her hood and finally revealing the beauty I knew I would find, was near blinding and a proven reason why I never allowed pale, golden haired beauties in my harem. The day I received word from the Oracle of Delphi telling me of the gift the Gods would bestow on me, the only vision given was whispers from above of the Golden Fleece that would follow her every step. I never understood it fully, knowing this could also mean so many things.

It was in fact, my own sister who had first given me the notion that it was most likely in reference to her hair. An idea that quickly seeped into obsession and it took me all but half a day to make the decision to have all golden-haired girls removed from the palace. And once I saw her, I knew I had been right in doing so, and the smug look I gave her was most likely taken for amusement at seeing her flinch when I touched her. Of course, when I had caught sight of her injuries, I quickly had to bite back the rage, watching her swallowing hard and making me fearful of the blade I still held at her slim, pale neck.

Asking her name was spoken as such that it was certain to

cast doubt in her mind as to my intentions. But she would soon find that my actions towards her would be far from harmful, for I was already looking for the reasons I could have her taken to my room. A private space so that this meeting was not being witnessed by my mortal court and I could finally get this damaged little lamb of mine…*alone*.

But this moment was stolen from me by that fat, pompous mortal Narseh, one I had witnessed who had caused the whole scene by his arrogant ego. To speak the truth, finding the first action committed by my Electus was her striking a man with enough force to bloody his face… well then, I shouldn't have been surprised. No, not given her nature, she would need to be with a King of my world, along with one of her own. The only thing that kept my wrath firmly under a horse's hoof, was that I didn't want to scare her with witnessing blood spilt by my blade so soon.

So instead, I used the opportunity to ease her fears by condemning the man who caused her current dilemma, letting her know indirectly, who I thought was rightly to blame. I will never forget her next words spoken to me, trying to prompt from me what her next move should be. It was the first time I had wanted to burst into laughter around her and the delightful knowledge was utterly heart-warming.

However, instead of divulging in the pleasure of continually teasing her, I put her worried little mind out of discomfort by whispering my reply to her. But even in this I was not to be disappointed as once again, she needed my guidance in something as simple as speaking his name.

Well I knew in this moment two things, one, she was clearly not of this land and the second was the strange urge to not only protect her body but also her mind. I wanted to help her. I had even felt compelled to do so, this along with knowing her name.

Something that felt like a gift in itself when she told me she didn't remember it, for here was my opportunity to take her as I saw fit…until Ranka stepped forward and spoke up for the girl. So, I took in that moment what I could, as I listened to my second in command speak of the mysterious discovery of the girl, one who unknowingly became mine when she first set foot in my palace. Lifting my hand to her face I felt at least comforted in the knowledge in doing so that I didn't scare her, for she did not flinch.

Even when letting my voice snap, lashing out when asking Ranka of the meaning for her damaged, delicate skin, she stood still for me. I found myself at least hoping there was someone left for me to torture for the fatal offense in touching her. I would have turned murderous had it not been an overriding emotion that took hold of me after Ranka's words…for she had fought back? This little lamb of mine had tried to defend herself the best way she could. Because of this I was quickly filled with admiration, respect, and pride of the likes I had never known. In that moment, I had never hated my duty, or felt the string of bitterness that I was burdened with when being King, as I knew for the first time, I could not just do as I pleased.

I hadn't been lying to Nāzanin when I spoke of being a selfish being that always got their way and nor was I ever sorry for such things. But this time I could not simply pick her up and take her as I would have liked. No, I knew to do such would have put her in more danger and until I could ensure her safety, then I would simply have to bide my time. A time that only lasted until the fading of the sun, for I found my footsteps cutting across my palace and taking me to only one place…*my mortal harem*.

I even recalled chuckling on the way there, just thinking back to the way that Ranka had to remind her of royal etiquette when calling me 'her King'. I didn't know how I hadn't laughed aloud at the time but this was quickly dampened when being approached about my current head concubine. I had nearly snarled at her servant girl for daring to speak of another female in the presence of my new-found treasure but then something curious happened. For my little lamb didn't yet know it, but her expressive eyes gave her away even when her mind frustratingly denied me the pleasure…*she was jealous.*

I could barely comprehend my own reactions to seeing this and asked myself many times, why I relished the idea beyond control. Which, shamefully I will admit, became the reason I was cruel enough not to give the servant my answer, one which would no doubt have enraged the spoilt hellion, Stateira. One who I only made my head concubine at the time as I knew such a strong character would no doubt keep order in a place I could not. No, for keeping my eye on the hierarchy of my harem was not something I deemed important enough for my time, so swiftly passed this on to another I deemed fit. But for once, I felt myself second guessing my past decisions the moment Ranka told me of Stateira's venomous reaction to seeing my Electus.

She felt threatened, it was clear and it was swiftly after this that I announced the next 'Choosing' to be within three days. This no doubt stirred the pot of gossip into a frenzy within the palace, as most had witnessed my first encounter with the golden-haired beauty. The first one to be seen for many mortal lifetimes.

Next was to issue Ranka a silent but firm order in which to protect the girl with her life and situate her in my harem for the time being, an order only issued in her mind. But I found I could not resist one more, little spoken promise to the sweet girl next to me, for her to stay out of trouble. Something she had frustratingly still failed to do since she first entered my kingdom I might add.

Which brought me back to the now and the next lot of

trouble she was in, this time at the hands of her King. Looking down at her now waiting with trepidation and panting, with her heart beating wildly in her chest. It was exquisite torture, one only made better when I got to tease my fingers along her soft sensitive skin. So, with that ideal set firmly in my mind, I began to gather up the damp fabric in my hands. I had wanted to rip the offending item from her body, for not only did it conceal her from me, but it was cold and wet, from her stubborn choice to wear it. Then hearing the way she spoke about 'catching her death', an offending quip, I had never heard before… well then, even said in jest I was murderously mad. So much so, I felt it best to remain silent as I watched her reactions after receiving my serious threat about speaking of such things again to me.

At the time, I found I could only stand there in some outwitted manner, watching her and finding it almost impossible to read what she was thinking. These were the utterly frustrating times that I found were near unbearable.

It was the hidden looks she expressed that told me enough to know something important was passing through her mind, but she would quickly lock it down before allowing me even a glimpse. So many times I had tried to force myself inside there but without success in the battle I had with her mind, as her strength in such things was astounding.

Staggering even, when I thought back to seeing the power she possessed when facing Pertinax, having never believed something like it possible. I would have been more inclined to believe it was a dream than the Hellish reality it had been. But then she spoke those words, declaring herself as the Electus and all thoughts turned to that of the Heaven half of my soul was branded too.

"You tease me," she said with lids heavy with the obvious lust I knew she felt for me. Just hearing her sweet, breathy moans building as she chased the storm of her release was enough to tell me that she was close to begging me for more. Something I was foolishly breaking my control over and all because when I took her I wanted nothing between us. Which included the web of lies which she continued to spin. But each time I tried to force myself the simple task, I would find it felt like the hardest. Because I feared she would try and run from me and I wanted her addiction to match that of my own before I could allow such a risk.

So, instead of doing what my Demon side wanted of me, which was to find the chains I had made specially for her, and shackle her to my bed refusing her to leave. Not until I got my answers so that I could finally sink myself into her. Well until then I was left trying to fill her heart, like I had told her I would. And this started with exploring one of the new discoveries I had made when first seeking her out in my harem.

"Wait, no…no…please…oh…" She started to moan and writhe beneath me as I dragged my fingertips softly up the side of her body, grazing her ribs as I had done that night in her small allocated alcove.

Thankfully this time my displeasure at seeing them bound in flax linen was overridden by the sight of her pale skin, no longer marked by her brutal attack. I hated that I couldn't have just healed her as I wanted to. I almost laughed at her defiance when disagreeing with Parmida on it taking a month before she was ready for my bed. I was far beyond pleased that she, as I, didn't want to wait for such a time and recalling that night, she was even saddened when I told her I had to leave. And I in turn warned her of a future she couldn't have foreseen, one that disappointingly, I was yet to make come to pass. But at the very least, it was certainly a start with where I had her now. I smirked down at her recalling my very words spoken…

'I can see that your hidden defiance will amuse me greatly and your reluctance to see me go is even more pleasing, but be warned my little beauty…once I have you in my bed, I may not want to let you out of it again.'

And above all…

I was a King of his word.

CHAPTER SEVEN

NĀZANIN

FINDING WEAK SPOTS

At first, I wondered what Draven was up to because he looked so heavy in thought, as if he was trying to decide what my punishment would be. But then I felt his hand gathering up my wet kaftan in his hands and I knew where this was heading. Especially when he had it pulled up so that it was all bunched up under my breasts. At one point, I thought he was going to rip the thing in half and have done with it, but then he seemed to think better of the action. I had to wonder if the reason for this was trying not to scare me and instead show me how gentle he could be after his outburst and tackling me unceremoniously to the bed. It was if he had seen me walking past and thought I was trying to leave, as the action seemed to be done out of panic.

But now, well he must have remembered my reaction to

when he touched my bandaged ribs back in the harem. And this was to be his revenge, because he started to trace his fingers along my sides.

"Wait, no…no…please…oh…" I started begging the second he started tickling me and I was soon lost to a fit of giggles. I started kicking out my legs, making him hook his foot over one to hold me down, as he was still straddling my body. Damn him but thanks to those big hands of his, he easily held me pinned to the bed with only one hand.

I could barely take in the look of wonder he gave me with thrashing my head around in some mad attempt at controlling the laughter. He was merciless with his fingers and the softer he touched me the more it made me howl with shrieks of joyful chuckles. But then he got closer to my armpit and I was lost in the worst way possible for someone trying to act sexy…*lost to my inner piggy*.

I snorted!

He froze.

I blushed.

Just as I turned a very unhealthy shade of crimson and slowly died of shame it made it all worse, when he suddenly threw his head back and laughed, loud, long and hard.

"Heavens above my sweetest one, for that was an adorable little sound you just made!" he told me still chuckling as if he couldn't help it. I tried to give him my best 'I am not impressed face' but this he seemed to find just as amusing, as once again he was laughing down at me.

"Yeah, yeah, I know…very funny Mr, now time to get off me," I told him exasperated and he smirked at me before saying,

"That is not going to happen little one, for I find myself greatly entertained and wish to hear more." Then he started once again and he was only satisfied when I had tears in my eyes and had snorted six more times. After this, he must have realised my need to breathe more freely, so finally took pity on me. I had to say it was the most fun I'd had in this time so far. It felt just like old times, between Draven and myself back at Afterlife… or was it new times?

"See, I told you it was a little funny," I told him once he had released my wrists and had joined me, lying by my side on the bed. We were both lay flat and looking up to the elaborately painted ceiling above that was concaved into a star design. However, my saying this prompted him to move. He turned on his side to look down at me and he started running his fingertip down my cheek in a tender show of affection.

"There is only one bright light in my life that I find funny and I just discovered she can even make animal noises, something to adore and become addicted to," he told me making me blush and roll my eyes in feigned annoyance. He pulled back a little and said,

"And what of that look, for it puzzles me greatly." Oh crikey, I guess he didn't get many people rolling their eyes at him.

"Don't worry about it, big guy," I said patting him on the arm before moving to sit up and pulling my kaftan down at the same time. The growl I heard made me smile before it soon turned into laughter when I looked back over my shoulder and saw his face. Now he looked annoyed and I couldn't help but find the humour in it. It was nice to finally be able to tease *him* for a change. His eyes softened when he saw that I was just being playful and I knew he was finding this difficult. After all, he had probably never encountered anyone like me before, so I knew I had to go easy on him.

"I jest with you," I told him making him grin.

"You will keep me on my toes, of that I can be certain," he told me and I wanted to say, 'boy, you have no idea!' But thankfully I engaged my filter. I was about to speak when the next embarrassing human trait beat me to it. My stomach rumbled, making me giggle when his eyes went wide.

"By the Gods! I must feed you!" he shouted, suddenly getting from the bed as though he had just committed a sin by lying there.

"Arsaces, it's fine, I'm…" I told him but he suddenly seemed really angry at himself. He sliced a hand through the air to cut me off before saying,

"It is not acceptable! You are mortal and I have not taken such into account. I need to take great care, as being around you renders me mindless to such things as your basic needs," he told me and I sighed before shifting off the bed and approaching him. Then without warning him of my actions, I wrapped my arms around his waist and hugged him to me, taking him completely off guard. I felt him first stiffen in my hold before he took a deep breath, releasing it on a sigh before relaxing into me.

"I am quite capable of requesting such things for myself, so the fault is not solely yours to bear. After all, I have been taking care of this mortal body a lot longer than you, so I have no excuse only for it to be your own…"

"What do you mean little one?" he asked me, looking down and bringing my chin up so that he could see my eyes.

"That you distract me from such things, just as I do you." I told him and the grin I received because of it was almost blindingly handsome.

"This pleases me to hear sweetest one, but the truth remains that the fault is still mine," he told me and I felt myself frown as I asked,

"Why?" He gave me a small smile as he took in my frown

BLOOD OF THE INFINITY WAR

and reached up to smooth the line in between my eyebrows with his thumb before answering me,

"Because, little lamb of mine, your body is no longer your responsibility, for it is mine and trust me when I tell you that *I take good care of what I own,*" he whispered this last part as he tipped my head back so he could end his promise with a kiss.

After this he decided to make it his new mission to prove what he told me, starting with getting me out of my wet clothes. This time he did rip them off me and by the time I was shrieking in surprise, he had picked me up and had me lay back on the bed, covered and warm. I looked to the windows to see that it was getting dark and now not only was I thirsty beyond belief, I was also starving and dying for a pee. Three things around Draven that I didn't ever want to admit.

"I will be back in a moment," he told me and I sat up, holding the covers to my naked chest and asked,

"Why? Where are you going?" Once again, he seemed pleased by the needy tone in my voice, and smiled because of it before telling me,

"I need to assign you a new hand servant and request that some food be brought." At this I panicked and he saw it, for he raised an eyebrow at me.

"There is something wrong?"

"I…um…it's just…" I didn't know how to say this without sounding whiney.

"Speak it my love and if it is in my power to give you, then it shall be yours," he said and I wanted to cock my head to the side and say 'aww' but thankfully didn't.

"Can Pip be my hand servant?" Okay, so from his expression this seemed to be one of those things he *didn't want* to give. Something he confirmed when he snapped out the question,

"The Imp!?" At this I forgot about my nakedness and dropped the covers to cross my arms making his gaze turn purple and intense.

"And what is that supposed to mean?" I demanded getting huffy. Of course, his thoughts were somewhere else, like most men when presented with a glimpse of bare breasts.

"Arsaces, focus." I told him catching him out and he grinned before looking at me and saying,

"I don't think that is possible when presented with such bountiful fruit for me to taste." I tried not to laugh as I recovered my breasts making him groan aloud, giving me cause to laugh louder this time.

"Can we get back to my request now?"

"I do not trust her," he told me calmly and at this my mouth dropped open in shock.

"You mean you don't trust someone who has saved my life countless times and would die for me…" I asked but then before he could answer I carried on, too far gone in my argument of standing up for my friend.

"…someone who has only ever aided me in trying to *find you*, going to extreme lengths as to leave her husband for such a journey?"

"Well I…" he started to say and I interrupted again,

"…Someone who I love and care for like a sister and who brings me such joy in my life, that I would forever feel an empty hole in my heart if she was ever taken from it…you mean that Imp?!" I asked finally finishing, making Draven look as though I had just cast aside a dog to sit in the rain outside for peeing on the couch. Something I should mention I would never do, because I loved dogs but Draven…well yeah, if he was 'verbally peeing on my Pip'!

Now if there was ever a time to see a mighty King looking sheepish and wishing nothing more than to take back the last few minutes of his own stupidity, then that time was now. Draven released a big sigh and then decided the best course of action was the one most men took…eat some damn humble pie and grovel. Something that I could honestly say, was a first for this man.

"Forgive me, for I knew not the level of loyalty given by such a creature," he told me and I screeched,

"Creature?!" This was when he realised his mistake and rectified it immediately, no doubt wondering where his royal status had run off to in dealing with me.

"Being, but naturally I meant *'being'*. But now I know that I have nothing to fear from such a noble…*being*…then I will permit such a union," he said carefully, making me roll my lips trying to hold in the winning smile I felt peeking out, I nodded and said.

"And I thank you greatly for it, *My King."* I said granting him some of his royal ego back, one he smirked at hearing. Then he did something really out of character for him. Teasing me he folded an arm to his waist and bowed low before saying,

"But of course, *my lady."* I burst out laughing and said,

"Can I ask for one more thing?" Then when I heard him groan I knew it was another tease and I think in that strange moment, I fell in love with him even that little bit more. Something I didn't think possible, with the amount of love I already had for him.

"I now find myself praying to the Gods that your request is for the entirety of my treasury, for I fear for anything else," he joked and I burst out laughing and said,

"You made a joke...A jest…and it was funny!" I added as he obviously didn't understand the word joke.

"What can I confess, other than you must be using your

sorcery on me, for I believe it has never happened before you." I laughed again and this time bit my lip.

"Have pity on your King sweet one, and ask it of me," he told me still teasing and I suddenly wished I wasn't human, so I didn't need simple things like food to stay alive. That way we could continue this playful time on the bed together like before. But before my stomach could rumble again and make him feel guilty, I put him out of his misery and said,

"I would like a kiss before you leave me." Now this really had him smiling and I loved seeing his eyes sink to purple depths because of it.

"Then lucky for me there is little I can deny you, for I will gain great pleasure in your request this time," he said before walking over and giving me what I wanted. Something that happily took longer than I expected it to.

It was nice to see that he was always reluctant to leave me and this kiss was no different. But in the end, it was once again my stomach reminding him of his current task and he walked away cursing himself, muttering about being rendered mindless once more.

I had chuckled to myself once the door was closed. I did however feel for the poor soldiers that no doubt received his wrath on their impulsive actions earlier. I had now wished my request had been to take it easy on them but then again, I knew there was only so much Draven could take and thought it not wise to push him too hard, too soon. And I very much doubted hearing me advising him against how he saw fit to run his kingdom was the best way. After all, I had made that mistake once before, after discovering his temple and angry Draven from this time was far scarier than the one I knew how to tame back in my own time.

"Well hello Toot ta, ta, tit buddy." Pip said happily when skipping into the room.

"That's a long-winded nickname, even for you Pipperlicious." I told her making her laugh.

"Yeah well you are naked, so if the panties fit," she replied winking at me.

"So, juice on the Parthian grapevine is I have just been appointed your super, uber bit'ach hand servant." I smiled and said,

"Well I don't know, I was thinking about conducting interviews but hey, you came in here without brandishing a weapon at me and trying to kill, maim and slash, so… huh, would you look at that, I think you got the job." At this she did a power pull in the air and said,

"YESSS!" making me laugh again.

"Well, I must say that your powers of persuasion are second to none, for not only did you have the King *request* I be your new servant, but I also received a hint of a smile and a royal thanks for keeping your Electus ass, sweet and safe. I think I nearly wept, I will tell ya!" At this I gave her a beaming smile. He had thanked her?

"Wow happy much? Jeez if I knew it made you this happy I would tell you more often how Adam always thanks me for steak and blowjob Thursdays, 'cause see I can do this thing with my piercing and…"

"LALALA Can't hear you!" I said slapping my hands to my ears like I usually did around Pip. After all, it was our favourite pastime.

"Right, so where do we start…oh yes, you go do your business in that pot over there and I will get some clothes. Kingy man said he had some made for you and where are…ah over here," she said, all the while looking around the room until finding a huge chest. Meanwhile I was still stuck on 'doing my business' in a damn pot!

"I can't do that!"

"Well good luck with peeing out the window then, because trust me on this, unless you're a dude with a big dick, then it don't work so well…even if you're a squirter…if you catch my drift."

"Ewww Squeak, way too much info on that one…jeez." This made her chuckle as she hunched over the chest hunting for fabric treasure. I took a moment to take in her own outfit and smirked when I saw her all in black and once again looking some kind of ancient ninja. It must have really pained her to have to dress this way as I don't think I had ever seen her in anything that could be classed as plain, back in our own time.

She even wore a turban style scarf, hiding all her green hair from view, because I doubted she would have been able to explain that one to Draven. This also went for her colourful tattoos, but at least her piercings were safe, as apparently that was something practiced in some tribes for thousands of years. Plus, she said something about just making her look harder, for only warriors did this as a sign of their strength. Well either way, I was just happy neither of her body jewellery had things like smiley faces on it or candy skulls, as she had swapped them for plain ones before we left. I even bet my thirteen- year old self's sticker collection that she had to go out and buy these specially, as Pip didn't own 'Plain' anything!

"Look if you have pee stage fright, then just take it behind that little lattice screen thingy," she told me and before my bladder thought to burst I did as she told me.

"How you doing back there?" she asked and I groaned,

"Oh, just peachy!" She started laughing and then stopped abruptly, so I added,

"Let's just say I am not a natural born squatter and leave it at that." And then I heard her burst into a fit of giggles, followed by a very male sounding, clearing of someone's throat.

"Oh Gods…please don't let it be true." I whispered looking

up and praying hard enough to make my forehead veins bulge. But this only managed to get me confirmation that yes, Draven had come back and in true Keira fashion, at the worst possible moment. Oh yeah, say good bye to that sexy Kaz, because it didn't just get up and fly away. Oh no, it just got shot out of a damn cannon and exploded mid-air into a 'poof' of feathers!

He cleared his throat, obviously trying to hide a laugh and said to Pip,

"I will wait for her out here." Pip laughed once and said,

"Yeah good plan that, My Lord." Making him cough back another laugh. The next thing I knew I had Pip popping her head around the screen, look down at me and saying,

"Well that went well I think." I growled and snatched the cloth from her so that I could wipe my embarrassed lady bits.

"Oh yeah, cause hearing me say that I am not a natural born squatter, *is a sure way to get him to have sex with me!"* I hissed this last part making her chuckle again and then said,

"Well just look at this way Tootie Pants, if he can overlook the fact that you suck at squatting on the pisser, then let's just call him a keeper and try and wow him with just the sucking part."

"Pip!" I screeched and said,

"Okay, don't get your pubes in a dreadlock! Jeez, what is it with you and blowjobs anyway?!" she said and I groaned, biting my lip. After I had finished and grabbed the material that she hung over the screen, I decided to come clean.

"I...I'm not very good at them, okay." I told her honestly. It was at this point that I had sort of expected her to start laughing but it was surprisingly quiet back there, so I just prayed that Draven hadn't decided to make another appearance, or I think I would have died, prophecy or no damn prophecy!

"Umm...Pip?" I said after pulling the top part of my outfit over my arms, barely taking notice of it other than seeing it was peach colour…cute Pip, trust her to take my 'Peachy' comment and make it an outfit choice.

"I'm thinking," she told me and I had to ask,

"About what?" I would have been lying if I didn't say that her answer filled me with dread,

"About where we can find a banana." At this I actually stopped midway trying to pull up my harem pants and muttered, 'oh God'.

"Look I know he is all powerful up there Toots, but in this, I really don't think he can help you," she said on a chuckle and I rolled my eyes as I tried to squeeze myself into the little bolero jacket, hooking the hidden clasps, after almost punching my breasts into it. Well, at least walking around the palace without a bra wasn't a problem as nothing said sexy like two watermelons in a pair of tights…*not.*

After this I stepped out and let Pip sit my ass on the bed so that she could attack my hair with a comb and believe me when I said, that with my big blonde mop, then it took some time. In the end, she growled in frustration and finished it off by plaiting it to the side after slamming the comb down on the bed with a huff. Welcome to my world I thought with a smirk.

"I know what you're thinking missy and when we get your ass back then I am buying your wavy butt some straighteners!" She vowed making me giggle. Thankfully, after spending most of the day naked, I was finally dressed and ready to be fed. Which I also almost thanked the Gods for as before long I was close to seeing Pip as a cartoon cooked chicken.

So, I took a deep breath, pulled up my big girl ancient belly dancing pants and walked into the sunken living space to find Draven there waiting for me. My eyes found his heated ones, as he looked me up and down with obvious arousal depicted in his flaming purple gaze. But then this was when it went all to Hell and back as I saw who else was in the room with us.

The person he had been speaking with before I had entered and it just so happened to be the only other person, not part of our time travelling family, who knew the truth about where we had come from.

I felt Pip stiffen next to me as one name escaped my lips…

"Lucius."

CHAPTER EIGHT

WRAPPING UP DEMANDS

When I walked into the room I saw Draven sat back casually, now dressed in a long sleeveless tunic that was open at the front, showing off his divine torso underneath. It was black with round gold symbols centred between two rows of thorns that framed the edges of his jacket style tunic. The sight of him was drool worthy, with his soft loose pants that tied to the side, ones I knew that all it would take was one pull so that one of my favourite parts of him would be free to come out and play.

But none of this was enough to take away the sight of him talking to Lucius who was sat in a seat opposite. Something that was the very last thing I had both wanted or expected. In fact, I had been in two minds whether to just look up at the Gods and shout 'oh come on!'

I heard Pip clear her throat next to me and all but nudge me into action as I had just stopped dead making my inner turmoil as about as obvious as neon flashing lights above my head screaming 'liar'. Draven had raised an eyebrow at me and Lucius…well Lucius just looked like he had found a tasty new treat to toy with. Damn him and his sexy ancient assassin ass!

"Nāzanin? Are you unwell?" Draven asked and Pip hissed next to me and said,

"Yes Nāzanin, are you well?" No doubt trying to prompt something from me, say a simple action of moving my lips, legs, arms…anything so long as it was something! Well, okay I think if I had broken out into the funky chicken dance then there might have been a few awkward questions thrown my way. But Jesus on a slice of toast! I think even then it would have been easier to answer than the time travelling shit storm headed my way.

"Umm…yes, sorry, I was…just…yes." I mumbled making Pip whisper,

"Smooth" next to me before walking past. I almost growled at her aloud, wondering when that had become a common response of mine. Talk about Supernatural Kings rubbing off on you or what!

"Come sit, little lamb," Draven said softly and Lucius shot him a look as if to say, 'Who the Hell are you and what have you done with my Warrior King?' I swallowed hard before doing as he asked. I was about to sit next to him when this obviously was not enough. He gripped my hips and guided me down to the space in between his legs, making me shiver with the feel of his fingers touching my bare flesh.

The wide waistband on my trousers was made thick and stiff by the spun gold flowers running down the centre of a pretty border. It lay flat and low against my hips, meaning that all of my belly was on show. The little peach jacket only fastened over my bust and stopped below it. So, it meant that when looking out over the feast in front of us that had been placed on the little table, I was going to have to be careful not to overdo it, as a little pot belly wasn't going to look good in this outfit… damn I missed my jeans.

In my stupidity, I suddenly felt like looking up at Lucius and saying, 'Look familiar?' as Draven pulled me back against him. Thankfully, I swallowed the suicidal urge and squashed down all memories of my time in Lucius' hidden German Castle.

Meanwhile, once Draven had me positioned how he wanted me, he reached forward to grab a gold cup that had two faces moulded either side. It was in this moment that I said the first thing that came to mind and blurted out,

"Oh, is that the God Janus?" I then looked to Pip who was walking to the door and had actually stopped to smack her hand on her forehead. Draven tensed behind me as I did the same thing. Lucius on the other hand seemed to be taking note of everything with extreme interest.

"You know of this Roman God?" he asked in such a way that I knew I shouldn't and I wanted to sigh, roll my eyes and then confess everything. I looked for a fleeting moment towards Lucius in panic as if waiting for him to say something that would mean the point of no return for us all…literally! Because after Draven found out about how I came to be here, then there was no way we would ever make it back. And realistically, all I had to look forward to was a life of imprisonment and brushing my teeth with a damn twig!

But this was when he shocked me and in true Lucius style, he casually leaned back and said coolly,

"I believe that is my doing Arsaces, for she is a curious little thing indeed." Hearing this I was suddenly glad that Draven couldn't see my face as I was still facing Lucius, because my mouth dropped. Lucius looked to be fighting off a grin at my reaction and I only snapped out of it when Draven spoke.

"Is that so? Umm, I am yet to encounter her questioning

mind, for I must confess to being the one asking most of the questions so far." Okay, so I knew this was a dig and I rolled my eyes knowing he couldn't see me. However, I did forget the big ass cocky Vamp who could. His eyes flashed crimson for a mere second as Draven looked down at me to hand me his drink.

"Try some, I can assure you that you won't find a better wine," he told me and I took it from him, soon finding myself almost downing the whole thing. I felt him chuckling behind me as Lucius commented,

"Upon my blade Arsaces, you will have your hands full indeed if you don't limit her cup."

"Thirsty perhaps?" Draven said laughing and taking the cup from me. I cleared my throat and said,

"Umm…just a little." Needless to say, this made him chuckle again.

"Now you need to eat, for I find myself partial to these enticing curves of yours, ones I intend to keep on this body of mine," Draven said, running the back of his fingers down the side of my breast. I felt my cheeks flame and looked to Lucius who was watching us with a steely gaze. But then Draven brushed some escaping wisps of my hair back to the side it was plaited and started to kiss my neck softly. I don't know why but I couldn't take my eyes off Lucius, who in turn couldn't keep his intense gaze from us. I bit my lip and saw him grip his own cup so hard, it started to disfigure the design, leaving an immortal hand print.

Then suddenly he downed that last of his drink and stood, as if he could stand it no longer. I had to ask myself what was going on with him?

"You take your leave so soon, Septimus?" Draven asked finally lifting his head from my neck and I had to wonder if this little show he put on wasn't made in the way of a King staking his claim. I mean, I knew that even the Draven of my own time cared little for what he did to me in public, or making it known to all how he cared for me, with his actions. But this just felt…*different*. Could it be since seeing me giving him my blood to save his life? Had he seen how I cared for him and for a life I had for all intents and purposes, not known for that long?

"I fear I must." Draven tensed a hand possessively at my hip and I knew he had taken this meaning as what it had sounded like. Lucius couldn't stand it any longer. But then he finally relaxed when Lucius added,

"There is still much to be done, even as the Roman army retreats…what is left of them." Draven huffed and said,

"That mortal empire will never learn, for by the time they make it to my lands, they are very near spent even before the battle begins. No, but you are right, you must go and find what their next move shall be."

"For whatever it shall be, I doubt it will be soon in coming, for they now have a new ruler to find," Lucius stated and this was when Draven made a sound in the back of his throat, as if he had just thought of something.

"And so they shall."

"My Lord?" Lucius asked as if bracing himself for it. Then Draven dropped a 'Emperor' sized bombshell.

"You shall become Emperor of Rome," he stated and I gasped, displaying the right reaction to such news, one I would have thought should have also come from Lucius. However, he simply folded his arms and looked to his King with slight amusement.

"I would enquire as to why, but I think I know," he said nodding down to me, but with a small shake of his head, Draven silently told him not to go there, which of course, had me questioning 'why' myself.

"And you are sure of this outcome?" Lucius asked and Draven laughed once and said,

"You advanced through the *cursus honorum*, the customary succession of offices and under the reigns of Marcus Aurelius and Commodus. If that is not enough to seize power then finding yourself with the biggest army most certainly will Septimus, they know this and will accept your rule without question," Draven told him and I was surprised to see Lucius was being reluctant.

"And this is your will, Arsaces?" he asked seemingly dejected and I had to wonder why…he was after all being given the chance of his own kingdom and be ruler.

"That it is my friend, for you know of my plans and that the Gods' decision, for our Supernatural rule over the Mortal world is quickly coming to an end…this way, when the time comes, it will come to pass with less bloodshed coating the life of innocents." Hearing this had me stiffening in his hold and he started to whisper in my ear,

"Ssshh, calm for me." I think he realised that he had shocked me with his plans and also speaking of the bloodshed of mortals.

"You believe the time to be near?" Lucius asked finally seeming shocked by this but even then, it was said with a steely reserve.

"We are all but puppets of the Gods Septimus, for this you know more than most." Now this reply was one that had Lucius reacting and for some reason he looked at me as if trying to find evidence if I knew of his past. I held my lip firmly in my teeth at the thought of what torture he went through, when he himself was but a mortal man.

I knew I had made my mistake, when his eyes turned hard and cold. He had seen for himself that I knew and boy, he did not like it! He looked so tense he was close to breaking something and I could only hope that deep down he wouldn't let that something be me. Okay, so it was at this moment that I wanted to point out that *I did* save his life, so, surely, he could cut me some slack…right?

"Fine," Lucius snapped making Draven raise his head and I was sure he wouldn't have let this snippy one worded answer go without reprimand. Which is when he surprised me and I realised something I never would have thought before…Draven loved Lucius like a brother and therefore treated him as such. I knew this when he started laughing heartily at my back before saying,

"Come now, my friend, is what I ask of you really so distasteful?"

"I am an assassin, Arsaces, not an autocratic Emperor of Mortals." Ah, so this was his problem, because I knew in about 2000 years he was going to feel very different about being a ruler over his own domain. No, it wasn't the ruling he had a problem with, it was *who*. I couldn't say that I blamed him all things considered. I remember hating Vampires myself after a certain blonde hunk had invaded my life and kidnapped me. Okay, so we had become friends after this, but I was still seeing his point on this one.

"That you are and the very best assassin at that, which is why I expect nothing less for the position you will now take. Besides, you rule well enough over your own kind," Draven argued and Lucius released a sigh, knowing he had lost this one.

"Very well Arsaces, you will have your way this time, my friend," Lucius said and I can't say that it didn't touch my soul hearing how close these two used to be.

"Good! In that case make use of the Black Gates to get back to Rome quicker and decree it possible with the help from the Gods. That way no one will deny your claim, for word surely got back to the capital of your involvement in

Pertinax's foolish campaign," Draven told him and Lucius nodded.

"A messenger was sent with news of our progress and lucky for me, none of the mortal men saw me fighting against him at the end," Lucius added looking to me when he said this, no doubt wanting to say more on the matter. Well, if his eyes could speak then that was what they were silently telling me. Of course, I was now questioning what the 'Black Gates' were and how they would get Lucius back to Rome so quickly? I knew I would have to ask Sophia this when I saw her next, which I hoped was soon.

"Then it is settled. Go and enjoy your brief relax from death, my friend." Draven laughed when he heard Lucius groan as if a holiday from his day job of killing people was the very last thing he wanted to do right now.

"Yes, my King," Lucius said, bowing respectfully and then saying,

"Little Keira girl, until next time." I swallowed hard and froze as if he had just pulled me from that damn lake all over again. His eyes flashed blood red so briefly that Draven missed it when he was too busy looking at me, and trying to find a reason for my reaction. Draven didn't seem to mind that he had called me this but then remembering back to earlier, he had admitted that he wouldn't call me Keira because another man had already done so. He wanted to keep Nāzanin for himself and Lucius knew this.

"Oh, and Septimus…"

"Yes, my Lord?" Lucius stopped by the door to turn back and inquire over his shoulder.

"Try and have some fun, after all, I believe the position also comes with certain perks, for there are many beauties to be found in the capital, is this not true?" Draven asked and I felt like growling at him taking about these 'beauties' when I was sat right there. But then it was Lucius' reply that had me dropping the annoyance and I felt the pinch of heartache I had no right to feel when he replied,

"I care little for Mortal women for my tastes, now and always lie elsewhere, you know this Arsaces." And then after one more intense look my way he nodded and then was swiftly gone, leaving a painful hole I couldn't understand. I hadn't missed that he had also taken the evidence of his silent rage with him, as the destroyed cup was still in his hand as he walked out the door.

Draven chuckled again as if he had enjoyed goading him before letting him leave.

"Ah alone at last, my beauty," he said running a hand across my neck and down, brushing against my ample cleavage.

"Are you sure you're alone with the right beauty, for I hear there are plenty to be found in Rome!" I snapped moving to stand up but I barely made it to standing before his arms were around me and he was laughing at my back. I huffed and folded my arms across my chest.

If I was honest with myself I wasn't just annoyed at Draven's comment but also irrationally, Lucius' as well. I knew I had no right to be angry and if this was the way he felt, then if anything, it made life in this time easier. But there was just something in the way he had said it that made me think there was a hidden meaning to be found.

"As pleasing and gratifying as it is to see the lashing of jealousy tail coming from you, my love, alas, it is this time unfounded." I frowned, then shifted around to look at him and the smile I saw there stemmed purely from how much pleasure he found in seeing me jealous.

"How so?" I asked and by his smirk, I knew he had both wanted and expected, me to ask this.

"Because, little protective viper of mine, I said this in jest as

Septimus is well known for his distaste of mortal women. *Unlike my very current change of heart on the notion,"* he said whispering this to me seductively, as his hand first caressed my cheek only to snake into my hair, before grasping me hard and pulling me into him for a kiss. I moaned into his mouth and was soon lost to his demanding touch.

"Now it is time you eat little one, before you faint... *as for what I have planned for you, will require your strength,"* he told me after ending the kiss and before nipping playfully at my nose.

"You're very bossy, you know that?" I told him as I shifted off him and he tilted his head slightly to the side and inquired,

"Bossy...I know not this term." I laughed and wanted to say, 'oh you will totally get it in the future' and wasn't this true considering that was exactly what he would be first introduced to me as...*My Boss.* But instead I decided to go with the safer,

"Domineering." A word he very much understood.

"But of course, as is my right...now eat woman of mine!" he ordered making me laugh at him 'jesting' once again. But to be honest he didn't need to ask me twice as I was starving and the ancient feast in front of me was making me almost salivating. I had briefly taken it all in before but now, oh my, just the sight of cooked chicken, lamb, flat breads, cheese, pots of honey, a small dish of some mixed spices and a kind of stew, all lay out before me. I felt as if I had stepped into Heaven's buffet and all that was missing was chocolate cake, a cup of tea and some French pastries.

Okay, so there were also some other things I wasn't sure of, like the mixed beans and lentils thingy, with green bits. Oh, and there were more vegetable dishes, along with fruit, small bowls of different 'sweetmeats' as they were called. These were sugar coated nuts, honey coated almonds, caramelised dried fruits, what they mainly ate as a dessert. I did want to point out that this was more of a snack in my world and introduce these people to the marvel that was cake!

So, with this in mind, I shifted to the floor, placing myself in front of the table after grabbing one of the cushions from the seat. I bit my lip wondering what to try first when Draven started laughing. I decided to ignore him, knowing he was doing so at what he most likely considered 'strange behaviour'.

Instead I went to it, starting with making a little room on the table for me to put the gold plate on. I had grabbed it after first trying to figure out where to put all the flatbreads, so decided on top of the pomegranates was as good a place as any.

"In all my years…" he then muttered to himself.

"What?" I asked as I started grabbing the things I needed, including one of those large flatbreads to start.

"I have never seen someone look so happy or ready for their meal and so very prepared, it seems. It feels as if I am laying witness to a ritual," he told me making me blush and then I told him in a shy voice,

"I like my food." This made him laugh once, shake his head and then give me a loving look as if to tell me that he wouldn't have had it any other way.

"I can see that, sweetness. Your eagerness is a delight to witness but I fear that I feel somewhat of an intruder on your private Heaven," he added, once again teasing me and making me laugh.

"Then why don't you join me, for there is room for two, Arsaces." I told him in a teasing tone myself. At first, he looked surprised by my challenge and I would have loved to pop inside his head and take a peek at what it was *he* was thinking this time. Then I decided to prove I wasn't bluffing and I did indeed want my King to sit beside me on the floor, a place I don't think he was used to. Of course, I knew that most meals were taken as such in this time and place but I also knew that Draven was another type of King, one who didn't conform to that culture. He liked his thrones, and he was usually positioned higher than most so that he could keep an eye on that which he ruled.

I remember him telling me this once after joking with him one night in the VIP. It was one of the many times he had simply walked towards me, plucked me out of my chair next to him and positioned me on his lap, so that he could 'play with me better', his words not mine. He had told me that he had never conformed to the ways of the mortal world in a lot of things and being King came with the perks of never being questioned for such.

I had teased him about his 'modern throne' the one we had been sat in at the time and this was when he had pulled me close and told me,

"Well how else am I to keep my eye on unruly little vixens that like to tease me so?"

The memory almost had me forming tears, for I missed him so much. And I know it sounded strange, considering I had the very same man facing me now but it was what it was. Draven, the man I fell in love with, was a world away and in his place, was someone that felt more like the reflection of Draven, when looking in the mirror. I loved them both, but in truth, I loved one just that little bit more than the other. And looking at him now, I felt cruel for even thinking it, no matter that I was simply being true to my heart… it still felt wrong of me.

In the end, my thoughts were taken from me at the sight of Draven smirking at me. Then, getting back to my challenge, I grabbed an extra cushion from the seat, placed it down next to me and patted it, saying,

"It's safe, I can assure you, my King." At this he looked to be fighting biting his own lip and the light and mirth in his eyes was stunning.

"Very well Nāzanin, I will forgo my advantage and play," he

answered me cryptically, making me ask as he knew I would. So, I let him shift his big body off the seat and slide in next to me. Bless him but he had to move the whole table just to fit, making me giggle before asking,

"Your advantage?"

"In height, so that I may enjoy the entertainment in watching you eat." I groaned making him chuckle and said,

"Then I am even more pleased you decided to…*play,*" I said trying to say this last word as seductively as I could. As soon as I saw his eyes flash momentarily I mentally high fived my inner vixen and decided to get back to the delicious task at hand… this time being food and not getting to wash Draven's amazing body.

So, I went to it and knew that I did so under the watchful eyes of a very curious King. First, I grabbed a breast off a whole cooked chicken and started to rip it into strips to place at the centre of my flatbread. Then I grabbed some cheese, crumbling it along as it looked very similar to feta or goat's cheese. Then I lifted the pot of spices and brought it to my nose to smell, trying to detect what it was before just sprinkling a load of chilli on my meal.

To be honest I couldn't tell but it smelled nice and after a little dip of my little finger, I decided a sprinkling would give it a good kick and complement my next ingredient…honey. I loved honey glazed chicken, so thought this would be like that as I loved the combination of sweet and spicy.

"Gods have mercy," Draven muttered behind me and I bit my lip, wondering what it was about seeing me do this that needed to be granted mercy?

I decided to ignore the comment and find my last ingredient. I had to go hunting under the flatbreads, as I loved pomegranates, so decided it might taste nice in the wrap I was trying to build. I knew if I looked back over my shoulder now, I would find Draven watching me with astonishment, so I saved my cheeks the heated torture and continued to finish.

"Umm…is there a knife?" I asked him, whilst peering over the table and moving stuff around, trying to find one. Of course, he produced one swiftly as it was his own and after taking the fruit out of my hand, he cut it in two in the blink of an eye. I couldn't look at him in the face, but I knew that all I wanted to do right then was suck the juice off his fingers. After all, pomegranate juice was sticky stuff indeed and would take a while to clean up.

"Now that look interests me greatly, for it looks *sinful,*" he hummed in my ear and I shuddered against him.

"Lucky for me then it is not something I will ever find myself punished for, for my thoughts are thankfully my own," I teased back making him growl and nip at my neck.

"Umm…not for long, for I will have my way with you, Nāzanin," he promised and I was almost curious enough to ask if he was joking or if he knew something I didn't. I decided to clear the lust from my throat and ignore the way he chuckled behind me. I then went back to my task and grabbed the spoon from the stew. I first cleaned the spoon with my mouth, nearly moaning at how good it tasted. And was that a groan I heard from Draven at the sight of me doing so?

I smiled to myself when he said,

"Now what are you planning to do with that, I wonder?" he asked and I resisted to the urge to tease him further, as it was obvious by the tone of his voice, that by watching me create my meal, he was getting turned on.

"You shall soon see. My grandmother taught me this trick when I was little," I told him thinking it safe enough to give him this little insight into my life. I then turned one half of the fruit up over my wrap, and started hitting it with the back of the spoon so that all the little juicy pink seeds could fall, like the scattering of jewels, over my meal. Then I discarded the rest of the fruit and started finishing my wrap, starting with folding in the bottom. Then I folded over one side, before rolling it over the other way to create a tighter wrap. Then I licked my fingers, something that granted me another moan and took a huge bite.

"Oh my…tis, sooo good," I said with my mouth full making Draven boom with laughter. I finally swallowed my bite and then held the wrap out to him with both hands around it and said,

"Here, try some." He smirked at me before looking down at my wrap like it was some great gift I was about to share with him. I nodded to him to take some and with a gratifying look, he held his hand over mine as he brought it closer to his lips. He took a big bite and nodded his thanks, making me lean back and continue eating as I awaited the verdict. I smiled when I saw his eyes go wide when all of the combination of flavours started bursting across his tongue.

"This is really good!" he said sounding surprised. I laughed once and said,

"I have my talents." To which he turned my face to his so that he could reply softly,

"Oh, of that I have little doubt in my sweet girl, most of which I think you are unaware of such." And then he took the opportunity to take me off guard by bringing my wrap to his mouth and taking another large bite. He tried not to laugh with his mouthful at the sight of my false horror.

"Oi! You stole from me!" I said pretending to be outraged and he just shrugged his shoulders, making me forget for a moment which Draven I was sat with.

"I believe this time you hold all the blame, my dearest one, for you can expect nothing less when presenting your King with such treasure and I did say I always took what I wanted, did I not?"

"Like me?" I challenged, one he readily accepted when his eyes flashed purple and he shifted closer to me. He gently tucked a stray part of my hair behind my ear and came closer before giving me his answer,

"Oh, I will take you, Nāzanin…" he said, pausing enough to speak the next words over my trembling lips,

"…And never let you go again."

CHAPTER NINE

TRUTH WHERE IT MATTERS

After this promise issued, he had no idea just how damning it sounded considering our plan was kind of crucial to us getting back to our own time. But for the time being, all I could hope for was to gain his trust enough to…well, for starters, let me out of his sight for more than an hour. Something that didn't seem likely for some time yet, not when on two occasions someone had tried to approach the door on what they deemed a 'royal matter' only to be turned away. Draven wasn't in any hurry to get back to his Kingdom and seemed far too engrossed in sitting with me whilst we shared our first meal together.

In the end, I had made two more wraps, one for him and another for me, for he continued to steal bites out of mine, quickly making it into a game. The rules had been easy, being only two to remember. The first, was distract me with sweet soft words, and the second was to swoop on in and attack my food when I was being lured into a false sense of security. The laughter had been worth every stolen bite.

It was amazing, because in the end we must have looked like a couple of teenagers sat on the floor, laughing, play fighting, and pigging out on ancient junk food. All we were missing was some corny slasher movie on in the background and a small child upstairs we should have been babysitting. At one point, he had teased me so much that I decided to get him back by turning the tables on him. So, I played the game by leaning in close, keeping a hand behind me and whispering up to him,

"You know my Lord, I find you quite handsome." The look on his face was perfect! He seemed so taken aback by my sudden flirty statement that I totally had him in the palm of my hand.

"Is that so?" he asked with a smirk and I nodded my head. Then I motioned for him to come closer to me and said,

"Although, there is something missing that I wish to see on you," I told him whispering behind my free hand, scooping two fingers he couldn't see in the pot of honey.

"And what is that my beauty?" he whispered back, totally playing along and I let out a little giggle and said,

"Something sweet to lick off you!" Then I ran my two dripping fingers down from his nose, over his lips and to his chin. I then burst out laughing at the sight of his utter astonishment. In fact, I was laughing so hard I had to put a hand to my heart, as I could barely breathe. Meanwhile he slowly lifted his fingers to his nose and caught the drip before it fell. Then he brought it to his lips and sucked it clean, suddenly making my mouth go dry at the sight. Holy mother of all that is sinful, could he be any sexier.

"Oh, if that is how you want to play...*then we will play, sweetness,"* he warned and before he could make his move I lost myself to my addiction and threw myself at him! I knew I took him completely off guard and for once, I became the uncontrollable one. I had jumped on his lap, straddling him and started kissing the honey from his face, like a woman possessed.

He growled low as his hands gripped my hips, holding me to him. I was doing the same with both my hands on his head, with my fingers in his hair, keeping him locked to me. I licked up his chin and over his lips before diving in there and letting him taste the honey on my tongue for himself. His hands fisted in the material of my trousers and I heard the first sign that he was close to losing control…it made me grin over his lips at the ripping sound.

"By the Gods woman! What is it you do to me!" he shouted tearing his lips from mine and panting like some overworked beast. Then I decided to take what little control I had over this situation and I *pushed it!* My fingers curled into fists in his hair, making his eyes widen before I yanked him hard to me and said,

"Why don't you show me!" Then I forced his lips to mine just as he released a growl. The kiss was so intense I felt as if I could have come from it, which made me shamelessly start grinding myself against his erection…one that *definitely* wanted to come out and play. I knew this when he pulled back an inch and snarled down at me before I heard the crash of our feast hitting the floor with a clatter. Draven had mentally pushed it from the low table, thanks to the power of supernatural telekinesis. Then he pushed me backwards, after wrapping his arms around my torso, so that he could lay me on the now cleared table.

"Now this is what I call a feast worth devouring," he said coming down on top of me and thankfully I found out the true nature of craftmanship back in this time, as the table held both our combined weight without breaking. And it was a good job for we were suddenly at it in some kind of wild frenzy, tearing

at each other's clothes like reunited lovers. Desperation became the true meaning of our actions and I knew that for the Draven of this time, it was certainly another first.

He panted as he both struggled to hold back but also to ensure he got enough of me. It was as if this was not how he saw our first time together but trying to find the will to stop it was pushing against the realms of impossible. Of course, this just drove me to push him further and the idea of this was sending me into a near frenzy. I wanted him with a sexual fever of the likes I had never known.

"More," I demanded making him growl and it was one that morphed into a deep groan as I reached in between us, pulled at his trousers, and took this hard length in hand, flesh to flesh.

"Gods!" he hissed between gritted teeth as I pumped his length and then I ran my fingertip across the top to gather up the drips of his pre-release. Then I let him go to bring my finger up to my mouth, so I could play him at his own erotic game. I pulled back from his kiss and just as he started to growl again, I put my finger in my mouth and sucked on it long and hard, loving the salty taste of him. This was all it took to sever that single thread of willpower he had left and it snapped with one word spoken,

"Fuck!" He swore with such an intensity that it made me arch my back and moan out his ancient name,

"Yes Arsaces!" Then I smiled when I expected any second now to feel the harsh tug of my harem pants being torn off me like paper, as he grabbed a handful of the material at my hip. Then just as he was about to enter me we both heard another crash from the other room and what sounded like a bull charging our way. With my head already thrown back I opened my eyes to the sight of a massive black creature racing towards us upside down and I screamed.

"No, Colossus!" Draven shouted but it was too late as the

massive animal was trying in vain to skid to a halt at the sound of his master's voice. Needless to say, it didn't accomplish the task, but instead it just so happened to finally come to a stop where most of the food now lay scattered along the floor. What once was our feast, had now swiftly become its own and from the happy grunting noises, it seemed more than pleased with its new bounty. I felt Draven release a deep sigh above me as he looked down at the animal with a disappointed shake of his head. I, on the other hand, found this whole thing hilariously funny and burst out laughing after shouting out the obvious,

"You have a dog?!"

"This isn't funny," he told me sternly, which only ended up causing me to laugh even harder and now add a long string of piggy snorts to the sound.

"By…Gods it…is!" I said in between my fit and in the end Draven was left with no other option but to join me in seeing the humour in it all. I don't know what I found funnier, that Draven actually owned what my world would have classed as a *'normal pet'* not some killer hybrid demonic bird or that it was in fact an *'Unruly'* one!

Finally, I calmed enough to try and get up, an action Draven allowed as it was obvious our sexual rampant moment had swiftly come and gone. So, he helped me up and I quickly turned around to face the 'black brute' as I was desperate to see what type of dog a man like Draven would have. I can't say I was surprised by the sight.

"Is that a Neopolitan Mastiff?" I asked remembering the breed from falling in love with 'Fang' from the Harry Potter movies. He raised an eyebrow at me in such a way as if to ask, how the hell I would know something like this?

"It is and was also a gift from my…"

"Sister?" I asked quickly, knowing this was totally something Sophia would get a kick out of giving him.

"Brother," Draven finished with an exasperated groan. At this I laughed again and thought back to their conversation about when Vincent had been complaining about Ava and her only behaving for her Master. I could imagine then that it was great pleasure on Vincent's side to see that his mighty, ruling brother couldn't seem to get his other pet to do the same and behave. But I suppose the same could be said for me, as I was still giggling as I took in the sight of his huge, black wrinkly dog.

I was too eager to meet his pet, much to his surprise as I crouched down and started making cooing noises.

"Here boy, here…um, what was his name again?" I asked looking back over my shoulder at Draven.

"Colossus," he stated folding his arms across his chest, probably still pissed off at being interrupted.

"Ha, figures," I said making him scoff before saying,

"And the meaning of that is?"

"Well it means giant statue in Greek right…I think it's The Colossus of Rhodes, isn't it? Anyway, what you have here is a pretty big dog, so it fits," I said talking away and not for one-minute stopping to see how strange me knowing any of this was. Of course, I could have said something stranger like, oh he's named after a kick ass metal skinned X-Men character, who just also happens to be Russian…do you know him? Yeah, no, I don't think this would have gone down any better. And speaking of going down, then that's precisely what our left-over food was doing right now.

"And how you know this, puzzles me greatly, I must say." I laughed nervously and then tapped my head and gave him a vague,

"Well read, remember." Then I decided to get back to the dog, who hadn't really seen me yet as it was obviously far too busy with the left-over chicken bones.

"Colossus, here boy!" I shouted him over and finally it looked up at me as if to do a double take.

"I should warn you, he doesn't usually like…" Draven's sentence trailed off after the dog bounded up to me and started fussing over me so much, he nearly knocked me off my knees.

"…women," Draven finished off softly as it was clear, I was one woman he made an exception for. He was so huge and I could imagine, quite intimidating to most and rightly so, given that he looked like he could have quite easily gone up against a bear! It was easy to see that he was unusually big, even for his breed and his fur was beautifully soft, like blue/black velvet. His head had too many folds and wrinkles to count and with his soppy droopy eyes, he looked at you as though he would love you forever. I grabbed his head, rubbed behind his ears and made cooing noises at him, telling him,

"You are so cute! Yes, you are…you're a handsome boy, yes, oh yes you are!" I heard Draven behind me clear his throat as if he was trying not to laugh and when I looked back at him, his dog whined in a way that told me it wanted to keep my attention. I giggled and then said,

"Oh look, Arsaces, it seems that you will have to share me and my attention with another intimidating beast," I said going back to the cutie pie that was a drooling Colossus and start stroking him down his back and the many folds around his large neck. Then suddenly I squealed in shock as I was picked up and thrown over Draven's shoulder. Colossus started barking in a deep throaty way that most big dogs do and Draven whipped round and snarled playfully,

"Mine!" making the dog back down. Then he turned and started walking us both into the bedroom.

"Aww…I still love you Colossus!" I shouted back at him, lifting myself up over Draven's shoulder, making him huff and then go back to his happy place…that being hoovering up the leftovers.

"I don't share," Draven said pulling my body forward and making me yelp as I landed with a 'humpf' on his bed.

"But he's so cute," I told him, this time making him playfully nip at me making me giggle.

"I suppose I should not be surprised at you being the first female he likes, considering the power you seem to hold over the opposite sex," he said dryly making me giggle again. Seriously though, all I seemed to do around this man was laugh, giggle, snort or moan in sexual frustration, for I feared that if I didn't come soon I would just self-combust after my next cheek caress.

"And does that power extend to you, my King?" I asked seductively and he gave me a pointed look and said,

"As you are well aware, my playful Lamb, for the proof is always easy to find," then he looked down at himself and I followed his gaze to find that, yep there it was and it was mighty and glorious! Of course, it would have been made more glorious if it was currently freed from its material confines and finding new comfort in that of my body.

"And I fear that because of such, you make me easily lose my mind and most of all, my focus." At this I frowned at him as he sat back putting space between us.

"What do you mean by that?" I asked folding my arms, knowing I would most likely not like the sound of what was to come next.

"It is now indisputable that you are my Electus but this fact comes secondary to the heart I gave you willingly and did so knowingly at the time, that the decision made could mean forsaking the future of my own kind." Okay, so far so good, as I couldn't say that hearing this didn't make me smile and one he reached out and caressed his thumb across.

"However, at the time nothing else mattered to me for I want you as I have never wanted another. But you must know that when I take you, I want not to only to own your body but your mind also…*I want everything you have to give,"* he told me, letting his hand fall to my neck and gently pull me closer to him before he uttered the very reason for these words spoken. Ones that I shuddered against, knowing my time for answering difficult questions was near.

"And I know nothing of you but the lies you told."

I hated that he was right but what I hated even more was the lies I would have to layer on top of the lies I had already cemented at the foundations of this relationship. But I knew that I had no other choice as I had made my time travelling bed already and there was no going back now…well, other than trying to get back to my own time that is, I thought inwardly cringing.

So, with this shameful truth in mind, it was time to lie.

"What is it you would like to know?"

"How did you come to know of my kind and learn of your place within it?" Draven asked and I knew exactly what this was considering he had already had his account of how I came to be from his sister Sophia. No, this was nothing short of a test, one that I could pass thanks to Pip…*or so I thought.*

Pip had told me that the story Draven had been given was that I was brought up by a secret society that believed in the prophecy and posed as priests in England. They groomed me from an early age after word reached them as to who I was. There I learnt all about his kind and the ways of the world. I supposed this was to explain all my worldly knowledge that Draven had been right, a simply merchant's daughter wouldn't know. Even when Draven had asked after my family, Sophia had told him that they had allowed me to remain in contact, so it at least explained where my passion lay when briefly mentioning my father to Draven.

All I could say was thank the Gods for Sophia's quick thinking and ability to hide her thoughts from her brother, something they all did with each other. Of course, having this same skill helped but not enough to defend myself from all of Draven's powers and he still had one or two tricks up his sleeve in getting the answers he wanted.

"Well I first learnt of…umm…" I started to tell him but soon stumbled on my words when he reached down and picked up my hand, so that he could hold my wrist, placing his fingers at my pulse point. He wanted to read my lies.

"You were saying," he said smoothly and I swallowed hard before thinking back to what Pip told me. She had said the trick was to believe in your own lies, morphing them into a warped version of the truth. Draven knew what he was doing and when he started stroking his thumb along the back of my hand it felt like he was trying to sooth my fears but also provide me comfort. I didn't know why he would do this other than to lure me into a false sense of security.

"I was…well, there were people and they taught…me…I…" I let my broken voice trail off and Draven frowned at me.

"Nāzanin?" He called my name but I was lost. I had turned my head and was looking out to the night and something just didn't feel right. It was as though something deep down inside of me was pulling at a thread I was desperately trying to hold onto but didn't know why.

"Just let go."

"Just let go." Both sentences were said at the same time but only one belonged to the room as the other belonged to another side of myself…*Katie.*

"I can't do this!" I suddenly shouted and pulled my hand from his, as I shifted off the bed.

"What, what can't you do?" he asked me and suddenly I had tears falling from my eyes as I knew that what I was now going to do could have the power to ruin everything. The very reasons for us being here now depended on this one point and the simple question I had to ask my soul…could I lie once more to a man who had declared to have loved me enough that he was ready to forsake his own kind to be with me?

Now the question remained, was I really about to reward that level of his love with the depth of my lies?

So, I took a deep shuddering breath, let my tears overflow and I gave him my answer…

"I can't lie to you…*anymore.*"

CHAPTER TEN

ANCIENT LESSON LEARNED

Soon after speaking these freeing words, things soon went from bad to worse. The bad started with Draven demanding to know why I felt I couldn't tell him the truth and then the worse ended with me just standing there with no more words to tell him. Then he had asked me the fatal question…

"And what of my sister, did she too tell me of your lies believing the truth was spoken?" I took a deep breath and told him,

"I lied to her also." As soon as I said this his anger was easy to see and I couldn't say that I blamed him. He stood from the bed and stormed over to me, making me back up and just as I was about to hit into a shield hanging on the wall, he got to me and steered me away from it. Well, at least even in his fury he cared enough about my wellbeing, so I guess that was something good to focus on.

"Tell me why?!" he demanded taking that last step and caging me in with his hands held above me. I knew he was trying to intimidate me enough to tell him and I would have said that most of the time, it would have worked…but not this time.

"I…I…" In truth, I had nothing.

"Tell me why you lied!?" he asked again and I knew with that harsh tone he was close to losing it.

"I can't…I…"

"TELL ME!" he roared at me making me flinch back. So, I gave him what I could.

"Because the truth is dangerous!" I shouted back and he jolted as if shocked by my reason.

"You believe I will hurt you if I know the truth?" he asked in a hiss as if even thinking this was abhorrent and utterly foreign to him.

"N…" I was about to speak when his hand shackled the column of my throat but not in a threatening way or a way to silence me but it was a gentle touch. One that meant to achieve only one thing…*detecting for my possible deception*.

"No, not dangerous *for me*." I told him, knowing that everything I said from this point would only be found as a truth. Because it would be dangerous for him and everyone else I loved if he knew the truth. If I failed to get back and complete my mission, what then?

"For me? But that is impossible, no…I… you must surely mean for yourself," he challenged and I hated where my current thoughts started to take me. Because if anything *I* was the only one in this whole thing that it *wasn't* dangerous for, not considering my fate had already been determined and my life… well it wasn't the one I was fighting for anymore. *It was his.*

"You felt it for yourself, for what I say is true." He narrowed his eyes at me and shook his head a little as if he couldn't believe what he was hearing.

"So, of what you speak, you wish me to trust that the

information you withhold from me is to keep *me safe*…is this what I am to believe, Nāzanin?" I bit my lip as it started to tremble, so I closed my eyes just as the first of my tears started to fall before opening them and telling him the truth once more,

"I swear to you… *on my very soul*… that everything I do is solely to keep safe those that I love and top of that list is…*is you, Arsaces*." The second he heard his name uttered from my lips he wrapped a strong arm around my waist and yanked me hard to him.

"You wish to save my life?" he asked me fervently and I let another tear fall before raising my eyes to his and whispering my answer,

"Always." Suddenly he put his hand to the back of my neck and eliminated the rest of the space between us in a heartbeat, to once more give me a piece of his heart,

"Then never leave it!" Then he took my lips in a bruising kiss. I gasped over his lips letting him glide his tongue in and taste me. The bitter sweet moment didn't last long and the sweetest part was when he lit up my soul by kissing me and the bitter, well that was when he left me.

I felt his lips leave mine and I opened my eyes, expecting him to be looking down at me but I was wrong…

He was gone.

It was at this realisation that I felt my legs buckle and I crumpled to the floor. I pulled my knees up and hugged myself as I cried, wondering how had I managed to mess things up this badly. In essence, it should have been simple. We all get here together, form a plan, get me in bed with the king and have Ari do her baby making mumbo jumbo, then get the hell out of Dodge! But from the very start it had felt like everything had been against us.

Now the big question remained, was this still all part of the Fates' plan, or was this simply what it felt like it was…me winging it and fumbling around in the dark? Because from the very second I woke up in that desert, all it felt like I was doing was making one mistake after another. All I wanted to do was tell Draven the truth and place my trust in him doing the right thing, something he refused to do back in my own time. But even thinking this, I knew it was something Draven just wasn't able to give me.

Because ever since we first met all he had done was make painful decisions based solely on my safety. I thought back to all the tears shed and I felt that I could have drowned in them for everything this relationship had put me through but at no point had I really said... *enough.*

Even when it started with his stern and harsh treatment of me when being my boss. Why hadn't I been repelled against him because of it? No, if anything it seemed to only add fuel to the fantasy and from this my obsession grew. And then he once against tried one last push, which was using that traitorous bitch Celina, to break my foolish heart. Oh, at the time I had tried to convince myself that I'd had enough but the reality was as it has always been, that no matter how I try I could never give up on Draven.

And now all I had left was asking him to do the same, to not give up on me. A girl he knew nothing about other than what I was supposed to mean to him thanks to what the Gods deemed so. But I never wanted any of that because stripping this down to its most basic form...

I was simply a girl, in love with a man.

"Oh dear, Houston we have a problem with one of our astronauts," Pip said to a concerned looking Sophia and Ari, who now stood at the bottom of the bed. I had at some point finally dragged my sobbing carcass off the floor and was currently huddled on the bed, hugging a massive dog. One that had just had to listen to all my problems for the last two hours. No wonder he looked depressed.

"Oh, honey!" Ari said coming over to the bed and receiving a warning growl from my new guardian, Colossus.

"Umm, he's a bit…protective, aren't you boy, good boy ssshh now, she's my sister." I told him making Ari smile at me as if she was touched that I still recognised her as such.

"Meh, yes, I remember that hound," Sophia said sounding unimpressed and I gave her a questioning look.

"He used to eat my shoes," she said with a shrug of her shoulders. Um, well I guess dogs didn't really change much, even after 2000 years, as they still went for what was usually most precious to a girl.

"Shame you didn't bring those 'Gods holding their noses' awful sneakers with you Toots, he would have had a field day with those bad boys!" Pip said laughing then walked over to me and plonked herself on the bed with a little jump. Strangely, Colossus didn't make a sound of protest.

"Hey, how come she gets the waggy tail treatment?!" Ari complained, as he started to sniff at Pip before rolling over on his belly for her to make a fuss, which of course she did, in her own Pip way.

"Um Pip…what are you doing?" I asked as she pretended to be a dog herself and start poking his belly with her nose and making snuffling noses. I had to say whatever her reasons the dog loved it!

"Communicating," was her only cryptic response.

"Oookay." Ari said making me smile.

"She's an Imp, so don't ask as this is her thing. But getting back to the reason we snuck in here and off the shoe eating mutt…what happened, Honey?" Sophia asked as she gently sat on the bed along with Ari, now that Colossus seemed to be relaxed enough. Well yeah, why not considering he was currently spooning a snuggling Pip. She looked like his new favourite toy as he kept licking her neck making her giggle.

"I just couldn't do it." I told them and Pip's eyes got wide and she said,

"Tell me you have not gone off that delicious man king candy and I am not talking about the wreck it Ralph variety!" Pip asked making Sophia and Ari look at each other with comical matching 'What the Hell' looks. I, however, had a little niece and knew she loved the movie, although it was questionable who loved it more, her or her father Frank.

"No, Pip, it's not that."

"Then what?" Ari asked putting a hand on my arm in comfort.

"I couldn't lie," I told her honestly and Sophia gave me a warm, soft look as though she was starting to see where this was going.

"But why not, I told you the trick and…" Pip started when Sophia stopped her.

"He wants you, body and mind, doesn't he?" I nodded and let my shoulders slump.

"I am confused" Ari said and Pip agreed,

"Me too, sister big booty." I had to laugh when Ari growled at her.

"I have told you to stop calling me that! My 'booty' isn't that big." Ari complained and then shifted to the side so that she could pull her Kaftan down, making Pip giggle.

"Don't know what your big panties are in a twitch about, it's not like Vinny boy isn't a big booty man! And besides, your ass is fine girlfriendly big bum and it gives you that sexy swagger that skinny bitches like me can't do without looking like we woke up one day and just forgot how to walk properly…you got it going on, so it's all good and *peachy*… hehe," Pip said finishing with a giggle. Meanwhile I had to laugh as Ari looked as if her eyes were about to explode from her sockets. It was in that moment that the look she was sporting right now was the very same one that had been glued to my own face years ago when I first met Pip. Talking about history repeating itself, for that was a mind-boggling joke considering where we were all now sat.

"Take it as a compliment," I whispered next to her after Pip had gone back to snuggling the dog, one that was now snoring.

"Oh, I am taking it as something, not sure I understand what though," Ari replied making me laugh.

"Well, if it makes you feel any better, she is like this about my breasts all the time and this may be hard to imagine, but one day, this will all just seem quite normal to you," I said making Sophia laugh and say,

"Yep, pretty much." And Pip lifted her head from the dog's belly and made a clicking noise at Ari along with a flick of two fingers like she was firing a gun. I took this as she agreed with my statement but really…who knew.

"So, what are we going to do about my brooding brother, who I might add is currently making his kingdom's life hell from his foul mood?" Now this peaked my interest. My back turned ramrod straight and I asked in desperate tones,

"Why, where is he? What is he doing? Why is he making the…?"

"Whoa, slow down there, Skippy!" Sophia said and I laughed,

"You have spent way too much time around Pip." I informed her, making Sophia blush, a colour that matched her beautiful red and gold dress. She looked like a sinful goddess and her ebony hair looked like glossy waves over one shoulder. I just knew that if Zagan was around in this time then he would have stopped at nothing to have her. The thought made me sad. And just as it did with Pip, I couldn't even imagine what it must be like for them both, being without their husbands and here was me acting all sorry for myself.

"Hey, come on now, I know that look," Sophia said reaching out and taking hold of my hand.

"We knew what we were doing and we all had a choice," she added making Pip say,

"Yeah, I was wearing my big girl pants and everything, so it's all good…Well, as long as no time has passed and we get back and my Adam hasn't done anything silly like destroy the Earth looking for me or anything," she added with a shrug of her shoulders and Ari's face looked as if she had swallowed a bug!

"Don't ask," I told her with a little shake of my head. Then she looked to Sophia and she did the same, telling her silently not to go there.

"So, getting back to Draven?" I asked her.

"Well it's obvious he is pissed, which was kind of a big indicator you would be here alone upset." Yeah, it usually was, I thought bitterly.

"So, you two haven't umm done…"

"The R Kelly?" Pip added making me laugh.

"The Bump and Grind, she means sex," I told Ari, who was looking more lost by the minute.

"No, we haven't but we came close," I told them.

"Oh, so that explains the mess in the living room," Sophia said making me blush.

"Alright Tootiesextornator!" Pip shouted giving me a high five.

"Yeah, well thanks to this big brute here, we kind of got interrupted. And then well, Draven has kind of got it into his head that he won't…you know…"

"Put in until you put out?" I laughed at Pip's 'nut shell' statement.

"Yeah. He wanted to know where I came from and I just knew that when he detected my lie, that would be it, game over. In the end, I couldn't bring myself to do it, so I told him that the truth would be dangerous for him." Sophia's eyes grew wide and then realisation dawned on her.

"Well that explains all the messengers."

"What do you mean?" I asked her.

"Well, he called forth all his messengers and had them spread word of a bounty for anyone who has information on the 'fair haired girl called Keira from Britannia'. I believe forty men are currently leaving on horseback." Hearing this I groaned aloud and buried my head in my hands.

"Well then that's no biggy, and all is good in the hood," Pip said and Sophia shrugged her shoulders and added,

"At least no one will come back with any proof and the only man who knew the truth about us has been sent off to Rome."

"Yeah to become a bloody Emperor! Pip did you know this?!" I screeched and she just shrugged her shoulders and said,

"Yeah, of course." Okay so it seemed to be common knowledge and I don't know why but the thought that *I didn't know* hurt a little.

"Okay, so the question still remains, what the hell do we do now, because if your brother won't 'put in' as Pip called it, without first getting to know the truth about me, a truth I can't tell him I might add, then what's our next move?"

"Oh, I know!" Pip shouted, suddenly getting excited by raising her hand up like she was in school. That image alone gave me shivers as I couldn't imagine the nightmare some poor teacher would have on their hands with Pip.

"You can cook for him!" she shouted out and in true Pip

fashion, it was the very last thing any of us ever expected. I think all our faces said exactly the same thing…

'Uh, what now?'

"Well, when Adam is in a grump with me I usually cook for him, I mean granted when I serve it to him I am usually naked but it always ends in food covered nookie, but still, my point being that if you show how much you love him, then he might just give up the goods without thinking about it…I mean you did say yourself that you nearly did it earlier over food…maybe that's his weakness…what…it could be." Pip whined this last part when I gave her a pointed look.

"Pip, I appreciate the…" Sophia suddenly put a hand on my arm and stopped me,

"You know, she may be on to something."

"What?!" I shouted in disbelief.

"Look we know my brother's weakness here…"

"Prunes?" Pip asked making me and Ari both laugh.

"No not prunes or any other dried fruit that makes you…"

"Shit through the eye of a needle?!" Pip again added on a shout as if it was a guessing game and me and Ari were soon in stitches.

"Focus Pip. No, I was going to say my brother's weakness has and always will be his Chosen One. It's you Keira and not just because the Fates deemed you the Electus but because of who you are in here," she said pointing to her own heart.

"He will always love you to the point that it will soon become unbearable for him not to take you to his bed and this notion of knowing your past, will soon become secondary to his obsession in joining his body with yours…all you have to do, *is push.*" I knew what she was saying and I found tears in my eyes once again at the thought of Draven's love for me. But she was right, I needed to use that to my advantage and push him until his limits snapped.

"Yes, well I tried that and he left, so how do I stop that from happening." I asked thinking back to earlier and how I had opened my eyes after that amazing kiss only to find him gone.

"Chain him to the bed…what, it works for me," Pip said after receiving looks from us all.

"I don't think you will have to worry about that for long, as Dom will soon find his limits pushed to the point of no return. Now, all we have to do is make sure we have Ari in place…"

"Umm…what now?" Ari said raising her hand and I had to say, I couldn't help but feel bad for her.

"Here, let me handle this one…so here's the skinny, big booty, you have been sent back here with us for a reason and the only one we can think of is that you have some kind of baby making mojo that will help in getting the 'Tootie no baker' into a 'bun in the oven Tootie baker'… Capiche?" At hearing this, we all had our own reactions. Mine was to smack my forehead, Sophia's was to ask the Gods for strength and Ari's was to swear…loudly. Of course, just to add to our shit streak luck, it was now that the door burst open and an angry Draven sibling stormed in.

"Vincent!" Ari shouted making him growl at her.

"Brother, what are you doing here?!" Sophia shouted in surprise at the sight of her brother storming in like a man possessed.

"I could ask this of you dear sister, for I remember not long past that our Brother forbade you to do the very same," he snapped making her look indifferent and shrug her shoulders,

"You know I do as I please."

"As do I. Now Ariana, *come here*," he demanded and I couldn't help it as my mouth dropped…was this really the same Vincent?!

"No! I am not a damn dog!" she shouted back and folded her arms across her chest.

"I warned you what would happen if I found you gone from my chambers," he said this in such a way that it was the first time he looked related to his brother in such a way that I almost warned Ari what was about to happen. In the end Vincent's actions were quicker than my lips.

"Ahhh! Put me down, you big ape!" Ari shouted as soon as he had her up and hoisted over his shoulder. Yep, and there was the family resemblance I thought with a smirk.

"Your unwillingness to follow my order is only adding to my enjoyment little peach, now keep still before I see you bound again." Vincent warned playfully smacking her behind, making her shriek out in fury. Then he turned to face us and bent slightly to bid us good evening, as if there wasn't a woman over his shoulder, desperately trying to hold on to him for fear that she would be dropped.

"Sophia, your being here is but a passing memory."

"As was yours, brother," she replied grinning knowing that this meant neither would be in a hurry to tell their brother.

I had to say he left in much better spirits than when he first arrived as the mad panic and fury was now gone from his face the moment he felt Ari in his arms. Oh yeah, he had it bad.

"Is it wrong that I was just glad it wasn't my one that just burst in here?" I asked making the others laugh as soon as the door closed.

"I fear both my brothers are experiencing things they never thought possible and obviously their way of dealing with it, is pretty much the same," Sophia said in their defence.

"You mean they both act like cavemen who all but drag their little women back to their caves?" I said making Pip snort a giggle.

"Yeah, pretty much," she replied.

"I hate to be the baring peach bum of bad news here but if we are trying to plan mission, get rocket into Toot's atmosphere, then how are we going to do that without our main astronaut here to press the launch button?" Pip asked and I complained,

"Hey but wouldn't that kinda be my job?"

"No, Toots," she said and I asked,

"Why not?!" This was when she leaned over and patted me on the leg and said,

"Because you're the one flying the shuttle."

CHAPTER ELEVEN

OPERATION 'WOO DRAVEN'

Soon after hearing Pip make this very cryptic point, Sophia had simply said,

"Leave it to me." And I can honestly say I was more than happy to as I had enough of my own problems to deal with, the main one being how to destroy Draven's willpower and have him give up the manly goods…or his 'man rocket' as Pip had put it.

"So, what about Ranka, can she help us in…what?" I had asked as the way they both looked now, it obviously meant they knew something that I didn't. I mean yes, I thought it weird how I hadn't seen her, but considering I had spent most of the day naked in Draven's arms, then I guess it wasn't surprising.

"Well you remember when we were taken?" Sophia asked softly.

"Yeah by Uber dick Pertinax, I mean what kind of name is that anyway, sounds more like a laundry detergent!" Pip added making me laugh.

"Yeah, but that wasn't her…right?" I said remembering how he had took on the image of her vessel to trick us.

"No, it wasn't her, but the thing is…"

"Warrior woman has gone incognito!" Pip shouted once again interrupting Sophia.

"What do you mean? She has gone missing?" I asked making them both nod and I frowned wondering what had happened to her.

"But Draven never said anything," I argued and Sophia, bless her, patted my hand and said,

"Well I hate to point out the obvious, but my brother hasn't really been very forthcoming in the past when divulging important information to you, has he?" Okay so she had a very good point there as in Draven's mind, it was just stuff that I didn't need to worry about.

"So, what do we do about that?"

"Dom has some of his men looking for her and when I say men I mean…"

"Your own kind," I surmised and she nodded.

"So, there is nothing we can do?" I asked and Pip shouted,

"We are a little early in time for 'WANTED' posters but hey, I could always start off the trend, do you think you could draw a picture of her?" I smiled when Sophia sighed.

"I don't mean to talk to the press or anything…jeez, I am using the good side of my brain you know. I just mean to do a little recon, lay of the land, shake of the bush…that type of thing…ask around," Pip added when we were both stumped on the 'shake the bush' comment.

"That's not a bad idea." I said and after arranging for my new art supplies to be brought to me thanks to Pip, I felt better that we were at least formulating a plan. Of course, next on that list was a little trickier.

"So how exactly am I going to sneak past the guards, down

into the kitchen and cook him a meal surrounded by servants, without Draven going crazy mad, and pretty much giving us a repeat show of what Vincent just did?" I asked, to which this time Pip replied,

"Leave it to me." After this we pretty much tried to come up with every plan possible for me to bombard Draven with as many sexy, cute, loving gestures as possible in the hope that one of them would work enough in one night as Pip was worried.

"Care to share with the time travelling class," Sophia said as Pip looked deep in thought, chewing on her finger.

"I just have a slight concern." Oh dear, well I knew that if Pip was speaking normally, then it was definitely something to worry about.

"And that is?"

"Well, once they have done the disco dancing deed…" Okay, so back to feeling slightly better, well that was until…

"…that he will be able to detect that her soul isn't recognised in this time."

"Yeah but I thought you were masking that?" Sophia said and now I was completely lost as these two started to discuss something I had no clue about.

"I am but it's easy when her soul hasn't been touched yet… now after they dance the mambo together, then who the frick knows!" she said banging a hand on the bed, making Colossus grunt and take notice.

"Can someone please explain?" I asked and just as both of them pointed to the other at the same time, Pip won by getting there first. I had to say I was glad as I knew I had at least a chance at understanding this better from Sophia.

"Alright, so one of our gifts as you know is seeing souls… you know, detecting a good, bad, or in your case a rare Pure Soul, so that when we feed, it's like…"

"Reading a label on your favourite brand of cereal," Pip added, making Sophia hold back a groan.

"Yeah, like that," Sophia said and when Pip went back to fussing the dog, she looked to me and mouthed the words, '*No, nothing like that,*' before continuing,

"It just tells us a lot about a mortal and this gift is something we all possess as it's how we feed or gain energy, if you will."

"Okay, so yeah, I remember Draven telling me that, but neither he nor anyone else could feed from me," I said remembering back to all that time ago on his balcony.

"And this is true, we can't but that doesn't mean that people can't still see it," she told me and I thought back to all those strange cryptic comments people in my past had made, about me being a 'pure soul' or about me having a 'light'.

"Well, as for my brothers and I, we can also detect other things," she said as if trying to tread carefully.

"Like what?"

"Well, we can detect whether or not they intend to do harm or even lie and no, I know what you're thinking, but you don't need to worry, as you are not easily read like the others...it is because of your mind's shields I think, as if you are casting the barrier far enough to cloak your soul as well," Sophia added when I gave her a panicked look.

"Yeah not like when you told me about what he did to that boy Justin when he knew...why are you doing that cut throat actiony thingy at me...ooooh...my bad." Hearing this I snapped my head round to Sophia and shouted,

"He didn't!" Sophia sighed and said,

"He might have detected his intent to try and kiss you, so he might have slipped a little something in his drink." The way Sophia said this was as if it was a tiny little harmless bit of playfulness on her brother's part...but for me and the way I remembered it, not so much on the playfulness!

"Look anyway, take it up with lover boy when you get back but for now, focus," she said after clapping her hands in front of my face.

"The point is we may not be able to get a read on you but Pip is worried that once he connects to your soul, that he will be able to detect that it isn't from this time. Pip can only mask so much but even she might struggle with that one."

"Hey!" she complained and Sophia shot her a look.

"Your words, Pip!"

"Oh…oh yeah, sorry I forgot," Pip said looking sheepish.

"So, what you're saying is as soon as we have sex, then he might know that I am from a different time?"

"Like we said, it's a possibility."

Well hearing this didn't exactly fill me with hippy happy thoughts that was for damn sure. In fact, shortly after this the girls left me, as Sophia had to go and show her face in the throne room and I laughed as she made a 'kill me now' face. I gave them both a hug and gained strength through their comfort, which meant after they left I didn't go right back to sobbing hopelessly. No instead I got up and decided to clean the mess we had made in the living space just for something to do.

Thankfully the dog had cleared most of the remains, which even included the honey and spices. Man, I just hoped the dog didn't start farting in the night, because after all that spice, I wasn't sure I would survive it! I certainly didn't envy his poor stomach tomorrow, or the poor souls that had to clean up after his mess, that was for damn sure. No, in the end all I had to do was pile up the dishes and place them back on the table. I had even been tempted to carry them all down into the bathing room and wash them clean. But considering this was where we washed, I didn't think it wise.

So, with nothing else to do, I lay on the bed and snuggled up to another new male in my life and he…*well he snored.* I must have slept, which was surprising with all the crap I had going on inside my head. But I knew I had, for I woke when I heard a noise and in my sleepy state I stroked across the dog's head and said,

"Ssshh easy Colossus…it's just the wind," as he had started to rumble as if not happy about something. He soon calmed and I put my arm around him to both comfort him and myself as Draven still hadn't returned to me. I didn't know how late it was but after waking twice and still finding myself alone, let's just say I didn't hold much hope for him coming back…or so I thought.

"Colossus, down." I suddenly froze at the sound of his voice in the dark as the only light was from the moon shining through the open arched windows. The dog released a deep 'humpf' sound before doing as it was told, begrudgingly. I turned to look up at him and the imposing shadow he made had me swallowing hard.

"I see you have already replaced me," he said and after releasing a sigh I smiled,

"Well he usually does as he's told and seems to understand the word *stay* best of all," I said trying to make my point and I saw him grin in the moonlight.

"And this is a word you think I need to learn?" he asked folding his arms and I knew he was trying to keep his annoyance at bay.

"No, just *practice*," I said telling him in three words what I thought about him keep leaving me.

"I have a Kingdom to rule," he told me as way of an excuse, one that was a total cop out.

"And I am not included in that?" I asked unable to keep the bitterness from lacing that question, one he could easily detect. He released a sigh and pushed his hair back in an agitated manner.

"In time, I would wish for you to be very much a part of that but…"

"But for now, you don't trust me," I finished off for him and there was no way of keeping the hurt from my voice or my reaction from turning away from him. I looked out into the night and wondered how did I get to this point in my life? Because if I thought going to Hell and back twice, was hard then the reality was that Hell had nothing on this mental torture!

I felt him sit down on the bed but I didn't look, not even when I felt the backs of his fingers caress down my back.

"You're still dressed," he commented softly and I snapped,

"Yes, and I would rather stay that way." Okay so I knew this wasn't helping my 'Woo Draven' plan but I couldn't help it. I just hated this canyon sized void between us. It felt as if my soul was a mere shell of what it could be and it was screaming at me to reconnect to its keeper. But for that to happen Draven would first need to trust me enough to get past not knowing my *past.*

"You're vexed?" he asked me and I felt like getting up and saying something sarcastic, like 'Gee, aren't you observant!' But in the end, I decided that this day had seen enough backlashes.

"I have no right to be, you are king and I am just a woman in your bed," I told him on a sigh.

"You say this to hurt me," he said sounding angry.

"How else am I to think when you leave me after I speak of my love for you," I told him, now turning to face him and it looked as if he had finally started to get it.

"You are right. I should not have left you," he admitted and I knew that until this moment he had never even considered how his abrupt actions had affected me. But I couldn't be hurt by this, because I knew it wasn't done out of selfishness or through lack of loving me. No, it was simply because for a man like Draven, who was only ever used to acting on impulse and until now, he never had the feelings of others to consider.

"I see now of the pain you suffered from my actions and for that, I am sorry little Lamb, will you forgive me?" he asked me sweetly, getting closer before leaning his face into my neck and breathing deep as if my scent calmed him.

"Always," I told him and I felt his smile against my neck before he started kissing me there. I moaned and let my head fall back as it felt so good.

"I missed you," I said on a breathy sigh.

"Good, for I felt the same void Nāzanin, have no fear of that," he told me coming back up to the level of my face. Then he ran a thumb over my lips and said,

"I missed your smile and being the one to put it there," he whispered and I smiled under the pad of his thumb making him grin because of it.

After this there were no more words needed as he quietly undressed me and lay me down, tucking me close to his body. Then he covered us both and we said goodbye to the turbulent day together in the best way possible…in each other's arms.

The next morning, I saw the day in by being licked and not in a way I would have chosen.

"Oi, behave! Come on now, get off me!" I said laughing and the loveable brute only stopped when he heard his master's voice behind him.

"Colossus, come to heel!" Draven ordered sternly but I laughed when he just looked back down at me, making all his wrinkles fall forward. He panted and licked his chops once, moving from the bed only when I said,

"Go on, do as your master says." Draven huffed when he did and said,

"I believe he prefers a far prettier master than I." This made me laugh before it quickly turned into a yawn. Now this had Draven chuckling as he walked over to me.

"Go back to sleep, sweet girl, for you are still tired and I have a matter to attend to but I will come back to you," he told me softly and I looked to the window to see that it was only just dawn. No wonder I was still tired and this was proven when I yawned once again making Draven grant me a soft smile.

"Come now," he said and when I didn't lie back down in time he smirked as he quickly snaked a hand under the covers, so that he could suddenly yank me down.

"Oi! That was a dirty trick!" I complained trying to keep the grin from my face at seeing his playful side was back.

"When means must, my little beauty. Now do as you're told and sleep, for I command it by royal order of the king," he said and this time I giggled before answering back,

"Well only if my king demands it." Then I sat up a bit and pretended to bow.

"Ah I believe you are improving, yes much better than the first time we met, as now there is no one behind me to prompt such an action." At this I laughed and said,

"I recall you never had me punished for the offense." At this he leaned in closer and flicked my nose before saying,

"And I recall that you soon found yourself in chains and at the mercy of my touch as I will never forget my first taste of you." I blushed hearing this and he liked it as his eyes flashed purple for a split second.

"Now do as you are told and be good for me," he said almost purring the words. I bit my lip making him growl,

"Be good, my Nāzanin." I giggled again before doing as I was told and lying back down.

"I shall not be long," he said to me and after one last kiss, he was gone and I found peace knowing that it wouldn't be long before he was back with me.

"Mission control calling operation 'woo King'…are you hearing me, over?" I moaned when hearing this and rubbed off the feel of someone poking my nose.

"Confirm status, over." I heard the voice and batted away the annoying finger that continued to poke at me, this time at my cheek.

"ENGINE FAILURE, OVER!" Suddenly I bolted upright as I heard the screaming and I grabbed my heart in fright. This was when I heard the giggling from one naughty Imp, who just so happened to be one of my best friends.

"Laugh it up skinny butt, and next time you're asleep I will shave off your eyebrows," I warned making her laugh harder.

"It's okay, I still have some comedy stick on eyebrows leftover from Adam's Christmas stocking last year…come to think of it, I don't think he has used any of them." Now this made me laugh and I sat up, shaking my head just trying to picture poor Adam and what he had to put up with on a daily basis with his crazy little wife. Although looking at the way he obviously adored her, it was easy to say that I doubted he would have ever wanted it any other way.

"So, what's with the wake-up call?"

"Time to get to work, starting with a bath," she told me and I frowned at her.

"So how is that going to…" I started to ask but she just placed a hand over my mouth and whispered,

"Trust me…this is what I live for…"

"Wwwhat?" I asked muffled behind her hand.

"Sexually teasing my husband." Okay, so I had to agree with her there, she did seem to be a pro in that particular art

form. So, I did as I was told and put on the sheer white kaftan she handed me.

"So, what's the plan?" I asked her as I covered up my nakedness.

"Come with me and I will show you." So, I did as I was told and followed her down into the bathing room, wondering how this would help me. We walked down the tunnel and into the same domed room I now had very fond memories of thanks to Draven and his delicious body.

"Now any second he is going to come back to the room and be in a frenzy wondering where you are."

"Okay so how is that going to help me?!" I shouted thinking it wasn't sounding like a good plan at all.

"He will race down here and just as he reaches the side of the pool, you will rise out of the water and flick your hair back like some erotic cock tease on steroids...And I don't mean muscles but you know…"

"Yeah, I get it, I'll be all naked and…" This was when she stopped me and said,

"Oh, he won't see you naked, but teasingly he will see you in a very wet, see-through kaftan that will tease him to the point of pain, that is our aim here. And when the mighty blue balls king sees you, he will ask why you bathe dressed and you say…

"I was fearful of anyone else seeing my body, as it is for your eyes only, my Lord?" I said filling in the void making Pip grin in that 'I am a naughty Imp, hear me roar' type of way.

"Now she gets it," Pip responded and then continued with,

"Then, as he sees you like this, I am hoping he can deny you nothing, so you ask him if, with a guard, you can go for a walk…then we go and make him a meal good enough to give up the goods for!" Okay so it wasn't a bad plan, I had to admit.

"Okay so this might work," I admitted and Pip looked towards the door for a minute and said,

"Good because here he comes!" she said before running for the door, unlocking it and disappearing out of sight. I was just about to panic about the locks when she must have used her powers to make them slide back into place. Then as I heard him desperately shouting my name I quickly slipped into the water, with my heart beating erratically. I then pushed my kaftan down as it wanted to float up thanks to the trapped air under it. I didn't think that would have been the sexiest of sights, seeing me struggling and surrounded by white balloons.

So, just before he could emerge in the doorway, I took a deep breath and dipped my whole body under. I gave it a few seconds, hoping that he was near the pool when I emerged as gracefully as I could given my clumsy nature. But I ended up surprised as that was precisely what I did.

I rose up taking a deep breath and pushed all my loose hair back. Then I gave him a feigned surprised look at seeing him but the small gasp that escaped was very real. This was down to the undiluted look of lust he gave me when he saw me.

"Arsaces, are you well?" I asked softly as I took in his masterful form stood there almost panting he was breathing so heavily. His dark eyes bled into purple fire, one that didn't extinguish as he drank in my dripping wet form. I could feel the material of my kaftan clinging to every inch of my skin and my nipples pebbled at the intensity of it all.

"I…I…" I wanted to smile as I heard him try to find his words, something that was very rare for Draven to ever struggle with. So naturally this response made me bite my lip, something he also found an erotic sight on me. I saw him swallow hard and his hands at his sides turned to fists as if he was fighting with himself.

"You're dressed?" he asked in a deep voice, one thick with restraint. I gave him a shy little smile and said,

"I didn't know if this room was off limits or not…" I paused after saying this and looked to the only door in the room.

"So, I didn't want to take the chance without you with me," I told him causing him to arch an eyebrow in question, so I continued,

"My body is for your eyes only, my Lord," I told him and this was when I knew I had him just where I wanted him.

"Come here," he ordered in a soft lure and I did as I was told, giving him what he wanted. I knew this was a big weakness for a dominant personality like Draven's, something that was proven when I saw his hungry demonic eyes take in every inch of me as I walked from the pool. I stopped just in front of him and the blush bloomed across my skin thanks to the intensity radiating off him in erotic waves.

"I fear that seeing the beauty as I do now, would leave little to the imagination as to what lies beneath your clothes, my dear, for it looks like you have bathed naked in milk," he told me and I looked down at myself to see that he was right. It just looked like someone had picked me up and dipped me into a vat of cream. I looked back up at him and gave him wide eyes, hoping he took this for embarrassment, as let's face it, I knew what I was doing.

"I am thankful then that the door remains locked and I have forbidden anyone to enter this space other than that of your servant. For I fear if anyone were to gaze upon this divine beauty you bestow…" he paused to caress my near naked breast with the back of his hand before continuing,

"…Well, then they would no doubt meet with a bloody end indeed, for I fear my wrath unstoppable, given what you deem for my eyes only…something that has never been in question, for you are mine and *mine alone,*" he promised making me shudder from both his touch and his words.

"Now ask of me what you wish, little lamb," he said, surprising me.

"I…um…" I tried to speak past my shock that he would know, when he put me out of my misery.

"As much as I enjoy this sweet look upon your face, I fear I would be classed as cruel if I did not put your mind to rest," he said clearly amused.

"My lord?"

"Your servant informed me of such." Ah, so Pip had set it up, no doubt so I couldn't back out in asking him.

"Well she, I mean I…wondered if I would be allowed to go for a walk?" I said approaching the subject delicately, but even that didn't hide the displeasure on his face on hearing it.

"After all, I am not a prisoner, am I?" I added and I knew the look on his face said it all. But it was his words that felt like they had damned my fate…

"I am afraid that you are."

CHAPTER TWELVE

TRUSTING YOUR STOMACH

"I am a prisoner?" I asked in utter astonishment, one on the verge of morphing into rage.

"You are not permitted to leave my chambers," he said as a way of answering and I suddenly felt like screaming at him but I knew that would not have been my best option right now. Now guilt, well that was definitely the way to go. So, I bit down on the string of arguments I had against this, my main being 'you cannot just lock up your girlfriend'. No, instead I released a big sigh. Then moved away from him and walked over to the marble table that had a fresh pile of linen. I heard him do the same as he too sighed, obviously feeling the weight of his words at the sight of my cold reaction.

"Nāzanin, I can explain," he started to tell me as I lifted the wet kaftan up and over my head, before wrapping my body in a large piece of cloth.

"You don't need to as I understand perfectly, my King," I told him without any emotion as I grabbed another piece to dry my hair with. I heard him grunt as if my answer had irritated him.

"It is not safe for you to leave." This came from directly behind me and I turned to face him and said,

"Not safe for *you* is what you really mean, for you don't trust me."

"You ran from me before," he argued.

"I did but that was different."

"How so?" he asked folding his arms across his chest.

"Because that was from a fear that you would break my heart, for it was after I heard you speaking of your current head concubine and how that would not be changing in the foreseeable future," I told him dropping this emotional bombshell, one I named, 'big guilty guns'. He looked so taken aback by this, that at first, he didn't know what to say other than to confirm,

"You heard that?"

"Yes, which at the time gave me enough cause to save my fragile heart and run." As soon as I said this you could see certain things starting to fit into place for him. I had never told him this before and I was hoping now was the right time in taking the first steps for him to start trusting me. I knew that if I could just prove myself to him that his fierce need to keep me locked away from fear of losing me was unfounded, then maybe he would start to ease off a bit…or at least this was my hope.

"It is true I said this but what you didn't know at the time was *why* it was said."

"No, but now I trust you enough to know that the reason was no doubt done so with my safety in mind." Oh, now this surprised him and I would have laughed under different circumstances. But this was also said as a tactic, as I could only hope that he would reward my faith in him with some faith of his own.

"Then I consider your trust in me a gift, one that I fear should not be shadowed by my impulsive decisions." I gave him a huge grin and said,

"Does that mean I can…?" He smiled at the pleasure he was granting me and said,

"You may go for a walk, *but* only if you are escorted under my royal guard," he told me and I squealed as I threw myself at him, shocking him. He went back a step as he caught me and I peppered his face with little kisses making him laugh.

"I promise, I will not abuse your trust in me, for I only intend to earn it further," I told him feeling almost giddy that I finally managed to do something right and on plan for once.

"I am happy to hear it, little lamb."

After this I kissed him and when it became apparent that it would go no further, thanks to his iron will, I let him go and rushed back up to the room to get ready. He had more 'King's' business to attend to so after Pip came back to get me ready for the day, we soon found ourselves being escorted out of the room and to the gardens of the palace.

"Wowzer."

"Wow." Pip and I both uttered our own versions of amazement when being faced with the beauty before us. It had to be said that the Persians were masters at gardening and this was the proof. We were both escorted through a series of open arches which led out into what looked like a private courtyard the size of a ballroom. It was surrounded by a tall stone wall that was topped with scalloped arches and marble pillars topped with mythological winged creatures, that for all I knew were real in the supernatural world.

Down the centre of the grand space ran a long rectangular pool with water so clear, it almost looked surreal. Massive lily pads floated on the surface with huge pink and white flowers and the flashes of huge orange and red fish could be seen swimming beneath. Framing this marble pool were flowering bushes in between large urns overflowing with trailing flowers, looking like red wine was pouring out of them.

At the very end of the garden was a pretty stone seating area in a half-moon shape, that was shaded by a domed roof, painted gold.

"You know that the word 'Paradise' comes from the Persian word for garden as they were known for the greatest gardens of the world," Pip leaned in and told me, sounding very informative and surprising me.

"What? I like The History of Gardens and read it whilst on the toilet, that is when I am not playing Bubble Witch," she added with a wink making me chuckle.

"There aren't many people around?" I questioned leaning closer to Pip and one of the guards next to me spoke up,

"My King thought it best to have the area cleared, ensuring you a peaceful walk." At this I laughed and said,

"You mean a royal 'peace of mind' walk." I looked side on at him to find him trying to fight back a grin and he cleared his throat to reply,

"A safe walk for you is no doubt a peaceful one for my King." At this I burst out laughing and agreed,

"I can imagine so." Then I continued to walk the grounds basking in the hot sun and fresh air. Of course, I had only been allowed to do this after Draven had instructed Pip that I was to be covered from head to toe, for fear of burning my skin. At first, I thought this a little overkill and probably more down to Draven not wanting anyone to see any of my skin but now that seemed like a bit of a joke, as there *was* no one around to see me. Draven had made sure of that.

"If it pleases you, my King thought you might need some refreshments," the guard said holding out an arm towards the seating at the end. I nodded my thanks and continued down the gravel path that ran alongside the pool. The amazing smell of roses filled the warm air and with the sound of birds singing in the trees, it made for an idyllic moment in time.

We reached the end and the guards all turned their backs on us, positioning themselves at four points, no doubt facing any potential threats that could reach us.

"Wow, talk about paranoia," I said to Pip who giggled as we sat down.

"I know, I am even surprised he used men to guard us. Mind you, I can't imagine a man known for his temper wouldn't paint a gruesome enough sight if any of them dared to touch you," Pip said, sounding surprisingly normal as she deflated onto the stone bench.

"Are you okay?" I asked taking a seat opposite her.

"Just missing my honey pot," she said and I reached across and gave her hand a squeeze.

"I am sorry, it must be horrible for you and Sophia."

"Not gonna lie, it sucks the big one and not in a way I like…but we are a team, we are the Tittanian and the three Boobeteers!" she stated enthusiastically and I had to smile.

"You know I couldn't have done this without you guys. I mean hell, half the shit I do, I would be lost if I didn't have you girls with me and I want you to know that I am looking forward to the day that life's drama for us all doesn't always revolve around me." At this she burst out laughing and said,

"Oh, Tootie Pie, I wouldn't hold your breath or plan a fasting anytime soon, because that is like asking for a snowman in Hell and trust me when I say, that singing Olaf shit ain't happening down, down, hotter than Aussie land, under." At this I burst out laughing and couldn't help but hear my sister's groan about stabbing forks in her eyes every time Ella asked for the movie Frozen to be played.

"Okay well speaking of drama, how exactly are we planning

on getting into a kitchen and cooking for Mr Royally Overprotective?" I asked leaning towards her so that the others wouldn't hear, which ended up being pointless as she just called over the guard that we had been speaking to.

"Is there anywhere else we have been permitted to go, for the King's head concubine wishes to surprise him with some culinary delights from her home land." At this his dark eyes looked thoughtful a moment as he dragged a hand down his black beard. He was dressed differently from the rest and his thick sash tied around his waist looked to have metal rings attached in gold. I wondered if this meant he was higher up the ranks than the rest.

"You wish to go into the kitchens?" he confirmed, seemingly shocked by this.

"I do," I stated.

"I cannot see a problem as I will need to clear it first and then inform the King." At this I was about to argue when Pip intervened.

"Oh, but she so wanted to surprise him." I gave him a pleading look and after a moment's thought he agreed,

"I can see no harm." Then he turned back to his men and issued an order for one of them to go ahead and clear the space.

"Well, that was relatively easy."

"Yeah but after that comes the hard part," Pip informed me and I frowned,

"What do you mean?"

"Oh, just wait and see." And this was all she gave me.

After this ambiguous comment made by Pip, I soon learned why the hard part came once we were in the palace kitchens.

"I have no idea what most of this stuff is!" I shouted as Pip was lifting up a hooked metal tool that looked better suited in a torture chamber.

"Well, this here looks like one of those things the Egyptians used to pull the brains out of people before they made mummies…and this here could be used to scramble them first," she said moving on to the next poker looking device making me give her a 'eww' face.

"I would ask if Sophia would know but…" Pip burst out laughing at this and said,

"I doubt she even knows where this room is, let alone what's in it!" I had to agree with her on that.

"So, what were you thinking of making him?" she asked and I sighed and said,

"Well, one thing's for certain and that is my layer chocolate and strawberry cream cake is off the menu!"

"Okie donk, let's see what we have to work with at least," Pip said skipping towards what we knew to be the larder. It was down a few steps and kept underground to keep food cool naturally. The guards were situated outside the doors and I was almost tempted to go and ask one of them what most of this stuff was used for, but I decided other than the blades, then they would have been as lost as we were.

"I would say lamb meat balls, but I don't think we have much chance at finding a mincer around here, do you?" I said nodding to the cut pieces of lamb's meat.

"Okay, I have an idea," Pip said after running back up into the kitchen and lifting up what looked like a rolling pin.

"Tada!" she shouted and I put a hand on my hip and said,

"I am not seeing it, Pip."

"Okay, so I saw this one recipe on Pinterest where you flatten a chicken breast, like this…" she said making karate chops with the wooden pole, before carrying on,

"…Then you make a stuffing, roll it up and then dip it in

egg then flour a few times and then fry it…it looked amazeballs!"

"Wow, that does sound pretty good."

"Yeah and we have everything down here to make it, plus you could make some saffron rice to go with it, as there is a bucket load over there," Pip added, pointing a thumb over her shoulder.

"Great, okay so we have a plan, now you get the chicken and attack its poor breasts, whilst I make the stuffing…oh but wait."

"What is it?" she asked backing up the steps of the food store.

"How do we know when Draven eats his dinner?" I asked making her giggle,

"Leave it to me." Then with a wink she disappeared singing 'Here, chicky, chicky'.

A short time after this and added to it a load of giggling, we had pretty much finished making our meal. In the end, I had stuffed the rolled out chicken with some of the goat's cheese stuff I had eaten the previous night with onions, garlic, more herbs and finely chopped tomatoes. Then I had rolled them up but after failing at it twice, we wrapped some kind of twine we found around each breast so that we could fry them in olive oil. Then we covered them in egg and salted, peppered flour to create a nice crust after first removing the twine.

Needless to say, we forgot the first time and we both ended up pulling cooked string from our teeth. It wasn't a pretty sight, but one we both howled with laughter over. So much so, one of the guards came rushing in thinking I had burnt myself or something. The smell had me near salivating, as all I had eaten had been fruit.

I think Pip's favourite part in all this was battering the chicken breasts like Bruce Lee as she pretended they were planks of wood she was hitting and all to the sounds of a fake audience. I only knew this when she started to bow and thank imaginary people for coming.

So now it was time for the big reveal and after shedding about twenty meters of fancy blue material from around my body, I was left with a small waistcoat style jacket. To this was added a pair of loose trousers that were tight round the ankle with a thick gold band of patterned fabric and low to my hips, showing off a lot more skin this time.

Pip had gone to get the King as I was laying out our second feast, this time one I had made from scratch. I just hoped she could convince him to come back before it went cold as otherwise it would all be a bit pointless. There wasn't much in the dessert department I could actually make, so in the end I went with honey roasted peaches with chopped almonds and some sort of cream that I added honey to and a sprinkling of sugar, so that we could spoon it on top later. Alright, so it wasn't my famous chocolate cake, but it was as close to a dessert as I was ever going to get.

I heard the knocking at the door and had to smile when I heard Draven speaking behind it.

"What is the meaning of this?!"

"Only a surprise for you, my King." Pip answered and I raced to the door to stand in the way for when he entered. Then, as soon as the door opened, I issued my demands,

"Don't look! Close your eyes!" He looked taken aback for a moment and thankfully was too focused on me to look ahead towards my surprise.

"Nāzanin, explain this to…" I suddenly cut him off by getting close to him and pulling his face down to mine.

"Please…don't ruin your surprise," I said tenderly making his features soften.

"Now close your eyes for me," I asked him and after a sigh, he did as I asked. Then I closed the door behind him, first winking at Pip and mouthing the words, 'thank you' at her. Then I took his hand and started leading him round to the living space.

"What are you up to this time, little lamb?" he asked making me giggle,

"You will see, now no peeking!" I told him, thankful that he was playing along. Then I shouted,

"Surprise!" To which he opened his eyes and took in the plates of food before him. Bless him, he looked really confused.

"I don't understand, you wish to eat with me again?" he asked making me laugh.

"Well yes, but the surprise is that I made it for you," I told him grinning and the shock on his face was priceless.

"You made this?" he asked, as if this was impossible.

"Yes, and well, I thought after you liked those wraps I made you that you might like my cooking as well…see we have chicken and… Arsaces? Is everything alright?" I asked because he just seemed stunned and rooted to the spot.

"You cooked for me?" he asked and I nodded, suddenly going shy and wondering if this was a big no, no in his time.

"You were down in the kitchens today making me this?" Again, he asked and I just hoped he wasn't angry about that so I quickly said,

"Yes, but no one else was there and I was under guard the whole time. Please don't be angry as I just wanted it to be a surprise and to thank you for trusting me today," I told him quickly and he looked to me and said,

"I am not angry, for how could I be?" I gave him a small smile and then took his large hand in mine and led him to the little cushioned seats I had set up.

"Then let's eat before it gets cold," I told him and as he sat down I dished up his plate first and handed it to him. Then I did one for myself and poured us both some wine.

"And you made this?" he asked again lifting the plate and looking at the wrapped fried chicken in nothing short of wonder. I laughed once and said,

"Yeah, I made it for you, so eat."

After this he shook his head as if trying to make sense of what was happening before he cut into his food to take his first bite. I knew when his eyes widened in surprise that he liked it but like him, I wanted his words, so I asked,

"Do you like it?"

"It is delicious!" he said with his voice rising as if he were shocked to find it so tasty.

"Good, you don't know how happy that makes me," I said smirking down at my food, unable to wipe the smug look off my face.

"It is I that finds such happiness in the gift you give me, for it not only comes from your heart but also from your hands," he said, picking up my hand and kissing the back of it sweetly, making me blush.

"I feel blessed indeed, Nāzanin," he added and I bit my lip before telling him,

"You are most welcome, Arsaces."

After these sweet sentiments were exchanged we ate and after a few moments of silence I looked to Draven to find him looking down at his food with a small smile playing at the corners of his lips. He looked deep in thought and I left him to his secret thoughts, until he enquired,

"How did you make it?"

I laughed thinking back to Pip smacking the shit out of a chicken breast and told him all we had done to make the meal. He had laughed as I recounted about the chicken unravelling and stuffing falling out. I told him of other foods I liked to make and he was amazed to find that I even cooked at all. We continued to talk the evening away and it was easy to get lost in the time we spent together like this. It was as if we both forgot the heavy burdens on our shoulders, his being King and mine the reason I was here. No, instead we just talked and I got to learn even more of Draven's personality than ever before.

He told me of the places he had been and the battles he had fought, both mortal and supernatural. He even spoke to me about his parents and their forbidden love, even admitting to having a deeper understanding of his father's obsession with their Heavenly mother. It was at this point that he reached out to my face to hold my cheek against his palm as he said,

"At least I am blessed enough to be granted the right to keep you." At this I leaned further into his palm and then turned my face to kiss his skin.

"And an eternal life of your cooking to sample," he added making me laugh at him. I very nearly blurted out about my chocolate cake and my spicy 'Devil's chicken' I had made him once but thankfully I stopped myself in time.

"So, this was the real reason for your walk today?" he asked and I nodded and said,

"I wanted to do something nice for you, to show you… you…" I started to get teary and I didn't know why as my words felt too thick to speak past my lips.

"To show me?"

"How much *I love you,*" I finished and just as I did I soon found myself in his arms.

"As the Gods are my witness woman, how I love you too!" he told me back and kissed me before I could say anything more. He lifted me up as he rose to his feet, doing so effortlessly. Then he gathered my legs under his arm and picked me up so that he could carry me into the bedroom.

"Arsaces?" I whispered his name on a breathy moan hoping this was it, our time had finally come.

"I need to make you mine…*now."* he said forcing the words out as if he was close to breaking his vocal chords with how tense his neck looked. Oh, yes, he was on the edge alright and I knew now nothing would stop us…well that was unless Pip decided at that point to sneak in my head and whisper five little words that would douse the flames of passion for anyone

"Stop! Don't do it yet!"

"Why not!?" I yelled back in my mind as Draven started to follow me down onto the bed. In fact, I didn't know how I would ever stop as the feeling of his hands spanning my body as he kissed my neck. I threw my head back and moaned, forgetting Pip for the moment, that was until she said the dreaded words…

"Because Ari is missing!"

CHAPTER THIRTEEN

SPANNER IN THE SEX WORKS

The second she said this my whole body froze and Draven knew instantly there was something wrong. He pulled back from my neck, painfully slow and just as he was about to speak, an erratic banging could be heard at the door. Draven looked towards the sound and then back at me, silently asking me how I knew. Thankfully I didn't have to say anything as Vincent burst in through the door and saved me.

Draven was suddenly up and after issuing me a stern order,

"Stay here!" he then left the room.

"Shit!" I hissed through gritted teeth. It only took a moment for Draven to shout my name and playing the good little concubine, I got up and went to him.

"Vi… Vardanis?" I said stopping myself just in time.

"Do you know where she is?!" Vincent shouted as if half crazed. Draven sighed and then came over to me and gently raised my head to look up at him.

"Your sister is missing, have you seen her?" he asked and I let my mouth drop and I repeated,

"Ari is missing?" I knew this was enough to convince him, as to be honest, I was still in enough shock to pass it off.

"Have you seen her?!" Vincent asked again, this time more desperate than before.

"No, no I haven't." I told him almost spilling about us all sitting together the day before but once more stopping myself. Christ, but I was looking forward to when I could get home and just say what the hell name I wanted and speak the truth with ease! Being here was mentally draining.

"Calm brother, she will be found for the city is still on lockdown…she couldn't have gone far." Draven tried to comfort his brother's fears and when he looked back at me, I realised he tried to do the same for me also.

"We need to go look for her, we need…!" I said shaking my head wondering where on earth she had gone and then something terrible occurred to me.

"What if she was taken! What if someone sneaked in and…" I started to think the worst when Vincent spoke up.

"No, this did not happen, for she left me a note," he told me and I looked down at him, finally taking in the sight of the piece of parchment he held firmly in his grasp in a destroying grip.

"What did it say?" I asked delicately. I saw him flinch as if I had wounded him and he tore his gaze from me. So, hating seeing my dear friend this way, I decided to help him.

"Vardanis, listen to me, there is something you need to know about my sister," I started and this was when he looked back up at me. So, I walked over to him, ignoring the way Draven tensed the closer I got to Vincent. I placed my hand on his arm and said,

"She doesn't understand who she is. It's hard to explain but she suffered a great tragedy at the hands of men and because of it she lost all memory of her life before. Now her biggest fear is getting too close and suffering once again. It's why she doesn't trust people and no doubt this is the reason she is running scared," I told him, knowing that even without her telling me so, this was why Ari never opened up.

Unlike anyone else in the world I knew how she suffered, but unlike her, I had at least been granted my memories back. I could only imagine what Ari was going through and for someone like Vincent to come along and try to force her through her fears, well it was most likely why the Vincent back in my time was being so patient with her.

But the Vincent staring back at me now, looking utterly stunned, well then, he hadn't known what she had been through. He looked thoughtful a moment as if he was replaying where he went wrong now he had this new information to go by. Then he covered my hand with his, one I still had on his arm and he said,

"I cannot thank you enough for sharing this with me, for things are starting to become clear and the shadows of her refusal to speak, are now understandable. I will find her and I will not fail her again," he told me as a promise.

"Arsaces."

"I will soon follow for I need moment alone with my sweetest one," he said without looking at his brother, as his intense gaze was rooted to me. I didn't even notice when Vincent had left as all my focus was on Draven, as if he had the power to suck all my mental ability and centre it solely on him.

"You eased his suffering," he stated as if in awe by the fact.

"Of course."

"But why, you owe no loyalty to my brother, but you do to your sister?" he asked me and I knew it wasn't said in a nasty way.

"He is a man in love and I know that deep down she loves him too, it is why she runs."

"As it was why you yourself ran from me?" he surmised. I gave him a small smile and said,

"Let's just say that I know how she feels, as there are certain things in our past that are hard to explain to another, even if the person facing us is the person we love, because sometimes, it makes it harder."

"Why do you say this?" he asked frowning.

"Because, it is said to the one person we hope not to cast judgement on us the most." This was when he finally understood what I was telling him as it wasn't just my sister who faced her own demons of the past but me as well.

"And what of you little lamb, do you fear my own judgement be cast upon you, if I knew the truth?" he asked stepping closer to me, and tracing my jawline with a gentle fingertip. I closed my eyes for a moment and tried to strengthen my reserve, but one look at him once I opened them again and I knew I had failed.

"It's what I fear the most," I whispered to him and he swiped away the single tear as it started to fall. Then he placed his forehead to mine and whispered,

"I will know you my love, and I will not let you down when I do." Then he kissed me and left to go and join his brother in the hunt for my sister. I thought about his words and wondered if I could trust in them? It was easy to claim to not let the truth affect you, but when you didn't know what it was, could you really make such a promise. But in this case, then I knew…

Only time would tell.

Thankfully I didn't find myself alone for long as all I was doing was sitting in the seating area with my legs bobbing and my fingernails turning soft on two fingers from being chewed on.

"Any word yet?" I asked standing the second Sophia and Pip walked in. Sophia shook her head and Pip came over to me and gave me a hug and whispered,

"No worries Tootie babe, we will find her." I gave her a small smile in thanks and sat back with a sigh.

"Do we at least know why she ran?" I asked and Pip shook her head this time but Sophia no doubt had an idea.

"I fear my brother in this time isn't yet used to showing restraint," she said sadly and I grabbed her arm and said,

"But surely he wouldn't…*force her."* I hated that the words even formed and her eyes widened for a moment before she swallowed down the insult, putting it down to what it was, concern for a sister.

"No, never but…" She stopped and I knew she didn't want to finish but I needed to hear this. I knew there were things about Vincent that no-one spoke of and that steely reserve and calm nature had to end somewhere and I had a feeling where…*the bedroom*.

"Let's just say he has a lot of our father in him and like Dom, demands control in almost every aspect of his life. But unlike our brother, Vincent battles against the Angelic nature embedded in his soul. Therefore, has to fight harder to suppress the darkness in him when faced with something he is passionate about." She sighed and then continued,

"After all, love is the most powerful of all, an emotion he has not yet experienced until Ari came into his life…and almost two thousand years is a long time to learn control for when that first happened." Well, put like this, then it was easy to understand why the Vincent from the now was so different to the one I knew and this was something I needed to explain to Ari before Vincent found her.

"I have to go look for her!" I said making Sophia shake her head.

"If my brother finds out then that would be disastrous! Our main goal here was to get him to trust you enough to…"

"I know, I know but what else can I do Sophia, she is like a sister to me, I can't just leave her to be dragged back here kicking and screaming without any understanding?" I told her and she gave me a sad smile.

"I understand, I do but…"

"You know I think it might work in our favour," Pip said after being unusually quiet and obviously deep in thought, which could sometimes lead to genius solutions from Pip…or other times, just crazy shit we had no clue or chance at understanding.

"How so, because if my brother finds out, he will shit harpies!" Sophia said and I had to agree with her there.

"Yes, but if he finds her coming back on her own free willy and bringing a compliant big booty back with her, then what right does he have to wig out?"

"You know she has a point," I said and Sophia look thoughtful for a moment.

"Alright say we let you do this, that might also mean that our one way out of here is going to be compromised," Sophia informed us and this definitely peaked my interest.

"So, there is a way?"

"Yes, but once Dom knows about it, then that avenue of escape is lost to us."

"Well either way it doesn't matter because unless we have Ari back, then we are going to be stuck here a long time and I don't know how long I can hold your brother off from…"

"Engaging his rocket?" Pip added helpfully and I rolled my eyes before saying,

"What she said."

"So, the plan is working then?" Sophia asked with a smirk.

"Well yeah, after our rad, mad cooking skills, then I

shouldn't wonder." I smiled, looking down at the empty plates wishing I was back on the bed with Draven and none of this stuff with Ari had happened. I wish she had just let herself fall madly in love with Vincent and feel the same happiness as I did with his brother. But I knew now that my only way to help her was to find her first before the royal Draven brothers did.

"There is one other thing we need to discuss," I told them as it was my other concern.

"And that is?" Sophia asked and Pip scooted closer.

"I know I may be jumping the gun here but how exactly are we going to get back, because unless you know of a Janus gate around here or a quick way to get back to England, then I don't see many options."

"I only know of the Black Gates that are in the mountains where we were kept prisoner. It was what Pertinax used to get his own kind here so quickly," Sophia told me and I remembered hearing about it when Draven was speaking with Lucius.

"That's what Draven told Lucius to use to get back to Rome," I told them.

"It is a portal to use in the mortal realm, not one to be used for travelling through our worlds, let alone using it to get back to the future," Sophia said sounding as deflated as I felt on hearing it.

"Well, I guess that is just something we will have to face when the time comes," I said, knowing we had more pressing matters to deal with, like finding one of our lost Boobeteers.

"Now we have to think about where in Persia Ari could be?" This is when Pip slapped her hands to her knees and said,

"Well that's my cue."

"Cue for what?" I asked and she gave me a little head pat and said,

"To shake the bush." Then she left, leaving me and Sophia to look at each other and say the same thing at the same time,

"Recon."

"Recon."

It took until almost dawn for Pip to come back and I found myself glad that Draven nor his brother had found her yet. Pip had heard word that someone had seen a cart full of goods leaving the previous night that had seemed a lot fuller than usual. So, was it possible that someone had helped her or had she simply snuck in there when no one was looking?

Either way, it was our only lead so it was all I had left to go on. The cart had left by the north gate and Pip had heard that Draven and his brother were looking outside the south gate, which was the main gate into the city. They assumed she would go this way as really it was the only way to anywhere. But Ari wasn't heading to anywhere she knew, she was just heading away from here and that was all that mattered to her right now. I didn't know what was going through her head but I knew that I was the only one to help her, as I was the only one who knew what she had been through.

So here I was, heading out down a secret passageway after using the door in the bathing room. Sophia told me that only her kind knew about these tunnels, so she would try and think of a viable reason that I would know of them as well. It turned out that the tunnels took me deep underground until finally they levelled out. It was dark and wet down here but thankfully Sophia had given me a flaming torch, one that made my hand sweat, making the wooden pole keep slipping in my palm. I certainly missed my handy phone at this point, as the flash light app would have come in handy.

I don't know how long I travelled down the narrow tunnel but I was getting spooked doing so when it felt like a black wall was following me close behind. That was the thing with being in the pitch black, it almost felt like something solid surrounded you. I would find myself spinning around every now and again just to check I wasn't being followed. It took me back to the Hellfire caves, and fumbling around in the dark. It almost felt like you were being buried alive!

I stopped and leant my body back against the curved wall just to try and catch my labouring breath. *I was scared.*

"Come on Kaz, get it together, now is not the time to lose your shit," I told myself, almost jumping at first with the sound of my own voice cutting through the looming darkness. I didn't dare close my eyes so instead I focused on Ari, and what she could be going through right now. After all, it wasn't like I had landed in the desert and had the best of welcomes. What if another band of thugs were out there too…what if…oh god no!

"Ari!" I shouted her name and knew I had to hurry. So, with this in mind, I started to run down the darkness, no longer caring about my fear as it was now being overridden by a greater one. I needed to get to her and fast. So, I continued to run as fast as I could, nearly weeping in happiness when I found the door at the end. Thankfully it wasn't locked otherwise it would have been a long walk back with me singing every curse word I knew.

I looked to the wall and found an iron holder for my torch, so that I could see what I was doing without burning the crap out of myself. Then, once it was safely attached to the wall, I turned my attention to the door. I carefully lifted the heavy metal catch, and slide it through the hoop, making it creak and groan, before I could pull open the door.

Sophia had told me that it led straight out into the surrounding fields and was made in case there was ever a siege on the city and they needed to get the woman and children to safety. She told me the only path for Ari to follow from this side would eventually lead into the mountains. But thankfully the passageway had cut out a lot of the distance between us, so I was hoping it meant I wasn't too far behind Ari. That was of course, holding out for the hope that if she had snuck out in a merchant's cart, that she didn't just stay in it until they reached their destination.

Okay, so as it turned out there was a lot that could go wrong with this plan but in the end, all I could hope for was that Ari had snuck out of the cart from fear of being caught and was now currently walking at an incredibly slow rate. I raised up the hood of the cloak Sophia had given me and went on my quest to find my sister.

I was thankful that it was almost dawn as there was a warm pinkish glow meeting the night sky over in the distance, allowing me enough light to see where I was going. I had been half tempted to take my torch but then I would have stuck out like a sore thumb and I wasn't sure where Draven and Vincent were looking.

I decided to follow the straight lines of the crops until I could see the farm land end and meet the harsh desert sands. Well, back to the desert for me then, I thought with a grimace.

I don't know how long I walked but by the time I turned back the city was small enough that I could have hidden it with my thumb. Thankfully, the hot Persian sun wasn't yet out in full force as the sunrise had only started about twenty minutes ago. It was as though someone had turned a switch on the world, casting the sky into a burnt orange hue, making it look almost on fire.

And there in the distance was a lone shadowy figure that could only be one person. So, with the last of my energy, I started to run.

"ARI!" I shouted her name and the figure stopped dead, turned slowly and then started running back towards me. My heart felt utter relief when I saw it was her and we joined together, catching each other's bodies as we collided. Ari sank to the floor and started sobbing uncontrollably and I was left holding her tight to me. I stroked back her hair, ignoring my own tears as they fell, telling her,

"It's okay, I am here, I'm here now." I let her cry for a good long time until her sobs started to subside enough for her to speak.

"I…I…so, so…sor…sorry," she started to say in between her tears and I pulled her head closer to me and whispered,

"I understand why, Ari."

"You…you do?" The sound of her voice breaking had my heart aching for her.

"I do. I was there, so I know how hard it is to trust again as Katie is still inside me, she is still with us both Ari," I told her, admitting it for the first time to anyone.

"What do you mean…she's still inside you?" I gave her a small smile and told her,

"When I received my memories back, it was as if we just switched places and the Katie part of me, the Katie I was, well the only way to describe it was as though she took a back seat and let me drive." Ari looked thoughtful as if she was trying to process it all before asking,

"Does she ever speak to you?" I gave her a smile and nodded.

"She guides me, it's how I knew I couldn't lie to Draven."

"She told you not to?" Again, I nodded and then told her,

"Just like she told me to come looking for you, our sister." At this she smiled through fresh new tears and then grabbed me for another hug before telling me the truth of why she was here.

"I feel so lost and just thought…I thought that I could make him see me, that I could make him find the real me."

"You wanted him to know what he was doing to you?" I asked finally relieved that she was opening up.

"He's so intense and what he asks of me I can't give him. I wish I could, but each time he tries I get scared and he doesn't understand." I frowned trying to make sense of what she told me and then she spoke again and it all made sense.

"How can I fully give myself to a man I love, when *even I* don't know who I am?"

"It will never make a difference to him who you were in your past, he only cares for who you are in the future," I told her but she shook her head.

"But that's not true and we both know it. Look at the lengths Draven has gone to trying to find your past or even back in our own time. He nearly sacrificed my life to have you back and would have done so had it not been for you or Vincent…not that I blame him," she added squeezing my hand. I thought about her words and knew that she had a point.

"But Vincent will love you no matter what," I told her and she winced and then came the next stream of tears when she said

"But what if…what if he falls in love with someone that's… that's…*bad?"* This opened the flood gates and I caught her as she fell forward into my embrace. Luckily, we were still sat on the sand or she would have knocked me over.

"Oh Ari, my sweet sister, is that what worries you? Listen to me…look at me Ari," I told her lifting her face up. Then I wiped away her tears and said sternly,

"Now you listen to me! You are one of the kindest, most courageous, caring, loving souls I have ever known and I can say this not because you are my sister but because I owe you my life for I would have died without the strength you gave me to carry on. All those times, every beating, every starving day and every over worked muscle I did it all finding a smile each day because of what you gave me!" I told her and when she tried to turn her face from me I wouldn't let her, not before I told her,

"So, I don't give a damn who you were before because that is not important...for it is who you are *now* that will only ever matter and if Vincent doesn't realise that, then he is a damn fool and does not deserve your heart." Hearing this she burst into more tears, placed her head to my shoulder and whispered the only words I needed to hear...

"But I love him."

After this I smiled, feeling my heart soar for the both of them, because I knew in the end they were destined to be together. So, I let her have the time she needed before telling her softly,

"Then it's time for us to go back and you must tell him that, for nothing else will matter to him, I promise you." She nodded and we both got up, laughing when we shook the sand from our cloaks. Then I took her hand in mine and we started walking back towards the palace.

"We can do this," I told her and she gripped my hand tighter telling me that she was with me.

"Together," she said looking towards our destination and it felt like that night all over again. The one where we finally broke free and made a run for it into the unknown. Well, this was the same, as we were heading towards an unknown future but like that night, we were together and back in that palace we were not alone. Which had me asking myself if even this, like back then, had also been in the Fates' plans and if it was, then why?

"Do you think we will ever get back home?" Ari asked me

as if reading my mind. I looked back towards the mountains, thinking of the Black Gate and said,

"I have no clue how, but I hope so because I don't fancy peeing in a pot until plumbing is invented!" At this she laughed and said,

"It's a shame we don't have one of those magic coins left so that we could just create our own doorway home." It was at this point I stopped dead and her hand fell from mine.

"Kaz?" My hand shot to my neck and then I looked out into the desert wondering how I could have forgotten everything about it.

"Okay scaring me now…whoa!" she shouted as I suddenly grabbed both her arms and shouted back,

"Ari, you're a genius!"

"I am?"

"Yes! I can't believe I didn't think of it before!" I said to myself, this time making Ari look at me in a puzzled way so I put her out of her misery.

"I know a way to get us home!" This was when her eyes widened and the biggest smile crossed her lips.

"Oh, thank God!" she said making me smile. Yes, thank God indeed.

The rest of the way back we started making plans and all I could hope for was there was a way to find what I needed to get us home. That's when we would need help, which meant our next mission was to find…*Ranka.*

After this we continued to walk until the palace started to get bigger, telling me we had about another hour's walk until we were at the gates. I didn't think it wise to use the tunnels again to get back inside and besides, I had got a bit lost and didn't think I would have much hope in finding the entrance again anyway.

"Are the girls angry with me?" Ari asked after a while.

"No, they were worried." Hearing this made her smile and she said,

"It's nice having people to care for you, isn't it?" I gave her a sideways grin and said,

"Yes, it is. They are family." And she nodded as her gorgeous blue eyes sparkled from unshed tears that held there from the sentiment.

"And speaking of people who care," she said and nodded towards the new sight in front of us. We both tensed as the riders got closer and I was left to hope that this was going to go to plan or we were both going to find two very angry royals on our hands.

So, we both took a deep breath and…

Faced our future head on.

CHAPTER FOURTEEN

FACE THE HORSES

The sight of Draven sat upon a massive black horse was one I would never forget for as long as I lived and hopefully beyond my short life. He was as stunning as the striking black beauty he was sat upon. His black armour reflected the hot sun making it look as though it had been dipped in crude oil and his helmet made him look like some dark knight, coming to deal out punishment. It was a simple design that covered most of his face, coming down his cheeks in two solid pieces that curved and a nose piece coming down like a dripping diamond shape. The top was a mohawk of jet black hair that stood up straight, getting longer at the back. It looked more Greek in design than the domed helmets that most of his men wore, men that now framed either side of him and his brother.

I could only see his purple eyes through his helmet and they were looking at me with an emotion I couldn't read from this distance. I looked to Vincent to see he looked the polar opposite of his brother, being that his armour was brushed gold and his helmet had a deep red mohawk of hair instead. Even his horse was a pale one and the differences between them both looked like yin and yang positioned next to each other. Like Heaven and Hell had both sent riders in search of us.

I decided not to look at Draven again for fear of his wrath, a rage that would have scared the shit out of me considering how menacing he looked. So instead, I squeezed Ari's hand and led her over to Vincent. The men thankfully seemed frozen at the sight of us as if the last thing they expected was to find us both walking back towards the palace hand in hand. And from the way they were dressed, then they looked to have been expecting trouble. I suppose I couldn't really blame their caution, not considering what had happened to me when first arriving here.

"It's okay Ari, he will take care of you," I said, loud enough for Vincent to hear me and he bowed to me after dismounting his horse.

"I am forever in your debt Nāzanin, for finding her and in bringing her back to me," he told me and then wrapped a secure arm around her waist, pulling her close to him. I watched as she released a comforting sigh and snuggled in closer to his embrace, one he seemed utterly shocked by.

"Come, let me get you home, little Peach." Then he lifted her up, so that he could place her on his horse. She gave a startled yet excited yelp and I bit my lip at seeing her looking happy for the first time in a long time. She loved horses and, sat upon one now, she looked born to do so. Vincent took a moment to look at her as if she had just been dropped from Heaven itself and just for him alone. I even noticed him shake his head a little as if trying to understand what was happening to him. It was a beautiful sight.

I watched as he mounted his horse behind her, pulled her close to him and then he took the reins, before riding off towards the palace. I then took a deep breath before having to deal with my own demonic rider.

"Leave us!" Draven demanded in a severe order directed at his men.

"Yes, my King," his general said, nodding in respect before he too ordered his men to leave for the palace. This left just Draven and I alone in the desert. I had no clue what he was thinking and even when he too swiftly dismounted his majestic steed, I found myself wondering which way this was going to go. So, I took a deep breath and held it in as he walked over to me with such purpose.

Once he was what he deemed close enough, which was inches away, he raised my face up to look at his, and then he tore off his helmet. His unruly hair added to the raw beauty and I couldn't help but gasp at the sight. He was devastatingly handsome and if I wasn't so unsure of how these next few moments were going to go, I would have thrown myself at him!

"You left me," he stated, his voice thick and hoarse.

"I…" I was about to speak but he placed two fingers across my lips to silence me and when he was assured of my silence, he then cupped my cheek with his gloved hand. I closed my eyes and leaned into his touch as he whispered,

"You were coming back to me." I swallowed down the emotion, but not until a single tear formed. Then I opened my eyes and told him the only words that needed to be said, with such desperation no one could ever deny them as being anything but the truth,

"I will always come back to you." This was when he dropped his helmet in the sand and reached down with both hands, framing my face before he pulled me in for a what felt like a desperate kiss. I reached up on tip toes, letting my hood fall back and wrapped my arms around his neck straining to get

even more of him. It was beautiful. It was sensual and raw but most of all, it was…

My perfect first desert kiss.

After this amazing reunion, he seemed reluctant to let me go but then after touching my heated cheeks it seemed to tell him something.

"Come," he said, and again with even that one word spoken, it sounded as if dragged from deep within him. I nodded and took his hand, but then I stopped.

"Nāzanin?" he said my name as I bent down to retrieve his helmet so that I could hand it to him. Even this small action looked to have touched his soul in a way I would never fully understand. Then, just to get past the moment without turning all shy with the look he was giving me I said,

"You look too handsome in it to leave behind." At this he threw his head back and laughed as if he needed it after such a long night. It made me wonder if he even knew I was missing? He grabbed me to him and then slowly led me over to the massive beast…another pet of his.

"Ssshh, easy boy," he cooed as his horse flicked his long wavy black mane around as if showing off. I backed up and into Draven's chest at the sight.

"Do not fear him," he told me, leaning down and speaking in my ear.

"Here, now!" he suddenly demanded and I was surprised that this worked better than the gentle coaxing he had started with.

"He's…he's exquisite," I told him, as it was true, for I had never seen such a beautiful creature in all my life. He was the darkest black horse I had ever seen, and I remembered the farms my mum used to take me and Libby to when we were little, as she loved the horses there. I think the breed was called

Friesian from the Netherlands, which begged the question, how one would have made it here in this time?

"His name is Arion and this time, a gift from my mother," he told me surprising me with this knowledge. Arion was as huge as a shire horse and like the breed, had a feathering of hair around his lower legs that looked so soft to touch. His long mane and tail was a mass of unruly waves of black and he was all elegant muscle.

"Arion?" I questioned.

"It means an extremely swift, immortal horse." Hearing this I laughed and said,

"Couldn't have been more fitting then as I guess he is fast?" Draven scoffed once and said,

"I believe I cursed him for not being fast enough when searching for my missing lamb," he told me, answering my earlier silent question if he had known if I had been missing.

"I am sorry I made you worry," I told him softly and he nodded, accepting my apology without words. Then he walked past me and grabbed the reins of his horse, pulling him closer. I took a step back at the sight and Draven raised a questioning eyebrow at me.

"You are afraid?" he asked.

"It's been quite some time since I have been round a horse," I told him without thinking about it. I knew my mistake the second I saw his eyes narrow. Stupid Kazzy! I mean I was now living in a world where if you wanted to travel anywhere then you could only do so by horseback. And was I forgetting so soon of being on the back of one with Lucius, in trying to get to Draven when he fought Pertinax?

"Well, I mean on my own riding one I mean," I said quickly but from the looks of his hard features I would be surprised if he believed me. I was just happy that he left it alone and didn't press me further on the matter.

"Plus, he is like the biggest horse I have ever seen!" I added, ending this with a nervous laugh. Draven huffed his own laugh and went back to pull something off his saddle, before handing it to me.

"Here, you need to drink. Your body is dehydrated," he said quickly going stern again. I took the black leather flask from him and started to drink, relishing in the cool water as it went down and soothed my dry throat. I decided to stop now before it was empty so that I could offer it back to him. He looked touched for moment by my gesture and then he frowned as if something had displeased him.

"No, drink it all, I brought it for you."

"Honestly, I'm okay, I have…" I started to say this but stopped when he growled at me, and sternly snapped,

"…*Not had enough*, now do as you are told and drink." In the end, I didn't 'do as I was told' but instead asked,

"Why are you so angry at me?"

"Why?" he repeated as if utterly astonished at my question.

"Yes, why?"

"Because, my naughty little lamb, I not only find you missing from a place you promised me you wouldn't leave, but I do so to find that you are out in the desert without a weapon and most dangerous of all… *without water!*" he snapped yanking me to him, lifting me up and then after this burying his head in my neck to take in my scent. I knew that this worked in calming him down as it was obvious he had been worrying like a crazy man.

"Oh…that," I murmured knowing he was right.

"Yes, *that,*" he muttered dryly against my neck and I couldn't help but giggle.

"Are you laughing?" he asked incredulously.

"Um…no?" I said trying not to laugh again but failing miserably.

"I fear that you are," he stated acutely.

"I am sorry that I made you worry," I told him again pulling back so that I could kiss him on the cheek. He eyes soon softened and I knew I was back where I wanted to be, which of course, was on his good side.

"You did, but as I have you back in my arms once again and I see that surprisingly, no harm came from your little endeavour, then we shall speak no more about the matter," he told me and I think this was his way of accepting my apology.

"Now let's get you home," he said, this time in more tender tones.

"Arion, here!" he shouted, and his horse, as before, responded by moving closer to us.

"Up you go." This was my only warning as Draven wrapped an arm around my waist and putting his foot in the stirrup, he gripped with one hand around a horn shaped handle at the front of the saddle so that he could pull us both up. I yelped as I dangled to one side before he got his leg over and then pulled me up the rest of the way with no effort at all.

I placed my leg over, which he helped me with and then he patted the horn in front of me.

"Hold onto this," he told me pulling himself closer to me and taking hold of the reins either side of me. I was suddenly transported back to less than a week ago when I was doing the very same thing with Lucius at my back. I had to close my eyes against the memory, forcing it from my mind.

"Good girl, now hold tight, for we will be travelling at speed," he warned me and I stiffened against him.

"Umm…can we not just, you know…"

"Alright sweetness, we will start off slow…alright?" I nodded my head making him chuckle before he gave Arion his starting command.

"Steady we go, boy." Then he clicked his tongue against the roof of his mouth and the horse obeyed.

"Whoa!" I made an uneasy noise making Draven place both sides of the reins in one hand so that he could place a hand to my stomach. There he gave me comforting little pats and told me,

"Try and relax, I'm not going to let you go." Hearing this I did what he said and he felt it on my belly when I took in a deep breath.

"Good, now just try and breathe with the motion he makes…feel it… now just swing your hips back and forward with his steps," he instructed me, as he tried to get me to move with him by gripping a large hand to my upper thigh making me swallow hard.

"See, nice and easy. Trust in your steed and he will have trust in you," Draven said humming words of encouragement closer to my ear.

"Like in relationships," I told him teasingly. Then he gripped on to my thigh harder and after nipping at my neck he told me,

"Behave, little lamb." I giggled once but did as I was told.

"Ah, but I already foresee that you will make a good pupil of mine," he told me and I couldn't help but repeat the question,

"Uhh…pupil?"

"Yes, I find myself very much looking forward to teaching you how to ride." I gulped and had to confirm with words that he meant what I dreaded he meant.

"You mean like, *on my own?*" I very nearly hissed the words making him roar with laughter.

"Yes, my beauty, *on your own,*" he whispered seductively, no doubt loving the idea of it all even more now he knew he could tease me with it.

"I think I will stick with you, if you don't mind." I told him firmly, making him laugh again, and with being so close to him, it ended up jiggling up and down next to him.

"She goes up against a Persian God and stabs him in the heart with his own weapon, but the idea of riding a horse alone frightens her!" he said as if speaking to the Gods.

"Well, what can I say, we all have our weaknesses," I threw back at him cockily. But then he took my reply as a challenge and his hand snaked down and covered my sex. Once there he tapped it twice making me shudder and whispered in my ear,

"Yes, that we do, my sweet tasting Electus." Then he continued to keep his hand there, cupping my sex and I had to say that with the motion of the horse, it was soon driving me insane wanting to come. I gripped his hand and tried to move it, quickly making him tut in my ear,

"I don't think so, no indeed, I believe it is time for a little... *punishment,"* he hummed in my ear making me press myself back against him and moan. Then his hand left me and I didn't know whether to protest or be thankful, so instead I looked round so that I could see him and asked,

"What are you doing?" he lifted a gloved hand to his mouth and bit down on the leather, pulling his hand free of the confinement. Then once free, he dropped the glove into his lap and came back to my sex. I would have lied if I had said it wasn't one of the sexiest things I had ever seen in my life!

"I want to feel your inner channel clenching my fingers," he told me smoothly, before ducking his hand into my waistband and placing his palm flat against my mound.

"Ahhh!" I cried out suddenly as he inserted two thick fingers like he said he would. I arched back against him, holding on to the horn, for fear that I needed something to anchor me to this world. The feel of him inside me was incredible and with the wild motions of the horse, it naturally set a rhythm for rocking his fingers against that inner bundle of nerves.

"Tell me Nāzanin, do you want me to grant you your release?" he asked me and I was getting so caught up in the moment that I couldn't speak. But then he gripped me harder and I cried out,

"Now answer me. Do you want me to grant your need to come?" he asked firmly.

"Yes, yes, please," I said as I would have given him anything to do just that.

"Mm, maybe you don't want it as much as I thought," he said cruelly and I suddenly gripped his arm to stop him from moving.

"No! Please, please I do, I want it! I need it! Please Arsaces…oh please." I begged enough to make him satisfied and if I didn't need his hand as badly as I did right then I would have turned around and hit him for chuckling.

"Ah, now that is better…such sweet words spoken when you beg for it. Now are you ever going to leave the palace again without my consent?" he asked and I suddenly knew what this was, it wasn't just about punishment, no it was about compliance. I wish I could have said my will was strong enough not to give into him but with being so close to the pleasure he could give me, then my will had evaporated the moment he put his fingers inside of me.

"No, I will not," I told him.

"There's my good little lamb, now are you going to come all over my hand like a good pet of mine?" he asked and his erotic words just drove me higher and I moaned again, as it brought me that extra step closer to chasing my orgasm.

"Yes, oh yes please." I asked of him and he growled low, demanding me to do as he said,

"Then hold on tight!"

Then he shouted another commanded and suddenly the horse took off at a faster pace and this drove his fingers in and out of me at greater speeds.

"AAAHHH!" I screamed seconds later coming in long hard waves, shuddering against him. Then as I could take no more, I begged,

"Please, no more." But at this he just laughed an evil, wicked sound and said,

"Only I say when you are done and I have not finished with you yet!" he told me and I cried out again.

"After all, *this is a punishment,*" he whispered down at me with sexual cruelty lacing his words.

"No please…oh Gods, I am going to come again!" I warned him without needing to but then he said,

"I can't wait to feel you gripping onto my cock the way you do my fingers. To feel your juices dripping down my length, holding me tightly connected to your body, for I fear I will never want to leave such a sweet, warm home for my cock." This once more pushed me over the edge and I screamed again. It felt like flash bombs had just exploded beneath my eyelids, for my eyes were still closed but I felt blinded by the intensity of it all!

"One more I think," he told me and soon I was sobbing.

"No! no, no, no, please! I will do all that you ask, but I can't take it…I…oh…please." He stopped listening to my desperate words spoken in breathy moans and instead he listened to that of my traitorous body, moving with him and not wanting to let go.

"I can't wait Nāzanin, do you hear me! I cannot wait until I am seated firmly inside of your core, for you will be a good girl for me won't you…?" he asked and I nodded frantically as he started flicking his fingers harder against me.

"Then tell me, for I want the words."

"Anything!" I told him and I felt him smile against my neck before he whispered the last words needed to make me come one last time.

"Say you will take all of my cock! Say it now!"

"I will take it all!" I shouted and thankfully he let me find my last release, one I nearly passed out from. I screamed long and hard this time and once it was over he finally stopped moving inside of me and commanded his horse to slow once more. I turned my head side on and rested it against his arm, as it felt as though I didn't have enough strength to even lift it.

"Alright little one, Ssshh, just breathe…let's calm that little fluttering heart of yours, shall we?" he said soothingly and when he gently removed his fingers from my now tender, pulsating flesh, I winced and moaned.

"I think you will remember not to disobey me again so soon, am I right little lamb?" he asked and I could merely nod as my answer. Then I watched as he brought his soaking hand up and lick his fingers and palm as if it was honey he took great pleasure tasting.

"Oh Gods." I muttered in a hoarse voice, rough from screaming. I was so embarrassed by the intimate and carnal act, that I felt myself spasm again.

"I see you blushing from here sweet girl, but you should know it is my gift to taste whenever I please and I will warn you…" he paused so that he could dip down again and gather up more of my release before sucking it from his fingers. I made small pleading noises at the sensitive feel of him touching me again.

He simply grinned down at me and said…

"I am Fucking addicted!"

CHAPTER FIFTEEN

KING OF KINGS

When I woke I realised that I must have slept the day away and I was pretty sure this started from the moment after my last orgasm on a freakin horse! I think I must have even beaten Pip with that one. I know it was crass and probably not at all 'pure' of me but I knew the second she made it through the door I would just shout it out at her. Which just so happened to be precisely what I did.

"I orgasmed on a horse!" I shouted the second she walked into the bedroom and thinking back, this sounded way too 'weird, wrong, animal abusive, sick, twisted, violating and any other words of utter disgust that needed to be thrown in there, so I quickly added,

"I mean on Draven's horse and he was there…not watching or anything but, you know, like he did it to me with his fingers and…what? Why are you looking at me like…?" And this was when my shame hit hellish new levels, one that had the ability to set my cheeks alight by the Devil himself! Because swiftly behind Pip was of course,

Draven.

"Okay, so here's your clothes...bye!" Pip said throwing me a bunch of material and legging it out the door. I could hear her roar of laughter from back inside a thick wooden door and past two stone walls. I think my mouth was still hanging open even after minutes had passed. Draven, on the other hand, was looking oh so pleased with himself and boy was he trying to fight a smirk.

I might add that he totally sucked at it!

"Would you prefer I send for the city's crier, for I fear your news didn't reach far enough?" Draven couldn't help but tease and I groaned once, fell back down onto the bed, covered my head and decided to stay this way and moan for the rest of eternity.

I heard Draven roaring with laughter and I groaned again and said,

"I am going to die of shame!"

"I don't believe that has ever happened before," he told me coming to sit next to me on the bed. I whipped back the covers and said,

"Yeah, well there is a first time for everything!"

"Like finding your release on the back of my horse?" he asked teasing me again, making me yell,

"Grrr!" Then I re-covered my head and hid from the world.

"Forgive me, for I find I am enjoying this greatly at your expense," he said chuckling and I said,

"Yeah and it sounds like you're really sorry about it!" The next minute the covers were yanked down and he was covering my lips with his. I let myself be lured into his kiss and once he pulled back I whispered,

"That was a dirty trick, my naughty King." He simply grinned down at me and replied,

"When means must my sweetest one…now ready yourself."
I frowned and asked,

"Why, where are we going?"

"Tonight, we celebrate, so I ask for you to join me this evening in the Great Hall." I looked down at the floor, where a pile of material now lay and said,

"That was my dress, wasn't it?" Draven laughed again and said,

"I will send your servant back in here to help you."

"You know, she's not really my servant…right?" I told him and he gave my chin an affectionate little shake before saying,

"Yes, little lamb, I know this." Then he pulled me closer for another kiss before he whispered sweetly,

"Soon I will have you but until then, I will see you at my throne, little beauty of mine."

Then he was gone.

For once I had to say I wasn't looking forward to Pip coming back as I knew the second she popped her head around that door the teasing would start and probably not finish again until I did the next stupid and embarrassing thing. Which, granted, could be within the hour knowing me. Speaking of which, I was currently picking the dress off the floor when I heard,

"So, the king gave you a wild ride, eh?" I mouthed the words 'give me strength' and turned to face our resident troublemaker.

"Haha, you could have told me he was right behind you!" Pip laughed once and said,

"Yeah well here's a tip for next time, Tootie Shame Maker, a thought comes to mind, you hold on to it for say, twenty seconds longer than you want to and then blurt it out at me when the coast is clear. I mean geez…I hope the horse isn't too traumatised."

"Whatever, laugh it up! And besides, it's a boy," I told her not really sure of what point I was trying to make.

"Wow, you do work fast, Mazel Tov!" she said, this time making me laugh.

"His horse, it's a boy."

"Oh well that's alright then, because it would have been like totally weirdo wacko if it had been a girl." I laughed again and then said,

"Come on woman slave, time to tackle my hair, for my presence has been requested in the throne room," I said this putting on a posh accent and trying to sound like the queen.

"Great, just the job for muggins here…seriously, can' t they just make the afro comb and have done with it!"

"Hey, my hair isn't that hard to brush!" I complained making her wink at me and say,

"Not when it's in a cute little bob it isn't."

"Oh no! You are not coming anywhere near me with a blade in your hand!" I warned making her giggle.

"Fine, well we'd better get started because the festivities have already begun and you wanna get your ass down there before all the half-naked, coin dangling ditties all start shaking their titties at your husband from another time!" Okay, so as weird as that sentence sounded, I had to agree with her, so I said in a panicked tone,

"Let's get a move on!"

I had no idea how much time had passed as without a clock to go by, days were all merging into one here. So, let's just say some time later I was being led by four armed guards down into the Great Hall, a place I remembered back from when I first arrived. It was the same large space that I swiftly found

Draven's blade at my throat and I had to admit, not one of my fondest memories, including my husband.

I don't know why but I was nervous, just like I had been when Draven had first chosen me as his head concubine. And for some reason, just like back then, this felt like a test. Was this all to see how I would deal with this side of his world? After all, since I had come here, other than that one time, he had pretty much managed to keep me separated from his kingdom.

Pip had told me of all the rumours flying around the palace as people were going crazy with gossip about me. She was halfway through pinning my hair up into barrel curls when she told me one story. It was that Draven had been so captivated by my beauty, he had locked me away so that no-one but him would ever be able to gaze upon it. I had blushed scarlet and thought, well at least that is one rumour that will be quickly put to bed after tonight. The same went for another one where someone heard that every day he had my whole body painted with gold flowers so that he would know if I had been touched by another. And these were the tame ones, as there were stories far more ridiculous, which was most likely why I found myself so nervous.

"Seriously, couldn't he have picked a more revealing dress, I don't think I can actually see any bare skin other than on your neck and head!" Pip complained and I had to agree, it was true. Although something Pip said did surprise me.

"Draven picked this?"

"Well I certainly didn't, that's for damn sure! I would have had you in one of those glittering bikini tops and some see-though harem pants, like those chicks over there," Pip said nodding to all the nearly naked dancers that were annoyingly beautiful and currently trying to entice their king into becoming hypnotised by their hips.

"Kinda makes your eyes go cross-eyed, don't it?" Pip said and I had to agree with her on that one.

"Okay, let's try and sneak closer so as not to draw atten…oh no." This genius idea of mine was cut short when suddenly what sounded like a bloody gong was hit and was currently echoing through the enormous space. Of course, everyone turned to face me and I suddenly wanted to grab one of the dishes filled with fruit from one of the servant girls and throw it up in the air. Then I would make my escape as people focused on flying pomegranates and raining grapes.

This was my most practical of ideas as the entire room parted in the centre like I was sodding Moses and had the power to plague them with flying cats or something.

"Pip, I can't do this…I can't…" I muttered to her wanting to turn around and run.

"Look, just pretend you're at your wedding and you're meeting your groom…just keep looking at the King…look, he is watching you," Pip advised, so I took a deep breath and did what she suggested. Well, if I thought looking at Draven was any better I was very, very wrong. Seriously, why did he have to look as though he was undressing me with his eyes. No, scrap that, why did he have to look at me like he was currently ripping my clothes off with his eyes!

I was now even more thankful for him picking my outfit choice as at least I wasn't doing this wearing about as much as Princess Leia in a gold bikini. No, instead I was wearing a long, deep purple dress that had two slits up the sides that reached just under my bust. Thankfully though, I had trousers on underneath, so there wasn't really much skin on show. The top part of the dress looked more like a long-sleeved kaftan design, only it had a large slit down the middle, one framed by thick gold embroidery that was at least four inches wide. The design spanned down to my navel and joined under my breasts in a tear drop shape, almost as if it was a gold arrow pointing the way to a woman's sweet spot. Not that Draven needed any directions where to go, I thought with a deepening blush, recalling this mornings 'wild ride' as Pip had put it.

The sleeves of the dress were made from a sheer material and tapered off into wide cuffs, stiff with the thick gold borders in the same design as the top part of the dress. There was only my cleavage on show as it was quite low cut and, thanks to my ample size, it was another dress I had to be squeezed into. The little mandarin style gold collar, completed the look and curled slightly outwards.

"You'd better get a wiggle on Chickey, as he looks ready to come and get you any minute," Pip informed me and I had to say, she was right. Draven had one elbow to his chair's armrest and the other hand was currently gripping onto the end, that being a snarling lion's head. And if I thought that wasn't intimidating enough, then where he was positioned in the room, certainly made up for it.

The Great Hall was as it sounded, full of colossal sized pillars, elaborately decorated arches and a pair of carved, monstrous sized doors at the end that looked as if they would have needed six men either side just to open them. But this was nothing compared to Draven's throne, as it was set back at the far end of the room and dominated the space with it grandeur and size.

It was, in true Draven fashion, raised up by seven steps and a platform high enough so that the whole room could be viewed from wherever you sat up there. It was almost like its own room and I smiled thinking back to the VIP at Afterlife. I was happy to see that even after 2000 years things didn't change that much.

The space wasn't only separated by the steps, but also by the huge intricately cut scalloped arch coming down from the balcony above it. From this hung two vast lengths of material, that framed the space in a royal purple shade that was decorated with a large gold emblem I has seen a few times in the palace. It was a picture of a full-length lion from the side, holding a curved blade with a sun behind him and all of this was framed in a circular vine of some kind.

Then, at the centre, was the man himself sat upon a massive throne which rose up high at his back in tiered tear drop shaped arches. Scattered carpets in lush colours gave the room its colour along with the crowd, no doubt all dressed in their finest. But every single one of them were just shadows in the background of the masterful figure that sat waiting for one thing...*me*.

He was dressed differently than I had ever seen him dressed before. His impressive torso was for once covered with a sleeveless tunic style jacket that could be seen underneath another layer of draped dark purple material. It hung down loose around his neck and covered his chest and abs, where it met length after length of leather, from the many belts that hung off to one side.

To this he'd added black armour to one shoulder that was covered in layered curved plates and this matched the wicked looking metal gauntlet he wore over one hand. In fact, it looked as though he had dipped his hand into Hell itself and pulled it back to find a demonic black glove. Sections of arrow shaped metal all overlapped one another to create free movement, but it was the deadly points that covered his fingers like demonic claws. Yep, I think I would be staying away from that hand I thought, swallowing hard.

I knew this was all done as a show of strength to his people, one that couldn't be shown for real considering if they saw Draven in his true form then they probably would have thought him to be the Devil. So, this was his way of dominating over his mortal realm, as fear of the wrath of a king was sometimes what was needed for his rule to remain as strong as it was. And there was no doubt in my mind that Draven was a good and fair ruler, one who put his people's needs first.

You could see that from the lack of poverty and all the riches of the land. Of course, you still had slaves but that happened all over the world in this time and unfortunately wouldn't change for quite some time. It was a hard fact to face and one I would be putting behind me along with the past, the second I got out of here.

So, taking Pip's advice, I decided it was best not to let him wait any longer as I braved the steps needed to take me to him. It felt strange like this, as though I was being led closer toward punishment rather than to a man who loved me. For when we were alone it was easy to be with Draven as a man, but like this, well there was no way of getting around the fact that he was *King.*

In fact, it was very much the same with Afterlife. Just sat in the VIP you could almost convince yourself he was just a businessman in charge of a nightclub. But when he had been down in the Temple, I had encountered my first real taste of what Draven really was…*a ruler over his kind.*

I continued to walk towards him, feeling as if my legs weighed twice as heavy as they usually did, as they no doubt filled my muscles with dread. I don't know why I was so scared, it wasn't as if he was going to hurt me, but one look and it was like he knew. I was starting to panic and I looked both left and right, as if trying to find my escape from it all.

"Easy, Toots, you're nearly there," Pip whispered to me, gripping onto my arm as if she too knew I was about to bolt. Draven watched the action and frowned before something seemed to click into place for him. The next thing I knew two things started to happen simultaneously, as I took my first step away from him, he in turn was up out of his seat. The crowd gasped at the sight of their King meeting a woman head on, instead of having her pay the right amount of respect and presenting herself to her King. But he didn't seem to care for this, as his only concern was getting to me.

I felt Pip's hand leave mine as she took a step back. I first looked down at my arm and then at her before her eyes told me where I needed to be looking...head on. I raised my head up just as Draven was nearing and before I could take a step back he had me in his arms, yanking me to him before kissing me passionately in front of hundreds of his people. Thankfully, they all cheered once it was finished and the second I was up in his arms I felt my body relax into him. It had been all that was needed. He didn't say anything to me as he walked us both back to his throne. I looked side on to see Sophia was smirking and Vincent outright laughing.

Draven ignored both and turned to face his people who all got to their knees and bowed in perfect sync. He nodded to them and then sat with me still nestled in his arms. They all rose and the evening for them continued as before. I was still speechless and I jumped when I felt Draven run a finger down my cheek, of course it didn't help it was by the gloved hand. He didn't hurt me but the cold metal was enough to bring me back to the room.

"Ssshh, calm yourself for me, my fearful little lamb, you are safe in my arms," he told me bending his head to my level so that he could speak next to my face. I took a deep breath and tried to control the hammering of my heart.

"That's it, now you can tell me what had you ready to take flight, little bird?" he asked me and I sighed back against him.

"I don't like being the centre of attention," I said making him tap a metal clad finger on my cheek to prompt me to look back at him.

"I find such a thing astonishing to hear."

"Why?" I asked frowning in confusion.

"Because sweet girl, it is rare to see someone with your beauty shy away from the world's eyes rather than…"

"…Taking advantage of it and using it as a means to gain?" I finished off for him, shocking him enough to shift back as if he wanted to look at me better. Then after obviously seeing what he wanted in me he gave me a tender look and smiled.

"I believe just then you granted me a glimpse of your soul and it was near blinding in its beauty as well," he told me and this time I really did blush, making him chuckle.

"Thank you," I whispered softly before I decided it was safer to look back at the crowd or I felt my flesh would melt from the bone, as was my usual reaction to Draven's compliments.

"You are most welcome to the truth in my heart, Nāzanin," he answered behind me and I couldn't help but close my eyes, wishing in that moment I had heard my real name coming from his lips. Had this been what it had been like for Katie back when she had control over my body? Had she encountered the same inner turmoil every time Draven called my name? I didn't know without asking her but I think I had I good idea as to the answer, for this felt like torture. In fact, I wished that he would just call me endearments like 'little lamb' or 'sweet girl', for that way I could at least pretend that he knew me as I knew him.

"My girl looks deep in thought." Draven's voice brought me back and I said,

"Um?" I heard Vincent laughing as it had been obvious he had been speaking to me.

"Oh, I am sorry, what did you say?"

"I simply wanted to inform you of your sister's wellbeing," he told me and suddenly I felt like a selfish bitch for it not being the first thing I had asked.

"Oh yes, how is she? Is she alright? Has she slept or eaten?

I can imagine she must have been hungry after…" I stopped when I saw him laughing and felt Draven doing the same behind me.

"I fear you ask too much of my brother to answer all but one question at a time," Draven told me and I bit my lip.

"Sorry, it's a bad habit of mine," I told them both. Draven pulled me tight to him, hugging me from behind and whispered,

"Cute and endearing, yes always… but never bad."

"In answer to many of your questions, your sister is well and is currently still resting. I thought it best for her to be close to you, so situated her in one of the rooms next to your own, after my sister suggested so." Hearing this I looked to Sophia and she winked at me when no one was looking. So, I bowed my head to show my respect, making her smirk.

"I cannot thank you enough for the kindness you show her," I told him making him bow at me as I had done to Sophia.

"But of course, and I in turn cannot thank you enough for not only bringing her back to me but also for granting me with your trust when communing with me about her past, for I will now take things at her pace, not my own," he told me and I gave him a beaming grin in return.

"Careful little one, for you will find a jealous king at your back if my brother is able to put a smile like that upon your face, where tonight, I have not yet accomplished such a task," he warned getting a little possessive. I turned around to face him and decided to be sexually brave and tease,

"Yes, but it is only you who can make me wet at just the sight of you." I knew this had worked when his eyes flashed purple and he growled low down at me, before playfully nipping at my ear, warning,

"Behave kitten or I will control the minds of all that are here and take your delectable little body with or without a controllable audience…in fact, *I think I am due a little play,"* he told me purring the words and making me shift on his lap just to control the sexual urges now inflicting my body. At first, I thought he was just teasing but then I soon realised two things, one the reason for his interference with my wardrobe choice and second, my sexual bravery had backfired.

His gloved hand snaked inside my dress from the high cut slits up the sides and I flinched at the feel of cold metal against my naked skin. It felt so dangerous yet erotic at the same time, it made me want to moan and writhe against him, which made me even more vulnerable to his actions.

"Ahah, take care now and be still for me, for my talons are sharp," he warned making me yelp against him.

"Then why…?"

"A test…I want to see how good you can be for me, *ready for later in my bed,*" he whispered this last part as a promise of things to come and I sucked in a sharp breath, knowing the time was nearly here. I had no idea what his reactions toward me would be if he could finally read that my soul wasn't from his time, or if Pip could hold on to masking that long enough. But I guess time would tell for I didn't have long now to wait.

And well it was a good job, given that Ari was finally in place and in the next room,

For tonight, time would change…

Everything.

CHAPTER SIXTEEN

ANNOUNCEMENT

After this sexual bombshell dropped I tried not to panic about what the night would hold for me. What exactly awaited me once we finally became one, I couldn't say but I had a feeling it would be explosive and I would…finally be exposed.

He started off slowly, taking great care with my body and the sexual high that surprisingly, I got from knowing something this close to hurting me was against my skin was confusing me. Then he started using the backs of his long talons to caress along my ribs and I tried to keep my breathing as steady as I could.

"That's it, deep, easy breaths for me," he praised before shifting me closer so that he could sneak his hand in further. My hand automatically went to stop his and I hissed,

"Someone will see you."

"Your body, it belongs to me…yes?" he asked sternly. I nodded and started to say,

"Yes but…"

"Good, now remove your hand," he ordered so as I did as I was told and tried to take comfort in the fact no-one seemed to be watching us.

"Now relax back against me," he told me and with a sigh I did as he instructed again, knowing he was getting off sexually with my obedience. Well, that was if the giant erection was anything to go by that was currently poking me in the back.

"That's it, now let me take care of you," he cooed and I took another deep breath before he continued to stroke my skin with his dangerous hand. He rested his other arm across my torso no doubt to hold me still this time, as he took my wrist in his hand. Then he left my ribs and flattened a hand against my stomach, tapping his talons against my skin. It didn't hurt but it was enough to know that they were certainly there as if someone was pressing the tip of a blade against you. Then ever so lightly he dragged his claws down, grazing my now hypersensitive flesh, creating little goose bumps along the way.

I shuddered against him, trying to hold as still as I could. It was more a mental torture than of the physical sense. Although, I had to admit that it was also shamefully hitting the right spot because I was near panting from it and could feel myself getting wet.

Had Draven just tapped into a new kink of mine? I couldn't say for sure but I knew how I felt and when he started scraping one talon directly under my breasts I suddenly wanted to be naked. I wanted him to be doing the same teasing around my erect nipples. I wanted him to take hold of my throat as he thrust into me, holding me still so that he could take me under his command.

Jesus! What was wrong with me, I was very nearly ready to come from the onslaught of erotic thoughts I, myself was placing there in my mind to play out.

"Now I am intrigued as to where your mind is heading to sweet one, for you are getting very hot and flushed," he commented and I bit my lip to stop myself from moaning.

"Tut, tut, do you think it wise to keep such things from me, when I hold such delicate, pale flesh at my mercy…come now, be good for your captor." His softly spoken dominant words added to the sexual euphoria he was creating and I was only left gripping his arm, shaking my head and telling him without words, to please accept my silence. Of course, he wouldn't.

"Tell me, what I am doing to you in your mind?" he asked again and when I shook my head, I felt him apply a little more pressure with a single finger under my breast. I released the smallest of little yelps and jolted in his hold.

"Now tell me, for I will not ask it of you again," he said, this time it was a strict command, one I knew not to push.

"I…was just…" I started to speak but he squeezed my wrist, one still held and said,

"Remember, for I will know if you lie and you remember your punishment from earlier, for I know you do after speaking of it so fondly to your little friend," he said reminding me both of my shame and the forced orgasms he had controlled. So, I decided it was better to grant him his wish and add even further to my shame.

"I…I wished I was naked," I told him, deciding to start off with the tamer side of my fantasy.

"Go on," he ordered and I swallowed hard before doing as he asked again.

"So that your talons could play more freely, circling my breasts, my…*my nipples.*" Hearing this he moved his face closer to my neck and breathed deep and said,

"Would you then wish for me to sooth the sting I inflict with my tongue, taking the pretty little bud into my mouth to suck?" he asked and I took a deep shuddering breath at the erotic images he started to paint. I nodded but like most times, this wasn't good enough for him.

"Words, give me your *fucking* words Nāzanin, for they are only mine to hear," he said holding me tighter and growling the swear words in my ear. He was getting off on this, just as I was, the deep rumbling in his voice told me as much.

"Yes, Arsaces, yes I want that," I told him and was rewarded with another tap of his talon in between the lower parts of my breasts where they met.

"What else would you have me do?" I swear it sounded as if his Demon had asked this of me. So, I decided to give him it all and see how much strength his will really had. I knew it was a dangerous game I was playing but my sexual need just wouldn't let me stop.

"I would have you clasp my neck in your metal hand and hold me down as you thrust your cock deep inside me, making me come, quivering around your full length, at the first feel of you connecting to my body, making me yours in all ways possible." As soon as the words were out I felt almost crushed as he pulled me impossibly close to him. He then gripped the back of my neck with his teeth so that no-one could see and I moaned as pain flooded into pleasure. I felt his fangs lengthen against me and for a moment I thought he would bite me. I could feel his laboured breathing behind me and I knew he was fighting himself for control.

Finally, after long minutes of not knowing what would happen he growled against me one more time before letting go of his prey.

"I can smell your need for me and I want nothing more than to make a meal out of you but for now, I will take what I can of you," he said snaking his bare hand up to my face, and turning my head so that he could kiss me deeply. His tongue duelled with mine and suddenly I had the dirty craving to taste my own desire from his lips, after he devoured his 'meal of me'. I think in the end our kiss was getting a little too heated as Vincent started to clear his throat, making Draven growl low when I pulled back from him.

"I think gossip will reach new heights with you two nearly making love on your throne and there is only so much protection I can provide brother," Vincent informed him sounding amused and also letting us know that he had been controlling the room's minds enough to protect our lustful ways from view.

"And I thank you for it Vardanis, for I fear my little lamb likes to push my limits," Draven said once again scraping his talons down my belly, making me arch against him and moan. I then sucked in a deep breath on a gasp, as he reached lower and started tapping his fingers against the inside of my leg before scrapping his metal nails across my covered mound. He chuckled and told me,

"I adore how responsive you are to my touch and the trust you show me now, is one I will never reward with pain…do you understand of which I speak?" he asked, his voice thick with lust.

"Yes," I replied on a breathy moan.

"I look forward to the moment I can tear this dress from you as I fear I can think of nothing else," he said as he removed his gauntlet from my hidden skin and instead dragged one finger across my cleavage, making me shudder against him. I had to smile to myself at the idea I was driving him wild.

"Half of me wishes I had you dressed in something more revealing so that I could play more freely. But then I look out into the sea of lustful gazes and I know I made the right choice, for this body is and always will be mine, for no other holds the right to your beauty." As soon as he said this I couldn't help my reaction, as I turned my face into his chest and moaned. I felt him chuckling before he raised my face up with a talon under my chin.

"Why, may I enquire, are you hiding?"

"Because I think I have turned the colour of a beetroot!" I told him and he raised an amused brow down at me.

"I know not of this 'beetroot' of which you speak."

"Think tomato, only redder," I said, making him laugh.

"You think my words affect you so?" he asked and now I was the one laughing as I replied,

"Ha! You know they do as I see the anticipation in your eyes as you wait for my response." I called his bluff and he feigned shock.

"I would never do such a thing, upon my word, am I not considered a gentleman, even from your own land?" At this I burst out laughing and had tears quickly start to form. I could see him smirking from making me laugh as much as he did. Even Vincent watched us as if very intrigued to see how funny his brother could obviously be, and he looked a little more than surprised by it.

"That depends, do you usually chain up your concubines, bite them in the bath, make them unwillingly come on horseback or sexually tease them with a deadly gauntleted hand?" I asked him and he looked taken aback by my brazen comment. Oh, and there was that bad boy grin I adored so much.

"Is that not considered gentlemanly behaviour in your lands, for I can assure you, it is surprisingly tame for a man such as I," he teased back and once again I got carried away with our game and smacked his arm and shouted,

"Humpf! Now it is I, you try to make jealous!" I don't know

if his people saw or not but the room suddenly went very quiet and I turned around slowly and saw that everyone was now in complete shock that I had struck their king. Each and every one looked on edge as if waiting for their King's famous rage to erupt and I turned back to Draven and whispered,

"I think I went too far, for I fear your people are ready to have me hanged, so try not to make any sudden movements as they might class that as the go ahead." Hearing this Draven threw his head back and roared with laughter, a sound that boomed through the hall and echoed so that most of his kingdom could no doubt hear it. It only took a moment for the rest of his people to catch on and soon they were all laughing as well, only I doubt they had much clue as to why.

"Upon my word, you are a funny girl! I bless the Gods again to have granted me not just a beautifully, intelligent girl, but also one ripe with humour, for I can only imagine the fun we will have. Which reminds me," he said after caressing my cheek affectionately.

"Reminds you?" I asked but he simply kissed me quickly and said cryptically,

"The reason behind the festivities that I called upon." I frowned and gave Sophia a panicked look, knowing it wasn't good when I saw her mouth the word,

'Sorry.' Adding to it, a shrug of her shoulders.

I was about to protest, but before I could Draven gripped me tighter as he stood, then let go of my legs. I bit my lip and shot Pip a panicked look but seeing that it hadn't helped when doing so to Sophia, then I wasn't holding out much hope for the naughtier member of our quest. And she didn't disappoint for she just started giving me the thumbs up. Oh god, but what could he be doing now!

"I will have silence!" Draven's command thundered out into

the crowd and I jumped, making him place a hand on each of my shoulders. The weight felt there was supposed to comfort me but facing the crowd now it just managed to root me to the spot so that I couldn't run from my dread.

"You do remember the part about me hating attention... right?" I hissed the question at him through clenched teeth. He gripped my shoulder once and then whispered down to me with amusement,

"But of course, my blushing little lamb" At this I growled low in response and he chuckled once before addressing the room.

"I grant all to enjoy this night's festivities, as we welcome another battle won when defeating the Romans, for hair would grow on the palms of our hands before we let Roman dogs into our city!" Draven shouted making the crowd cheer and go wild, rejoicing at their King's victory. I looked back to Vincent as he hammered a staff against the floor making his own echoing boom. But then my head snapped back to the room when I felt Draven's hand squeeze my shoulders as it was clear he wasn't yet finished.

"But now I speak of another battle won, that of my heart, for it was quickly captured by a lost beauty, with that of a golden fleece!" he stated loudly and I bit my lip and desperately wanted to turn around but he wouldn't let me. The crowd cheer again and I thought I would die of shame.

"Please Arsaces, that's enough." I pleaded. I heard him chuckle behind me and whisper back,

"Not yet it isn't."

I stiffened in his hold trying to figure out all the possibilities to what it could be but nothing prepared me for what it actually was.

"For on this night I deem it known, this pale goddess

bestowed on me from the Gods, is on this coming moon's cycle to become…" he paused turned my face to look up at him and with all the love in the world, he wholeheartedly declared to the kingdom…

"…My Queen!"

CHAPTER SEVENTEEN

RELIVING THE PAST

"My Queen!" He shouted this last part and just as the words registered, I felt my legs buckle beneath me as he turned me back to face the celebrating sea of people.

"Brother!"

"Arsaces!" Both Sophia and Vincent shouted and just as I crumbled he wrapped his arms around me before I fell. He picked me up as the room continued to cheer and rejoice. Then, instead of turning back to his throne, he dismounted the steps with purpose. His people bowed and congratulated him as we passed, which he acknowledged with a slight nod of his head. But it was clear that his sole focus was on being alone with me as he swiftly walked us from the Grand Hall.

We headed down an empty passageway and I looked over his shoulder to see that his guards were cutting off access to this part of the palace. It was a beautiful wide hallway, with walls covered with square cut panelling, each inlayed with a paisley pattern in a droplet-shape. The bottom section of the walls were larger carved panels, each displaying a carving of different plants and all were framed with colourful tiles.

We walked through a huge archway in a teardrop shape and I realised that this was heading towards Draven's private chambers. Of course, what I didn't understand was that they had been far vaster than the few connecting rooms I had been staying in. It quickly became apparent that Draven had thought it safer to keep me contained to one place than giving me free rein to wander around his private home.

I didn't speak and neither did he as he walked me through this new space but my mind was reeling with questions. Where we were going being at the very top of that list. I knew it wasn't where I had hoped it to be when I saw him reach a large circular staircase that led straight up. It was like a massive turret and I quickly found that it led to the rooftop as I gasped at the first view of his immense city.

"It's…it's so…" I was just about to say beautiful when suddenly Draven filled the space and I looked up at him to see him looking down at me with purple fire in his eyes.

"You trust me?" he asked and an action drew my eyes down to see him pulling free a long sash from around his waist.

"Answer me," he ordered softly and I looked back up to him and nodded, making him smirk no doubt at my fearful gaze.

"Good girl." Then he raised the long length of silk to my face and I stepped back. All he needed to do was raise a brow in question at me and I knew what he wanted…my compliance. So, I took a deep breath and stepped up to him. My reward was a grin and a nod of his head, telling me silently that he accepted my trust and was pleased by it. Then once more he raised the material to my eyes and tied it securely at the back of my head. He lightly smoothed it out over my eyes and whispered,

"Time for my own surprise."

After he said this I ended up making a girly squealing noise as I felt my legs go from under me as he lifted me into his arms once more.

"Hold on." This was my only warning as he started running. Now, from the brief glimpse I got of the rooftop, I knew there was nowhere for him to run to so when I felt him jump up, I knew what was coming next…*wings.*

I first heard the loud whoosh, before a swishing sound of them erupting and opening to their full span. Then I felt the shiver that usually followed before I found the air blowing back against me.

"I should probably tell you that I don't like heights!" I shouted over the sound of his wings hitting the wind.

"Then it is fortunate for you that I chose to blindfold you, my fearful little lamb," he replied and chuckled when I yelped and gripped onto him tighter when I felt us start to descend. I had to ask myself if I would ever get used to this and then the painful truth hit me…*I might not need to.*

I quickly pushed that thought from my mind as otherwise he would be removing this blindfold to find me in tears.

"Ready?" he asked me after I felt him land and I nodded before he placed me back on my feet. Then he reached around and untied the knot so that it fell away, revealing what looked like a private Arabian paradise. Suddenly I was transported back to another rooftop and I gasped at the sight. It was back when Draven and I had split up. A painful time to look back upon yes, but one I still held with fond memories as it was my first night spent in his arms after so long apart. Which begged the question, had this been where Sophia had stolen the idea from…the past?

"Do you like it?" he asked and I turned back to face him to see something I hadn't seen on him in this time…*he looked vulnerable.* That's when I finally understood what this place meant to him and what I was seeing was another version of

Draven's cave. His secret place. I looked back to his tranquil hideaway and smiled.

"I love it!" I shouted, turning around suddenly to hug him, holding him tight to me for a moment before looking back at the space that obviously held all the things dear to him. He hugged me back, looking surprised at my reaction but happy with it nonetheless.

"You like to read?" I asked him as I saw all the scrolls, ones that looked well used and I giggled wondering if he was a 'Dog ear' folder.

"You're not the only one who's 'well read'," he teased coming up closer behind me. I had expected this place to be filled with treasures and it was, but just not of the gold and expensive ones you would have expected from a king.

His 'secret space' consisted of an Arabian style tent, layered with endless lengths of fabric in rich sunset colours. But around the walls in between small pillars, were small water features that spouted from demonic mouths. These all fed into a surrounding channel that framed the space, connecting at its centre to a large hexagonal pool.

Inside the covered space was a comfortable seating area with giant sausage shaped cushions used for back supports on the flat square cushions that were scattered on the floor. At its centre was a small table which was simple in design, like most things in his little slice of hidden hideaway heaven.

Other things included a small shelving space with maps, well-worn scrolls, a carved figure of what I thought looked like Ava and a small bust of a woman's face, who looked like a Goddess thanks to the startling white marble it was cut from. But what was most strange of all was that I recognised her face from somewhere but I couldn't place where or how.

It looked flawless and I had no idea when owning something so beautiful, that he could find me so. He must have seen me looking because he took my hand and pulled me closer. Then he picked it up and looked down at it, smiling.

"It is an image of my mother," he said, surprising me.

"She is so beautiful," I told him, making him grin and he replied,

"Yes, my father would also agree." Now this made me grin and suddenly I knew where I had seen it before…it was in the last place it should have been but in the only place it needed to be, with Draven's father, in Hell. I couldn't help but wonder what he would think if he knew that I had been introduced to both, in very different ways and one more intimate than the other. Although a foot rub from the King of Lust was what I would call a tad overfriendly when first meeting a potential daughter in law for the first time. But then again, so was taking over someone's body in the middle of a battle and basically kicking ass. Not that I was complaining as she did save my life and well, she *was* really nice to me.

Draven raised it to his lips and kissed her forehead before placing her gently back on his shelf. I smiled at the tender gesture and couldn't help but wonder where the small marble bust called home back in my own time?

"I have never shared this place with anyone before," he told me softly and I bit my lip, trying to contain the massive grin that wanted to erupt. He sat down and I followed him, then turning to face him I placed a hand at his cheek and told him,

"Then I feel honoured that you do so with me."

"I never felt inclined to do so before there was you, but then I saw you that day from my throne, sneaking through the crowd," he said as if watching the memory playing back in his mind. I blushed thinking back to it myself.

"You scared me."

"Oh, of that I have no doubt my little lost lamb, but I wouldn't have hurt you, not for all the power in the world and especially not when I intended one day to make you my wife." Hearing this I sucked in a sharp breath and said,

"You meant what you said down there…you…you wish to make me your queen?" My voice started to break a little and he smiled, pulling me close. Then he reached behind him and pulled something from beneath the cushions that had been hidden there. It was a long piece of scroll wrapped up and for a moment I had no idea what it was.

"I believe it was when I saw you drawing this that I was ready to declare you my queen, but first I had to declare you my head concubine." He paused a moment and laughed to himself before letting me in on his thoughts,

"I will never forget as I had you sat on my lap with thoughts of making you my queen filling my mind, when I had you saying the opposite, speaking of only doing so if it was expected of you for the man you loved…you know not how deeply you shocked me that day." I had to confess I was stunned at the idea that he was thinking in such a way at the time. In fact, I remember this was shortly after I had made the major mistake of calling him by the wrong name and after hitting the roof and promising murder to anyone named Draven, he soon stormed out.

Oh, but not before he cruelly told me how I'd better impress him at the 'Choosing' as he was still undecided. Now I knew he had just said this to piss me off and get revenge, but then again, in his mind I had said another man's name in the bedroom. So, thinking about it like that, then if it had been the other way around, then he would so still be sleeping on the couch!

"I waited to open this as I wanted you to be here with me when I did so."

"I promise not to take it from you this time," I said smirking as that was precisely what I had done not long ago.

"No, I should think not, otherwise I would have to find

something else to tie you up with…for I find myself without any shackles to ensure your good behaviour," he teased and I challenged him back by tugging on his leather belts and silk ties saying,

"Well, you do have quite a lot of leather and silk here, so I don't think you would have to look too far." At this he burst out laughing and in turn hooked a talon down the front of my dress near my cleavage and tugged me closer to him.

"Now I do believe you are trying to distract me once again from my mission, my clever little lamb." Then he kissed me, making me melt into him and I decided to knock him off his game again by pulling up my dress so that I could straddle him. He groaned as I lowered myself down rubbing against his obvious arousal.

"I am sorry my Lord, did you say something?" I asked playfully, making him growl this time.

"How is it one so seemingly innocent can be so mischievous and full of trouble, for you could easily make this King lose his mind and most of all…*his focus,*" he said squeezing my hip with one hand and running the backs of his metal nails down my face with the other.

"I think a King like you needs to be kept on his toes or on his back, either one," I replied with a smirk and a kiss on his nose, making him chuckle before shaking his head.

"And I thought I was the one with a demon inside of me." Now I was the one laughing and then replied,

"Yes, and lucky for me your demon seems to like my naughty side."

"More like fucking adores it!" This time it was his *demon side* that answered me and I couldn't help the breathy sigh I released at what each side of this man did to me.

"Now behave whilst I opened my gift, so that I may give

you yours," he told me and then smirked when he saw the shock on my face.

"You have a gift for me?" I asked with my voice rising as I got excited.

"Ah, I see my sweet girl has a weakness for surprise gifts… this pleases me," he said as he obviously liked the idea. It wasn't exactly surprising as he also enjoyed spoiling me in my own time and even though his great wealth meant little to me, it did mean something to me when receiving gifts from the heart. Something he did often.

"Only if they are from you and not too expensive," I told him and once again he roared with laughter and had to hold me still as I bounced on his lap.

"Upon my word, I fear you are not real for it must surely be impossible for such a woman to exist…by the Gods it must be!" he shouted up at the night sky and I growled at him this time, making him laugh again.

"And what do you mean by that, um?"

"Simply that you are unlike any other I have ever met, for you have no ambitions of power by becoming queen and in your own words, doing so only for love, yes?" I nodded, knowing now where he was going with this.

"You never shy away from danger but instead face it head on for those you love and wish to protect."

"Well yes but…" He cut me off and continued.

"And now you speak as though the riches of the world mean nothing to you and for all you care, my treasury could be empty." I grinned at him and said,

"No, not empty, for the space could be filled with enough food to feed a city and a bag of rice goes a long way." Hearing this he gave me a soft affectionate look as if I had touched him with my words.

"What a sweet heart you have given me, I feel truly blessed

for this combined with an intelligent mind and such a sweet tasting body, then if I found my treasury empty tomorrow, I would still consider myself the richest beings alive."

"Oh Arsaces," I said putting my hand to his face and placing my forehead to his, so that I could whisper,

"You are the only treasure I will ever need." Then I kissed him.

I don't know how long we kissed but this time it was slow, soft and tender. I pulled back and then whispered gently,

"I still want my gift though." Once again joy bloomed within me as he looked at me first with wonder and then laughter quickly followed.

"Now let's take a look at my gift, for I believe it was given first," he mocked with a grin he couldn't keep from his face. I suddenly became nervous as to what he would think of my drawing and I bit my lip as he first unravelled it from the cloth.

"It's, well it's not my best…I mean I…in the time I had and…" He gave me a sweet, knowing smile and covered my lips with two of his fingers. Then he pulled off his gauntlet and said,

"I am not risking such a treasured gift with an unforgiving hand." Then it was the moment of truth as my image of the man himself was revealed. Looking down at it now, I didn't think I had done too bad a job with what I had to work with. Of course, it had helped that, thanks to Draven shocking the room and lending me his blade to sharpen the charcoal with, I had found it easier to use or I think it would have turned out quite differently. It was done in quite a rough way thanks to the texture of the paper as it was harder to get the finer details but his eyes, they were all Draven. They were dark and brooding, that seemed to tell a hidden story within their depths.

"Tell me my talented beauty, is this how *you* see me?" he asked and I bit my lip before thinking of my next words.

"This is only how I saw you in that moment, but not what I get to see of you daily, for that is a secret I would never share with the world, even if to immortalise it on paper...for that *is for my heart only."* The smile granted me was worth every stroke made and every word said, as it was clear that he loved both.

"I will treasure this forever, along with your sweet words, for I will never forget them." Then, after running a fingertip along his jawline, he rolled it back up and added it to the shelf along with the rest of his personal treasures. After this he pulled out a hidden box from a place I couldn't see. It was modest in design and I was happy to report not covered in gold and jewels. It was a long rectangle shape and it held a single simple image carved on the top...A single feather.

I opened it up and gasped.

"It's...it's beautiful," I said, never before expecting to say that about a weapon.

"I told you that you needed a dagger, and this only belongs to the one whose hand first wielded it to take life in order to save another." My head snapped up to stare at him wild eyed.

"It's Pertinax's spear tip?!" He smiled as he lifted it from its silk bed and held it up to the moonlight as he spoke.

"No, Pertinax was just a man; a vessel used to gain power first among mortal men with the sole purpose of defeating me, in both battle and in single combat."

"It looks now to be filled with blood," I said looking at the crimson hue it cast against his skin as the moonlight reflected through it.

"It is now, thanks to you. The glass spear was stolen many years ago by the Persian devil Ahriman, for he believed it had the power to defeat any God and thought it easily used against me. In the end, it was used by a mortal girl who declared herself my Electus and who drove it into the chest of the beast, now gaining his blood as spoils of war." I shuddered at the thought and took the dagger from him as if any moment it would shatter in my hands. He laughed and said,

"I can assure you it is as sturdy as my own blade, for it was forged in the very deepest levels of Hell and is not like any glass you will have encountered before," he informed me and I was surprised seeing as it hardly felt it had any weight at all.

"And you had it mounted into a dagger for me?" I was so touched by the gesture that when he nodded I reached over to grant him a kiss on the cheek, one almost covered with his thick beard. I looked back down at the dagger and marvelled at the beautiful craftsmanship it must have taken to make it.

It was like looking at a giant shard of blood red crystal as though it had been chipped off a glass boulder. It was held in place by a band of gold secured by six hooked claws to the metal it appeared forged to. Added to this was a deadly element, not letting you ever forget it's story, for whose blood it now housed. For its T bar held a fan of claws reaching outwards on either side, which looked like lethal spikes ready to injure anyone who didn't wield it right.

The handle itself was decorated with embossed gold lattice work and its pommel end piece looked like an Aztec sun, arching round like some Sun God's headpiece.

"It's as stunning as it is dangerous," I told him and at this his lips quirked and he gave me a look I couldn't place, that was until he replied,

"It is, as is its new owner." I blushed and said,

"You're the dangerous one, remember." Then I nodded to his discarded gauntlet. He looked thoughtful for a moment and replied,

"I hold no danger to you or the truth you keep from me, for both will not be judged." I would have laughed at this if I could have gotten away with it, along with saying, 'Yeah, wanna bet on that!'. Thankfully I went for the less damning response and just gave him a sceptical look back.

"You don't believe my words?" he asked looking offended. I released a sigh and shifted off the cushions to go and stand near the wall, so that I could look out over his kingdom. It was a stunning sight at night as though the blanket of stars above had started to trickle down to earth, thanks to the flickering flames seen in all the small windows in his city.

"You don't know of which you speak, so therefore you can't make promises of that you do not know," I told him after taking a moment to collect my thoughts.

"This is true, but I can speak of the matters of my heart, for I know the truth you keep must be for reasons to keep others safe, for you would not do so for your own gain, or to purposely hurt another." Hearing this I spun around to face him and asked him incredulously,

"You can't know this! You just can't!" This was when something inside of me just snapped. It was the ultimate torture, knowing the heart I would have to break when I returned and here he was right now thinking it an impossible truth! I didn't deserve his kind words and the pain of knowing that ripped through my soul as if he himself was tearing it apart with his bare hands.

He got up from the cushions and I held my hand out to stop him coming any closer, for I didn't think I could do this anymore. Especially not when he uttered my name in such a tender way...*the wrong name.*

"Nāzanin." The way he said his given name for me, well it finally broke me...

"My name is not Nāzanin, my name is *Keira* and your name isn't Arsaces...no, to me it's Dra..."

"Actually, I don't care!" he suddenly shouted and before I could react, his hands were either side of my face and his lips were crushed to mine. I sucked in a startled breath, one he took advantage of as he swept his tongue inside. But it wasn't the sudden action that took my breath away…no, it was the memory.

We were in Draven's chamber before it became known as ours and Celina had just been asked to leave. It was before I knew what Draven really was as he feared that if I did, I would run from him. It was a point in your life that you face one of the biggest decisions to make. You could chose knowing a past, and in doing so, let it affect your future or you could simple pick that future and have faith in where it would take you.

I had made this same decision when facing Draven back in his room that day and in fact, said the very same words that he himself had said to me in this exact moment in time, almost two thousand years into the past.

That was when it hit me and I knew…

It was fate.

CHAPTER EIGHTEEN

I SEE YOU, SOUL OF MINE

It didn't take long after this for our kiss to quickly spiral out of control and I soon found myself once again in his arms.

"Close your eyes for me little one, for I fear this may frighten you." I did as I was told as I knew what was coming next and I held on tight, linking my fingers behind his neck. Instead of thinking about what we were doing and the potential deadly heights I could be faced with, I concentrated on the man who was shortly to take me to his bed. I had no clue what would happen after, but for now all I knew was how much *I needed it*.

It wasn't just down to sexual urges or the fact that this man could seemingly light my nerves on fire from a single touch. No, it was almost as if I waited any longer, I would feel physical pain. Of course, it was widely known throughout his world how I was born to be with their King. But putting that all aside was easy, for I knew I would have felt the same if Draven and I were merely a man and a woman in love. I craved him like no other and even when we were apart, it still wasn't enough to douse the flames of the fantasies my dreams would torture me with.

Which was why I had my head buried in his neck and was almost getting a sexual high from just the natural scent of the man. At first, I very much thought we were just going to do it on the rooftop but then something finally clicked in my mind. Ari was already situated in the room next to Draven's and thanks to Sophia, things were already in place, ready for us to do the baby making deed.

Thankfully, I didn't have to come up with a reason why we shouldn't take things further as it seemed Draven had his own ideas of what he envisioned for our first time. Thinking back on the night, I believe taking me to his special place was his last attempt at getting me to open up to him. But instead of choosing to discover my past, he decided to choose living a future with him. A decision that meant the world to me.

"I want to make you mine in a bed I can finally call our own." This was all he had said, growling the words into my neck before picking me up and walking me to the edge. Which brought me back to the present as I felt the way Draven folded in his wings at just the right moment. I knew this as I felt him tighten his hold on me just before we started to freefall. I gave a little yelp as I felt myself being jolted when we landed hard. Suddenly, I was starting to feel nervous again and it wasn't just from the unknown that faced me.

"Your cheeks are red sweet girl, any reason for that?" The sound of Draven's voice directly behind me made me jump but the feel of his hands rubbing down the length of my arms added a shiver to the mix.

"Come with me," he said taking my hand and entwining his fingers with mine. Then he squeezed them once before pulling me along with him into the bedroom. I don't know why but I kind of felt like a teenager again, being led into my boyfriend's bedroom ready for my first time.

He swung me around and after placing a hand on my cheek he pushed my hair back before embedding his fingers there. Then he tilted my head up and started to walk me backwards towards the bed.

"I will wait no longer," he said, his words coming from him in a rumble, as if his demon was also trying to have its say. So, this was it, this was our time.

"You look so scared little one, why?" he asked and just as I tried to hide my red cheeks by looking down he raised my face up to his.

"I will take care of you, have no fear of that," he told me softly, running the back of his fingers down my heated cheek. Then, before I could say another word, he wrapped an arm around my waist and lifted me up so that he could take possession of my lips. This was all I needed to feel as my nerves started to dissipate with his kiss. I could tell he was trying to hold back for fear of scaring me by going too fast and I wished in that moment I could have told him that it wasn't his desperate touch that was the cause of my worry. No, I wished I could have told him it was fear of rejection that was the root of my concerns because after this, he may think differently of me.

I decided I needed to cast these thoughts to the back of my mind with the rest of the mountain of worries I had and was trying to keep under lock and key until we returned home. Oh, then they would all come flooding out whether I wanted them to or not, because the second I saw Draven, I just knew there would be no stopping it. There would be no stopping the true depth of what I had done from coming into the light, as let's face it, there was only so long you could hide a pregnancy.

Thankfully these thoughts were taken from me whether I wanted to let them go or not because Draven turned, still holding me and lowered me down to the bed. The way he kissed me felt as if it could have been the last, as though any moment he half expected me to just disappear, as if the Gods were cruel enough to take me from him. Well, that statement was a little too close to home for me and in more ways than one.

Then just when I thought my need for him couldn't get any greater, he started to undress. It was painfully slow as he pulled at the straps of leather binding armour at his arms and shoulder. Then once free of metal and animal hide, he reached up, grabbing handfuls of material at his back before pulling it forward and off his torso. Sun kissed skin over hard muscles came into view and suddenly my mouth went dry at the sight. I found myself even licking my lips and curling my fingers into fists so that I could hold myself back from reaching out to him. He was utterly perfect and in this moment he couldn't have looked more God like, that was until he removed the clothing from his lower half and I was quickly gifted with the sight of him naked…and very, very, aroused.

I was just about to speak when he lowered to me once he was free of his clothes and started to kiss along my collar bone and up my neck but it didn't seem enough for him. I had to agree as I wanted his lips on my breasts like never before.

"By the Gods, you're beautiful," he told me pulling back so that he could look at me. The look I gave him, which I could feel was a bashful one, only made him smile even more.

"But there is something missing," he mused running a hand down his beard as he studied me.

"My lord?" I questioned nervously and my only warning was the bad boy grin before suddenly he gripped both sides of the front of my dress before tearing it down the slit swiftly making it into a jacket.

"Much better," he said as he flicked both sides back, now

baring my naked body to him. Then he ran a flat hand all the way down from my throat to my lower belly.

"All this lovely pale skin to play with, I am looking forward to seeing it bloom a crimson blush the way your cheeks do when I speak of your beauty," he told me and as if on cue, I could feel the heat invade my face.

"What are you…?" His actions cut off my question as he quickly gripped my hips and spun me so that I was now on top straddling him.

"Now let down your golden fleece for my pleasure," he ordered in a gruff voice, one thick with lust that became proof of his restraint. I gave him what he wanted and reached up with shaky hands and started removing my pins so that one by one the barrel curls sprung free. Literally, the only sounds to be heard were pins dropping on the floor and Draven's heavy breathing.

Draven and I had become experts at mad passionate lovemaking, as usually it only took a simple kiss before we found ourselves in the nearest bed or on any surface for that matter. But this, well it was painfully slow and for some strange reason it only ended up adding to the erotic recipe that Draven and I always created when together sexually.

A recipe I only wished I had an eternity to taste.

ARSACES

By all the Goddesses combined she was so beautiful that the very image of her stole my breath. Just as her kindness, warmth and witty mind had quickly stolen my heart. I hadn't thought it possible for a person to continually surprise me, but what the Gods had granted me was a being that went beyond the realms of perfection, for every action committed and every word voiced was like encountering a fresh new discovery. And looking at her lush little body now was no exception.

She was full figured, even for her small frame, she had curves that were just begging to be gripped tight and used to hold her steady as I thrust into her at pace. Even now, as she released her golden gift to me, the one the Gods spoke of, I couldn't help but hold onto her, spanning her ribs with my hands. And watching her as she did my bidding, obeying me, not just as her King but as the man who owned both her body and her heart, I couldn't help but crave more. I had made a vow, one I knew I would soon be breaking for I found it an unbearable torture I was inflicting upon myself.

But I had wanted to do so knowing I owned all of her, every single piece of her soul, but so far, I was yet to be granted a glimpse into her mind, for this was something she was keeping from me. It had pushed me close to the hellish lines of insanity trying to discover what her past could hold that she feared would make me look upon her differently and the only painful reason I had was a single name…*Draven.*

I almost growled just thinking upon the name. She did not know the true depth of my murderous thoughts on this matter, for she had only sampled a taste of my rage, one tamed greatly for her benefit. She also didn't know of the lengths I had gone to, to try and find this man, one who I knew meant a great deal to her. I didn't know what it was about her or the way she had spoken his name, but it was enough to tell me that this was the reason she was keeping things from me. She was protecting this man, I could just feel it.

Thinking this, I couldn't help it when my hand squeezed possessively at her hip and I could feel my demon's need growing. If I didn't take her now I wouldn't have enough control left to stop him from taking over and I had to remind myself how breakable her sweet little body was in my hands.

"Mine!" My demon growled at her and before I knew it my hand was embedded in her silky locks, pulling her closer to me. I looked at my hand as though it were foreign to me but there it was, as though it had been dipped in liquid gold. Just breathe, just breathe Arsaces. By the Gods, but I felt like a rutting buck near ready to flip her over and mount her from behind. I was holding on by a mere thread and with only two words spoken she unknowingly severed it.

"I'm yours," her gentle voice ended, being the exact opposite of my actions, something I could no longer control, for I was ultimately lost, so I did all that was left to do, bury myself deep within the confines of her body.

Inside my own taste of Heaven.

NĀZANIN

I don't know what had changed in Draven but as soon as I let down my hair it was as if someone had fired a starting bullet. The next thing I knew was a possessive hand embedded in my hair pulling me forward into his kiss, one less gentle this time.

"Mine." This single word came from his demon side and I said the only thing he needed to hear right then, thinking hearing it would help calm him but like many times before, *I was wrong*.

"I'm yours." As soon as the words were out of my mouth he growled at me before yanking the dress hard down my arms but not pulling it off all the way. It ended up restraining my arms behind my back as the material caught tighter around my elbows, something from the looks of things he had been counting on.

"Yes, you are and you are going nowhere, little lamb of mine." This was nothing short of a promise, one backed up when he took one naked breast into his mouth to feast on. I arched my back, crying out and tugging at my arms, trying to free myself. I didn't know what I would have done had I managed it, hold him to me or try to get away from the onslaught of beautiful pain his tongue, teeth and lips were creating.

He would scrape a fang across the sensitive nipple before soothing the hurt by circling his tongue around the aching bud. Then he would suck me in and start the maddening combination all over again.

"I can feel how wet you are for me, girl," he said after letting the swollen nipple fall from his mouth. I nodded unable to find my voice as it felt that if I opened my lips I would have shamelessly begged for more.

"You're ready for my cock so soon?" he asked and hearing the crass word coming from him had even more of my juices flowing. He was so raw. Like the Draven from my time only without years on top of years of etiquette and manners to conform and adapt to at the time in which he lived. But here, he could do as he pleased and had no one in the world to answer to. However, in modern day, he knew that if you wanted power in a mortal world as well as that of the supernatural one you owned, then you had to converse with mortal men. And even without the aid of Heaven and Hell, for humans weren't without their own powers…money usually at the very top of their list.

So, instead of an expensive designer suit, that spoke money and authority the very second he stepped in the building, the Draven of this time fought to gain that power with a sword in hand and an army at his back. Which was why the hands that gripped me now were rough and hard and most of all, unforgiving. He was merciless as he told me,

"Well, I am not finished with you yet for I don't just want you wet, I want you *fucking drenched."* He swore at me on a growl and I threw my head back as he started my delicious torture all over again, this time with my other nipple. One that I will admit, was starting to feel neglected.

"Please, oh God please!" I said twisting and trying to get free so that I could get my hands on him.

"And this God you speak of in my bed, prey do tell me his name?" he asked releasing my now matching abused, red nipple. When I didn't answer him quickly enough he ran a finger gently around my rose-coloured flesh, making me shiver before crying out when he added his thumb so that he could apply enough pressure to sting.

"It's you! You are my God, Arsaces!" I shouted and he pulled my head forward and kissed me before praising me,

"Good girl." Then he gripped my hips, lifted me up to position himself at my core and I held my breath waiting for what I needed as if it was my next lung full of air.

"And you are my Goddess, keeper of my heart and soul, for I finally make you mine, *for all eternity,"* he said as an absolute. Then, with a firm hand at my hip, his other moved to wrap around me to grab hold of the gathered material pinning my arms down. Once satisfied with his hold on me, he then thrust up into me at the same time pulling me down onto his solid length.

"AHHH!" I screamed out at the intensity of it all and quickly found myself shuddering around him, my inner muscles quivering along his length as I came quickly.

"By the Gods! My cock has found Heaven inside your tight little body!" he told me, gritting out the words in my ear as he gave me a moment to come down from the high he had launched me to with only the first feel of his glorious shaft.

"I will have you over and over again, for I will never get enough of you…do you hear me? Tell me you understand my needs, my Electus," he said sternly and all I needed in that moment was my hands free to touch him.

"Let me go."

"Never!" he snarled the word right over my mouth and I smiled before nipping at his bottom lip and putting his mind to rest,

"I want to touch you, for that is my right as you are mine also," I reminded him and he growled once but his kiss told me that he liked this more than having me restrained. His grip left my side to finish his earlier task and he tore the rest of the material from my body in such a way, it was now in two pieces. The second my arms were free, I tore the remaining sleeves off before I threw my body into his.

I don't think he ever expected to receive the same desperation returned from me so at first it was as if he didn't know what to do. I placed my hands down on his solid chest and rocked my hips, almost in the same motion as he had shown me when on his horse. I rode him with a frenzied need I had never known before.

"Fuck woman, what is it you do to me?" he shouted, grabbing my hair covering his face and forcing his head back, so that the muscles in his neck looked strained. Suddenly something started happening, something unexplainable as it had never happened before. It started when I began to chase my next orgasm and with each roll of my hips, it took me a step closer to not only my release but also something more. I felt the tingly feeling start to grow from the centre of my chest and span outwards as if using my nerves to travel along like some organic highway.

I felt a new strength tug at my muscles as if they needed to be stretched, to be used. I felt my heartbeat pound faster and faster as if it were my blood that couldn't keep up with it. But it was looking down at him now, seeing his neck bared for me that made me lick my lips and I was surprised to find something sharp there…*fangs had grown.*

Rapidly, I was catapulted back through time in my mind as I was staring at myself in the mirror. It had been the morning after I found Draven's Temple and I remember first seeing myself with tired red eyes from crying. But then I had splashed water over my face and looked back to find a very different Keira looking back at me.

Two eyes filled with crimson pools of death, as if frozen in time. Full bloody lips and the same purple fuelled veins of stolen power fanning out across my skin. And last of all a pair of gleaming white fangs, out and ready for the feast. This was what I had now become and I knew without looking, as I didn't need a mirror this time…*all I needed was blood.*

So, I took it.

Before I even fully registered my movements as being my own, I placed my hands to his wrists and was holding him down as I latched onto his neck. I felt my new extended canines pierce his skin with such a force that blood overflowed into my mouth, making me slurp at him so as not to waste a drop. The first taste of him bursting over my tongue was like taking the first sip of life's elixir and I felt my hold on him harden.

"Fuck!" he hissed and I knew it wasn't in pain. Oh no, he was getting off on this just as I was, which was why his Demon was the one to finish this curse off with a hellish snarl. I felt him trying to sit up and get from under my control. I don't know how it happened but I quickly found myself growling around the flesh I had in my mouth, like a kill I wasn't ready to let go of.

It startled me so much that suddenly my fangs were gone and I jolted back from his neck as if worried I had hurt him. What had been happening to me? I suddenly let go of his wrists and pulled back to look down at him, ready to say how sorry I was. In the end, I never got the chance as I quickly found myself underneath him.

"My turn," his demon told me as his eyes sank into purple depths followed by a wave of power as he erupted into his other form. Great wings burst from his back just as he gripped my hair and yanked my head to one side. Then he sank his fangs into me just as he started to power into me. I cried out as the second I felt that first pull of blood leave my body I was lost. I came so hard my back bowed up and I screamed as I felt the strength of it heat my insides. It was as if someone was setting my nerves alight starting at the base of my spine.

"You are mine!" he shouted pulling back and licking my blood off his lips.

"Yes! Yes! YES!" I shouted back at him as once more he started to build up the delicious pleasure and I soon found myself again chasing the white rabbit down the endless tunnel named euphoria. Then he lay down over me and put both hands to either side of my face, making this moment one of the most intimate of my life. He started to move slower, less frenzied but no less powerful as the connection started to burn ever brighter. It was as if our souls were joining for the first time and the beauty of it nearly had me in tears. I felt that in that moment we were…

Creating life.

"I can feel you… I can feel you touching my soul," he whispered over my lips and I nodded unable to speak the words as I knew they would only come out trembled.

"Come with me, we shall find it together," he told me and I placed a hand on his cheek and said,

"Always." And we did. We both continued to move as one, joined in the most beautiful way two people in love could be. His body framed by feathers and mine by a fated golden fleece, one whispered to him from the Gods. It was a single moment in time, one that only belonged to me and the man I loved. For it no longer mattered what time we were both in, what mattered was that our souls were being reunited and finally…

We had the power to change the world.

I came in an explosion of white light and so did Draven as though the force of our connection was trying to blind the world from seeing it. As though it was ours alone and not even the Gods had the right to witness it. Draven roared, something that managed to drown out my screams and we seemed to ride the wave of rapture for what felt like infinity.

"I see you, *soul of mine,*" Draven said and I closed my eyes at how beautiful those words made me feel.

It was one of the most amazing experiences of my life and I couldn't help but pull his head down to mine so that I could place my forehead to his. Then my wonderland started to disappear in a dark storm of regret for I made a grave mistake when whispering what was in my heart, as though it was just bursting from me.

I couldn't stop it as it was out before I could take it back and it was the first time I was to ever call those four words spoken *a mistake*. For it wasn't how it started that had him freezing above me, but it was how it ended that had him snarling down at me in anger…

"I love you, *Draven.*"

CHAPTER NINETEEN

WIFE

For long moments, neither of us moved and it broke my heart to see all the painful thoughts flicking across Draven's face. I swallowed hard and spoke first,

"Let me explain," I told him but it meant nothing to him as he was no doubt still playing another man's name over and over in his mind. I knew this when he tore himself away from me and suddenly my perfect moment was over as I was left frozen from his icy treatment.

"You *dare* speak of love for another man whilst my cock was still buried inside you and my release still dripping from your core!" he threw at me and I closed my eyes against the cutting sound. It was the first time I'd heard this tone from Draven and heartbreakingly it sounded like hatred. He grabbed a length of material from a nearby chest and tied it angrily around his waist. I couldn't help but cover myself with shaky hands, trying in vain to regain control.

"It wasn't like that," I said in a small voice knowing he wouldn't understand but still, I had to defend myself.

"IT WAS THAT!" he roared at me and I flinched back, feeling tears start to emerge. I looked up at him to see he looked purely murderous with his fists clenched and white knuckled by his sides. His chest rose and fell heavily as he panted through his rage. Then as if having a few moments longer to think and process what had happened he came to a decision when he snapped,

"Get out!" This was when my heart sank and it felt as though my body had been plunged back into that icy German lake. I bit my quivering lip so as not to let out the crying sob I felt lingering there. So, instead of arguing against his decision, I simply nodded. I then looked around for something to cover myself with and was cruelly awarded an angry sigh before he walked over to another chest and grabbed something from it. Then he threw it at me and said,

"Cover yourself!" Again, I wanted to get angry back but I had no right to, as in his mind I had whispered words of love to another man's name after our first time making love. There was nothing worse and no greater betrayal as the sin committed was beyond measurable. I didn't know what to do now. Would he just cast me out as if I meant nothing to him? Well, from the looks of him with his arms now crossed and waiting for me to leave his sight, then I had no choice but to see this as the end of my journey. I never wanted it to end this way, but what choice did I have? It was obvious he couldn't see my soul as Pip had thought, so he still knew nothing of who I was.

Even if I tried to explain, I very much doubted that he would believe me, not when in this amount of rage. So, I did the only thing I had left and that was to try and leave with what dignity I had left. I wasn't going to beg him, as there was little point. No, instead I simply pulled the long kaftan over me and shifted slowly to the edge of the bed. Then I walked to the door but stopped knowing that this was it, the last time I would ever see him like this. Well then, I just had to say something. So, with tears now streaming down my face I looked back over my shoulder and took in his angry glare, one I knew was masking the devastation he felt. I wiped away some of my tears and told him,

"I will never say sorry for loving you, Arsaces, in this world or my own. But I am sorry if my words hurt you. Thank you for the beauty you gave me, for I will treasure it always…Good… goodbye… *My King."* I finished with my voice breaking along with what felt like my heart. Then I turned away and pulled up the latch, ready to walk away from him.

Ready to go home.

"NO!" he suddenly shouted from behind me and the next thing I knew the door slammed from my hand. I jumped at both the sound and from quickly being manhandled from behind. He grabbed my arms and spun me round so that he could press me back against the door.

"You will never leave me! NEVER!" he shouted and then his lips were on mine, kissing me in a way he had never kissed me before. At first, I let him have his way, hoping to calm the beast but then it got too much to bear.

"Stop! I said stop!" I shouted when he wouldn't, so I pushed him back. This time he listened and for another moment we just stood breathing heavy as we were both at a loss on what to do next.

"I should just go," I told him and he growled at me before shouting,

"NO!"

"I think it's…it's for the best," I said again trying to get him to see reason.

"If you ever leave, I will hunt you down and lock you away from the world," he threatened, one I knew was only said in anger.

"You mean from a man who is impossible for me to get away from!" I snapped making his demon roar before punching his fist clean through the solid door. I just turned my head away from the sight and closed my eyes, feeling more tears fall.

"Do you understand what I will do when I find him, for you belong to me?" he told me and then he gripped my chin and made me look at him. He didn't hurt me but his soft touch became the polar opposite to his next words spoken.

"I will kill him Nāzanin and there will be nothing left for you to love!" he promised looking at me with purple fire and that was when my will to keep quiet any longer snapped. I pushed myself away from him and laughed once without a single shred of humour to be found. Not when it was bred from bitterness as I told him,

"Well, good luck with that for it is an impossible task!"

"Then you really do underestimate my strength and power for I can guarantee you, Nāzanin it stretches out far beyond these city walls." This was when I knew what he was saying and I asked incredulously,

"You have people out there looking for him?!"

"You are mine and the world will know it, for no man touches what is mine and lives to speak of it," he told me as his answer and this was when I lost it completely and started laughing. Oh, and boy this made him angry.

"You dare to mock me!"

"Yes!" I snapped back making him snarl.

"Then you are not of right mind," he told me and I released a sigh and told him,

"Why, because I know you won't hurt me, you never could?" I challenged, shocking him by my statement.

"I may not have it in me to hurt you, but surely seeing this…*this Draven* dying by my hand would cause you pain, for surely so if the love in which you speak is true!"

"I am not worried," I said dryly, one he took for different reasons.

"You foolishly believe I will never find him, don't you?" His cocky response made me shake my head and I replied,

"Finding him won't be the hard part but killing him surely will."

"Then you truly are a fool and hold not the intelligence I thought you did, if you believe me incapable of killing one man!" he snapped back venomously.

"The only foolish act I make is staying in this room with you when you are in this murderous mood!" I threw back at him, silently asking myself why I was taunting the beast. This was when his eyes narrowed before he asked in a dangerous tone,

"You know where he is…*don't you?*"

"I…I…don't…" I tried to think of my lie as his question took me off guard. However, I never got that far as faster than my eyes could trace he was at me and before I knew what was happening he had his hand shackled around my throat. His thumb tapped my pulse point, telling me silently that he was waiting for my lie. And like always, there wasn't an ounce of pain from the aggressive act.

"Tell me little Lamb of mine, where would you have run off to if I had let you leave?" he asked.

"I don't know!" I snapped back and then tried to pull from his hold.

"Ssshh, easy now, for I do not want to hurt you, so do not fight me," he said, in softer tones this time as he didn't like seeing the distress in my eyes as I tried to pry his fingers from around my neck. Again, he wasn't hurting me but if I started fighting him, then we both knew it could happen accidently.

"Would you have fled the city?" he asked next and I

panicked as I knew I couldn't lie but that didn't mean I didn't try.

"No." Oh yeah, his snarl said it all.

"You would have left!?"

"You told me to get out, what do you think I would have done?" I shouted back, telling him that he was the one who drew that line, not me.

"You are *never* to leave the palace, do you understand?" he ordered after thinking about what I told him, feeling no doubt somewhat better that that had been my reason.

"So, what then, I go back to spending the rest of my days locked up in your damn harem as now you don't want me, but you keep me from the world so no one else can!?" Hearing this he wrapped an arm around my waist yanking me hard to his chest. Then his hold on my neck loosened as he tilted my face up to look at him.

"What a foolish little Electus I have found myself, for indeed if you think I would ever simply let you walk out of here and straight into another man's arms. Your beauty is for my eyes only, your body only mine to touch and your soul destined for me to own by the Gods themselves. Yes, you are foolish, if you think I am a man who would share you with the world, let alone the one you call Draven, for you will never see him again!"

"And what of my heart?" I asked him after straightening my back. My question took him by surprise but I could see it the moment he chose to use anger to mask his true emotions.

"What of it!?" I flinched at his harsh question.

"Do you not wish to own that as well, for everything else I have maybe taken as easily as you say, but a heart has to be given freely and can only be owned after love has been earned," I told him thinking that I was getting through but then his eyes hardened and he asked me the dreaded question, one I should have foreseen.

"And this Draven, do you give *him* your heart as freely of which you speak?" I sucked in a sharp breath and hated how far this had gone and knew this was the time to confess…*the point of no return*. I felt tears start to build as I thought back to my Draven. The man I had left behind waiting for me in naive bliss as to what I was doing now. A woman who should have been drinking champagne getting ready to put on her wedding dress, spending time with family and surrounded by my bridesmaids. I should have been stood in front of a mirror looking at my reflection and telling myself that I wanted nothing more than to walk down the aisle with my arm nestled inside my father's as he gave me away to the only man I'd ever loved.

No, I could never lie about that.

"Yes." I said that small word as if it held the weight of the world upon it and the reaction was as I knew it would be…*rage*. He erupted into his other side and I slumped down on the floor crying as he destroyed the room around me. I saw little ricochets of things that should have hit me but he must have been putting a protective barrier around me because everything just bounced off in the other direction. Even as I broke this man's heart he still protected me but just because he would, it didn't mean he would protect the ones I cared for. So, once he had finished he issued me a promise,

"Then I will leave you nothing left to love for *I will find him* and I know exactly who to ask!" he said before storming over to the door and nearly pulling it from its hinges.

"Get me the Imp!" he snarled out his order and it made my blood go cold.

"NO!" I shouted getting up and facing him.

"Yes, my King." said the guard who had been nice to me in the private garden. He gave me a sad look, that told me he had heard everything of my turmoil, telling me that he wasn't just a mortal guard as I had first thought. Draven then slammed the damaged door and turned back to me.

"You don't have to involve her in this, I will tell you everything!" I told him, almost begging now, for I had no idea what he would do to my friend or the lengths he would go to.

"You left me no choice Nāzanin, for you have lied to me from the first moment I saw you and I will have no more. Your lies can no longer protect you and neither can your friend," he told me, this time in a softer tone and no doubt this was at the sight of the tears streaming down my face. The next thing I knew Pip was being escorted through the door and she looked at me with concern. She knew with only one look what had happened. The kind eyes she gave me were like a lifeline to me and I couldn't stop myself from running to her. Draven had no time to stop it, only to clear a path on the floor so that my feet didn't get cut. Then I threw myself into her and whispered,

"I am so sorry! I'm sorry. I ruined everything!" She tenderly brushed back my hair and told me,

"Ssshh, you have nothing to be sorry about my friend… ever." Draven let me have this moment before I felt his hand on my arm pulling me gently from her. Then, after making sure there was enough distance between us, he looked down at Pip and demanded,

"Where is the one she calls Draven?!" Pip never looked at him but just kept her eyes on me when she said simply,

"I refuse." I swallowed hard and waited for his next play.

"You will answer me, for I am your King!" he demanded angrily, obviously getting frustrated now dealing with the two people in the world that would say no to him.

"Yes, but she is my Queen and therefore I answer to no-one but her," Pip stated back, keeping calm and I bit my lip, letting the tears fall.

"Very well. Guards!" he shouted and my eyes widened in panic as two of them came into the room. I looked from them to her and back again.

"Toots, look at me," she told me and I did.

"It will be okay, trust me," she said as if secretly trying to get something across to me that I couldn't see.

"Take this woman down into the dungeon and lock her in chains until her trial, for she will be charged with treason."

"NO!" I shouted stunning the guards as they were about to step forward. I couldn't let this happen, I just couldn't!

"Take her!" Draven demanded and suddenly I screamed,

"Touch her and I will kill you!" I told the guards with deadly intent, and this time they seemed even more stunned at being threatened by the King's concubine.

"Keira it's okay, I will be fine," Pip told me softly but I was too far gone to listen. I could feel the tingling in my fingertips and knew that even if they touched her, I wouldn't be able to stop what was coming next. Draven looked down at me and raised his hand to stop them from approaching. He knew I was on the edge.

"Are you going to tell me what I want to know?" he asked in a quieter voice this time and I could tell it was because he didn't think it wise to set me off. I could feel my fists shaking by my sides, getting ready to unleash whatever this was.

"No, she will not, now take me away!" Pip answered for me and I cried out,

"NO! No, don't please, I will tell you!"

"Keira, you don't need to do this!" Pip pleaded but I ignored her pleas and told her quietly as even more tears fell,

"But you're my best friend." This time she gave me such a warm look before nodding and her own tears formed before falling from her beautiful forest green eyes.

"Leave us!" Draven nodded to the door and the guards

bowed and swiftly left. He didn't look happy or satisfied that he had got his way, but instead remorseful that it had come to this.

"Now I will ask again, where is he Nāzanin?" I sucked in a shuddering breath trying to hold back a sob and looking straight at Pip, I answered him,

"He is here." I don't think in that moment I could have done this without my friend here with me, as Pip gave me strength when she nodded her acceptance.

"In the city?" he asked again, only this time sounding shocked.

"Yes." I answered again, only this time hoping this was where the questioning ended…

It didn't.

"Tell me, for I find myself at a loss to understand why one would be so willing to meet death if this be the truth, but where in the city would I find him?" he asked after holding the bridge of his nose for a moment as if he couldn't believe what he was hearing or preparing himself to hear next. An answer this time that didn't come from me but from Pip,

"He is right here in the palace." At this Draven closed his eyes a moment as if he had just been told the impossible. Even his wings shuddered and the muscles on his torso tensed.

"Then your love for him will die sooner than I thought!" Draven said looking disgusted with me and I suppose from his point of view then it was disgusting. I was a woman he had fallen in love with and brought to his bed only to find that I had sneaked another man into the palace, a man I was in love with. No, I couldn't blame Draven's action in this moment for he didn't know the full story. But that would soon change as I shouted,

"My love for him would never die for it is impossible because I am staring straight at the only man I have ever loved!" Hearing this he frowned and shook his head as if trying to make sense of my words.

"I don't…" This time I cut him off and shouted,

"You are Draven!" Pip took a deep breath and released it as a sigh.

"What…what did you say?!" he asked taking a step back as if he didn't know what he faced.

"You are Draven and I am from…" I paused and saw Pip nod at me knowing I couldn't go back now, so I finished that sentence, one I never thought I would ever have to say to the man I loved,

"…I am you're wife, from the future." Draven sucked in a staggered breath and looked as if I had just shot him with the truth, not simply whispered it like I had.

"What trickery is this!?" he snapped not believing me and really, who could blame him.

"It's not a trick, I can assure you of that," I told him bitterly. Draven looked from me to Pip and then snarled,

"If you both think me foolish enough to believe even greater depths of your lies just to save this man's life, then you are surely mistaken, for I will tear this city apart in finding him!" Hearing this I knew nothing but proof was going to get him to believe me, so I made the final decision and said,

"Pip, drop your guards." Draven looked to her, curling his top lip in anger, knowing that she had been keeping him from seeing all of me. You could see the cogs starting to turn and play back all the reasons he hadn't been able to get a read on me.

"Are you sure about this?" she asked and I knew what she meant as this could mean us being trapped here for far longer than we ever hoped. But knowing what the alternative could be, with Pip being held in chains in some prison somewhere, well then, I couldn't chance it.

"Do it," I told her and Pip closed her eyes for a moment and inhaled deeply before nodding in acceptance. Then I shivered as if shaking away an invisible cold veil from my body, one I had only felt for the first time since she had unknowingly put it there.

The second the last shreds of it were gone Draven took in a startled breath and said,

"I can see you, I can see your soul and it...*it is not of this time.*" Hearing this I felt a part of my heart break for him and the tears I shed were for him and what he now faced. But then my concern quickly shifted and it was seeing my friend looking utterly exhausted that held my attention right now. I ran to her just before she would have fallen.

"Pip!" I shouted her name just as I caught her, cracking my knees hard against the floor as I landed. I felt the pain there but didn't care, not when my friend's head lay in my lap.

"Pip, speak to me! What's wrong!?" I asked in a panicked voice. She could barely hold up her hand let alone her head.

"It's...ok...ay," she murmured in a small voice, one that spoke of being anything but.

"What's wrong with her!?" I demanded looking up at Draven, who for a moment looked as if he was still trying to process it all.

"Please help me...*please Draven,*" I asked him, no longer caring about what name I called him. He registered it but in the face of what was happening now, he ignored it. Instead he came down to me and placed a hand on Pip's head, as if trying to get a read on her.

"The power being absorbed back into her body has simply tired her vessel, for she needs rest and days of it at that," he told me and I bit my lip as I cried for my friend. I felt my chin being raised and Draven told me softly,

"Don't fret, for she will be fine...I promise you, *Keira.*"

Finally, he said my name and on hearing it being spoken in such a tender tone I closed my eyes at the overwhelming pleasure it brought me.

"I will take her back to her room and call a healer to care for her," he told me as he took her from me, lifting her small frame into his arms.

"Wait, can you…can you ask your sister to care for her?" At this he paused and raised an eyebrow in question before realisation hit him.

"She came with you?" I hated that I was getting her into a world of trouble here but I knew that if I was going to be honest, then I wouldn't be able to hold anything back. So, I nodded and said,

"I'm sorry." He took a deep breath and replied,

"You and I will speak of this when I get back and be warned little lamb, for I *will* know everything, for this time, nothing will be between us." Then he looked down at his new little sleeping burden and I knew what he meant, as Pip had taken away any defence I once had.

"I will explain who I am… I promise you," I told him and for a moment my heart soared as the look he gave me was utter relief, for I had eased his worrying and heartbreak. He bowed his head to me and then before he left he closed his eyes for only a moment and I watched in amazement as the room righted itself again. It was like watching the carnage in reverse. Weapons flew to walls and remounted, what were scattered splinters reformed into wooden chests and broken pottery puzzle pieces found their way back together again. I looked down to see the floor clear and free from any dangers.

"I won't be long," he told me and for a moment it seemed as if he didn't want to go.

"And as always, I will wait for you, *my Husband,*" I told him softly and his eyes widened hearing it. At first, I thought it had been the right thing to say as the warm look he gave me could speak a thousand words. But then he abruptly walked out of the door, now leaving me thinking the complete opposite and that I had offended him. And as he left me standing there like some lost soul, hugging myself, I was just about to let my misery overwhelm me when suddenly he reappeared through the door.

I was about to speak when his actions stopped me as he stormed over to me and taking my face with both hands he whispered the sweetest two words,

"My wife." And then kissed me with such tender passion I found tears streaming down my cheeks and overflowing onto his hands. It was a blissful end to such a turbulent turning point in our parallel lives that I found myself melting into him and not wanting to let go again, for fear of who I would find myself facing when he came back. I wanted this Draven, the one who loved me and didn't look at me with utter betrayal. But after this kiss I realised that the real root of his anger had solely been focused on jealously and his belief that I had loved another but him. I couldn't say that I could blame him for look what I had done when faced with Aurora, back when I thought that he had picked being with her over me.

In fact, I had very nearly killed the bitch and if I had known of the part she would play in our future then I would have done so without an ounce of regret or a single moment's thought. But that had been beside the point, for at the time all my actions were all focused around jealously and nothing more. And with his next words, I knew he felt the same as I had done.

When the kiss ended he placed his forehead to mine and said softly,

"Have no thoughts of worry, for when I return, you will not find me angry." I think after he said this he could tell that I was relieved because he smiled when I released a big sigh.

"I am sorry I have caused you pain," I told him and in return he pulled me in for a hug, holding me close as he whispered in my hair line,

"Ssshh, for we will speak on matters soon. Now I must go and attend to your friend." I nodded and let him go, knowing that when he returned, it would be as he said,

Nothing between us…

But the future.

CHAPTER TWENTY

TIME TRAVELLING TRUTH

I don't know how long I waited but I must have fallen asleep on the bed in my emotional exhaustion for I felt my subconscious being tugged at by a soft, gentle touch down my cheek.

"Draven?" I murmured his name forgetting where I was and as soon as I said it I internally panicked as memory assaulted me of where in time I was. My eyes snapped open and I was momentarily surprised to find him looking down at me with a small smile playing around the edge of his lips.

"Easy sweet one, for I find I no longer loathe to hear the name, not now I know who owns it," he said smirking and no doubt remembering each time it had slipped from my lips. I let go of my held breath feeling relieved. I looked outside to see it was still dark and he took this action as a silent question.

"I wasn't gone long but my sister now looks after your friend at your request."

"I am glad Sophia is with her," I said without thinking and he raised a brow at me before saying,

"Ah, yes, Sophia is her name in your time." I winced just thinking of what she'd had to endure from her brother now he knew, which was why I was surprised to find him suddenly laughing.

"You're not mad?" I asked disbelievingly.

"Not when she told me of her reasons for being here and from what I understand it was lucky she was." I thought back to the Sophia of this time and knew that was certainly the truth, as I doubted I would still be breathing now.

"Are you ready to tell me how and why it is you came to be here?" he asked me in a gentle way and I knew it was so I wouldn't worry about telling him. After all, he could no doubt imagine what a difficult story it would be to tell. So, I nodded and after first pushing the covers back, I put my hand in his after he stood from the bed. Then I followed him to the sunken living space and took a seat, shifting sideways so that I could face him as he too sat down.

"Just take your time," he said after I released a sigh wondering where on earth I would start explaining any of this.

"Time…seems like such a funny word now," I said, more to myself and he gave me a small smile before asking,

"Would it make it easier if I were to ask you questions?"

"No lie detector tricks?" At this he laughed and held up his hands before putting them to his thighs saying,

"I promise they will stay right here, for I have no need not to trust you now." I gave him a small laugh in return.

"Alright, I think I could do that."

"How did you get here and from which time did you travel?"

"I used the Janus Gate, the one that powers the rest and after seeing you in my dreams from this time, it…well I thought of you and it brought me here." He looked surprised for a moment and then said,

"So, you believe it was fated to be this way because you saw me in your dreams?" I nodded and then told him,

"I do, for why else would I dream of the man I loved from nearly two thousand years earlier?" Now this really shocked him to the point that he looked as I usually did when faced with the impossible. I swear his mouth almost dropped and I tried not to laugh trying to put myself in his shoes. What would I have done if faced with a Draven from the future in some kind of silver space suit telling me of flying cars and super computers that get implanted into your mind. Okay, so this was going to be a long night that was for sure.

"Two thousand years?!" I placed a hand on his arm and said,

"I am from the 21st century." His next question nearly broke my heart.

"No…no, please…please don't tell me that I had to wait another two thousand years before I met you." I scooted closer and placed my forehead to the top of his arm and muttered,

"I am sorry to tell you this but I only met you when I was twenty-three and now I am twenty-five." Hearing this he closed his eyes as if in pain and I could imagine finding out that decade after decade millennia after millennia, and still nothing, was depressing enough. But then knowing that was what faced you in waiting, well then it was nothing short of torturous.

"Then I find myself thankful that fate brought you to me now, for many lifetimes in waiting will no longer face me," he said and I winced without thinking about it but he surprised me when he said in such an easy manner,

"You are planning on leaving me, little lamb?" I swallowed hard and tried to speak,

"I… well I…um you see…" His laughter stopped my lame attempt at explaining.

"I am not angry, for I doubt I have changed enough not to be as demanding as I am now…ah, but that look tells me something different," he said cutting himself off and shaking his head a little before confirming his suspicions.

"I know nothing of this back in your time, do I?"

"Okay, so no but technically you can't get angry with me because I didn't…umm, why are you laughing?" Suddenly his booming laughter cut me off.

"Because if you ever think me foolish enough to be angry with you doing something that brought you to me sooner, then I fear you have lost your beautiful mind to the realms of madness." Well I had to give him that.

"No, I find myself thankful indeed that I knew nothing of your plans and only thankful that Ranka found you as she did, bringing my lost lamb home to me," he added and I found myself amazed that he seemed to be taking this so well, which was why I had to ask him,

"So, you're not worried about me trying to get back to my own time?" His grin told me enough but his words only confirmed it.

"Why would I be for there is no way for you to return?" he told me and my heart dropped.

"What do you mean?"

"There is no Janus gate of which you speak, as it has not yet been discovered in this time," he told me and now I knew why he seemed in such good spirits…*I was trapped.*

"But there are gates…right?" I asked him and after giving me a small pitying smile, he told me,

"There is but one, the Black Gate, but that only works in the mortal realm." I didn't know how to feel about this as he didn't know what I had brought with me and was yet to find back in the desert.

"I will not lie and tell you that I am sorry, for I now look forward to an eternal life waking up to meet the rising sun with you in my arms." Hearing this what could I say. Hell, I was even tempted to say what was so wrong with being faced with all those lifetimes ahead of me with Draven by my side. But of course, it did beg the question that when I came to the point of being conceived, what then? Would there then be two of me in the world or would I simply disappear as though I had never been born?

Besides it was a moot point as I would never stop trying to get home, not when I had three people with me who all had loved ones back in my time and a prophecy to fulfil. But this wasn't something I needed to explain to Draven.

"But, I have to ask, why did you risk your life in doing so?"

"The Oracle sent me back here," I told him and he didn't look as surprised as I would have thought but he did want to know why, which put me in a difficult position.

"I don't really know but she told me it was all part of the prophecy and that I would know my purpose when I got here and found you." Hearing this he looked thoughtful for a moment as if he too was trying to find the reasons for himself, other than what he gained in finding me sooner.

"Then why did you hide yourself from me…your true self?" Okay, once again I found myself having to bend the truth, as what could I say. That I wanted to make a baby with him from this time because he refused to give me a baby in my own time as he knew it would be the cause of my death! Umm…no, didn't think so. So instead I went with something a little more cryptic and less…should we say, doomsday, stabby, stabby.

"Because the Oracle told me that as soon as you knew who I was that I would have failed." Okay, so it was nearly true as no-one knew how Draven would have reacted to any of this. For the first time during this conversation, Draven had heard something he didn't like.

"And you believe this to be true?" he asked and I shrugged my shoulders and said,

"I feel as if I don't know anything anymore but as you know, the Oracle cannot lie," I replied making his frown deepen and it was when he was looking down, that he finally noticed something. He suddenly picked up my arm and lifted it, bringing it closer to him.

"What are you…?" My question trailed off when I saw him pushing up my sleeve and I froze when I realised something. Pip had been hiding my scars all this time, as well as my soul to no doubt to save me from lying about how they came to be. I couldn't say that I blamed her given the extent of my lying capabilities, as it was probably on the same level of a child with a stolen cookie behind it's back telling a parent that they didn't do it.

He pushed my wide sleeve all the way up baring all my scars on one arm and I suddenly felt like crying. It had been so long that I had been bothered about them, as being next to Draven from my own time, just felt as though they had long ago faded. But like this, I felt painfully naked and I dreaded the next question out of Draven's mouth.

"Who did this to you and why was it hidden from me?!" He sounded angry and I tried to tug my arm out of his hold but he wouldn't let me.

"Please…don't do this to me," I asked him, trying to keep the emotional vibrations from my voice, a voice that told him how vulnerable I was.

"Ssshh calm now, I am not angry with you," he told me pulling me closer and gently caressing over my scars, trying to sooth my fears.

"I need to understand, did you think showing them would have made you less beautiful to me, for you have to know now that nothing could accomplish such an impossible task." I gave him a small smile of thanks for his kind words and to be honest I hadn't even given it a thought. Of course, I had wondered why he hadn't seen them but then knowing that Pip was masking who I was from him, then I just thought that would have had something to do with it. Obviously, I had been right.

"It isn't that but more the difficult story that follows," I told him honestly and he must have taken note of the way I looked down at both my arms, because the next thing I knew he was taking the other one in his hands.

"I…no, please, you don't need to…" My pleas went unheard as he started to push back the sleeve on the other arm.

"Oh, my precious girl, tell me who this did to you and please tell me that they are no longer allowed to breathe free air." I took a deep breath and knew I couldn't get away from it any longer. Pip had saved me from telling the painful story up until now but knowing Draven as well as I did, then finding out was top of the list of his next obsession. It didn't matter what era he lived in, it was the same in any time, for if it was something to do with me, then just like the Draven back then, he would do everything in his power to find out what happened.

So, I took a deep breath and told him the painful truth,

"I did this to myself," I told him, shocking him enough to drop my arms. I had to admit the rash reaction stung but not as much as his words,

"You tried to end your life?!" I closed my eyes and swallowed hard the hateful lump that felt as if I was choking on my own past.

"No…*I did not!*" I almost snarled the words at him and my reaction must have surprised him. I decided I needed to put space between us, so I shifted a few seat spaces down and lowered my head in my hands just to try and find the right words.

"It will be all right Nāzanin, you can…"

"Keira, my name is Keira and have no fear my Lord, for

you are the only man who ever called me it," I told him and hated the bitter tone that laced it.

"I care little for such right now, for nothing is more important to me than you and clearly you are in pain, a feeling I have forced upon you and for that I am sorry," he said sincerely and got up and walked over to me so that he could then kneel in front of me. Then he took my hands in his as I raised my head to look at him and I watched a King on his knees start to kiss each of my scars. It was such a profound sight that it took my breath away!

"I would rather not know how they came to be if it causes you such distress in telling me, for they would never dampen the love I have for you, as that fire burns eternally." Hearing this I couldn't have stopped my reaction for the life of me as I threw myself into him locking my hands around his neck.

"You don't know what that means to me!" I whispered fiercely in his ear and then suddenly, holding him wasn't enough. So, I started kissing him, feeling as though if I didn't I would self-combust with the love I felt overflowing for him. Like this it felt so natural, no longer having to hide and being free to do and say whatever I wanted, as he knew this was the real me.

"By the Gods woman, you know not what it is you do to me!" Draven said, his voice thick with lust. I smiled against his neck before I continued to kiss along it, sucking and nipping at him. At the same time, I ground myself against the erection I could feel and because it wasn't enough I reached down between us so that I could take his length in my hand. The sound of his groan was like music signalling a green light and I knew I had to have him, right then and there. It took me back to that day we nearly made love for the first time like this, only to find ourselves being interrupted by his dog, one that was no doubt now locked out of our room for fear of the same thing.

"I need you." I told him and this was all he needed before he tore up my long kaftan, along with ripping his sarong off. Once we were free of our restrictions he pulled my legs apart and surged up into me making me cry out. He held on to the back of my neck, anchoring himself to me and I held on to his shoulders as I arched back. The scorching intensity became overwhelming and I found myself scratching at his back, raking my nails along his skin as the building orgasm felt as though it would consume me whole.

"I have to taste you!" he told me applying pressure to my neck in a way that had me baring my neck to him in submission. After this he took no time at all before he had me under his dominating hold and I cried out as I felt his fangs biting down into my flesh. The second he took that first pull of my blood I was plunged into a sea of sensations that had me drowning in pleasure. I came so hard that I felt almost blinded from it and I felt my core fluttering around his length as he continued to thrust into me, over and over again.

Then he tore his fangs from my neck and with my blood still dripping from his lips he looked down at me. The sight was dangerously erotic and my eyes widened at the dark and horrifying beauty of it all. Then he yanked me to him hard and my surprised cry ended in his mouth as he took control. My own blood burst across my tongue and together we experienced the carnal taste together.

"Mine!" He pulled back enough to snarl at me before taking my bottom lip in between his teeth and then sucking it hard, making me moan out. It was as if he knew how addicted I became to feeling that tinge of pain morph into a pleasure of the likes I had never known before him. It was like making love to a wild beast that knew no bounds and the sexual thrill of it only managed to drive me higher when chasing my release…

something I quickly found again when he took a nipple into his mouth and feasted upon it.

"YES, YES! Don't stop! I...I...need to come!" I shouted as I tugged at his hair, something that made him growl around my heaving breast. The sound vibrated around my nipple and he bit down harder just as he slammed into me one last time and I came again like a rocket, weeping my release down his length as I quivered around him.

This was enough for him to find his own orgasm, and he let go of his bounty as he tensed back, roaring at the ceiling with his head thrown back. The sight had my insides clenching around him as I felt him bathing my channel with his cum as he pumped into me. It had been rough, hard and beautifully erotic in this moment of raw pleasure. My head fell forward on his chest as I was barely able to find the strength to keep it up. I panted, dragging air into my lungs and I felt him hold the back of my head to his chest as if he too took comfort in it being there.

"Did I hurt you, for I fear I lost my head?" he asked me softly and I lifted my head up, feeling as though my hair must have looked like an untamed lion's mane around my face. The daft, happy grin I gave him was obviously enough to tell him that I had enjoyed myself. He gave me such a tender smile in return as he pushed all my unruly hair back from my face.

"You look so beautiful right in this moment that I fear it would cause me pain to gaze upon you if I was not still nestled inside your tight little body." Hearing this I blushed and he ran the backs of his fingers across my burning cheeks. Then his eyes narrowed on my lips and he placed a gentle fingertip to them.

"I was too rough," he told me as if scorning himself. I felt the sting and smiled, as I realised he must have bitten them too, only I had been too deep in the throes of passion to care about the aftermath. I had only thought of the pleasure the pain brought me at the time which was why I grinned at him now and stopped him when he went to bite his own finger, no doubt to heal me.

"No, I want to remember and every time I lick my lips and feel the sting, I will get wet thinking about what you did to me," I told him shamelessly and his eyes widened in astonishment. I watched as a range of emotions flicked in his eyes until purple heat was the last one to remain.

"And I in turn with think of how my cock has found its eternal home when seated in your tight sheath whenever I see you biting that pretty, red lip of yours…one I very much enjoyed abusing, along with other parts of your beautiful body," he told me caressing my very red and bloody nipple. I shuddered against him at the sting, and his eyes flamed brighter when he felt my inner muscles throb around his length, one still hard and buried deep.

Needless to say, we quickly found euphoria together shortly after for the third time that night.

"How did we first meet?" His question came many minutes after our next round of the sex triathlon, which events included, front, back and me riding him like I was back on his horse! We were back in bed together and I was still coming down from my sexual high when he asked this question.

"Well, I'd just moved to the area to live with my sister."

"And what of your parents?" he asked and I couldn't help but smile as the tables had obviously turned considering I was usually the one asking all the questions.

"My parents stayed in England," I told him and almost laughed at the strange look of confusion he gave me.

"I know not of this England."

"It's what you now call Britannia, I believe in this time it is ruled by the Romans," I said and he nodded, now knowing where I came from.

"That explains the pale skin, for I believe their weather to be quite cold, yes?" I smiled and said laughing,

"And very wet, which is very similar to where I met you." Hearing this interested him greatly.

"It was not in Parthia I take it." I laughed again and told him,

"No, think less sun and more snow…we met in a place named Evergreen Falls in a country called America and somewhere that won't be discovered yet for quite some time."

"And how did I meet you in this new land I wonder?" he asked pulling me closer and picking up one of my hands so that he could play with my fingers.

"Well, you were my boss…I worked for you, as a…um…a server." I told him, trying to explain it better when I saw his confused look as he clearly didn't know what the word 'boss' meant.

"You served me?!" He sounded so shocked that I burst out laughing.

"Well not you directly, but where you lived, well it was a place that people go to and pay to drink…I am not sure if you have something like a tavern?" I asked.

"Yes, I know of which you speak, but I must confess, for I am confused as to why I would feel the need to own one." I laughed and told him,

"Let's just say that power in the modern world isn't held by kings and queens but by rich businessmen and you are very rich and own a lot of businesses, one of which is in a small town where you find it quiet enough to rule over your people in a more private way," I told him thinking this the best way to describe it.

"Ah, I see. It is similar in Rome as great wealth equals power and ruling is gained not by birth right, like royalty."

"So, you say you worked for me, I have this correct?" he then asked, taking a minute to think about it. I grinned and told him,

"I served the mortals in your club to begin with and then Sophia intervened and ensured I worked upstairs with your own kind, to be closer to you, something you were not happy about at the time." His face was a picture, as I knew it would be.

"I don't understand my reasoning behind this, why would I have you working in this way, if I knew who you were to me? No surely your true self was being hidden from me as it was now." I laughed and surprised him further when I said,

"You knew who I was but I believe your reasoning at the time was concern for my safety, as you didn't want me around your kind…you weren't very nice to me at first." He scoffed at this and replied,

"Then I fear I must have lost my head along with the rule of my people for if I had known who you were, I would have taken you as mine the moment I first saw you and killed anyone that dared question me on the matter or presented a threat to your life." Hearing this I couldn't help but smile. Looking back and trying to picture how his version would have gone wasn't exactly practical in modern day and would have quickly been labelled as kidnapping.

"I am sure this was what you would have preferred to do but things are very different in my time and besides, you had an extra two thousand years of learning patience," I said winking at him, an action he didn't understand the meaning of. Boy, did I have a lot of explaining to do and it seemed that he wanted to start with the most difficult. He ran his fingers softly over my scars and asked,

"And these, can you tell me why you would do this, for I know now you would not try and end your own life." I sighed knowing that for the second time in my life I would be reliving those painful steps that brought me nothing but traumatic memories and fading white lines along my skin.

Scars that I now knew didn't define me...

I defined them.

CHAPTER TWENTY-ONE

THE FALL

The rest of the night consisted of hours answering questions and blowing Draven's mind about what awaited him in the future. I tried not to lie to him about anything but for obvious reasons, I did hold myself back as to the depth of what I told him. For example, I didn't think it wise to mention too much about the prophecy or the long list of shit that had happened to me because of it. After all, there was me pretty much dying to save Lucius' life after he had kidnapped me, then there was the whole Draven faking his death heartache. Oh, and not forgetting me going to Hell and back before getting blood poisoning from some scum of the earth rapists. Oh yeah, I could just imagine the can of worms that would open...

Then there had also been Alex, which would have been a big no, no to mention around this extra jealous and murderous version of Draven, especially when hearing about how he too had tried to kill me. And of course, after that there were old enemies being released from prison, the near fatal attempt at releasing the Titans, a few demonic battles, spending eight months with a cult of vampires and not forgetting a few parties thrown in here and there for good measure.

So, all in all, there was probably more I couldn't tell him than there was *to* tell him. Like the bloody long list of people that had tried to kill me. Talk about a way to give a girl a complex I thought wryly.

But my decision to hold back turned out to be a good thing for more than one reason, as we would have still been chatting a week later and still have lots left over for a raging encore! But thankfully for me, the stuff he wanted to know was mainly centred around how we got together and more about my life in that time.

There had also been the difficult conversation about my past and I could see Draven trying to rein in his temper for my sake, something that looked close to exploding by the time I had finished. Telling him about Morgan for the second time was just as hard as it had been the first.

"If it helps, you did get to kill him in the end." I had told him, something he thankfully *did* relish in knowing. However, when I then explained all the ins and outs about how it happened, he complained at how quick a death it had been, going on to say,

"Death found him too swiftly, for I would have made it last the weeks he took from you and I would have enjoyed watching his torture at my hands for the suffering you endured at his." The tone in which he said this was a deadly promise and one that was the complete opposite to the soothing touch he granted me as he ran his fingers up the column of my neck.

"I will never let anyone hurt you again, this I can promise you," he then told me and I turned my body to his and snuggled in close, gaining comfort from his soft tender words of care. He pulled me even closer and wrapped his arms around me. I blissfully fell asleep that night in his arms as he whispered adoring words in my ear.

The next morning, I had happily woken to the feel of lips at my inner thigh and ended up arching my back at the first swipe of his tongue against my aching clit. I came screaming his name before I had even opened my eyes. Soon after this I found myself screaming again after he took my body in ways only Draven knew how.

After our delicious morning sex, I had asked him if I could go and see Pip, something he had no hesitation in granting me. I had been curious to ask why he suddenly felt so at ease with me coming and going as I pleased, as long as I stayed within the palace that was. But in the end, there had been no need to ask, as I quickly found out why.

I was now dressed in harem pants the colour of raspberries that were edged with a gold border in a grape vine design that was thick around the ankles and the low waist band. There was also a little bolero top to match that fastened under my bust and had capped short sleeves that flared off the shoulder. The whole of my belly was on show and I had to wonder at Draven's choice for my outfit, as it was the most revealing yet. I think he particularly liked the low neckline that showed a lot of cleavage as he continued to stare and touch me there whenever he felt the need…which turned out to be often.

Of course, the answer to that soon came as well, as eventually I had to ask,

"Where is everyone?" I said looking around trying to catch sight of anyone as we walked from Draven's room.

"I had this part of the palace forbidden to enter, as there is only a few of my most trusted guards allowed." His answer shocked me.

"But why?" I asked going slightly high pitched.

"Because I knew you would want to walk freely about your

new home and now you can do so at ease." My eyes widened before they narrowed at him.

"What you really mean is *you* can be at ease with me doing so." I mocked and he glanced at me side on and smirked, before agreeing,

"I must confess it was somewhat for my benefit also." Then he gave me a lustful look that started at my face and travelled the full length of my body.

"Ha! Yeah right, it is all for your benefit!" I teased, smacking him on the arm and making him growl light-heartedly at me.

"You want to play my little pet, for I find I am in the mood for something sweet and dripping once again?" he warned me and I took two steps from him and said,

"You will have to catch me first!" Then I giggled as I ran away from him down the large corridor. Of course, I didn't get far and I shrieked out, making it echo around the large empty space as he scooped me up into his arms.

"Okay, so I didn't get far," I admitted laughing.

"And you never will, for I fear for my mind if ever you accomplish the punishable task," he teased lifting me higher and biting my neck playfully. I giggled as it tickled thanks to his long beard.

"Punishable you say…mmm, that sounds interesting, tell me more my demanding King." I asked jovially. Hearing this he threw his head back and laughed, making me jiggle in his hold.

"Behave yourself my pet, for remember, I still have your chains, and after last night, I know your weaknesses and am not beyond exploiting them for my amusement." I had to say, hearing this had me soon squirming in his hold and the sound of the deep rumble rising from his chest told me he could shamelessly scent my arousal.

"I like the idea of being chained to you all night," I told him after pulling myself closer to his ear.

"By the Gods woman have you no pity on your King's manhood, for I fear by your words alone I could come undone like a young cock at the first sight of a naked girl spread ready for him?" he warned with a heavy grate to his voice that spoke of his waning restraint. So, what did I do, what I always did…*I pushed,*

"I know where I would like my large King's manhood to *come undone,"* I said whispering the last two words seductively. He growled at me before snapping,

"Enough, for I cannot wait!" Then he kicked in the nearest door which thankfully turned out to be an empty storage room, as there were folded linens, large jars, small pots and even chopped wood and filled sacks of god knows what. To be honest neither of us cared and I was sure it was no doubt Draven's first time in here, as it was mine. The thought made me giggle, a sound that was quickly growled at light-heartedly. He kicked the door closed and sealed it shut with a flick of his wrist.

"You mock your King's choice of rooms in which to take you?" he asked as he let my legs go, only to seat me at a high work bench, one he first swiped clear of the piles of cloths.

"Not at all, it's a very sexy room…tell me, my Lord, do you take many a woman in a place as grand as this?" I joked making him smirk before then yanking my pants down, making me cry out in surprise.

"No, but then there are none as special as you and as you know, I do love to spoil you so," he teased back and I was amazed at the ease in which he joked with me, hardly believing it was the same ancient, stern King I had met not that long ago. I giggled again and it soon became a sound that faded to a moan as his mouth took possession of mine. Then I felt his hand spread my legs and after tugging at the ties of his trousers, he thrust up into me, making me cry out in pleasure.

It turned out to the be the very last place I would have thought I would have had sex with a King, but was wonderful to know that it was a first for us both and three orgasms later, I found myself very grateful for the 'special room'.

"How is she?" I asked Sophia, as soon as I was led into the room by Draven, one who was even more at ease now, thanks to our little romp on the way here.

"She is still sleeping and she keeps calling for Adam in her dreams, which keeps breaking my heart but at least she is smiling in them," she told me making me tilt my head and say a girly, 'Aww'.

"Adam is her husband and a basic bad ass demon that all of Hell is scared of." I told Draven who gave me a look of disbelief…I soon found out why when he asked,

"He has a rotten behind?" I burst out laughing and then reached up to kiss his cheek for being unintentionally funny.

"Bad ass means the fiercest of our kind, strong and fearless among others," Sophia said translating for me.

"Ah, I understand and he is in love with this Imp?" At this I coughed out a laugh and said,

"More like adores, worships and obsesses over, oh and of course loves dearly…she is also the only being alive who can tame his demon side before it destroys the Earth so, needless to say, they are made for each other," I added and Draven must have thought I was joking as he turned to his sister for confirmation when he asked,

"This is true?"

"Yeah, pretty much," she agreed nodding. Now when

Draven looked back at Pip, he seemed to do so with a look of great respect rather than the disdain he had shown her the last time he had seen her. Although I could see his point on that one for at the time she had basically given him the verbal middle finger by telling him that she wouldn't take orders from him, but only me. And for a man like Draven, I couldn't imagine that was something he was used to hearing all too often.

"I fear I must say goodbye for a short while, as I have…"

"I understand, after all you have a kingdom to rule. It's okay, I will see you when you're ready for me," I told him cutting him off.

"I am always ready for you, my little time traveller," he told me softly pulling me to him and cupping my cheek.

"I think you proved that not long ago by spoiling me, my demanding king." I uttered back reaching up on tiptoes so that I could speak in quieter tones. He growled low and nipped at my nose, warning,

"Behave wife of mine, or you will find yourself back there and I will find my kingdom in ruins from lack of care, for you will make me lose my head as I have already lost my heart willingly." His sweet reply had me grinning like a mad woman and I beamed up at him before pulling him down for a kiss. If anything, it was the sound of Sophia clearing her throat that finally broke our connecting lips, as it was starting to get heated once again. Jesus, but I felt like a damn teenager again!

"It's alright, don't mind me or anything," she commented sarcastically making me laugh. Draven was about to speak when Sophia held up her hand and said,

"You don't need to ask Brother, for I would protect her with my life." Draven looked relieved and nodded before walking over to his sister and pulling her head forward so that he could bestow a kiss on her forehead.

"I am proud of you, my sister," he told her gently and

released her. Then, with her still looking flabbergasted, he simply kissed me swiftly before telling me,

"Try and stay out of trouble this time, little lamb, for I wish not to worry for longer than a day." Then he winked at me, like I'd taught him to do earlier that morning. I rolled my eyes at him, something he also now knew the meaning of, which was why just before he left he smacked my bum playfully, making me yelp.

After this I released a big loved up sigh, just as I usually did around Draven from any time.

"I see you two are finally getting along," Sophia commented, bringing me down from my cloud 9. Realisation soon hit me that my rash decision in telling Draven the truth could have cost us everything, so in that moment I threw myself into her arms.

"I am so, so sorry! I tried to hold back telling him but then I made the stupid mistake of saying the wrong name and then he got angry, and then when I refused to tell him, he called for Pip and…" She started laughing and said,

"Whoa there, take a breath honey, I am not angry and I knew you did what you felt you had to…besides, Dom has obviously taken this better than we ever expected he would or you would be locked in the tallest tower he could find right now, growing your hair and singing about floating lanterns." I laughed and said,

"Okay, you have been spending way too much time around Ella."

"Nah, I love that kid and besides, it's mainly Pip who makes me watch that crap, but getting past all that, it looks like our only problem now is finding a way back home…congrats by the way," she added nodding down at my belly and my hands flew to my stomach, as my eyes went wide.

"You really think I could be…I mean, can you sense it or

anything?!" I asked in astonishment and hope combined. Sophia gave me a soft, kind smile and took my hand.

"I'm afraid I can't but don't be discouraged, as I wouldn't be surprised if the guards you have protecting your mind also feel the need to protect the life that may grow inside you." I bit my lip and nodded, hoping that she was right. The first thought that I could be pregnant right now brought me a warmth in my heart of the likes I had never known. Of course, feeling the slight sting on my lip also made me think of what Draven had done to me that morning, like I told him it would. I don't think my smile could have gotten any bigger.

"That reminds me, where is Ari?" I asked, thinking that she would have been here. Sophia grinned and said,

"I am afraid she is too busy being wooed by another brother of mine, for after your desert escape, I fear he has taken it upon himself for the first time to try and make a girl fall in love with him." I chuckled once.

"So, how's that working out for him?"

"I think he is making progress." Hearing this made me smirk.

"Oh really."

"Yeah, I believe he is out there right now teaching her how to ride his horse."

"Yep, that would do it," I told her laughing and shaking my head at the thought of those two. It was just a shame that the Vincent from our own time wasn't getting the chance at 'wooing' her and I could only hope that this would mean her cutting him some slack when we got back home. Speaking of which,

"I haven't yet had chance to tell you, but I think I might know a way to get us all home." Hearing this had Sophia's full attention.

"Oh, good because I really don't want to be around when the

other version of me wakes up and Dom has to deal with that shitstorm sister!" After this Sophia explained how she told her brother the reasons for her coming through the Janus gate were to keep me safe. And after describing how her younger self had tried to murder me, well, let's just say after that he didn't have much to argue with. She also told me that her other self had been moved to a separate part of the palace and been made secure, along with having supernatural guards constantly keeping watch. I, in turn, told her my plans for getting us back but that first we needed to find Ranka.

"She is the only one who knows where she found me that day and I doubt we can just go hunting around the desert for bloody patches in the sand and rotting body parts," I added.

"Good point and plus eww." I gave her a half-cocked smile and said,

"I thought you were a demon?"

"Yeah, give me fresh body parts any day of the week, but even I think anything that has had chance to start decomposing is gross, do you know what that putrid shit does to your clothes?" she informed me, quickly planting images of Sophia in a biohazard suit in the desert looking for our ticket out of here.

"I can't say I have been around many dead bodies, let alone rotting ones, so I will take your word for it," I said with a little shiver.

"So, any ideas on where she could be?" I asked after looking back down at the sleeping, green haired beauty that was curled up on her side. She looked so young and childlike that you just wanted to wrap your arms around her and protect her. Sophia came to sit down next to me on the edge of the bed and tucked a curl behind Pip's ear, one now full of holes thanks to having taken all her earrings out.

"Honestly, I have no clue and I feel bad for saying this now, but I never really cared to find out much about her." I found this amazing seeing as she had been with them all from the beginning.

"I know what you're thinking and yes, evidence would suggest that I was an uber bitch back then, but I was also utterly faithful to the Fates and the second I heard about you, then I kind of made it a bit of an obsession," Sophia admitted shocking me. Okay, so I knew that she was willing to kill me just because she thought I would get in the way of the prophecy by being with her brother. But to hear that she was as obsessed with finding me as her brother was, well that was a bit of a shocker.

"So Ranka's obvious love for my brother didn't exactly sit right with me, which was why we never really saw eye to eye," she said almost wincing as if feeling guilty for all those times she had been less than kind to her. I knew it was strange and I should have hated her myself considering she was in love with my husband, but for some reason I just couldn't find myself disliking her. After all, she had protected me and saved me from a horrific death out in the desert. Which also begged the question…*why*? Why, if she knew who I was to Draven? Well I guess these were on the long list of things I needed to ask her when I finally saw her next, after the main one of course…like could you draw a map to the place where I almost died and you killed a load of guys? Yep, that would be a big one and top of the list right now.

"I get it, as I felt the same way when I first met her, but I don't know now, as it's almost like her love for him comes secondary to the prophecy," I told her and she nodded, as from her actions it couldn't be denied.

"I wonder if there are any clues as to her whereabouts in her room," Sophia mused aloud.

"Only one way to find out," I said slapping my hands to my thighs and getting up.

"Let's go," Sophia said and we both looked back at Pip and said together,

"She will be fine."

We both walked out of the door and I quickly found myself glad that Draven had this side of the palace cleared out as it certainly made sneaking around a lot easier. Ranka's room wasn't far from the room Pip was in. It was also close to the one Draven had ordered me to be placed in until it became known who I was to him. I remembered it from when I first woke after being attacked and it was the same door we were slipping into now.

"Wow, well this is boring," Sophia said taking in the relatively plain room that held nothing but a cushioned bed, a large wooden chest and a few bows of different sizes on the walls.

"What did you expect, a David Hasselhoff Night Rider pinball machine and a Darth Vader alarm clock?" I asked making her roll her eyes at me.

"I don't know, but I expected after a few thousand years the girl would have at least collected a few possessions." Okay, said like that I guess she had a point. But this wasn't what I said because the second I heard even a hint at how old they were I jumped on it,

"So, few thousand years eh…does that mean Draven is…?"

"Oh no, nice try blondie but I am not falling for that one, he already warned me not to tell you how old we are," she said cutting me off and making me fold my arms to sulk for a few minutes.

"Fine, but I do have a right to know at some point!"

"Who knows, maybe Dom is planning on telling you for a wedding present," she joked making me groan.

"Right, well getting back to the room, or should I say lack of, I don't think we are going to find much here, do you?" Sophia said and I had to agree with her, as there was nothing in there. I also had to say that the more I looked around the more it began to seem suspicious, as the lack of 'stuff' was almost a massive clue in itself.

"Do you think she could have another room somewhere, like one no one knows about?" I asked making her shrug her shoulders.

"It's like I said, I didn't really know much about her as it was clear who she was on this Earth to obey and it wasn't myself or Vincent…she was only loyal to Dom."

"But what about friends?" I asked and Sophia winced telling me,

"She didn't have any." I frowned thinking this was getting weirder.

"What about guys…lovers, surely she would…?" My question died when Sophia once again shook her head.

"Wow, that sounds depressing," I commented, feeling sorry for her.

"Well, I don't think we are getting anywhere here," Sophia said walking back to the door and I had to agree with her. I turned around about to follow her out when, in true Keira fashion, I tripped over my own feet. I ended up knocking over a pottery jug that must have been there for her morning routine, as it was next to a large matching bowl.

"Yeah, yeah, I know, you're bad," Sophia said as I bent down to pick up the broken pieces, placing them all into the bowl, but that's when I started to notice something odd.

"Hey…that's weird," I muttered to myself as I noticed all the water started to drain away down in between some large joints in the stone floor. I had to wonder where it went to and was just about to ask Sophia when I reached out for what looked like a strange symbol that started to appear in the corner of one of the stone slabs.

"What's weird?" she asked just as I reached out and touched the mark to see if I could rub it off but the second I put weight on it, something happened. The stone slab I was knelt on started to move and tilt up, which in turn sent me flying forward.

"Keira!" Sophia shouted my name, one that ended when I fell down the person sized hole it created and then it quickly shut back up above me. I only noticed this briefly as I continued to roll down what was a secret staircase. I cried out as pain shot through my knee, elbow and ribcage before I came to land at the bottom with a painful thud, knocking the side of my head on the last stone step.

"Oww," I moaned as I tried to move my body, but I quickly found out that this was the least of my problems as a male voice spoke my other name,

"Electus?" I looked up and the second I saw the horrifying sight I started to panic.

Piles of mangled and dismembered bloody bodies lay all around me and there was only one thing left for me to do…

I screamed bloody murder!

CHAPTER TWENTY-TWO

SECRETS

I wasn't ashamed to say that the first thing I did at the sight of all the decaying bodies was to paint the floor with vomit. I heaved and heaved until it felt like there was nothing left but bile. I heard the big sigh from over in the corner where a figure stood hidden in the shadows. I felt the panic quickly build the second I saw him moving closer towards me. I tried to scramble backwards up the steps but felt the pain at the side of my body where I had banged it on the way down.

"Ah! D...don't come any closer!" I told him with fear making my yelled warning start out garbled.

"It's all right, I won't hurt you...I will just stay over here but please, you are hurt and bleeding, please don't injure yourself further for fear of me," he said and it was a soft voice I didn't recognise.

"Who...who are you?" I asked after deciding there was little I could do but trust in what he was telling me. Again, I heard him release a heavy sigh as if this was the very last thing he wanted to tell me. And considering the revolting state of the room, I couldn't say I was surprised.

"I am someone you know but for now, I think it's wise to get you from this room, for there is little doubt that Saphira is informing the King of your disappearance right now and this is not a place I want anyone to find." I looked around the dark stone walls that were only lit by the few candles that were situated around the room. But it was enough to show me the carnage of death that lay piled in bloody sacks around the edges of the room. It smelt like, well like you would imagine what a rotting corpse would smell like and not surprisingly, it made me gag.

Well would you look at that, so much for telling Sophia I hadn't spent much time around dead people, let alone rotting ones. So, I had to ask myself what were the chances of finding both just minutes later. I was thinking more like close to winning Hell's version of the lottery, that's what!

"Come, for if you stay here it will only make you sicker, I promise Electus, I will not harm you, for I never could…come with me," he said holding out a hand to me. I looked down the centre of the room and noticed a small seating area at the back, where he had been sitting. And sickeningly, it strangely resembled a small dining room table. I didn't even want to think why there would be one, so after a revolting shiver wracked my body, I took a deep breath and weighed up my options.

I quickly decided there was little option left, as in Zero, so I did as he instructed and slowly walked towards him. He pulled a hood up over his face, hiding himself from me for the time being as he motioned me closer.

"You promise not to hurt me?" I asked knowing it was pointless as it wasn't as if the Supernatural couldn't lie. But for some reason I had to hear it first.

"I swear to you Electus, I am no threat to you or the King."

I didn't know what it was about the way he said this but I found I could do nothing but believe him. So, I nodded and moved forward until the small table came into view.

"What is this place?" I asked after I sucked in a horrified breath and coughed through the nausea, when seeing pieces of body parts on large plates on top of the table. I was right, it had been where someone was eating a meal…one where human was on the menu.

"Not a place for human eyes that is for certain…come," he said, first making sure I followed before opening a small hidden door, one that was a low enough archway that he had to duck under as he entered. Once inside he gave me a wide berth, no doubt not wanting to scare me by getting too close. So, I took a few steps further in so that he could close the door behind us, thankfully locking out the smell.

"There is some water on the small table over there, please help yourself," he told me as he went about bolting the door. I looked to where he had said and walked over to a small seating area that this time seemed cosy enough. Although, with what I was comparing it to it didn't exactly take much to make it seem 'cosy'. Just minus a few knawed bones, bitten flesh and chopped organs was really all it took.

Well, at least this room was the complete opposite to the slasher movie set I had first found myself in. Strangely the small space looked to be filled with a world of artefacts and unlike ones back in my time, none of these looked all that old. It looked as if someone was a pack rat or compulsive hoarder as my mum liked to call them. There was stuff everywhere, statues, scrolls, paintings, instruments of all different shapes and sizes, large precious stones and even what looked like an ancient board game or two, that involved little wooden counters on Chinese looking markers.

All these things seemed to climb the walls on shelving that

looked close to collapsing from the weight. Then on the other side were all things mounted, like hunting trophies and weapons, some still looked stained with blood. Which was when I started to make sense of what I was looking at, each kill was paired with the weapon used to take it down. To be honest it too made me want to gag again, so instead of looking any closer at the poor unfortunate souls that used to roam the land, I sat down in a comfortable looking half-moon shaped chair and poured myself a goblet full of water. I downed the whole thing and all the while the hooded figure said nothing but looked at me. Once I had finished the water I placed it down and wiped my mouth on the back of my hand, feeling better now that I had rid myself of the bitter taste of bile.

"So, I think it's now time you tell me who you are," I said as I watched him and if I didn't know any better I would say he looked nervous. He started playing with his fingers and then wiped his sweating palms down his cloak.

"Look, if it helps things I can promise to keep your secret and if you can get me back without anyone seeing, then I won't tell anyone that you're down here."

"You would do that?" he asked sounding astonished. To get myself out of this gruesome Hellhole and away from a human eating demon, then yeah, of course I bloody would, I thought secretly. Needless to say, I didn't say this.

"Of course, if you can first explain to me what it is you are doing down here," I said nodding to the locked door of death and quickly needing some more water so as not to be sick again just thinking about it.

"I don't kill for food," he said abruptly and I nearly spilled the water I was pouring. I placed the jug down slowly and said,

"Oookay, well that's good that you didn't kill them at least."

"I did kill them," he admitted, causing my eyes to grow wide and suddenly I was wishing there was something stronger in my goblet than just water, preferably something made from potatoes and could give you a mean hangover.

"That sounded bad," he said as if having time to digest what he said and play it back to himself.

"Uh…yeah, kind of," I agreed and again he released a heavy sigh, something that seemed to be a habit of his.

"I killed them to save another and it is not in my nature to waste the meat I kill. Their heads however, I was ordered to display on spikes by the King as a warning to all other travellers that think about attacking our people," he told me and just as I finished processing his words I was suddenly up and out of my seat. The goblet clattered to the floor, making me flinch. It hurt, thanks to the split in my knee and sore ribs, but I didn't care because if what he was telling me now…well surely it was impossible, wasn't it?!

"That…can't…you…surely…no." I couldn't seem to form a sentence as it was too unbelievable, but only managed to keep shaking my head.

"It is I…*Ranka,*" he said pulling back his hood and showing me a very male version of the warrior woman I knew…*or the one I thought I knew.*

"But you're a man!" I shouted and he swallowed hard before telling me,

"This is my true form and yes, I am male."

"But you're in love with Draven!" I blurted out without thinking and I felt like an utter shit when I saw him wince. He looked down and off to one side as if his greatest secret had just been cut from his heart and now he was watching it spill onto the sandstone floor. He even closed his eyes as if the pain was near unbearable.

"I'm sorry! I shouldn't have said that," I said quickly, unable to contain my guilt. Hearing this his eyes suddenly snapped open as if he couldn't believe what he was hearing.

"You're sorry?" he asked with a small shake of his head as if this helped in testing his hearing or something.

"Yes, it was inconsiderate of me to just blurt it out like that."

"But why would you be sorry, you should hate me," he admitted looking away as if disgusted with himself.

"We can't help who we fall in love with and I would be a fool to believe otherwise," I said thinking about all the years Draven had been on this earth and knowing that the list of hearts broken by his lack of love returned must have been as long as my body.

"I would have never…" he started to say on a whisper and then his words trailed off as if unable to finish the sentence. Because let's face it, could you really say you wouldn't have when faced with your heart's desire, no matter what price you had to pay? Look at what Draven himself would sacrifice by turning his back on the prophecy just to save me. Loving someone wasn't as clear cut as following your heart and looking at Ranka now, I would say he would have agreed with me.

"I…I…don't know what to say," I told him or her, oh God I was so confused. He shrugged his shoulders before walking cautiously over to the empty seat near where I had been sitting. Then he held out a long slender hand for me to sit back down. I did but I also couldn't help staring at him in awe.

He was a beautiful man in an exotic feminine way. He had the same almond shaped eyes the colour of hazel and honey that were framed by thin arched eyebrows. Even his triangular shaped face was the same as the Ranka I was used to seeing. His hair was the same mohawk design, one braided back down the centre. He had darker mocha colour skin that was speckled black around his hair line and ears, that were also slightly pointed. It reminded me of tattooed war paint and just like the female version of him, he looked ready for battle. His attire was leather trousers, strapped with numerous wicked curved blades, and tarnished leg armour that looked to have been made moulded to his frame. He was tall, with a slim but fit build that looked made for skill and speed, not for brute strength.

"Does anyone know?" I asked softly, trying to sound as sympathetic as I felt. He shook his head and I swallowed down the hard lump of pity.

"Not even Draven…I mean, Arsaces?" The look of panic he gave me had me holding up my arms and saying,

"Don't worry, I won't tell him, I just wanted to be sure." He quickly looked relieved.

"The King does…*not know,*" he said confirming it with a sigh that caused half his sentence to come out as a whispered confession. I couldn't help my reaction as I reached across the small space between us and gave his hand a reassuring squeeze.

"Hey, it will be okay, no one needs to know, not if you don't want to tell them." He first looked down at my hand on his and then up at me in shock. Had this really been the first show of friendship he had been given by another?

"I am not surprised he is in love with you, for I think he would have given his heart willingly even if you weren't destined for him," he told me giving me a small smile, one that reflected back in his warm coloured eyes.

"You love him, don't you?" I came out and said it. For a moment, he looked panicked until I said,

"It's fine and like I said, I understand and I am not angry or anything. It's just our little secret… along with how handsome you are instead of pretty," I told him with a smirk, one that thankfully put him at ease.

"I am happy he found you, even if you do not think I would be."

"Well that's what happens when you care deeply for someone, that despite who they choose, you at least find comfort in knowing they are happy…that is what real love means," I agreed and he nodded, giving me the biggest smile.

"Yes, I think you are right."

"Which comes to my next question, why are you down here hiding, Ranka?" This question looked once again like a difficult one for him to answer and he looked back at the door for a moment, as if it held the key. This was when I was transported back to that day when Pythia told me about Ranka and it quickly started to make sense.

"You are regenerating your cells by eating their flesh so that you can get your old form back, aren't you?" I said making him snap his head back to look at me in astonishment.

"How…how would you know about such a thing?" he asked frowning and I gave him a small shrug of my shoulders before telling him the only name he needed to hear,

"Pythia told me about you back in my own time."

"I see," he replied sounding sad as if I must be sickened by the idea.

"Hey, it's cool…"

"You are cold?" he asked interrupting me and I held back a giggle.

"It means it's fine, that I am not upset or anything about knowing this about you. It's your nature and you can't change what you are and nor should you want to. But I would like to know what happened, if that's alright?" I asked and instantly felt bad when I saw him hang his head in shame.

"I was not strong enough to fight him," he said after a moment of looking uncomfortable and now I knew why as this was obviously not something easy to admit.

"You mean Pertinax?" he nodded and told me,

"Pertinax had spies in the city and on the day of your choosing he not only saw you but I also as I stepped up for you, when you decided to draw the King's image. I believe it was then that not only you caught his eye, but I did as well." I remembered back to seeing someone in the crowd that looked like he had been spying. This was when I started to understand the layers that me being here had added on top of the past that *should* have happened, not the one that mistakenly *did* happen.

By me being here, well I had changed everything.

"He attacked you?" I asked in a sympathetic tone getting back to my questions.

"He found me, yes and then stole my form, leaving me bare and as you see me now," he said nodding down to himself as if ashamed with the way he looked.

"Well, if it helps I think you look pretty good as a man," I told him making him blush and try to hide a small smile.

"And I thank you greatly for the kindness you show me, for I do not deserve it, not when you know my reasons for preferring a female form over one birthed to me as my true vessel." I gave him a small smile in return as I knew what he meant. Draven was only ever going to find a woman attractive being that he wasn't gay and Ranka clearly was. I knew it was a deception and I should have been angry on Draven's behalf, but looking at the utter shameful agony on Ranka's face, then I could find only sorrow for such a lie.

"I know why Ranka, and although I don't think you should feel the need to live life as a lie, I am not going to judge you for your decision to do so," I told him honestly and he nodded, accepting it for what it was, friendly advice.

"So, you have been hiding down here since then?" I asked moving on and getting back to what happened.

"Yes, until my strength is great enough for the change and of course the men that attacked you are helping with that," he admitted with a smirk, letting me know who it was that was acting like a human protein shake. Well, I couldn't say I was half as disgusted now, not knowing how those raping bastards ended up as a demon's 'all you can eat' buffet.

"Well, I am happy the assholes are helping with that," I told him and he gave me a horrified look before saying,

"By the Gods, I don't eat that part of them!" Then he shuddered and I couldn't help but burst out laughing. Then I grabbed his hand and told him chuckling,

"Calling someone an asshole is just an insult, don't worry, I never thought you would eat one." Hearing this he too burst out laughing and I never thought in a million years I would be bonding with someone I once thought as a girl in love with my husband, discussing them possibly eating an asshole after just discovering they were really a man. Wow, I think even Jerry Springer would be stumped at that one!

"Ah, I see," he smirked and then looked above as if hearing something I couldn't.

"Come, we need to get you back above, as the King is searching for you." I looked up, straining my hearing ability to try and listen but there was nothing.

"Wait, I need to ask you something, it's why I was in your room in the first place, trying to find you." Ranka gave me a questioning look and nodded to a door behind me that was half hidden by a long hanging curtain that looked to be handmade Chinese silk print.

"I will answer your questions on the way," he told me walking past and sweeping the beautiful silk aside. I got up out of my seat and followed behind, but jumped when I heard a roar of anger from above, one that even my puny human's ears wouldn't miss.

It had me wondering what Sophia had told him as I doubted it was how I had been swallowed up by a stone slab. I don't know what she had said but if it had been the truth then I doubt there would have been much left of Ranka's hideaway, unless…

"Is there some kind of magic on this place?" I don't know why I thought of this but it was strange, as if I knew I was right. He looked taken aback and no doubt wondered how I knew this.

"It is hidden from all my kind, which is why it only opened for you, although I am curious as to how you would know this?" he asked and I told him honestly.

"I am not really sure myself." Then I ducked through the low passageway, one that was pitch black until he lit a torch he first unhooked off the wall.

"The King will not find this place unless he knows of its existence," Ranka said and gave me a look over her shoulder. Once again, I found myself holding up my hands and saying,

"Don't worry about me, I am not going to tell him...but I do however need to give him some reason as to why I suddenly disappeared and got all bruised up. I know being with him makes me heal quickly but not quick enough that he won't notice," I said muttering *'Unfortunately'* after it with a wince of pain.

"I will think of something before I let you go up, now ask me your question."

"When I arrived in this time back in the desert, I lost something," I told him putting a hand to my neck as if feeling it there for myself, the one I had put around my neck before stepping into the Janus Gate.

I remembered when I found it, knowing for some reason it meant something important. It wasn't like the other coins I had used before as it looked more like a piece of gold jewellery or large pendant than something we could have used to get here. Which was why I had never thought about it until out in the desert after finding Ari.

But now, well what else did we have to lose. So, I told him,

"It was something the Oracle gave me and I believe it is the only thing that could get us home. It is a large gold pendant that has a lion holding a curved blade sat inside the sun on one side and on the other is some kind of bird, with the head of a panther." This was when Ranka's eyes widened and recognition flickered in his hazel coloured eyes.

"And what of symbols, does it also have these forged in its design?" he asked and once more I recalled that day, back in my broken-down truck that had ran out of fuel. It was after I had gone to the library to see if Pythia had any more answers for me. Instead all I had found was Lucius and a book, 'The Time Machine' by H. G. Wells. But it wasn't the book itself that gave me any clues as what to do next but it was what she had put inside it. I remember picking it up by the cord, letting it spin around slowly at eye level and there it all was, symbols and all.

"Yes! Yes, it did...but wait, how did you know that?" I asked and that was when he hit me with a 'Time travelling' sized bombshell,

"The King is the one who gave it to her as a gift, telling her that one day she would need it to aid her in fulfilling the Prophecy." Hearing this my mouth dropped open in utter shock. It was almost an impossible fact to face knowing that even back thousands of years the building blocks of destiny had cemented the foundations of what I must do by the Fates themselves. But then I had to ask, knowing that with his answer, I had my sign,

"And who gave it to the King to give to her?"

"Her Father, the God Janus."

CHAPTER TWENTY-THREE

LOST AND FOUND

After making my way through numerous narrow tunnels with Ranka, I finally found my way back up to the surface of the palace. Of course, it would have to be outside what Draven had considered the 'safe zone' and one he had forbidden me to enter. After cutting off his private wing of the palace I had to ask myself how I would get back in and just hoped that the guards would know who I was or what I meant to him. Well, I was no doubt just racking up the number of disapproving looks I was going to get from one angry king. I hadn't even been able to give him one worry free day, like he asked for, I thought feeling guilty.

The tunnels had led into a servant's quarters, where people were busy preparing food and wine for the night ahead. I had told Ranka along the way where I thought the pendant might be and he promised me that as soon as it was nightfall he would sneak out unseen and go and look for it. He said that thanks to the blood he had consumed he would easily be able to home into where he first spilt it, back where I was attacked. It was crazy to think, but even that seemed to be part of the Fates, as I could only imagine what Draven would have thought if he had found me wearing it that day.

So now here I was, trying to make my way through the busy palace thankfully covered by Ranka's cloak, so at least I didn't stand out like a sore thumb. I walked along the halls looking around and for the first time since being here, doing so freely. This was when it hit me, I could have probably walked straight from the palace and no one would have been any the wiser. Had I really just found my way out of the palace when the time came?

I decided to try and test the theory and followed the others as they busied themselves with their chores. I heard one woman barking orders at a young girl, handing her a big basket and telling her to go to the market place. So, I followed her. She looked back at me and I smiled, trying to act like just some other friendly servant, going about her business. I don't think I achieved it as much as I hoped as she was frowning at me. After this I thought it best to hang back a bit, keeping my distance until she reached a side door that I knew led to the Great Hall. This of course, was when I heard one very angry King issuing his masterful orders.

"Find her and bring me the head of anyone who dared try and take her from me!" I groaned aloud letting my head fall back against the stone wall I was leaning against and thinking this didn't look good for me. Sophia had obviously informed him of my disappearance, no doubt being worried about what had happened to me herself. The only chance I had left was that he clearly didn't know about that secret trapdoor into Ranka's private hideaway, so we might still have a chance at getting out that same way when the time came.

Of course, what would help me now was to speak to her first, so that I could get my story straight. Ranka had at least been helpful enough to speak of hidden tunnels that had been closed off and could have made it easy for me to slip into the unknown after the battle only days before. After all, the Earth had certainly shifted after Pertinax's destruction and I was sure it wouldn't be too farfetched to believe it enough to make these hidden access panels to become unstable. Well that was the theory we were going with anyway. So, I took a deep breath and forgot about the girl I was following to go in search of Sophia… or so I thought.

I had only just turned my back when the young girl I had been following dropped her basket and ran into the Great Hall screaming about being followed by who she thought they were all looking for. Well so much for my stealth skills, I thought wryly. I decided I couldn't exactly put it off forever so was just about to step out into the Great Hall when suddenly I was grabbed from behind.

I was just about to fight against it when I felt something I was unfortunately becoming accustomed too.

A blade at my neck.

"Come quietly and you won't be hurt but make yourself known and I will slit your throat." A voice hissed from behind me and I wanted to actually roll my eyes at this fool.

"Listen up buddy, if you think for one minute we are getting out of here without being seen then you are so wrong, it's almost funny." I told him in a tired voice but then I felt the blade nick my skin and I sucked in a painful breath at the sting.

"Now that got your attention," he told me with a snigger and then just as I heard the commotion coming from the Great Hall I felt myself being pulled back before being pushed hard against the wall. The man wasn't exactly what I would have called a kidnapper's lackey as he was annoyingly handsome… in fact, stunningly so.

He wore a turban that had a long length hung down so that it could conceal half his face, leaving just his unusual light olive-green eyes on show. They were incredible and unlike any I had ever seen before. It just made me want to get closer to him to see if the emerald green and orange star that seemed to burst into lighter shades around his pupil was really there. Added to this he had a strange shadow around his eyes that gave him an exotic hard edge to his serious glare.

"Now stay," he told me sternly, pulling the large blade back and waving it in front of my face as an obvious threat. Then he turned his attention to the wall next to us and I had to wonder why…what was he waiting for? Well, it turned out that I didn't have long to wait as he started to reach out to the wall and I looked on in amazement as it started to move. I narrowed my eyes as if what I was seeing wasn't possible and by all mortal accounts it shouldn't have been. But there was no denying the truth of my situation as the wall in front of us started to liquify.

A sandstone droplet started to drip outwards as if defying gravity and being drawn to his fingertip. Then I looked at his eyes and saw that the olive-green starburst was no longer there as his eyes had seemingly caked over with what looked like a cracked rock iris. It was the strangest thing, as if he had somehow mimicked the substance in front of him so that he could control it.

My head suddenly snapped back towards the hall to see soldiers coming around the corner and I could hear Draven's commanding voice with them.

"Where is she?!" he snapped obviously speaking with the servant girl that had alerted him to my whereabouts.

"In…in there… my Lord," she stammered out fearfully.

"Time to go," the man said and suddenly I found myself being yanked back to a place that should have been impossible to travel…*through the wall.* At first it felt as though I was drowning in sand and I was just thankful that I had at least had the good sense to take a deep breath before I felt myself falling backwards. I closed my eyes the second I felt the sand burying me alive.

"Ahh!" I shouted finally opening my eyes and mouth, as I felt myself about to land, only it never came. The man had grabbed me with a fist full of my cloak at my chest, stopping me just before I landed on the unforgiving hard ground.

"What the hell?!" I shouted after he yanked me to my feet. I was looking around and saw that we seemed to be in another room in the palace, one that I hadn't been in before.

"Quiet girl!" the man snapped, swinging me around and once again manhandling me into another wall, this time the one opposite to the one we must have just passed through. It gave me a chance to take a good look around and I was at least happy to see that it looked to be an armoury. It was a long room and further down from where we stood were lines of spears and swords. I knew I couldn't just take a skip and jump over to one of them so that I might defend myself, but that didn't mean I had nothing to work with where I stood.

So, I lowered down ever so slightly and reached for one of the baskets that was only a hairsbreadth away from my fingertips. Thankfully, where we stood were thousands of bundled arrows all piled ready in baskets and all I needed was one. I kept my eyes on what the man was doing now and this time I couldn't help but flinch as I saw him pulling a long thick needle from his turban. It looked just as deadly as the blade that he had thankfully just tucked back in its sheath attached to his leg.

All I could hope for was that one, that lethal looking pin wasn't for me and two, I could reach the only weapon to hand before he remembered I was still there. Thankfully when I saw him stabbing his own hand with it, I knew that I was in luck but unfortunately for me, it was short lived. I saw him tighten his fist around its length before letting it go so that it was dripping crimson.

I had no clue what he was going to accomplish by doing this but his eyes started to change once more. Only now, where they were once like solid rock, they were now bleeding liquid sand, just as the wall had done before we travelled through it. Then suddenly he thrust the long needle though the wall, as if he had been trained in an ancient version of Hogwarts. I expected him to shout 'Liquidoso' or something.

Just as this happened I finally managed to grasp the arrow's feathered end. I had been trying to get a good enough grip on it to pull free from the others attached to its bundle, only up until now it had been slipping from my fingers. This, of course, was also when I became the other part of his plan and I was grabbed roughly by the top of the arm and yanked closer to him. I let myself be dragged towards him just as I pulled the arrow up the sleeve of my cloak, so that it was out of view. Once I was close enough he spun me around to face what now looked like some kind of sandstorm vortex that had taken up most of the wall. It looked like a portal into another world or something and I quickly backed up, not wanting to get anywhere near that thing!

"No! Let me go!" I shouted as I felt him taking steps closer towards it, which in turn made me take forced steps closer as well. Then, just as I was about to turn and stab him with the arrow's end I held tight in my fist, he reached up with one hand to the slight cut at my neck and pulled it apart making me cry out. I felt the blood start to drip down my neck and he flattened his palm against it, bathing his hand in my blood.

"Let me go!" I shouted and just as I twisted, he put his bloody hand out in front of me leading the way and pushed us both through the portal. I had no choice but to take a deep breath and close my eyes as I felt the power of the small storm engulf us. It felt like walking through a wind tunnel and I felt the pressure of it push against the skin at my cheeks. Then my world started to spin before I felt myself being thrown forward with enough force that it propelled me through to the other side.

This time there was nothing to stop me from landing hard and I almost choked on my own cry of pain that shot through my damaged ribs from falling down the stairs.

"Get up!" he snapped as he followed me through and I gripped the arrow, one I blessed the Gods of war I hadn't dropped coming through the damn sandstorm. I felt myself snarling at his back as he walked past me before I begrudgingly did as I was told. I got up, trying not to wince as I did, but with this much pain, I had to wonder if I hadn't fractured a rib or two, as it was getting harder to breathe without it hurting. Which begged the question again, why hadn't I healed yet?

Once I found myself on my feet, I looked around to see I was no longer in the desert as I thought I would be, but instead on a ridge of some vast mountain range. What the hell had I gotten myself into now I asked myself? Well whatever it was, it was starting to look even worse when I saw my captor walk towards a group of men with horses. Suddenly my little single arrow wasn't looking quite as promising as I had hoped. So, with this in mind, I decided to tuck it further up my sleeve and out of sight, knowing that it might just come in handy later.

"Come girl!" he shouted over to me and I looked back to see the portal was long gone and in its place an impossible escape thanks to the sheer drop over a cliff face. No wonder he wasn't worried about me being this far away from him, 'cause let's face it, where was I going to go? I wanted to scream in utter frustration. I had finally just worked out a plan of getting the four of us out of the palace and back to our own time, when suddenly I found myself once again, plucked from my path and at the hands of another's mercy.

The man looked back at me expectantly as if waiting and I

looked down finding a rock that would have been better suited to bashing his head in than just sitting there for the rest of eternity doing nothing useful. But instead of giving into this vengeful impulse, I decided not to push his temper and walked over to him, with the hate pulsating from my gaze.

"I care little for your venom girl, now get on the damn horse," he threw back at me, matching my attitude for some of his own.

"I can't ride, so unless you want your journey to take twice as long, I suggest you think of something else, like letting me go for example," I told him sarcastically. He rolled his eyes at me before looking over at the horses and the men that had started to mount them.

"Women," he muttered after a moment and then walked over to one of the men to issue an order, telling me he was the one in charge at least.

"Pack some of the supplies on the horse, the woman cannot ride so will travel in the cart," he told him and the man slid off his horse without question to do as ordered. I waited and watched as the man in charge stormed off to his own horse to grab something out of a leather pouch hanging at the side of the saddle.

"Great," I muttered scathingly as I saw him coming back towards me with a looped length of rope in his hands. Meanwhile two of the other men had been busy making room on the rickety cart that was being pulled by two mules. They moved a few sacks and strapped them to the sides of the horse that I gathered should have been for me.

"Jeez, rough much!" I snapped as I was grabbed by the arm again and pulled towards the cart before being shoved onto the back of it.

"Get in and sit down," he ordered ignoring the way my hand went to my side as I yelped in agony.

"Alright asshole!" I snapped back and did as I was told, climbing up into the space that had been made for me. Thankfully, I had some of the sacks to sit against and I strangely asked myself what they were filled with. Well, at least I hadn't come full circle as it didn't smell like body parts

"Hands!" he shouted and I froze knowing this was when he could possibly find my arrow. So, I deliberately pretended to fall backwards further into the cart at the same time pulling the arrow free from my sleeve and tucking it in between the sacks. He sighed as if this was all very taxing for him and then grabbed the side before hauling himself up into the cart. I quickly pulled myself forward and scooted over where I had hidden the small weapon so that he wouldn't see it.

"Now give me your hands," he told me, this time dropping some of his attitude and I knew why when he looked to where my cloak had opened on one side. My little bolero top left little to the imagination as all my belly was on show as well as my bust, but this wasn't what he was looking at. It was my injury and I looked down to see what he saw. I had an angry red mark all along my side and a graze from where the stone had taken some of the skin off my ribs. No wonder it hurt so much.

"You're injured," he said as if shocked. Maybe he thought I had been faking all those painful little sounds I had been making since he took me. I wanted to say, yeah, no shit Sherlock, but refrained. Because one, he wouldn't know who Sherlock was for quite some time yet and two, well he wasn't looking at me in asshole mode any more, which might swing in my favour.

"I fell down some stairs before you took me," I told him dropping my attitude and trying for something a little softer and labelled 'damsel in distress'. He didn't look happy about this and said,

"He will not be pleased," he informed me sounding

concerned. I frowned at both what he had said and the fact that he was currently tying my hands together, leaving a long length at the end.

"Who's he?" I asked as I then watched him throw the long end over the side of the cart before jumping down. He walked around near the waiting mules and grabbed the rope he had thrown before tying it off to a place I couldn't reach. I didn't think he would answer me at first as I watched him walk back towards his horse and mount it in one swift action. But he trotted it over to me and grabbed a leather water flask from his saddle and threw it to me.

"Be sparing with it, for we have far to journey."

"But wait, who is not going to be pleased?" I asked again and he looked first to his men and nodded for them to start moving. Once they were out of earshot, telling me they were human, he told me.

"The King." I frowned and asked,

"What King?" This time instead of looking annoyed with me he pulled back the length of material from the lower half of his face and smirked, showing me just how handsome the rest of him was. Perfect lips set in a perfectly square jaw…damn him!

"You will find out soon enough, little girl." I frowned being called this and just before he could ride off as he turned his horse to face the other way, I shouted,

"My name is Keira!" to which he replied,

"And Dariush be mine." Then as he passed he smacked the back of the mule making it pull forward suddenly so that I lost my balance and fell backwards into the piles of sacks. I made an unattractive 'Umpf' sound and growled when I heard him laughing.

At some point, I must have fallen asleep because the next thing I knew I awakened to the feel of my leg being kicked and the sound of someone growling.

"I told you to wake her up, not kick her like a fucking dog!" I heard the one I now knew was called Dariush say angrily and I opened my eyes to see the guy that must have been kicking me being dragged backwards off the cart.

"Time to get up, Princess," he said sounding agitated. Then he grabbed the length of rope from near where I lay that he must have released from the other side first. I watched as he wrapped it around his hand like a lead and tugged on it a few times to try and get me moving.

"Okay, okay," I grumbled, first stretching my stiff limbs and rubbing my eyes before taking in my surroundings. I waited for him to turn his back before I reached down and slipped the arrow back up the wide sleeve of my cloak. I quickly stood before the rope became too taut and I ended up being dragged from the stupid cart.

I gingerly climbed down, surprised that he allowed me enough space to do this. Which is why I found myself asking the question, what had changed with him from how he had treated me in the beginning? Also without knowing I put a hand to my neck to touch the small cut that he had put there.

"I didn't cut you deep," he said and my head snapped up to find him watching me in an almost guilty way. Then he looked to my injuries and I knew that seeing me so bruised and broken had affected him. Now if I could just understand why, then that would be half the questions I had floating around my head answered. Maybe he had simply realised how breakable I was after all. Either way, something in him had changed and it was why he was growling at the other men as they came closer to the cart. They backed away a little and it was only when I was off it completely that they quickly started to unload the sacks they had been trying to get to.

I looked around and was shocked to find it didn't look too different from the sight that had met me at the beginning of this journey. The mountain range still surrounded us but other than it being darker, the landscape hadn't really changed. It was surprisingly green up here, which was strange considering we were surrounded by the vast desert that could be seen for miles.

I had not slept the whole journey, but I had to admit, I watched the sun get higher in the sky before falling asleep as it lowered again. The rocky mountain path had seemed endless and after spending hours running every escape scenario in my mind, in the end, the large open space had made each one impossible. It wasn't the getting loose aspect of my plan I had a problem with thanks to the sharp edge on my arrow, but more the running for my life without looking like a zit on a supermodel.

So here I was, unable to make my move too soon for fear I would screw up my only chance. Of course, thanks to the cryptic musings of my new guardian/captor Dariush, I had not only kept my mind busy trying to think of new interesting, but unrealistic ways of escaping, but I had also been wracking my brain wondering who could be after me now?

I mean I wasn't stupid as I knew a royal figure like Draven didn't get where he was without creating his fair share of enemies. Pertinax was evidence enough of that little supernatural megalomaniac ploy to take over the world. So once again I was right back where I had started and being placed on the damn chessboard as a sodding pawn! I will tell ya, I was getting tired of this macho man bullshit! Which was why I asked,

"So, who wants to use me this time?" Dariush looked taken

aback by my brazen question, giving me a quizzical glance over his shoulder as he led me off from the rest.

"The Parthian King has many enemies, some of which still remain in the shadows lying in wait and remain unknown until the time is right to strike and take control of his empire," he told me and I frowned before snapping,

"Oh yes and how very mighty of them to use a woman to accomplish their ambitious goal in conquering lands that aren't theirs to own!" Hearing this he started to laugh, which wasn't the reaction I was hoping for.

"You are mistaken if you think the reason for your capture is to use you to bargain with the King in giving up the city and I know not of which place you come from but here, in my world, wars are never fought with women," he said sounding amused that I would think so and this time my frown was for a different reason.

"Then why take me at all, what could this King possibly gain from it other than to use me as a blackmailing tool?" I asked moving quicker so that I could catch up to him. He looked down at me side on and said,

"I don't know why but at a guess, I would say he must like collecting small, pretty things… although if you ask me, I would also warn him that he might be better continuing his collecting of coin, for gold doesn't speak and ask annoying questions." This was finished with a smirk when he heard me growl at him in annoyance. Seriously, he was freaking joking with me now?!

"Yeah well I also have claws and teeth so you might want to warn him about those things as well!" I returned making him look down at me again, focusing on my clenched fists.

"Consider it known," he told me nodding and I could have sworn I saw a glimmer of respect in his unusual green eyes. He looked very much of Persian decent, with his warm bronze skin tone and slight slant and almond shape to his eyes. Dark stubble covered the lower half of his face that framed his full lips, lips that were currently flat as his features hardened. I looked to where he was aiming his annoyance to see a band of men coming towards us on horseback. I watched him place a hand at the hilt of his sword as if readying himself for trouble.

"Get behind me," he ordered and looking at the four men all armoured and coming at us at speed, I couldn't say it was a bad idea.

"Yep, sure thing," I said with a high pitched lilt to my voice. I did as I was told and he let go of the rope that he had twisted around one hand. Then he looked behind him at his own men to see them falling back.

"No questions needed as to how they knew we would be here," he said before snarling at them and then spat at the ground in his anger at being betrayed. The men swiftly approached and Dariush quickly directed his menacing snarl.

"We come for the girl," one of the men said who was dressed like someone in charge as he pulled off his rounded helmet. I didn't recognise the armour as being one of Draven's men, so I knew that something wasn't right here.

"Scythians, I think you find yourselves too far across the border, for I recall seeing the heads of your brothers upon pikes at the Ctesiphon city gates," Dariush said confidently and their reaction to this was to draw their weapons. Well that explained who the rotting corpses were down in Ranka's Hell's kitchen.

"You foolish dog fucker! Fight as you may, for we will take the girl bathed in your blood if we have to!" The one in charge said before raising his arm and charging his horse forwards to fight. Dariush didn't look the least bit concerned as he whipped back his cloak, showcasing a body strapped with weapons. He threw one knife to one of the men charging him before pulling his large sword free. And just as it was about to clash with the other man's sword, I noticed his eyes changing once more. This time instead of sandstone like before, they morphed into black speckled granite and I watched the flow of power branch off down his cheeks out of sight. Then the unbelievable happened in mere seconds. The true source of his power was unleashed as it shot from his hand and seeped into his weapon, creating a deadly granite blade.

He swung his gleaming black weapon around onehandedly and the second it hit the other man's sword, it created a rippling affect. The power shifted as if transferring the opposing breakable material to his enemy's sword before smashing through it like glass. Clear shards exploded outwards and with his free hand he caught them with an invisible force, before using them as small projectile weapons. He shot them forward with a flick of his wrist.

The solider soon found himself writhing on the floor in agony with a face full of large glass splinters. Not surprisingly, the other three men tried to stop their own horses from continuing on into the fight after seeing their leader going down by an impossible force. However, Dariush wasn't planning on letting any of them leave alive, so after cutting down the next two in three swift moves, he ended up making chase. He started running and then grabbed onto one of their fleeing horses from the side before swinging himself up on its back. Once there he took control of the reins so that he could catch the last one currently running for his life.

I was watching this all play out when I was suddenly grabbed from behind.

"AH! Get off me!" I shouted trying to twist in his hold and fight against him. I just managed to get free and I turned to face him to find that he had his own weapon. I noticed it was the man that had kicked me awake moments before.

"More will come and I will not die here on this mountain or

leave without my promised gold!" He spat out his words as he held his blade towards me as if he was getting ready to strike any minute. Then I heard the rumbling behind him as if many horses were now charging towards us. He took this opportunity and sliced out at me, missing me by less than an inch. I jumped back just in time but fell on the rocky ground. I screamed in pain and felt one of the sharp rocks hit the side of my head, along with my injured side. But I didn't have time to fully register the hurt as the man jumped on top of me. He tried to grab the length of rope as I kicked out against him and when I caught him hard in the leg, he decided to get his own back by kicking me in the damaged side of my ribs.

"AHHH!" I screamed, louder this time and despite the pain, anger flooded my system until my next action became a blur of real time. I felt my body rising up and just as I threw myself at the man, I jerked my bounds hands up with enough force that the arrow shot out from my sleeve. I caught it just at the right moment and drove it into the man's shoulder as my body's weight propelled into him. We both went down, crashing to the floor and I lifted my head to see that both my hands were still wrapped around the arrow that was now half embedded in the howling man's flesh.

I then felt myself being pulled from the bloody man and set back on my feet by Dariush. He looked down at the damage I had caused, raised an eyebrow and said,

"One of your claws I presume?"

"Damn straight! Just be thankful," I said pausing to push my hair from my face, which wasn't easy with hands still bound.

"Why?" he asked as I walked past him to reach for the blade my attacker had dropped to the floor. I picked it up awkwardly and replied,

"Because it was meant for you." This made him roar with laughter and I had to admit, it was a nice sound.

"Now cut me loose," I ordered him, passing him the weapon, one I was surprised he took from me to do as I asked. He sliced through the rope without a word of protest. But then what was even more surprising was when he handed it back to me and said,

"Use it, for I fear you might need it," he said hearing now what I had, more soldiers approaching.

"Well I guess you found your traitor," I commented dryly looking down at the bleeding man.

"Indeed, one I will come back to finish off later, but for now, we must hurry to the gate before more Scythians reach us."

"The gate?" I questioned thinking this didn't sound good but saying that, then neither did the sound of what now looked to be a small army of men heading our way.

Of course, Dariush only confirmed my fears when he replied…

"The Black Gate."

CHAPTER TWENTY-FOUR

BLACK GATE

Dariush and I ran towards some of the largest rocks that jutted out of the earth like giant hands reaching for the stars. It sounded like the small army was closing in behind us at speed and strangely there also sounded like fighting had broken out amongst the ranks. I tried to look behind me but Dariush grabbed me and pulled me in between a small gap in the boulders out of view. Then he faced the rock as he had done with the wall back in the palace. I didn't think it was the best place to hide as it wouldn't have taken a genius to figure out where we were but this was where I was wrong.

"I have to say, I am really starting to appreciate your unique set of skills...well after you kidnapped me of course," I said adding this last part when he gave me a questioning arch of one eyebrow just as his eyes started to change again. This time they started to seep into stone grey the same as the rock in front of us and like the sandstone wall, it started to liquefy.

"Will this work in time?" I asked in hushed tones after

looking back over my shoulder at the sound of some sort of general issuing orders to look around the area for us.

"It will if you silence your tongue long enough to let me concentrate," he informed me irritably.

"Oh, right, sorry…shutting up now," I said biting my bottom lip to stop from asking any more annoying questions. I heard him groan as if this was all very taxing on his nerves before he went back to doing his…well I didn't really know what to call it other than, eye changing, stone melting, portal mojo. Which was what it looked like right now as the rock started to become like dark smelted silver being stirred against the stone. It spun around and the effect was a dizzying one. Looking at him now, it seemed the power of it was mirrored there, giving new depth to his eyes.

"Blood my King, on the rocks!" I heard someone shout and then just as Dariush ran his fingers along the cut on my head I sucked in a sharp breath at the sting.

"Oww, that hurt!" I shouted without thinking about trying to keep quiet but then he grabbed my arm and I didn't know why until I heard his voice…

His desperate voice, calling for me.

"KEIRA! Where are you?!" As soon as I heard it I knew Dariush had tricked me into believing the army after us was the same as those that had attacked us. I screamed out just as I was pulled into the portal, reaching out a hand just as his figure came into view.

"DRAVEN, I'M HERE!" My last sight was his hopeful face quickly change into one of sheer devastation at finally finding me, only to lose me just as quickly. I felt myself surrounded by darkness and I reached out, fumbling my way in the drowning shadows that felt as though they were trying to consume me. I was trying everything to reach him but no matter how much I tried to swim through the dark, an invisible force pushed me further back into the abyss. Finally, I felt a hand reach for me but unfortunately it wasn't the one I wanted it to be.

"Are you trying to get yourself killed!?" Dariush's harsh voice snarled down at me as I fell backwards, but this time at least he caught me before I found myself even more broken than I already felt.

"He was right there! You could have let me go! I want to go back!" I shouted, only when I turned the portal was gone and in its place was the rock face we had travelled through. I ripped myself from his hold and pounded on the wall but little good it did me other than bruising the sides of my fists.

"You can't go back!" he growled at me and I whipped round to face him and bellowed,

"You lied! You made me believe it was more of the others chasing us!" I accused and he simply shrugged his shoulders and admitted,

"My only task is to get you to *the King*, which means taking you from another… and I did not lie, for the Scythians were behind us but were swiftly killed by Arsaces and his men." Hearing this I gave him my best 'I will kill you in your sleep' glare, one he didn't take seriously or if he did, he didn't look worried. And another thing, I couldn't help but notice how he had said, 'the King' instead of *'his King'* as surely that had to mean something.

"Now come on, we must reach the Black Gate before the river rises." I frowned unsure of what he meant and only now taking in my new surroundings. We looked to be in a massive cave and when I started to follow him, I saw the vast network of walkways that had been cut into the rock. This is when things started to fit into place.

"I have been here before," I muttered frowning and now, minus all the Gorgon leeches, I had to say it looked far safer. That said it still looked creepy, just with less teeth and the sound of screaming for my life echoing off the coarse stone walls.

"Yes, so I heard," he replied coolly as if he had read it in some weekly newspaper or something. I could just imagine the headlines now, 'Time travelling Concubine saved by moody Vampire assassin from Demonic horde'. Jesus, I think I even preferred it back in the spa from Hell, also named Draven's 'Slut Harem'. Okay so it wasn't really full of sluts, but as a jealous wife faced with a room full of her husband's wannabe bed buddies, then yeah, it totally was named his 'Slut Harem'.

"So, I have to ask as I am not sure whether you also heard about the Demonic horde that also play house down here, along with some scary ass dudes that play prison guards with them." I said looking around nervously and hating the way my eyes played tricks on me.

"Scary ass dudes?" he repeated the words questioningly, words that were obviously utterly foreign to him. I felt like smacking my forehead and muttered,

*"Get a grip future girl, they don't do slang yet...*Scary men that want to kill me and eat me, and not necessarily in that order," I corrected.

"Nothing is down here, so you have nothing to fear," he told me and I scoffed a laugh.

"I beg to differ on that one," I said receiving a vacant look as he didn't understand me once again. Jeez, it was easier dealing with Ranka!

"I disagree...someone must be here, or did the torches light themselves?" I said nodding to the long row of flaming lights that lit our walkway, one I was currently walking along practically hugging the rock face. You would have thought after dating someone with wings and going through the amount of shit I had been through the last few years, that I would have been used to it by now. But no, that edge was still screaming danger to me and trying to convince the irrational side of my brain to jump off it.

"Since the death of Pertinax, all under his rule perished along with him, so as I said, you have nothing to fear…and it was *I* that lit the torches," he said adding this last part when I was about to speak again, beating me to my repeated question.

"Oh." I muttered making him smirk as if he had won a round or something.

"So where is it, this gate you're taking us to?" I asked making him release a frustrated sigh.

"Do you always ask so many questions?" he complained.

"Yes, but I will let you know if I am ever in a situation where I don't need to know important shit about myself, like where the hell you are taking me!" I snapped getting tired of this being kept in the dark bullshit. Again, this outburst granted me another sideways glance as if he was trying to silently figure out how to deal with me.

"All will be revealed in…"

"In time, yeah, yeah, so they tell me but just so you know, time isn't really on my side at the moment," I told him and for once, I was the one who sounded cryptic.

After this we continued to walk on in silence and I only complained when the side of the stone walkway started to narrow.

"I don't like heights," I told him when he glanced my way over his shoulder.

"Give me your hand," he said stopping and holding out his hand for me to take. I looked at it as though he was luring me into a false sense of security or something, prompting him to tell me,

"I will not let you fall." So, after looking down to what could be my death and at the very moment was one of my worst nightmares, I looked at the only possible safe option I had left open to me. I took his hand and let him lead me slowly on, pulling me to his side, close to the wall and putting a barrier between me and the edge.

"Thank you," I whispered softly and at first, he looked as though he didn't know what to do my thanks but then decided to go with a simple bow of his head in acknowledgement.

"How are your injuries?" he asked me as if being this close to me just reminded him of the fact I had been bleeding. I reached up and touched the tender side of my head and I felt the dried crusted blood matted into my hair. Well at least the bleeding had stopped, the headache however was a different story.

"I'm sure I will live," I told him making him huff out a laugh.

"I have a feeling that it would take a lot to keep you down for long," he said and this time I laughed thinking about all I had been through in my own past. I had been stabbed, sliced, punched, kicked, pushed, drowned, starved, bitten, scratched, sold, poisoned, branded, gone to Hell and back and nearly burned alive… and that's not even including how many times I had been bloody kidnapped!

"What makes you think that?" I asked smirking as he, like most people, had no idea of any of it.

"You have a strong will to survive. I can see it, for most in your position would not have fought but ran away in fear. Yet you found the only weapon available to you and used it when it was needed…I respect that," he told me and this time that respect he spoke of was easy to see.

"You respect me?" I questioned as if I hadn't heard him right the first time and also wanting to know why.

"I admire anyone who chooses to fight for a life, whether it be their own or that of another. Even I can appreciate a mortal soul as it clings to hold onto this realm." Wow, it seemed my kidnapper had a soft, mushy side. Now if it was just mushy enough to let me go with a handshake and a map outta here, that would be just peachy, I thought wryly. But instead of pushing my luck I just nodded, accepting what he said and continued to follow him, now hand in hand around the cavernous space.

"Through here," he said nodding to his right before leading me through a small gap, which turned out to be a narrow tunnel that held some kind of symbolic plaque above the entrance. The tunnel didn't look to be manmade but more like formed this way over the centuries. It was only big enough to fit one person at a time so I wondered, after the danger of me falling was long gone, why did he still hold my hand the way he did?

Maybe he thought it best to continue to keep a hold of me in case I decided to do something stupid, like run off and take my chances with getting lost in the maze of caves. Or maybe it was because he felt the need to offer me comfort, making me feel safe by making sure no harm came to me. Either way, he didn't let go of my hand but instead let it fall behind him so we could both walk down the tunnel without losing contact.

Once we made it through to the other side, I sucked in a startled breath at what I was now faced with. The once formidable looking cave had been transformed into a thing of beauty. It opened out into what looked like a hidden temple had dropped from the sky and then swallowed up by the earth, creating a protective jagged shell to encase it.

"This...this is incredible." I said in utter awe. It looked as if row after row of huge stalactites hanging down from the ceiling had met the gleaming floor we stood on and each one had been carved and moulded into shapes at the bottom, to create natural looking pillars half way up. In fact, if the craftmanship had been continued all the way to the top, you wouldn't have known they weren't originally manmade at all. The room was at least three times bigger than Draven's Great Hall back in the palace and it was so long it was difficult to see the end without squinting.

It didn't house anything else other than at its centre was a slightly arched stone bridge that connected to a large platform of rock. One that seemed to be attached to the rest of the cave not from the bottom, like you would have thought but from the carved stalactites above. It looked almost like a floating island of stone and not something I was looking forward to ever setting foot on. Of course, this was me we were talking about so naturally this was the way Dariush started to lead me towards.

"Uh…I don't think I can do that." I told him in a shaky voice, one he could easily read as fear.

"Then I will carry you across," he said firmly and before I could utter a word of protest, I quickly found myself up in his arms heading towards the bridge.

"Oh, bloody hell!" I shrieked making him chuckle.

"I can assure you that there are places in Hell far worse than this, girl." I rolled my eyes at him taking my cursing so literally and was half tempted to tell him that, 'yes I know, I have had seen it first-hand thank you very much'. After all, I doubted even most demons could claim to have been inside Tartarus and lived to tell the back stabbing, cowboy saving, banshee fleeing, tale. Which is why in the end I went for the simple,

"I can imagine."

I found myself soon gripping on for dear life, grabbing his cloak in a white knuckled death grip as he started to cross the bridge.

"Oh God, oh God, oh God." I muttered over and over until he forced my head to his chest so I could no longer look suicidal heights in the face.

"You can breathe now, we are on the other side," he told me softly, which added a nice comforting lure to his usually gruff, accented voice. He removed his hand from the back of my head, one he had kept there so I couldn't look and essentially have a panic attack over. I raised my eyes and I must have looked up at him like a blinking doe after staring at the headlights too long. Not that he would know what that looked like of course, but it didn't stop him from giving me a kind smile before nodding to what I should be looking at.

I let him go just as he placed me back on my feet and looked towards the centre of where we were now stood. The small platform was no bigger that Draven's bathing room and was used for only one purpose…

The Black Gate.

I had to say it wasn't how I had pictured it in my mind. I was tempted to ask if it still worked as it looked more like a shell of what it used to be. The half crumbling stone block arch was made from what looked like solidified lava. Black, coarse rock that was so full of tiny holes and looked so porous that it could have easily crushed to dust in your hand with only a small amount of pressure. It looked as if it had once belonged to a dilapidated castle that had been set alight and what was left was the scorched remains.

One side of the arch was thicker than the other as if it had once been attached to a great wall and the only remaining decoration was a wider keystone at the very top. It was depicting a picture of Janus, the God of doorways. I knew this, as his symbol was of a two-head man, one that faced left, the past and the other to the right… *to the future, if there was such a thing left for me?*

I remembered back to the first time I had set foot in his temple and all the doors that filled the space. Which had me asking the question, where were they all now in this time but more importantly, could this be the first Janus door to be created?

"Are you ready to face your fate?" Dariush asked me and I

frowned thinking it strange how he knew anything about my fate, let alone asking if I was ready for it. Well, considering it felt like all I had been doing since I met Draven was stumbling blindly down its path, then what did I say to that question other than the answer I gave him,

"No, but then again, I never am, so unless you are going to let me make my own decisions and let me go, then let's just get this shit over with," I told him before facing the gate and like he said, with it my doomed fate.

"Very well," he said flatly, sounding as he didn't care for the way I answered him. Did he feel guilty for what he was about to do? I never found out as he walked past me and this time, instead of just his eyes changing, his whole body did the second he reached out and touched the empty space in between the stone frame. It was like some invisible force had just lit the fuse at the end of his veins because his fingertips sparked before black soot followed up the entirety of his skin. It was like watching Draven's purple fire fuel his body only on Dariush it was in reverse and it was black. I watched the spark disappearing under his clothing only to re-emerge by his neck, followed quickly by what looked like dark demonic poison flooding his bloodstream. It only ended once it travelled up his face and the spark of fire found home in his eyes.

The second it made it there the gate erupted into life and the shadowed abyss looked endless as it swirled inwards. The rest of the stone suddenly took on new life and became the stunning craftmanship it always should have been. It was like watching its destruction through time in reverse and what was once a crumbling archway was now one worthy of the Gods to step through. Stone filigree started to grow and branch out over the blocks, joining up until it grew into something that looked closer to living than dead dark, volcanic rock.

"Your path awaits," he told me nodding for me to step

closer and I swallowed down the large lump labelled fear before nodding back. Then I straightened my shoulders and took the next step towards what was obviously my destiny. A place I would soon find out to be further away in the world than I would have ever thought.

Stepping inside wasn't like I expected, but then again, nothing with this gate ever was, including the new beauty I was looking up at as I passed through. It wasn't like stepping into the shadows or even a vortex of power like it looked to be created from. It was more like walking into the centre of a twister and finding a calm piece of the world being protected by the most violent of nature's forces. I looked up to see a night sky filled with a blanket of shooting stars as if I was looking at it from space not the earth I felt beneath my feet.

"What is this place?" I dared to ask myself and the second I did, I felt myself falling as if the land had suddenly turned into water. I felt the cold liquid engulf my body and I opened my eyes to see the surface shimmering above me. I reached up for it just as I had done that night in the lake when I was searching for Lucius to rescue me. And just like that night a hand reached in and grabbed me.

My body broke the surface as I was pulled up out of the water, coughing and spluttering the second I could start dragging air back into my burning lungs. Then there was pain, thanks to my damaged ribs.

Arms grabbed me around the waist and thankfully not too hard as even the smallest amount of pressure there had me wincing again. I was being tugged towards what looked like a river bank and I could just make out Dariush swimming us both to the edge. Thankfully the current didn't seem too strong, or I am not sure he would have managed to get us both there. At least I now knew what he had meant about the river getting too high, although the heads up that we would be bloody landing in one would have been nice!

Once at the bank he gripped onto the grass and heaved me up before following me out. He didn't even seem out of breath. On the other hand, I flung myself on the grass, lay on my back and panted for air, trying not to moan in pain.

"That wasn't what I expected," I confessed sounding breathless.

"And what did you expect exactly?" he asked sitting next to me and dragging his now ringing wet turban off his head and slapping it down on the grass next to him. His hair was black and shoulder length with the shorter bits now curling around his ears.

"Oh, I don't know, maybe stepping gracefully through to the other side without falling on my ass or half drowning to death for once…yeah, that would have been nice," I said making him chuckle.

"Then next time, I suggest you don't speak, that way it might be kinder on your fall," he informed me and I groaned and replied,

"And you think now is the time to tell me this…how did I know the damn thing was going to get pissy when hearing my voice!" He merely shrugged his shoulders and got up, holding out a hand for me to follow. To be honest I felt so tired that I could have stayed there all night but I knew the likelihood of being allowed to do so was lower than zero, if there was such a thing. So, with this in mind, I forced my tired aching limbs to work and got up from the grass after taking his offered hand, holding onto my side as I went.

"Okay so the only question I have now is, where in the world are we?" I asked and he scoffed before commenting drily,

"The only question…I sincerely doubt that."

"Ha, ha…I suppose you would be just fine not knowing

where on earth you were," I threw back at him and again he just shrugged his shoulders, which I was half tempted to explain to him how this wasn't an answer.

"Right well getting back to my question, where have you brought me?" I asked again and this time he turned me around from facing the river towards a gleaming white city of columns, that was bathed in the moonlight.

Then he told me calmly,

"We are in Rome."

CHAPTER TWENTY-FIVE

TOUCHY SUBJECT

"Rome!" I screeched making him look at me as though I'd left some of my brain cells back in Persia and to be honest I might well have done considering the crack to the head I had received when I fell to the ground. Well, it had been that or getting sliced by Mr dagger happy gold digger.

"Yes, Rome," he responded in a deadpan tone. Then he started to make his way up the river bank, glancing behind him and giving me a 'Why aren't you following me' look. In return gave him my best 'I am not a dog, so don't treat me like one' glare but from the looks of it, it completely went over his head and was half way to the city by now. Oh well, maybe someone would get it there, I thought with a smirk at my own private silly joke.

I followed him up the rolling green bank and just as I was about to reach the top something unexpected happened. Suddenly pain burst from behind my head before blackness overwhelmed me as I passed out to the sounds of weapons clashing and death echoing in my mind.

I vaguely dreamed of reaching the top of a hill and seeing men in the shadows approaching my friend...no, wait not my friend, or was he? I felt confused and tried to recap on what had just happened. It felt as though it was only minutes ago but when I finally opened my eyes I saw daylight. I didn't know where I was but I started by having the strangest form of déjà vu. I had done this before, I was certain of it. In both my own time, back in Germany and this one, only in Persia.

"Persia!" I shouted bolting upright as my memories started to piece back together in the right order and then came the pain. Seriously, I was starting to think I wouldn't survive another blow to the head. I fell back with a groan, which alerted someone to my presence. The fog in my mind had a hard time trying to get my eyes to work and I found myself trying to blink back the blur.

"Nihil; maiori, mane in lectulo!" ('No, young one, stay in bed.') An old woman's voice started speaking to me in what sounded like Latin. It also sounded like she wanted me to stay lying down as her frail hands started fussing over me.

"I have to get up and find...find my friend...a man, did he bring me here?" I asked but she just kept shaking her head as if she didn't understand me. This was when I realised, what Ranka had given me back in the desert must have been so that I could understand people in this time that only spoke Persian...*Not Latin.* Great, just great! That was all I needed. Not only was I now stuck in Rome, but I was here with no guide, no translator and absolutely no clue as to why I was here! As if things couldn't get any worse. But in true Keira fashion, I spoke too soon as I felt the throbbing pain start pounding once more in my head. Jesus, but was it split open and currently leaking parts of my brain because that was what it felt like!

I tried to look around the room only to feel my eyes start to roll back into my head and a heartbeat later I was falling once more.

I must have passed out shortly after this, as the next time I woke it was still dark outside. Thankfully though I could now see without looking as though I had just tried on some old person's glasses and was trying to read a newspaper with lenses that resembled jam jar bottoms.

The room I was in had whitewashed walls and housed nothing but the bed I lay in and a small table to one side that held a bowl full of water. The window didn't have glass in it and I could feel the cool night breeze wafting in scents of jasmine and sweet-smelling roses. I leaned across as the bed was close to the window and looked down over the ledge to see a small walled garden below and beyond that was what seemed to be the street.

Looking back to the room I noticed a cloak lay across the bottom of the bed. I recognised it as belonging to Dariush and all I could hope for was that it meant he was the one who brought me here. I then looked down at myself to see I was still wearing my skimpy harem outfit, which also offered a view of my wrapped ribs, sending me hurtling straight back to when I first arrived back in this time. I touched the tightly wrapped length of linen and sucked in a painful breath at how tender they felt. I reached back and felt the other throbbing pain, this time at the back of my head, only to find blood encrusted in my hair.

"Fantastic, just what I needed, another bloody injury," I complained aloud, shaking my head and wondering how I managed to get myself into so much shit.

And speaking of shit, a commotion outside drew my attention back to the garden as I heard horses coming to a stop just on the other side of the wall. I peered over and saw I was right, as now there were at least ten armoured men that looked to be Roman soldiers dismounting horses. There was even a covered cart, one a lot nicer than the rickety old thing I had been forced into the first time. No, this one was painted gold and was tented with a deep red material that hid who or whatever was beneath it.

I watched as whoever was in charge walked with two of his men to the side and I heard the banging on the door from up here. I also ended up hearing him order something in Latin,

"Huic autem puella, in quo est?" ('We've come for the girl, where is she?') I didn't understand the words but I knew enough to know that it was most likely about me, especially when I saw them being allowed into the house.

"Shit, shit, shit!" I complained looking around the room and knowing there was no way of escape other than out of the window. I looked down and noticed that there was a tall stone trellis that didn't look too far to reach but first I needed to make sure to slow them down. So, I grabbed the cloak as I gingerly got out of bed, groaning in pain as I did. I had to brace myself against the wall for a second as it felt like I would soon pass out again and that would have sucked the big one! Thankfully though, I must have had at least a smidgen of luck left on my side as the fog in my mind started to clear. After I felt steady enough, I pulled the bed from the wall, struggling against it as I started to push it across the door. Once there I heaved it up as much as I could with my ribs screaming at me to stop. I was nearly sick from pain and had to take a few deep breaths to get the nausea to pass.

I was just happy that it wasn't a big bed or very heavy so at least I managed to block the doorway with it. Now all I had to do was climb out of the window. Yeah piece of cake, I thought sarcastically before wrapping the cloak around my shoulders. I then went about trying to get out of the window and down to the gardens without being seen by the other guards. I nearly freaked out when I heard the sound of many feet bounding up the stairs, as I knew my time had quickly run out. I rushed to the window ignoring the pain in both my head and my side, then after making sure I had the top of the trellis lined up, I cocked a leg over the side and lowered myself down until my feet could feel the stone beam.

I heard the banging on the door just as I popped my head under the sill and bent down trying to balance on the garden structure. I heard them above trying to force their way into the room and my panic started to double. I cried out in agony just as I launched myself off onto the grass, trying in vain to fall on my feet…of course unsurprisingly, I didn't manage it.

No instead I fell sideways and my screech of pain echoed through the night, alerting the soldiers on the other side of the wall to my position. I had no idea what they wanted with me but I knew it couldn't have been good if someone was sending so many men to come and retrieve me.

"Prohibere!" ('Stop') I heard shouted from the window and I looked up at them before getting to my feet and legging it out of there. I was just happy that the wall was high enough that the ones on the other side couldn't manage to jump over it. I followed the path that was framed either side by the roses I could smell and just as someone was coming out of a side door I barged passed them, feeling bad that it was the old woman no doubt coming to see what the commotion was.

"Sorry!" I shouted as I ran passed her through what looked like a cushioned living space. I slipped through the narrow hallway just as one of the soldiers was coming down the stairs, and the only place left for me to go was barrelling out the front door. I burst from it, knocking into one stunned guard and lucky for me it was the last thing he was expecting so he didn't have time to grab me.

"Prohibere!" There was that word again being shouted at me, just before they all started to make chase. I knew I had blown it the second I was seen coming out the front door. Not only was I a girl with shorter legs than these guys but I was also injured. A fact that was starting to become an ever-increasing problem. My will to survive finally crashed into my need to stop the excruciating pain in my side and chest, as it was obvious which one was going to win.

Even breathing hurt and I fell forward placing my hands on my slightly bent knees as if I couldn't even hold myself up anymore. I felt too weak and after only a few seconds of coming to a stop, the first guard caught up with me, wrestling me to the ground before he realised I had given up the chase. This time I screamed in my suffering and he was quickly yanked off me roughly by the one I had seen in control of this hunting party.

He was literally dragged backwards and flung off to one side as if he weighed nothing at all. I watched him roll and then looked back at the man in charge with shock. I knew he was their leader, as he had been the one issuing all the orders and along with this, was the difference in their appearance. The rest all wore the same plain chest plates, with long red capes but this dude had his chest plate adorned with a winged beast either side at his ribs and a horse's head at the centre. He also looked bigger than the rest and not exactly fresh out of Roman soldier school like the others.

He tore off his helmet that was also highly decorated and higher than the rest. He looked down at where I lay curled on the floor, holding my tender ribs, no doubt looking more like a wounded animal.

"Eice hanc a me et in raeda!" ('Get this woman up and in the carriage!') he barked an order at his men who quickly stepped forward to get me. I shouted at them to stay back and tried to shuffle away from them.

"NO! Don't touch me!"

"Prohibere!" The one in charge said holding up his hand making the men stop, which was when it clicked that this must have been what it meant. The general then crouched lower and approached me slowly, so as not to frighten me. He was an older gentleman, one that had a greying beard, along with lines around his eyes and mouth that told me at least he smiled a lot. I don't know why but I trusted this man when he started speaking softly to me.

"Noli timere: exaudivit nos flamma non ardebit in te." ('Fear not, we will not hurt you') He reached out a hand and gave my shoulder a small squeeze before nodding, as if silently asking if his men could approach. I shot a panicked gaze between them and him before weighing up my situation. It didn't take me long to know that this could only go one of two ways. I could either be taken by force or go willingly but either way, I wasn't getting out of this mess any time soon, so I went with the easy way.

"Alright," I muttered, nodding as well, just in case he didn't understand. He gave me a warm smile and motioned for his men to come forward once more.

"Custodite animas vestras ad deterioratus est." ('Be careful, for she is injured') He told them sternly. I frowned and tried to sit up myself, when he shook his head at me as if he knew I was in pain. The soldiers all gave me easy smiles as, like their commander, they too knew I was fearful of them. They carefully lifted me up and carried me over to where the cart was, making me wonder how they knew they would need it in the first place. They gently laid me back down and one of them muttered what must have been an apology when I winced as my weight was transferred onto my injured side.

But I couldn't complain as the covered cart was more like a luxury carriage inside as it was lined with furs and pillows. I made myself as comfortable as I could and had to ask myself, would they really treat a prisoner this way before they planned on killing one? Well the signs were looking good at least, now I just wished I had known that before jumping out the damn window.

Not surprisingly it didn't take me long before I had nodded off again thanks to the rocking motion, combined with one killer headache. I could have been sleeping like a baby by the time we arrived to wherever it was they were taking me. I put it down to the effects of banging my head twice in the space of thirty minutes as I remembered how I had felt when I had done it outside the cabin.

It felt like an age ago, especially when it had been back before Draven and I had even got together. It was the first time he drove me home and I remembered how nervous I had been, convincing myself at one point that I was possibly still dreaming. Which just so happened to be exactly how I felt again now as the carriage came to an abrupt stop.

The next thing I heard was the sound of many men moving as one, like a wave of soldiers all saluting.

"Ubi puella?!" ('Where is the girl?!') I heard a voice growl out a foreign demand and the ferocity that laced those few words had me sucking in a frightened breath.

"Imperator." I heard the commander say, addressing the newcomer respectfully and telling me that I was about to face the man who had ordered my capture. I jumped when I heard the whoosh of the material above me being ripped back and the face that met me was one that I never expected to see.

"Lucius!" I shouted his name in astonishment and without thinking about it, I shot up, only to cry out as pain stabbed at my side. Hearing this Lucius didn't hesitate in his actions. He swung himself up into the cart effortlessly, coming down on one knee next to me with a thud.

Holy shit but staring up at Lucius now looked as though some dark avenging angel had just dropped from the Heavens. Or like some kind of demonic centurion used to stand guard at the gates of Hell, killing all that tried to escape. A body made for sin, concealed by ancient armour made for destruction of those that stand against him.

He wore a black breastplate brushed with copper that looked like it had been chiselled in his torso's image, as I knew firsthand what lay beneath the metal. Rippling muscle after muscle, just like the deep ridges forged on his chest and stomach that faced me now. I even found myself raising my hand and reaching out to touch it, just to see if he was real. Then his harsh words stopped me and my hand fell back to the furs beneath me.

"Quomodo haec deterioratus est?!" ('How was she injured?!') Lucius snapped in what I assumed was still Latin. He sounded furious and barely keeping a lid on his rage. I couldn't help but flinch back, as like this, even *I* was scared of him. That was until he spoke to me this time.

"Ssshh, be still," he whispered, leaning down closer and softly proving that his anger wasn't directed at me. Well, that was until the commander spoke.

"A fenestra saluit haec domine mi." ('She jumped from a window, My Lord') After he was informed of something, Lucius growled and this time, it *was* directed at me. So much for not being the one to piss him off! Way to go Keira, I thought with an inward growl of my own. This time I tried to scrabble back only his hand whipped out, circling my throat in a split second. He followed up the action by shaking his head slowly, silently telling me no and it was enough to get me to take his threat seriously. Unsurprisingly, I stopped moving immediately and had to ask myself what had been said to him to make him shift his anger towards me so quickly. Unfortunately for me, I didn't have long to wait until I found out.

He leant down even further until he dominated the space around me and I couldn't help but hold my breath as I waited for what he would do next.

"You jumped from a fucking window!?" It wasn't very often I heard Lucius speaking to me from the depths of his demon side and trust me when I say that I was more than thankful for that fact. Because right now, I was close to peeing myself with fear from hearing it.

"I...uh..." I started to try and make my excuses when his actions stopped me, as he peeled back my borrowed cloak. It was no surprise to me what he revealed but for him, well you would have thought what he was now seeing was me half dead from being mauled by a blood thirsty bear. He very slowly reached out with his free hand and with a feather light touch, he ran his fingers across my strapped ribcage. I sucked in a startled breath, snapping him out of the moment.

The demonic snarl that rippled up from his chest had me once again trying to get away. However, with my neck still firmly in his grip, all he had to do was tighten his hand for a few seconds, cutting off my air supply as a way of telling me to be compliant. I stilled quickly and once I did and he was satisfied, he eased his hold on me once more. He made sure not to hurt me but the control he had over me was rolling over me like an invisible wave of domination. Even the gentle feel of his thumb grazing up and down along my chin was something that felt more like he was luring me into a sense of false security.

It was messed up, I knew that. As one hand held my life at his mercy, the other was gently examining my body and the two forces became warped together, creating something dangerous. Something my laboured breath told me with certainty.

"Next time you run, I will be the one chasing you, do you understand, Keira girl?" he asked me with formidable weight behind his words, words that I could only nod to for fear my reply could anger him. I even had to close my eyes against the sound of him calling me by the nickname he had christened me way back when he first took me from Draven.

I think if he had called me his I would have found tears forming behind my lashes. Even his voice sounded like the Lucius I knew and it was a difficult thing to face. This near cosmic pull that connected us together throughout the ages. Now if all I could do was understand it, I might have had a hope of how to defend myself against it.

He continued to stare at me for a moment longer as if trying to rip my thoughts from me and then without taking his eyes from me, he barked out another order,

"Volo erro mundatum inuenies!" ('I want the hallways cleared.') I don't know what he said but his commander certainly did as he nodded before issuing his own orders to his men. Half of them saluted Lucius by hammering a fist over their hearts before saying in unison,

"Caesar!" Then they swiftly left, moving as one to a place I couldn't see thanks to Lucius' imposing body that was still leaning over me. The next thing I knew he was pulling my focus back to him when he started to cover me back up with each side of the cloak. It was such a tender action that once again, it didn't match the deadly hold he still had on me.

"Take a deep breath, for I am going to move you now," he

said, only now releasing his commanding hand from my neck before it caressed along my chest. Then I felt it snaking down from my collarbone to the back of my shoulder. I did as he said just as he started to lift me into his arms. I whimpered, sounding like a wounded pet of his and he cooed over me, offering me much needed comfort.

"There, easy now, just take light breaths, for your ribs are broken and deep breathing will only hurt you," he told me tenderly and I found myself falling deeper under his spell thanks to the sensual lure in his voice. Then he raised up from one knee as easily as if he had been carrying a sack of feathers. He even made sure not to jar me too much when he jumped gracefully from the carriage. The commander stepped forward making Lucius release a low, predatory growl.

"Si vis me ad viros...?" ('Would you like my men to take...') His question ended with what first sounded like a snarled demand and then a deadly warning,

"Nemo tangit eam!" ('No one touches her!')

"Et omnis, qui tetigerit eam non occidere me ... sum, ut patet Marcus?" ('And have it be known that if I find otherwise, that offending hand will find itself severed, *along with its owner's head*...do I make myself clear, Marcus?') Lucius said, and the dip in his voice only added severity to the obvious threat, one the commander named Marcus took very seriously.

"Bene ergo de verbo" ('Good, then I suggest you spread the word of such.') he added before walking past Marcus and his men, leaving them both looking shocked and fearful. This was when I was granted my first real look at where I was and even the blanket of night couldn't diminish its ethereal beauty.

"Ww...where are you taking me?" I asked, first trying to find my voice and forcing the words out, embarrassed by the nervous quiver that told him everything he needed to know...

My fate was at his mercy.

"Into my home," he said confidently and I looked up at him as we mounted the endless steps that would take us through the tallest row of columns I had ever seen. They stood all in a line like heavenly stone soldiers all gleaming white in the moon's rays. It was the most imposing entrance I had witnessed and I couldn't help but reach up and curl my fingers over the rim of his breastplate around his neck. I gripped on tight just so that I felt safer. He looked down at where my hand now gripped him and something unknown passed across his face.

"Your home!?" I hissed as if needing confirmation on this one as it was too insane to believe. It was one thing studying the time of the Romans and that of ancient Rome's architecture, seeing most of it in ruins, but seeing it here and now in the flesh, was more like stepping into a dream than into my forced reality of the past.

Lucius looked down at me and with a slight smirk playing at the corners of his lips, he told me something I already knew but still found unbelievable.

"But of course, I am after all, now…"

"Emperor of Rome."

CHAPTER TWENTY-SIX

A NEW RULER

After he said this I didn't know what to say in return, so decided the best course of action came in the form of silence. I mean what did someone say when finding yourself being carried through a Roman palace by an Emperor Vampire overlord that had seemingly kidnapped me for the second time...or would this be classed as the first? Nope, not going to venture into that time warp minefield, as I might not make it to the other side without my brain oozing out of one nostril.

We walked the massive marble hallways in silence and I simply marvelled at how the ancient world had managed to create such beauty without the aid of modern day technology. It was mind blowing really, which was why most of the journey I looked over his shoulder simply staring in awe.

I would feel his eyes watching me as if he too were discovering it all over again through my inexperienced eyes. I could barely get over the sheer scale of the place and there was a definite theme going on and that would be massive, marble pillars. They were simply everywhere, along with every other shape you could think. Arched doorways, square recesses cut out of walls that were brightly painted, intricately carved panels sectioning off rooms and lush deep materials made from the finest of silks. It was almost like the rest of the world had been laid out for the picking and they had simply plucked pieces from each culture and mixed it with their own.

The one aspect that remained a constant in all this was the distinct lack of people one would have expected roaming the halls. I had to wonder if Lucius hadn't made it this way, almost as Draven had done, so that no one would see me?

I don't know how far we had walked but it seemed like no time at all before we approached a pair of massive double doors. They were huge, so big in fact that I couldn't help but speak my mind…or at least try too.

"It's all right, you can put me down so that you can…" I was cut off when he lifted me up slightly so he had space to kick forward, hitting the centre of the doors with a thundering boom.

"Or not," I muttered and when I felt the slight rumble from beneath his breastplate I looked up to see he had found my sarcasm amusing. He looked so handsome it was almost painful to look at him. His sandy coloured hair was longer in this time, but was held back from his face with a strip of fraying worn leather. If anything, this gave his face that meaner edge to it and you couldn't help but take him seriously just from his bone structure alone. But if this was not enough for you then his intense eyes would have been. They were like grey ice, or smoky quartz with blue flecks sparking out from his pupil. This combined with the exotic almond shape and thick, long dark eyelashes casting shadows around them, didn't marry up with the unusual colour.

Oh, he was still the cocky and confident Lucius I knew, but

with something more. Even when I first met him back in the cave prison and the sight of him killing the guards had me throwing up in the corner, I still hadn't found myself afraid of him. Okay, so I hadn't exactly known it was him and it was obvious that he had been there to free us. But even seeing him for the first time as the renowned assassin I had briefly heard about still hadn't been enough to get me to look at him any differently than I did back in my own time. But now, dressed like this and ruler of the entire Roman Empire…well then yeah, that was a totally different Lucius and not one that I had been counting on *ever* seeing.

Even when Draven had ordered him to go back to Rome and take his royal place, I still had held onto the idea that when he left that room, our time meeting in the past had swiftly come to an end. Well, like Draven once said and I had numerous times preached back to him,

'Assumption was the mother from which all mistakes are born' or most commonly known as, 'The mother of all fuck ups'. Well this was definitely one of those times I thought as he walked us both into what looked like a bedroom. And my reaction to this was to physically gulp, an action Lucius didn't miss if that damn smirk was anything to go by.

"You know back in Persia I just had one of those little tent things, so there's no need to put me up somewhere this fancy," I told him forgetting which time I was in when he repeated,

"Put you up?"

"I mean sleep," I told him and he nodded once before informing me sternly,

"Yes, well I am not putting you in a fucking tent! This is my private bedchamber and one you will be staying in until I say otherwise…am I understood?" Okay so there was that gulp again, only this time one I thought I might possibly choke on… did he say, his…*his bedroom?*

Oh no, I was in big trouble, unless he planned on sleeping somewhere else…yes, that must be it, I thought with a shit load of hope and a sprinkling of 'Oh please God, please'. He cleared his throat and I soon realised he was still waiting for something.

"Oh, right sorry…umm…I..." I told him trying to go back and wrack my brain for what he'd said.

"You are not to leave this room unless I state otherwise, now am I clear?" This time his voice told me to take this more seriously than I had the first time, so I thought it safer to simply nod.

"Good," he said just as he walked to the large bed and placed me down at its centre. I took this brief opportunity to look around the enormous room, one that even dwarfed the huge bed I was now lay on. The high ceilings were adorned with panels of artwork painted straight onto the stone walls. Pictures of Gods and Goddesses sat in Heaven, waiting no doubt until their judgement on the Earth was called upon. Garden scenes with overflowing fountains being admired by beautiful ladies in togas. Two arched, carved doors situated at the centre of one of the side walls looked as though they opened out onto an enclosed garden that mirrored some of what was already painted inside.

Well at least it wasn't a balcony, I thought nearly rolling my eyes as I played out a small montage in my head of all that had happened to me on one in the past few years. No, I had to say I wasn't sad to see one missing. Besides, we were on the ground floor, so it wasn't really all that surprising.

The tall windows might have been narrow but the room had many and each were covered with latticed wooden shutters, decorated with tiny star cut outs. Then there was the bed itself that had a rolling headboard which curled around back in on itself. The edges were painted gold against the dark wood. Above there was a circular canopy covered in crimson red silk that flowed down around the side of the bed, just waiting to enclose those that lay underneath.

The other parts of the room included a comfortable looking seating area, with wave shaped couches that matched the yellows and reds in the woven rugs they were sat on. Each of the armrests curled in just as the bed did and each were rich in colour and gold. The room didn't exactly scream Lucius' dark nature but considering he had only just risen to power, I doubt very much he'd had time to redecorate. Shame really, as I think I preferred the manlier Gothic Lord of the hidden castle look.

Which brought me back to the man himself and now we were both in a room bathed in candlelight, thanks to the dozens of candlesticks, I finally got to see more of him than just his face and breastplate. Large silver shoulder pieces bent over in three connecting metal strips attached to the top of his chest. Attached to this was a burgundy coloured cape that reached the floor.

Like the rest of the men I had seen, his strong legs were bare, with only a knee length tunic seen beneath strips of leather. These looked attached to the bottom of his chest plate, one that curved down past his stomach. Each strip of leather held small arrow shaped pieces at the top, each adorned with the head of a lion in what looked like forged bronze. Straps of thinner leather across his torso finished the look as these seemed to hold his weapons either side of his body. A brushed copper eagle at his chest was left uncovered and the bird was one with outstretched wings and carrying a plaque in his claws that held a single word written…SPQR.

I don't know why but like before I reached out to touch it, this time actually managing to make contact.

"What does this mean?" I found myself asking, and from the look on his face, one that was completely unexpected. At first, I thought he wouldn't answer me as he just seemed to be looking at me with a quizzical stare. But then he spoke.

"Senātus Populus Que Rōmānus," he said with a deep purr to his voice. The way the foreign words just rolled easily off his tongue had my mouth going dry. Jesus, but how was it that the sound of three words could turn a person on! I felt ashamed of myself as I always did when feeling this way around Lucius, but it just couldn't be helped. I didn't know what it was between us and had even resigned myself to never fully understanding it, but if I had to give it a name, it would simply be 'An invisible pull'.

"What…what does it mean?" I asked having to clear my throat after the first word and rising slightly, leaning back on my bent arms. He at least tried to hide his smirk this time, as he tapped two fingers on his lips before answering me. I knew it wasn't a gesture done out of thought but more like one done out of amusement and the knowledge of this made me blush. He knew how much he was affecting me.

"It means 'The Senate and People of Rome'…you will see it a lot among Roma" Okay, so that made sense as a nation's moto and also why he, as the Emperor, would be wearing the Empire's emblem.

"And now you wear it as their ruler…does it…?" I let the question fade having second thoughts about asking it. However, a man like Lucius wouldn't let something like that drop, I knew this when one honey toned eyebrow rose.

"Continue and ask it of me."

"I…well, I guess I just wondered if it bothered you?" I forced the question out to the end this time, one that I found myself having to elaborate when he asked,

"Bother me?"

"You know, being here and having to wear a symbol that you don't believe in? Rule an Empire you never asked to rule."

Oh yeah, asking this was a mistake, I could tell the second he started to shut down as his expression turned cold.

"I make my own decisions, make no mistake of that. Now no more questions…lie back," he told me sternly and added a hand to my chest so that he could slowly push me back, making my arms flatten to my sides.

"I umm…" I started to mutter as he situated himself on the bed next to me before peeling back my cloak as he had done on the carriage. Then he stopped and leaned down closer to my face, making me think for a split second that he was going to kiss me.

"Why not try and exercise the art of silence?" he whispered over me and I rolled my lips, holding onto them with my teeth so that I wouldn't be tempted to say what I wanted to say… which would have been along the lines of, 'Why not try and exercise the art of not being an overbearing asshole?' For obvious reasons, I decided to go with silence. He only moved when he looked satisfied that I was taking his advice and the smirk was one this time, I wanted to wipe from his face with a swift kick to the balls.

"Now hold still while I discover the extent of your injuries," he ordered firmly. I wanted to roll my eyes and if I had been facing the Lucius I knew from my own time, then I knew I would have. However, this Lucius wasn't yet my friend and now strangely he also seemed like a far cry away from the assassin who had helped me in the desert. Which had me asking myself, what had happened to him since to change him this way.

Okay so asking myself this question was quickly followed by a mental slap to the forehead as I counted the things down. He had not only been forced to face off a Demonic God, hellbent on taking over the world, (Pun definitely intended) he had also nearly died because of it and had to have his life saved by a mortal girl. Something that had to sting considering he didn't even like mortals, especially the female variety. Then after this he was ordered by Draven to take a position as Rome's new Emperor and pretty much spend however many years surrounded by beings he didn't like. So yeah, that was enough to put anyone in a shit mood for the next decade.

Which then begged the question…*did he blame me?*

It wasn't surprising that the second his hands came in contact with my skin all thoughts fled from my mind. He was looking down at me as if he could see past my damaged flesh and fractured bone and straight into the darkest shadows of my fragile soul. It was as if he was plucking strands of secrets from my heart and laying them all out for his personal view. I shuddered at the thought and mentally put a lockdown on my mind, slamming closed any doors he had tried to open.

It had been a long time since I had needed to think about doing that, after so long it was more like second nature to me. Almost as easy as breathing but then someone came along who suddenly has to remind you *to* breathe and you realise that you are not as immune as you once thought.

I looked to Lucius with wide eyes and when I saw his own narrow in annoyance I knew he had been locked out and was less than happy about the fact. Although, it seemed he hadn't walked away empty handed.

"Tell me, for I am curious… do you usually hold your mortal life with such little regard?" he asked me as he reached out and started examining the damage to my head, causing me to frown in confusion.

"What do you mean?" I asked quietly.

"What I mean is this!" he snapped, snarling down at my injuries and losing his false cool exterior, one I had foolishly started to place trust in. I sank back as he suddenly produced a blade from his side.

"Be still girl!" he demanded as he pulled me back and then after forcing my compliance, he grabbed a handful of the linen bandage and cut it in one swift move, slicing its length up my torso. Then just as quickly he had it back in its sheath freeing both hands to peel the binding from my ribs. I looked down and now saw what he saw… *and it was a mess.*

The whole of one side was deep red surrounded by deep blue and purple bruising. It looked as though I had come off a motorcycle and folded my body around a damn tree! A nasty line of raw missing skin had me wincing. My mouth then dropped open making a little O shape and I looked up at him with shock. I hadn't realised it had been that bad but looking at it now, well then, no wonder I was in such an amount of pain.

Lucius obviously saw my shock for himself and released a deep sigh.

"It wasn't my fault!" I blurted out and in return he gave me a sceptical look.

"It wasn't, I mean it started when I fell down some kind of trapdoor and then down the stairs. And then I was…" Lucius stopped me mid flow by raising his hand in what looked like exasperation.

"I know what happened after that, which is why I ask you again, you thought it best to jump out of a fucking window whilst inflicted with such an injury?" He all but growled the question at me, which had me asking myself…why did he care? I felt the anger bubbling up inside me and before I could think about what his actions might be, once faced with my attitude, I unleashed it.

"I am sorry, next time I have a small army outside looking for me I will just stick my freakin' head out the window and ask them if they plan on killing me first, before I decide to run for my life!" I snapped back sarcastically after pushing his hand away from touching me. He snarled back at me and said,

"And it didn't then occur to you upon finding yourself in Rome that I was now ruler here and would have sent my men to come and retrieve you?!" he argued making me frown and I tried to shift my body up as I was getting sick of fighting this battle on my back.

"I swear to the Gods, if you move before I heal you, I will tie you to my bed!" he warned, stopping me with a firm hand back at my throat.

"Fine!" I shouted up at him and then it started to register what he'd just said.

"Uh, wait, what do you mean? You're going to heal me?"

"Learning of such disregard for your own life, then I am sure you're now accustomed with the act, as I doubt this is your first time," he said sneering. Jeez, what was his problem?! He seemed so pissed off with me and for the life of me I couldn't understand why?

"I already have the King's blood, so I don't need you to do that," I told him making him bare his teeth at me. This was when I hit my limit,

"What the fuck is your problem!?" I shouted, lifting my head against the hold at my neck. He looked taken aback for a moment as if surprised I would challenge him this way. To be honest, maybe he was right, as I did seem to keep putting myself in danger and screaming at an obviously angry Vampire King probably wasn't the best of ideas right now.

"You are my problem!" he shouted back at me, his chest heaving as if he was holding himself back from something I couldn't see.

"Then here's an idea, let me go and I will get my ass back to Persia…there, problem solved!" Okay, so this was definitely the wrong thing to say and I knew it the second I saw his eyes flash crimson and his fangs extend past his bottom lip.

"Mine!" he snarled and this was my only warning before he

was at my neck threatening my life with nature's weapons. His teeth held me immobile and ice filled my veins as I froze. My heart beat wildly in my chest, a fact he could probably feel with his lips against my pulse point. I felt the sparks of pain as his fangs nicked at the skin but didn't fully pierce my flesh. He could have quite easily ripped into my neck but yet he hadn't and again I was asking myself why?

I don't know how long it was before he decided to let me go but I found it must have been long enough for my lungs to hit their limit as the second he did, I dragged in ragged breaths so as that I didn't pass out. I felt him licking my neck, sucking away at the tender flesh before pulling back and issuing me some advice.

"I suggest not pushing me again little Keira girl, for I find myself on edge around you and trust me when I say, you do not want to see what happens when I step from it…am I understood?" he told me and when his eyes nearly turned to black blood, I nodded my head in frantic little nods.

"Good, now do as you're told and don't fight against me again," he added, now satisfied to see I was compliant once again. Well, no wonder as I might have had a few screws loose but I wasn't damn suicidal! And one look at the beast above me screamed only one answer and that was submission equalled survival.

I wanted to reach out to him and explain of our connection back in my own time. I wanted to tell him of how we cared for each other and that it didn't have to be like this. Not after all we had been through together but this man, this handsome, misunderstood Vampire King, well how could I reach him the way I did back in Germany? How could I make him see me the way he did back then?

I was so confused as one moment it was almost as though

he seemed to hate me and then in the next moment he seemed almost possessive over me. I just didn't get it?

Meanwhile, in the midst of my musings, Lucius had risen from the bed and started to shed himself of his armour. He had walked towards a large chest as he undid the straps at his sides, after first pulling his weapons free. He kicked open the lid and dropped his chest plate inside with a clatter, one I jumped at. He continued to take each item off until it left him in just his burgundy tunic. He then grabbed a pair of loose fitting trousers from a drawer and started yanking them up his legs. He pulled at the cord and tied it before making his way back to me. Then when he was closer to the bed, he reached up over his shoulder and pulled his tunic off, baring his wide muscular chest to me. He threw the material casually to the bed and I tried not to look like I was drinking in my fill of him.

It couldn't be denied that seeing Lucius half naked was a thing of beauty. Ripples of muscles along his ribs joined those mouth-watering, deeper indents of his six-pack abs. It was true that he didn't have the same intimidating muscle mass as Draven but he was still just as ripped and looked made for stealth and speed. Of course, his wide shoulders and large biceps looked more useful for wielding heavy weapons with great precision and not delicately lifting damsels in distress into his arms.

"Now I am going to move you, try not to tense or it will only cause greater pain. Ready?" And there it was again, a slither of kindness breaking through the dark clouds and blinding me with tender words. I nodded for him to do as he wished and was surprised when he first brushed back a few strands of my hair, tucking them gently behind my ear. Then he hovered over me and started to sit me up with a hand at my back. I sucked in a startled breath, one that caused pain like he said it would. I tried to relax but then he pulled me the rest of the way and completely upright creating space behind me for him to slip in between my back and the headboard. Once he was where he wanted to be, he gently pulled me back against him, so I was now sat in between his outstretched legs.

Sat like this with him felt so intimate I could barely breathe without it hitching in my chest. How was it possible that with my back nestled against his chest and now that I couldn't see his face, it still seemed more sexual than when he had been holding himself above me? Of course, this was made even more so when he wrapped one arm around me as if first securing me to him.

He then lifted his other hand to his lips and I looked back enough to see him biting down hard at his wrist, tearing through the thin veil of skin there like it was paper. I watched as blood seemed to almost burst to the surface as if it had been waiting all this time for the chance to escape. All the while he didn't take his steely gaze from mine and it felt as though he did this so that he could judge my reactions. What he found would have been concern for the pain he could have been inflicting on himself and I knew he saw it. He raised a brow in question but he didn't ask me why I cared, he only showed me how deeply he did, when he placed his bleeding wrist in front of me and told me softly,

"Please drink." I reached up, watching it drip to the bed like tiny red bombs hitting the material covering my legs, inking my trousers and soaking them with crimson stars. I took hold of his thick wrist in both hands and brought his offering to my lips, knowing the depth of the gift he bestowed upon me. Then I did as he asked and drank from him, straight from the vein.

The second the first drop of blood touched my lips his essence burst across my tongue. I wished I could have said it tasted awful and the metallic bitterness made me want to gag, but I would have been lying. No, it tasted like it usually did, like liquid sin and life combined. It was hard to describe it as anything but, as the taste was too addictive to give familiarity to. To compare it to anything else just didn't seem right, so it could only be described as a feeling and that was like…

A warmth to my heart.

A comfort to my body.

And a blanket for the soul.

I shuddered in his hold and felt him react by holding me tighter to him as if he never wanted to let me go. And then came the side effects to such a gift and he too felt it as he started to growl against my sensitive neck.

"Just let it go," he told me as I felt the heat invade my belly as it started to coil and tighten. My inner thighs tensed and the base of my spine tingled, waiting for that euphoric moment of release. I swallowed him down over and over again, feeling the pulsating effects tug at my feminine core as if invisible fingers spread me open before plunging deep.

I finally tore my bloody lips from his wrist and I cried out from mind blowing pleasure, feeling as though it was powerful enough to consume me whole. Somewhere in the midst of it all I could hear Lucius roar before I felt the pain of teeth invading my own flesh. The agony only lasted a single second before it quickly morphed into another crashing wave of pleasure. This time I heard more than my simple cries of release, no this time I hear screams of ecstasy ripped from a place so deep, I barely recognised them as belonging to me. Almost as if I was experiencing an outer body experience without once ever opening my eyes. I felt as though I was floating on the wings of rapture and delirium. I could have simply drifted to another world and I wouldn't have known it but then I felt that strength envelope me, anchoring me to the world I didn't know…

His world.

"Ssshh, calm for me now, Keira girl," he cooed and only

then I realised he must have finished making his own meal out of me. I was still quivering against him and I felt the heat of embarrassment invade my face as I thought about what had just happened. Oh god! What had I just done! I had just come in Lucius' arms after feeding from him, that's what!

I felt Lucius looking down at me over my shoulder and when I tried to hide my shame he reached up with the hand that he had been holding flat against my belly. He then tipped my chin up, so I had no choice but to face him.

"You blush for me?" he questioned as if surprised. Well, what type of girl did he take me for? After all, I wasn't some blood sucking hussy! I would have told him this but his sweetness knocked it clean out of me. He then reached up with both hands and swept my hair back before kissing my forehead and whispering,

"Fucking addictive." I sucked in a sharp breath at the intensity of his words and this time, I marvelled at how it no longer hurt. I looked down to see that my bruising was long gone and I reached up, feeling that the bumps on my head had also disappeared.

"I feel strong," I admitted, making him chuckle behind me, a sound I had yet to hear coming from this ancient version of Lucius.

"I am glad to hear it, along with the fact I no longer have to play witness to your pain," he informed me and now I had to ask myself if that had been part of the reason for his foul mood. Had he cared that much for my wellbeing? Maybe he felt responsible after I had saved his life and to him, this was simply him returning the favour?

"Now explain that look to me." The sound of his voice quickly brought me out of my inner turmoil and alerted me to the fact that he had been watching all these silent questions playing out in my mind.

"I am confused," I told him and once again, I had him chuckling behind me.

"As I can see, for this line tells me as much," he said with mirth, running a thumb in between my frowning eyebrows and smoothing the line he spoke of. He seemed so at ease now and I wondered if tasting my blood had released some of his tension.

"Why am I here, Lucius?" I just came out and said it, turning around in the small space I had so that I could face him. He bent up one knee quickly and it was almost as if he had done it without thinking. Like he was scared I had been about to try and escape off the bed and he did this to stop me, as it was now a solid support at my back.

He looked thoughtful for a moment, almost as if he was contemplating whether or not to tell me. He went with the latter when he said,

"That is enough for tonight, your body needs rest and I am not in the mood for another battle with you on the matter." Well that shot me down, I thought with another frown, one he laughed at. He then ran the back of his fingers down my cheek and shocked me when he said,

"I am glad you are here." I didn't know what to say but I guess my blush spoke for me again. His hand travelled from my now heated cheeks to the crusted blood at my hair.

"However, you do need a bath," he teased and this time I couldn't help but grant him a smile, one that made his eyes brighten at the sight. He liked to see me smile?

"A bath would be good," I agreed on a breathy whisper, too afraid of my own voice right now and what this tender side of him would reveal in the emotions it provoked.

"Very well, I will have one brought to you," he told me shifting me to the side so that he could remove himself from the bed. I found that I could finally breathe easy once he put the much-needed space between us. He was just making his way across the room when something stopped him. A thought must have tugged at his now clear mind for he froze mid step before looking back at me over his shoulder.

"You are not to leave this room, understood?" And just like that the other side of Lucius was back to full commanding Keira mode. So, I replied,

"That's not really a way to treat a guest."

"That's because you're not," he informed me pragmatically making me narrow my eyes at him in annoyance.

"No? Then please enlighten me, what am I exactly?" I asked this time folding my arms across my chest. He took a moment to look at my small display of attitude before issuing me my next big shocker, one more serious than all those before it.

My reason for being here…

"You're my prisoner."

CHAPTER TWENTY-SEVEN

HOW TO OWN A HEART

Lucius left straight after informing me of my part in all this and not surprisingly he did so leaving me with my jaw nearly touching the floor! He said that I was his prisoner but surely not? How could he say that, we were all on the same side weren't we? Jesus, but suddenly I wasn't so sure of anything anymore! It was like stepping back to a time when I first met Lucius and finding out that he was none other than Draven's mortal enemy. I had no clue as to what game he was playing, but I knew one thing, I intended to find out!

I decided to climb out of bed as sitting waiting was starting to drive me mad. Asking myself over and over what the hell was I supposed to do now? Would Draven come for me when he found out where I was? Would he start a war? I surely hoped not as I wasn't planning on being the next Helen of Troy anytime soon.

Thankfully, I wasn't given much time to continue asking myself torturous questions I had no answers to, as the echoing of the doors being pushed back had me almost jumping out of my skin. In walked Lucius, taking large confident strides and coming at me with purpose.

"What do you mean, I am your prisoner?" I blurted out my first question and from the looks at his mouth quirking up at the corners, then he knew I had been stewing on this a while. However, he didn't answer me, but instead simply took my breath away when he placed a shoulder to my belly and hoisted me up, bending me over him as he stood straight.

"Ahh! What are you doing?!" I complained as my legs dangled over his chest and my torso down his back. As before, he didn't answer me but simply held an arm across my flailing legs, pinning them to his chest. He quickly walked me over towards the other end of the room. Then he unceremoniously dumped me back on the bed, yanked the curtains around and issued my only warning,

"Stay." The tone of his voice knocked all the fight out of me as I knew when to take his threats seriously, and now was one of those times. He waited until satisfied with my compliance and when he saw me nod in acceptance, he too gave me a curt nod. Then he moved back pulling the curtains the rest of the way, hiding me from view. What did he have, a jealous wife lurking in the shadows or something? I don't know why that thought suddenly had me placing a hand to my heart as if it caused me pain. It was almost as if I secretly knew there was only one soul out there for him, now if I could just discover who it was because no matter how much I loved him, I knew it would never be me.

I shook these strange feelings off me, like shedding a weak skin and replacing it for one thicker, something I had a feeling I was going to need in the next few minutes.

"Nunc intraveritis!" ('Now enter!') Lucius' booming voice echoed around the large room and I scooted closer to the curtains so that I could peek out between the join. I watched as servants all started piling in the room, the first two carrying a huge bucket that I was gathering was going to be used as a bath. I knew that in Rome they didn't have single baths but communal bath houses, so I guessed this was the best Lucius could come up with on such short notice. Well if he was trying to keep me hidden for the time being, then this fact at least told me that my arrival hadn't been planned for long.

I watched as they heaved the thing into the centre of the room and then a line of people all carrying large urns followed with the water. Lucius meanwhile, stood back with his arms folded and watched them work. I also couldn't help noticing that he situated himself between the bed and the people, as if standing guard and ready in case trouble should arise.

Once full or at least until Lucius was satisfied, he waved the rest away, dismissing them after first motioning for a wooden box to be placed down on a small round table that also held a decanter of red wine. They each showed their respect for their leader and left as quietly as they had arrived. Only one girl had made the mistake of being too curious and looked towards the bed, something Lucius had snarled at like an angry possessive beast marking his territory. Not surprisingly, the girl fled from the room with the rest.

"Your bath awaits," Lucius said after the sound of the doors closing had sealed my fate. The curtains were roughly yanked back and I was surprised to see them still intact and attached to the canopy above with his careless treatment.

"Thanks, now answer the question," I snapped now we were alone. He didn't look at me as he walked back over to the bath, but merely ran his fingertips through the water as if testing the temperature.

"It is a simple concept. No doubt you want to leave and I forbid it, therefore making you my prisoner. Now get undressed." He finally decided to answer me and I nearly choked on it. Was he serious?!

"I do want to leave!" I shouted and he glanced over his shoulder at me as if he knew I would say this. He shrugged his shoulders and told me,

"And as I said, I forbid it, now get undressed, for I won't ask again," he warned, one I stupidly didn't take his threat serious enough.

"But you're…you're loyal to Draven, to the King…how could you just keep me from him?" I stuttered out the question and this time, I got more than feigned indifference.

"I *was* loyal to the King and he rewards such with lies and deceit. Therefore, my loyalty shifted to another," he told me with a hard, unforgiving tone, one that had me gasping. How…? How had he found out about the spear so soon? This shouldn't have happened for almost two thousand years and I couldn't think of what could have changed to make it now known to him. What had I done in this time to make it so? But then something he said has me questioning him once again,

"You say your loyalty has shifted to another…?" he didn't answer me this time and it looked as though he didn't think I was ready for the truth. Instead he gave me a pointed look and raked his gaze down my revealing outfit.

I couldn't help but hate the way he looked at me as though he was displeased by what he saw. I suddenly hugged myself, trying to hide what I could from him and unable to stop him from sneaking a glimpse at my insecurities. He dragged a frustrated hand through his hair, as if he knew and I hated that he did.

"Bath. Now!" he ordered and I felt my shoulders slump in defeat.

"Fine. You can leave now," I told him but he scoffed at this.

"I am going nowhere," he told me, crossing his arms over his chest and by doing so, he looked indestructible.

"But…but I am not getting naked in front of you!" I hissed making him smirk back at me.

"I am well accustomed with the female form Keira, for I have seen many. You have nothing I have not seen before," he told me and I all but growled, not really knowing why. Well that was a lie, I knew why as I wasn't exactly about to do jumping jacks to hear Lucius bragging about all the naked conquests he had enjoyed over the years.

Just looking at him and I knew that his body was made for sin and lust. So, just feeling like another meat sack and a soul in any unimportant form, I decided to give him what he asked for. It wasn't like he gave a shit, as I clearly disgusted him anyway. He, no doubt, just wanted me clean before I slept in his bed and this was his way of making sure. That or he thought I might drown myself just to get away from him! Right now, I was so angry it was a thought, but to be honest I would rather it be his head I was holding under the water!

He seemed to be watching all these different emotions play out over my face and I wished I could have slapped the satisfied smirk off his face when he knew he had got his way. I stormed towards the bath, turned my back to him and unhooked the small raspberry coloured top, peeling it from my body. Then I dropped it next to me and took a deep breath before pushing down my pants. Thankfully he couldn't see that my eyes were closed and I was half destroying my lip with nerves. By the Gods, but I hated the way my heartbeat hammered in my chest just knowing I was in the same room with Lucius whilst naked.

I didn't dare look back for fear of the disappointment I would see in his eyes and my thoughts nearly crushed me. I didn't know why this was important to me for admittedly, I may have cared deeply for Lucius but it was Draven who owned my heart and always would. So why then did I continue to feel the way I did around him? It was almost as if this had been part of the Fates' doing and if that was so, then I felt sick because of the cruelty of it all. Seriously, did they know no bounds in playing with my life?

"Oh..." I whispered on a breathy gasp that escaped me when I felt Lucius coming up behind me. The feel of his naked chest against my naked back, the skin on skin contact, was nearly enough to undo me. I sucked in a sharp breath when he lowered his head to my neck.

"Here, let me help you," he whispered against my neck and I felt his satisfied grin spread over my skin after I shuddered against him. Then I felt his hand reach up and pull my hair free from the braids and pins used to secure it back and out of the way. I hated that Draven too had done this for me, feeling ashamed that I didn't have the power to just turn, knee Lucius in the balls and run back to him. Okay, so I knew that I wouldn't have got very far but at least I would have tried.

Of course, these thoughts quickly fled my mind when Lucius went a step too far and started running his long thick fingers through my hair, massaging my aching scalp with his strong hands. I couldn't help my head from falling back as if my neck had turned to jelly and the blissful moan slipped out before I had chance to bite it back. I felt the rumbling in his chest as he must have liked hearing the sound.

"Here," he forced out, his voice a thick and heavy timbre. I looked down at his offered hand and I tried to get my own to stop shaking as I placed it in his. He released a sigh the second I touched him and his fingers curled around my hand as though he was claiming me and never wanted to let me go. I bit my lip as I lifted a leg and stepped into the bath, just so I could get him to let me go before he took things too far.

I didn't understand any of it, why would he behave this way, unless this was his idea of fun? To play with me this way, making me think of nothing but disdain for my body and then contradicting it with soft, gentle touches and kind gestures. I was so damn confused and I hated myself for even caring!

"It's perfect," he told me after I had both feet in the water and as I lowered myself all the way, I agreed with him, saying,

"Yes, the water is just right, thank you." I sat, cradling my legs now thankful I had the water to help cover my modesty. But Lucius had other ideas as I felt his hands envelope my shoulders so that he could pull me backwards. Then still standing behind me, he bent at the waist so he could speak directly in my ear again. But this time, his spoken thoughts stunned me to silence and if I thought I was confused before then now I was dumbfounded.

"I wasn't speaking of the water." My breath hitched and caught in my chest and I found myself gripping onto the edge of the tub just so that I wouldn't sink.

"I care little for the water that keeps your beautiful body from my view…now relax, whilst I tend to you." Then he raised himself up and finally gave me a minute to breathe as I felt him walk away from me. I looked back over my shoulder to see him retrieve the wooden box and a small stool for him to sit on. He swung the stool around in a swift motion and positioned himself directly behind me, sitting so that he was at the right height to reach me with ease.

"Wh…what are you doing?" I asked, having to clear the golf ball sized lump from my throat first. He had opened the box and took out a strange tool that had me shifting from him and quickly looking fearful.

"What is that!?" I shouted at the sight of the long, hooked tool that was concaved and looked like a blade, only one that thankfully was void of a sharp end. Lucius took in my look of horror and couldn't help himself when he started to laugh.

"Don't be afraid, it is only a strigel, do you not have these in your time?" he asked, clearly amused by my reaction and adding such a beautiful light to his usually serious grey blue eyes. I moved further away from him and held myself in a protective ball, hugging my knees to my chest once again, a position he looked on with curiosity.

"Gods no!" I shouted making him laugh again.

"Then what do you use to clean yourself?" he asked sounding very interested.

"That's to help clean you!? Jeez which part, because that looks painful," I complained and the second I saw the mischief in his eyes I knew what part of my sentence he had focused on.

"Come and I will show you," he challenged, one I didn't accept.

"Uh no thanks, I think I am good." Hearing this he threw his head back and laughed heartily. I can't say I hated the sight of his corded neck straining against his amusement and I felt my mouth get dry as I tried to swallow down the urge to touch him.

"I can assure you it doesn't hurt…*or get inserted into any bodily orifice,*" he told me, whispering this last part and making my cheeks flame with a burning blush because of it. Seriously, did he have to purr the words with a sexual intent?

"Then how does it work?" I asked, quickly moving on from the 'bodily orifice' comment. He grinned at me before he turned it back on himself so that he could then scrape it up his arm, as if removing imaginary dirt. I couldn't help but look fascinated as the historian in me was amazed.

"That doesn't look like it would be very effective," I told him on a laugh, moving closer to him of my own free will. He held the object out for me to take so that I could examine it myself.

"We first rub oil into our skin and then use this to scrape it off." My eyes widened and I didn't even realise I was edging even closer to him, quickly getting lost in learning about his ancient ways. By the look of things he seemed to latch on to this fact about me, now knowing my weakness.

"What do you use?" he asked, trying to keep me in this easy manner and continue the conversation.

"Soap, which is like a bar we rub on our skin, we even have a liquid form that we rub on with a sponge or flannel. Oh, and then there is soap for our hair called shampoo and conditioner for making it softer." I told him and he seemed to enjoy hearing me talking about it, as his eyes widened but then he reached back in his box and pulled out something that made me squeal with delight.

"Soap!" I shouted making him laugh.

"I see it doesn't take much to please you," he teased making me laugh.

"Where did you get that?!"

"It comes from Egypt," he informed me and I couldn't believe that here we were having a friendly chat about soap. Not after he had informed me that I was his captive and demanded I have a bath. Talk about the strange situations I found myself in.

"Well knowing how clumsy I can be I think I will take the soap, as it's no doubt safer that way," I told him making his lips twitch as if fighting another grin. He nodded for me to come closer still as he held it out for me to take. I don't know why I felt like it was a trap, maybe because of how predatory he always looked.

It was certainly easy to see him as the great assassin everyone painted him to be. I could just picture it now, that stealth body lurking in the shadows, just watching with his steely gaze, waiting for the right moment to strike. Even now, as I reached out, trying to stop my hand from shaking as I did, with fingertips barely grazing the square bar of soap in his hand and then…

He moved.

It was so fast, I never would have seen it and I squealed as his fingers took my hand in an unforgiving grip before he yanked me towards him. I shot through the water and just before I hit the edge, he spun me so that now I found myself with his arm banded across my naked chest with my back to him, just as I had been on the bed.

"Tell me Keira girl, do you still think it safer?" he asked me, humming the dangerous question with his lips again at my ear, finishing it off by nipping at my lobe.

"With you in the room, nothing I do is safe," I confessed on a whisper, closing my eyes against how wrong those words felt being voiced aloud. This time it was he that sucked in a sharp breath and I knew by the tightened grip on my hand that it had meant something to him. For long moments neither of us spoke and the only sound was our combined heavy breathing as if the weight of how we felt for each other had the power to suspend time.

"I won't hurt you," he said, his voice gruff and thick with emotion as if it had been dragged from somewhere deep. So, I told him the only thing I could, something that I knew had the power to stop this. And something that had me soon hanging my head in shame after I did.

"You already do by keeping me here." As soon as I said it, I knew I had hit the intended nerve, but I couldn't rejoice in my mission accomplished when he let me go. I had wounded him and I had to bite back the guilt that would have made me say something to get him to stay. But in the end, all I was left with was the pain I gave myself as way of punishment. Because I heard the stool he had been sat on grind against the stone floor as he moved back.

I heard his heavy deep breaths from behind me, but I didn't dare look for he would have seen the tears in my eyes. Tears that were his and his alone. But I couldn't do that. Because then he would have stayed and I would have wanted him to. No, Lucius was too much of a temptation for my fragile will to endure. So, I needed to put as much space between us as possible and being naked in the bath with his hands on my body was like delicious torture. Like a last meal to a starving man before he dies. It was bitter sweet cruelty and all I needed to do was resist a taste.

"Then it is unfortunate, as I intend to continue... *for I am not letting you go,*" he said firmly and I finally let my bottom lip free on a gasp. So, I tried one last time and thinking back to our final goodbye back in the library, surrounded by the broken remains of written mortal words. I had to wonder and ask myself how many of those torn books and flyaway pages had held broken stories of love?

"You already did... back in my own time," I told him softly and his growl made me flinch.

"Then I was a damned fool!" he snarled before I heard the slamming of the door, a sign I was now alone. I let my head fall back onto the rim of the tub and turned my head to the side. Finally, it was safe to let my tears fall.

"No... you just knew the truth," I answered the empty room on a heartbroken whisper.

After this I washed my skin through my misery as if trying to scrub myself free from it. But no matter how much I tried, the betrayal still clung to my skin, like an invisible layer only I couldn't see. Why couldn't I break away from this hold that Lucius held over me? I had always thought it had something to do with my prophecy but what if I was wrong, *what if it was his own?*

I went to sleep that night with only one thought plaguing me and that was who was I to Lucius? Who was I to his own fate? I had no answers as usual, but at least I found comfort that this was all meant to lead somewhere. Like a story being told before it was even written.

I don't know why but after I had cleaned my body and hair, ridding myself of the day's turbulent events, I unconsciously picked up Lucius' discarded tunic and placed it over my head. I didn't want to sleep naked and I was fooling no one by pretending I didn't find comfort sleeping wrapped in Lucius' scent. Of course, I hadn't been planning on him coming back to the room that night, but come back he did.

He silently slipped beneath the covers and gently lifted my head so that he could slip an arm beneath me. Then he pulled me closer, cradling my body with his as he wrapped himself around me. In that moment I had to ask myself if he too had needed the comfort as I had?

"You saved my life," he said in the dark as if he could no longer contain it. I swallowed hard before letting a whispered response from my lips,

"Yes."

"Why?" he asked, obviously seeing it all play back that day. The day we three combined beat Pertinax. The day he almost died and I had saved his life by giving him my blood. The Venom of God. Did this mean he knew of the darkness I now held inside of me?

"It wasn't the first time I saved your life," I told him, hoping this would be enough…*it wasn't*. He released a deep breath and then shifted so that he was on his side half above me.

"I asked you why," he growled and I knew with the sound

of his voice that this was eating him up inside. He smoothed back my hair from my forehead, waiting for me to tell him.

"You know why, it's because I care for you," I said forcefully and he pulled me from my side, so I was now on my back looking up at him. He had left some candles burning in the room as it now cast a warm glow, giving the space a romantic aura to it.

"You gave me your blood and I saw it," he told me and I frowned in confusion. I shook my head a little, telling him silently that I didn't understand.

"I saw it all. I saw the future." I sucked in a sharp breath of shock and that's when it started to click together like ancient puzzle pieces combining with those of my own time to create the picture in *his mind.* It was that single moment that had changed for him. The moment I gave him my blood and showed him a different life, one that was private and solely belonged to me and the Lucius I knew. Now he'd had a taste and he wanted more.

"What…what did you see?" I asked as I needed to know. I had to know the depth of the levels I faced. And this time it wasn't a frozen lake I was pushed into, no in return he gave me an abyss of feelings to drown in.

One I had unknowingly jumped into,

"You gave me my humanity back and taught me…" he paused before lowering his lips to mine so he could whisper the last part as the start of a forbidden kiss…

"…How to give my heart to another."

CHAPTER TWENTY-EIGHT

FAMILY CONNECTIONS

"Wait, this is wrong, we shouldn't be doing this," I told Lucius just before he could kiss me and his answer was,

"I'm a vampire Keira, *wrong is all I know,*" he told me and the heart-breaking way he said it made my guard slip, enough for my hands to stop pushing against him, which was all the encouragement he needed. He crushed his lips to mine before I knew what he was doing and for a shameful moment I allowed myself the sin of getting lost in his bruising kiss. He ran his hands in my hair, holding me to him for the onslaught. His lips, his teeth, his tongue, they were everywhere, my mouth, my neck, along my jawline and all the while, nipping, sucking and kissing me in the most delicious, mind consuming ways. It was as though he couldn't get enough of me and the feeling of power that evoked was intoxicating.

"What are you up to this time, little wife of mine?"

Draven?

I heard it and I almost cried out his name. A voice from a

different time, speaking not *to* me, *but of me*. It was all I needed to tear myself from Lucius' lips, and I vowed it would be the very last time we kissed.

"No!" I shouted and rolled myself from under his hold, making him growl as he tried to reach out and grab me but surprisingly, I was too quick for him. Well, I guess there was a first for everything. Although I had to say the whole thing would have looked a lot better had I not just rolled out of the bed and landed on the floor in a mass of covers and with a very unsexy 'Umpf' sound.

I felt one corner of the covers being lifted off my face to find Lucius above me, now lay on his front and leaning casually on one elbow looking down at me with humour lighting up his eyes.

"Comfortable?" he asked teasing me and I growled up at him before snatching the cover out of his hand and placing it back over my head to hide my shame. The sound of his laughter had me biting my lip to hold in my own. The next thing I knew I was squealing at the feel of him gathering me up in my cocoon and placing me back on the bed. I then felt him join me and start to unwrap me, as I no doubt resembled a burrito. Not that he knew what one of those was…which was when my stomach must have reminded me of what food tasted like. Jesus, but when was the last time I had eaten, let alone gone to the bathroom!?

"I think that means something important," Lucius teased pulling the last of the covers off me and revealing my red cheeks.

"You think?"

"Often, you?" was his comeback and it made me giggle.

"When was the last time you were fed?" I looked up as I thought about it and then shrugged my shoulders, saying,

"I don't remember." Hearing this he groaned and swore to

himself. Then he got out of bed and I couldn't stop myself from shouting,

"You're naked!" he looked back at me over his shoulder, now with his muscular back and perfectly shaped ass on view for me to openly gawk at. Obviously, he smirked when he saw my face and said,

"As should you be." At this I snorted and quickly wanted to smack myself when he looked far too intrigued at hearing it. He was half way between pulling his trousers back on, when he stopped.

"Did you just snort at me?" he asked and I bit my lip, shaking my head quickly.

"I think you will find that you did," he said playfully narrowing his eyes and I laughed, releasing another snort. This time it was one I followed by slapping a hand to my mouth. The grin he gave me was all bad boy intent and he finished pulling up his trousers before stalking back to me. They hung dangerously low on his hips, and I couldn't help but follow the light speckling of blonde hair that travelled from under his bellybutton into a place I liked to call, 'The Forbidden Land'.

"And this little animal in you, is that to be denied to me also, for I am sure I know a way to get you to repeat such a sound, after all…*I know of your weaknesses.*" I was about to comment with some witty retort when he lunged. The next thing I knew he was straddling my body and had my arms pinned above my head. Then he transferred both my hands into one of his and used his other hand to inflict his torture.

"Don't! Don't you dare!" Okay, so with my giggling tone it was a stadium sized empty threat, one he raised a brow at before giving me another bad boy grin full of mischief.

"Do I hear that right… did you really just *dare* me to try and extract such an adorable sound from you again?"

"Uh…no?" I said before biting the side of my lip to stop myself from smiling.

"I didn't think so..." I released a relieved breath too soon as he finished his sentence leaning down, over my cheek,

"...but I'd better make sure." Then his free hand started to snake up my tunic, dancing his fingers gently along my sides. Needless to say, I burst into a fit of giggles and the snorts came thick and fast. Seeing this side of Lucius had me completely blown away and I knew that he was showing me what a life with him could have been like. But deep down I knew something he didn't and right now, I knew it also wouldn't have been something he would have accepted as truth…

I wasn't destined for him, someone else was.

Well whoever it may be, I hoped for two things, that first, he didn't have to wait too long until he found her and second, that she was a strong character, because she would need all of it to be able to keep up with this man.

"Okay, okay, I give in, you win!" I shouted just so that he would stop tickling me.

"I always do," he told me acting cocky, which had me questioning…was a man like Lucius ticklish?

"And what about you?" I questioned looking up at him breathlessly.

"What about me?" he asked not understanding what I meant by the question and I laughed again. I tapped his hand that still had hold of me, telling him to release me. He did so without hesitation, no doubt wanting to see where this was going. So, without thinking anymore about it, I ran a gentle fingertip down his musclebound torso and asked,

"Could it be possible for this big, bad macho, Vampire King to be ticklish and giggle like a girl?" His lips twitched before he feigned shock. Then he let himself fall to the side and flopped down onto his back next to me. Then he motioned a hand down his body and said,

"Have at it." Oh my, what an offer and if I had been single, I would have jumped at it. However, I very much wasn't and was now questioning my sanity for starting such a game. Talk about playing with fire, I was doing it with fire *and brimstone!*

"What's wrong little girl, scared of losing?" I knew he was baiting me and I wished I could have said I was big enough to just shrug my shoulders and give up but this was me we were talking about. So instead I tapped a finger to my lips and looked him up and down wondering where I should start. He faked a yawn, making me laugh.

"Close your eyes." I told him and his eyes widened at the request.

"What's wrong big man, scared of losing?" I threw at him and he scoffed a laugh before doing as he was told. Now, if I could just find some indestructible shackles, tie him to the nearest marble pillar and make a run for it, I thought with a smirk.

"Put your arms up." I ordered and now it was I who issued such a command with a voice sounding thick with lust. This is just a game Keira. This is just a way to get him to trust you. Just a way to get a chance at escape. I told myself all of these things as I reached out and started to touch him. I saw him flinch the second my fingertips made contact with his soft skin, like a fine veil of satin over stone. Then using only one finger, I let it skim featherlight along the skin on his sides and I smiled when I saw his lips twitch as if fighting a grin. *So, he was ticklish.* Um, interesting. Well, this will give me something to tease him about when I get back, I thought with a deeper grin, wondering what his reaction to that would be.

I continued my journey, reaching the inside of his underarm, the light speckling of honey colour hair, tickling my own fingers as I gently brushed through it to get to the skin and this was where I had him. He jerked and made a small moan of protest, rolling in his lips quickly after, so as not to make another noise. It made him look beautifully innocent and for the first time, incredibly human.

"What's the matter Lucius, getting too much for you?" I asked in a seductive voice, one laced with confidence. He smirked, but kept his eyes closed. He then tensed his arms, making his muscles bulge, which turned out to be a contradictory action, when he said,

"Not at all, please continue for I should be asleep soon." I couldn't help but snort a laugh at his teasing, one he raised a brow at without needing to look at me.

"Was that my favourite sound I just heard?"

"No, it was the wind." I told him faking a bored tone and making him laugh easily this time. The sight of his stomach muscles tensing had me licking my lips, thankfully a response he couldn't see, as he still had his eyes closed.

"Well unless there is a sow out there, trying to escape that wind, then I think you must be mistaken…that or something far more sinful, *like lying."* I couldn't stifle a laugh like I tried to, as I was having way too much fun to stop it. But what was nice to see was that every time he did hear me laugh, he too couldn't help but grin.

"Who me…*never.* Now hold still so I can get a girly giggle out of you, like I intend to," I said before upping the game and this time as I made my next journey up his ribs, I added something a little extra. I got down low on the bed and started to blow over the same spot my finger travelled and this time I knew it was going to work as he shivered. The higher up I went the more I could see him fighting against it, and the second I got to his underarm, I paused cruelly, making him wait for the unexpected…then all my fingertips attacked at once. A laugh erupted out of him and I don't know who looked more shocked because of it, him or me?

"You cheated!" he shouted bolting upright and I burst out laughing.

"You can't cheat at tickling!" I told him with a shake of my head.

"You used your mouth!" he complained again and soon I had tears of laughter rolling down my face. I couldn't believe I was sat there arguing with a Vampire King because he had lost the tickling game. It was priceless.

"Oh, and you wouldn't have?!" I challenged back and his look said it all, he so would have!

"Oh, I would have used my mouth alright, but now I am also thinking about teaching sinful little girls a lesson…*with my teeth,*" he promised with dark intent and I replied with sass,

"So, you would fight sin with sin, that makes sense…*not.*"

"It doesn't have to make sense, it only has to go my way," he informed and again this made me giggle. I swear but his smile was infectious.

"You don't change, do you?" I commented, referring to his cocky nature, one that was just as prominent to this day…or should I say, back in my day.

"Tell me, for I am curious…what is our relationship back in your time?" he asked shifting his body against the headboard and raising one knee to rest an arm on. I had to admit he surprised me by this question.

"Well, we are friends," I said and he looked sceptical, repeating,

"Friends?"

"Good friends," I added but even this didn't sound good enough for him.

"Oh, come on, give me a break here, this *is* like the second time you have kidnapped me and one of the first times I met you, you did try and kill me," I told him, letting it all spill out without thought. Now this really got his attention.

"No! For surely you are mistaken. Why would I ever try to kill my…" he let the sentence trail off, shutting down before he went too far. Obviously, I wasn't the only one keeping secrets.

"Your?" I prompted, not letting it go as I knew if the shoe were on the other foot, then he wouldn't either.

"What happened when I tried to kill you?" he asked, skipping my question completely. I released a heavy sigh, knowing this was a road I really didn't want to travel down.

"To be honest unbeknown to me at the time, I was trying to kill you also… only in my defence, I didn't really know that was what I was doing." I added this last part when I saw the shock about to seep into rage.

"What were you doing?"

"I was burning you with the sun," I told him in a small voice. He gave me a thoughtful look as if he was trying to make sense of why this would hurt him, which was when multiple things occurred to me.

"Why doesn't the sun hurt you in this time?" I asked and he looked as if he was giving the question some thought.

"The only answer I have is that I am still a young vampire, if not the most powerful, I still have many years ahead of me to fully develop my demonic powers and reach my full potential. Maybe losing the sun is simply the price I must pay." Okay so that made sense but there was one other thing he needed to explain,

"But what about all the times I had shown you the sun when we kissed, how come that never burnt you?" I asked him totally forgetting that he had no clue we had ever kissed before tonight, which was why his eyes grew wide and his grin even wider.

"Just friends um…then pray, tell me sweet girl, just how *sweet* are you to the rest of your friends or is it just Vampire

Kings you hold in greater esteem above others?" I couldn't help but roll my eyes at this and then said in a whiney, outraged voice,

"It was you who kept kissing me!"

"Yes, and by the way you kissed me back tonight, then I can see that I was solely to blame for all this," he mocked and my mouth dropped open at his cocky bastardy! Okay, so I knew it wasn't exactly a word but there was just sometimes in life that when somebody said something really shocking, then inventing new words was needed. And this was one of them!

"I think you will recall I was the one that stopped the kiss… *just like all the other times I might add."* I said this last part muttering to myself. Lucius threw his head back and started laughing, as if this was the most fun he'd had in years and well considering his career choice, then not being too big headed but then yeah, maybe I was right.

"Yes, in your mind you might have stopped the kiss but I also know what your writhing hot, little body was telling me," he said, being a cocky ass again and I rolled my eyes and replied sarcastically,

"What, that you needed to open a damn window?" I thought this was pretty funny and so did he from the look of things but then I realised he was grinning for a different reason. I let out a high-pitched yelp when he suddenly grabbed me by the arms and pulled me into his embrace, sliding me up his outstretched body.

"You were saying, pet?" he asked seductively running a fingertip down the apple of my now, very heated cheek. He chuckled when I struggled for words.

"In answer to your question, I don't know why it is you show me the sun back in your time when we kiss, nor do I know why it doesn't burn me…but perhaps it is because the first time you did so fighting against me and the next…well maybe you were always supposed to show me my salvation." Hearing this my body froze against him. I think it was one of the sweetest things he had ever said to me and through our time together, I wasn't ashamed to say that there had been many. But hearing him calling me his salvation had me biting my lip and tears springing to my eyes. The intense look he gave me told me that he was taking in every detail of my response to his sweet words.

And it meant something dear to him.

In the end, my reaction to this was one I was never going to try and hold back. For I couldn't do it, not around Lucius. So, I placed both my hands to his cheeks, framing his handsome face and pulled him as close as I could, placing my forehead to his. Once under my mercy, I simply whispered a heartfelt,

"Thank you," I was about to pull back when his hand shot out and held on to the back of my neck, locking me to him and keeping me close. A startled breath left me on a faint whoosh sound and my hands dropped like dead weights to his shoulders.

"Keira, I..." he started to whisper back to me only it ended with a deep growl emitting from his chest as it rumbled with displeasure. I was about to ask him what was wrong but when he turned his glacial stare towards the door, I knew it hadn't been about me. No, it became clear what had him so angry…

We were being interrupted.

"Wait here." He snarled out the command and it wasn't one I was going to argue with. I knew his anger wasn't directed at me but more at the person on the other side of that door. He shifted from me, making sure I wasn't just going to face plant into the bed with him moving so quickly. Well, I had already showed him my ungraceful side, so I didn't think he needed to see it a second-time round.

I watched him stalk to the door, nearly ripping it from its hinges as he tore it open, before slamming it shut behind him. I jumped at the bang and then counted to all of five seconds before I was off the bed and at the door listening to what was being said.

"Why the fuck did you have her moved, I told you I would handle it!?" I heard the familiar voice say and seriously, I never knew up until now that Dariush had a death wish. Well, that answered my internal question of where my kidnapper had run off to.

I half expected in the next instance to hear the sound of him choking or having his throat ripped out by Lucius, but what surprised me wasn't what I didn't hear, it was what I did,

"Yes, and you were taking too long to do so."

"Yes, because I was out there fucking hunting the bastards that thought to rob us by the Tiberis and I couldn't risk anyone seeing the girl," Dariush snapped back venomously. I was left wondering why Lucius hadn't killed him yet. Oh, and secondly, (because this was me we were talking about) the next random question that popped into my head was…*is Tiberis the name of the river?*

"So, you thought to hide her in a whorehouse!" Lucius ground out shocking me enough to drop the river question and lead straight onto, 'Eww what the hell?' upon finding out that was what it had been. I thought back to the old woman and shivered but then the rational part of my brain kicked in and I thought that she must have been a servant, not a 'working girl'…and I use the term 'girl' loosely considering she must have been pushing on eighty.

"She had been knocked unconscious! What was I supposed to do, just wrap her in my cloak and walk her into the palace full of fucking dignitaries and senators, looking like I'd just dragged a dead body out of the river!" Dariush had a point if you asked me, although the sounds of Lucius' growl told me that he didn't agree.

"It is of little consequence now as I had my men take care of it," Lucius told him matter of fact and this time it was Dariush's turn to growl.

"Yes, and how did that go, because from what I heard she jumped out of a fucking window terrified!" Again, he had a point.

"Back off Decarabia, for she is no longer your concern," Lucius warned with that deadly dip in his voice that spoke of violence. Now I was asking myself what Decarabia meant?

"That maybe so but my dirty work isn't exactly done yet, is it?"

"It is where the girl is concerned," Lucius informed him coolly.

"And another thing, speak to that bitch in heat, Lahash and sort her shit out." The second I heard the name I knew I had heard it somewhere before.

"Why, what has she done now?" Lucius asked as if sounding casually bored now they were no longer arguing over me.

"I overheard her telling one of the senator's wives again how any day now, there should be an announcement made of your impending marriage." This time both my and Lucius' reactions were the same, as we sucked in a staggered, surprised breath. Okay, so his was more of a hissed-out sneer but unfortunately for me, both of which were heard. The next thing I knew the door was yanked open and because my cheek had been pressed against the panel, I therefore had no choice but to fall forward. Lucius had of course planned for this and was stood there waiting to catch me…and catch me he did.

"Well, well, look what I found," Lucius said in a reprimanding tone as my face was now plastered against his bare chest. I looked to Dariush to see him with his arms folded, smirking.

"Uh…would you believe I needed to use the bathroom?" I

said looking up at him, making Lucius' lip twitch. Then he lifted me up so I was no longer stuck to his chest and I looked up at him once more, no doubt looking like a kid caught stealing sweets.

Once I was back and steady on my feet, he nodded to the door behind me and ordered,

"Inside, *now!*" I looked back at it and then at Dariush before hearing Lucius sigh as if this was all very taxing on his nerves. Then before I could move and comply with his stern command, he started walking me backwards, leading me as I went, with a hand held possessively at my hip. Dariush followed us in and closed the door behind him.

"Keira," Dariush said with a nod and I frowned at him and answered in return,

"Kidnapper." He grinned hearing this and replied,

"Just following orders from this broody son of a bastard!" I quickly shot a look to Lucius, half expecting to see rage bubbling up at the disrespect but all I found was a face of indifference. I had to wonder then who Dariush really was to Lucius to be able to get away with talking to him like that as I had never met anyone other than Draven who could do so and live long enough to make the claim.

"Yes, and if I am to be called as such, then you also must stand against the claim, considering that bastard you speak of is one we must share." Hearing this I would have fallen back on my ass had it not been for Lucius' hand holding me steady.

Was he really saying what I thought he was saying?! No surely not, surely that wasn't possible…was it?! Lucius must have seen the disbelief for himself and he looked intrigued to the fact I obviously didn't know, something he quickly confirmed with his next sentence,

"Keira as you know this is Dariush Decarabia…" Then he paused and tapped his chin before adding,

"…but what I find odd and it's clear to me you obviously don't know is…"

Lucius never finished off the sentence as Dariush himself walked forward, hit Lucius on the back and dropped a nuclear sized, family bombshell…

"I'm his brother."

CHAPTER TWENTY-NINE

OH BROTHER

"Your brother!" The sound of my high-pitched voice was almost loud enough to be heard back outside the grand entrance.

"Yes," Lucius said, his jaw tight. I looked off to the side and shook my head before looking back at him again.

"A brother?" I repeated.

"You know, I think she's getting it now," Dariush commented, clearly amused by my stunned disbelief. Well, he should be considering I knew nothing about him, in this time or my own. Holy shit, Lucius had a brother! Lucius shot him a glare but refrained from saying anything in response to him. Instead he kept his steely blue eyes on me and folded his arms.

"You have a brother?" I asked Lucius this time, needing to hear *him* say it.

"I do."

"On our father's side, of course," Dariush added in jest and Lucius finally snapped.

"That's enough," he snarled, looking round over his shoulder, as Dariush was still stood behind him by the door.

"Leave us," Lucius said after taking a deep breath and this time he looked over at his brother, conveying something silently between them. Dariush nodded and left without saying another word.

"Does Draven know?" I blurted out the question the second the door closed.

"It's complicated," he answered after running a frustrated hand through his hair.

"Then uncomplicate it for me," I replied haughtily and I couldn't understand why I was so upset. Well okay, so that was a lie as I knew why. Lucius and I were close and at a level I knew was a single thread away from being wrong. But as always that fact couldn't be helped as it seemed to be forged in our destiny's making. However, this wasn't what pained me now, no it was that this was something huge and it had been kept from me. Now the next question was why?

"It is not that simple."

"I disagree," I told him and we quickly found ourselves at loggerheads. He took another deep breath and then held his arm out towards the seating area.

"Come, sit with me." I followed him over to the plush looking couches and sat opposite him, hoping I could take this as a sign that he would explain things to me. However, at the sight of him bent over, with forearms to his knees and as he continued to remain silent, I found that I could take it no longer.

"I am sorry Lucius, but you have got to give me something here." He looked up at me and for a minute, he looked so deep in thought, almost as if he had forgotten I was even in the room.

"I don't know why my brother was never known to you in your own time, for that I cannot answer." Okay, so that was fair enough.

"But I assume you know of how I came to be...yes?" I thought about this question and I was mentally transported back to my house, sat with Draven on the couch hanging onto his every word as he told me of how Lucius came to be, well...*Lucius.* I nodded unable to keep the sadness from my face. Lucius had felt betrayed by Jesus and by the God he believed in, so with his dying breath, he renounced his faith, quickly finding a new god to worship instead...*Lucifer.*

King of the Underworld.

"Come now, you shouldn't look so sad, for as you see, it turned out well enough for me," he said, motioning down his body and trying to ease my sadness with a glimmer of his cocky side. But what Lucius didn't know was that I knew the true depth of his feelings on the matter and this feigned acceptance wasn't going to fly with me.

"Tell me," was all I needed to say. In response, there seemed to be only one thing that Lucius needed to say in return.

"Dariush was the one who buried me." My mouth dropped open right on cue as shock quickly replaced my 'tell me now' attitude.

"You mean...*the day you died?*" I uttered as if it was a sin to speak of it.

"The day I was *killed*, yes," he corrected. His answer was a grim one and mirrored the hard, thin line that had become his lips.

"By the other disciples?" He nodded and I couldn't help but notice the way his hands turned to fists as if he could still see the pain of it all.

"I was no traitor." He hissed out these words as if he had done the same back when being hung from that tree. I closed my eyes for a few seconds before telling him softly,

"I know." He looked as though those two little words of acceptance meant the world to him and for long moments he

was silent as if digesting them whole. Consuming my belief in him and keeping it safe with him always. At least that was what it looked like.

"Once I drew my final mortal breath, the last face I saw was Dariush. He told me that the end of this life would only mark the beginning of my next. The last thing I remember was the sun turning red just before the moon eclipsed it from sight… that was when my eternal night captured the day." I swallowed hard and then bit my lip just to stop it from shaking.

"What…what happened next?" I asked, forcing the sentence out on a shaky breath.

"The next time I awoke, I was in Hell." I quickly sucked in a sharp breath and my hands flew to my mouth. I don't know why hearing this affected me as strongly as it did, as it wasn't like I didn't know this part of the story.

"And there you met Lucifer?"

"I did and I was given a choice. Live out my death paying for my one and only committed sin or rise above it all and take the first step along a new path." Well when he put it like that, then yeah, I couldn't say that I blamed him.

"So, you became a Vampire King." It was a statement not a question and one he grinned at.

"This Draven from your time has told you much about me, I presume?" *Now this was a question.* And a hard one at that.

"Well back when you were his enemy and wanted to take me, I kind of asked about you," I said feeling suddenly embarrassed about saying this.

"And why was I his enemy then and not sooner I wonder… tell me, for I am curious, was it when you happened to stumble into his life?" Wow, okay so where in the world had that question come from?

"I…um…" I 'um' didn't know what the hell to say, that's what I *ummed!*

"I will take that as my answer," he told me with a smirk and this time, it was one that I was thankful for as it meant I was off the hook. I mean what could I say exactly…*No, it had nothing to do with me, it was all to do with finding out your lifelong friend and King had lied to you since the first day you met. Oh, and that lost relic that you have been searching for your whole, immortal life, well yeah, he has it!*

No, I didn't think so somehow. Which now begged the question… why on earth did he no longer consider Draven his ally and was it because of me? What had he gotten into his head this time?

"So Dariush buried you, how does that make him your brother?" I asked moving swiftly on from the long list of crazy questions I wanted to ask.

"Cause' I gather you don't mean he is like a blood relative…right?" I added, trying to make sense of so many things right now, my head felt like mush…mush named Lucius!

"But that's where you are wrong as we *are* 'blood brothers' just not in the mortal sense you understand it to be." I frowned at him and said,

"Okay, your gonna have to help me out with that one." He chuckled and said,

"To turn me into what I am now, Lucifer had to gift his blood to me. That same blood is what keeps my heart beating as its essence and power never leaves me but in turn it transformed my own blood, granting it the ability to gift a diluted form of it back to others." He gave me a small smile when he saw my confused look in return.

"It enables me to turn others into my kind," he elaborated.

"Oh."

"But Dariush… I still don't see…" I was about to carry on when Lucius interrupted me.

"As far as I know, Lucifer has only gifted his blood to two people in his existence, one was me and the other…"

"Dariush," I uttered his name, this time finishing off for him.

"It was his payment for retrieving me. I became the ruler of all Vampires and Dariush became the Great Marquis in Hell and King of the shifter portals. He was also granted thirty legions of demons under his command."

"What are the shifter portals?" I asked wondering if they had anything to do with all those walls he had pulled me through.

"Shifter portals are summoned doorways." Yep, so I had hit the nail on the supernatural head…*for once, my subconscious muttered at me.*

"Doorways to where?" I asked fascinated.

"To anywhere of his choosing," he answered with a casual shrug of his shoulders.

"But how?"

"He can manipulate the power gained from Hell and use it to temporary create a gateway, sometimes this gateway could be to the next room say, or another building. Then sometimes, he can summon one to a far greater distance."

"Like a mountain trail," I said thinking back to my journey here.

"Yes. Although the further he travels, the more energy he uses. In fact, the easiest places for him to travel to are back in his home," Lucius informed me and when I asked my next question he smirked as if he was waiting for it.

"And where is that?"

"Hell."

"Oh…right." Of course, duh Keira! So now I was wondering what a penthouse apartment looked like in Hell and how much they went for? Ten, twenty souls a month with a serial killer deposit!

"The summoned portals he creates are much stronger when they connect to the place his power still remains rooted to. However, on this plane, the portals he creates are only substantial enough to hold for one or two people and even then he must use the blood of his companion, so that they are accepted to travel through… unless of course he wants them to be ripped apart like the Aeolus' eyes he can summon," Lucius said, as though thinking back on a particular gruesome time with a grin. I thought about what he had said, thinking about the cut on my neck he had inflicted and the same blood he had used to touch the portal with. He had done that to protect me? Of course, this wasn't the question I asked,

"What is an Aeolus' eye?" Lucius threw his head back and started laughing as if talking about such things was his idea of a rootin', tootin' barn dance for a cowboy.

"Upon my word but I have never known so many questions to be asked by a female, and one with such dangerous curiosity." I crossed my arms over my chest and gave him my best 'I am not impressed' look. He simply ended up laughing at this as well.

"It is a simple but deadly vortex originally created by Aeolus, the God of wind and Perses, the God of destruction. They were both given the task by Zeus to create such a deadly force. There aren't many that can wield such power as easily as Dariush can but it makes for a torturous weapon, along with an effective prison…or so I am told." The second he said the word 'prison' a horrific memory hit me.

I was locked in the centre of a storm, one raging around me and keeping me from escaping. I braved reaching out, testing my fingertips against it and not understanding the true nature of the destructive force that faced me. I was then left to watch on in horror as my skin and flesh were stripped from bone in mere seconds.

"Tartarus." The word slipped from my lips before I could stop it and Lucius hadn't missed it.

"Now I have to wonder what you would know of such a place." My head shot up and I struggled on what to say next.

"Only…uh… what I have been told," I replied, hoping this was enough.

"There are not many who venture to the deepest level of Hell and make it out again to tell the tale…something you're not telling me perhaps?" he asked, obviously not trusting my blustered words. So, I told him a few facts, starting with the main truth of it all.

"Look, there are a lot of things that have happened to me since I met you and Draven, most of which I really can't tell you about since it could affect the future…I just don't know. But I can tell you this, you have saved my life more times than I can count and you have helped me without question whenever I needed it. You are a good and loyal friend, who always has my back, no matter what and…" I never got chance to finish as he was looming over me in a pounding heartbeat. He placed a bent knee in between my legs and caged me in with his hands gripping onto either side of me on the couch.

"Now listen to me and listen carefully, for I will not repeat these words again…understand?" I bit my lip and nodded, feeling out of depth in seconds and silently asking myself what had happened to set him off. I didn't need to ask myself this for long.

"I am not your friend," he all but snarled at me.

"You're not?" I asked on a breathless whisper, one almost none existent from heartbreak.

"No," he stated firmly making me flinch back. It felt as if I had been slapped and for a moment I was contemplating pushing out of his hold and storming out of the room. Not that I would have got far of course. But then I found he wasn't finished as I thought. No, he continued to speak and this time, he made sure that I listened…

"I. Am. So. Much. *More.*" He enunciated each word with each inch he eliminated between us. I swallowed hard, forcing myself not to choke on the intensity he had ignited between us.

"Lucius…don't…don't do this…*please.*" I pleaded with him, placing a hand on his chest to stop him from taking possession of my lips again. To be honest, I didn't think I would survive it a second time.

"Then I suggest you never speak of such things again, for if I hear you mention 'friendship' to me once more, then I will prove otherwise through very actionable means and little Keira girl…" he paused so that he could lean in closer, whispering his lips against my neck before drawing his nose up the length making me shudder. Once he reached my ear he nipped at it before finishing his threat…

"…You will fucking love it!" I closed my eyes against the sexual urges building to near crescendo level and by the time I braved opening them again,

He was gone.

Shortly after this a servant knocked on the door and brought in plates of food. I nearly wept with joy. She was a young little thing, with a sweet face and chubby cheeks that made her eyes disappear when she smiled. I watched with curiosity when she walked behind a large screen in the corner of the room and walked out holding a large empty pot. As soon as I saw it, I raced over to her, took it out of her hands and held up one finger, indicating for her to give me one minute. She blushed and smiled, nodding. Then I took what felt like a gift from the Gods and released my pained bladder into what was commonly known as a 'Piss pot'. It felt almost as satisfying as gorging myself on the food after she had left.

There was every meat imaginable and everything was cut into small bite sized pieces as there wasn't a fork or knife in sight. Which made eating the fish in a delicious sauce somewhat of a messy sight but seriously it was just so good, I couldn't help myself. I was just about to pick up something that was dripping in honey and poppy seeds when Lucius stepped back into the room.

I was just thankful to see that leaving the room and giving us both the space we needed hadn't been in vain.

I quickly looked down and licked my lips, in hopes I didn't have sticky food around my mouth as Lucius stalked towards me, watching my actions like a hungry wolf.

"I see you're enjoying my hospitality," he commented with a one-sided mischievous grin. Then he stopped right in front of me, lifted up my face with one hand and then gently wiped some honey that had dripped down my chin. He raised it to his lips and licked it clean off the pad of his thumb. I was almost panting from the sight and the cocky bastard knew it!

"The food is delicious…I was just about to try these but I am still trying to figure out what meat it is," I told him holding up the honey coated morsel and trying to keep my voice even and not as strained as it felt. Besides, it seemed like a good way to change the 'you have a sticky sweet substance dripping down your body, here let me lick it off you' vibe he had going on.

"Ah, a Roman delicacy…"

"Oh, okay," I said lifting it to my lips and just as I was about to put it in my mouth he continued with,

"A dormouse." I dropped the dead skinned rodent back in

the golden bowl with a splat of honey. My mouth hung open in horror before I swallowed down the bile I felt about to rise.

"A…a what now?" I asked hoping that I had heard him wrong.

"A dormouse. Here we catch them from the wild in autumn when they are at their fattest…here, try one for they are quite good," Lucius said picking one up and holding it out to me to bite. I slammed my mouth shut and shook my head in little jerky motions. Then I swallowed again and again. Oh god, were those little feet I could see sticking out…Oh Christ no!

Here it came…

I was suddenly up and out of my seat like my ass was on fire. I dashed behind the privacy screen just in time to throw up in the now empty piss pot. I heaved and heaved until all my lovely meal was now wasted at the sight of one little honey covered mouse…oh jeez, here it came again.

"No, no, really I will be…" I tried to say as I felt Lucius come up behind me and lower to his knees at my back. Then he gathered up all my hair and held it back for me as I continued to vomit. He started rubbing my back in big circles with his free hand and once he thought I had finished, he then picked up a goblet of water he had brought with him, passing it to me. I swallowed again, making sure nothing else was going to come up. Then I nodded my thanks before taking the cup and nearly downing the whole lot. It felt like heaven sliding down my burning throat.

"Easy, or you will soon find yourself sick again," he said taking it from me. I felt so embarrassed I lowered my head and wished I could have buried it somewhere.

"Better?" he asked, tucking in his chin so he could catch sight of my eyes. I nodded and bit my lip, not trusting myself to speak. I usually blurted out random crap when feeling this way, so decided silence was definitely golden and not vomit coloured. Seriously, I hadn't even eaten any bloody carrots!

"Put your hands around my neck," he told me softly and when I didn't do as I was told quickly enough, he reached out and grabbed my wrists in his hold. Then he lifted them up and once he felt me holding on, he tucked an arm under my legs and lifted me off the floor. It was done with so little effort, it was scary to think of the strength and power this man held in a single hand, let alone all of him. It was also a thought that had me shivering in his hold, an action he put down to me being ill and not the real reason of me shamefully being turned on.

He walked back into the room and instead of walking us back to the seating area he turned away from it.

Then I asked the dangerous question,

"Where are you taking me?" receiving an even more dangerous answer in return…

"I am taking you to my bed, Keira girl."

CHAPTER THIRTY

THIRD TIME'S A CHARM

Standing in front of the mirror now and I barely recognised myself. My hair had been brushed so many times, I was surprised I had any left. But this, combined with the strange oil they had first rubbed on their palms and then smoothed through the strands, made it look like spun gold.

And this had just been the start.

But I am getting way ahead of myself, as it all started that morning when waking up in a Vampire's arms. The room had been dark, with just the slightest cracks letting in the light around the windows. It then occurred to me that at some point in the night Lucius must have left my side to lower the reinforced shutters over the windows. It seemed as if he still had an aversion to the light after all.

He had carried me to the bed last night and when he felt me tense in his hold he tenderly pushed back the hair from my forehead and whispered,

"I will have you…you can be sure of that but that time is in our future, not our present. Now sleep, for you will need rest for tomorrow." I had been about to ask him what he meant but with a small shake of his head I knew now was not the time. So, once he had rolled me to my side, he nestled me against him, tucking me into his strong body. I had to admit, it wasn't the worst way to fall asleep.

However, that night my mind didn't sleep as easy as I would have hoped as it was filled with nothing but death and destruction. For I found myself stood imprisoned in my own nightmare of what I prayed would never come.

A War.

It raged all around me like a storm I could neither run from or control. It was like finding yourself trapped by your own doing. No one seemed to notice me but there I stood, in the middle of a demonic battlefield watching both sides dropping like flies. I didn't even know which side I was on, for both looked just as monstrous. Winged demons, attacked from the dark sky. Some falling onto their prey as if fired from catapults and other swooping low and plucking soldiers from the battlefield like mice in the clutches of eagles.

I didn't know why but my knees gave out and I hit the floor just as the first sound of death reached my ears. The sound of death for us all. Those who had been imprisoned in Tartarus had been merely used as pawns, placed at the front line as a prelude to the main event. Their lives didn't matter. No one's did. We would all die and there would be nothing left to save.

No Heaven, no Hell and no Earth to call home for any of us. A new start, a new birth...*a cleansing*...that's what he called it. But first to cleanse the land, you had to destroy the weeds that infected it,

And we were the weeds.

Angels classed as the righteous wrongs and corruption in Heaven and Demons the vile filth coating the surface of each level of Hell. And then there were the humans...

Humans he classed as the *rot among the earth.*

This is what he had told me. Whispered in my ear like some promised secret he spoke of before all the rest. He wanted me to know first. He wanted to torture me with the future, a future that no matter what I did now, I couldn't change. He laughed in the face of the prophecy and cursed out the Fates, taunting them to prove their worth. Challenging all who stood in his way…*including me.*

I felt him approach through the blood and flesh of the fallen. He parted the field of death like a tangible wave he could control. Everything I now knew, all my thoughts of doubt, planted there by this being. This master of eradication…

"Cronus!" I hissed his name, spitting the blood I felt pooling against my bitten lips, aiming by his feet as they approached me. All of these thoughts of powerless means, whispered to feed the doubts of my mind. I needed to breathe free air. I needed to hold on to the hope that not all was lost. But he made such a task nearly impossible to fight against.

"You cannot win against a war that has already been won," he told me calmly as though we were not standing at the mouth of a Hell he had created. But no, that wasn't true. For when he knelt next to me I felt his talon under my chin, forcing my face up to meet the born cruelty in his eyes. He leant closer to my ear and whispered the sickening truth in my ear. This was his secret kept and now passed on, it soon became mine. A secret to torture my soul until my dying breath.

I sucked in a sharp breath, feeling the tears fall with my back to the mountain, for I could not watch what I had done.

I couldn't watch the…

War I had created.

After this I had started screaming and thankfully found myself not alone. Lucius had me in his arms and for one moment my tears weren't solely from my dream, but waking and finding the wrong arms around me. I didn't remember what Cronus had told me in my nightmare but the effects of it stayed with me like a poisonous veil no-one but I could see. It felt as though it was dripping from me, sticking to the ground and trying to pull me under. I knew it was something important, those words he spoke. I knew they held the key to something but what, I didn't know.

"Ssshh, it will be alright, it was just a nightmare," Lucius cooed, before kissing the top of my head. He had a hand to my cheek, cradling me to his chest. I absorbed his comfort like a child would to a security blanket, but deep down I knew it wouldn't be enough.

"I need to know," I whispered in the dark and I felt him pull back slightly so that he could look at me.

"What…what is it you need to know, Keira?" He asked me so tenderly, this too even felt as if it could have been a dream.

"I need to know what was whispered in my ear…a man, a being…someone in my nightmare…I felt like, well like it could be something important," I told him with a voice that was strained and close to pleading with him. I heard it myself and almost felt ashamed by how weak it sounded. But, however Lucius had heard it, it had been enough for him to say yes.

"Lie back." I did as he asked and feeling his presence looming over me in the dark didn't make me feel half as uneasy as it should have done.

"I need you to open your mind to me." As soon as he said this I grabbed his arm and told him in panic induced words,

"You can't…I can't."

"Relax, I promise only to look for the lost remains of your dream," he told me but even then, my fingers gripped him tighter and I was now asking myself what was more important. There was so much he couldn't be allowed to know but then on the other end of the scales was the fate of the world, hanging there like a promised doom. I knew I had to chance it. I knew if there was anything that could be learned from this, then now could be my one and only shot. Lucius could obviously see my inner turmoil of what I should and shouldn't do, so knowing that I needed it, he eased my fears,

"I give you my word. I will not pry into the vault of your mind, I will only reach out to the surface of thoughts, in hopes that fragments of the dream remain. If I find nothing, I will see nothing…*trust me."* I nodded as after hearing this, then I knew he was right, I needed to trust him. So, I did as he asked. I tried to relax and nodded my thanks to him, when he lit some of the candles with his mind, so I was no longer doing it in the dark.

Then it began and I tried to visualise allowing access to my once impenetrable fortress, one I had spent years building. I knew I wasn't destroying it, I was merely creating a door, one that I knew I could slam shut with but a single thought.

I knew the second he was in as I felt a warmth surround me as though he was still trying to sooth my worries and ease my mind. He didn't make it feel as though an intruder was trying to break in, but more like a friend was just casually having a look around. I know it sounded weird and a whole bucket load of crazy but there was no other way to describe it. Or was there?

I guess the only other way I could think about it was like looking at someone you kept a secret from and seeing them give you a single look that had you questioning yourself. Could they hear your thoughts…? Did they see your guilt for themselves? Could they read the lies on your face or hear you soundlessly whispering of your desire? Well, that was what it was like having someone access your mind. As though someone could see what you never intended them to see.

I didn't feel it in my mind when Lucius finally found what he was searching for, no it was his eyes that told me. They bled into crimson fire and I flinched back out of reflex. The second I did he snapped his eyes shut and once he opened them again, they were back to grey stone with flecks of blue.

Lucius shocked me when he explained he hadn't seen anything of my dream or heard of the whispered promise spoken in my ear. My disappointment had been clear to see but he assured me that if I had another, then I must tell him straight away, for he may have another chance at seeing it for himself. I made him that promise and fell back asleep in his arms, clinging on to new hope.

Which brought me back to now and after the team of girls, none of which I could understand, had all left. Of course, what they had left behind was a mere shell of what I usually looked like, for as I said, I could barely believe my eyes. My hair had been braided in such a way that it had become like a band over the top of my head, framing the gold crown that sat there, before it's length coiled round to one side, where loose curls sat over my shoulder. The crown itself was a delicate and dainty piece that fanned out in a band of gold, inlayed with filigree rose gold and speckled with tiny jewels. It was beautiful and matched the dress was wearing.

It was pure white chiffon and it floated around me every time I moved. It almost looked as though all my movements were being made under water as it danced around my skin. The skirt was long and hid the gold sandals that were wrapped up my ankles. All the material was edged with a thin gold border in the same design as the filigree on my crown.

It was as if a huge square piece of chiffon had been crossed over a tight silky underdress, one that at least managed to keep my breasts firm and secure. The overlapped parts of the chiffon then gathered at my shoulders, creating a plunging neck line and the excess flowed down my back, draping like a cape that followed me. A thick gold belt pulled it all in under my bust, tying into a knot at the back. At first the girls had wanted to keep it knotted at the front but I thought it looked silly, so I spun it round once they had left.

Now I had no clue why I was dressed this way as Lucius hadn't told me anything before leaving. The only thing he had done was open the doors for a team of girls and issued some snapped order at them in Latin. Things had seemed tense for him since waking and I didn't know whether it had anything to do with my nightmare and his failed attempt at trying to get a read on it or...well I didn't really want to think about the 'or' bit.

It had started when I woke to find him staring down at me, my torso encased safely in his embrace. But then once conscious thought started to become clearer in my head and the fog of sleep had left me, I realised exactly what he was looking at. I instantly tried to pull my arm from his hold and the fingertips that were softly caressing my scars. However, he wouldn't allow it and merely tightened his hold on me as I struggled.

"Easy now for I am not hurting you," he informed me softly and I quickly gave up the fight.

"Who did this to you?" he asked me gently and I wanted to groan out my frustrations as I really didn't want to be doing this again.

"It was a long time ago...*for me anyway.*" I added this last part as that time hadn't arrived yet and wouldn't for too many lifetimes to count.

"Then I only want to know one thing," he said surprising

me, as unlike Draven, Lucius wasn't interested in all the details. No, he only wanted to know one and something he classed as the most important,

"Did he suffer?"

"Yes." I forced the word out through gritted teeth, thinking back to the day he died and *I almost died with him*. This one worded answer told Lucius the two things he wanted to know, one was if he was dead and the second was it painful enough. I would say first being flung across a cabin, having a knife plunged into his heart and then finding himself at the bottom of a ravine could be classed as suffering. But then again to these guys, if it didn't include some medieval looking torture chamber, then it was probably not what they called '*suffering enough'*.

"Good, my only regret is that it was not by my own hands and I wasn't there to care for you after the ordeal." I raised my hand to his cheek and whispered a sincere,

"Thank you." Then I reached up and kissed him lightly on the cheek. To be honest I was just grateful that I didn't have to explain it all again and I could just marvel in the fact that seeing them bare like this, didn't seem to affect the way he looked at me at all. He just continued to stroke along each line as if he had the power to erase it with just his simple caress.

Of course, now I looked down at them and no longer saw the shadows of my past looming over me but more the journey lines that enabled me to walk towards my future. I took that decision from Morgan that day and chose freedom, whether that be death or life. I took away his control and all this time I should have looked at these scars feeling proud, instead of ashamed.

It was like Vincent had said to me that day, the scars are only skin deep, they don't connect to my heart or my soul and they don't define me, I defined them. And he was right. All this time I had been defining them as a sign of weakness when in actual fact, I should have been defining them as strength.

A strength I certainly needed when the door suddenly flew open and in walked someone who had tried to kill me twice before.

"You!" I hissed, balling my fists in anger. I should have known that she would have been slithering around this time and trying to cling onto Lucius. I knew when I heard the name Lahash that something was tugging at my memories and now here she was in the slutty flesh. Even now in this time, she was dressed like a hooker, with a dress that looked barely covering her breasts. It was made of two measly strips of silk tied at her shoulders and gold braided thread coiled around her body, and bare sides. Her blonde hair was pinned as high as she could get it and her lips curled in anger, snarling at me like an aggressive dog.

"Tu putas turn te non tantum ut est hic et uxores peregrinas?!" ('You think you can just turn up here and take him from me!') She shouted something furiously at me in Latin and I actually rolled my eyes thinking, 'Christ, not this shit again!' Seriously, was there even a place left for me in the world where there wasn't some asshole trying to kill me?!

"Do me a favour and fuck off, Layla I don't have time for your shit!" I snapped and her mouth dropped and nearly hit the floor. It looked as though I was the first person to ever speak to her this way and I revelled in the idea. Good, it was about time for some payback…now if I could just find my 'angry powers' to follow it up with then that would be just peachy. Preferably before she tried to kill me this time. But unlike last time, I decided not to make the same mistake twice and do something that I should have done every bloody time she had approached me with death in mind. Well, that's the good thing about hindsight…I now finally had some good sense to use it. Oh, and there was the whole, travelling back in time thing, so that helped.

"I will kill you…" she started to say, meaning she did so in Persian for I could now understand her. Well, at least she got the hint and so did I when she started to pull a deadly looking blade from behind her back. She raised it high ready to run at me. But that's when I unleashed my best weapon against her,

"AHHHH LUCIUS SHE'S TRYING TO KILL ME!!" I screamed with everything I had in me and I wouldn't have been surprised if glass had shattered from the force of it. She looked back to the door with panic clear in her eyes, no doubt trying to judge how long she had to get the job done. But in this time, I reached off to one side and grabbed a big gold statue of the eagle that Lucius had told me symbolised Rome. Then I stormed over to her as she was still looking at the door.

"Hey bitch, miss me?!" I said getting her attention and the second she looked back at me I swung the heavy beast by the legs and let it smash into her face. I could not express the satisfaction I felt when I saw her eyes grow wide with shock before the gold wings connected with her head. Lucius ran through the door just in time to see her hit the floor like a meat sack but he didn't miss the blade that fell from her hand as it skidded across the marble floor.

"For the Senate and People of Rome, bitch!" I snarled down at her the words I now knew were written on the plaque before dropping the big bird with a cracking thud on the floor beside her. Then I looked up to Lucius and said,

"You know that's the third time that bitch has tried to kill me, so you have no idea how good that felt." His eyes widened in shock and then narrowed down at the writhing Layla, who was now looking very worse for wear. But I had to say, the blood looked good on her. Man, he looked pissed.

"Master, look what she did to me!" Layla started to moan,

holding her bloody jaw before reaching out a hand to Lucius. He looked down at it before taking it in his own. I was just getting ready to step up to him and kick him in the balls for being so blind stupid when thankfully he proved me wrong. He yanked her up hard enough to pop her arm from her shoulder and her screams died when he spun her round and in a single second, he had her slammed against the wall with his hand encasing her throat.

"You dare come here and attack her!" He threw the words at her and she flinched before trying to defend herself and when I say defend herself, what I actually mean is lie through her asshole with the amount of shit that spewed from her lips!

"It was her that attacked me! I came here to merely congratulate her on your upcoming wedding!"

"Umm…my what now?" I asked but no one was listening to me as he just gripped her neck in a tighter hold, one that had her desperately trying to tear his hand from her. Then he looked towards the knife on the floor, one she didn't know he had seen fly from her hand just before she hit the floor.

"Is that right?" he asked her dangerously, luring her into his false acceptance.

"Yes, yes my lord. She must have attacked me out of jealously, for I only wanted to wish her well," she said adding even more layers to her mountain of lies. I couldn't help it but I snorted a laugh, one Lucius snapped his head at, giving me a dark look. I wanted to roll my eyes at him but seeing him this way, nearly on the verge of dismemberment, well then, I thought it best not to add to his pissed off killing state right now. Thankfully, he turned his attention back to the bitch at hand and asked her in a murderous tone,

"Then tell me Lahash, do you usually bring a blade with you when offering such happy sentiments or did you suddenly find yourself fearful of mortals?" Layla knew that she had fucked up when she shot a panicked look to the blade on the floor and then back to him.

"My lord I…" She never got chance to finish as he pulled her head back a bit so that he could then hammer it back into the wall, cracking it with the force. Then he roared mere inches from her face,

"YOU TRIED TO TAKE HER FROM ME!" Now, unlike my own mighty scream for help, his bellowing rage did smash glass as a wave of power emitted from him, smashing shutters, pottery, mirrors, and even cracking one of the posts on the bedframe. Oh shit, but Lucius hitting that level of anger was enough to make a person pee themselves and beg for a forgiveness they didn't even know they had sinned for.

After roaring this in her face he flung her body off to one side making her roll a few times before hitting into the furniture like a human sized bowling ball.

"Get her out of my sight!" Lucius lashed out the order and for a crazy second I thought he was talking to me but then I saw Dariush step into the room followed by the general he had called Marcus. Dariush strolled over to the whimpering Layla and hauled her up by the back of her dress. Then he passed her over to Marcus and said only two words,

"Carcer Tullianum." ('Tullianum Prison') Even Marcus looked stunned and I had to wonder with both his and Layla's reaction, what that place was. Layla let out an almighty scream and started trying to twist free, frantic eyes pleading with Lucius.

"No! You can't do this! Don't…not there! Not there please, my Lord!" but Lucius wasn't listening, no instead he walked straight up to me and took me by the shoulders.

"Are you alright?" he asked me tenderly. I bit my lip and nodded, momentarily stunned to silence at the sight of his worry. I looked over his shoulder to see Dariush nod once for

Marcus to take her. He did and when she started to try and fight against him, I was surprised to see that he too wasn't without his own powers. Marcus simply placed a hand inches from her face and after muttering something I couldn't hear, she quickly passed out. He hoisted her up into his arms and left with his burden, now a little more compliant.

"Dariush, go and make the necessary excuses and tell them we won't be long," Lucius ordered without looking back at his brother.

"It is typical for the woman to be late, or so I hear," Dariush commented strangely and I frowned, making him chuckle as he left the room, closing the door behind him.

"Did she hurt you?" he asked again as if he had to make sure.

"No, not this time."

"You said that this was the third…am I to believe that she attempted to take your life twice back in your own time?" he asked, his voice dropping dangerously low.

"Yes. She stabbed me the first time and then pushed me from your balcony into a frozen lake the next," I told him, quickly flinching back when he growled. However, he just stepped back into me and wrapped an arm around my waist.

"My balcony?" he questioned and I nodded.

"Yes."

"What happened?" he asked clearly curious, as it was obvious I didn't drown or become a Keira popsicle sitting at the bottom of the lake like she had hoped.

"You saved me."

"Good…and then I killed her I presume."

"Ah well, not exactly…she escaped and is currently still at large." Okay so he *did not* like the sound of that if his sudden crimson stare was anything to go by. So, I decided to brave calming him down by reaching up my hand and cupping his cheek.

"But if it makes you feel any better, this is the first time I got chance to finally hit her back…" I then reached up on my tip toes and whispered,

"…And it felt oh so gooooood." I was happy to report that this finally had him grinning again and I wondered if it had anything to do with the comical way I dragged out the word 'good'.

"I am glad to hear it, little one," he said tapping me on the chin.

"Where is he taking her? That place Dariush said…"

"Carcer Tullianum." Lucius repeated his brother's words cutting me off.

"What is that place?" I asked quietly.

"A place reserved for Rome's fiercest enemies, an underground prison that is as old as Rome itself and has more tales of horror there than any other place on Earth. It also holds a direct portal to Hell itself and therefore serves my needs when faced with a traitor of a different kind," he said and I shuddered even thinking about it, remembering all too well where Draven had kept her under the unsuspecting grounds of Afterlife.

"But enough talk of such dire things, not on this day." I was just about to ask him what he meant when he suddenly paused.

Then his eyes grew wide as if he had only just noticed something. I was about to ask what as I looked up at him with a frown, but he took a step back so that he could take in all of my image. He gave me a leisurely look up and down, making my cheeks heat as he scrutinised every inch of me. It was only when I finally braved meeting his eyes that I saw the animalistic lust staring back at me.

He liked what he saw…*very much.*

"The Gods will envy me on this day, for I have no doubt," he told me, making my blush deepen. So, I asked him,

"Why, what happens today?" He gave me a bigger grin, one I knew to be wary of especially when he told me,

"Today I make you mine…" Then he paused, yanked me forward and finished his sentence in whispered torment by my ear.

"…By marrying you."

CHAPTER THIRTY-ONE

ONE WEDDING AND A DEATH THREAT

After this Lucius kissed me lightly using my stunned reactions against me and then whispered, *"Don't keep me waiting, little Keira girl."* And then after that he was gone. I was left standing there alone and utterly speechless. Could he be serious! He wanted to marry me!? I mean was the guy insane!? Okay, so these questions continued like this for some time as I had no clue what to do next. It was obvious Lucius had lost his ever-loving mind if he thought that he could just kidnap me one day and then marry me the next!

And seriously, what was it with men back in this time? Did they even bother to ask a woman if she wanted to marry them? Or did they just announce it to the world or worse, plan the bloody thing, stick them in a dress and then spring it on them at the sodding altar! Was I going mad or was this as seriously messed up as I thought it was?!

Well, there was one thing I was sure of and that was I wasn't leaving this room, not unless he wanted to marry someone bound and gagged...okay, definitely not going down that road, not with a kinky ass vampire like Lucius. But still, surely the bride had to be A; conscious and B; somewhat compliant, neither of which he was going to get from me.

Finally, this mental surge of questions and arguing with myself was enough to pull my finger out my butt and act. I needed to escape and after walking through the usual pointless first steps of checking the doors, only to find them with guards outside, I then had to have another rethink. After, of course, mumbling something about leaving my handbag back inside and I would just be a minute. Their vacant looks were enough to tell me they had no clue what I had said. Well, that was good because I wasn't even sure handbags were a thing in this time. Now, maybe if I had said something about, 'Oh I just fancy another honey dripped mouse' then maybe that would have been more believable.

"Eww, don't go there again, Kaz," I told myself aloud as I slumped back on the couch trying not to gag. Okay, so I had to do something as I couldn't just sit here and wait for mould to grow on my ass in hopes then he wouldn't want to marry me. So, I got up and checked the small walled garden area outside. Well, unless some ancient version of Spiderman was currently looking for his Mary Jane and happened across me instead, then I don't think I had much chance getting over that thing. I released a sigh looking up at the ten-foot wall and suddenly wished for ivy. I'd had some luck with ivy. Damn it but why couldn't there have been ivy!

"I see you didn't get far with that escape plan."

"Sophia!" I shouted her name before I even turned around to face her as I would recognise her voice anywhere!

"The one and only...Umpf" she commented drily before I launched myself at her.

"Wow, it's been what, three days and you miss me this much?" she said on a chuckle as I clung to her.

"You know I may be a demon but my vessel still needs to breathe," she added which made me finally let her go. Sophia was dressed as a servant girl, which explained how she managed to sneak inside the palace and then inside this room.

"Oh, sorry, my bad…speaking of which…?"

"She's not here," Sophia said interrupting my question, knowing instantly who we were talking about.

"You came alone?" I asked and she shrugged her shoulders and said,

"Not exactly but come on, I will explain on the way."

"On the way to what?"

"What do you think, the Black Gate of course," she told me with a wink and then grabbed my hand and pulled me towards the door. I pulled back a bit and asked,

"But the guards, what will…"

"Already taken care of," she replied with a mischievous smirk and then she opened the door to reveal four guards all slumped over one another. Oh, so that had been how she had got in here then, good old-fashioned assault and battery, I though wryly. It made sense, considering this was Sophia we were talking about. In fact, I was just surprised to see them unconscious but still breathing as they seemed to have all their vital body parts still attached and in good working order…or was that at least one bone I could see popping out of flesh…Ewww!

"I…I…Oh god, I have to be sick!" I shouted letting go of her hand and having nowhere else to throw up, I did so over the poor unconscious guards. Projectile vomiting was never a pretty sight but waking up just in time to see it being rained down on you was quite possibly the worst. That and a sandaled foot just before it connected with your face…yep, that was a bad day in anyone's books.

"I am not even going to comment right now," Sophia said looking down at her foot with utter disgust before then dragging the sole against one of the guard's tunic sleeves, trying to rid it from vomit.

"Next time can I suggest less gory means of incapacitating the guards before the human with a fragile stomach needs to step over them?" I said making her roll her eyes at me.

"And can I suggest you try and stop getting your ass kidnapped for more than a week…ergo, no guards in need of stepping over?"

"Good point, let's go," I replied as yeah, it *was* a good point. I mean hell, it was as if people had score cards or something, although I had to say I think if that were the case then Lucius would be winning so far.

Sophia started to walk down the hall and I had to catch up with her in time to say,

"Wait, what about them? Won't anyone see them?"

"Well, I was going to drag their asses in the room but that was before you vomed all over them, so there is no way I am touching them now." Sophia was wrinkling her nose in disgust again.

"Vomed?"

"Puked, vomited, hurled, spewed, discharged, look I don't care just pick one!" she said making me laugh and say,

"You have been around Pip too long."

"I have been around Pip too long," she agreed and then we both laughed. I couldn't express how happy I was to see Sophia here as it could only mean one thing…

I was finally going home.

We made our way down the halls and even though people were staring at us, there seemed to be no soldiers in this part of the palace. Although from the looks of the way they kept whispering as they walked away from us with added pace, I had to say I didn't think it would be long before we had trouble.

And I was right.

"Dariush!" I said his name just as we turned a corner and found him stood at the centre of the hallway with his arms folded…oh and did I mention he did so with a small army at his back.

"Fuck!"

"I gather this wasn't part of your plan?" I asked leaning a shoulder into Sophia after hearing her hiss a curse.

"That would be a no."

"Looks like the diversion didn't work as planned Princess, although I must confess to being surprised to see you here at all, as last I heard it was you yourself that tried to have her killed," Dariush said looking intrigued and I gave Sophia a sideways glance. One she understood pretty quickly, as she merely gave me a small shake of her head in return. It seemed the only knowledge Lucius had of me being here in this time was that I did so with some of the others he rescued that day, but obviously didn't think this included Sophia. Which meant Dariush must have thought this Sophia was the one who had tried to poison me that day.

Maybe we could use this to our advantage…now if only I could make a T shape with my hands and call time out, as I needed a moment alone with her so that we could have a private conversation. And then of course it hit me and I felt like slapping myself…*I could* have a private conversation with her!

I quickly catapulted myself back through time and soon found myself sitting next to Draven in the VIP. It was when I had just got my period and needed Sophia's help with some girly things, like pain killers and a box of white torpedoes. (I swear that I will never be able to call them white mice again, or even think about 'mice' in any other scenario without feeling sick!).

I had tried to focus my mind and open it up to allow messages to get through, which I had been amazed to find after a few attempts of me foolishly screaming 'hello' in my mind, I finally got a response back. Which is precisely what I did now. Although I had to say looking back at all the times it would have come in handy, I was surprised that I was only thinking about this 'little gift' now.

"I can hear you, only not sure why you're talking like a commando?" Sophia's voice spoke in my mind and her reply was referring to me shouting, *'Keira to Sophia, do you copy, over?'*

"Just playing the part, seeing as this is quickly turning into a covert mission. So, what's the plan, 'cause he doesn't know you're not who you are...if that makes sense."

"I don't know but I think he is going to figure out something quick if we don't just stop looking like a couple of deaf mutes trying hard not to move our lips."

"Good point," I said again trying to refrain from moving my lips or worse shrugging my shoulders for no apparent reason.

"Just follow my lead."

"On the contrary, I am not here to steal her from the Vampire King, I am here to make sure she marries him."

"What?!" I screamed at her and I could almost see her rolling her eyes at me in my mind.

"Work with me here," she muttered back in my mind.

"Well, my outrage could be easily believed if that helps!" I all but snarled the words back.

"Oh really? Now I am curious."

"It is true, for it is my brother's men out there creating the diversion, I was just simply intercepting his retrieval of her and ensuring she could not escape her new husband to be," Sophia said adding a higher authoritative lilt to her voice, one that sounded haughty like the spoilt Saphira I had encountered before we…well before Sophia drugged her and the three of us stuffed her ass in a trunk!

"And why exactly would you do that?" Dariush challenged.

"Because I do not believe her to be his chosen Electus," she replied and I couldn't help my reaction. I sucked in a sharp breath from the pain hearing that sentence caused me. I knew she was only playing a part but just hearing the words…well let's just say she was making it easier to act my own part out.

"No? Well then I have to wonder what reason you have to think so, for I am sure the King should know this for himself." I knew Dariush was just testing her and I couldn't imagine what her response would be to this.

"Because the Oracle told me that he would only meet his Electus many years from now and as you know, the Fates are never wrong. Therefore, she stands in the way of my brother ever finding his true Electus, for you know it is forbidden for our kind to…well, to commune with such a being." The way she said this last part was with a sickened hiss directed at me and I had to give it to her, she was a pro. So, I decided it best if I at least tried to match her acting skills.

"You lied to me!" I shouted hoping that I looked as outraged as I tried to sound.

"Quiet girl!" Sophia snarled at me and brought back a hand as if ready to slap me…I released a relieved breath when Dariush stopped her before she could make the swing.

"Enough!" Sophia dropped her hand and the look we exchanged was one I would never have thought to see in a million years. Well okay, so I had seen her hate me but that hadn't been the real Sophia, not the one I knew.

Not the one I called sister.

"So, what makes you think she is right for Septimus Severus?" Sophia laughed at the question and said,

"I really couldn't care if she is or not. No, my only purpose in all this is served to my brother in getting rid of the girl, whether that be dead or with your precious Vampire King. Either way, she is out of my hands and more importantly out of my brother's life. So, do with her as you will, but just make sure you do it fast, for you will not have long before he tries to claim her!" This seemed to do it for Dariush as he nodded his acceptance. Sophia did the same as something silent passed through them and my jaw nearly hit the floor when I saw her start to walk away.

"Don't worry, I will think of a way to stop it…just go with them and pretend to be compliant," I heard Sophia speak in my mind and I had to be careful as a massive sigh of relief wanted to slip out but then I replayed her words and almost screeched out in my mind,

"You want me to pretend to go through with it!?"

"Just act like your fate is already sealed and there is no other option left for you," Sophia replied more calmly and I knew I had no choice but to trust in her words.

"Sophia…you…you will come back for me, won't you?" I felt Sophia smile in my mind before telling me sincerely,

"Always…my sister."

"Come on little bird, time to get your wings clipped," Dariush said gently and I scowled up at him, no matter how calm he sounded. But I didn't say anything. No, instead I did as Sophia told me to and walked alongside him flanked by an overkill of guards.

Even if Sophia hadn't of told me to do this, really, what other option did I have? Also, if Dariush believed Sophia as he obviously did, it meant that they hadn't yet discovered the puke covered guards piled outside the door like rubbish on collection day. And how long that would be was anyone's guess considering they were a bit of an eyesore.

I could almost hear Darth Vader's 'Imperial March' music as I was accompanied through the vast hallways on my way to meet Lucius at the altar. Surely, he couldn't do this? I mean once I explained this wasn't what I wanted, that it was a mistake, then maybe he would listen and call this whole thing off…yeah right! I mean, who was I kidding, this had Alpha male bullshit written all over it!

Swallowing hard I realised we had arrived at a huge archway that had double pillars each side. I looked up and saw a great marble eagle with outstretched wings with the same word I had asked Lucius about…

SPQR, meaning 'The Senate and People of Rome'. Well I doubt him marrying me now had anything to do with the good of the people, because surely an emperor was expected to marry into wealth or power? Although this was Lucius we were talking about here as, other than Draven, I had never heard him taking orders from anyone.

"Just keep walking, Keira," Dariush told me looking down at me as I'd not realised, but I had stopped on the threshold. I knew with every step that this was wrong and my entire being was screaming at me to run. I even looked behind me, over my shoulder and as if Dariush knew where my thoughts lay, he cleared his throat and informed me softly,

"You wouldn't get far…he wouldn't allow it."

"No, I don't suppose he would," I muttered back before swallowing hard and taking another dreaded step closer. The massive hall was covered floor to ceiling in the whitest cut stone and flawless marble I had ever seen. It was as stunning as it was cold. With a floor that looked like white water, made that way by turbulent rapids swallowing up the blue. The first step I made I was half expecting to apply weight and sink. Hell, it felt like I was drowning anyway.

I looked up and half expected to see a room full of people all there to celebrate such an occasion as to witness their emperor getting married. But no, there was only about ten people, and that was including the robed priest that stood waiting for me like the Devil about to cast judgement. I didn't see Lucius at first and my heart skipped a beat in the hope that something had happened to detain him.

I looked to Dariush but was quickly left feeling deflated as he didn't look worried. So, I tore my eyes from him and took in the rest of the room. Connecting arched doorways all lined the walls with a balcony corridor situated above, with a long line of balustrades all looking like small white soldiers standing to attention. Above this was another floor of arches set further back and it mirrored the ground floor level. The third level looked to be simply a homage to the Gods, fallen warriors, mythological beings and past emperors. As above each second-floor arch there were massive plinths atop marble Corinthian columns holding these mighty statues all standing tall and immortalised in action.

And at the centre of it all, the Emperor's Throne.

It was situated up at least twenty steps in a massive domed recess, making it look as though part of a Temple stood at the head of the great hall. I couldn't make out the throne itself as it was still too far away but the two colossal Roman Centurion statues that crossed long spears above would have been hard to miss.

I would have thought that walking the full length of the room would have taken forever but in the situation I was currently in, it didn't take long enough. At some point the rest of the guards stopped following us as it seemed it was left only to Dariush to deliver me.

"It looks as though I will be playing the role of the father in this," Dariush said and I wasn't sure if it was to me or himself.

"You're giving me away?!" I hissed making him laugh.

"Trust me, it wasn't ever a role I envisioned for myself either, little bird," he replied before nodding ahead at someone and I turned just before we approached the steps to see Lucius stepping from the side and joining the priest. He was an old man, swathed in a deep purple sash that covered most of his long white tunic. When Lucius motioned towards him he started filling the hall with the echoing sounds of some Latin prayer.

"As I once said, the Gods will envy me greatly, for your beauty is breathtaking," Lucius said once we had made it up the stairs and I was now by his side. I bit my lip and looked up at him with wide eyes. I hated what I had to do next but I knew I had no choice. I couldn't be allowed to marry Lucius, even if it didn't count legally, as it was not of my own time. To me, it would always symbolise my greatest betrayal. One I would never forgive myself over.

"Thank you, but Lucius I…" I started to say when he stepped closer to me and spun me to face him. Then he reached down and gripped my belt in his hands.

"What are you…?"

"This should be shown at the front, for it is the Nodus Herculeus, the united knot that symbolises both our union and the virility of Hercules," he told me, spinning the belt around and making me suck in a sharp breath.

"And this is the flammeum, a veil both representing our combined blood and that of the Eternal Flame," he continued motioning for a servant to come forward so that he could take the crimson rectangular veil from her and place it just slightly over my crown, so that it didn't hide my face.

"Now come, it is time to make you mine in all eyes of

Rome," he said and I looked back at the empty room, making him chuckle.

"Figuratively that is." Again, I bit my lip and hated that I was about to destroy this man's happiness by trying to gain back my own. He looked so handsome and carefree, it felt as though I was about to take a dagger from behind my back and plunge it straight into his heart.

He now wore a golden breastplate over a deep red tunic, that was half hidden by the matching crimson sash that fastened at one shoulder by a round emblemed clasp. It held the symbol of two swords crossed over a wreath and this matched the golden crown of leaves he wore on his head. Oh yes, he was painfully handsome alright, and looked as though he had moments ago passed through the gates of Heaven themselves.

Looking at him like this, it was almost impossible to think of him as a vampire, let alone the King over them all. But then again, I had seen many sides to Lucius and I knew more than most just how ruthless he could be. But it was the hidden tender side to Lucius which scared me more. The side that seemed to make it his mission to keep me safe and had even reconnected past alliances with Draven after decades of being enemies, something I wasn't at a loss to know why he did this for…or should I say *who*.

But unlike then, when I had been the cause for their reunion, now I seemed to be the reason for its breakdown.

He took my hand and led me to the priest just as wine was being poured into a golden goblet he was holding out. He gave my hand a squeeze as if trying to ease my unspoken fears.

"Wine is offered to the Gods so that they may bless this marriage," Lucius whispered down to me, translating what the Priest was saying. Even the way he did this was thoughtful and made what I was about to do even more heart-breaking.

I pulled my hand from his and whispered,

"I'm so sorry Lucius but I…" I never got to finish as suddenly a booming voice echoed through the vast room and it was loud enough that I was surprised to see the walls didn't crack. I looked back at the same time as Lucius did and the snarl of anger coming from him made me take a step back. I looked back at the others to see that they had been frozen, every one of them now paying witness to nothing as they became living statues. Lucius had done this no doubt to save the audience from seeing what could come next.

Then a mighty roar, followed by a commanding voice I would know anywhere, drew my attention back to the entrance. There was no mistaking him and I cried out his name, almost falling to my knees for the strength shouting that name held,

"Draven!" He strode towards us with furious purpose and suddenly my happiness at seeing him was being quickly replaced with fear.

Something he confirmed to be justified when he issued his first threat…

"And now, it's time for me to kill you, old friend!"

CHAPTER THIRTY-TWO

TWO KINGS

Seeing Draven again had me taking the first steps in running to him but Lucius had other ideas. He snagged me just as I took off and hauled me back against his chest. Then he banded an arm around my waist, holding me back and making Draven snarl at the sight.

"No, let me go!" I shouted and tried to struggle free.

"Not this day, little Keira girl," Lucius whispered down to my ear with purpose and promise adding strength to his words. I closed my eyes against the pain of it all. It was tearing me apart being in the middle of this raging conflict and all I wanted to do was scream at the top of my lungs before running from it all. I wanted to tell them both that I belonged to no one in this time. That there was only one who I was destined for and he wasn't named Septimus or Arsaces. No, the one true keeper of my heart was and would always be named…

Dominic Draven.

But what had I done? What had being here in this time cost me…what had it cost them? I couldn't even comprehend what faced me when I returned and the weight of dire possibilities nearly crushed me. Would Draven know what I'd done? And if not, then how long did I have before he found out? I don't know why I chose now to dwell on the consequences, maybe it was at the sight of the two men I cared for coming head to head with only my flesh in between.

Draven cut the distance between us like a man possessed and at first, I didn't think he would stop until he had torn me from Lucius' arms. But stop he did. Then he issued his threat, one that came straight from his demon.

"Give. Me. The. Girl." I swallowed down the hard lump of panic at what Draven would to do to Lucius if he didn't comply with his demands.

"She doesn't belong to you!" Lucius snarled back, tightening his hold on me instinctively. Draven roared at him and let his demon form take over. Purple flame pulsated under his skin, and travelled down the length of one bare arm, up his neck and seeped into eyes as black as night. He looked indestructible and dressed the way he was, you could add demonic warrior to the mix.

His other arm was covered in overlapping black metal plates that looked tipped with silver at the points. Silver…another thing Lucius didn't like. It couldn't kill him but weaken him, yes. This was down to the thirty pieces of silver it was rumoured he took as the price for performing the 'Kiss of Judas'. This was the signal he used for the Romans, so that they may seize the Son of God. Of course, I knew that this never happened, as did Jesus but unfortunately none of the rest of his disciples did as they made him choke on the silver when they hung him. Hence his aversion to the precious metal. Draven knew this of course and looked to be using it to his advantage. This included the silver tipped, wicked looking talons attached to the end of the gauntlet hand, that also seemed to be part of his armour.

Oh yes, he had come here ready for a fight all right and I hadn't missed the hint of chest armour beneath the black hooded cloak he had draped across his torso and over to one shoulder. A deadly blade hung down by his leg, one long enough that if straight, it would have touched the floor. Black trousers strapped with leather and knee-high metal leg guards completed the formidable look.

"That is where you are wrong, for she is *my Electus!*" Draven replied and I looked down to where the sound of metal grating against metal could be heard, not surprised to find Draven clenching his gauntleted fist.

"And you get this information from where, I wonder?" Lucius asked, donning a calmer voice this time.

"You know where!" Draven snapped, only Lucius didn't bite back with anger, no he remained in better control.

"Enlighten me for I want to hear you say her name."

"I know not this game you play Lucius but I grow weary of it all the same, however, if it is a means to end this farce then so be it, for you will have your name!" Draven replied barely holding on to his rage enough to speak.

"But my price?" Lucius asked, beating Draven to it. He raised a brow in question and Lucius scoffed,

"Come, come, you look surprised, but do you so soon forget how well I know you?" Lucius replied with untrusting ease and again Draven nearly shook with fury and spat out,

"Yes, but that knowledge died along with your loyalty!"

"Yes, and back then my loyalty was earned, *not betrayed,*" Lucius replied now with an icy cool demeanor, only his last two words held the biggest clue to the root of his actions…he felt Draven had betrayed him?

Draven looked taken aback by this and for a moment I

thought I saw regret. But surely it was impossible, for Lucius couldn't have known what Draven was hiding from him and would continue to do so for almost two thousand years.

The Spear of Longinus, or better known as the spear tip that had pierced the side of Jesus, had rightfully been seen as belonging to Lucius. For he had been responsible for his death just as Jesus was responsible for his. So, in order to get back what he thought was owed to him by right, he wanted the spear so that he could gain more power from both sides…just as Draven had.

So, he had been searching for the missing piece since his rebirth. But according to the Fates, Draven was told to withhold it from him until the right moment and that only presented itself when I died so that I could save Lucius. It had all been prophesied but right now, in this time, Lucius didn't know any of this. Which then begged the question why exactly had their alliance crumbled now?

"Ah, but you seem surprised, for surely you must know of which I speak?" Lucius commented and Draven crossed his arms over his chest and asked cautiously,

"What is it you want Septimus?"

"First, I want a name," Lucius replied and I frowned not understanding what was happening.

"Fine, you know my price, now let her go!" Draven barked and Lucius took a deep breath before I felt his arm loosen from me before dropping to his side. Then he took hold of my hand and spun me so that I was now behind him. I sidestepped about to go to Draven but one look towards him told me not to move as he gave me a small shake of his head. It was a warning?

"Now say her fucking name!" This time Lucius lost his cool and his demon broke through. Draven looked torn for a moment but then one more glance at me and it was all he needed to

make his mind up. I didn't understand what was going on? Why was it so hard for him to just speak her name?

"No Arsaces! Don't do this brother!" I heard Sophia shout just before he could open his mouth. She revealed herself on the balcony, stepping out from one of the arches and then jumping down from the balustrades, landing as graceful as a cat.

"If you do this, then there will be no going back, for none of us know the consequences of such a force," Sophia warned as she mounted the steps slowly.

"Then the girl is mine by rights, for if you refuse to summon her, then you have no choice but to accept the truth *from me,*" Lucius told him and Draven first looked to Sophia and then back to Lucius as if trying to seek the right answer.

"What do you mean by truth? What claim over her do you think you hold rights to?" Draven asked and Lucius grinned before informing him and the rest of us the reasons why, dropping another prophecy sized bombshell on us all.

"She is my Electus." I sucked in a sharp, disbelieving breath and for a second all that could be heard was the echo of my shock.

"Impossible," Draven hissed. I shot a panicked look to Sophia to see her pause and close her eyes as if she knew this was coming.

"So, you doubt the Fates now?"

"The Fates, what have they…?" Draven questioned but was quickly cut off.

"Who do you think it was that told me of such things?" Lucius stated firmly.

"You lie!" Draven threw at him, slicing his armoured hand down through the air. Lucius released an annoyed sigh and then let him have it.

"No, it is you that lie, to none other than yourself!" Lucius snapped taking a step closer to him, circling him as he stated what he knew.

"Do you really believe that I would act on such at a mere whim? Do you honestly believe that I had gone to such lengths as these for merely a passing fancy? Now you know what to do if you require your proof! Say her name and summon her here and hear it being spoken from lips that cannot lie, even when you believe that mine still would!" Lucius snarled this at him with a deep-rooted venom that had me doing as Sophia had earlier…but no matter how I closed my eyes I couldn't blind myself to the pain I'd heard in Lucius' voice.

"No! Don't do it brother, for you know we are not of this time and none of us can say what such a thing may cause." Sophia again pleaded and Draven was once again left with no other option than to believe in Lucius' words, as he didn't want to chance it. So instead he asked him,

"How…how did you…"

"The day I left the palace I didn't return to Rome as you had instructed," Lucius replied.

"You went in search of the Oracle?" Draven finished for him filling in the blanks and sounding outraged that his order had been disobeyed.

"I did," he said with a mere shrug of his shoulders.

"But that is impossible! No-one but I know of her whereabouts," Draven said but Lucius made a tut, tut sound and informed him,

"You're not the only one with spies Arsaces, or even greater power at their disposal." I quickly thought to Dariush and wondered if he had something to do with this? Then I looked around and it was the first time I had noticed that he had disappeared. So, Draven wasn't the only one keeping secrets it seemed.

"But why, what made you seek her out…why now

Septimus?" Draven asked in a strained voice that had been found in the shadows of their lost friendship.

"She saved my life and gifted me the Venom of God. For you know what that means as such a thing can only be given, not taken simply by feeding on her." Well that explained one thing I hadn't even thought about until now. Why had I never questioned why Draven hadn't ended up with the Venom of God when feeding from me?

"I know that she holds the blood of the First. How or why I do not know," Draven said and this was obviously something that he had held back from asking me. But I couldn't get away from the look he gave me as it felt like a back-handed slap given to someone through betrayal. Sophia shot me a look of concern as if silently asking if I was okay. It gave me strength.

"She knows of Tartarus, for I heard her speak of such, but I do not know what happened back in her own time. All I know is what the Oracle told me and the way I feel about her," Lucius admitted and it didn't look as though it came from him easily.

"She is mine," Draven stated and this time it wasn't done so in a furious or dominating way. It was merely said as a fact.

"Yes, well if that be the way of things then it would also seem as though she is mine as well, so there is only one solution I can see in all of this." Lucius didn't argue the fact but just accepted it and was moving on with a solution. Well, I felt like raising my hand up at this point and saying, 'I know, if you want a solution why not try asking what the girl in question wants'. Yep, I am sure that would have been the smart thing to do right now, I thought sarcastically.

"And what is that?" Draven asked crossing his arms as he waited. I, on the other hand, held my breath as if waiting for doomsday itself…and then it came when he spoke,

"We each fight for the right to claim her."

"What!? No! You can't…you can't do this!" I shouted,

horrified by the idea but they both ignored me. I had been expecting it from Lucius, but Draven?

"Done," Draven said without giving it a single second of thought. I felt my tears start to build as I shook my head in mute disbelief. This couldn't happen...I couldn't allow it!

"Then we fight at dusk at the Flavian," Lucius added with his mind made up.

"You want to make the fight public?" Draven asked, clearly surprised and to be honest so was I. How exactly they were planning on fighting with the powers of both Heaven and Hell on their side without the mortal world noticing was beyond me.

"I do, for I think the only way to settle this is if we fight as mortal men." Okay, so that was how then! Was Lucius serious? They were going to fight as mortals?

"Unless of course you would like to see if I am now strong enough to tap into your mind and have you fight against yourself for me?" Lucius added and the question made Draven growl. Of course, he knew he was right, Lucius did have the power to do that but honourably, it looked as though he didn't want to. He wanted this to be a fair fight.

"Careful Vampire, for you are still young and I have many years on you," Draven warned adding a threatening depth to his voice.

"Yes, but you are forgetting something, King."

"And that is?"

"Thanks to our Electus, I now have blood of the First running through my veins, for I sincerely doubt that you can claim the same." Draven shot a stern look to me and I flinched back a step. I bit my lip against my inner turmoil and had to close my eyes just to escape that disappointed look. It seemed I wasn't the only one who needed a few deep breaths to calm frayed nerves. As Draven knew Lucius was right, he was now stronger and because... well, because of me.

Unbeknown to what I was doing at the time, I had managed not only to save Lucius' life but also to upgrade it in a way I had no knowledge about. I felt like I was being buried alive under the mistakes I continued to make. As though I was trying to swim in the dark and find the shore I couldn't see. Was I even getting close or was I just going the wrong way, only delaying when I would drown after my time was spent and I had long given up ever making it home?

"If you want to fight as men then so be it, but you will also meet my terms," Draven said after giving himself a minute to think.

"And they are?" Lucius asked not sounding surprised.

"The girl, she stays with my sister and does not leave her side."

"You think I can't keep her safe?" Lucius snapped, obviously not liking what Draven implied, but what Draven said next couldn't be denied.

"I heard about the attempt on her life Septimus, so do not have me believing myself a fool! She stays with my sister or we will find this fight happening sooner than you think and without Rome at your back!" Lucius didn't look happy about this, but after releasing a deep sigh, he agreed, adding his own terms.

"Very well, but she does so at the Imperial Box, for there she will lay witness to the victor before he gets to claim her as his own," Lucius bargained and I was outraged. I wanted to scream at them both that I wasn't a piece of damn meat and that I had a say in who I was going to be with! How dare they!

In fact, I was about to step forward and give them both a piece of my mind when Sophia intercepted. She had silently made her way around to me and now she was close enough that she could place a hand on my arm. She gave me a squeeze and when I looked at her she shook her head, telling me no. I decided to take her advice and remain silent.

"Then it is set, we meet at dusk… and I warn you Septimus, that this time, only one of us will leave its walls of a blood soaked past alive," Draven said with deadly promise, then after granting me one last look, he turned and left, walking with purpose to meet up with his band of men he had left waiting near the entrance. I nearly crumbled to the floor as I was left only to watch the man I loved turn his back on me and I was left asking myself why?

"I will explain later," Sophia whispered next to me obviously reading the devastation on my face.

"Yes, but then it could be too late," I told her and before she or Lucius could react, I ran for it. I didn't know how I managed to get as far as I did without being held back by Lucius but the second he came within grabbing distance, I whipped back to face him before he could touch me.

"NO! You don't get to stop me this time!" I shouted at him holding a hand up, stopping him before he could do the same to me. My demand echoed around the room and reached Draven's ears before he had chance to leave. He turned to look back at me and waited to see where my standoff with Lucius would lead to.

"Just…just give me this," I asked him in such a way he knew my voice was close to breaking.

"You have until my men arrive," he told me before nodding behind me towards his enemy. I didn't waste any time as I turned and ran the rest of the way. My veil came off and floated away behind me, landing at Lucius' feet. But I didn't look back to see the pain etched on his face of what that symbolised.

I just ran.

Draven held a hand up, signalling for his men to stop at the sight of me approaching.

"Keira." The way he said my name could have been an embrace or almost made up for the lack of one.

"Draven, don't do this!" I blurted out and his once soft features hardened upon hearing it.

"It is done," he stated in a voice that brooked no argument.

"But it isn't, not yet and it doesn't have to be…I will make him see, I will try and convince him to let me go and that way…" I never got chance to finish.

"We cannot both live in the same world as our Electus and stand by whilst the other claims her…it just isn't possible Keira," Draven told me as if he would have preferred to have choked on the words than see them be true.

"But you don't understand." This wasn't the right thing to say. He took a step closer to me and his eyes narrowed down at me.

"What…what don't I understand? How you never told me of his involvement in your other life or what he means to you in it? How you fear for his life and would plead for me to spare it, just as you would do the same to him, pleading for my very own? Or how by telling the truth for once you could have prevented all of this?" Draven said, nearly growling the words at me and they hit me hard enough that I had to tear my face from his, as my tears started to fall.

I swallowed hard, knowing that he was right and I said the only thing I had left in me,

"I…I am trying to fix this, Draven," I uttered on a broken whisper and he left me utterly heartbroken with his icy cold reply,

"My name is not Draven…my name is Arsaces, King of Kings and you would do well to remember that, for it will be a name you will be spending many a year speaking of, once I have killed your Vampire lover!" After this he turned his back on me for the last time and walked from the room without once looking back. He didn't want to know about the sob that escaped my quivering lips or ask himself why my body collapsed to the floor. He didn't see the hand I reached out to him and he didn't witness my tears as they fell to the floor like exploding crystals.

He didn't get to hear me.

He didn't get to hear anything but the sound of his own footsteps taking him far from what he thought of as a betrayal.

But most of all,

He didn't get to hear the truth.

He never got to hear my last whisper to him…

"But he has never been my lover."

CHAPTER THIRTY-THREE

ANOTHER WAY

After that I let myself be led back to Lucius' bedchamber until it was time for the main event. I felt numb and even as Sophia walked beside me, holding my hand in comfort, it was as though I couldn't feel it. I just kept replaying Draven's words over and over on a torturous loop. He thought I had slept with Lucius.

I mean, by thinking that then I could see why he was so angry at me but for my part, I was angry at him for thinking that I could. Okay, so I knew I wasn't perfect as I had let Lucius kiss me and not slapped his face because of it, but sleep with him? Did he really think so little of me?

"My brother is just angry that's all. He will calm down once he…"

"Once he what, kills Lucius!? You do understand how we can't let that happen…right?!" I shouted, interrupting Sophia once we were back inside and the door was closed behind us. For once she didn't look as if she knew what to say and that in itself only ended up adding to my heartbreak.

"What…what…have I done?" I asked her as my voice hitched and broke on a sob.

"Oh, Keira!" Sophia came and caught me before I sank to the floor. Instead, she led me to the couch and held me to her as I cried into her shoulder, shaking with the force of my tears.

"You didn't do anything wrong, this…well this just happened and there was nothing you could have done," she told me softly, smoothing back my hair and trying to comfort me the best she could. But really, deep down I knew there was only one comfort left for me and he had turned his back on me.

I knew why. Because it was easier that way. Easier for him to turn away from the hurt and betrayal he felt, but one he had no right to. Okay, so I hadn't told him about Lucius, but really, what could I have said, for even I didn't understand it myself. All I knew was that something deep within my soul told me to keep him safe. It almost begged me to and such a thing couldn't be denied just because someone wished it. I knew better than anyone how much easier life would have been if I had been able to do as Draven had done. If I had been able to turn away from Lucius and never look back. My conscience would be as clear as crystal and the heavy weight of guilt that kept piling on top of me every time we kissed, would have been none existent.

But wishing for something that could never be wasn't going to get me any step closer to achieving it…any closer to achieving the impossible. It felt as though I was somehow keeping his heart safe and getting it ready to love for when his true Chosen One made herself known. But Draven would never see it like that. At least not the Draven of this time. For he only saw Lucius as one thing and that was a threat that needed to be eliminated. If only he knew that his greatest threat to losing me…

Was me.

Because I couldn't stay here. I didn't belong in this time and just the same as Lucius and I, because he wished for it, it didn't make it so. If only he knew the real sacrifice I made by going home. On one hand, I could choose to stay but then what life would I be condemning the rest in my own time to live. It may not have made sense in my head but it only ever had to make sense in my heart.

I needed to get home. If only to live for a short while longer, so that those I love could live on beyond me. I had so much to lose…so much it hurt to breathe, for no one knew. No one knew the Hell I was burying myself under and the one person who deserved to know more than anyone, was also the one person who could never know…

Not until it was done.

I remember seeing him cursing me in my dreams once. I remember seeing him holding my dead body in his arms and cursing me for ever leaving him. Was that how it was going to happen? Was that really going to be my last memory of him before I died? By the Gods and all their will, I sincerely hoped not, for if it was then they would find me cursing them right back.

Because I deserved more than that. I deserved my last breath to be taken with only love looking back at me. I deserved…

Draven's love.

After this I must have passed out or something, as the next thing I knew I was being awakened with a gentle caress running down my cheek. But I didn't open my eyes for fear of who I would find.

"She has been crying." I heard Draven's beautiful voice and I half wondered if it was a dream?

"And do you blame her, considering what your last words to her were?" Sophia replied cuttingly. I heard Draven sigh in response before admitting,

"I was angry."

"Yes, and she was scared and in need of the only person that could have comforted her but what did you decide to do...you turned your back on her when she has never done so to you!" Sophia replied verbally lashing out at him on my behalf.

"You may have lashed out at her in jealously for saving the Vampire, but you know nothing of the lengths this girl has gone to for you!"

"What...what do you mean?" Draven asked in a hushed voice that nearly broke.

"If you think Lucius was the only one she saved then you are a damn fool, brother! For you may not know this but this girl...this amazing, strong hearted girl has gone far beyond the ends of the Earth for you. The things she has done...well you couldn't even comprehend."

"Tell me." It was a demand.

"If I told you it all, then you wouldn't waste your time fighting but instead you would be worshipping at her feet and praying to every God we know that you never lose her." Hearing this I had to stop myself from reacting the way I wanted to, which was biting my lip to hold back the quivering I felt would soon inflict them. Her words, her beautifully kind words, were like someone wrapping my fragile heart in a blanket and nurturing it back to health.

I felt Draven shift on the bed and he said again more forcefully this time,

"Tell me!"

"Very well, I shall tell you and maybe then you will understand not only the depth of your love for her, but more so the depth of her love for you," Sophia told him and I heard her approach. Then she must have been leaning forward for the next thing I heard was her whispering to him, telling him a slice of our future together,

"This mortal girl travelled to Hell and back twice… so she could save you." I heard Draven suck in a sharp breath of disbelief and his look must have said it all because Sophia's parting words were,

"Ah, so now you get it…I guess it is how they say… *understanding love, it's better late than never."* I heard the door close seconds after this, signalling that we had been left alone. I felt the back of his knuckles caress down my cheek. The pad of his thumb ran under my eyes as if trying to take away the remaining tears that had left blotchy skin in its wake.

"Is what she says true, did you…did you really do that for me?" Draven's voice sounded both so pained and yet also astonished. I held my breath and felt him whisper above me,

"I know you heard everything, now open your eyes and look at me, so that I may see the truth for myself." I did as he asked and he instantly looked guilty, no doubt at the sight of past pain that had turned the whites of my eyes to red.

"You went to Hell for me?" I nodded and then told him,

"I would do anything for you." This was all it took for him to crush his lips to mine and for one long minute all was right with the world. But then his lips left mine and I was left feeling lost once more. Because no matter the power he held behind that kiss, it could never be strong enough to change where I was and what he was about to do.

"And the Vampire?" He asked the question and I knew he didn't do it this time to inflict a mirrored hurt he felt, but he really wanted to know.

"You can't kill him…you can't kill him just for loving me," I told him feeling the tears rising again and trying everything to hold them at bay.

"And what of your loving him, should I kill him for that?" he snapped and I took a deep breath, shifting myself up so that my back was to the bed.

"You don't understand and you never will if all you do is let jealousy cloud what I say."

"Then try and explain it to me." I took another deep breath and thought about what he was asking of me.

"I am not his Electus." Draven liked hearing me say this, that much was clear, but his response was one of arrogance all the same, even if his eyes told me something different.

"I know that."

"But he's doesn't deserve to die just because *he doesn't,*" I said, emphasising this last part, trying to get through to him.

"Then the Oracle, what of her words?" he asked me and I shrugged my shoulders and told him,

"I don't know what she spoke of but the only thing I can think is that he is confusing me with what he has been looking for all his reborn life…*something I know you are keeping from him.*" This last part I whispered and his eyes widened before he shot off the bed. His surprise was clear.

"That is…I…I don't…" For once Draven couldn't find the words and thankfully for him, this time he didn't need to. I held up my hand and stopped him.

"You don't have to explain…I already know why you keep it from him." Draven looked as though he was about to say something more but stopped himself, deciding to say something different instead.

"Yes, and now I must keep something else from him… but first I ask you, if I promise to spare his life, can you also promise never to see him again in return for such a vow?" I sucked in a startled breath the second he finished such a request. It would have been so much easier to just say yes and lie, because in this time, if Draven managed to take me away from here, then I very much doubted I would have seen him again before hopefully getting through the Janus Gate.

So, I wanted to tell him yes but then I knew I would have been making a promise clouded by the shadow of breaking it before I had even finished the vow…and I just couldn't do that. Because it was impossible, but I first had to make him understand the depth of what he asked of me.

"And this promise, you think by me making it will somehow make our lives easier?" I asked grimacing at just the thought of a final goodbye with Lucius.

"And you think that by agreeing to this that *it won't* make his life easier? Tell me Keira, for I know you are not a cruel being, how do you think it would feel for him seeing you with me, for him to know that you can never be his…do you not think it best to let him go, so that he can be free of the chains your heart represents?" On hearing this, I covered my mouth as a sob burst free. I knew he was right but I just couldn't do it…I couldn't let him go.

"I am sorry if this upsets you, but there are only two choices to make and both are yours." Draven told me, this time having the patience to do so in a softer tone.

"And…and if I chose a third?" I asked in a quiet voice trying to control it through my tears.

"There isn't a third choice to be had, Keira," he said, after getting up from the bed and slashing a hand through the air.

"You're wrong," I told him firmly.

"I am not…"

"Do you know that without him, I wouldn't be here," I blurted out stopping him. He flinched back as if I had slapped him with the truth.

"What are you...?" Again, I interrupted him.

"It's true. He helped me get here, even though he didn't want me to, even though he was ready to try and stop me, in the end he helped me… just like all the other times." Okay so I might be stretching the truth, but considering he had covered for me with what happened in the Library, choosing not to blow my plans by telling Draven. Then yeah, he had helped.

"Other times?" Draven questioned.

"Look, I know this is going to sound crazy after he kidnapped me and everything, but he has helped me and I know you have no idea what I mean when I say this but I have to say it anyway…"

"Go on," he pushed, folding his arms across his plated chest. So, I took a deep breath and hit him with the truth of his future actions. I knew it was cruel but considering what I was fighting for, then he gave me little choice. I had to make him see.

"You have not always been there for me, Draven." I whispered sadly.

"But surely I would have had I known…" I cut off his logic with fact,

"Through choice…you weren't there for me through choice, Draven."

"No, that isn't possible, I would never have left you!" he sounded outraged and not surprisingly in complete denial.

"Be careful of the word '*never*' Draven, for you don't know the future I speak of, nor do you understand that when I say I wouldn't be here without him, what I also mean is…*I wouldn't be alive."* Okay, so I was hitting him with the big guns but he was leaving me little choice now.

"He saved your life?" He sounded surprised.

"Yes, more than once and sometimes he even stood by your side, aiding you in trying to do the same…so do you see why you can't kill him…because there is no getting away from the truth?"

"And that is?" Okay so here it was. The biggest gun of all and I was just hoping that it wouldn't be a misfire.

"That Lucius *is* supposed to be a part of our lives…that it's fate. It's prophecy. It's whatever you want to call it but there is no getting away from the fact that…*it is what it is."* Draven looked almost as lost as I felt, only he was drowning in a sea of knowledge whereas I was drowning in a sea of desperation. I needed Draven to believe in my reasons, Lucius' life depended on it.

"And if he holds a blade to my throat and I one at his heart, what then? Should I let him spill my blood without doing the same? Should I fall on the sword for *his life*, giving *my own* in return?" Draven asked me sternly and I closed my eyes against the deep-rooted pain that image brought me.

"Of course not!" I hissed.

"Then what would you have me do Keira, tell me?"

"I would beg you not to fight at all and ask you to take me from this place, to steal me away like he did from you." Now it was Draven's turn to close his eyes against the image I painted.

"I am afraid I cannot do that, little lamb." he informed me sadly.

"Why not!? You don't have to fight! I beg of you please… please don't do this!"

"I have no choice." Was his own sad reply and I hit my limit hearing this.

"Bullshit!" I shouted making him look at me in shock.

"We all have a choice!"

"And what of my choices Keira, did this Dominic Draven have a choice when you left him? Did he have a choice when you sneaked out of his world and into mine? What of his choices?" He threw at me and I knew he was right. I had given *my Draven* no choice at all.

"Your look tells me all I need to know."

"Yes, but what I did was for the good of others but this… this fight is for nothing but the egos of two men in love!" I threw at him and in response he shouted back at me,

"It's for you!" I got up from the bed and stormed over to face him. Then I let him have it.

"No! It's not for me! Because if either of you were making decisions based on my happiness then you would have given *me* the choice! But instead you fight over me like children fighting over a damn toy! No-one is considering my feelings in this, not at all! Because if you were, then you WOULDN'T FIGHT!" I bellowed this last part at him. He looked as though he wanted to throttle me and right now, I couldn't have cared less. I was fuming mad, quickly replacing my hurt for anger and my pain for frustration. His deep breathing made his chest plate rise and fall and I looked up into twin purple flames, burning hot with raging emotion. We seemed locked in this silent fight, each of us trying to understand the other.

In the end neither of us won.

We both lost.

A knock on the door made me jump and Sophia allowed us a few seconds before walking through the door. Draven tore his gaze from me and looked down at the floor ready for what she had to say.

"It's time," she informed him in deflated tones, obviously hating this as much as I did. He gave her a nod and she took the hint, giving us the space we needed by staying near the door.

"Once this is done, I am taking you home," he told me without looking directly at me. It was almost as if he knew it would be too painful to see the tears welling in my eyes. He was about to turn from me when I grabbed his metal coated arm. I then stepped into him, raised both hands to his cheeks so that I could pull his face down to mine.

"Don't do this, please Arsaces, please, there must be

another way." I pleaded with him one last time in a voice that was barely more than a whisper. But it was enough. He heard it. And my answer was two words that held the weight of a thousand.

"Forgive me." I sucked in a shuddering breath and barely felt him kissing me on the forehead before walking away. He paused three feet away and without looking back at me, he spoke,

"There is no other way." It was said in such a way as though he was trying to get me to know how difficult this was for him, but that it was too late. I felt too far gone in my own misery to see this from any other angle other than one that led down a pointless road of death.

"Go to her and keep her safe." I heard Draven speaking to Sophia but again I didn't care because as I heard the door close, he was sealing the fate of someone I loved. Because no matter how powerful Lucius had become thanks to my blood, I knew it would never be enough to beat Draven.

Not in this time.

Because it wasn't the Venom of God he needed to become powerful enough to match Draven.

No, it was the blood of Christ…

Blood that was on the Spear of Destiny.

CHAPTER THIRTY-FOUR

A SHOW OF DEATH

After this Sophia led me from the room and I soon found a small army of soldiers escorting us through the palace. I knew we were being taken to where the fight would happen and my dread increased with every step I took closer to it. It felt as though I had been made to swallow dead weights as any remaining food I had in my belly just felt like it wanted to come back up again.

I didn't take in any of my surroundings as we walked through the dead hallways, feeling it mirroring my empty shell. Sophia held my hand firmly in hers but it could have belonged to a ghost for I barely felt it. If anything, it just felt as though I was being lured to witness my own death for I was sure my hand was shaking through fear.

"It will be okay, I have a plan," Sophia told me as she could obviously see how much I was struggling with it all and felt like she needed to give me something. But really, what could she do? I knew there were only two people on earth that had the power to stop this fight from happening and they were both as stubborn as each other.

We continued to walk until it seemed we were heading out of the palace and down a long corridor leading to another building. I didn't know what to expect. But when I heard a rumbling sound I instantly held back.

"What...what is that?" I asked, stuttering at first. It sounded like the thundering feet of an army of thousands. I could see the dim light at the end of this tunnelled walkway and the closer we got the more the army started to sound like something else.

"This is Rome," Sophia answered me as we stepped out into view and I gasped at the sight. She was right, it looked like the entire city was now crammed into one space.

"It's the Colosseum!" I exclaimed in utter shock. I had never seen anything like it before in my life. The arena itself was no bigger than a football field but the utter marvel of ancient architecture it sat in was nothing short of breathtakingly incredible. I think my jaw must have dropped as Sophia chuckled next to me.

"Not what you imagined?" she asked and I mutely shook my head. It felt as though someone had just dropped me in the middle of the Gladiator movie with Russell Crowe. Only instead of a half-built set filled with extras, this was as solid and real as they came and filled to the brim with thousands of people. Hell, there must have been at least 60,000 people here at least.

"I thought they were fighting somewhere else? They mentioned some about the Fla...something." Sophia laughed before helping me out, with both the name and an explanation.

"You mean the Flavian Amphitheatre, well it is one and the very same. The building was constructed by emperors of the Flavian dynasty, following the reign of Nero."

"So why is it now known as the Colosseum?" I asked unable to help myself.

"It's known now as the Colosseum thanks to that colossal statue of Nero nearby. I believe Lucius' arch will only find itself completed and dedicated in his name in 203 AD to commemorate the Parthian victories," Sophia added and I knew she was doing this to try and get my mind off what we were about to witness, along with the rest of Rome.

"Lucius has his own arch!?"

"The white marble Arch of Septimus Severus stands close to the foot of the Capitoline Hill…or at least it will do."

"And it's still there?" Okay so clearly, I was shocked to find that Lucius had a monument dedicated to him and his reign as Emperor of the Roman Empire.

"It is and still stands proud…and fares better than this place I should say…did you know they used to flood this place so that they could put on shows or re-enactments of sea battles?" she told me as we stepped closer to the edge. We were currently standing in a large open room sat on a raised podium at the centre of the narrower side of the arena on the north side. It gave us the perfect view to be able to see all of the space below. I shuddered at the thought of what that view might be shortly.

There were four columns, each surmounted by a statue of victory which supported a canopy in rich colours over us. Gold tassels hung down like golden dew drops travelling down branches and I looked around the vast space to see that no other part of the Colosseum looked so grand. I glanced behind me to see a large marble throne with a huge lion's head at it back and its sides were rolling marble curls that ended at the floor with giant paws of a beast. The cushioned seating pads were thick and lush deep purple with gold embroidered wreaths at the centres.

It certainly looked fit for a King, or in this case, a Caesar of an Empire. Even looking at the rest of the Colosseum, it had me believing that if ever such a fight between Lucius and Draven were to happen, then they couldn't have picked a grander stage to house such a fight. However, looking at all the cheering thousands, I was sure that I was only one of two people that didn't want this fight to happen, as Sophia looked as grim as I did.

Collectively they all looked like ants gathered around scraps of food like a swarm.

"All of these people," I uttered and Sophia stepped closer to me.

"See the top tier, near the awning..." She pointed to the very top row where people looked on, stood under a sloping red cover, one that looked as if it retracted. It was obvious its purpose had been to cover the audience from the elements as it must have covered at least two thirds of the arena's roof.

"That's where the common women are and as you follow the tiers down, so do you rise higher up the social ladder. The third was originally reserved for ordinary Roman citizens, the plebeians. Seating was then divided into two sections, the wealthy of these and the poor. After this came the second seating level that was reserved for the non-senatorial noble class called the Equites, or knights," she told me and now I knew she was definitely trying to keep my mind occupied and considering we once took history together, let's just say that she knew my weakness.

"And the last tier?" I asked looking at those closest to the great wall that surrounded the arena.

"The first tier, called the Podium, which also means place of honour, well that's reserved for the most important Romans. The Emperor, the Vestal Virgins, the important priests and members of the Roman Government including the Roman Senators." I looked all the way around and you could easily see the differences between social classes even by the way they were dressed. The Podium she spoke of was like a flat platform, or terrace, measuring at least 15 feet wide. Parts were covered like ours, no doubt protecting the precious and important people from getting too much sun as they watched the brutal killings of others.

To think how much blood went into building this place only for its sole purpose was to have blood spilled freely within it. It was a sickening thought wondering how many lives had been lost so that others may find some entertainment. I felt bitter tasting bile rise up in my throat just looking down at the sand coloured arena floor, wondering how much blood of the poor lost souls it had soaked up and how much of it left was tightly packed earth and how much of it was invisible death?

Flaming torches framed the outside wall and rose high like beacons as, unusually for the people of Rome, what they were going to witness tonight, was going to be done in the small window of the dim light of dusk. So, no wonder giant bowls of burning oil had been placed around the arena floor, as well as massive torches attached to the pillars that framed the outside space. It certainly managed to give it a more menacing atmosphere and considering who they were here to see fight, then I wasn't surprised. Although, none knew the true nature of these two as I did and I knew that no grand fight in the day would have been fitting for two that were far more connected to the shadows, one more than most.

And speaking of him, I felt everyone else with us in the imperial box straighten up and I knew someone important had just arrived. Then I felt his hands on my shoulders and I flinched.

"Easy, little Keira girl," Lucius hummed in my ear and I wanted to turn around and slap him, but knew I would probably only get myself arrested for the offense. Good, then maybe I wouldn't be forced to witness this pointless display of ownership!

But then I knew showing him my anger wouldn't get me anywhere, but maybe pleading with him would. So, I turned to him, the tears in my eyes there without even needing to try.

"Please Lucius, call this off...don't do this." I pleaded and instead of meeting angry eyes, I was met with ones of deep sorrow.

"I wanted to marry you so that *I didn't need to do this,*" he confessed, which was when things started to make sense. He was hoping to claim me without the bloodshed. That was why he had rushed me to the altar. I had to say that if it would have spared lives then I would have made the sacrifice and married him. Better running back to the future from a living husband then a dead loved one.

"And what of now, don't you have the power to stop this?" I asked and he raised a gentle hand to my cheek and pulled me closer to him.

"I wish I had the power to do anything you asked of me...to be able to give you anything you want, which is why I hope this will be the one and only time I say *no to you.*" He knew the second his answer crushed me as I closed my eyes and let the tears escape beneath a fan of lashes. I'd had just a slither of hope, one that was quickly crushed.

"Have no fear sweet one, it will all be over soon," he told me kissing my forehead just as Draven had done. Then I decided in the middle of my utter anguish, to issue him a warning, one he could also deliver to Draven.

"Then if you do this, if you both fight, then know this..." I wouldn't meet his eyes before but I finished my sentence looking up at him and he couldn't miss the pain in my eyes, nor the pain in my voice...

"I will never forgive either of you."

"Then that is our burden to carry and for one of us, to our grave," was his only reply and heartbreakingly, could be his last goodbye. I couldn't allow that, so just before he approached the edge of the Imperial box, I grabbed his hand holding him back. As Draven had done, he didn't look back at me but instead looked down at his hand now entwined with mine.

"Please be safe, I care too much about you...*about both of you.*" He took a deep breath and nodded, telling me silently that he had acknowledged my words. Then he gripped the edges of the side and vaulted over it making me cry out. I ran to the edge to watch as he gripped onto the long banner, allowing it to help in his fall. It wasn't very far and he did so as the crowd went wild around us at the show Lucius made of entering the arena. He landed gracefully and his people cheered for their Emperor as he walked into the centre of the empty space.

I could now make out that he certainly looked ready for the occasion as he was no longer dressed as an Emperor. No, this time he looked more like a mighty Gladiator. He wore a tarnished looking golden breastplate, this time void of any elaborate moulding as it was simply a sculptured representation of what lay hidden underneath. Armoured Pecs, a tapered waist and a rippling display of solid abs. Then all the indented lines in between the muscle were lined with a copper thorn vine, giving it an edgy badass look. This was finished off with two large curved shoulder pieces connected with thick leather straps.

His biceps were on show and they bulged as he rolled his shoulders, limbering up, ready for the fight ahead. His forearms were protected by leather bracers, one of which covered the top of his fist, whereas the other was shorter and finished at the wrist, like a thick band. His legs were bare, as was the usual fashion in ancient Rome, and thick leather strips finished above the knee. His manhood was saved from view by the red material attached to the bottom of his chest plate.

A line of servants stood by holding a weapon, a shield, and a helmet in readiness for his use. Suddenly a booming voice started speaking in Latin and Sophia came up behind me and said,

"He is announcing the fighters..." Just then the crowed started cheering and Lucius put up an arm, acknowledging his people's support. Then with the next few foreign words out of the announcer's mouth Lucius pointed to where I stood and suddenly the crowd all turned to look at me.

"Oh dear." I heard Sophia mutter next to me.

"What, what is it? Why are they all staring at me?"

"It's just been announced that the reason for the fight is to win your affections as the victor gets to claim you and your hand in marriage," Sophia said with a wince, ready for my freak out.

"What!?" I hissed. Oh great, that's all I needed.

"I think I need to sit down," I complained, feeling as if I was once again going to throw up. Sophia led me over to the seats either side of the throne and just as I was about to sit down, Marcus stepped forward. I hadn't even realised he had been behind us.

"The Emperor wishes for you to take his seat, where you will be more comfortable." I was shocked that I understood him this time.

"Thank you," I said letting Sophia lead me to his throne.

"He is one of us and like our kind, speaks many language," Sophia whispered to me as my face must have said it all.

"But that night he..."

"If he was in front of his men, then he would have no doubt looked odd speaking Persian, seeing as in their eyes he is born and bred here in Rome." Okay, so I had to agree with her there.

The next announcement drew my attention back to the arena and my heart sank as I knew there was only one thing left...

Draven's arrival.

My eyes shot to massive grated doors at the end, interlaced with massive metal spikes. Almost as you would have imagined the gates of Hell to look like and for the poor gladiators and slaves that were forced to fight, then I suppose it was…as they were certainly walking into Hell on earth by stepping through them. And the next person to step through them now, like some dark avenging knight was,

Draven.

The gates were framed with four large pillars and topped with mighty statues of fallen heroes. And speaking of heroes, my own was about to emerge. The gates opened and a lone figure walked from the spiked gates with deadly purpose. I hated it when the crowd started to boo and hiss their displeasure, my anger reaching new levels. Sophia placed her hand on mine, one that was trying in vain to claw at the marble beneath my fingers.

"Calm down, you know what getting yourself worked up can do," Sophia warned and I knew she was right. I couldn't chance doing something stupid in front of all these 'mortal' witnesses.

"But they're booing him," I said in a pained voice, one that Sophia looked heartened to hear.

"My brother has thick skin, trust me when I say that hearing such would not affect him in the slightest."

"Well it affects me!" I complained making her smirk.

"And I would expect nothing less."

I watched as Draven strode from the entrance, dressed as he was earlier only now he wore a black helmet, the same one I had seen him wearing that day he came to get me on horseback. Plucking me from the desert like an eagle after circling its prey.

Lucius looked to see his opponent approaching and then motioned for his servants to come forward. He took hold of his own helmet, one that matched his golden armour but looked more elaborate. It was the head of a demonic beast with its mouth open wide and it fangs hanging down past his forehead. It was finished with a gold mohawk of metal, unlike Draven's one of black hair.

He then took hold of his shield and sword and I couldn't help but notice that Draven had chosen against having a shield.

"Why doesn't Draven have a shield?" I couldn't help but ask.

"Who says that he doesn't," she answered cryptically, winking at me. I was then forced to watch as the two men I cared most about in this world, other than my own father, approach one another. You could see them exchanging words and as if on cue, they both looked up to where I sat, bowing their heads to me, as if this was what I would want to see.

I tore my gaze from theirs, letting each of them know how I felt. Something they both knew seeing as I had pleaded with each of them.

I didn't want this.

I never wanted any of this.

All I ever wanted was to spare the lives of those I cared about, but all those sacrifices, one soon to be my own life, would all be in vain if they did this!

"Sophia, we can't let this happen...I have to...*do something,*" I said gripping onto her arm in desperation, angry hopeless tears falling freely, for I no longer cared who saw them.

"Be strong and *be ready,*" she replied whispering this last part, squeezing my hand as if trying to relay a secret message. I gave her a look and she shook her head slightly, after first motioning to the guards behind her with her eyes. I knew she had something planned but why did I get the feeling it was one for us than for them.

The thundering sound of many feet banging on the floors of the tiers sounded like the Devil himself was knocking at the gates and I looked back to the arena, ready to watch my own private Hell play out.

As this was it, the time was now. I took in a ragged breath as Draven and Lucius faced each other. Then Draven whipped off his cloak, throwing it to the ground in a fan of crimson before it landed on the floor, leaving Draven looking like a demonic gladiator ready to fight his demons. Lucius in return reached up and pulled down a section of his helmet, now covering his face for one of death. A metal skull plate was now in place and proving my earlier thoughts true,

Draven was in fact, face to face with his demons.

He then drew his sword and Lucius held his ready for the attack. They both pulled back, spoke once more and then…

The fight began.

CHAPTER THIRTY-FIVE

ARSACES

STABBED IN THE BACK

Approaching the iron gates and grand entrance into the Flavian's arena, one built only to cast dramatic effect as the gladiators emerged, I snarled my anger at the servants leading the way. I knew the fucking way! Not many knew but when this place was first built, I came here dressed as a slave posing to be one of the first gladiators, so that I may experience it first-hand.

I remember walking from the dark tunnels and up the corridor through those gates before seeing the unimaginable in the capability of what mortal hands could create. Having it spread out before me was almost like looking up the centre of a great beast with its mouth open trying to swallow a piece of the Earth.

But unlike then, now I found no joy in its thundering walls or spectating eyes. The thrill of it back then, well it was like being once more on the battlefield and seizing victory with a single slice of your sword directed at the right commander. Like cutting the head off a snake, its body may still move for a few moments after but it doesn't take long for death to swiftly follow.

Well, right now I faced a new snake, one that had tried to claim what was rightfully mine. But, as I faced those doors ready for them to open, I didn't feel as I should. I didn't feel the warmth of excitement coursing through my veins or hear the murderous need of whispered words of encouragement coming from my demon side. And why, well I knew why…

Forgiveness.

That one word held me shackled like a chain around my neck pulling tighter the closer I got to the arena. She had begged me to spare his life as she had no doubt done the same to Lucius for my very own. But it was done and there was no going back on it now. We both knew the price of his actions and whereas before I had been eager to tear him limb from limb, now I was eager for it to be done with. So that I could face the aftermath and start to rebuild the broken pieces my own actions would cause.

The doors opened and I walked through with even steady strides, holding myself back from running in there, drawing my sword and getting this show over with. Lucius was there ready and even he didn't look as though this was something he relished the idea of. But as I, he knew it had to be done. One Electus for one King and to have it prophesied for both was simply not possible, yet neither of us was prepared to give her up to the other.

However, what my sweetest one had said to me did grant food for thought. Was it possible that Lucius had mistaken the words of Pythia for another prophecy? One I was to play a hand in some time in the future. The problem with that was even if it was fact, it still didn't enable me to tell him so. Not without giving him knowledge that I held the Spear's broken tip from him, for the blood of the Son of God could not fall into the hands of another. Not until those hands were granted worthy in the eyes of the Fates and washed clean of the sin and blood that remained there.

"Arsaces," Septimus said in acknowledgement and I nodded my own.

"I see Rome had no issues accepting you as their new ruler," I commented dryly as I looked around the thousands that cheered for their new Emperor.

"It was as you said it would be," he replied coolly, showing his usual calm demeanor, one he was even famous for on the battlefield. Septimus didn't kill or strike at the end of an enraged battle cry like most. No, he simply killed silently, slicing through his victims with not even so much as a heavy breath or a whispered warning. It was why I had assigned him first as a spy, then an assassin and after this, positioned him as right-hand man to my enemies. His skills of such would most certainly be missed and above all this, his loyalty as a friend could not be overlooked.

But that all changed when he stole from me my most precious gift bestowed by the Gods themselves. One I had been waiting for longer than Septimus had known life, both mortal and immortal. But even now, I was yet to discover how he managed it? I would be the first to admit I was arrogant enough to have thought the task impossible as I had gone to enough lengths to make it so. I had turned my home into a fortress and cleared the halls so that she could have the freedom and no longer feel like a prisoner in her new home. But, in reality, a prisoner is very much what she was and would remain. For the fear of losing her simply outweighed that of any discomfort she may have found in the over protective orders I issued as law.

Outside the walls of my private chambers was also a different matter entirely. No one could merely come and go as they once did, nor could anyone but myself and a few chosen others be admitted into this section of the palace. And all my men had been given strict instructions that if my new Queen had been found lost wandering where she should not be, then they were to surround her. They were then ordered to turn their backs to her and inform me at once of her whereabouts so that I could retrieve her myself. She was for my eyes only and if I were forced to share such a beauty then it would only be done so whilst in my presence. It was the only way to ensure that all who gazed upon her knew who she rightfully belonged to. Irrational thoughts it may be but I was King and after all this time with hopes of finding her, then I wasn't about to let her go by the hands of another.

But in the end, none of this had mattered as the one who took her from me, ended up being one I would have least expected. But his loyalty ended up being a lie and it is as my sweet one had once said, 'assumption is the mother from which all mistakes are born'. Wise words indeed, and some I wished I had listened to more intently.

"Do you wish to know what our last regards from our Chosen were?" Septimus asked, still looking to the crowd. I growled thinking that he too as I, had spoken with her, something we both agreed we wouldn't do. Well, if loyalty was completely fucked then neither of us would be surprised at the others disloyal actions. But that was the unknowing power of the Electus and it seemed as though it continued on, as I nodded for Septimus to tell me in which regards she spoke of.

"She informed me that if we fight, then she will never forgive us." The thought of this pained me indeed and I knew that I would have another battle on my hands the second this one was over. Each of us turned to the girl who held both our hearts in her hand and bowed, unable to miss the painful way she turned away from us.

"Then one of us will fight for her forgiveness when this is done," I said as I ripped my cloak from my shoulders and drew my sword. Septimus nodded and said,

"Indeed, we will." Then he held up his own sword and brought down the face of death in place of his own.

And so, it began.

I swung my sword around in my hand just as Septimus did the same, then we raised them once more together and hit out, clashing our steel. This soon became the signal for Rome's citizens to release the echoing of their bloodthirsty cries. I wanted to glance once more at my wife but I daren't. Not whilst I had a sword in my hand and was currently swinging it towards the King of Vampires.

For some reason, I chose this moment to think back to how it felt when first hearing that she was my wife. Even if it was in another life, the depth of hearing such near brought me to my knees, after of course it was proven true. At first hearing such things, things that sounded like the impossible, well surely, I could be forgiven for thinking it as lies. As it was something I had believed at the time to be said only to save the man she loved... *this Draven*. But then the Imp had lowered her guards at her queen's request and I had seen it all.

I had finally seen her soul and to know that I owned it, well the elevation to my own was of the likes I had never known. Which is why it was mine to protect and the reason that I now fought for it.

I swung my sword up and over aiming for his head, knowing he would block it all the same. It was difficult fighting as a man but somewhat liberating all the same. But it would have been harder still had I been fighting a man I hated. Hatred is harder to control the other side of me. Harder to control the beasts of Hell that want to lay waste to any enemy that may stand in my way. But the one I was fighting now, well his only crime was loving the wrong woman...

My woman.

A crime he must now pay for with his life.

So, as I spun with my sword and then I aimed high for the killing blow, getting it over and done with so that I didn't have to prolong her pain...

Or his.

KEIRA

I didn't want to look. I even hated myself for looking but I knew I would have hated myself even more if I would have turned my back on them now. So, I watched. And I hated every second of it. Every clash of their swords, every hit, block, parry, swing and dive I winced in fear that it would be the last ever needed. Because as long as they were still fighting then it meant they were both still breathing.

Draven was unstoppable. He swung the sword like it was just an extension of his arm and I guess knowing the other side of him, then this wasn't far from the truth. Even watching them fight as mortal men still seemed impossible. How fast they would move, at times almost quicker than the eye could see. Lucius was better at dodging the coming blow than dishing it out. He was the faster of the two but Draven was the stronger. You could see this every time their swords would meet, and Lucius' hold would be forced to bend just that little bit more. In my own time, they were equally matched. But now, in this world, Lucius was still young and had lots of catching up to do.

"Sophia, we have to do something! We can't just sit here and let this happen!" I almost shouted at her in my grief.

"After the next few hits, we are going to stand up and go to the edge…I will explain there." I listened as Sophia leaned next to me and whispered, pretending to comfort me by patting my hand. I nodded letting her know that I understood and after a few more gruelling hits, I got up, rushing to the side. She followed me.

Once there, I watched Lucius spin on his heel twice and each time he came back to Draven swinging his blade upwards. One of the blows actually managed to catch Draven unawares and sliced into his bare arm. He roared in rage and I was so caught up at the sight of blood trickling down his arm that I hadn't even noticed Sophia was trying to get my attention.

"When I give the signal, I want you to pretend to faint," she muttered next to me.

"But what will that do?" I asked in hushed hopeless tones.

"It will help us get out of here." Her reply confused me, how exactly did she think we could accomplish such a thing. And besides, how was leaving now going to help them.

"What! But we can't leave and…" I started to argue but she cut me off and gripped onto my arm to get her point across.

"Keira, this might be our only chance, everyone is here and the guards are preoccupied. This might be our last shot."

I thought about her words, glanced around us and knew that she was right. Every important person in Rome was now here. Which meant if we managed to leave, then the palace halls would be empty and anyone who could know who we were, were also here watching the fight. But then what if something happened to one of them…what if I didn't know? What if Draven killed Lucius and I wasn't there for him, there to say goodbye? Or even thinking about how Lucius had momentarily got the upper hand, what if Draven found himself distracted enough not to see his own killing blow coming?

The sound of clashing steel made me jump out of it and I looked back to see this time Draven was gaining the upper hand. He lashed out with new fury, slicing his blade one side and then the next, each time Lucius was left only to defend against the attack. They managed to get closer to the wall and after Lucius managed to trip Draven up the crowd went wild.

Draven snarled up at Lucius and then in retaliation, kicked up one of the large flaming bowls in Lucius' direction. Thankfully, he still had his shield, so managed just in time to deflect most of the flying flaming oil. Then he threw his shield to one side and charged at Draven. The fight seemed to be increasing for both of them and I actually felt my head start to spin because of it.

"Now!" Sophia hissed and I put a hand to my head and didn't have to fake the dizziness I felt, as the lightheaded sickening feeling was very real.

"Help, she is faint." Marcus stepped forward and helped me onto the chair. I barely just noticed as Draven looked up at me as if he had heard, which meant letting his guard down for a second...one that could have meant his head...not if I hadn't screamed,

"LOOK OUT!" He ducked just in time because of it, making the crowd boo. Then he came up from the dodge and elbowed Lucius in the face, making him stumble back a step. Before he could regain his balance, Draven was on him, hammering down with his sword. Lucius just managed to bring his own weapon up to fend off the blow, but with him still lay on his back and Draven above him, well let's just say gravity wasn't on his side.

Lucius brought his other hand up to grip onto the blade, no matter that it sliced into his skin. He needed the extra power to stop Draven's sword from going down any closer and I held my breath at the sight of it mere inches from his face.

"No." I uttered wishing my words had the power to stop this but that's when it hit me, maybe my words were never going to be strong enough. Not unless backed up with something stronger. A statement like no other.

Backed up by action.

"Come on, we can slip out," Sophia said, urging me up out of the seat, as everyone had raced to the edge to watch the end. I let her drag me up and pull me towards the entrance when I pulled back. My mind was racing at what I knew I had to do.

"Keira?" She questioned my hesitation with a worried frown.

"I'm sorry, but I can't allow this to happen." Then before she could stop me, I yanked my hand free and raced to the edge, pushing people out of the way. I was just in time to see Draven kick out at Lucius' sword, making it skittle off to the side, leaving him defenceless. He tried to roll out of Draven's way, but he wouldn't allow it. No, instead he stepped on Lucius' injured shoulder and raised his blade high, ready to hammer it down into his heart.

I didn't know whether it would kill him or not but I couldn't take that chance. I knew there was only one thing in the world that could stop that blow right now and that was…

Well, it was me.

Draven had closed his eyes, as if what he was about to do was too painful to watch and I screamed as loud as I could just before I launched myself over the edge. I didn't think the drop would kill me but it certainly would have enough force to break something. I watched just in time as Lucius shouted my name, something that must have been enough to get Draven to stop his attack. I braced myself for the landing and when I felt the impact it wasn't half as hard as I thought it was going to be. I opened my eyes after feeling no pain and the second I saw Draven looking down at me, I knew my plan had worked. Draven had forgone dealing his death blow to Lucius to save me instead.

Lucius got up from the ground and after retrieving his sword he walked over to us. Draven let my feet go and the next thing I knew I had two angry men on my hands, now shouting down at me. Well, as long as they weren't fight each other, then I considered this a vast improvement.

"What the fuck were you thinking!?" Lucius snarled and Draven yelled,

"You could have been killed!"

"What if we couldn't have saved you!?" Again, this was Lucius, followed swiftly by Draven once more,

"You could have seriously injured yourself!"

"I don't care, I am not letting you just kill each other over me! And I promise you, if you value my life at all, then you will stop this shit, or I swear the next thing I do won't just be jumping off a wall, but it will be a damn cliff!" I threw at them both and Draven's and Lucius' reactions were the same. They both flinched back at merely the thought.

"One of us will save you." Draven was the first to argue.

"Yes, but you don't know that, what if you're not there or what if I manage to sneak off?" I challenged.

"Then you would find yourself quickly living out your days locked away!" Lucius snapped and I rolled my eyes as Draven looked in agreement.

"That maybe so, but you can't force me to eat! You can't force me to live or be happy!" They knew I was right but for good measure I added one more threat.

"I swear to you, as the Gods are my witness, if either of you kills the other I will make your life so miserable, that you would envy the dead! I would make you witness each day as I faded away, so stricken by the grief and pain brought on by what the other took from me, you will regret this day for the rest of your life!" Alright, so now they were listening to me. Good, I was finally getting through, no matter how dramatic I sounded.

"Then what would you have us do?" Lucius asked as if pained by the idea.

"I would have one of you forfeit me to the other, so that I may be happy. Because if you both love me as you claim, then you would want that for me." Lucius looked as though I had struck him and turned away because of it. However, Draven looked to be trying to control the impulse to snatch me away from this place and never look back.

"Neither of us are prepared to choose that," Draven gritted out. I took a deep breath and informed him,

"Yes, but it was never your choice to make." They both looked hurt by this so I continued.

"Neither of you ever asked me what I wanted, you never even considered that my feelings mattered! That's not how love works! You don't just take what you want, like some stolen treasure you think belongs to you because you want it more than its owner."

"Then tell us, what is love about if you claim we don't know!" Lucius threw at me and Draven looked ready to agree with him. I took another deep, shuddering breath and placed a hand on each of theirs that were covering the hilts of their swords.

Right at that moment they had never looked more like brothers. Night and day. Each other's balance.

And they didn't even know it.

So, I told them.

"Love is about sacrifice… and there is always another way," I said knowing that Draven would understand my words more than Lucius as they referred to the last time we spoke. But

the second the words were out all I felt was hurt. I screamed out in pain as I felt the impact in my back, one so powerful it brought me to my knees. I briefly took a moment through the sheer agony of it all to look around and all I saw was chaos. People were screaming in the crowd, Draven and Lucius were issuing orders as they had me in their arms. Sounds seemed to fade away and I felt my clothes become wet and sticky. I tried to take a deep breath but something was trying to stop me. That's when I looked down as if I would see the problem for myself.

And I did...

I saw the arrow in my chest.

I had been shot.

CHAPTER THIRTY-SIX

A KISS FROM THE DEVIL

I never imagined this was how it would end. I thought my death would be at the hand of Draven, not by the hand of his actions...not by choices made to fight Lucius. But was this what the Fates had meant all along? Was I always supposed to come here and die for nothing? No, surely there was some way I could stop this?! Surely one of them would save me? Which then begged the question...

Why weren't they?

I didn't even know who it was behind the bow that fired the arrow. Although I shouldn't be surprised, after all, it seemed there was always someone out there trying to kill me.

"We have to do something! She can't fucking breathe!" I heard Lucius snarl and I felt hands grip my shoulders,

"Keira look at me! Open your eyes!" Draven's voice was shouting at me in sheer panic.

"Why can't she look at you?!" Sophia shouted.

"Find her! Bring me her fucking head!" I heard Lucius roaring in the background.

"Keira listen to me!" I couldn't speak and as one of them had said, I could barely breathe. It hurt so bad. It felt like I was drowning and trying to breathe underwater…was I choking?

"She is drowning in her own blood! Just open a fucking vein, let me deal with the people!" Lucius ordered and I felt Draven place something to my lips. My nose still worked as whatever it was, it smelled metallic. Was it blood? Oh good, that was a good idea. Soon, soon and I would be healed. And the pain, the agonising pain I couldn't even scream about would fade. Oh God, but the pain!

"She's not drinking!" I heard Sophia yell and her voice sounded strained as if upset. Well, I guess looking down on what state I was in would do that to you.

"Lucius help me rip out this fucking arrow so I can put my blood on the source, quick!" I felt hands start to move me and my hair being pushed back from my face.

"This will hurt little lamb, but try to hold still." What they didn't know was that I couldn't move my limbs even if I wanted to. I was frozen and unable to do what I wanted, not understanding why. I felt myself trying to scream at what they were doing to me, like silent torture. I only felt the liquid in my throat gurgling up and I tried to open my mouth to spit it out but I couldn't manage it.

Why couldn't I move?

Even when the pain was unbearable. Even when I felt them snapping the arrow and yanking it back through my chest. Why wasn't I screaming. This very question was asked by someone else.

"Why isn't she screaming?" Sophia asked and I felt hands come to my face and then to the rest of my body.

"She isn't moving!" Draven shouted and then I felt him shake me,

"Keira! Keira speak to me, open your eyes, Keira!" I wished

that I could but I felt trapped in my own body. Even in my head I was screaming at them to let me out. Then I heard the cause and it felt as though my blood was the next to freeze inside my veins…

"Why isn't she healing? Why doesn't your blood…" Sophia was cut off when Lucius snarled a venomous,

"Fuck!"

"What?! What is it Septimus?!" Draven demanded and I would have done the same had I been able to move my dead lips. Of course, I would also have gasped had I been able to when I heard the next sentence out of Lucius' mouth.

"The arrow head, its…its Achlys…*she's been poisoned."*

SEPTIMUS

After helping Arsaces pull the arrow from her chest cavity, I watched helplessly as he placed his slit wrist over her wound, ready to cut him in half if need be. It was only when the Princess' voice cut through our hope that I looked down at the broken arrow in my hand. I lifted it to my nose and one sniff was all it took. I could smell the foul stench of misery and sadness that represented the only one powerful enough to create such a poison…

"Achlys?" Arsaces hissed snapping his head back to me after I had informed them of such.

"The one and the fucking same!" I replied with such violent rage, I could feel my eyes seep with the blood of my victims. The ones I had fed on, the ones I had taken to give me strength and life. But what was it all for if my blood was useless now!

Achlys was the Greek Goddess of Eternal Night. She was

the mother of Chaos and her weapon of choice was the 'Mist of Death'.

According to Hesiod, the Greek poet, she was the personification of misery and sadness. She was a pale, emaciated, and weeping creature, one with chattering teeth, swollen knees, bloody cheeks, and her shoulders covered with the eternal dust of the deathly remains of all the lives she took. But more importantly right now, she was the Goddess of deadly poison…one that had no cure.

"No! There must be something?!" the Princess cried out as she, like myself and her brother, knew what this meant. Our blood couldn't save her…

But what if *his* could?

Could this be what it was always meant to be?

"I am not losing her! Do you hear me? DO YOU FUCKING HEAR ME?" Arsaces roared up at the Gods, ready to curse them as I once did.

"There might be another way," I uttered trying to hold on to my sanity and convince myself that this could work. Arsaces snapped his head up and the hope I had planted there was easy to see.

"What, tell me?" he demanded, but right now he was not my King. I was doing this with or without his acceptance. So, I did not reply, for it would only be wasting time. No, he would soon know what I had planned.

"Come, bring her, for this is something I cannot do here." I ordered Arsaces, knowing that he would do anything to save her right now…or he would find death at my hands for trying to stop me. For if I was not successful, then she was lost to us all.

"Easy with her." I looked back over my shoulder to see the Princess crying as her brother hoisted Keira's deathly still body into his arms. Anyone else seeing her and they would have believed her dead but I knew different. I had tasted her blood, so would always know with just a thought, if and where it still beat through her heart. Which was also how I knew she didn't have long.

"Everyone is being evacuated, Imperator," Marcus said after I had jumped back up into the Imperial box, knowing such a thing would not be seen in the eyes of mortals. The second that arrow had pierced her flesh I'd started concealing what was really happening. Then I planted the thoughts of an earthquake and soon the whole place was being evacuated, taking care it was done so at an orderly pace. Thankfully, the place was built for such a thing to be done with ease.

"Did you find her!?" I snarled the demand, knowing nothing would ease my rage other than seeing her blood on my hands. The blood of the killer being spilled in return for the blood they tried to take from me. I would pierce her body with over a thousand poisoned arrows in return. That was if I could restrain myself and my rage from just ripping her head slowly from her neck!

"Not yet, but we will."

"Good, see to it that you do, for I want Lahash on her knees begging for her life at my feet before sunrise. Now go!" I knew Marcus could see how on edge I was and it was an unusual sight but then so was the sight of the only girl I have ever cared for bleeding in the arms of another man. Oh yes, I was on edge all right.

We all moved with pace through the tunnel that connected directly from the Flavian into the Palace of Domitian and we didn't stop until we were back in my private chambers. For what we had to do next couldn't been done in front of any witnesses. Not even those of our own kind. It was utterly forbidden and for once, both Kings would have to choose to break the rules.

Now, all I had to do was convince the other one to cut me open and help me do it.

KEIRA

I couldn't speak, all I could do was hear the desperation in their voices and feel the pain...*so much pain.* I would have passed out from it long ago but this uncontrollable force in my body wouldn't even let me do that. So, the only thing I had left was to try and reach out my mind to speak with them. But even that seemed utterly useless.

"Speak of your plan Septimus, I can feel her slipping further away!" I heard Lucius taking a deep breath before laying it all out on the line.

"She will die and there is only one way left to save her."

"Then fucking do it!" Draven roared but Lucius didn't shout back in the way I would have expected. No, it was Sophia who must have seen what her brother was missing.

"He needs your permission, isn't that right Vampire?"

"I need *his help,*" he reworded, obviously not liking the idea of him needing his permission for anything, especially when it came to saving my life.

"I allow you to break every rule I know, just save her!" Draven snapped back but this was when Lucius said,

"And what of those that you don't, are you willing to break those also?"

"What is it of which you speak!?" Draven demanded. I would have held my breath if didn't already feel as though it was already stuck there. But either way, nothing prepared me for what Lucius would say next as, after a deep breath, he told us precisely what rule needed to be broken in order to save my life.

"I must change her…I must change her into *a Vampire.*" Hearing this must have snapped something inside me as it was enough power to open my eyes but nothing else.

"NO!" Draven roared and just before he could react even more by giving into his furious impulses, Sophia grabbed his arm.

"Look!" He snapped his head down to me and his eyes softened once he saw that I could now see him.

"Oh, sweetest little lamb…" he whispered down at me, placing his forehead to mine.

"She is losing too much blood! If we are to act, we do so now!" Sophia shouted and both Draven and Lucius looked up at each other.

"We can't do this to her!" Draven argued and Lucius growled back,

"Then she dies!" I would have flinched at the harsh reality. Draven closed his eyes against the pain, hearing that caused him.

"What you ask, does it have the power to save her?" Sophia asked, obviously not so opposed to the idea.

"I would be gifting her with the blood of the Devil, right now it is the only thing we have left to fight against this," Lucius told her sounding more in control than anyone else in the room.

"NO!" Draven argued again and said,

"There must be…!"

"What, another way like she said?!" Lucius threw back at him my words just before I was shot.

"Well, what if this is it!? What if this *is* the only other way? I know it is hard to ask you to trust me but something is telling me this is it… this is what she has come here for." Lucius finished and I couldn't help but feel as though he was right. The Oracle had spoken about something I needed from Septimus, something to help defeat the Titans…what if this was it? What if everything happening now was for a reason…or at least part of the reason I was here? Could it be possible that even at the face of my death, could that too really be part of the prophecy?

"What do you mean?!"

"Last night she dreamed of Tartarus, she saw it all as if she had been there before…" Draven snapped his eyes accusingly to Sophia who was looking grave. She merely nodded confirming without words that it was true.

"But how, how is that even possible, she is mortal?" Draven argued and Sophia placed a hand on his arm and said,

"I think we both know she is much more than that." Draven lowered his head as he accepted her words, before coming to terms with it and asking Lucius,

"What else did you see?"

"When she woke, she asked me to delve into her thoughts and see for myself what she had seen."

"And?"

"I saw Cronus," Lucius stated and I wished in that moment I could have cried. Lucius had seen my dream and not the empty void like he claimed…*but all of it.*

"No…*impossible,*" Draven hissed as if hearing that name held enough weight to tell them all they needed to know.

"He was there. He was walking towards her as if he knew her. As the great war battled on around her, the Titans bursting free from their eternal chains, he taunted her with the truth and whispered in her ear…" Lucius said replaying it all back to me.

"Tell me."

"He said, 'You cannot win against a war that has already been won' Then he lifted her face and whispered in her ear, 'For I am a God and you are a mere mortal girl…what could you ever do to me?' Then he left her dreams," Lucius said and then went on to explain his own thoughts,

"What if I was always meant to do this. What if this was the reason she came here?" I looked to Sophia to see her looking as though she was fighting with herself.

"You think she would want this!?" Draven sounded outraged but Lucius threw his own outrage back at him,

"You think she would want to die, knowing how far she had come? I don't know why she came back here but it wasn't for you or I to gain her heart for our own…for she clearly already has ours in the palm of her hand back in her own time." Draven looked deflated as he turned to his sister.

"You know her best of all Sophia, for you have been with her longer than Septimus or I can claim. You are the only one who knows her reasons…would she want this…would she, *forgive us?"* Draven asked his sister, almost pleading with her to make the choice and take that responsibility from them.

"I only know one thing and that is she would do anything to protect those dear to her…*including her unborn child…your child, brother."* The second Draven heard this his hand shot to my stomach and his eyes to my own. The power and strength in his gaze was like nothing else in the world.

"My child?" he repeated in utter shock as if such a thing wasn't possible. He looked so happy for that short moment as if nothing in the world could crush it…well other than me dying of course.

"Then do it!" he vowed with such strength I knew he no longer made the decision just for me but for the child as well and I couldn't have loved him more for it.

I looked to Lucius who tried to mask the hurt that hearing such news must have caused him. It was only small, but I knew Lucius better than most. It was like being allowed that tiny glimpse into his soul, only one seen through his eyes and the pain found there.

"I will need your help. The blood of Lucifer never leaves my heart," Lucius said sternly, all business.

"Then how…?" Sophia started to ask but was quickly interrupted.

"I need you to help me cut it out." My eyes widened and in that moment if I could have screamed NO, I would have. I couldn't have him sacrificing himself for me and cutting out his damn heart!

"Right at this moment this is not a task I will find difficult." Lucius chuckled at Draven's response and said,

"I thought you would say as much." Then he drew his blade and said,

"Cut through my chest but take care, for I only need to access the heart enough for a single drop." Lucius then spun the blade round and handed over his knife.

"Sophia, take my place," Draven said leaving my side and even though I couldn't feel it, she placed my hand in hers. I couldn't bear to watch. But then seeing as he was doing this for me, I knew I also couldn't look away. If he had to endure the pain, then I would also endure it by watching.

"Ready?" Draven asked.

"To be cut open, what do you think?" Lucius asked sarcastically as he pulled off his armour making Draven smirk. Then Lucius lay down next to me on the bed and Draven gave him his reply.

"Yeah, you're fucking ready!" Then he pulled back before plunging the dagger into his chest, taking care not to go too deep but also, deep enough.

"AAAAHHH!" Lucius roared, and I had to say, I felt his pain. If I had been able to move I was sure I would be currently adding vomit to the pints of blood that were now pouring from the large gash in his chest. It overflowed his torso, onto the bed, until we were both lying in a pool of blood, his and mine combined, as we were in this together.

It was a sickening sound, hearing someone cutting into flesh and knowing that it didn't belong to some dead carcass of an animal. No, it belonged to someone I cared deeply for and knowing that he was enduring all of this to save my own life… well it was like receiving another arrow to the chest, only this time, one to the heart.

"Now…ho…hold…back…the sides," Lucius gritted out as Draven had cut him enough, then what I saw would haunt me to my very core. This was no fake body parts made of rubber and stage blood. Or anything you would find on some hospital show, where actors dressed as doctors had their hands inside a dummy pretending to do surgery. No, what I witnessed now was heart stopping real and it had the power to do just that.

Lucius reached his own hand inside his body and that's when I started to lose it. I felt myself starting to fall to a place I had no control over and the next thing I knew I was screaming inside my mind.

"Hurry up, we are losing her!" Sophia shouted as Lucius lifted his hand up before delving it back inside his own chest, reaching in to find his heart. Blood spewed up around the invasion and he screamed as if he had found what he had been looking for.

"Keira listen to me, give me a sign, anything that tells me this is what you want, that you are ready for this? Because once you taste this blood, it will change you…it will change you forever!" Draven said looking to me and with the last of my conscious self, I did the only thing I had the power left to do. I told him with my eyes that I was ready. That I would do anything for us to be together and that I would do anything to save our unborn child.

"She is ready," Draven confirmed with a nod.

"Well she'd better be, because this is going to hurt!" Lucius said before tearing his hand from his chest and curled inside of his fist I saw a single talon. He shifted over to me the best he could with a gaping hole in his chest and brought his bloody hand to my mouth.

"Ready to be a child of the Devil?" he asked me and I could barely believe he was smirking down at me. I blinked once, telling him 'Hell yes' and so he nodded before uncurling the talon and letting the blood it had cupped inside drip into my mouth. It was as if time stopped as we all watched that single large droplet fall from the end of his deadly claw. The second it landed on my tongue, I felt the power of it rip through my body as though it was trying to tear it apart.

I heard screaming. Screaming so loud it felt as though my ears would burst. At first, I thought my body was still trapped as I couldn't move but then I realised that I was being held down by my arms as the rest of my body fought to be freed. I thrashed and turned, trying to twist in their hold but it was useless.

I couldn't get free of this pain.

"Calm! Keira, Calm down!" Draven shouted down at me before asking Lucius,

"What's happening?!"

"This is how it is, it is how I remember it was. Just give it time," Lucius responded and just as he said it, Sophia shouted,

"Look! She has already started to heal!"

"It's working!" Draven shouted as if all his prayers had been answered at once. I had to agree with him, it was certainly working all right as it felt like my veins had been pumped with lava! Like my blood had been replaced by liquid Hellfire and my skin was melting from the bone because of it.

"She's burning up!"

"It's fighting off the remaining poison, trying to regain control back over its new host…just give it another minute and it will calm," Lucius promised and I was only left hoping that he was right, because it felt as though I was being burned alive.

"Here, this may help." Draven said striping off his own armour before pulling off the rest, uncaring who may see. Then he lay down on the blood-soaked bed with little care and turned his body to ice, before encasing me with it. His skin felt as if I was being touched by Heaven and I moaned wanting more.

"More…please more." I begged.

"Get on the other side," Draven gritted out as if hating himself for asking. But looking at Lucius' blood soaked skin, he now at least seemed fully healed as his chest no longer showed the marks of such brutality. I half expected him to say something cocky, as I knew the Lucius back in my time would have. But instead he got on the bed on the other side of me and wrapped an arm around me, tucking his front to mine.

Now I had ice from both sides and I sighed as the pain started to subside.

"Better?" Draven asked and I nodded snuggling closer to both of them, trying to drain from their ice-cold skin.

"So, it is done. The change is complete." I heard Lucius say somewhere in my fog filled mind. I felt my eyes rolling back in my skull as the dark pull once more started to take hold.

"Now what…what does she need?" I heard Draven ask in the shadows of my mind.

"Rest, plenty of rest and then when she wakes…" Lucius paused as if trying to think how best to word it. In the end, he just came right out and said it after Draven snapped,

"What, what then?!"

"Well then…"

"…She feeds."

CHAPTER THIRTY-SEVEN

FOLLOW THE BLOOD BRICK ROAD

Waking up I felt a thirst of the likes I had never known. It felt as though baking hot sand had been poured down my throat followed by acid. The last thought I had was lava flowing down the mountain into that of an icy lake. An indestructible force, raging war against the body that contained it, only to find it tamed by the love of two men.

"Th…th…thir…sty," I said reaching out to see if anyone was there. My voice sounded raw and haggard, as if screaming for hours on end when you suffered from a cold. I felt someone taking my hand and the second they did I was assaulted by the pounding in my head. It was a beating drum, telling me that blood was near.

To take it. It was mine.

"She needs to feed and that…" Lucius' words were cut off when, before I knew what I was doing, I had reached out and grabbed someone. With a speed I never thought possible I had the body half over my lap and had sunk my teeth into a warm neck. I felt my fangs growing as they had done that day I had been on top of Draven. The second his blood bathed my tongue, I felt as if I was drinking straight from the immortal well in Heaven. As though I had found the fountain of youth and drank from it using the Holy Grail as my cup.

It was incredible.

"Well, that would do it." I heard Lucius chuckling.

"Oh dear, should we stop her?" Sophia asked and I opened my eyes to see I was locked on to a familiar neck.

"No! No, it's alright, let her drink," Draven said holding out a hand to stop anyone from trying to intervene. I gulped him down without much thought of anything else but quenching what felt like an eternal thirst.

"When you feel the pull start to cease, that is when you must release," Lucius told me stepping closer. I nodded around my prey and the second I felt sated, like Lucius said, the pull and need for blood started to fade. I pulled back feeling the flesh around my fangs do so with a pop. Draven slowly lifted his head and gave me a questioning look. I covered my mouth and shouted,

"Oh my god, im' ssso, sssorry!" I said stuttering and asking myself why. It felt like my mouth was too full. Sophia giggled and Lucius looked to be fighting a grin.

"Whath wrong witttth me?" I slurred.

Draven gave me a soft gentle look and reached up to tap on one of my new fangs. It felt strange and I couldn't help but shudder at how sensitive it felt.

"You will get used to it in time," Lucius told me with a smirk.

"Dith you?" I asked feeling myself getting annoyed with the way I sounded but he just shrugged his shoulders and said,

"I suggest for now trying to practice retracting them, instead of speaking with them." I felt like growling at him and then asked,

"And how doth I doth ttthhat ethaclly?" I felt like I had to keep swallowing just so I could speak without drooling. Talk about embarrassing.

"Well, I am sure we all have our different techniques but for me I simply think of something I find distasteful," Lucius replied with a grin playing at his lips.

"Like wthat?!" I snapped folding my arms across my chest and giving Sophia an evil glare when she started laughing again.

"I'm sorry…it's just, oh by the Gods, it's too funny!" Sophia said again bursting out into a fit of giggles before having to walk away.

"If you really want to know, I think of vegetables." Hearing this, like Sophia, I couldn't help but burst into a fit of slurred giggles and thankfully, it relieved some of the worry I felt building up. I was way out of my depth and could barely believe what I now faced.

I was no longer human.

I was a freaking Vampire!

Holy shit! I was a Vampire? Okay, so first things first, get rid of lisp creating fangs *and then* start freaking out. So, Lucius said to think of something distasteful, well after being here I didn't have to think too long. I felt a tingling sensation in my mouth and I reached up to feel that they were gone.

"Hey, I did it!" I shouted enthusiastically and Draven looked pleased for me.

"What did you think of?" he asked but I wasn't the one that answered him, Lucius did.

"At a guess, I would bet on it being a dormouse dipped in honey."

"She doesn't like this delicacy?" Draven asked sounding

surprised. Seriously, was a dead mouse dripped in honey some kind of ancient version of caviar or foie gras? Not that either of them were nice thinking about it, so maybe it was.

"Let's just say I had an incident of illness on my hands," Lucius replied and I blushed ten shades of scarlet and Draven's reply didn't help,

"Ah, I see."

"How long before we can move her?" Sophia asked, now over her giggling fit and getting back to business…which was something I was now out of the loop on.

"The blood will help her gain her strength. I would say she would be ready to leave shortly," Lucius answered coolly.

"Why, where are we going?" I asked looking from Lucius to Sophia and then back to Draven. He was still sat next to me on the bed and it was only now that I realised the bed was void of blood and so was I. Someone had obviously washed me and re-dressed me, something I was more than thankful for. He brushed some of the hair back from my forehead and said softly,

"I am taking you home."

"But wait a minute, what about what happened between you guys?"

"We have come to an agreement," Lucius was the one to answer me.

"What, that each of you get to share me? You will both have me every other weekend and alternate Christmases?" I asked, causing them both to give me the same confused look.

"I don't know what that means," Draven said and Lucius agreed,

"Me neither."

"It means that they have found a truce," Sophia told me stepping forward and adding,

"Lucius has forfeited his claim to you as he believes this

was his destiny, the one the Oracle spoke of. Of course, now that you are also classed as one of his *made,* it also means…"

"That you can't kill him! Ha…well would you look at that, guess you two have to be friends again after all…um…I knew there was always another way," I said feeling quite pleased with myself because I knew for a fact that if Lucius died then so would all of his 'Children'.

"I hardly call almost dying being 'another way'!" Draven said angrily.

"Yes, well I didn't exactly fire the arrow, and speaking of which, is the bitch dead yet?" I asked pulling myself further up the bed and as I felt the deep-rooted ache in my bones, Draven helped me. As if he knew I was silently struggling.

"Easy little lamb, your body is still adjusting." I gave him a smile in thanks.

"And Layla…I mean Lahash, what of her?" I asked again. Lucius emitted a low growl which was all the answer I needed. He spoke anyway.

"Her time is coming to an end, have no worry of that." So, I guess history was repeating itself then, I thought gritting my teeth. The bitch got away again!

"Come, it is time you rest some more, for shortly we will leave and you will need all your strength for the journey," Draven told me softly placing his hand at my cheek. I reached up and covered it with my own and asked,

"Can I have a moment alone with Sophia?" He gave me a small smile and said,

"But of course, Septimus and I need to speak with one another, but we will not be far." Then he kissed me on the forehead before leaving with Lucius. Once the door was closed Sophia was by my side and in panicked tones we both said,

"What are we going to do!?"

"What the Hell are we going to do?!"

"Okay, so we need to think about this…" I said after our initial freak out.

"Yeah, I would say because once my brother has you back in Persia, well let's just say I hope you like confined spaces." I groaned and let my head fall back.

"Surely it's not that bad."

"Oh, you think?" Sophia argued.

"Okay so what am I facing here, a pretty giant bird cage, a life in gold chains with matching gold bikini, or tallest tower type of gig?" I asked only half joking.

"Knowing my brother, maybe all three but if you're lucky, with maybe a walk around the courtyard for your birthday… with an armed guard of course," she joked back.

"So, the way I see it, is that we have one shot at this," I said making her raise a brow at me.

"And that is?"

"We use the Black Gate from the Persian side." Sophia started shaking her head and reminded me,

"But it's impossible, unless you magically have Pythia's coin with you or managed to send a damn homing pigeon to tell the other two to meet us there, then we…wait, why are you looking at me like that?"

"Because you're a genius!" I exclaimed excitedly.

"Well yes, but that's beside the point when I have no clue what my genius has gotten me into this time," she responded dryly.

"Ye of little faith…Okay, so in theory, being changed into a Vamp now has increased whatever power I had…right? I mean that's how it's supposed to work…yes?" Sophia thought on it a moment and agreed,

"Yes, in theory, why?"

"Because we have work to do and not much time to do it."

"So, no rest for you then," she commented and I winked at her before saying,

"There is no resting...*not until we are home.*"

After this Sophia and I made what little plans we could from this end as the main goal was to see how far I could stretch the powers I already had. This was our one and only shot as we both knew that when Draven got me back to his palace, he wasn't going to let me out of his sight again. Sophia told me that Draven had no choice but to allow Lucius access to me as I would only weaken if I didn't. As was the same with all of his kind. Although granted I was the first and only human to be turned, so it was anyone's guess at what could happen. Either way Lucius had sworn a vow to do all in his power to help me through this.

Something I was also hoping for once we made it back... which begged the question, what was he going to think about me returning only to find he had turned me into a Vampire in the past. But more importantly...

What was Draven going to say?!

This thought had me in near panic, one that Sophia had to deal with.

"Now is not the time for a meltdown, now is the time to form a plan, so let's deal with this current shit storm should we and deal with the other, commonly known as my brother, later." This had been her advice and I had to agree with it, for I wasn't going to get anywhere by freaking out now.

So, instead I did what I had to. I reached out my mind further than I ever thought possible. At first it was pretty much the same thing, me shouting 'Hello? Can anyone hear me?' in my mind and feeling like a grade A idiot for doing it.

"Try and focus on your memories of Pip and..." she started saying when suddenly something started to happen, someone started speaking back to me...

"Katie?" I uttered her name and Sophia looked at me as though I had finally gone mad.

"Oh Gods, not this again!"

"Ssshh, she's trying to speak to me...quick I need a mirror or something!" Sophia looked as if ready to shake me out of this craziness but instead went with it and grabbed me a mirror.

"Alright but if you start asking who is the fairest of them all, I am so outta here." I rolled my eyes and took the mirror from her, trying to keep a straight face, as to be honest, it was pretty funny.

"Katie...are you...um, there?" I asked in unsure tones.

"Oh brother," Sophia muttered.

"Keira, can you hear me?" Okay so I don't know what was freakier, waking up with fangs and talking with a lisp or looking at myself in the mirror as someone else speaking back to me! Someone who looked exactly like me! Take about enough reasons for therapy! Can anyone scream mental asylum?

"Holy shit, you weren't going crazy," Sophia said after sucking in a sharp breath. I rolled my eyes and muttered back,

"Thanks for the vote of confidence there, Robin."

"Oh, we are so discussing this when we are done here," Sophia threatened and I released a sigh. Yep, we so were.

"Uh, hi Katie, how's...um Keira's head?" Sophia asked giving the mirror a little wave and wincing when I shot her an 'Are you serious' look.

"Really? How's Keira's head? That's what you went with?" This time Sophia rolled her eyes and said,

"Maybe we should leave the arguing until after this conversation with your sub-conscious is done." Okay, so I had to give her that, my timing sucked.

"You two are funny." Katie said on a giggle.

"Can you help us? I gather you know what I am trying to do?" I asked.

"Well it's kind of hard to miss the twenty minutes of screaming 'hello, can anyone hear me' gig. Besides, I think the furthest you got was some poor confused hand maiden in the next room, who now probably thinks God speaks to her and sounds like a woman," she answered making me laugh.

"What am I doing wrong?"

"It's not what, but who." I frowned and shook my head a little.

"What do you mean, who?"

"You're reaching out to everyone around you, hoping someone is open enough to hear, like casting a net blindly.... but what you should be doing is focusing on just one person, someone who is connected to you...*like Ari."* I knew what she was saying. I was wasting all my energy on trying to reach out to everyone instead of trying to home in to someone I knew would listen.

"Alright, focus on Ari...gotya!" I said and after saying goodbye to my other self, that being Katie, I tried again. This time though I doubled my efforts and when I did, I felt myself casting out in a straight line inside of throwing my powers over everything, like a blanket. It felt strange but it was the only way to describe it.

"Okay so not to freak you out but your eyes are turning black and what's that...?" Sophia said and I looked in the mirror to find she was right.

My eyes had changed.

But they weren't blood red like Lucius' were when using his powers. Or glowing like Draven's. No, they were unlike any I had seen before. They were onyx black, with a white light spreading out around where my iris should be, but then in the centre of my pupil was something flaming. I couldn't quite make it out as I had never seen it before.

"What is that?" I asked and Sophia spoke in hushed tones,

"The Infinity symbol?"

"What does it mean?" I asked just as confused as her. We looked at each other in the mirror and after a few fearful seconds, I received her answer and it scared me....

"The War, its begun."

After this Sophia explained that the infinity war was one prophesied as being an everlasting war between a new powerful race and the elders. She confessed that she didn't know much about it as it was always a myth in their world. But then I asked about what new race it spoke of and with her answer it all started to make sense. The new race was human hybrids, ones forbidden to be created but ones prophesied all the same.

Well, considering I was now the only human Vampire out there, it didn't take a genius to guess that it was no longer a myth. Although I couldn't exactly put Sophia's fears of such at ease considering I doubted I was going to be around long enough to keep that claim. But it did make me wonder, what would our child be when it was born? Would it be human, Demon, Angel or this hybrid she spoke of?

Well, either way I would love it no matter what, just as I knew Draven would.

After this I also had to explain briefly how Katie had never really left me that day. Although, I had to say that Sophia didn't look quite as surprised as I would have expected her to be. She also mentioned something cryptic about a cloned soul, about which I had no clue. I had tried asking her but shortly after this

Draven and Lucius came back and it was time to act out the first part of our plan.

I fell back to the bed dramatically and let Sophia go to work. Well, let's face it, knowing my bad acting skills, then one look at my face and they would both call bullshit...that was if they ever called anything bullshit in this time. For all I knew the term was mouse shit...oh no Keira, don't go there again, as I think the last thing I needed right now was to see what vomiting blood looked like.

Sophia went on to pretend that I needed longer to rest and to postpone our journey back for a day or two. This, unbeknown to Draven and Lucius, was so that it would give Pip and Ari time to reach the Black Gate. What Katie had suggested worked and after a few confused screams, Ari finally understood what was going on. After I first convinced her that A; I wasn't hiding in the room somewhere, trying to creep her out, B; I wasn't dead speaking from the grave trying to creep her out and C; I wasn't a ghost come to haunt her because of B and also doing so to try and creep her out. I mean seriously, what kind of sick sense of humour did she think I had?

I explained the plan and told her to be ready as Pip would know what to do. Of course, this helped immensely when she explained that Pip's favourite Mohawk had been found, oh and that it *was* a woman. She didn't tell me this of course, but I gathered as much as Ari hadn't yet started shouting about Ranka being a man. Something I think would have been on the front page of the 'OMG News'.

Well, at least it looked like after Ranka's human scum chow down, he found himself enough energy to change back. And just in time too because I'm not sure he would have helped me if he hadn't.

So, now the plan was set and after a day of 'resting' we soon found ourselves travelling through the streets of Rome on horseback. It was after sunset and the streets were quiet, which made the sights of Rome even more striking under the moonlight. I wished I had seen more of it but to be honest, since being kidnapped, nearly getting married, shot with a poisonous arrow, turned into a Vampire and then plotting to get home, I had found time for little else.

Lucius and his men were to accompany us for a while so that we didn't run into any trouble. What trouble we could get into considering the soldiers that had followed Draven and Sophia through the Black Gate were of the supernatural variety, then I didn't know. To be honest I just thought this was Lucius' way of saying goodbye.

I had already spoken with Lucius alone that day, as I obviously had questions. Ones like, is it a bad idea to try and get a sun tan and should I wipe Hawaii off my bucket list. Also, should I stay away from granny's silver and forgo the garlic bread as a starter…? Basic need to know things like that. All of which had him howling with laughter once I had explained what most of the stuff meant.

Thankfully, he put my mind at ease with the biggest one…*the sun.* He had picked me up out of bed and carried me outside, even if I was screeching like a girl about to be dunked into an ice bath. Let's just say he proved his point…I didn't become an overcooked roast on Thanksgiving.

He said he believed it would all be different with me as I was still mostly human and so far, other than that one initial thirst, I felt no different. Oh, but then there was the added reaction to any overemotional outbursts…fangs. For some reason, the second I was getting teary saying goodbye to Lucius in the bedroom, my fangs popped out and I was now not only a crying fool but a lisping one too.

"Don't worry little Keira Girl, you will get a handle on it… in time." I had wanted to add, 'yeah, I hope I do get a handle on it in *my own time*, as that was precisely where I was headed.'

"If you want to know the truth, I used to practice speaking with them alone in front of a mirror," Lucius admitted and I swear I saw a slight blush added to that confession. I couldn't help it but it made me love him even more!

But before our private goodbyes, I found myself blurting out the question,

"Why did you agree to this, why are you letting me go?" He released a big sigh and laid it all out for me.

"Because, I knew that although I had a claim to your heart, I now know that I would never have a claim to your unborn child." His reply had been a heart-breaking one as I knew he was making the decision to give me up out of his love for me. After this I threw my arms around him and whispered through my tears,

"I will always love you."

"As I you… My Little Keira Girl." He hadn't realised it but until then he had never said the 'my' part of the nickname he had given me, as before now he had never called me his in this time. But now, I guess he did have the claim to do so as after all, I was now one of his vampires. It made me wonder if this was subconsciously where it had all begun, but then I shook off the thought as that wasn't a can of worms I was ready to open yet.

We made it to the river and I felt sorry for Draven having to witness my emotional goodbye to Lucius. But it couldn't be helped. At first, I didn't think he would let me off his horse, but one pleading look up at him and well, he was putty in my hands. I ran over to Lucius as he too had dismounted and then I hugged him to me.

"Thank you for all you have done," I told him, knowing now that this had all been prophesied. It just had to be.

"Are you thanking me for kidnapping you, little one?" he teased and I nudged him and teased him right back,

"It wasn't all bad."

"Then I seriously must question what you class as a good time, for you were shot, near to death and then made into a child of darkness." I laughed, shrugged my shoulders and replied,

"Yep, just a regular day in the life of the Electus." At this he burst out laughing and after kissing my forehead he wished me farewell, bidding me to take care until next time. Unbeknown to him the next time we spoke would be nearly two thousand years into the future.

After this he left us to continue to the river alone and I think once Lucius was out of sight Draven could finally breathe more easily. You could tell he was eager to get back to his own land and was probably already planning for my eternal 'lock down'. No doubt already constructing a Fort Knox type building in his head, one to be built with no windows and only one door! I grinned to myself a little at the thought but then sadness swept over me as I was getting closer to another heart I would soon have to break. This one, much more difficult than the first.

Draven dismounted and then reached up and pulled me from the horse. A few of Lucius' men had continued on with us, no doubt to retrieve the horses once we were finished with them.

"So where is the Gate?" I asked as I looked up and down the river bank seeing nothing. I knew it was dark but the moon provided enough light to be able to see that there was no gate like we had stepped through in coming here. He took my hand in his and started walking me down the bank towards the water's edge. I looked behind to see the soldiers all followed but it was Sophia my eyes sought out. She gave me an encouraging nod, as only she knew what we had to do once we reached the other side.

"It needs immortal blood to summon it," Draven said pulling me from my depressing thoughts of my upcoming betrayal. I then watched as he pulled free one of his smaller blades he had strapped to him, for he had many hidden there. Then he sliced clean across his palm before holding his hand over the water and making a fist, letting the blood flow. At the first droplet, something started to happen. The water started to create little waves and then it grew in speed, swirling around faster and faster. It started to rise up out of the normal water level of the river, as if a tornado was picking it up. I stepped back at the sight but Draven grabbed my hand and pulled me back to his side.

"Don't be frightened!" he told me, having to shout over the sound of tons of water spinning and creating a vacuum. As it rose up, it started to tilt so that soon it became fully upright and presented itself as a liquid portal. It looked darker than all the rest and more hostile.

"Allow me brother, let her see me go first as it may ease her fears," Sophia said winking at me and I knew this was so she could go first and warn the others. I watched her step onto the water without sinking and then into the portal, quickly disappearing from sight.

"We go together!" Draven shouted and then tightened his grip on my hand before we followed Sophia through the wet abyss. Like before, it felt like I was falling, but upright, not down as I expected. Almost as if someone had a rope tied around my waist and was yanking me forward through space.

I would have fallen forward flat on my face once on the other side but Draven managed to spin quickly and catch me before that happened.

"Easy there, I have got you and you're safe," he comforted me and I gripped onto his forearms a little longer just until the world stopped spinning. After this he moved me out of the way so that his soldiers could follow us through.

"Scout ahead and wait for us outside the entrance…I don't want to take any chances of an attack from the Scythians," Draven ordered firmly.

"Yes, My King." His general answered with a bow and then marched his men out of there. I looked around and couldn't see anyone, knowing that Sophia was keeping them hidden until the men had gone. The last thing we wanted was a small army of men forcing us out of here at Draven's command.

"Come, let's get you home." Draven said as he started to grip my hand and pull me towards where his men had disappeared to. Then we heard Sophia's voice.

"Well, look who I found!" she said faking surprise.

"Tootie bear!" Pip shouted before launching herself at me, meaning Draven had no choice but to let me go. Her green hair had been braided back and it whipped me in the face making me laugh.

"Miss me?" I asked.

"Sure did, Buckaroo! *And so did this,*" she said, whispering this last part as she reached down between us so she could place something in my hand.

"Mohawk says hi, oh and bye-bye." I smiled and whispered, back,

"Thank you, my friend." I then gripped my hand around the large coin protecting it like the lifeline it was.

"What are they doing here?" Draven's stern mistrusting voice brought me back to our situation. I pulled back from Pip and nodded to Ari and Sophia before then turning to Draven.

Then I told him the heart-breaking truth.

"We are going home." Then I threw the coin and…

Unlocked the Gate.

CHAPTER THIRTY-EIGHT

HOMEWARD BOUND

Before he could act, I turned and threw the coin into the Black Gate, praying to every God that it worked.

The coin flew through the air and just at the last second, when Draven registered what was happening, it seemed to land in the empty space between the rumbling stone. It stayed suspended there for a few moments before it started to dissolve.

"What...what have you done!?" Draven cried out in anger taking a step closer to the gate as if something could be done. But it was too late. The portal was already starting to change. It had started to suck in all the rock around it, breaking it up into tiny fragments until a vortex of fine, spinning dust was all that was left.

"I'm sorry Draven, but I have no choice." I looked back at the girls to emphasise my point, as it wasn't just me I had to go home for.

"You *do* have a choice, Keira!" he told me and my heart broke for him. I knew what awaited me on the other side but for

Draven, he had an eternity to wait for me. He pulled me off to one side and his grip told me that he never wanted to let go. This was it, there was no other way but to tell him the truth. I looked back to Sophia and she nodded for me to do what needed to be done.

"I came here for the prophecy Draven, *because I had to,"* I told him with such fervency that he had no choice but to feel the magnitude of my words.

"What do you mean?"

"Back home, back through there…" I paused and looked behind me.

"…that's where I belong. It's where everyone is counting on me. So many people I care about, my friends, my family and most of all, you, my husband…they don't know it yet but they are all relying on me to return and save them from the war that is coming," I told him with such fierceness, the truth of what I was telling him couldn't be denied.

"The dream? It's true, isn't it? It's what awaits you in your time?" I nodded, swallowing hard.

"I'm the only one who can stop it." This time I couldn't keep the sadness from my voice.

"No! That's all the more reason for you to stay!" he argued and as far as arguments went, it was a good one. It would have been so easy. To stay with the man I loved, to be with him for longer than what little time awaited me back through that portal. But what type of person would I be if I chose my own happiness over the happiness of those I cared for.

"I know you, Draven. I know that you don't have it in you to condemn me to a life of misery and pain. Both of which stem from knowing that I have left everyone I've ever cared for behind to face certain death. To face the end of days, knowing there was some way I could have stopped it. *You would never do that to me,"* I told him, then I looked down and placed both hands over my belly and said,

"You would never do that *to us."* He closed his eyes against his utter anguish and I hated myself for doing this to him.

"But I can't lose you," he told me with his voice nearly breaking.

"You will never lose me…*never,"* I told him, framing his face with both hands and pulling him down to me.

"I could never forget you, I could never forget our time together…I could never forget falling in love all over again," I said with tears streaming freely down my face and he sucked in a shuddered breath, one I felt rock me to my core.

"I…I don't want to let you go," he whispered placing his forehead to mine and I could feel his own tears landing on my skin. Each one was as beautiful as it was torturous.

"I know," I told him, leaning up to kiss away the tears left on his cheeks.

"But I also know that if I don't go, then I wouldn't be the person you fell in love with and this soul, my soul…well, it wouldn't be worthy of your love." This whispered confession was something he knew and in the end, it was reminding him why he had fallen in love with me in the first place. Why, even when he thought me just a mortal girl, not his Electus or Chosen One, he was still ready to give up everything just to be with me.

And now, knowing what he did, it was also the reason he had to let me go.

"I will miss you," he whispered once before pulling me to him, where I let myself cry freely in his embrace. He placed his hand to the back of my head and held me to his chest where great heart-breaking sobs erupted.

"Ssshh, don't cry for me, for I want the last time I see you to be your beautiful smile, to see your enchanting eyes light up as they look at me. I want to see your soul and heart one last time, so that I may remember it and…*and keep it with me for always…for the eternity I must wait."* Hearing his beautiful goodbye was too much to take. I gripped onto him as if I never wanted to let go and it felt like I was saying so much more than goodbye for now…it felt like I was saying goodbye forever…*our forever.*

Because he was my temptation…and this…well, this was my sacrifice.

Instead of the lifetime we could have together, I was exchanging it for a together that could only stem from a shorter life with little time.

Oh yes, it was my sacrifice indeed and one I had to make.

"I love you," I said looking up at him and he granted me a smile that both warmed my heart and almost crushed it.

"And I love you, which is why I am…*I am willing to let you go,"* he told me and I nodded, biting my lip to stop it from quivering.

"I know," I replied and then granted him his last wishes. I smiled up at him and gave him a sight he wished to remember me by.

"Thank you. And now something for you to remember me by," he said placing his lips to mine and kissing me one last time. I felt him pulling at something before he reached inside my cloak, then he wrapped his arms around me and pulled me close. We both deepened the kiss and it was one I felt tugging at my heart, branding the memory to my soul for the rest of my life and hopefully… *far beyond.*

I don't know who broke the kiss first, but I knew that neither of us wanted to. *We had to.* I grasped his hand, entwined his fingers in mine and just held onto him a second longer before I stepped away. I kept my hand in his until it was far enough that my steps wouldn't allow it any longer. My fingertips grazed slowly along his until the connection was broken. I let my hand linger there for a second before it fell and his did the same.

"Ready?" Sophia asked me softly placing a hand to my forearm. I couldn't speak, so nodded, as I wanted to reserve all of my words left for Draven…*for my King.* I saw her nod to her brother as did the rest of my girls, before one by one they stepped through the portal until all that was left was me and Draven.

"Wait for me?" I asked on a shuddering breath and I wiped away my tears so that I could see him more clearly and not through a watered veil of sadness. I took a step back and I knew only one more and I would be gone from this land…Gone from him.

His last words granted him another of my smiles,

"I will wait for you always…*my wife."* I mouthed the words 'I love you' and he did the same in return and then I closed my eyes and took that last step back…

Back home.

Draven…
(The Present Day)

Standing in the window of one of Brockencote Hall's feature suites I looked on to the lake and thought about my bride to be. Truth be told she was already my wife and had been for some time. But I wanted to make her mine, not just in my world but also her own. I needed to make her mine in every way possible.

But her emotional reaction to saying goodbye this morning

was unsettling me. It felt like so much more than a simple, 'goodbye for now' and much direr. Hell, if I hadn't known better, I would have said it felt like she was saying goodbye for a small eternity. The way she had clung to me, the way she had been trying to hold back the tears. I knew a bride's wedding day could be an emotional undertaking but this…well this felt like so much more.

It felt as though she held the weight of the world on her shoulders and because of it she was now being forced to do something she didn't want to do. Now I know that could have just been my paranoia speaking and considering how many times I had almost lost her, then no one could blame me for such. But it wasn't just her reactions, the way her heart pounded in her chest, or the way her breathing hitched on her words. The way her fingers bit into my flesh, as though trying to anchor herself to me. No, even without those things, if nothing else, it was that kiss.

It was the way she had grabbed me to her as if my own farewell hadn't been enough. The way small bumps broke out along her skin and the way her tongue duelled with mine, as if trying to burn the memory of my taste to her very soul. I hadn't lied when I placed my forehead to hers and told her it felt like another gift. But now, as I looked down at the ring she had given me to hold on to, it felt more and more like a long goodbye.

To say it was a disconcerting feeling that was quickly taking hold of me, was somewhat of an understatement. I knew something was wrong. I could just feel it.

'Take care of my heart and my wings, Dominic,' had been one of the last things she had said to me. At the time, I had found such sentiments a beautiful reminder of the gift she was giving me…her tender, loving heart. But now, it felt as if it had been said to mean so much more. I had made her promise me

that she would be at that altar and I had believed her wholeheartedly when she replied with,

'I promise you I will be there. I vow nothing in this world would be able to stop me'.

Now, looking back those seemed like choice words indeed and I was now asking myself, had she been planning something behind my back? I knew deep down we were both keeping something from each other. Mine done so out of protection, for there was nothing I wouldn't do to keep her safe. But what if she had somehow found out about the prophecy?

Not that it mattered as there was nothing she could do to change the actions needed to fulfil it. I had seen to that, for as much as the idea elevated my soul, I would never be able to give her a child. There was too much at risk and her life was too precious to me to ever take that chance. I knew one day I would have to tell her. The Gods knew how I had tried, but the truth of the matter was simple. I had taken a coward's way out and used the excuse that every time such a conversation was interrupted, I took it as fate.

She deserved to know, I knew this but not yet. Not until we were married. Which in itself, now seemed like a worrying prospect, if my little Vixen was indeed up to something. So, this was why I stood at this window and waited. Waited to see her limousine arrive, which I knew from the tracking device I had on my phone, would be any minute now. Looking down at the GPS app I watched that little blue dot getting closer and closer, until finally it pulled up the long driveway, coming to a stop outside the main entrance.

And finally, I could breathe.

I couldn't see them from this angle but I allowed them enough time to exit before making the call to the front desk.

"Hello Mr Draven, how may I help you?" a generic voice answered, one trying to sound overly helpful. Not surprising considering they knew that I was the insanely rich man that had booked all of the rooms in this place. And at late notice had to also find other accommodation for any guests they may have had booked. But money talks as it always has done and more importantly, it got me the results I needed. It was rare in this world I didn't get what I wanted and now was no different from any other.

Or so I thought.

"I am enquiring about my bride to be, has she and her party checked in yet?" I asked allowing my voice to seep into undertones of great authority, as was usually effective when dealing with the human world.

"I am afraid not, although we are booking in some of the wedding party, there seems to be four guests missing, your bride being one of them, Sir." I had to repress the urge to growl. Especially as I watched the limousine coming back into view before driving down the lane and joining the main road.

"Very well," I said hanging up and forgoing the pleasantries...after all, it looked like I now had more pressing matters on my hands. I tapped my phone a few times, placed it to my ear and issued only one order,

"Bring the car round." Then I placed a hand to the window as I watched their car go out of sight and asked the question aloud...

"What are you up to now, little wife of mine?"

Sat in the back of the limousine I quickly found myself wishing for any one of my Ferraris, so that I might be able to put my fucking foot down and catch up with them. This traffic had me nearly pulling my hair out. I looked down at my phone once more and followed their progress. I had tried ringing my sister, knowing now that she, along with the Imp and Ari, my brother's chosen, were also with her. However, my sister wasn't answering her phone and that fact alone was enough to scream trouble.

I don't know why I felt the need to get to them with such urgency, but I just did. I could feel it, and that combined with Keira's goodbye to me this morning, then I knew something was happening. Something big.

By the time I saw where their blue dot had arrived I released a sigh of relief, knowing that in all likelihood, Keira could not wait to see the venue. I allowed myself the gratification of a smirk at thinking of such but then started to ask myself the important question, one I knew I should have done so long ago…

Why here?

Why had Keira asked to get married here and so quickly? At the time, I had simply found myself delighted that she wanted to marry me with haste as it seemed, like myself, she couldn't wait. But now, well now I was giving into paranoia and near praying that was all it was.

I wasn't long behind them, however I was cursing our current situation as we were stuck behind an old Ford hatchback that would have been better served on the top of a scrap heap about fifty thousand miles ago. What was worse was being in a limousine. It wasn't as though my driver could overtake the old fool on these winding country roads. So, in the end I did the only thing I could think to do. I accessed the senior's mind and had him pull into what looked to be a garden centre, so that the long line of traffic stuck behind him could now move more freely…but more importantly, with greater speed.

By the time we pulled onto the private road into Witley Court, I knew they had been there almost twenty minutes and by the time I exited the car my heart was pounding. I looked up at the huge dramatic shell, remembering the day it was ablaze. Of course, the ones responsible had paid dearly for the offense as, unlike what the mortal history claims, it was no accident in the bakery that caused it to burn to its bare bones.

I couldn't help after witnessing it again and seeing the result at such a deception, I found myself pulling my phone from my jacket and placing another call.

"My Lord, I am sorry but you wish me to do what?"

"As I said Lauren, I wish you to break into Keira's truck and tell me if you find anything she might have left. Call me when it's done." I waited for the call back, not wanting to be seen inside until I was given the sign to do so. I hated it but I had a gut feeling that just wouldn't go away no matter how I tried to digest it. I even found myself flinching when I heard the buzzing of my phone, becoming as jittery as a human.

"Speak to me."

"There is nothing here, my Lord." I released a sigh and closed my eyes looking up at the sun and silently thanking the immortal Lords above. I started to walk back towards the limousine ready to go back to the hotel and leave my wife to be to her pre-wedding plans… then Lauren continued,

"There's only some cds, some fuel receipts and a couple of dollars…oh and some old book." I stopped mid step and froze, then I gripped the phone so hard it nearly shattered in my hand.

"Wait! Which book?" I asked sternly and when I received her answer it felt like someone had kicked me in the chest for I couldn't breathe…

"The Time Machine, by H.G. Wells." At this I dropped the phone and ran towards the fountain as though every second counted. No, she couldn't! It was impossible, for no one could! That maybe so, but she was foolish enough to try and that alone would mostly likely get her killed! What had Sophia been thinking?! Had she been tricked? For surely so, as she knew the dangers of such an undertaking as much as I, as much as all our kind.

But then how, for she would need…

"A coin…no! Please by the Gods, no!" I ran faster, harder and the mere seconds it took felt far too long. I reached the side of the fountain, looking around for any signs of them, silently pleading to any God that would listen that I must be mistaken, that it couldn't be. I turned around and that's when something crunched under my foot. I looked down to see broken glass and when I followed the source I bent down and retrieved my dreaded answer. For there, in my hands, was the broken remains of a gift I had given to her.

Its message was still there.

The coin was not.

'I will always bring you home.' That was what it said and now it became a mockery of what it was supposed to symbolise. For it might have once brought her back to me, but now it had been the very thing powerful enough to take her away…

"And I was the one who fucking gave it to her!" I snarled down at the remains in my hands before crushing it until nothing remained. Then I roared in anger before producing one of my own coins from my vault and throwing it into the fountain. I cursed the path for taking too long in appearing and once it had, I stormed through to the doorway caring little for the water that rained down around me. I ran down the tunnel and into the Janus Temple, cursing its very existence.

"Ranka?!" I shouted her name in utter shock, one that quickly morphed into rage.

"My Lord?!" Her own shock was clear enough to know I was the last person she expected to see. I looked around and when I didn't see Keira, my reactions couldn't be helped. I grabbed Ranka by the throat and applied enough pressure to cut off her air supply. Such a thing wouldn't kill her but it would make her vessel pass out if I wasn't careful. I tried to get a hold of my fury enough to ease off slightly or I knew I would never get my answers.

"Where is she?!" I demanded, seething.

"Mmmy...my...Lord...I..." She scratched at my hand in vain, trying to remove the current instrument of her torture.

"WHERE?!" I roared, bringing her face closer to mine and her fearful eyes looked behind me. I dropped her and she fell to the floor gasping. Then I turned to the main Janus Gate, the one that powered them all and the one utterly forbidden to be used. For certain death was all that awaited those foolish enough to try it.

"No! You cannot fool me Ranka, now tell me, where is she?" I demanded knowing it was a trick, that she had travelled through one of these doors, I just needed to know which one.

"I do not lie," she hissed though a ragged breath.

"WHICH DOOR?!" I roared again having done with her games! I looked left and right down the endless corridors that branched off from the octagonal shaped room, with only one that remained centred at its core.

"She didn't walk through any door, My King," Ranka said with a severity that couldn't be denied, one that added with but a look and I knew...By the Gods,

I knew, it was true.

"NO! No, no, no. What...what has she done!?" I shouted first up at the Heavens and then threw the question back at Ranka. Someone I had once thought as loyal to me as my own blood. I stormed back over to her and let my demon have its say, letting it growl down at her,

"Why didn't you stop her?!" She looked back up at me like a wounded animal receiving another lashing before strengthening her resolve and telling me,

"Because there is no stopping the Fates." I snarled and then turned my back on her, storming over to the cause of all my anguish. How could she do this to me!? What in all of Hell's levels could have possessed her to do this? I looked up and down the forbidden gate with a hatred of the likes I had never known. I hated its very existence, for it stood here all this time like a taunting beacon, attracting those stupid enough to think it could grant them anything but death.

And she was but a moth, where usually…

She was the flame.

I tried to recap all that she had said to me in these past weeks, to give me any clue as to why she would do this? I knew she was plagued by nightmares, but I didn't think that enough to guide her to…

"The book," I uttered aloud to myself, for what else could have been the cause of such a foolish notion. Did she really believe that heading into the past would have the power to change the future?

But it wasn't just the title of the book that held my interest, for it was where that book had come from that was more cause for concern. Yes, it was all making sense now. Lucius had told me of Pythia being there, could she have gotten to Keira before he intervened? Could she have told her everything that I would not? Well, seeing where I now stood, it seemed a likely cause for who else was strong enough to plant such a poisonous root in her mind?

The same root strong enough to get me to deceive her in some foolish notion it would save her life. She was like some demonic puppet master playing us both for the Fates' entertainment.

Well, in this she had gone too far…

No! I couldn't be led to believe that she was gone, for no one entered into the eternal fountain and survived. And yet, there was no body to suggest her death, for that was what would be left if a mortal tried to cross over into its path. My own kind would simply disappear and cease to exist, but a mortal?

To be honest I didn't know, but I knew one thing, if she was in there then I was going in there too, and I would rather drag her back with me or die trying!

"NO! My Lord you cannot! You cannot go in there!" Ranka shouted trying to stop me. I looked back at her over my shoulder and snarled only two words…

"Watch me."

CHAPTER THIRTY-NINE

KEIRA

AN AUTUMN DAY IN JUNE

PRESENT DAY

Stepping through the Janus Gate was like being suspended in time. It wasn't like it was before when I had simply woken up on the other side. No, this time using the Janus Gate was explained to me. Personally, I thought it a bit late to do so now, considering I had already done the deed and stepped back through.

But when I first found myself stood in an empty, white endless space looking all around waiting for something to happen, I had no clue as to why I was here. Had I done it wrong? And if so where were the others?

"Hello?!" I shouted and nearly jumped a mile when I heard a calm voice behind me.

"Hello." I spun around to face a man in white robes and with white curly hair. He smiled at me, showing me a set of perfect white teeth but none of this was why I sucked in a sharp breath. It was his clear white eyes that unnerved me the most. He placed both his hands together in front of him and they soon became hidden in the huge sleeves that covered them.

"No need to fear me, for I would not harm one such as you," he told me in a kind, warm voice that was soothing.

"Who…who are you?" I asked after having to find my voice.

"Why, I am the God Janus and I am very pleased to meet you, Keira." he said shocking me. Holy freaking Moly! I was talking to a God!?

"You're Janus?!" I screeched making him wince.

"Sorry," I said and he shook his head telling me it was fine.

"I am indeed and I am very pleased to meet you," he told me and once again his voice was like a sweeping lullaby blanketing me in trust.

"It's umm…well it's nice to meet you too…I have never met a God before," I told him making him smile again, one that caused sweet crinkles to appear around his eyes.

"Then I am pleased to be the first," he informed me, this time smirking. Well, he certainly was a happy fellow for a God, that was for sure.

"Where are we?" I asked looking around at…well, a whole load of nothing.

"We are in the Void," he told me looking around at the same nothing.

"What is the Void?"

"It is a place in between worlds, a place where I can keep watch over the gates." I looked around again not exactly seeing any windows.

"You're here alone?" I couldn't help but ask. He gave me

another warm smile, this time cocking his head a little to one side as if pleasantly surprised by my question.

"I am, for no one has ever been here before." This surprised me.

"Then why me?"

"Because you are the first. The purest soul and the only one that was fated to cross." Well, that made sense considering what I'd heard about this gate, all had died trying.

"But my friends, they came in here…" He held up a pale white hand and stopped me.

"Your friends are fine. They made it back to your time." I released a relieved sigh.

"And me? Will I make it back?" I asked making him grin again.

"Yes, but for the moment, will you walk with me…it has been a long time since I have conversed with another…in person that is?" he asked me, holding out an arm and the second he did a beautiful scene appeared. It was a long leafy lane framed either side by trees that over hung and interlocked above like a canopy. The ground was covered in fallen Autumn leaves, like a blanket of yellows, oranges, and reds. A fake sun shone through the trees above, casting beautiful rays of light on the sunset colours on the ground.

"It's beautiful," I uttered. He nodded deeply at the compliment and I took a step closer, falling in by his side as we walked together to nowhere.

"Do you ever get lonely?" I asked him and he looked truly as though he had to take a minute to think about the question. It was almost like being with a robot, one programmed to being happy, kind and softly spoken.

"I guess I do, for I am enjoying this meeting with you very much," he answered making me smile this time.

"I hear whispers, from the other worlds and it keeps me

comforted but there is much to be said in being heard and you ask such nice questions…you have a caring heart, that I can be sure of."

"Thank you." I replied thinking it was sweet to hear a God complimenting you on what he thought of your personality.

"I always knew you would come," he then shocked me by saying.

"You did?"

"Why yes, it was fated." Of course, it was, duh Keira, he was after all the God of Time.

"Can I ask you, what do you know of the Fates?" He smiled at this and patted my hand.

"I am the God of past, present and future, so yes, I know much of the Fates."

"And is it true, what is in my future…I am really going to… *to die?*" I asked after first swallowing hard and forcing the last two words of my question out.

"Oh yes, that too is fated I am afraid." I sucked in a sharp breath, one that felt almost too painful to release.

"And…and my child and Draven and the rest…" I started to say holding on to my belly and looking down as if seeing it all play out for myself.

"Now, now, don't upset yourself child, for everything has its reason. Life, death and the sacrifices in between. It is what brings power to the worlds and with it yours especially, but these are not the things I wish to discuss with you." I tried to pretend that his words hadn't cut me as deep as they had and managed to ask a broken,

"Then…then what do you wish to discuss with me?"

"I heard you whispering your sad goodbye…tell me, why were you so sad?" he asked me about when I'd left Draven in the past and once more he tipped his head to the side. His voice was so soft and calming and his naive questions almost reminded me of a child.

"Because I knew Draven would have to wait thousands of years before he saw me again and it breaks my heart to think of him missing me for that long," I told him, wiping away my stray tears the thought evoked.

"Oh, I see. Then there is no need to be sad."

"What do you mean?"

"Anything that happened in the past, anything you changed, will not stay that way." What?! Could he be serious? Well looking at him now and I doubted he knew what it was like to joke around.

"What? You mean, it will be as if I was never there?"

"But of course, your journey there was a sacrifice, no one else needs to suffer the actions of such, for change one thing in the past and it ripples through the ages, changing its current destination forever. As the God of Time, I could never allow such a thing. So, I paused it…"

"You paused time…for me?" I could barely speak I was so shocked.

"Yes, because you were worthy. So, I created an alternate path for you in the past and now you have left that path, it no longer exists. So, you see, your loved one will not suffer as you fear…for it will be as if you were never there," he said in gentle tender tone and I couldn't help my reaction. I threw my arms around him and hugged him. Well, he certainly didn't see that coming.

"Oh my," he whispered in surprise.

"Thank you, thank you so much!" He laughed and chuckled as he hugged me back, gently patting my back as if this was what he knew was customary. I was so overwhelmed. But most of all I was so happy to know that I wasn't leaving Draven behind, knowing what he faced. For there was one thing saying 'it was better to have loved and lost than never loved at all'… but then, to have loved and know how many lifetimes you must then wait until you get them back. Each day would have been torture.

"You are most welcome." I pulled back from him and started to carry on walking but then came to an abrupt stop when he muttered,

"Oh dear."

"What is it?"

"I fear our time is at an end, for those whispers are becoming quite loud and your future husband does not sound pleased." Oh my god, he was here!

"He's there, on the other side?!" My smile soon faded at the thought. Oh dear, this wasn't going to be good if he was and now knew what I had done.

"He waits for you. He loves you dearly and would also sacrifice much for you." I smiled at hearing this and he grinned back.

"The eyes are the windows to your soul but someone once said that if this is true, then your smile is the window to your heart and it is very clear to me that you hold beauty in both," he said making my heart melt for him.

"Thank you. But, I have to ask, who said that?" I was curious but never would have guessed his answer.

"My daughter, Pythia." I sucked in a shocked breath.

"She is angry at me. I can't say I blame her, for she feels the Fates have cursed her, but one day she will find happiness, for she doesn't know it yet, but once your day is done, then so shall hers be." Okay, now hearing this really shocked me!

"She will die?"

"No, but she shall live…for the first time. Please tell her that I love her and miss her dearly. Now it's time to fly away home little bird, for you're missed terribly," he informed me turning to look at the end of the lane.

"Thank you, for all that you've done for me," I told him reaching out and taking his hand. He looked down at it as if it was the first time he had felt such a touch, then his white eyes found mine.

"You are most welcome child, for the Fates chose wisely indeed." Then he held out his arm for me and suddenly there was a door at the end of the path.

"I will never forget you," I told him, looking back over my shoulder as I started off towards the door.

"No, I believe you shall not. Now run child, run back to your destiny." I did as he said and broke out into a run. Soon the trees were blowing in the wind and started to spin and before long I was falling through the door just as it started to open.

A pair of strong arms caught me.

"Draven?"

"Keira?"

We both uttered each of other's name in a frozen moment of sheer happiness. I looked up at him and for a second it felt more like a cruel dream, one lingering on to taunt me.

"Is that really you?" I asked as I needed to be sure. Then I threw my arms around him and my cloak slipped from my shoulders. I held him tight as he did the same and for a few blissful, short moments, I was in Heaven. I felt the tears rolling freely down my face as I took in the most beautiful sight. My heart's keeper and my soul's saviour, the man I fell in love with. He nodded as if too afraid his voice would break the spell as well…but in the end, it was neither of us. Because the girls all came running.

"You made it!" Ari shouted,

"We did it!" Sophia remarked,

"Woo freakin hoo RA!" No guesses needed for who this last

remark came from as all three of them started jumping around in utter joy. And who could blame them considering we had done the impossible.

Well, it seemed as though one person could,

"SILENCE!" Draven suddenly roared in anger and everything stopped. I took a step back and before I could move away, he gripped my arm. Then he shifted me around so that I was further away from the Janus Gate, one that was still a huge circular fountain that flowed upwards in the centre of the huge room.

"How could you do this to me?!" he threw at me and I flinched at the anger twisting his voice into something dangerous.

"Come on girls, I think it's time we left them to…" Sophia never got to finish.

"I am not done with you and your betrayal, sister but I will deal with you later!" Draven snarled and I let my own anger rear its ugly head because of it.

"Leave her out of this, I was the reason she went and she has done nothing but keep me safe and saved my life!" I told him but this wasn't the right thing to say. Clearly not if his twisted features were anything to go by.

"Oh, of that I have no doubt and in turn by your careless and foolish choices you have endangered theirs!" he shouted back at me making me flinch again. Well, it wasn't exactly what I had in mind would happen on returning but then again, I didn't expect to find Draven waiting here either.

"What by the Gods, Keira were you thinking?!" he asked me and I hated how disappointed he sounded. As though he had found me in bed with another man or something.

"I was thinking about our future, you know, the one you refuse to let happen because you turned your back on the prophecy!" I threw back at him and this time he was the one flinching from it.

"She did get to you?!" he snarled, referring of course, to the Oracle.

"As you can see, you weren't the only one keeping secrets!" I snapped, quickly losing my temper as he tried to play the innocent party in all of this.

"Yes, but I was the only one keeping them in order to save your life!" He threw an arm out behind him at the mass of gravity defying water and shouted the question,

"What did you do?!" I started shaking my head and walking backwards,

"I…I…"

"WHAT DID YOU DO!?" This time he roared at me and Ari was the one who stepped in between us.

"Don't you dare speak to her like that!" Ari shouted, standing up for me and for a moment Draven looked ready to explode again but at the sight of Ari protecting me, he must have seen the situation for what it was. He took a deep breath, trying to calm himself and told her,

"I could never hurt her."

"There are more ways to hurt someone than just physical abuse." Draven took a moment and after a few more deep breaths he looked past Ari and straight to me. That's when it felt like a second arrow had fired through my chest, only this time it didn't miss its target.

"Yes, you are right and now she knows that more than most, for through her actions… she…*she just ripped out my heart.*" I sucked in a painful breath and he in turn, tore his gaze from mine before walking past us all and leaving the Temple.

Leaving me shot through the heart.

I crumpled to the floor and Ari caught me before my knees could crack on the ground. The girls were all around me in seconds and I soon felt my tear soaked face being held by two hands and raised up.

"He is just angry and upset...give it time," Sophia said and I looked back over my shoulder at the doorway he had disappeared through and said,

"But time is something we don't have..." Of course, I said this more to myself as no one else knew about what awaited me in my future, one that had been confirmed thanks to my new friend Janus. I looked back at Sophia and with the last of my heartbreak I muttered through my sobs,

"....it was supposed to be our wedding day."

"Oh honey!" Sophia had me in her arms and I cried, letting it all out on her shoulder.

"He just needs time," she told me again and I looked over at the Janus Gate through blurry eyes and said to myself,

Yes, and thanks to what I did, those I loved could be gifted with time. Mine however was only ever to be,

Time sacrificed.

After crying until all my tears were spent and again trying to suppress my fangs that had popped out, thankfully not in front of Draven, the girls convinced me to move. So, we left the Temple and after re-using the umbrellas so we wouldn't get wet, we crossed the fountain. I looked all around but it was when Sophia placed a hand on my forearm that she nodded over to a tall stone pagoda with a domed roof.

"Go to him," she said softly and I knew she was worried about us both. Now I'd had time to calm down I couldn't say that I could blame him for his outburst. After all, I had put myself in so much danger, it was no wonder he was seething mad, and that was without knowing the half of it but he knew enough. He was from that land, Hell it *was his land* and he knew the dangers it could hold.

I hadn't seen Ranka as she had left swiftly after the others had arrived, no doubt already finding herself on the receiving end of Draven's fury. Sophia told me that when they came through she found Ranka trying everything in her power to hold him back from coming through the gate to get me.

Only once we started to emerge, he waited all of about thirty seconds before deciding to go in and get me anyway. That was why he had been the one opening the door and that was why he had caught me. He was willing to risk his life to come and get me. I wasn't surprised by this, but it did make me understand the level of worry that must have been going through his mind. And why it had quickly manifested into anger.

I knew better than most that Draven didn't handle feeling helpless very well and when something like this was taken out of his hands he lashed out, quickly morphing his hurt into rage. But I knew deep down the truth of where all this stemmed from, which was why I did what needed to be done now.

I nodded to Sophia and the others before making the long walk around the massive fountain and then across the vast grassy area over to where I could see a lone figure sat on a wall. It was the first time I had seen him look so lost and the sight tugged at my soul.

He didn't look up as I approached and that in itself hurt.

"Hey," I said sitting down next to him.

"Hey," he replied softly, mimicking me.

"So, I guess we need to talk," I said after a long minute of silence.

"Yeah…I guess we do." But neither of us did. No, instead we just sat there and looked out over the grounds and on to the massive house that from this distance, almost looked whole again.

"How long were you gone?" Finally, he broke the silence with a question. I thought about it a moment, counting up the days and told him the truth,

"Seventeen days."

"Gods, Keira!" he hissed on a harsh breath then looked away from me in disbelief or disgust, I couldn't tell which one.

"Pythia put you up to this?" he said as it wasn't really a question.

"She told me what you refused to tell me, yes…the rest I figured out on my own," I told him hating that it had come to this.

"Yes and no doubt she told you why I kept this from you!"

"I know why, the same reasons you lied to me the first time, but Draven don't you see how something like that can do more harm than good," I told him and he snapped his head back to look at me.

"I just found you walking back through the Janus Gate, Keira! You know, the one that is said to rip people a fucking part!" he shouted and I knew it was done out of worry.

"I survived, doesn't that tell you something," I tried to reason with him.

"It tells me that I should be worried you have a fucking death wish!" he snapped back and I felt my own anger bubbling to the surface,

"You know that isn't true!"

"Then enlighten me Keira, tell me why I am wrong, because right now, it feels like I am the only one that doesn't know about half the shit you pull or why?!" He threw at me and I hated that he was right. It did seem like I was always conspiring against him lately. So, I went with logic.

"Think about it Draven, if I am the only one to have used that gate and survived, then it means it was always meant to be…it was fated this way."

"Fuck the Fates!" he snarled furiously.

"You don't mean that."

"Oh yes I do! Look at what they have done to us, look what they nearly…" He couldn't finish that painful sentence, so I pushed. I wanted to hear it, I needed to right now.

"What?"

"What they nearly took from me…*again,*" he said softly this time, now his anger was being spent and all that was left was the cruelty of my decision.

"We all have a choice and we both at one time chose to listen to them," I reminded him.

"Yes, and each time it nearly ripped you away from me… what if you couldn't have got back, what if something had happened to you there? What if…" I placed a hand on his arm and told him,

"But I did get back…*I came back to you.*"

"Yes, but for how long Keira, because what we face with Cronus, you think I can do that not knowing what you are doing behind my back…what about the next time you get some foolish idea in your head, one that might get you killed! You think I have the strength to deal with that, because I will tell you now that I don't!" I closed my eyes and took a moment to let his words sink in. Then I gave him what he needed to hear and yes, it was done so in anger.

"Well, I don't know, are you planning on keeping me in the dark about my future or the prophecy or are you just going to continue to hunt down the Oracle again so she can't tell me what you don't have the courage to!" I snapped back and I knew when I saw him jerk that I had hit a nerve.

"Everything I do is to keep you safe."

"Yes, but it still doesn't mean you have a right to take my choices away from me. We could have faced this together but instead you forced my hand, Draven."

"Yes, and what of the outcome?! Did you find what you were so preciously looking for?" he threw at me and in that moment, I knew that I should have told him. Told him about being changed into a Vampire, but more importantly, told him about the baby I could be carrying.

But I couldn't.

I couldn't because I was scared. In fact, I was terrified that he would simply get up and walk away and I couldn't let that happen. Besides, I didn't want to tell him about the baby, as when the time came I wanted it to be viewed as a joyous thing, not done so in the aftermath of anger or bitterness. Because I knew that telling him would only send him over the edge. And because my being pregnant right now would only mean one thing to him, that the prophecy was coming true and that I would in fact, die.

"I let it lead me down a path and can only hope that along the way it was done so because it was fate…the outcome is yet to be known," I said feeling that this would be enough. He took a deep breath in relief and I hated myself for being the coward that I knew I was. The very cowardly act I had accused him of, when not telling me the truth. And now I was a hypocrite and no better.

"How did you know?" I asked getting off the subject of what had happened there.

"I saw you arrive at the hotel and then drive away again, so I followed you." I raised an eyebrow at him, one he knew the meaning of.

"Don't give me that look, for under the circumstances I think I was well within my rights to be suspicious. Besides, after that kiss this morning, well I knew something was wrong." I thought back to that day and it seemed like a small lifetime ago but for Draven it had been hours. It was like Janus had said it was, my time in the past hadn't affected this time at all.

"I was on my way here and a thought occurred to me. I had Lauren check your car for clues and she found your book."

"Oh." I said thinking back to Pythia's book, one I had casually tossed in the back seat of my car without a single thought.

"That told me enough but even if it hadn't, what I found by the fountain certainly confirmed my fears." I looked to him and asked,

"What did you find?"

"My gift to you, it was broken…along with my trust," he added and I nearly sobbed hearing it.

"You lied too," I said, reminding him of that fact.

"Yes, but you kissed me and you said goodbye, knowing that it could be the last time. You made me a promise you had no idea whether you could keep…you didn't just lie Keira, you put our love on the line and then pushed." I looked away from what he was saying hating the sound of his cruel words right now. I got up and decided to throw some reality back at him.

"At least I said goodbye! What did I get from you that day, a friend of yours I hardly knew, turning up at my door and telling me you were dead!"

"Yes, and now you have your payback because I too thought you were dead!" he said hitting me with his harsh words. I was astonished and beyond furious.

"Is that what you think this is! Fucking payback!?" He flinched at my anger and after his shoulders slumped he said,

"No, I know you are not cruel but you don't know what it was like…" I staggered back a step and said,

"I didn't know?! You dare say that to me! What did you have Draven, twenty minutes to worry and what did you give me…months Draven, fucking endless months thinking you were gone and there was nothing I could do to get you back!

So, excuse me if I say I think in the grand scheme of things you fared better than I did!"

"Yes, and you are also forgetting that I had nine months of not knowing where you were or what was happening to you, so don't speak to me of worry, for since I met you then you can be damn sure I have had my fill of fucking worry!" He lashed out again and well, to be honest, I knew this was true but still, he wasn't getting away with his words so easily.

"That may be so Draven, but this isn't a pissing contest! I think we can both admit to making mistakes and breaking promises but now what's important is now we have a choice to make…"

"And what is that?!" he hissed obviously expecting another argument thrown his way.

"To move on from this and learn from those mistakes that all stemmed from lies or kept secrets." Okay, so I would have liked to have been brave enough to make the first step in telling him all he needed to know but I wasn't.

"You don't understand my world," he answered with a small shake of his head. But again, with this last comment, it only managed to fuel the flames of my own angry response.

"I don't understand it? Are you serious, I just spent over two weeks emerged neck deep into it! You have no idea what I went through and nor would I want you to but then again, if you did, then you might stop seeing me as a weak little human that could get hurt by your world!"

"I never said you were weak and I certainly never even thought it! But Keira, don't you see that it is my job to protect you and how can I do that when you fight against me, instead of with me."

"Because you're not asking me to fight by your side Draven, you're asking me to stand safely behind you, whilst I watch you fight it alone." He knew it was true and he raked a frustrated hand through his hair.

"And what other choice do I have when all the Fates tell us is that in order to beat this, you have to *die* along with that threat." And there it was, his greatest fear spoken aloud.

"If that is what it will take, then I do so fighting it by your side, as I always should," I said after closing my eyes against the pain the image caused me.

"NO! I will not allow it!" I jumped at his sudden outburst.

"Draven, you can't condemn the world just so that you may keep me in it, one that may not even survive long enough for one last kiss," I said trying to get him to see reason.

"That is where you are wrong, for I can and I will, with every selfish beat of my heart! For I will not lose you again!"

"And where do we live Draven, for the world you speak of may die right alongside everything we hold dear. Are you willing to sacrifice everything and everyone just so you may hold me a little longer?"

"I do whatever it takes to keep you safe," he declared and I knew that in sight of all I had said, he was only saying this now as a way of not accepting the truth of it.

"Then maybe…*you should stop trying,"* I whispered gently, one that wasn't received that way.

"What?!" he snapped.

"I have come to terms with possibility of my death Draven, what I am saying is, that maybe it's time you do too," I said tears flowing down my cheeks as it seemed there was always room for more. He stood up and gripped me by the arms and pulled me to him, then he whispered a fervent,

"Never!" Then he crushed his lips to mine in our first kiss and I melted into him, holding on and never wanting to let go. It was as if I was back in the Void where time stood still and nothing of the outside world could touch us. His taste, his scent, the feel of his tongue duelling with mine…it was all as I had remembered and it was,

Magnificent.

"I missed you…god I missed you so much!" I told him once the kiss had finished and I uttered these words over his skin, needing him to not just hear them but feel them as well. He wrapped both his arms around my waist and held me so tight, it was as if he was scared a storm would roll over us and blow me away.

"I've never been so scared" he admitted sincerely.

"I know, and I am so, so sorry I did this to you," I told him because I was sorry. Sorry that I put him through any of this, just like he too was sorry for all the things he had put me through. He placed his forehead to mine and said,

"I know sweetheart…as am I." Then he took my hand and entwined it with his.

"Come, it's time to go."

"Why?"

"Because this is one promise I am not letting either of us break," he said pulling me towards the house across the gardens.

"Promise?" He looked back at me and gave me a smile before spinning me back into his arms, then over my lips he let me feel his own beautiful words…

"To meet at the altar."

CHAPTER FOURTY

DING DONG THE FANGS ARE GOING TO DINE

Standing here now in front of the mirror and I had to confess, I was having a mini meltdown.

After Draven had walked me back over to the house I was ready to just grab his hand, run to the nearest church and ask the vicar to marry us right then and there. I even told Draven as much and he looked down at me and said,

"Well, you're certainly dressed for it." And he was right. I had come through the portal still wearing a roman goddess style dress, that was gathered up over one shoulder, leaving the other exposed and it was tied tight with a thick gold belt just under the bust line. Above this had been a dark red cloak that was huge and wrapped up across my torso and attached to one shoulder by a large round brooch that held a pin through its centre. And now, it lived in the Janus Temple, cast aside in sight of Draven.

But I looked as though I had just stepped out of a historical documentary.

However, one glance over to the three girls all waiting for

me by the car and I knew I couldn't skip out on the wedding and do that to any of them. Sophia had worked extremely hard on planning this wedding, that much you could tell by all the people running around carrying flowers, chairs, tables, and some other things I couldn't actually tell you what their use was. It even looked as though some guys had turned up ready to erect a big marque.

When I first arrived Sophia had made me promise not to look, but after returning and the turbulent events that quickly followed, then all promises went flying out the window. I think the fears of the wedding being called off were enough to have any prospective bride freaking out.

I had tried not to look, as I wanted it to be a surprise and if truth be told, it was still a working progress but even then, it was enough to see that it would be stunning. After this Draven had pulled me along the side of the building, not wanting to let go of my hand. We all piled into the limousine and Draven tucked me close next to him. Then he took a deep breath and said,

"We have twenty minutes before we get back to the hotel, so who wants to start first?" I tensed in his hold and he rubbed my arm up and down in a soothing motion no doubt trying to ease my fears.

"I will start," Sophia said nodding and I felt my eyes narrow in her direction. What on earth she was going to tell him I had no clue, hence my first meltdown…one definitely subtler than my current one as it consisted mainly of me quietly asking myself a million questions and coming up with excuses ready to blurt out at a moment's notice.

But in the end, it didn't go as badly as I thought it would. Sophia was precise and chose her words very carefully, telling him only the facts she thought he needed to know. Like how we went there, met his younger self, followed the clues we hoped would lead us to something, they didn't and we left. To give her credit, she didn't lie, she just left out a whole bucket load of truth, one I knew she would unfortunately pay for at some point…*myself included.*

You could see that Pip was almost ready to explode at trying to hold back on all the details. She even spent the car journey sitting on her hands, biting her lip and rocking back and forth like an old lady on a rocking chair. Even Ari kept patting her hand and comforting her. I also think that she was nervous and rightly so. Because Pip had never kept anything from her husband before and I very much doubted she would be able to keep something like this secret. I didn't particularly want to be anywhere near that shitstorm when it hit…and I was thinking desert island might be the way to go with that one. Talk about potential tsunami!

Hell, even Vincent and Zagan were going to hit the roof when they found out, as I doubted this was something we could just keep from them all. Draven turning up out of the blue had seen to that. Because he wasn't going to lie to his brother or his brother in law and no one was brave enough to lie to Adam.

Well, there was one thing for sure and that was this wedding party was going to be a riot, literally! I think my face said it all and so did Pip's when she started biting her nails.

"I think I can speak for all of us when I say I think it's prudent to keep our… little adventures, should I say, to ourselves for the time being, or I don't see this wedding being the event we hoped for." Sophia said and Pip started laughing nervously, as if she was also going slightly crazy. Ari put her arm around her shoulder and whispered,

"It will be okay Pipper, you will see."

"I think that's wise," Draven agreed and finally Pip took a deep breath, finally relaxing slightly. Well, considering my own experience with Draven, then let's just say I didn't envy them in their task. Our men were as scary and as badass as they came!

And I knew that my own explanation wasn't yet over, it was simply postponed until after the wedding. I knew this when Draven held me back after we had all got out of the car. He wrapped an arm around my waist and pulled me back against his chest so that he could whisper down to me,

"I will be waiting to hear your own version of events after I make you my wife… and Keira, I WILL know all." This last part was emphasised in such a way, I knew I didn't have as long as I had hoped to keep my secrets. Which was why I was now looking at myself in the mirror and was currently going through my second meltdown, one far more daunting than the first. Because no matter how beautiful I looked all done up ready for my big day, there was one major catch…

Fangs.

But before that…

I had half my hair swept back at the sides and twisted into the mass of tumbling curls that had been heated into shape. Each big bouncy curl that cascaded down my back looked like spun gold, and for some reason highlighted lighter strands of blonde as they caught in the sun. The shorter parts of my hair had also been curled and then softly pinned back, creating body. My makeup had been done to create ivory skin that looked near flawless, with just the hint of pink blush at the apple of my cheeks. To this was a sweep of neutral shades of eyeshadow that had a slight shimmer to the powder, one that was applied with a dark shade to the crease line and outer V of my eye.

My lips were tinted pink with a slight gloss to them and I had to say the look suited me. It didn't look overdone but was just enough to know I had make-up on. Even my naturally long eyelashes had been given extra umpf, making them curl upwards thanks to the mascara. Hell, even my eyebrows had been brushed.

And then there was my dress and boy, what a dress! I had nearly cried just seeing it on the hanger, something Sophia had started fussing over for fear it would mess up my makeup. Well, too late for that now I thought bitterly.

After that she had then helped me get into it with extra help from my own sister. The rest of my family had been in full swing of getting ready by the time we made it back and now Libby, along with Sophia was wearing a beautiful purple gown. Each of which were a different design and a slightly different shade but Sophia assured me at the time that this would go well with the theme.

And besides, we didn't think it possible to get Pip into what you would call a conventional dress, not when the one she chose looked like a purple disco ball, then yeah, conventional was way out the window.

My own stunning dress was an ivory, off white tone and the bodice had a sweetheart neckline and was covered in a luxurious beaded applique and lace embroidery. This continued up over the shoulders in a downward V shape, like delicate pearl and crystal encrusted vines were curling over my skin, making them shimmer.

The delicate design continued down over the bodice and past the waistline. It finished off to one side where it was at its thickest and overlapped where one side of the skirt was gathered up. The whole thing was pulled tight at the back thanks to the corseted ties making it fit me like a second skin. Then the skirt flowed out around me making me feel like a fairy-tale princess wanting to twirl, which was precisely what I did after I got it on thanks to layer after layer of rippling chiffon.

So now here I stood, alone at my own request, seeing myself as someone else…

A Vampire bride.

My fangs had come out the second I had started to get emotional and panicky over Draven finding out the whole truth. Then what followed was my eyes turning demonic and I started to cry as I just didn't know how to get it to go away this time. I had tried what Lucius had told me but no matter how many bloody honey dipped mice I thought of, I couldn't get it to go away. It seemed the more I started to freak out, the worse it got. Now, I could add a small network of black lines around my eyes that looked as though someone was injecting my veins with ink. Seeing this only managed to send me over the edge and pretty soon I found myself screaming in my mind for the only person who could help me.

"Keira! What is it, what's wrong…oh," Sophia said running back into the room and pausing when I turned my face to look at her. The next thing I knew my dad was following behind and Sophia quickly shut the door, leaving it open a crack and saying,

"Sorry Mr Williams, girly crisis." Then she shut it, locked it, and ran over to where I was shaking. I looked down at my hands I held out in front of me and said,

"I can'th…can'th get itth tho…tho sthop." I said trying to force the words out like they were getting stuck. I didn't know what was happening but it felt like I was close to having a fit.

"Okay, okay, let's just calm down and think about this, we will figure this out. Did you try thinking about something disgusting like Luc suggested?" I nodded and said with a heavy lisp,

"Yesth, I tryth that."

"Okay, well there is only one thing left to do," she said nodding to herself as if her mind was made up.

"And wthat thatht?"

"Time to ask the experts," she said and then was gone before I could ask her more about it.

I don't know how long I had to wait, because to be honest it could have been five minutes or twenty, either way every scenario of cancelling the wedding had gone through my head. The difference now was that I was sobbing. I had promised Draven I would be at that altar and it had been the one and only promise I really didn't want to break. But then how was I going to do that as a Vampire?

Pop my head from under the veil, look at the crowd and then shout 'Surprise, oh didn't you know it was fancy dress?' Then turn to my husband and silently beg his forgiveness? I was lucky enough that he couldn't sense I was pregnant, as Sophia must have been right about my shields, they were strong enough to hide a pregnancy and my new Vamp self.

But seeing me like this…? Well, I was hiding that from no-one! Hell, my reaction to feeling overwhelmed just by looking at myself in the mirror had brought it on…so even if I could get a handle on it this time, what about when I was walking down the bloody aisle?!

I nearly jumped a mile when I heard the door opening and hid my face behind a sofa cushion.

"Okay, so I brought a solution but you have to trust…" Sophia started to say as she walked back into the room but the sight of who swept her aside and stormed in after her had me crying out in shock mid sob and dropping the pillow.

"Luc…th…ius!" The sight of Lucius in a suit was a drool worthy sight indeed, but Lucius in this suit was jaw droppingly gorgeous and downright beautiful. It was a dark grey material that had a silver sheen at the collar, matching his tie. Two buttons pulled in the jacket in a delicious way that showcased large shoulders and a muscular torso that tapered in at the waist. I could just see a waistcoat underneath and a crisp white skirt. His hair was smoothed back and it was clear that he was ready for a wedding.

Me, however, well I clearly wasn't and his face said it all.

He stormed over to me as Sophia said,

"I will give you two a minute alone." And then she shut the door behind her. Lucius' eyes took a moment to scan my body and finally reaching the root of the problem, the second he did, his steps faltered. He was in complete and utter shock.

Sophia hadn't told him.

"Lucthius I…" Damn my inability to speak, which only made me break out into another sob. The next thing I knew I was in his arms and he was looking down at me, with a gentle hand at my face. He still hadn't said a word but so many emotions passed through his eyes, shock and concern being the main ones.

"Tell me sweetheart, how did this happen?" He didn't seem angry or upset and now his initial shock was over the only concern he had was for me. I burst into another snotty nosed mass of tears until I was a sobbing mess as I shouted,

"Sthe trith tho kill me…again!"

"Alright, Ssshh, you're safe now. Let's try and start this at the beginning," he said leading me over to the sofa and sitting down next to me after unbuttoning his suit jacket. It's when I noticed the one gloved hand.

"But first, as adorable as it is hearing you try to speak as a youngling, let's see what we can do about those pretty little fangs of yours," he said softly, skimming a gentle fingertip down one and making me shudder.

"Sthensathtive," I lisped making him smile.

"I know," he replied and I rolled my eyes at him making him chuckle.

"I gather I didn't just do this to you and then leave you to your own devices?" he asked as if the very idea angered him. I smiled and shook my head.

"You sthaved my lifthe." He gave me a grin and said,

"I thought as much, although if you mean to say I 'shaved' you in anyway, then I think we are talking at cross purposes, as I am not really into stripping a woman of her hair." I rolled my eyes and growled, making him chuckle but I knew what he was doing. He was trying to make light of my situation and ease my mind. No doubt in an attempt to get this to work more easily.

"Ha, ha!" I said at least grateful that this didn't come out in a lisp. He flicked my nose playfully and said,

"Did I tell you to try and think of something distasteful, like Pip's dress sense?"

"Oi, be nicth!" I shouted seeing him trying to fight a grin.

"Yesth, youth didth." I told him answering his question and again hearing me speak was making him smirk.

"And?"

"Ittth worthked, but…" He held a hand out to stop me and said,

"It won't work now," he finished off for me and then went on to explain,

"Heightened emotions usually bring out your other side and are hard to control in a youngling. Anger, sadness, nervousness…" he said nodding to me and my current meltdown. But then he said another emotion and I very quickly started to panic again, thinking of what would definitely happen after getting married,

"Arousal." Jesus, but did he *have to* purr the damn word!

"I'm sstho sthcrewthed." I had tried to say, 'so screwed' but with a lisp it was surprisingly difficult to say that one word without sounding like a swearing Sylvester the cat, from Loony Tunes. In fact, I was very tempted to try and say, 'You're despicable'. But thankfully decided against it as I think I had hit my quota of making a fool out of myself for one day. And after all, it was my wedding, surely, I should be trying to look as graceful and beautiful as I could. And I very much doubted that fangs, demonic eyes, black veins and me impersonating a lisping cartoon cat was the way to go with that one.

"Let's not call off the wedding just yet, love," he said standing so that he could take off his jacket. He then resumed his seat and started rolling up his sleeves giving me a clear view of the one tight, black leather glove that went up his forearm. You would have thought the sight would have looked silly but it was the complete opposite in fact, as it looked sexy as hell. Actually, the sight had me swallowing again and again just so the excess saliva having fangs produced wouldn't just start dripping down my chin.

Damn fangs!

"Now this might feel strange, as being one of my own I now have a..." he paused and sighed as if he didn't know how to describe it without it sounding intrusive, which in the end was exactly what it was.

"…direct line into your mind." My eyes grew wide at the thought.

"Don't freak out Pet, it's not like I will be making you my sex slave any time soon, I do prefer my heart where it currently beats and not in a certain possessive King's hand squeezing the life out of it…although…" he paused a moment and tapped his chin before adding,

"Now that I think about it, I think I will find the King less enthused about murder, considering ending my life would also now mean the end of yours."

"Oh, Sthit," I muttered making him laugh.

"Don't worry, I think we both know by now who your heart belongs to,." he said softly and I don't know why but I snorted and said,

"You werethn't sthaying thath when you kiddthnap me andth wanthed tho marry me." Then I swiftly slapped a hand over my mouth.

"Come again?" he asked but I shook my head. So, he said,

"Very well, this will explain it all better anyway." I was about to ask when suddenly he placed his un-gloved hand to my cheek and the next thing I knew a blinding white light had me closing my eyes before the last seventeen days started to play out in my brain like a flicker book of time. Everything I had been through, the harem, the attack from Pertinax, his rescue, the battle, destroying a God, saving his life, Draven and I, his brother kidnapping me and the list went on and on until the very last time I said goodbye.

He had missed nothing.

But he wasn't done, for at the very end on the side of that river saying goodbye, the memory lingered. It felt as though I was right back there, only this time it was in the middle of the day and the sun was shining over our heads. The white gleaming ancient city of Rome in the background but not a single soul around us for miles.

I looked up at Lucius to see him looking as he did now, in a suit, no jacket, rolled sleeves and a waistcoat and tie.

"You have been busy, my little Keira girl," he told me and I nodded.

"Retract your fangs," he ordered softly and I felt them going smaller without even a thought.

"Eyes," was his next order and I blinked a few times, knowing that even without the aid of a mirror they were back to normal.

"Good girl," he praised and I couldn't help but blush.

"Why… are we…?" I could finally speak at last.

"Because I wanted to know what you had been up to," he told me and I frowned reaching up to feel my mouth.

"You mean you could have ordered me to do those things without accessing my memories?" I asked starting to feel myself getting annoyed.

"Yes, I could have," he admitted.

"You tricked me!?" I exclaimed and he shrugged his shoulders and said,

"Means must, my dear and now I know what the King does not."

"And what's that?!" I almost snarled the words.

"That half of you belongs to me and the other half belongs to him." I frowned and snapped,

"What are you talking about?!" Which was when he hit me with the truth,

"You are half Vampire and the other half, well in that you will have to speak with Dom, for I already know you haven't told him."

"Haven't told him what?!" I asked wanting to be sure before I admitted to anything but this was when he snapped his fingers and his answer came back to me back in the present.

He leaned closer to me resting an arm at the back of the sofa and said…

"About the baby."

CHAPTER FOURTY-ONE

MINE AGAIN

"Wait, you know about the baby?!" I shrieked going high pitched.

"Yes, I know about the baby," Lucius responded calmly, much more so than I would have expected.

"You can feel it, I mean when you did your…handy touchy thing?" I asked placing a hand on his forearm and he flinched as it was his gloved hand. He gave me a small, uncomfortable smile and picked up my hand placing it back down onto the sofa. Okay, so note to self for the future, Lucius didn't like having his damaged hand touched…good to know. He gave my moved hand a pat and enquired,

"Handy touchy thing…seriously, that is what you want to call it?" I grinned once and then replied,

"Well, what do you call it…badass King Vamp Voodoo?"

"No, but now I am, it has a nice ring to it," he said making me laugh again.

"Ha, ha."

"And getting back to it, then no, I can't feel your baby." My face must have said it all because he looked as though he regretted it right away.

"That doesn't mean to say it's anything bad, just that your protective mind has now got another focus. I can only access your mind because you are one of mine, one of my made," he told me quickly trying to ease my panic.

"Then how did you know?" I asked deciding to focus on this question instead.

"Because the second I got that damn Oracle out of town I forced her to tell me what fucked up idea she spun you this time," he all but snarled at me. Oh boy, he did not like Pythia. I remember seeing how terrified she was of him that day in the library and now, well it was starting to make sense.

"She told you of the prophecy?" I guessed.

"Yes, but her idea of the prophecy and mine are quite different, I can assure you," he said sounding pissed off.

"What do you mean?"

"What I mean is they may not be able to lie but that doesn't stop them spinning the fucking truth!" he shouted getting up and storming over to the window to lean on the frame and stare out over the beautiful grounds. I got up and walked closer to him. I decided that considering I already had him in this bad mood thanks to mentioning the Oracle, then I might as well continue down this road and get it all out.

"Lucius, why didn't you tell me that you had a brother?" I asked him and he snapped his head back to me. Man did he look pissed.

"Because I don't...! *Not anymore,*" he said sounding angry and this last part was uttered back at the window. Okay, so it was clear that their once brotherly bond in blood shared, was now classed as 'bad blood shared' as something had obviously gone on with these two for him to not even count him as such...*unless,*

"Is he…dead?" I asked tentatively.

"No, but he fucking should be!" Well yep, there was my answer.

"Did you guys…?" I never finished my question because he looked back at me and said,

"Is this really what you want to spend your wedding day doing, talking about *my* family problems, when its clear you will soon have your own to deal with?" I narrowed my eyes at him as I knew what he was doing and it was called deflection.

"Fine, you don't want to talk about it, I get it, but it doesn't mean you have to be a dick about it!" I snapped making him expel a sigh.

"It is a touchy subject, I will admit and the reasons for such I don't discuss matters with anyone. So, I would appreciate your…" I held up my hand and stopped him, saying,

"Like I told you back in Persian time, I won't tell anyone. It was clear Draven didn't know then and as far as I am concerned, he doesn't need to know now…not unless he is planning on kidnapping me again and sticking a bullseye on my back for Layla," I added dryly. Lucius raised an eyebrow in question and I shrugged my shoulders not needing to explain as he had seen it all anyway.

"Man, was there ever a time that girl wasn't a raving lunatic, murdering bitch face?" I asked making Lucius smirk.

"Not that I recall, no." I had been tempted to ask what he had ever seen in such a crazy bitch, but I didn't think now was the time. Besides, I caught my image in the mirror and nearly freaked. Black lines streaked my face and my makeup was well and truly ruined.

"Shit, you could have told me that I looked like a racoon!" I shouted rushing to the mirror, grabbing some tissues my mum had left on the table and dabbing at my mascara tears.

"But a beautifully cute racoon at that," Lucius added

making me shoot him a sideways glance.

"Yeah right."

"I think that is my cue to leave you to your feminine devices," he said walking over to grab his jacket.

"You're leaving?!" I don't know why I sounded so panicky…oh wait, yes, I did!

"What if I, you know, take one look at that wedding aisle and Vamp out again?!" He gave me a small smile and chuckled, murmuring a 'Vamp out,' and then strangely, a 'Persian Time' to himself. Then he walked back over to me, leaned down and gave me a kiss on the cheek. Then he lingered and whispered,

"That is why I will be right there with you."

"Now tick tock, My Little Keira Girl, you wouldn't want to be any later for your own wedding."

"Crap! I'm late? How late?!" I said in a panic as he casually strode to the door, he opened it, paused and told me,

"Only seventeen days."

"We are so late!" I whispered as we arrived at Witley Court. We had all travelled in the Limos and I had spent the time trying to convince my parents that all was fine and we had plenty of time. Then the second I got out the car, I grabbed Sophia and hissed my own concerns so that my parents wouldn't hear.

"Its fine, look we are here now and besides, I don't think worry is really something you should be focused on right now…*do you?"* she said stressing the importance of maintaining a calm state, one for obvious reasons.

"Besides, Dom knows we're here now and can stop stressing as well."

"You mean he was stressing?" I asked straightening my long flowing skirt.

"Well, there was the small incident of Vincent and Zagan having to hold him back when he got it into his head to come and fetch you himself, but it's all good now," Sophia assured me and my face said it all.

"What? We are an hour late," she replied as if this was obvious behaviour.

"So, when did this happen?" I asked and Sophia looked sheepish.

"About fifty minutes ago...okay, okay, so my brother is now going to be a little paranoid for a while...we can't really blame him, considering we did run off to the past for a quick spell."

"You're calling seventeen days a quick spell?" I hissed so my family wouldn't hear and think I was having some Bridezilla freak out.

"I'm immortal and you just spent time with my two-thousand-year-old, younger self...what would you call it?" Ah well, put like that then yeah, I had to give her that one.

"Okay, so point taken."

"Which reminds me, because he reminded me, I have something for you from Dom, something he wanted you to wear," she said walking to the passenger side door and getting out a black gift bag. I took it with a shaky hand and then pulled a royal blue velvet box from the bag. It looked expensive and I hadn't even opened it yet. No one else was watching us and I was hoping to do this without attracting a load of attention.

"Gone on, it won't bite."

"I think you once said that about your brother...*and you lied,*" I told her making her giggle.

"Well, yes I did, but can you blame me considering I was trying to play matchmaker at the time?" she reminded me and I grabbed her hand and gave it a squeeze. She was right and I loved her for it.

"Open it before your first anniversary comes around," she teased and I did as I was told. I opened the lid and unsurprisingly, gasped.

"Oh my, Sophia!"

"Dom wanted you to wear a crown but I said you would never go for that so instead we came up with a compromise… do you like it?" she asked and I looked up at her with unshed tears filling my eyes.

"Okay, I know it's beautiful but please don't ruin your makeup all over again." She laughed as I held the box to one side and hugged her with my free arm.

"It's stunning." And it was. It was a beautiful wedding tiara that was shaped slightly higher at the peak, so that it resembled the shape of a crown. It was encrusted in diamonds, not crystals as there was no mistaking them for anything else and stunning flawless pearls that matched the necklace that framed it in the case. It also had rich deep purple amethysts as the larger stones, and the whole piece was swirls of platinum so fine it almost looked like lace.

Then there was the pearl necklace that was so unique I had to run my fingertip along the length just to check it was real. It was quite simple in its design but very effective. It was a long line of pearls that came down into a V shape and above the V was a cupid's bow shape of purple sapphires that matched my ring. Altogether it made a perfect heart shape, with one half white and the top a startling purple.

I was so mesmerized that I hadn't realised the next car had already pulled up and soon everyone was out in the courtyard all staring at mine and Sophia's exchange. All my bridesmaids, mum and dad and the cutest flower girl in the world, were all stood at the front of the massive hall, one where only the shell remained. Then started the cooing. Everyone came around and looked at Draven's gift, my mum with tears in her eyes, my sister with tears in her eyes, my dad whistling and Pip shouting about it being the bee's knees and then asking if anyone actually knew if bee's had knees.

After this Sophia helped place it gently in my hair before doing the same with the necklace. Then she snapped a picture with her phone and showed it to me.

It was now official, I looked like a princess.

"Oh wow! This place is incredible!" My dad shouted and my mum agreed, only as she had done all morning, started getting teary yet again. I looked around to see that all my bridesmaids together looked stunning and Sophia had been right, having all the different shades of purple and each of them being so different, it really did work.

RJ with her purple mini tartan dress, patterned with black velvet roses and skulls, suited her in both style and body shape. It was kind of a gothic 1950's style swing dress, so she had her hair done in a matching style. It was pinned high, with a huge curl on the top of her head making her look like a Gothic pin up girl. In the words of Pip, she looked 'Woozer hot' and I had to agree, poor Seth didn't stand a chance.

Then there was Sophia who looked like a Grecian Goddess with her deep purple A-line dress with a sweetheart neckline, tight bodice and floor length floaty skirt.

Libby also was wearing her 'gift' from Draven, which was another deep purple shade, one almost verging on indigo and one which complimented her red hair perfectly. It had a strapless top encrusted with tiny crystals, an A line skirt that reached the floor and a small belt of larger crystals under the bust line.

Then there was Ari, and I had to say I had very nearly found myself teary again at seeing her. She was stunning and even though all my girls were, none of them brought me to tears because I had seen everyone in a dress before…all but Ari. In fact, the first time I had seen her dressed up was my Hen do and that wasn't exactly what I would have called a dress.

But now, here she stood in the perfect, cute light purple

dress that finished just above the knee and was a wrap over design with off the shoulder straps. It had a sparkling diamond clasp at one side, where both sides of the dress met. Dainty strappy shoes that tied with ribbon the colour of the dress, making a bow at each side of her ankle. All three of my 'sisters', were wearing their hair twisted and curled to one side, with big ivory roses held at the twist. RJ and Pip also had the same roses and Pip, not surprising had upgraded hers to be dipped in rainbow white glitter.

This of course matched her crazy dress, one she had found in the mall that day. It was short, it was tight and it was covered in sequins, ruffles and what now looked like added rhinestones in every shade of purple. As if this wasn't enough, the skirt was made from a purple leopard print with a strange rainbow metallic effect. To this she'd added crazy heels that were purple velour platforms, in a peep toe design. They also had purple snakeskin straps, finishing in big bows that connected the bottom of the pointed heel, then to the rest of the wider rim of the platform. Big gold sparkly clasps secured them tight and the same snakeskin strappy theme continued up her ankles, finishing with an even bigger, glittery bow.

They were quite simply a work of art.

"Wook, wook, aunty Kazzy, wook how pretty I am!" Ella said twirling her adorable little ivory dress which had a thick purple sash tied into a big bow at her back. It was so cute and I loved watching the way she kept swinging her large puffy skirt as if she was in her own princess land. I grabbed her hands and swung her around, telling her,

"You are the most beautiful princess ever!" Then I stopped swinging her before I got caught up in my own skirt and leant down to whisper a secret,

"Even better than Bella." I told her, knowing she was going

through a Beauty and the Beast phase…man but that kid had a thing for wild beasts!

"Wow, Mommy, did you hear that!?" she shouted running off to Libby.

"Well, we had better get moving, we will meet you and your dad around the other side, okay?" Sophia asked obviously getting anxious, after looking at her phone.

"Is he okay?" I asked referring to my obviously impatient husband to be.

"Yeah, yeah, I just resent him that picture we took at the hen party, you know the one of you trying to pin rude parts to the carboard cut out we had made."

"You didn't!" I shouted on a half laugh.

"Oh yeah, I totally did."

"Way to go, me bootilicious, time busting, sister!" Pip said over hearing Sophia. I giggled at the thought of him currently looking down at his screen and seeing me blindfolded, with a penis in hand trying to pin it to anywhere but his head.

After this I watched them all walk around the side of the huge building and I waited behind with my dad. He stepped up to me and gave me a kiss on the cheek.

"You look so beautiful Kaz and I am so proud of you." When he said this, he looked down and I hadn't even realised that he had both my bare arms in his hands. I hadn't even flinched. I gave him a huge grin back and I knew what he was telling me without words.

He knew how far I had come to get here as a human girl, but he had no idea how far I had come to get here as Draven's Chosen One. But he wasn't telling me now how proud he was for battling enemies or surviving attacks, kidnappings, cults, or even Hell twice. No, he was simply telling me how proud he was that I was his daughter and how far I had come in surviving my own personal demons.

He knew this because this was the first time anyone in my family had not only touched my scars, but even seen them, as I hadn't shown my arms once in all this time to my family. And now, here I was displaying them to all the world, and even on my wedding day. He was proud of that and I loved that I could give it to him and my mum, especially on a day like today.

"Come on, let's get this party started."

"That's my girl," he replied and we walked along the same path the rest of my family had, because that was precisely what they were…

Family…every last one of them.

So, with my arm in the crook of my father's, we joined them. We walked past the place I remembered with a smile as it was where I had been trying to convince a badass biker to give up his jacket. Jared had helped me with my disguise after helping to get me sprung out of the joint. That joint of course, being Tartarus Prison in Hell with the help of a cowboy demon. Not exactly a sentence you say very often but there it was. Because that was now my life and as scary as it was at times, I wouldn't have had it any other way.

And walking around the corner to see what awaited us now was beyond incredible…it was paradise.

"Wow," my dad said as I sucked in a sharp breath in utter shock. I even went back a step at the sight. I can understand why Sophia had wanted to have a later wedding, as even as the sun was just going down the hundreds of fairy lights that lit up the venue was out of this world. Each of the eight huge pillars that framed the massive steps up to the house were now aglow with millions of tiny lights that had been blanketed by miles of strands.

Giant flower wreaths draped in swags above on the long line of balustrades at the top of the pillars and I remembered the place well. It had been where Draven and I had made love after being reunited at Pip's birthday party. Oh yes, I had fond memories of that time indeed.

But of course, making love isn't all we did. No, this was where Draven had proposed to me. He had waited until the sunrise before telling me how he had waited for me for so long. Then he had got down on one knee and asked me to be his wife before gifting me with a stunning ring. A flawless purple sapphire, encased in his wings, that would wrap around my finger and after this day, remain with me forever, even in death.

"You ready, kid?" my dad asked me and I looked toward the others all waiting to be escorted up the aisle first, giving Sophia the nod. We walked around the side and saw the most beautiful setting as a purple carpet was down the centre covered in white rose petals. Either side were rows of white chairs that were tied with purple sashes down the aisle, finished off with bundles of upturned white, wild flowers in a country style.

Oh, and even better a sight was that each chair was filled with the most beautiful array of people. Half of them looked as if from a movie set and the other looked like every day normal people you would have found at any wedding. A mortal side vs the immortal side…and I couldn't keep the biggest smile off my face from seeing it!

It wasn't dark yet but if I had been any later then I would have missed it in this stunning setting. Even the beautiful central fountain of lovers Perseus and Andromeda had lights and flowers floating on top of the water and off to one side stood, like I suspected, a huge open marquee as it was a lovely warm summer's evening. It looked as if even the English weather was blessing the day.

Even the huge sweeping staircase that lay as a back drop to the flowered arch symbolising the altar, had been covered in purple carpet and rose petals, with a cascade of flowers rolling down either side.

I watched from the side and out of view as everyone got in a line, waiting for the ceremony to begin. Then suddenly the music started to fill the air and I bit my lip at the sound of Etta James singing our song…

At Last.

It was a beautiful reminder of all we had been through and how we had finally reached this point. And one by one the people I cared most about in this world walked down the aisle, after all the others stood.

First was Libby and Frank and ahead of them was their daughter Ella who was skipping and throwing fists full of white petals on the floor like she was throwing balls in a ball pit. All the guests cooed over her and every now and again she would get embarrassed and keep stopping for her mum and dad to catch up.

They were then followed by Sophia who had her arm in her husband's, Zagan. Then there was Ari with Vincent and one look at Draven's brother was enough to tell me that he was making Ari feel uncomfortable, as he didn't once take his eyes off her. After them came Pip and Adam.

I giggled as I saw her trying to sweep along the floor gracefully but overdoing it as if she was in some period drama, holding out her skirt, which was far too short to do but look adorably cute all the same. Of course, Adam didn't care for he too couldn't take his eyes off his sweetheart of a wife.

Then there was RJ, who looked about to walk down the aisle alone and I stepped forward hating the idea. But then, out of nowhere, Seth took her by the arm and without saying a word he walked her silently down the purple carpet. He was the only one who wasn't dressed as one of the wedding party but he obviously didn't care, because he wasn't there for us…

He was only there for her.

It turned out that all the males in the wedding party wore the same dark grey suits as Lucius' but then I stepped up to be the next in line and that was when I saw him, my very own…

At last.

And he was breath-taking.

"Draven." I uttered his name on a startled breath at the first sight of him. He, unlike the others, was in a black suit and my word did he just know how to wear it! I think if the tailor had been here right now I would have kissed him for helping create such a feast for the eyes. In fact, I felt like running down the aisle just so that I could get to him sooner, so that I could run my hands over it and see if it looked as hard beneath that soft material as I remembered.

A black jacket, square to his massive shoulders, tapering down to his waist, with an ivory coloured waistcoat underneath and a purple tie at his neck. And as I stepped into view he too looked to have suddenly stopped breathing. His eyes swept over me from head to toe and suddenly it looked as though I wasn't the only one that wanted to run down the aisle. It was a look filled with such intensity that I blushed and had to look away, smiling. I heard my dad chuckle beside me.

"That fiancé of yours looks about ready to come and get you if we don't get a move on.," my dad whispered to me as we made our way closer to him and it was true. I would have looked at all the people as I passed who came to celebrate this day with us but I only had eyes for Draven. So, when I braved another look from the floor, I was granted with his smile. He wanted me to look at him, this much was obvious, so I gave him that and didn't look away again.

A few more steps was all it took and my dad was soon gifting him with my hand to take.

"Take care of my girl," my dad said and Draven took my hand, gripping it tight as he made my dad a promise.

"I will protect her life as well as her heart with my very

own, for it means everything to me," he told him and my dad nodded, cleared his throat of the emotion settling there and said,

"Aye, I know you will, son." Then he shook Draven's free hand, before stepping back to allow me and Draven to now face each other.

"Sorry I'm late," I told him quietly making him smile down at me.

"Worth the wait...*always worth the wait,"* he said taking a step closer to me.

"Shall we get started?" the Vicar asked and Draven held his hand up and said,

"In a moment, first I get to tell my girl how beautiful she is," he told him and I blushed again. Then he pulled me to him, lifted my face and in front of everyone he simply looked down at me.

"Draven, everyone is waiting," I whispered.

"Let them, for the world can wait...everything can wait when I am looking at you," he told me and I think it was one of the most beautiful things he had ever said to me. So much so that I no longer cared about the world either, for right now, there was only Draven and myself. So, I reached up and cupped his face.

"Then let them also wait whilst I tell you that I love you." Hearing this he smiled down at me and then gently lifted my hands to kiss them.

"As I love you, my beautiful bride." I smiled back and then leaned closer and whispered,

"Oh, and I like your suit, handsome." Hearing this he threw his head back and laughed, before turning to the Vicar and nodding his head.

Then he turned back to me and whispered down at me...

"Time to make you mine again, sweetheart."

CHAPTER FOURTY-TWO

SPEECHES

Standing there was one of the most surreal moments of my short life so far but that didn't mean that it wasn't also one of the best. No, because without a doubt, other than the first time Draven really kissed me, this was the greatest moment in my life. Because there is nothing more spectacular, other than seeing your child being born into this world, than that of seeing the man you loved desperate to make you his wife.

And as he was instructed to turn to me by the vicar and speak his vows, that time was now.

"I, Dominic Draven, take you Catherine Keiran Williams to be my wife, to have and to hold from this day forward, for better, for worse, for richer, for poorer, in sickness and in health, to love and to cherish, till death us do part, according to God's holy law. In the presence of the Gods, I make this vow." Draven said, then turned and retrieved the wedding bands from his brother. Then he slipped it on my finger and I noticed it was made in such a way that it fit perfectly next to my engagement ring, one he slipped on straight after.

"Vena Amoris, the vein of love," he said and I remembered him saying the same thing when he first slipped my engagement ring on my finger.

I looked down at it briefly to see that it was platinum with half a symbol etched into it. The inside of the ring was a soft curve making it very comfortable to wear but the unusual part about it was that the inside was coated deep purple.

"And do you, Catherine?" The vicar prompted and suddenly I was trying to think about what Draven had just said.

"Oh yes, I mean…" I started to fumble for words and the second I felt Draven's hand squeezing mine I knew what I needed to say.

"I, Catherine Keiran Williams, take you Dominic Draven, to be my husband, to have and to hold from this day forward, for better, for worse, for richer…" I smirked when saying this next part, knowing we didn't exactly have to worry about the 'poorer bit, or the sickness for that matter, and it made him smile back at me as he knew what my secret grin meant.

"…for poorer, in sickness and in health, to love and to cherish, till death us do part, according to God's holy law. In the presence of the Gods, I make this vow," I said surprising myself for remembering it all. Then Draven nodded behind me and I turned to find my beautiful friend Pip there waiting to give me my own ring to bestow on my husband. This time the band was black, with the same purple inlay. I twisted it round to notice the same half symbol design etched there.

I placed it on his ring finger and said to him,

"Vena Amoris, the vein of love." I looked up at him and the sheer joy and love that passed between our eyes seemed to freeze time for us. It was a perfect private moment, even though it was witnessed by over a hundred people.

"Then I pronounce you husband and wife, congratulations, you may..." The vicar was about to say something when Vincent stepped up and told him,

"It's okay, I think I have got this bit Vicar..." Then he turned to his brother, slapped him on the back and said loudly,

"Brother, congratulations, you can kiss your..." But Draven didn't wait until he was finished, as he would never need permission from God, Man or Beast to kiss me. He pulled me to him, tilted my head and kissed me in a way that could have almost been classed as indecent but he didn't care. No, all he cared about was me and the piece of me he wanted to take.

Because I was his, now and always and he, well he was...

"Mine," I growled over his lips making him nip at mine before growling the same promise back,

"Mine, always."

I hadn't even realised but everyone was on their feet cheering for us and we smiled against each other's lips before pulling away and facing the crowd. Then suddenly I was crying out in surprise as Draven picked me up in his arms and walked us back down the aisle. Flower petals were thrown as confetti over us and I giggled as Draven kept turning me so that I would catch most of them.

It was then that I noticed everyone. I smiled and laughed and waved to each of those dear to me. I even noticed faces I hadn't seen in a while, like Percy, Liessa, Caspian, Ruto and even Hakan all stood looking happy for us. This made me finally look for Lucius and I was surprised to see him standing at the aisle with the rest of the groomsmen, Vincent, Frank, Adam and Zagan.

Then there was Jared's crew, Marcus, Smidge, his big ass scary brother, Orthrus, Chase and his husband Otto. Now adding Ragnar, Sigurd, Seth, Takeshi and Rue into the mix, and I could definitely understand why they were being stared at by the mortal side. For starters, most of the men on Draven's side looked so big, buff and handsome, they could have been the entertainment for ladies' night at Vegas! I think I even saw my old neighbour Betty openly drooling and she was in her seventies!

But Draven didn't stop so that we could greet anyone, no instead he just kept walking with me, until the point where I had to ask,

"Where are we going?"

"Somewhere," was his vague answer and my argument came out in a giggle,

"Draven, we have guests and…"

"And like I said, the world can wait, *I however, cannot.*" And he was right, he really couldn't. He kept walking until we were at the fountain and then he sat down, placing me on his lap and sweeping the long skirt of my dress over his outstretched legs.

"I don't think I will ever forget the joy in my heart when seeing you walking down that aisle, Mrs Draven," he told me tenderly and I reached up and ran my finger along his lips.

"Well I did make you a promise, Mr Draven," I replied with a giggle.

"It looks so beautiful here," I said looking around and back over his shoulder at the fountain.

"The only beauty I see is the one I hold in my arms and can now proclaim you as my own to both my world and now yours."

"Oh, you smooth talker, you," I said cupping his cheek and pulling him down for a kiss. Then next thing I knew someone was snapping a picture of us, making Draven growl against my lips.

"Oh, don't mind me, I am just the photographer," said a young lad who had about four different cameras hanging around his neck. I looked from the guy to Draven and we both said the culprit at the same time,

"Sophia."

"Sophia."

"It will be nice to have pictures," I mumbled against his cheek, ignoring the way the guy snapped shot after shot. Draven decided to agree, or ignore him either way as he became far too engrossed in me nibbling and kissing my way up his neck…or so I thought.

"That's enough, please take some pictures of the guests, our niece especially," Draven ordered, making the photographer stop in the middle of taking one, he pressed the click button as he raised his head in a comical, 'Oh shit, this man is scary' type of way.

"Yes, yes Sir."

"Hey, wait, what's your name?" I asked before he could run off, probably to use the bathroom and relieve himself thanks to my husband's abrupt immortal manner. He looked shocked at first and then shot a panicked look at Draven before answering me, so I intervened

"Don't worry about him, he's a pussy cat…I'm Keira and you are…?

"Oh Ben…I mean I am Ben, pleased to meet you and congratulations."

"Thank you, Ben, I think most people are heading into the marquee, so I would love some pictures of that."

"Oh, yes certainly," he said then nodded before leaving us alone once more and doing so without now running in fear for his life.

"Pussy cat?" Draven growled and I smirked.

"Would you have preferred, big scary but slightly tamed lion, because I thought that would have been too wordy," I teased.

"Tamed?" he repeated with a raised eyebrow and I lifted his hand and tapped on his ring finger.

"Yep, and now owned…hey maybe I should get you a collar with a little bell on it, so I know when you're coming," I added with a giggle and a wink. His eyes got wide at the sight of my playfulness and he suddenly stood with me, warning,

"Right, that's it, you have gone and done it now!"

"Wait, where are we going?" I complained as he started to look as though ready to take me somewhere.

"Wait, we can't leave our guests!" I yelled, also slightly panicking because it hadn't been long ago that I had Vamped out and Lucius had told me that arousal would do the same thing. Well, if there was one thing I knew about teasing Draven, then it would usually end up with arousal being top of the list. Especially seeing that when he was making me come, I could almost see stars and thought fangs might not be welcome in the mix.

"I am going to show you just what this 'cat' can do to make you purr! But yes, I agree, I like the collar idea."

"You do?" I asked clearly shocked,

"Yes, for you, not me of course… then maybe with a leash attached I can wrap around my fist to stop you from sneaking off like you seem to do far too often." Okay so this thought shouldn't have had me getting wet but it so was. Then Draven stopped dead and sniffed the air.

"Oh, you like that idea I see," Draven growled and to my utter shame, I realised that he could smell my arousal. Well, if he carried on much longer he would be able to see it for himself, just not in the way that he would have planned. I blushed scarlet making him run his nose along my heated cheek.

"Draven as much as I would be begging for you to make

love to me now, I can't do that to my family...*our family,"* I reiterated. He looked thoughtful a moment and said,

"I did tell you my heart is selfish when it comes to you as I don't like to share you, but on this occasion, I know I must."

"Thank you and I…"

"At a price, of course," Draven added interrupting me.

"A price?"

"A kiss and a dance," he said making me smirk, more about the kiss and not the dance because I was hoping to make him forget about that one.

"Deal." Then I reached up and gave him a kiss, one he started to deepen. It was dreamy.

"As lovely as that was, that wasn't the type of kiss I was speaking about." I frowned not understanding what he meant and then it hit me,

"Oh…OH…well we can't…"

"Don't panic sweetheart, as tempted as I am to ravish you here and now, I can restrain myself for our wedding night, but make no mistake, that when I finally get you all to myself, then I am tying you to our bed and feasting on you until I can claim your sweet tears, begging me to stop…" He paused for my mouth had dropped open and then he added…

"…And stop, I might not do."

After this 'alone time' which mainly consisted of Draven sexually teasing me into a near frenzy, one where I was close to saying, to hell with the fangs. But the truth was that it was our wedding and people were there to celebrate it with us and well, an important factor in that plan was that we should actually be there.

So, we walked back to the marquee hand in hand and the

second we did the whole place erupted into cheers and applause, with everyone on their feet. I laughed and blushed as was my natural response along with granting everyone a little wave. And this was my first time in seeing everyone all grouped together.

Each round table on the right side was like one for a King and his council. As on one you had Jared and his motley crew of misfits and another was Lucius and his own council. Then there was the crownless Kings, Sigurd and Seth, who both refused to take their rightful places in their world. These two were also seated on the same table that was closer to the top table, that held other important people in Draven's life, Takeshi, Leivic and Ragnar.

There was also another table close to these on the other side, that had Adam, Pip and RJ who seemed to be shooting daggers at a brooding looking Seth. Then there was Ari, who like RJ, seemed to be shooting her own silent weapons of mass destruction at a smirking Vincent at the top table. Frank was also sat at this table with a squirming Ella who was desperately trying to get out of her high chair to reach something.

Then there was the other side of the room that was filled with distant family members, a few old school friends of Libby's and mine and then people my parents had known for years and therefore *I'd* known for years.

Needless to say, this was the side that was openly gawking at the other. And could I really blame them? I mean there was more eye candy in here than a romance novel book signing, filled with front cover hotties! Even my nan looked to be drooling and strangely, or more worryingly, for a certain someone. And the object of her affections was none other than scary massive mountain of a man, Viking Ragnar. My poor grandad had no hope…or should I say Ragnar didn't.

The top table and the one Draven was currently leading me

to was long and was the only one that looked fit for royalty. Large free-standing candelabras made from twisted wrought iron, framed it either side, each holding five church pillar candles. It was the only table in the room that had a luxurious rich purple table cover, that was half hidden by the long flower arrangement of white flowers which ran the full length of the table.

The whole place was stunning and purple and ivory definitely worked as a theme. It looked regal and classical at the same time, with hints of gothic thrown in there for good measure. Well, what did I expect, my husband and I did meet whilst I was working in his gothic nightclub!

Everyone was still on their feet, except my dear nan, as we walked to take our places and they only sat once we had done the same. Well, as I did because Draven remained standing, as it was clear he had something to say.

"I would like to start by thanking you all for being with us on this day…"

"Well you did send out your private jets, so it was the least we could do!" Marcus heckled and I was surprised to see him looking quite normal, for him that was anyway. He was quite handsome in a striking kind of way, and now he didn't have his hair in a creepy jester style or clown makeup on, he just looked like a slim, fit goth in a black suit. Although his red hair was still stare worthy, no matter how much he had styled it and secured it at the back of his head with a black ribbon… you couldn't exactly miss it.

"Actually, that was all my idea, Dom wanted to steal her away to a desert island," Sophia quipped back making everyone laugh.

"As true as that maybe, I am still thankful for the day, for I am now blessed with my bride's unwavering smile and seeing her happiness by being surrounded by family and friends…so for that I must thank you all." I blushed and bit my lip.

"But what I say next is for my wife." Draven then turned to me and I swallowed hard, knowing this was going to be emotional.

"Catherine, what I say to you now, I once said when I first asked you to be my wife. I do so again, to tell you that my feelings have not changed, but instead that the impossible happened…*they only grew stronger."* Hearing this I had to swipe away a single tear that emerged.

"We are here tonight with the sole purpose of saying goodbye to all the yesterdays spent apart and now welcoming a new forever of days together. For I promised you once to never let you fall and in doing so, ask you once again to place your trust in me, as I have placed my trust in you. And all I ask in return is that you believe these words of love and know that I will never let you go…I will fight for you until the end of days and beyond." Then he leaned down and kissed me, making everyone start clapping. Then he took his seat next to me.

However, I started to get even more teary and the second Draven looked away, I couldn't help but look at Lucius. He hadn't taken his eyes off me as if waiting for when I would need him and in that second, I felt it coming. I looked to Sophia in panic. I felt my fangs starting to slip past my lip and I tried to hide my face but not before Zagan and Vincent had seen. They both couldn't hide their shock, but before they could act on it, I heard Lucius' voice in my head,

"Retract your fangs, young one." The second he did my gaze shot to his. I quickly felt my body doing as he commanded and my fangs disappeared just in time as I felt Draven taking hold of my chin so that he could reclaim my focus. I gave him a shaky smile and the second he raised a brow I knew he was

trying to get a read on my strange behaviour. So, I did the only thing I could think of,

I blagged it.

"My turn," I whispered up at him before pushing my seat back and getting up to deliver my own speech…what exactly that was going to be, I didn't know yet. But I knew how I felt and unfortunately, I couldn't speak of trust like Draven had done, not knowing what I now was and what I had kept from him.

Because in the end it had been his last statement that held the weight of the truth of my actions. His words, *'…and know that I will never let you go…I will fight for you until the end of days and beyond.'* It was the reason for all of this. Because Draven would always fight to keep me, prophecy be damned. And looking around the room now, at all we cared about, I knew that at least one of us couldn't condemn them…

So, I condemned myself.

"Hello everyone…" I started nervously.

"Okay, so I am not great at this and don't have a flare for public speeches as my husband does, so please try and refrain from any heckling…Marcus…oh and you Pip…" I added making people laugh when Marcus held up his hands and said,

"I wouldn't dare, your husband is one scary demon!" This made everyone laugh, and thankfully the humans didn't get the inner meaning. Even Pip stood up, stuck two thumbs at her chest and said,

"Who me? As if I would Toots...okay, so only maybe a little." Then she winked at me before sitting again, making everyone laugh.

"First, I would also like to thank everyone for being here today as it means the world to me that I get to share this day with not only my family, but my friends as well." I paused to look at all those that meant so much to me.

"To my mum and dad, I owe the happiest of childhoods to you and you both taught me what it meant to love. To Libby, who wasn't ever just a sister to me but also a best friend and to her wonderful husband Frank, who became my brother after about five seconds of meeting him. I can't thank you both enough for giving me another home, one that brought me closer to finding my *final home,"* I said looking toward Draven's side and my other family. Draven gave me a warm smile and I knew he was thinking about something he no doubt wanted to add to this, only I could tell it was for my ears only.

"Which brings me to the important ladies in my life. First RJ who welcomed me into her town with open arms and gave me her friendship without question." I nodded to her where she sat blushing. Seth had turned in his seat so that he could fully stare at her, making her look close to squirming in her seat.

"Then there is the matchmaker herself, Sophia, who was always a sister to me but utterly determined to make it more official by setting me up with her brother. We wore him down eventually," I commented on a laugh, making everyone else do the same.

"Yes, and I bet it didn't take long, all of ten minutes, eh Dom!?" Jared shouted cheerfully hammering a fist on the table with the rest of the supernatural men surrounding him.

"Less than a second!" Draven responded, making me blush and the whole room chuckled.

"To Sophia, who made this wedding utterly perfect for us and all I ever dreamed of it being…but also to all my beautiful bridesmaids, who have all been there for me in ways I never thought possible and I can only hope that I can do them proud, as they have done me." Each of them smiled and I nodded especially to Ari, who tipped her glass my way.

"And then there has to be a mention of all the men in my husband's life, who have also been there for me in one way or another. You all, now and forever, will hold a dear place in my heart, for this journey could not exist without each of you helping me along the way to my husband's heart." They all knew what I meant and I didn't care for those that didn't. It needed to be said and I was glad that I finally had the opportunity to do so. I looked to Vincent, Sigurd, Ragnar, to Jared and his men and then to Lucius, who had helped me more than most. Each of them tipped their chin to me, acknowledging my thanks and love.

Then I looked down at Draven and placed a hand to his shoulder to gain his focus. He looked up at me and I told him

"And last of all to my handsome, loving husband who made me the happiest soul on earth today by taking me as his wife. I simply say this…" I took a deep breath and looked him in the eyes,

"Dominic, you will forever be my world, forever be my heart and forevermore…*be my everything…I love you.*" Hearing this he was up and out of his seat in seconds. His lips then captured mine and he kissed me to the backdrop of cheers, rowdy shouts and wolf whistles, mainly coming from his side of the family.

"I love you," he told me after our kiss, but not moving away from it. Then as I was still smiling he grabbed my hand, raised it up and said,

"To my beautiful Queen!" making me blush to the roots of my hair. Then everyone from his side started banging on the tables and stamping their feet on the boarded floor like something out of a medieval tavern…

And it was glorious.

CHAPTER FORTY-THREE

GOODBYE SALVATION

After the speeches were all said and done, we were served a delicious three course meal, which Sophia told me later that evening that Draven's only request was that the dessert be something that included chocolate. This made me giggle. The evening was in full swing and once dinner was finished, coffee, tea and even more chocolates (again at Draven's request) were served.

After this came even more speeches. The one from my dad had everyone almost in tears with laughter as of course, he told the coffee/gravy story where I had made all of his business clients cups of gravy with milk and sugar instead of coffee. Other embarrassing stories like that followed, which had me turning every shade of red in the spectrum, along with some new ones in there as well, one I think strong enough to be seen from space.

But then he finished it off with the mushy stuff, telling the whole room how proud he was of me. Again, I had Lucius in my head telling me, *'Easy Pet, just breath and keep it locked down.'* This helped as every time I started to get emotional, his voice was all that was needed to keep it at bay.

Then came the best man's speech and Vincent stood up and the room went silent. I think I even heard a few 'oh my' from some of the ladies, and one of my mum's friends was actually fanning herself with a folded napkin.

"I know custom has it that the best man's speech should be filled with embarrassing stories about the groom and as his brother, then I assure you, I have many but I am not going to do that…" There was a few boo's, mainly from the men.

"…because he paid me handsomely," Vincent joked making everyone laugh.

"Not enough it seems," Draven added dryly, again adding the comedy.

"But in all seriousness, what is there to say about my brother that everyone who knows him, doesn't already know? Well then, I say this, until he met you Keira, I had never seen him smile the way he does when he is with you… I had never seen him laugh, the way he does when you say something funny…which we all know is often," he added getting more chuckles.

"I had never seen his soul light up, the way it does when you simply enter a room but most of all, I had never seen him love the way he does now after he met you. Simply put, you complete him and because of that, *you also complete us."* After this I got up, walked over to Vincent and threw myself into his arms, whilst the whole room cheered. Then I pulled back, feeling my eyes filling with tears and I reached up and kissed him on the cheek.

"Thank you, brother."

"You are most welcome, my sister." He told me and before I moved away, I told him,

"I will tell him, just let us have today." He knew what I

referred to as he had seen it for himself, so without letting on, he simply nodded his acceptance.

After this was all said and done, a screen was moved to one side now allowing the room access to what was essentially a party room, looking more like a mini nightclub.

I found out quickly, (Because Pip popped her head up and told me) that this was Pip's doing and one look at the room and you could tell. The room had square U-shaped seating that surrounded the room so that people could sit more comfortably in the space. There was even champagne bottles chilling in glass coolers at each table. The dance floor was black gloss that was currently lit up thanks to the expensive looking system that was making everywhere glow with moving purples, pinks, and blue lights. Even where the DJ was set up looked like something you would have found in a high-class nightclub, not something for hire found in the back of a bridal magazine.

Of course, there was also the crazier side of Pip's vision, which included the 'Pip Pits' which was the sign painted on another closed off section. I found out this consisted of a network of smaller marquees, with rooms of the likes of, The Foam room, The Paint room, The Ball room (a room full of different sized balls, not the grand version of where you would dance) and the Bouncy room which was just a massive bouncy castle with an in-built slide.

I did ask why Pip had felt the need but she just nodded to Ella and some of the other children in my family and said,

"Well duh, it's for me and the tiddly winkers." And then she gave me a wink and made it her job to round up the kids and play babysitter. I didn't know who was more thrilled, the parents or Pip. Adam grinned at me as he came over and kissed my cheek, then said,

"I'd better go supervise." I nodded back and said,

"I think that's wise."

"Congratulations to both of you," he added and then followed his skipping wife, who was currently collecting children like the Pied Piper. I then scanned the room and started giggling.

"Do you think we should warn our friend of what danger lurks ahead?" I said leaning into Draven as I saw my nan now making a beeline for Ragnar. Draven followed my gaze and laughed,

"Hell no! If I intervene now she might turn her attention to me and I think my backside lay victim to your grandmother's wandering fingers quite enough to see me through my many lifetimes." I smirked and replied,

"Well she is fickle that way." He chuckled and we both watched the funny scene play out before us. I never thought I would have ever seen my colossal friend looking so fearful before, but there it was, Ragnar was terrified of a little old lady who was clearly making a move on him.

"I'd better go and save him," I said about to shift from my seat when Draven stopped me.

"Save me instead…for he will survive but I fear that I will not if I don't get you alone soon," Draven whispered in my ear with a sexual rumble. I gave him a grin and before I thought about what I was doing, I let him pull me up from my chair and guide me through the marquee but half way there Sophia intercepted us.

"Oh no you don't, not yet, it's time for the first dance and then you have to cut the cake. After that, I promise, the rest of the night is yours." Draven growled and I couldn't help but chuckle.

"Come on, I promised you a dance and then after that…"

"A kiss," he finished on a purred whisper in my ear as we both knew what kind of kiss he was referring to…and I couldn't wait.

"Now would you all please put your hands together in welcoming Mr and Mrs Draven to the dance floor." We both heard Vincent's voice coming over the speaker system. Everyone had already started moving towards the 'nightclub' part and I smirked thinking the setting couldn't be more perfect, considering where we had first officially met.

I let Sophia pull me along as I watched Draven being patted on the back by Lucius of all people. Then we were both led into the smaller marquee that once you were in, didn't seem that small. In fact, it opened up and was quickly resembling a small ballroom after all.

The lights had turned into a soft glow, like candlelight and the room was transformed into a romantic setting in seconds. I was pulled to one side of the dance floor and I watched as Draven was dragged to the other. Then he stepped onto the floor confidently commanding the space and Sophia, Ari and Libby all gave me a nudge for me to join him. Everyone smiled and laughed at my obvious nervousness and he nodded to Vincent for something. His brother then jumped down from the DJ's raised platform with a microphone in hand. He gave it to Draven, who raised it to his lips and said,

"Mrs Draven, if you would be so kind in doing me the great honour of granting me this dance." Then he handed the mic back to Vincent who was grinning like a loon. Draven held his hand out to me and I took a deep breath before joining him, placing my hand in his. The second he made the connection, his fingers tightened their hold and he spun me around into him, making the room cheer.

Then he raised a hand to my cheek and said,

"Don't worry sweetheart, I will take care of you." He nodded to Vincent who obviously knew what to do. Seconds later a familiar song started to play and I knew that if I could have the guts to dance to it in front of Draven's kingdom, then I could do so now in front of my family and friends.

"The night I declared you my Queen to the world," Draven told me as if also remembering it for himself. The night of the Venice Masked Ball. It had been after our first kiss when Draven was trying to win me back from Alex. To be honest, he hadn't had to try very hard.

"You're still my 'Salvation'," he told me placing his forehead to mine and he took a moment to bask in having me in his arms. Then as if he had all the time in the world, he took one of my hands in his, then placed a hand at my waist before he started to move me gracefully around the room. We soon lost ourselves to the song and its beautiful words, that meant something deeply rooted for the both of us.

Then as the song came to an end, he lowered his head to mine and said but one word,

"Always." I swallowed hard knowing that no matter how much I wished for it, that and 'always' wasn't ever going to be in our fates. But for today, I could give him my own vow, it just wouldn't be one of life but one more of heart.

"And forevermore."

After this we found ourselves back at the top table after a huge wedding cake had been brought out for us to cut. The other quirky part about this wedding was that each of the table's centre pieces was in fact a smaller version of this cake and a member of each table had to cut the cake at the same time as we did, to symbolise their blessing of the marriage.

It was a beautiful four-tier, round wedding cake that was covered in black fondant and then decorated in a lacework of purple icing that looked as though a master artist had spent weeks creating it. Each tier was then separated by a ring of delicate edible white roses that I couldn't tell whether they were also made from icing or white chocolate…I was hoping for the latter.

Draven raised up the knife and I placed my hand on top of his before we cut it together. Everyone did the same thing, and after Draven and I fed each other a bite, it took Draven all of about two minutes before he was whispering once more in my ear.

"I think you will find all human wedding customs are fulfilled but one." I smirked and then replied,

"Mmm, can't imagine what that is," I teased making him growl and nip playfully at my ear.

"Enough! You owe me a kiss unless you would like me to collect right here," he threatened and my mouth dropped before hissing,

"You wouldn't!" Then he pushed his finished napkin off the table, making a show of it.

"Oh…how clumsy of me, let me just get that," he said accepting my challenge and as he reached down to retrieve it, he brought his hand back up, caressing the inside of my leg, gathering up my skirt as he went. My hand shot to his to stop him from getting any further, making him laugh.

"Draven, you can't… not here!" I said through gritted teeth and fighting him under the table.

"Then come with me before I throw you over my shoulder and turn this delectable pale skin of yours a lovely shade of peach…or should I try for crimson and smack your lovely behind as I go?" he said and I was suddenly up and out of my seat like someone just lit my ass on fire. I heard the cocky bastard chuckling as he followed me.

"Keep an eye on my grandmother," I said to Vincent as we walked past making him laugh, as we all looked to see Ragnar trying to get away from her. I had already seen him be suckered into the whole, 'Would you help an old dear as she sits down' then as they stand to do so, that's when she goes in for the attack. I had almost been in tears at Draven's shoulder when I saw Ragnar's face as she grabbed a handful of his Viking bottom. Sigurd hadn't missed it either, hence his own tearful, booming laughter.

Vincent slapped his brother on the back and said,

"I will hold the immortal fort, as I believe our sister already has the mortal one eating out of the palm of her hand." Oh, and I could believe it, as half the guests were ready to declare their love for her, no matter how scary her husband looked. To be honest, he looked so used to it and found himself smirking more often than not as she floated her way around the room and conversed with all my family and friends.

"And for that I owe you greatly, brother." Then without another word to anyone, Draven grabbed my hand pulling me from the rest of our guests, obviously in a hurry. I laughed when I could barely keep up with him and was about to complain when he must have agreed with me being too slow. He stopped long enough to swoop me up into his arms and then continued on to his unknown destination.

"Where are we going?" I asked and he lifted me enough to say,

"You will see."

We continued back to the fountain and when he put my legs down I frowned in confusion.

"What are we…?"

"Seeing in the new future together," he said cryptically. Then like magic, he pretended to suddenly produce a coin from behind my ear. I giggled like an entertained little girl. Then he kissed it and threw into the water. I knew what would happen but I still stepped back into him when I felt the rumbling of the walkway that would soon appear.

"What if someone sees?"

"No one will see, I have seen to that…come," he said holding out his hand to me to take. I did without hesitation and walked with him across the small stone path towards the door at the end. I was about to complain about getting wet when Draven put out a hand so that the water was deflected by an invisible force he'd created. I looked behind me to see that not a soul saw us disappearing into a secret world, one I had only earlier this day come back from. But I trusted Draven and whatever he had planned I would follow him, even it ended up going to Hell and back. After all, I knew that there were enough doors to get there where we were going…

The Janus Temple.

Once inside the main room it felt strange being here with just Draven. It seemed to be even bigger if that was possible. As if I half expected giants to start walking down one of the large corridors or something.

"Draven, what are we doing here?" I asked looking back at the large waterfall at its core, wondering if Janus was in there somewhere looking down at us, hearing us as part of his whispers? I even noticed my cloak tossed off to one side that had fallen from my shoulders when I had first seen Draven.

"You don't know this but I own one of the doors here." Now this shocked me.

"You do?"

"Yes, no-one but Vincent and Sophia know of it, and now you do, *my wife.*" I smiled when hearing him call me this as the warmth that washed over me everytime he did was like a blanket being placed over my heart.

"Where does it lead to?" I asked.

"Come and I will show you," he answered smirking at my curiosity. So once again I let myself be pulled along down one of the corridors that was filled with row after row of every type of door possible. From the grandest, most elaborately carved wood, to the truly bizarre and downright weird. I swear I passed one that looked covered in stone snakes and I jumped back a step and said,

"That one just moved!" Draven stopped and looked to where I was looking. He scoffed and said,

"The Amazonian tribal lord of the Chuyachaki."

"Uh…the what now?"

"Do you know what a Satyrs is?" he asked instead and I frowned.

"You mean like the character from 'The witch the Lion and the Wardrobe'?" He smirked and said,

"Well read I see." I laughed and said,

"I liked the TV show as a kid."

"They are a race that lure the foolish to become lost, first in the jungle and then in their minds. They started to see beasts become men before begging to die and offer up their souls as a sacrifice." He laughed at the sight of my screwed up face.

"You tell the sweetest stories, my love," I teased making him smirk back at me.

"Come, it's not far now." And he was right, we passed a few more doors and he was stopping next to one that looked more like a bookshelf filled with every famous classic known to man. Jesus, but was that even Jane Austin? Well, I wonder what she would have thought to know that one of her books ended up on a shelf in a place like this. Well, for starters I think her stories would have turned out quite differently if she had ever met someone like Draven.

"It's a bookshelf," I stated.

"Such an observant little vixen," he commented with a wink. I rolled my eyes and cocked my hip to one side, throwing him some attitude.

"What I mean my cocky husband, is that it doesn't exactly look like a door now does it?"

"And this one next to it, that looks like a stained-glass window, or the one we passed covered in snakes, seen many doors like that where you grew up?" Okay so he had a point.

"No, didn't think so…pick a book," he told me nodding back to the shelf and I scanned the books doing as he asked. There was everything from Don Quixote, Robinson Crusoe, Dangerous Liaisons, even Mary Shelley's Frankenstein. I ran my finger along all the ones at eye level. The Count of Monte Cristo, The Scarlet Letter, Moby-Dick, Alice's Adventures in Wonderland.

"Little Women, Huckleberry Finn and The Strange Case of Dr Jekyll and Mr Hyde?" I chuckled asking Draven and making him shrug his shoulders and smirk back at me, as he casually leaned against the frame watching me. My eyes went back to reading titles like the The Great Gatsby, Catcher in the Rye, The Lord of The Rings. To Kill a Mockingbird and even The BFG but it was none of these I chose, nor was it Shakespeare's, Romeo and Juliet. No, I went straight to the one I would always choose and pulled on the spine of Charlotte Brontë's, Jane Eyre. The book didn't give but only tipped, creating a door as the book case started to split before opening on one side.

"Now how did I know you were going to choose that one, I wonder?" Draven said in a mocking tone tapping a finger on his lips.

"I don't know, must go back to your stalking days," I

replied with a cocky grin of my own. Then he snagged me around the waist and yanked me to him.

"Must be," he mused making me swoon. Then he opened the door and walked me backwards through it. The next thing I knew I was gripping onto him as I was stepping back into the dark.

"Draven?"

"Not far now sweetheart," he assured me and he was right. A few more steps was all it took until I felt something solid at my back. I felt him reaching around my waist so that he could open the door behind me. I turned around and let my eyes adjust to the light before I gasped in utter shock.

"Afterlife?!" I said stepping into the room and seeing a familiar sight…*Draven's library.* Actually, we hadn't just walked through a door into Draven's library but through the massive fireplace that always looked like a door to the gates of Hell. Its two iron statues that stood like sentinels guarding the room were what greeted us and I turned to find Draven grinning at me as I studied the room.

"Is this real?" I asked making him laugh before shaking his head.

"I can assure you, it's quite real, my dear."

"So, we are really home?" I asked getting excited by the idea of it. Hearing this Draven gave me a different kind of smile, this time one that was warm and tender. Oh yeah, he liked hearing me saying that.

"Yes sweetheart, we are home."

"Well, in that case…" I started to say, hopping on one foot as I removed my strappy heels before casting them aside. He raised a questioning brow making him look sexy as hell whilst doing it.

"…time we get a move on," I said turning around and running for the door. I heard him laughing from afar and when I thought I was putting some distance between us the next thing I heard was directly in my ear.

"Run little white rabbit, for the wolf is on your tail." I shrieked out in surprise but when I turned he wasn't there. He was doing what he did best…he was stalking his prey. So, what did I do…? I gave him what he wanted and played the game.

I ran.

I ran back to our room and just as I was rounding the corner, looking behind me to see if he was there, I ended up running straight into the arms of my pursuer.

"Mine," he growled before grabbing my face and taking my lips in a possessive kiss. I reached down and gathered my skirt up my legs by walking my fingers up the material until it was high enough to serve my purpose. I then hitched one leg up on his thigh, grabbed hold of his shoulders and jumped up at him, so that I could wrap my legs around his waist. His hands left my face and moved to hold my behind, grinding me into his long hard length.

Then I felt him rear back so that he could kick his door in. He stepped us through the splintered wood panels that hung limply from the broken hinges in his haste to get into our room. I finally came up for air long enough to look over his shoulder to see him cast a brief hand behind him to fix the door. However, any other thoughts fled me as I threw my head back giving him even greater access to my neck as he started kissing, sucking, biting along my tender taut flesh.

I felt him putting a knee to the bed before he lowered me down.

"I have dreamed of this moment and thought of little else," Draven told me, running a hand down from my neck over my corseted dress, down the centre of my heaving breasts.

"To see you in this beautiful dress, looking like the goddess you are, walking down that aisle towards me…I will forever hold that sight with me like the vow you made in giving yourself to me *forevermore,"* he said using my own words back at me and I closed my eyes, as I let his own sweet words coat my mind in utter comfort. Then I opened my eyes and asked him,

"Make love to me Draven, as I have waited far too long... *don't make me wait any longer,"* I whispered up at him and he didn't need to be asked twice. He kissed me deep before he started moving the kiss down my neck, the cleavage of my breasts and then he ran his hands down my sides, framing my body with his touch. He started to shift further down and I grabbed his hand, to stop him.

"What are you..." he snapped his head up and looked at me with a purple heat in his eyes,

"Your payment and I am taking that which is owed to me... your sweet body's kiss." And that was precisely what he did. He shifted down the bed and pushed my skirt up until it gathered around my waist. My white stockings and suspenders were a big hit with him as he started to kiss the thick lace around the top of my thighs before pulling at the straps that connected to the ivory Basque. One he couldn't see yet.

"As pretty as this is, it is in my way," he said snapping the fastening underneath and with a snap, I was bared for him. I felt him getting closer and instead of just diving straight in, he took his sweet time, blowing along the seam first, making me shudder against the tickling sensation. Then he ran the back of one knuckle down against my folds and I nearly jerked off the bed at the feel of his first touch.

"So responsive to my touch, it's as if I am being reunited to the soul I own, one housed in this delicious body of mine...my gift." I bit my lip at what his words did. Then he dipped his head in further and ran his nose there in place of his finger.

"You smell so good." Then he suddenly grabbed my legs

and spread them as far as they would go. I yelped at his sudden rough treatment and the sweet kiss he bestowed there was the opposite to how his large hands gripped me. At the first feel of his leisurely swipe of his tongue I moaned long and loud.

"You taste so good…so fucking good," he told me swearing on a growl. And then he'd had enough of teasing me, and went in for the kill and started to try and devour me whole. He sucked in my tight little bundle of nerves and I nearly came undone at that first scrape of his teeth.

"Ahhh!" I moaned, crying out and pressing the back of my head into the bed and arching my back like a bow. Draven allowed me the small movement before then hauling me back to his mouth on a growl. A sound that vibrated through his chest as much as it did through my clit. Then he doubled the pleasure when he inserted a finger. I almost shot off the bed and I wanted to curse him when he started chuckling against my tender wet flesh.

"Fuck me, but I love watching you! I could do this for hours just to see you squirm against my fingers and tongue," he said and as if proving himself right he added another finger.

"Please…" I pleaded as I could feel it coming but I just needed that extra push, that constant touch and rhythm, I knew he would soon have me coming like a rocket…that was if the bastard stopped teasing me with it.

"Please…mmm I like that word coming from you. All breathy and full of need, full of want but I have something else in mind of what to fill you with," he told me, pulling his fingers from me and making me cry out at the loss. He crawled back up my body and placed a hand against my forehead before whispering over my lips,

"You will only come when I am seated firmly inside you as I want to feel your release tightening around me and caressing my length as I spill my own release buried inside you, claiming you from deep within." Then he sucked in his two fingers before placing them by my own lips.

"Open," he ordered me and I did as he commanded. Then he placed them inside my mouth, for me to suck them clean as he had done. His eyes grew intense at the sight, and sparked a deeper purple.

"Tell me how you like the taste of your arousal dripping from my fingers." I couldn't tell him, I could only nod. Thankfully, it was good enough for him but oh my god, his erotic words nearly had me coming already. Unfortunately for me, this also came with an added extra, one I didn't want. I felt a tingling in my gums and I slammed my mouth shut, hoping it didn't mean what I thought it could mean.

Thankfully, he flipped me over so that he could start freeing me from my dress.

"This is one gown I do not wish to ever see ruined, no matter how eager I am to see what beauty hides beneath," he said pulling at the long corset ties and I could feel it getting looser with every pull.

"Unwrapping my wedding gift brings me great pleasure, my sweet wife," he whispered against my shoulder blade after he peeled back the first loose part. Then he continued down until soon the whole dress was being dragged down from my body. Then his hands were back and running down my sides and over the curve of my cheeks.

"Stunning. Utterly stunning, my love," he told me softly as he looked at my underwear set. But then he wanted to see more.

"No, please, like this…I want you to take me this way," I told him before he could turn me back over as I knew this way I could at least hide my face in case something was to happen.

"As you wish." He granted me this as I doubted with my pleading tone he could have denied me anything. Then I felt myself being lifted by the hips and before I had chance to take in a breath, he was thrusting himself inside me.

The second I felt his full length seated there, nestled within my core, I came undone and in more ways than one. He started to move and all it took was a few strokes along my inner nerves in that delicious way, and I was close again. But then he managed to touch my clit with one hand curled around to my front and I was screaming back against him. I started to ride him faster and faster through wave after wave of rippling pleasure. One so powerful it felt as though it was continuing to grow from the base of my spine as it bloomed outwards affecting the rest of my body.

Endorphins exploded and released into my body like someone injecting a drug. I was so lost to them that I hadn't realised my fangs must have retracted back, so when Draven suddenly flipped me, he wasn't faced with his new Vampire bride.

"I want to see you…I want to look into your eyes as I make you come again and we find our final release together," he told me and I arched into his touch as he freed a breast from the cup it was held behind. He pinched and pulled at my nipple and that sweet torturous action sent me into overload. I raised my legs up as far as I could and he quickly got the hint. He grabbed my legs, lifted them up over his shoulders and started hammering into me at such speed I could feel another release on the way.

"Together, we come together!" Draven demanded and in the end, it was only one thing that sent Draven over the edge and that was the answer to one question…

"Tell me who you belong to…say it!" he snarled in his demonic voice and I just had enough time to shout my answer before I came undone again around him, quickly milking him of his seed,

"I'm yours! I'M YOURS!" I screamed louder and he threw

his head back and roared up to the ceiling as he came deep inside me. And that's when my theory of showing my vampire side went completely out the window. As, no matter how strong my orgasm hit me, what followed this time was my fangs. I quickly grabbed a pillow and covered my face before he could see me.

"Keira, what are you doing?" He chuckled thinking it was done from embarrassment but before long he realised that it wasn't as he could hear me sobbing.

"Keira?! What's wrong, did I hurt you?" he asked and I shook the pillow telling him no. He slowly withdrew his still hard length from me and when he tried to take the pillow from my face I only held on tighter and shouted a muffled,

"NO! Dothn't look ath me!"

"Keira what is it, speak to me!" It was obvious he was getting worried as his voice had taken a more serious tone. And I knew, I just knew there was no getting away from it this time. So, I started crying harder, knowing he would just hate me for what I had done and all I wanted was to give him this perfect moment…

"I…I…I hath ruined ethery thhhing!" I told him through my lisp.

"Keira, your voice…what, what's happened?" I decided it was now or never. It was time to come clean and tell him the truth, or more like show him.

"I'm ssso ssso sssorry." I told him and then…

I moved the pillow.

CHAPTER FOURTY-FOUR

RUNNING FROM THE DANGEROUS TRUTH

The utter horror on his face had me releasing another heart wrenching sob, one that felt as though it was being ripped out of me.

"I'm ssso ssso sssorry, I didntth mean for thhhisss tho happen, iths all my fthault!" I shouted covering my face and crying so hard I was finding it hard to breathe. Then, after a few short moments, I felt a pair of hands on mine trying to pull them from hiding my face.

"No! D...d...dothn't look ath me! I'm a monttthser!" I shouted trying to fight him but he was much stronger than I was. He pulled my hands away and then lifted my chin up. I closed my eyes as tight as I could and winced, waiting for his harsh words.

"Look at me," he demanded softly and it was the tender tone of his voice that had me doing as he asked. I was expecting to see such pain, such disappointment but I was granted with nothing but concern. He looked into my eyes, that I knew had

also changed, then he raised a hand to my cheek as he touched the black veins that no doubt framed them.

"Why don't you tell me how this happened, sweetheart." His tender voice had me shuddering again as I tried to hold back another sob.

"Yourth not… athgry wwwithh me?" I asked still shaking.

"That depends, did you ask for this to be done to you?" he asked me, trying to keep his tone even and no doubt his temper at bay.

"NO! I certthhertenthly didth not!" I said firmly after first struggling way too much with the word 'certainly'. Draven couldn't help but give me a small smile in return as to be honest, it must have been comical to hear.

"Then no, I am not angry with you, however the one who did this to you will most certainly pay," he said with a demonic promise to his voice, one that was definitely scary.

"No, you can'tht! He sathved my lifffe as ith wasth Laythla's faulth asth sthhe sthhot me wittth a poithsonths arrwow made by sthome Goddessth of hate or sthomething and well…" he stopped my lisping rant with a hand and said,

"Let's make this somewhat easier, should we?" he said smirking and then ran a gentle fingertip down one fang, silently making it retract. Then he did the same on the other side.

"Hey, how did you do that?!"

"You are a youngling and although I am not your master, I can still inflict my will on you."

"Oh…well that will come in handy then when I am nagging you," I chuckled making him raise an eyebrow at me.

"Indeed, now please continue" he said dryly.

"Okay, so like I was saying, both you and Lucius tried to save me but you couldn't and I would have died but then Lucius had heard in my dreams about Cronus mocking that I was just a mortal and what could I do, so he thought that turning me was part of the prophecy! So, you helped cut him open so he could reach his heart and give me Lucifer's blood… so now I am a Vampire and you can't kill him because that would then kill me, but the good news is I can still be in the sun and eat garlic bread!" I said having to take a deep breath. Draven closed his eyes a moment and pinched the bridge of his nose with his finger and thumb.

"Do I dare ask what else happened whilst you were gone, something else you are no doubt keeping from me?" he asked and yes, now would have been the time to say, oh and congrats, you're gonna be a daddy, but I didn't. No, instead I told him,

"Well, there was the small matter of Pertinax kidnapping me but Lucius freed us, but then you needed help in fighting the demonic God, so me and Lucius kind of stepped in and killed him, well *he* didn't because he sacrificed himself to save us both, but I kind of brought him back to life…well after I turned all demony and powerful, then I stabbed him with his own spear, Pertinax not Lucius…and he died after that, again Pertinax, not Lucius and then you found out I was your Chosen One and didn't want to let me go and…" Draven held up his hand again to stop me and I didn't know if it was possible for his kind to get headaches but if it was, then I would say that one just hit.

"Are you telling me, that in the seventeen days you were back in time, you managed to get yourself put in my harem, nearly killed by another Concubine, then by a younger Sophia, then got yourself kidnapped by a demonic God, before escaping so that you could run towards the danger and kill him when trying to protect me. And then, after all this, get yourself kidnapped again only to have another attempt made on your life, to then be turned into the first human hybrid Vampire…all in seventeen, fucking days?!" Okay, so yeah, he was mad and well, put like that then who could blame him. I mean jeez, was I a liability or what? To be honest it was a bloody miracle I was still breathing!

"Yes, that is what I am saying, so please don't shout," I asked him in a soft voice trying to calm him down. He closed his eyes again, stood up and zipped up his pants.

"Where are you going?" I asked thinking this was it, he was going to leave me. I sat up ready to throw myself at his mercy and beg him to stay, when he surprised me. He placed a fist either side of my hips, leant down to command my personal space and said,

"I am going to go into the bathroom, get a wet cloth, come back to take care of my wife, as from now on, that is how it is to remain…do I make myself understood?" His stern voice had me nodding silently and biting my lip. He then pushed off the bed and walked to the bathroom where my voice stopped him.

"Please, please don't hate me, Dominic," I asked him with a voice that barely made it above a whisper. I watched as his shoulders slumped and he took a deep breath before storming back over to me. He then caged me in and forced me back onto the bed.

"Do you really think for one minute that I could hate the woman who has done nothing in this life but sacrifice herself for the safety and love of others? Do you really think I could hate one of the most selfless beings on the planet all because she sneaks off to another world in an attempt to try and save the world she comes from?!" I was about to speak but he snapped,

"I have not finished!" The tone of his voice may have sounded angry and on the edge, but the hand that gently caressed my cheek and hair, was anything but.

"And do you really think that I could hate the woman that has shown more bravery than anyone I have ever known, just so she can face impossible odds in hopes of saving my own life or find herself die trying?" I bit my lip and felt the hot tears roll down my cheeks at the intensity of it all.

"Keira, how could I ever hate you when all I want to do is spend an eternity worshipping at your feet and laying down my life as payment to every God out there, if that is what it takes to keep you." I swallowed hard and then said,

"So just to be clear..." I never finished as Draven had his mouth on mine in a mind consuming kiss. It felt raw and beautiful all at the same time, like he was branding me to him, chaining my soul to his in just one loving action.

Then he told me...

"Just to be clear, I fucking adore you! *And always will.*"

After this I found out from Draven that Sophia and he had had a little chat where she went into more depth of our time away than she had done in the car. However, the parts she had kept out were me facing off a demonic god, me being pregnant, me being shot with a poisonous arrow and lastly, me being turned into a Vampire. Everything in between, she had told him.

But now he knew it all...and he, in his own words, 'Fucking adored me'. So, all was good in the world, well other than the impending doom and world destruction that was going to hit at any point, thanks to a megalomaniac, Cronus and his band of imprisoned pissed off Titan buddies.

Oh, and not forgetting how Draven didn't yet know that he had knocked me up... 'cause that was kind of a big deal too. I knew that I should have told him and even as we made our way back to the Janus Temple, I was regretting my decision, as I should have just got it all out in one big hit.

But I couldn't.

I couldn't because I was a coward and I wanted to give my

husband hope that not all was lost. Because I knew the second he thought that I was pregnant then that would mean the prophecy was coming true…and that my death would swiftly follow.

Because according to the Fates our child would be the next powerful being that could put a stop to the end of days. I didn't know how but I did know one thing, that no doubt I would not be around to see the fight. As it was obvious that it wasn't by Draven's hand that I would die but by his actions…his actions by giving me a child. Something he had refused to give me in our own time and something he knew nothing about him giving me in the past.

We were back in the library and I was just trying to put my shoes back on when I saw Draven opening the door. We were back to being dressed for the wedding as it might have looked odd had we turned up in different clothes.

"Have you always had that door?" I asked wondering why I never knew about it.

"No, I had it created after Pip's party, after you were taken.," he informed me, sounding grim at the reminder.

"You wanted to be sure you could get to the Janus Temple quickly, didn't you?" I asked, getting it confirmed.

"As you can see, it came in handy, as I always intended to consummate our vows in our own bed," he told me making me grin at the sentiment.

"That's why it's Jane Eyre that opens the portal, because it's my favourite book…" I mused to myself making him nod.

"I too have fond memories of that book, after I borrowed it from you shortly after you arrived," he reminded me of when it went missing.

"You stole it!"

"*Borrowed it*…after all I did bring it back, with an added message." I remembered him attaching my lost hairclip to it.

"It was about being home. About Jane admitting to Mr Rochester that wherever he was, was where she called home," I said making Draven grin.

"I thought it was fitting considering I had just found you," he told me, holding out his hand for me to take, so that we could walk back through the door together.

"You will always be my home," I told him in the dark, thinking back to how even as Katie, I had been drawn to finding this place.

My Afterlife.

"As you are my home also, little wife," he replied making me growl as we got through to the other side.

"Please don't tell me that's to be my new nickname," I asked making him chuckle,

"I think it has a nice ring to it."

"You think anything with the word little put before it, has a nice ring to it," I said making my point with an added little growl. I felt my hand being snagged and pulled back so I had no choice but to follow. He loomed over me and said,

"Sweetheart, I hate to point this out but I am a whole foot taller than you, so to me, you will always be my little wife." I tried to hide my smirk as to be honest, it was a sweet picture he painted. He was bigger than me by quite a lot, but it didn't mean the endearment was demeaning in anyway. And besides, I thought it was hot how much bigger he was…especially when he was pinning me to the bed and I was writhing beneath him, something we had managed to do again before we came back here.

Oh, and sort out my hair and makeup as after two rounds of

sex and a soberthon, well let's just say that neither hair or face had survived.

I reached up and kissed him quickly and told him,

"It's lucky you're hot, that's all I am saying." He started laughing as we walked back down the massive hallway towards the main Temple when suddenly something happened. I didn't even know it was coming but Draven stopped dead as he knew.

He felt it before I did.

But it was too late. We couldn't stop it.

We couldn't stop it as…

Our world was torn apart.

Draven screamed my name before pushing me out of the way just in time before one whole side of the hallway's wall of doors exploded. I was tossed aside just in time, so that the explosion didn't harm me but hitting into one of the glass doors certainly did. I was momentarily stunned and I started to move each limb slowly until my mind focused on what had just happened. Then my head shot up as I looked at the destruction and screamed,

"DRAVEN!" I couldn't see him and my panic started to set in. I got up after needing to hold onto the wall in between doors just to steady myself. There was now a massive gaping hole on the wall that looked like one massive black gateway. It was like a swirling void, an abyss of nothingness…a place of oblivion.

I stumbled around over the mass of rubble trying to find him as that was all I could focus on.

"Draven!" I shouted his name again but there was nothing. Had he been sucked inside that thing? Jesus Christ, I hoped not, in fact I was convincing myself of that very fact and I stepped closer readying myself for stepping inside. I would do anything to find him. But then a hand grabbed me from behind and I screamed.

"Draven!" I shouted and flung myself into his arms.

"Oh, thank God," I muttered into his chest as he held me tight with one arm banded around me.

"Are you alright?" I nodded into his chest and then looked behind me at the giant portal, one that looked big enough to fit an entire army through it.

"What is that thing?" I asked.

"I don't know, but I must inform the others," he told me which brought me back to what was above us.

"Oh God, my family, Draven they can't…we can't." I started to panic and now my worry had shifted to all the people above us that had no idea what was happening below.

"I know Keira, don't worry, we will protect…"

"Oh, how touching!" We both stilled in each other's arms and Draven emitted a low demonic growl.

"I hear congratulations are in order," said a voice from within the swirling mass of hollowness.

"No, oh God please no," I uttered on a cry as it felt like someone had pumped my veins with ice. I turned around to face what was now coming through the portal and Draven shifted me so that I was behind him. But there was no getting away from it.

Getting away from him.

"Jack."

"Not anymore, my dear," Cronus said using Jack's body, the one I hadn't recognised until now but had seen in my dreams. But he had changed him into something dark, something terrifying. It wasn't Jack anymore. Not the happy go lucky guy that always had a smile for everyone. Not the same guy that had given me rides home. Or who I had sat in the crummy diner with laughing at his jokes about macaroni that looked toxic enough to get up and walk out the door. Not the same guy that had taken me to the Halloween dance or had sat with me on my porch steps telling me about how he loved a woman.

Celina. I fucking cursed the name, along with that of Aurora!

The ones who had betrayed us all just so that they could get to me, get to Jack, get to every single puzzle piece needed for this one and only moment. Where had my friend gone, because this one, this Jack looked as though he had just stepped through the gates of Hell and not a single shred of him had survived the journey.

His once honey coloured hair was now as black as night. His once hazel eyes had turned milky white with a tiny black dot at their centre with a red ring of blood. He had a thick layer of what looked like infected skin crusted around his hairline, cheeks and neck, in a sickly yellow colour. If I didn't know better I would have said that his host was fighting against him. Turning itself into something that would soon be useless to him. Was it possible he was running out of time? Was Jack in there somewhere, fighting him?

Maybe it was wishful thinking, but I had to hold onto hope, if only for RJ alone. Draven suddenly pulled me aside as Cronus seemed distracted, looking behind him ready for something else to appear.

"Keira, you need to listen to me, you need to get back through the door. I can't fight with you here..." Draven started to say but I cut him off.

"No Draven, I am not leaving you!" I told him making him growl.

"Do you trust me?!" he hissed and I took a deep breath and looked back at Cronus.

"Yes, but I am not..."

"Now Keira, do it! Go or we will lose this fight! Use the door and don't look back. Close it and run, run as far away from Afterlife as you can...do you understand?!" I shook my head as tears started to fall.

"I...please Draven I…can't…"

"Go Keira and don't look back…go and live, my love...live for me," Draven said both breaking my heart and his as he pushed me aside before he erupted into his other side, transforming his once suited body into something truly demonic. He looked magnificent. Like some dark warrior from Hell dressed in armour forged in the deepest flaming pits by demon hands. I don't know what material had been used that now covered his body in interlocking plates but he looked indestructible. His chest plate was far from the fancy ones I had become used to seeing on him in the past. No, this was made for one purpose and one purpose only, to aid in killing.

But he wanted me to run. He wanted me to run from the fight because to him I was still a mortal. I could still get hurt. But most of all, I could still die. After all, that was the prophecy, one he was trying desperately to avoid. So, I did as he asked letting my feet take me towards the door.

The door back to Afterlife.

But Afterlife wasn't just bricks and mortar. It wasn't just fancy furnishings and expensive fabrics. And it wasn't just its grand hallways and ancient artefacts and priceless antiques.

It was family.

And Draven wanted me to run from it as fast and as far as I could.

But I couldn't run from my family.

And I couldn't run from my heart.

So, I stopped running. Instead I looked behind me to see Cronus stepping further into the room and a mass of shadows wasn't far behind. I didn't know what it was but I knew it didn't look good. We needed to get word to the others but how.

Wait, Lucius?!

I was connected with him now! So, I did the only thing I could do, I got his attention. I thought back to what Katie had told me and I channelled all my energy into casting out in just one direction.

"Lucius! HELP US! We are in the Janus Temple, Cronus is here! It's just me and Draven and I…" The sound of Lucius' voice didn't reply in my head as I thought it would. No, it replied in person.

"I know, Pet." I looked down the hallway to see our own army had arrived…and everyone was here ready to fight.

So, instead of running away from it, I ran towards it.

I ran towards my destiny…

And it was time for battle.

CHAPTER FOURTY-FIVE

IMAGE OF DEATH

I raced back to Draven's side, jumping and hopping over the rubble. He was approaching his army and when he saw Lucius nod behind him, Draven looked over his shoulder to see me coming. But when his eyes grew wide I knew it wasn't out of shock at seeing me, no it was out of concern. That's when I felt it. Like something shifting in the air around me. It was like being in the dark and knowing someone was behind you because you used your other senses to guide you. We relied too much on our eyes to see, so that we sometimes ignored the importance of what our feelings saw for us.

It was like watching all their faces in slow motion. Shock, horror, worry, care, love…it was all there in each of them, and each one was already taking their first motions in saving me. But I didn't need saving, not yet. Because it didn't end like this for me. No, I knew that because I had a baby to protect and family above and below to fight for.

And fight I may not know how to do as well as the others.

But I knew one thing that was just as important and that was I knew how to get angry…

Very, very angry.

So, I closed my eyes for not even a second but what felt like minutes. I felt the familiar tingling in my fingertips and it was like reuniting with an old friend…but with it something new. My fangs emerged and this time, I welcomed them. I felt power in my eyes, in my cheeks, rolling down my neck to join with that already in my hands and then when it reached its peak, I simply turned around and lashed out at everything in my path.

And it was a glorious chaos!

A invisible wave of such destruction crashed into those behind me that by the time I turned to take in what damage I had caused, I could barely believe at what I had done with a mere thought. That great looming shadow behind Cronus had been his own army coming through the portal, only now the first wave had been laid to waste by a flick of my arm. Cronus himself had seen it coming and had unfortunately managed to get out of its path in time before he too found his vessel in pieces like the others. But he didn't come out of it unscathed either.

All those broken limbs, twisted, now burnt flesh, should have sickened me but it didn't. No, it was like something deep inside me was trying to claw itself to the surface and it was rejoicing at the sight.

"Impossible!" Cronus hissed and in return I felt my lips curl back over my fangs as I snarled at him. Then I calmly turned to face the others and walked slowly towards them, back to *my mate*.

I don't know where that thought had come from but that was what it felt like. This sort of possessive need I had to claim him that way. Was this what it was like for them? The Alpha in them? The tugging need to claim what they knew was theirs?

Draven watched me with his jaw clenched, but then his eyes scanned for any potential threat behind me, only easing when I curled myself next to his body. He snaked an arm out, seizing my waist and yanking me hard to him.

"Do you ever do as your told?" he asked me and I winked and said,

"No, but you should be used to it by now…besides, we fight together, side by side as one, now and always."

"Well, I think it's clear she can handle herself," Lucius commented with a smirk and I looked to him to see that he too was now dressed for the fight. In fact, everyone here was ready for battle. Out of all of them I was the only one that didn't exactly look dressed for the occasion, as I wouldn't have exactly said a wedding dress was practical fighting gear.

"What's the plan? What about all the people above, my family?" I asked trying not to sound as shaky as I felt when voicing that question.

"Don't worry, we have Adam standing guard at the entrance, anything comes through and Pip will know what to do," Draven informed me. Okay, so big scary unstoppable beast sounded like a good plan as much as it didn't.

"Is that safe?" I felt I had to ask.

"Rue is protecting the humans. We have them inside the mansion, Rue isn't to let anything in or out of there until she knows it's safe…we planned for this Keira," Draven told me and my mouth dropped,

"You planned for this…*on our wedding day!?*" Draven shrugged his shoulders and said,

"Well, they didn't exactly get a welcome invitation if that's what you mean. It was done just as precaution…of course, I also planned for you to do as you're told and get through that damn portal and stay there!" he snapped and that's when it all started to make sense.

"You always knew it would be here and that's why you had the doorway made…in case you had to get me out." Well it looked as though I hadn't been the only one planning things behind my partner's back.

"Uh…guys, I hate to interrupt the first marriage tiff here, but can it wait, only we have a demonic army to kill," Marcus said, and Sigurd and Orthrus both clashed their massive swords together and said,

"Fuck, yeah!" Orthrus' idea of battle gear was biker leathers and Sigurd's was a long black jacket and a chest strapped with weapons. Although to be fair, most of Jared's men did turn into hounds of Hell so you couldn't really blame them for not suiting up.

I looked to where Marcus had nodded and saw what everyone else was now seeing. Cronus was heading this way and the first wave of the army I had knocked out, well it was nothing compared to these guys!

Chained faceless beasts with hammered metal skulls were being dragged in snarling through the portal by tall skeletal demons that wore leather masks. When they started to come closer I realised that everything they wore was made from the skin of humans and I soon wanted to vomit. The tops of their masks had been covered in sewn eyeballs and the lower part covered in dead dry lips. It was a mask made only to mock what lay beneath it, for they couldn't see or speak. In fact, I wasn't even sure that they could smell but then the only holes in the masks were for their nose bones that were void of flesh.

"Looks like the beasts are up first," Jared said rolling his shoulders and stepping forward getting ready for the change. Orthrus, Chase and Otto followed suit and Sigurd nudged Ragnar and said,

"I think that means you're up too, old man." Ragnar growled and made his way to the front.

"I think he's just thankful to be out of the clutches of the old woman…no offence, little Queen," Caspian joked as he too made his way to the front.

"What can I say, it runs in the family." Then I winked at him making everyone chuckle.

"My old friend," Draven said looking to his side and I looked back to see Leivic grinning as he was the last to join the frontline. He gave me a tap on the nose and whispered down at me,

"Time for the teddy bear," making me smile and I knew all these jokes were said to try and ease the tension because this wasn't just a fight.

This was a fight for the world.

A fight to prevent the end of days and it was here…on our fucking wedding day of all days…Bloody typical!

I watched as seven men all took the front before us and one by one they started to change. Black sand rose up from the earth to engulf Orthrus, leaving behind a beast with the skin of cooling molten rock that cracked, showing the glow of hot power beneath the surface. Chase became the sleekest of the four, like a panther covered in shiny thick red oil and his husband became a beast of deadly skin, covered in spikes.

Jared shrugged out of his leather jacket and he held it a moment and said to me,

"I would ask you to look after this but I remember the last time and even though I don't see a red nose in sight, I think I will take my chances…no offense, doll." Then he winked at me and tossed the jacket to one side where the likelihood of it surviving was slim to nil. But he was right, they were probably even worst odds with me, as I wasn't exactly reliable for keeping out of trouble.

Jared was next in line to change and as he bent forward his back quickly moulded to triangular shaped scales. His body became something so ancient it could be considered Jurassic as his skin turned into hardened clumps of cemented fur, tipped with silver.

Caspian turned into his other self and became that of the stuff of legends…the Minotaur. Mighty horns grew as did Ragnar's when he too started to make the change, growing triple in size. But whereas Ragnar's encased his skull in a helmet of horn, Caspian's grew large and wide, ready to use them as a battering ram.

And here they were…

Afterlife's beasts of the battle.

They met the overwhelming odds head on and they might have been few against the masses but they were mighty and each took out the larger beasts with a brutality that had only ever been witnessed in fantasy movies…but this was no story, *this was real*.

Leivic started off running as a man but the second he leapt through the air, he landed on one of the beast's back as a wild demonic bear. He started tearing into the skull beast as if he was playing his favourite game.

The Hell beasts seemed to be enjoying themselves just as much as they tore into the bigger beasts, working as a pack and surrounding their prey. Great howls of pain and anger echoed along the halls as each of the chained beasts fell one by one, their many keepers alongside them. The flaw in Cronus' plan started to become clear as the portal would only allow so many in and like this, they were easy for the picking. But this was when things went from achievable, we might actually win this, to shit street in a heartbeat.

"You think that is all I have to offer, Son of Asmodeus!?" Cronus bellowed before laughing and the second after he finished a rumbling started, only it didn't come through the floor, it came through the remaining walls.

"Fall back to the Main Temple!" Draven shouted then grabbed my hand and pulled me with him. The beasts heard the calling and must have trusted Draven enough to know something else was coming.

"What…what is it?" I asked as we ran to where the Janus Gate stood still flowing at its centre. The beasts all fell back after finishing with their kills but the walls kept thundering.

"He is opening all the gates, calling forth more of his army and summoning them from the other lands," Draven told me as one by one all the doors burst open as if a bomb had been placed behind each gateway. A rippling wave of destruction travelled along the hallways until out of sight.

"Jesus!" I hissed and Sigurd walked past me and replied sarcastically,

"I doubt he can help us here, darlin'." Then he started to suck in all the shadows around him, using the darkness that came from the portal against itself and harnessing it as a weapon. It swirled around him in such a way that it kept growing in size, until soon the shadowed serpents I had been used to seeing were ten times as big. They both lashed out ahead of him like something that had risen straight out of 20 Thousand Leagues Under the Sea. The massive tentacles hit out at the walls just as creatures started to emerge. He looked like the master of shadows all right, he looked powerful enough right now to take on a God and win.

"He must have more than this planned," Sophia said stepping up to Draven along with Vincent and Zagan. Seeing Vincent in his angelic form was always a masterful and holy sight. Massive gleaming white wings curled by his feet and framed his strong powerful body, one that was dressed in silver. His arms were completely covered in elaborately engraved silver plates that all joined to one massive shoulder piece, that curved up around his neck. Scrolls of symbols and a piece of his forearm gilded with gold inlay displaying the elements of the sky. The armour was completed by a connecting piece at the inside of his elbow that curved round to promote movement.

Both arms were covered, yet his torso wasn't and was currently bare, displaying a strong muscular stomach rippling with hard abs and hard pecs. This was covered in strapping of black leather crossed over so that a massive sword held at his side could hang freely. Small deadly looking silver throwing stars tipped in gold were also attached in leather holders down one side. Talk about the Avenging Angel, he looked as if he had just dropped down straight from the gates of Heaven.

But as one was from Heaven, the other was from Hell.

Sophia was also in her other form, with her smoky wings following her every move and half of her face demonically changed into something terrifying. She too was dressed more like a warrior than the graceful and glamourous girl I remember seeing for the first time at college. The second she had first stepped inside that classroom, everyone there was half in love with her and without needing to do no more than grant them a smile. But that was part of her allure. No one would have expected her to be what she was, but I didn't care because to me she was beautiful inside and out, no matter what 'out' I was looking at.

"I agree, he is planning something more," Draven said looking back to Cronus through the shadows of battle Sigurd was currently single-handedly waging against the walls. But he could only cover one of the hallways and there were eight in total.

"LOOK!" I shouted just as more of the doors started exploding within. Creatures of every type imaginable started to jump down from the higher rows and others started running our way surrounding us from all sides.

"Zagan, call forth your legions to cover that passageway.

Hakan can you cover the right with Liessa and Ruto?" He nodded as he was always a man of few words. His painted eyes looked to where the other threat was headed our way. Then he started to uncurl his wired body ready to unleash his wrath onto the foolish oncoming wave of bodies.

"About fucking time I got some action," Ruto said before releasing his metal wings in a deadly show of power and flying up to start attacking the ones trying to climb down from the top balcony of doors.

"Let my husband know I am getting all oiled up, he gets to lick me clean later," Liessa said winking at me before dropping her jacket and showing us all her naked body underneath. The entirety of her body was covered in suckered skin like on the tentacles of an octopus and each had started to secrete a deadly ink.

By the time she had swaggered her curvy body over to the hallway, she was covered in black ink from head to toe as though she had been dipped in the stuff. Only her hands remained clean. I watched as all three of them quickly started to dispatch the enemy one by one. Hakan sliced out with his razor wire, cutting them in half before they could even get close. Ruto rained down his deadly tipped spearheads from his wings. And Liessa fired out her poison of death in a great mist.

"Vincent, Sophia, go and wreak havoc next to our friends." They both smiled at each other and Sophia hit her brother's arm and said,

"Don't cheat this time." Then she pulled the loaded guns from her holsters and aimed before taking her first shot. Vincent drew his massive sword that looked to have been forged in Heaven by Zeus himself.

"I make no promises, little sister." Then they were off.

"Takeshi, if you please." Draven nodded and I almost asked wouldn't he need back up but then I quickly found out that he wasn't going in alone. He drew both his samurai swords and they ignited in blue flames, and he nodded to Marcus for some strange reason.

"Jester, if you please, I think your master summons you." I had seen him once before fighting and he was now dressed the same. He was dressed like a modern-day pirate. His long dark red leather jackct had black metal buttons down its length and large cuffs folded back, only this time added to this was a faded 'Welcome to Vegas' T shirt and a thin red scarf wrapped around his neck a few times.

"As you wish My Lord. Do me a favour dolly, keep my dear Smidge out of trouble." Then he bowed in that over dramatic way of his before joining who surprisingly was his master. He pulled his sword free and as Takeshi had done, he lit it on fire.

"It is as I taught you, Master Mareo." I heard Takeshi say and Marcus bowed to him in return, this time out of respect and not with any theatrics. Then they both ran at each side of the wall, holding out a sword and cutting through not only the creatures coming from the doors but also, setting the entire wall either side ablaze.

"Cerberus!" Draven shouted and pointed in the direction of one of the other halls. He got the hint and roared to call his men and once again they went in for the kill.

"Ragnar!" he called out and it was clear who the general in all this was. Draven was a master at this and I shuddered to think of how many battles he had fought and armies he had commanded.

Ragnar's head snapped up after dispatching a large demon that had human skulls incorporated in its armour. Thankfully, its head was currently being ripped from its neck and Ragnar dropped the now bloody body part and swiftly stepped on its skull as he made his way back to us.

"Hey, big guy," I said making him wink at me in acknowledgment.

"Take Leivic and Caspian, I need you to cover the hall on the left." Draven said and Ragnar growled his acceptance. Then he made a demonic call, notifying the others. The three of them went charging at the oncoming horde.

"One hallway left." I said.

"And lucky for us, we have one badass left," Draven informed me.

"Draven no!" I said getting fearful he would take one alone when he said,

"My job is protecting you…Seth go and deliver your judgement!" He called out and Seth who was the only one still dressed as he had been for the wedding stepped up to us.

"I will aid you in whatever it takes to keep my Chosen safe but you must know, this will not end well unless something is unleashed," he said cryptically, nodding down at me.

"Go, do what you can." Seth nodded and then he started to transform into something utterly terrifying. I had never seen it in my own mind before as it was Katie who had witnessed it. However, I knew this memory wasn't my own but it was freely shared so expected. His face warped from handsome into death before it truly started to change and it was a monster of the likes I had never thought possible. An abomination many would have called him, I on the other hand just called it lucky that he was on our side.

Elongated and misshapen bone looked to be made from blackened stone and it erupted from the centre of him as he doubled over. Eyes that had once been white had now changed to dark holes in the skull with a tiny white dot lit in the centre. Pointed teeth and long fangs were rooted all the way from either side of the open nose bone and he snapped his jaws at the emerging enemy.

Then he unleashed that dark power on the entirety of the hallway and in seconds, there was nothing but raining ash.

"That's all of them, but what now?" I asked knowing it was like Seth had said, we couldn't hold them back forever.

"Now I cut the head of the fucking snake and watch as his army falls!" Draven snarled and unleashed his own power. His two swords grew from the insides of his wrists and I wanted to hold him back and beg him not to go. But I knew this was what he did. This was who he was. And he was an unstoppable force.

"Smidge, watch her…Lucius, protect her." I looked to see that she wasn't the only one that remained as Lucius was also now at my side. I looked back at Smidge and found myself amazed to find that she was an angel. Her flaming orange hair now looked like rose gold and a pair of beautiful shaped wings were white and tipped the same rose peach colour. They looked so soft I was almost tempted to reach out and touch them. But it was Lucius' voice that brought me back to our War.

"I will protect her," Lucius said stepping closer to me as if he knew that this was his role all along. Then Smidge nodded and I watched as Draven started to go to battle, walking through the shadows Sigurd produced.

"Will he…?"

"Succeed? I don't know, after all he is now fighting a God," Lucius said and there was something that struck me about the way he said it. He was fighting a God, we never thought possible to kill one before. Yet I had done it. Was that what I was always meant to do with my powers. Was that my path, my prophecy to take?

"But there must be a way, for he hasn't unleashed the Titans yet and to do that…what would he need Lucius?" I said taking hold of his leather straps, ones that held rows of throwing knifes against his own armour, one subtler and more fitting for an assassin. A hood and cloak gave him that dark appearance I knew he used well when sneaking up behind his prey before silently slicing their throat.

"He would need to open the seven seals, once that happens he would bring forth the…"

"The what, the Titans?" I asked in a strained desperate voice.

"No, *the four Horsemen,*" he replied and I looked around at all the chaos and knew that we couldn't fight much more. Even Zagan, who was bringing forth his own army of Hell out of a mighty hole in the ground, looked to be evenly matched against the other army coming his way.

"Oh god."

"Where are these seals Lucius, where would he find them?" I asked looking around the room as if I was going to find them just lying around here somewhere.

"It is said that opening the seven seals which secure the scroll that John of Patmos saw in his Revelation of Jesus Christ, will bring forth the start of the end of days. In John's vision, the only one worthy to open the scroll is referred to as both the 'Lion of Judah' and the 'Lamb having seven horns and seven eyes' but there are some who believe it is not true, but the one that harnesses the power of Seven…" He started to think about what he was saying, giving more severity to the thought.

"But who could…?" He turned me to face him, taking my shoulders before hitting me with the truth.

"It's you Keira," he stated and I took a step back and uttered a whispered,

"What…no…that's not possible?"

"The only one here that can harness the power of the seven is you. You're the Light that guides us to follow you. Our Electus. The power of the Seven is the six Kings and one Queen. Dominic, Vincent, Sigurd, Jared, Seth and I…you are the Seventh. He is going to try and use you somehow to unleash the gate."

"What gate?"

"The gate to the Horsemen as they will await their calling. They will then have the power to destroy us all and the door to Tartarus will be open for his reborn Gods to take over this plane…to take over every plane," Lucius told me and I didn't know if what he spoke about was right, about me being the Seventh. But then considering what part that number had played in my life, well I couldn't exactly deny it.

"Well, if it helps I am not exactly going to be opening any doors for him anytime soon."

"You may not have a choice," Lucius said sounding grim and nodding for me to look behind me. What I saw made me take a step closer just before I nearly went running.

"No…oh God please no." The prayer came out of me in a trembling breath. Cronus had Draven with a blade to his throat and was currently forcing him forward and Sigurd back.

"Withdraw your Ouroboros, shadow King or I will slit his throat and bleed his vessel dry with help from the poison coated on my blade," Cronus said forcing Draven forward and in sight of me.

Sigurd didn't exactly do as he said but instead he moved to the side, pulling back his serpents but not his shadows.

Draven staggered forward another step, clearly bloody from the fight against Cronus. I wanted to cry out at the sight. I felt my body starting to shake as both anger and fear merged into one. I wanted to lash out at Cronus for doing this. For daring to threaten the life of the one I loved. But I couldn't. It was too dangerous with that blade against his neck. And I wasn't exactly without my own knowledge of what poison it could be or what it could do.

So, what did this mean?

Was this really the end? Was this what we had come here to face, impossible odds and lose at the first hurdle?

For if Draven fell then all would be lost. But nothing could have stopped what came next and never would I ever rid myself of that image…

An image of Draven dying at the hand of his own blade.

CHAPTER FOURTY-SIX

GLASS AND BLOOD

Cronus smiled and I hated that he was twisting a smile I used to love seeing, into something vile and truly evil.

"Now send the Electus my way or your King is no more," he snarled and just as I was about to take a step towards him Lucius stepped in front of me.

"What are you doing, I have to save him!" I shouted up at him.

"And I have to save you, *trust me and watch the shadows.*" This last part was said in my mind and I looked back to Draven to see him winking at me. For some reason, the action didn't seem like it belonged to Draven and looked odd for a moment but it was clear Lucius and Draven had a plan and this...

This was part of it.

And I soon found out what this plan was.

The next thing I saw was a purple glowing blade placed to Cronus' own throat as a figure emerged from Sigurd's shadows...

"Draven?!" I shouted in question as I was clearly confused, now there seem to be two of them.

"Lower your blade, Cronus!" The Draven at his back ordered digging his sword into his neck to further stress his demand. Cronus did and the Draven that had been threatened by his blade stepped forward. The next few moments happened so fast that one second I found myself smiling at our imminent victory and the next crying out in horror.

"Drop the blade," Draven said and Cronus did but he did so smiling. Why I didn't know, not yet, not until suddenly Draven thrust his other blade deep through Cronus' heart and out the other side. I could see it pierce its way through and Cronus cried out with his back bowing against it. But then instead of dying he started laughing.

The sound chilled me to the bone.

"No, something's wrong, this is wrong," I whispered as I felt it before it happened. Like an invisible veil of death was sweeping over me, past me, and straight to Draven.

"You really think that is all it would take?" he asked and before any of us could react quickly enough he grabbed the Draven in front of him from behind and pulled him back onto the protruding blade from his chest, impaling him on the same glowing sword.

"NO!" Draven cried out behind him and instantly pulled his blade back, drawing it into his arm freeing both pinned bodies.

"NOOO!" I screamed as I watched Draven's body quickly morph into the body of Ranka before she hit the floor with her knees. Then Cronus turned to the Draven at his back and roared,

"I AM A GOD ON EARTH!" Then he lashed out all his power hitting out at Draven and flinging his body back so it smashed into the wall of demons. The sight of both Ranka on her knees waiting for death and Draven being hurled into the prey sent me over the edge. I stepped around Lucius, felt my power rising up quicker than ever before and let it rip in Cronus' direction.

But someone was ready for it and this wasn't the first time they had felt the wrath of my power. Aurora stepped in from nowhere and with Cronus' hand on her shoulder she took the hit. I was expecting her to go flying backwards like most people did. But with Cronus standing behind her, touching her he seemed to be helping her absorb my power.

"KEIRA, NO!" Lucius bellowed in my direction as he knew…

He knew what I had done.

My mistake…and it was fatal to us all.

I let my hand drop the second I realised it. I had somehow given Aurora some of my power and with one whispered word from Cronus in her ear she nodded and took off running. I didn't know where she was going but I didn't have long to find out as Cronus issued only one warning in my direction.

"My turn!" Then he let rip his own powers at me and neither I or Lucius were powerful enough to stop it. Lucius threw himself in front of me but it wasn't enough to leave me untouched. My body flew backwards as did Smidge's and Lucius' from the blast of power he threw at us like a sizzling blue wave of electricity.

It shot through my body and even as I was travelling backwards towards the Janus Gate, I could feel it immobilize my body as it attacked every nerve. It felt as though it was singeing every cell inside me, making me useless for a short time. Lucius was the first to recover and pulling his sword he ran at Cronus and attacked from the front. I blinked a few times just to clear the fog of pain that had clouded my head only what I saw was beautiful. Draven had reappeared from nowhere and joined in the fight against him.

Both Draven and Lucius attacked from each side and

Cronus was left to fight them both, unleashing his own weapons. Long glowing chains that looked as if made from Tartarus were like lava and dripping with power. They were wrapped around both arms as he lashed them out, snapping them against anything they hit, leaving nothing but destruction in their wake. Lucius hit out his mighty sword Excalibur against them, moving with power and speed. Draven did the same against the glowing snakes, using both of his swords in great sweeping motions.

But no matter the sight. No matter the bravery. No matter the strength, neither of them together or apart were strong enough to defeat him. They needed something more.

"Damn it, think!" I shouted but the answer came from the most unlikely of sources.

It was Janus.

"Look to the past," he told me, speaking in my mind and I did. I looked to the Gate first thinking is that where he wanted me to go…back to the past and try and change this. But how? Anything that happened back there didn't change the outcome of the future here, so that would have been useless. But he said look to the past, well the only thing in this room that belonged to the past was me, me and…

"Oh my god, it can't be!" I uttered as I quickly looked towards my cloak. But it was what I could see inside it that has me gasping. I quickly got to my feet and ran over to it and the second I reached it I flipped it open to see that I was right. My eyes hadn't been deceiving me. I had seen the hilt of a dagger. The hilt of my dagger.

Then a memory played back to me…

'Something for you to remember me by.' Then Draven from the past had kissed me as not his only way of saying goodbye, as that wasn't all he had been talking about. It was all starting to make sense now. The reason I went back in time wasn't just to

get pregnant as I thought. There was a reason to the time I picked, the dreams, the visions had all led me to pick that time for Pertinax. The only time I would ever manage to defeat a God and gain the one weapon to defeat Cronus.

This was what they needed to kill a God.

I needed to tell him!

"Smidge, I need a distraction, do you have any ideas how we do that?" I asked her after getting up now I had the Glass Dagger firmly in my grasp.

"I have an idea, yes," she said in that knowing tone and before I knew what she was doing her eyes started to roll back until her irises were gone and milky white remained. Then a great white fog started to rise from the ground as if the floor had millions of tiny pores. It started to fill the space with a white-out, and then split creating a clear walkway for me. I ran down its path not questioning my actions any longer. I just followed my heart and my instincts. So, I ran towards Draven who I could see looking around for me.

"Draven!" I shouted and after he looked beyond relieved, we met in the middle. He grabbed me, held me to him as if it gave him strength.

"Keira, you need to get out, you need to…"

"There is no time. Listen to me, you have to use this against him. It is the only thing that can kill him!"

"Is this what I think it is?" he asked as he took the dagger in hand as if it was the first time he was seeing it in two thousand years. The spear he too had used once.

"It's what I used to kill Pertinax. It has his blood in it, maybe if Cronus is stabbed with it, it will be enough to stop him," I said.

"You believe this is the prophecy?" he asked me and I nodded.

"Yes, I think it's the reason I had to go back," I told him and it was enough for him. He gripped the handle tight and after giving me a nod, he promised me.

"Time to end this." Then he walked back to Cronus who was nearly winning the fight against Lucius. Smidge sucked back the fog and not one for being wasteful, she pushed it all towards the demons behind the two fighting. Once it hit them she twisted her hands around and her eyes turned into that of dead flesh. The second they did this all the demons started to scream in high pitched death cries. I watched each one being stripped of their flesh like the fog carried acid vapour. An effective weapon indeed.

"Nice," I nodded in her direction making her smirk.

"I have my uses," she said cocking out her big, curvy hip and placing a hand to it. This now gave me a clear view of two things. The first was that Draven relayed in just a nod his plan and after Lucius saw the dagger he knew what to do. It was just like it was in the past I had stepped in on. Lucius was acting as a distraction whilst Draven silently went in for the kill. But that wasn't the only thing I saw.

"Aurora," I hissed her name as I saw her walking over to a door surrounded by demons. No, it wasn't just surrounded, it was being protected!

"The seven seals, where are they?" I asked Smidge who shot me a terrified look. Then she shot her head towards where I was looking to see what I did. Aurora was glowing with new power...

My stolen power.

The demons saw her coming and parted, revealing the massive door behind. It was sectioned into four panels and each had a horse and rider engraved on it. One white, one red, one light grey and one black. I knew what it was and what those panels represented. Three great locks ran down each side and one from above. All seven locks connected to the centre of the huge door and all were attached to a metal scroll that I knew unlocked them all.

"Oh, Gods no! She is going to unleash the Horsemen!" Smidge cried in horror.

"But how, she isn't the Seven…she doesn't have the…" Smidge started to say but I interrupted her, playing the scene back in my head of when I was trying to hit out at Cronus in anger.

"She does now," I replied dryly.

"But how?"

"Because I just fucking gave it to her!" I said in anger knowing that what was behind those doors was enough to destroy us all.

"Tell me of them." I said quickly, knowing that if I knew what we faced there might be a way to stop it.

"The first Horseman, the white, is Pestilence, inflictor of infectious disease and plague. The second is the Horseman of War, the red representing the blood of mass slaughter." Okay so none of these were sounding like people we wanted to invite to the party but then it got worse.

"The third is black like the land he kills, The Horseman of Famine and death of the earth."

"Christ, what's that last one?" I said knowing it was no doubt going to be the worst and I was right.

"The Pale, he is the fourth and final Horseman and his name is simply *Death*."

"So, what you're saying is that we are totally screwed if she manages to open that gate."

"Yes, that is what I am saying." I looked towards everyone fighting and I knew that if I had the power of seven like Lucius thought I did then it was time to use it! And right now, I needed my Kings more than ever. So, I did what I did best, I closed my eyes and called out in my mind.

"Vincent, Jared, Sigurd, Seth, I need you. Aurora is trying to open the gate to unleash The Four Horsemen of the Apocalypse…she needs to be stopped at all costs!" I heard Jared's beast roar in acceptance and saw Vincent flying overhead. Then Seth let out a mighty battle cry, which was a weapon in itself. It destroyed even more of the doors and the current wave of demons inside them. Then he turned around with the destruction behind him to come to our aid. Last of all was Sigurd who was the only one that said,

"Yeah, sure thing darlin, never liked the bitch anyway." He did this next to us and shrugged off his long jacket to show a large muscular body covered in spinning tattoos. He rolled his shoulders before letting loose. Four Kings, for four Horsemen. It was all starting to make sense now. Every single step I had taken was to ensure for this day. This Battle.

My Kings.

Sigurd was the only one that would be able to fight disease without it touching him. Vincent was one of the greatest warriors known to this world, so he would be able to fight against the one called *War*. Jared was a beast of the Earth and would therefore fight against Famine. And then there was Seth who was Death himself, and therefore would fight the Pale Horseman…the worst of his kind.

"And that leaves…" I looked to see Lucius was fighting Cronus but after taking a hit in just the right moment, he dropped to one knee. I knew it was now or never, as Draven was just getting in position to strike. But then Aurora turned and saw it.

"CRONUS!" she screamed and just before the others could reach her she threw all her stolen power into the scroll unlocking all bolts at once. Each lock twisted inwards to release the door and at the same time, Cronus twisted away from Draven's oncoming blow. The second the door opened, Cronus must have felt a wave of power coming at him because he seemed to suck in an unseen energy.

"Lucius get back!" Draven roared trying to save his friend and he did just before the killing blow could come down on his head. Lucius rolled out of the way with the last of his energy but it wasn't enough to return the favour.

"I think it's time for a little payback," Cronus said and he suddenly made a fist with his hand, which started to control Draven's body, making it taut. Draven still gripped the dagger and I could see him exerting his will on Draven. He tried to fight it, you could see him trying to use all of his own willpower to push Cronus out of his mind. To push him back. But as the dagger continued to get closer towards his own chest I didn't think.

I just acted.

I ran towards them and screamed,

"NO! GET AWAY FROM HIM!"

"Keira no!" Draven shouted back but I wasn't listening. I was just running. I needed to get to him. I needed to save his life as if this was my only purpose. As if this was the only reason I was here. Maybe it wasn't to stop this. Maybe it wasn't to prevent the end at all. But what if I was his Chosen One, his Electus just to stop him from dying. To protect him so that he could stop it!

So that he could stop the end of days. Even if that meant doing so without me in the world with him.

Well, I no longer cared.

The one and only thing in that moment in time I cared about was stopping Draven's death. Nothing else mattered. So as the battle raged on around me I ran. I ran to the man I loved knowing there was no going back now. This was it.

This was my time.

My time to die.

Cronus saw me coming and at the just the right second he forced Draven's mind against not only himself but against me. Draven stepped towards me and before he or anyone else could make a move to stop it,

Draven plunged the dagger deep into my chest as he cried out his own pain for being forced to do it.

"NO!" he bellowed out in sheer agony just as Lucius did. He let go of the dagger embedded in my chest, one put there by his own unwilling hand.

"NO, NO, NO!" he screamed again and grabbed my body as I started to fall backwards.

But it was no use.

The prophecy was complete. It was never about me having a baby and bringing hope to the world. A new saviour. No, it was only about this moment.

My Death…*At Draven's hands.*

For Draven had killed me.

CHAPTER FOURTY-SEVEN

UNLIKELY GODS

It was different this time.

Death.

It was different than last time. Now there was no Heavenly presence to take over my vessel and claim victory on the day. There was nothing but the feel of my soul as it left my body. I looked down at it, at the sight and I wanted to weep for it. As it was clear now it was all for nothing. I had sacrificed it all and for what? The battle still raged on and now the door was open for great demonic Horsemen to emerge. Ready to wreak havoc on the Earth and destroy all I loved.

All hope was lost.

Oh yes, I wanted to cry out as one of my nightmares now played out in front of me. But it was no longer a vision of my fears, it was now the reality of my death. I was currently being held in Draven's arms, as he cradled my body to him. He cried out to the world, cursing it and the Fates for all of this. He cried out my name and cursed me for leaving him. But in the next moment after cursing me he was then placing his mouth to mine and whispering words of love over my still, dead lips. It was a bitter sweet memory for me to take with me into the Afterlife.

My forever Afterlife.

I felt myself rising up to impossible heights until suddenly the sight of everyone I loved still fighting, fighting until there was nothing left to fight for…

Well they all disappeared.

A blinding white light enveloped me and at first, I wondered if I wasn't back in the Void. I wanted to plead and beg the first person I came across, but I never expected who that would be. I soon found myself as I looked on Earth. A stunning white dress, in what was supposed to symbolise the first day joined to my husband in the eyes of God, now symbolised nothing but my death by his hands. I knew he would never forgive himself, no matter how anyone tried to tell him it was my fault. I had been the one to run into that blade, no matter whose hand was behind it.

Because the truth was I had been blinded by my love for him and I didn't regret it. For he still lived, even if I didn't. My only regret was that I wasn't the only life I sacrificed. I looked down and placed a hand to my belly and then fell to my knees and cried. I cried for not only everything I had lost, but all that Draven had lost also, more than he would ever know.

But I knew there was only one destination left for me now. I looked up and saw the gleaming white steps in front of me. I wasn't certain where they led, but I knew there was no road left to take but this one. I could see nothing up at the top but maybe that was the point. One last leap of faith into the unknown. There was no pearly white gates ready to be swept aside and opened, granting the righteous access. There was just me in a white dress ready to take my first steps to the end.

The end of my days.

So, I picked up my long skirt and I raised my foot, closing

my eyes ready for it. Not welcoming it like you always hoped you would when the time came. To find that strength. But just ready.

However not everyone was.

"You don't want to do that." I felt a hand at my shoulder holding me back and heard a familiar voice, one that had been with me since I first learned to speak. I turned around slowly and saw her.

"Katie?" The complete double image of me was smiling back and she said,

"Don't you remember our warning. Don't raise your skirt and walk up the steps."

"The girl on the plane!" I exclaimed as I thought back to when she had said it all that time ago. I had completely forgotten.

"She foresaw all this?" I asked her, wondering how she knew.

"I don't think she knew exactly where those steps led to, only that you shouldn't take them." I looked back behind me as if the sight of battle would still be seen there, not the nothingness there was.

"Then what now? Because I don't think they are just going to let me go back there without…"

"Sacrifice, no I don't think so," she finished for me and my shoulders slumped and I said,

"Don't they know by now how much I have already sacrificed?"

"There is only one more thing to sacrifice," she told me and I closed my eyes at the pain of it and held my hands to my stomach.

"No, I couldn't…I…" Katie took my hand and gave it a comforting squeeze.

"That is not the sacrifice they would want." I frowned and asked,

"Then what, if not my…"

"They want your soul," she finished and I felt myself shudder. Then I nodded and was about to do what was needed when she stopped me with only seven words spoken.

"And they will have it with…*mine.*"

"What…what do you mean?" I asked her.

"That day you were dragged through the mirror…did you ever ask yourself why?" I frowned not understanding.

"It mirrored your soul and created me." I sucked in a harsh ragged breath at this. Could it be possible?

"But wait, so you…you are just another version of me?" I asked and she nodded grinning.

"By why, it makes no sense, none of it…it…"

"They needed a way to control you so that when the time came, they could use you to open the gates. To release the Horsemen, to open the gate to Tartarus…they needed the Power of the Seventh as was prophesied. So, they created a duplicate of a soul they could use."

"But how? How would they even do something like that?" And then she said the one name that nearly crushed me.

"Ari."

Our sister.

"What…no! She couldn't have done that, she couldn't have done that to me."

"She didn't know. She was used just as you were. She doesn't know the truth of what she is and that is her journey to discover, but I know this, the second you broke away from her was when your true self started to come back to you. She was the lock you had to break away from to get home. But don't you see, it has all been written in the Fates, for now I can take your place," she told me and I grabbed her hand.

"What? No! How could you? I mean even if it's possible why would you do that?"

"I would do it for Draven. The first man you and I both fell in love with. I would die for him just as you would and now I know that this has been my fate all along."

"And mine, what is mine?" Katie looked behind me, away from the steps and gave me my answer.

"Yours is to become what you were always fated to be."

"And what is that?" Her answer came to me as she let go of my hand and started to walk away from me. Then, before she took her first step, what she told me shocked me to my very core…

"A God on Earth."

"Katie!" After that I saw her turn to face her own destiny and just as I called out her name, she turned to me one last time as she placed her foot on the first step. Her body started to float away and she smiled at me, her last words to me were of love.

Our Love.

"Take good care of them all."

"I promise," I told her with tears I could feel but wasn't sure were real. Then, the second her face was the last thing to fade away I was suddenly plunged back into my body with such force I couldn't breathe from it!

I blinked my eyes a few times and slowly my senses started to come back to me. First my sight and then sound. It was like a howling echo, almost as though I was listening to what was going on around me through water. Then it started to clear. Then I started to listen.

Chaos surrounded my dead body.

My vessel.

Her name was Keira and I loved her. I needed to protect her. She was mine to care for but I needed more. I was a Vampire with the blood of both Heaven and Hell in me thanks to my mate, but I was also something else. I looked down at my hands and saw blackened fingertips coating my skin in something deep and dark. It travelled along my veins up my wrists and circled around my vessel's scars.

It was the Venom of God, but even this wasn't enough. I needed to become more. The other mirrored half of my soul had told me I was to become a God. Then if that was true I needed the blood of one.

I needed…I didn't need to finish that sentence as when I looked down what I saw did it for me. The glass dagger still remained locked in my vessel's heart, all I needed to do was unlock the key. I gripped the hilt with both hands and then I pushed. I pushed it further into my chest and I didn't stop until I heard it crack, then I twisted. I felt the blood start to seep from its captured glass and I felt it surge up inside me the second that first drop of blood was absorbed into my heart. A few more seconds and it was pumping around this body.

I knew that if I hadn't been a Vampire with the added strength needed I would have been ripped apart from the force of it. I remembered a story once told of a beast so mighty it nearly killed its host if it hadn't been for Lucius.

Adam was his name.

Abaddon is his beast.

Keira is my name.

Electus was my beast.

And I had finally awoken.

Oh, and I was pissed!

I started to move, so slowly at first as if testing out my new power. I could feel it coursing around my body, like a current. It hummed and sizzled through me as if waiting, no, begging to be released. It wanted out and the strength of that alone had me grinning. Something dark and sinister wanted to play with those that had dared to hurt people I cared for. My vessel had wept.

She had cried and people had hurt her. They made her love stab this knife into her heart…

No, not they, *him.*

The one called Cronus. He had called himself a God on Earth!

Well, now it was time to show him what a real God on Earth looked like! For he didn't have the combined blood of the three inside him. No, he just had the blood of the first but so did I, that…

And more…*so much, more.*

I started to stand up and the sight I took in around me made me react. It made me roar!

"AAAAHHHH! ENOUGH!" I screamed out and the second I did, it caused a wave, crashing into my enemies as they were about to lash out at my friends. They looked back in shock but no one looked more shocked than the two still fighting against Cronus. He had been close to winning against them, with one bloody on his knees and the other behind, held by the throat against a wall. A burning chain wrapped firmly around his neck, trying to rid him of his immortal life.

The one we call Draven. Our mate.

His life was mine! And no one took that from me!

I simply raised my hand up and the chain was gone, evaporated into dust. Cronus looked first at the chain and then back at me before Draven suddenly cracked his head forward, smashing it into Cronus' face, so he had no choice but to drop him. The other I cared about, my Vampire master Lucius, also had a chain around him and with a flick of my wrist that too was gone.

Then they both tried desperately to get to me but found a horde of creatures in their way.

I started to walk towards the cause of all this pain and suffering as Cronus roared back at me in anger. Then he issued a command for his minions of Hell to come after me. Good, let them come. I wanted a test to see if there were any limits to my power. But first, I needed to get those I cared for out of danger. So, I started taking them against their will. Their bravery and loyalty was strong, an unwillingness to crumble honourably…and they were about to be rewarded with a show.

A show of death.

A show of revenge.

A show of blood.

I started to pull back at the beasts, one by one they had no choice but to be dragged back behind me, no matter how much their claws dug in. I forced the change upon them, quickly becoming men again. I flicked a hand to the jester, I liked him. He was funny, entertaining as he was now trying to fight his way free of my control.

"What the fuck!" The one named Caspian said as I forced him back to his human form. I smirked at him as he passed and when a memory hit me I said,

"I told you it was in the family." Then I smirked as I took with him his wife Liessa. Then I plucked a young looking boy from the air, and forced him back as well…Ruto, I knew his name to be. Takeshi, Hakan, Smidge, they too all went behind me. I had to secure them as I couldn't let them get hurt in the crossfire.

They were my people.

My sister. I heard her voice calling out for me.

"Keira! By the Gods you're alive!" She sounded so happy but she had lost her concentration. A demon soldier behind her raised his weapon, one I would take from him. He had a massive axe above his head ready to bring down on hers. Then I took his arms, making them burst from their sockets. The axe quickly finished the job as I had intended and fell into his head, crushing it. Sophia looked around in shock at the sight of what I had just done.

"Hello, my sister," I said before forcing her along with her husband, Zagan back to the wall, quickly taking control of Zagan's legions for my own use. They continued to battle back the army but now without their master leading the way. Next was the scarred bear and Ragnar, my giant protector.

"Yield to your other form," I told them both, after first cutting down those they fought with a sweep of my arm. They first fell to their knees as they were forced to relinquish their demons. They soon joined the rest.

Next came the biggest threat…

The Horsemen.

But first I had to get my men away from Cronus also. In seconds, I put a knee to the ground and a single fingertip along the cool broken marble floor that had been damaged in the battle. I made the cracks widen, lengthen and then they shot out at speed towards Cronus. As soon as he saw it coming he had no choice but to try and run from it. But I was quicker. Soulweed grabbed him, the roots of Hell taking hold of him. It wrapped around him, keeping him busy for a moment, long enough for what I had planned.

I walked towards the two warriors and when they saw me I raised a hand and clenched my fist. They were both pulled towards me and I only stopped them when they were close enough for me to touch.

They were beautiful and my heart ached at the sight of them. Which was when I realised why.

"Keira, you're…you're alive?! Oh, thank the Gods, my love! Keira…" Draven said in utter shock and the light in his eyes, the emotion was clear to see. I raised my hand up to stroke down his face, capturing his single tear still not letting him move.

"Can it really be…can you…Keira?" Lucius spoke and I reached out to him and touched him. I had to touch them, as if drawing strength from them both.

My mate and my master.

I loved them both, one that was tied to my soul and the other that owned it. Draven. He was my everything. I remember now. I walked closer to him and his face fascinated me. I ran a fingertip across his lips and he closed his eyes against the intense feeling I knew it brought him. To know the woman he loved was no longer gone. Well I could feel it beating in his chest. His heart pounding in both love and concern. He cared deeply for me. They both did and now it was time to make them proud of what they had created.

"Look at me," I ordered them both and they did as I asked without question. I didn't need to assert their will against them. But then Draven looked down at the dagger still in my heart and I followed his gaze. Then I reached up and pulled it from my chest. He had done this to me.

"Cronus!" I snarled his name. He would pay for this.

"Wait, no, where are you going?! You can't do this alone!" Draven started to shout.

"He's right, you need us, all of us!" Lucius added in panic but I wasn't listening. Because I didn't need them in this. This was no longer their fight. It was mine and mine alone.

"Now it's my turn," I said dropping the glass dagger beside them as I walked past them both towards my prey. Then I flicked out a hand making them join the others. The Horsemen were in my way next but first there were others I needed to save. Vincent, Seth, Jared and Sigurd were all currently fighting the demonic Lords and Watchers of the Apocalypse.

And all were currently losing.

But they were trying to keep them back as was their only aim. They knew that they couldn't beat them. The Watcher

Lords couldn't be killed. They only existed so that when called upon they could cleanse the Earth when the time came. It was the Gods failsafe, created long before humans were ever created. But today was not the end of days. And today they weren't needed.

So, the four Kings battled on, their sole purpose in all this was simply to stop them reaching the top. To stop them reaching the mortal world. They protected my family and now it was time for me to do the same. And I would do so with only a simple command spoken.

"KNEEL TO ME!" I barely recognised the demonic voice coming from my lips. But one by one the Horsemen stopped their attack and not only lowered their weapons, they lowered their horses.

"Keira?!" Vincent said my name and I felt myself smile.

"Angel," I responded before I had him under my control, flying back with the others. Jared, I forced him to change along with Seth, the King of Death. He was the only one that took some energy to force back to himself but I did it after another command.

"ENOUGH!" he stopped fighting then and as his demon retreated back into himself I decided I liked that one. He was defiant but he was also reckless and he fought for only one, not the many like we all did. He only fought for one mortal.

RJ…*his mate.*

I flicked my hand back with a smile and then walked slowly to the last one. His shadowed serpents snarled at me until I held out a hand, bringing them quickly to heel. They whined at me but before long I had them purring in my hand, stroking them gently.

"Lille øjesten…is that really you?" Sigurd asked bringing my head up and away from his pets. I then reached up and cupped his cheek before telling him.

"Your Chosen One helped save my life." Hearing this he stumbled back a step and sucked in a startled breath.

"One day I will get to thank her…but for now, I will keep you safe for her." Then I clenched a fist making his shadows disappear before sending him back with the others.

"Now for you four," I said when all was clear and after I had looked back to see my army was safe. Held against their will at the Temple wall with no choice but to watch this play out. I looked at the Horsemen that responded now to me, *not to Cronus.*

The white Horseman named Disease was a rotting figure of what represented man. His horse too looked to suffer from its curse of powers bestowed as infected flesh hung from black bone. The red Horseman of War was painted in blood, the blood of the masses he could bathe his body in with all the lives he butchered. His horse dripped crimson with eyes of Hell's fire.

The Black Horseman brought famine to the land sucked dry any goodness to be found deep within the soil. His skin was wrinkled and worn, like leather left to bake in desert sand in need of water. And last of all was Death. The Grey Horseman. He was a ghostly figure of nothing but a cloak to his souls collected. His horse void of any flesh was nothing but bone and shadows.

And now, they were mine.

"NO!" Cronus roared behind me as he broke free of his Hellish bonds.

"They are mine! Destroy her!" He commanded them but I started laughing. It was a cruel twisted sound, I knew that but it was one I relished hearing when aimed at him.

"They are no longer your puppets Cronus, they belong to me now!" I said making them rise up behind me and follow me over to him.

"It is no matter for I have had my use out of them!" he

spat back at me and my head shot to a room I knew. The doorway to Tartarus was open, unlocked and Aurora was nowhere to be found. Cronus started laughing as if he had won or at least soon would if the Titans ever made it through that portal.

"She is there now, with the blood of the first, the blood carried on a blade I struck across your son of Lucifer, the one that I know carries the stolen blood of my people, my Titans!" he told me and I looked back to see it was true, Lucius had a deep gash across his chest that had yet to heal. I snarled back at Cronus.

Then I walked over to him, with my Horsemen following behind. I looked back over my shoulder and issued them one order,

"Kill all that follow him, cleanse this place for their sins against us." They nodded silently and each separated taking a hallway. The creatures saw them coming and knew what it meant...They had lost this part of the fight. So, they started to retreat and many did, but there were those that didn't make it.

"NO! Get back and fight! Fight for your God!" he demanded in vain.

"Your army has forsaken you. The Gods' Horsemen are no longer yours to control," I told him as I cut the distance between us.

"I still have my Titans, for they are coming!" he snarled at me and I grinned,

"Then we take this fight back to Hell…back to Tartarus but first, you have something that belongs to me and I WANT IT BACK!" I bellowed in his face before I plunged my hand inside his body and took hold of the darkness I felt there. Once I had it firm in my grasp I yanked it out of him until I was left with a black soul without a vessel. I saw Jack slump to the floor as slowly his body became his own again. Then, still with my prisoner in my grasp, I walked his dripping oily form towards the massive portal.

"NO! Keira no! Take me with you! You can't do this alone, let me fight by your side!" Draven shouted and I paused. I felt sad at what I must do and I hated what I was to say next, but I had to get him to understand…

It wasn't his fight.

Not anymore.

"Not this time, My Chosen One," I told him before continuing on.

I then grabbed a weapon off the floor and walked straight…

Into Hell.

CHAPTER FOURTY-EIGHT

HOME

Walking into Hell felt strange this time. Not like the other times when I was just a mortal girl. No, this time, it felt like I was coming home. And when someone was home it was when they were at their strongest and here, I wasn't just a God…

Oh no, I was so much more.

I knew where I wanted to be and I moved between the levels of Hell as if I had been granted access by all the Lords. All the Princes were on my side. Because none of us wanted to see the end. None of us wanted to see the Titans freed and Cronus at the head of such an unbeatable army.

They all knew I was here to stop it. And stop it I would. Because I had already seen this fight. Cronus had too, but in his mind he had unknowingly given me the key. The reason I went back in time. The sacrifice of the Septimus, helping me to get the blood of Pertinax. Then I saved his life after gifting him with the venom of God in order that when the time came he could then do the same. That was what the prophecy spoke of.

Which was why I had seen this moment in my dreams and it was a sight I was now seeing play out like the Fates had deemed it. I was stood on the edge of the cliff face overlooking the vast space to Mount Tartarus. I dumped Cronus' dark form on the ground, as the second we stepped back into Hell he had taken another form, one stolen as a creature walked past us. He looked like a soldier clad in black fighting gear. I could have stopped it but it was of no matter to me which form he was in, as long as it had eyes and it could witness the destruction of his plans. Then that was all I cared about.

He wasn't the only one that changed once we stepped foot in this place, I summoned my own fighting gear. So, gone was the bloody torn wedding dress. No, for now I looked the part. Black leather fitted me like a glove and moulded to my mortal form like a second skin, pulled tight like a corset. Armoured shoulder pieces connected with straps across my chest which were spiked and deadly. A cloak attached to this with a hood I wore up over my loose hair. Thick leather straps covered my forearms that matched the thick belt at my waist, one that held my weapon at my side. Finally, high black boots with metal heels completed my fighting gear.

The second I let Cronus go he tried to fight but with a single thought I soon had soulweed roots shoot up and take hold of him once more. I drew my sword and held it at his throat. I could have killed him but no, as I said, I wanted him to see. His fight was already lost, now he just had to lay witness to the fact. The army at my back should have told him that. An army I needed to face the Tartarus army heading our way. They swarmed out of the mountain, all the inmates that had been imprisoned there were now free, on one condition, to fight for Cronus. He had told me this when I had first found myself faced with the sight.

But it didn't matter.

I had already started assembling my own legions the second I stepped foot back home. There were those that I had entrusted to Zagan, back when I killed Malphas. There were even those that belonged to the other Princes that wanted to join the cause. Ones rallied together thanks to my new father in law, the Prince of Lust.

"Are you sure you have the power to beat them daughter of mine?" Asmodeus asked me, stepping up to my side and surprising me with his presence.

"We shall soon find out," I said in reply.

"And we shall do so together." The voice I heard behind me had me snapping my head around and when I saw him I couldn't help the human side of me coming through. My vessel and I both loved him.

"Draven!" I shouted his name and he came to stand next to me, taking my hand in his.

"We fight this together. We fight as one…now and always," he told me, repeating my words back to him and I gripped his hand tighter. I nodded and we both faced the tens of thousands as they started to race towards us.

"Besides, I am not without my uses," Draven said tugging on my hand and smirking down at me. Then he looked behind him and I followed to see that thousands more had joined our army. My husband's Legions.

"It is no use! The Titans are coming! They are coming and then you will all DIE!" Cronus shouted and Draven growled down at him and said,

"Can I kill him yet?" I laughed and said,

"Not until he sees for himself the fall of his people," I replied and then added,

"But after that, then sure, why not." This made both him and his father chuckle.

"Didn't I tell you she was a keeper, son."

"That you did father."

"Are you ready?" Draven asked me and I looked up at him and replied,

"I was born ready." Then the ground started to rumble and I knew that Aurora had done it. She had released the Titans.

"See you on the other side, my love." Draven said yanking me to him and kissing me. I felt my vessel's heart soar and I relished the feeling.

"On the other side," I repeated and he winked at me before taking flight with his massive wings, ready to help me lead this army into battle.

So as the head of this war, I raised my sword and bellowed my own battle cry into Hellish eternal dark red skies.

"ATTACK!" I roared my command and watched as everyone ran down the cliff face, swarming past me with my husband leading the way in the air. Giant beasts, now on our side, charged forward. Generals on top of eight legged horses also led their men forward as I stayed on the cliff face because my place was here. Ready to do war from afar so I could see, so I could watch and face the biggest threat of all.

"MY BROTHERS, THEY COME AT LAST!" Cronus cried out just as the top of the mountain burst open spewing bellows of fire and lava out into the sky like an untouchable bomb had just erupted in the centre of a live volcano. But I wasn't scared. I didn't feel fear, not in the sight of these ancient beings that thought themselves invincible.

Because what they now faced was something new.

The Infinity war had begun and it started with me.

"Yes, and you may say goodbye!" I told him as the first one to erupt out of the mountain had grown to almost the size of it. They may have been imprisoned as men-sized Gods, captured by flowing lava but when they were freed they would only grow to the size of colossal monsters the size of our tallest buildings.

They would lay waste to everything in their path until nothing remained. But I wasn't planning on letting them get that far.

I wasn't letting them escape. Their mountain had once been their home…Mount Olympus. And Zeus had defeated them making it their prison. Now I was about to make it something else.

I was about to make it their crypt.

I bent to the ground and touched the dirt beneath me. Then I let my humanity feed what no one else had ever done. I merged it with the demon inside me…with the God in me. I was different because I chose to be. I could have let power consume me long ago but I felt too much love to do that. I could have let my visions of this world send me mad, but I had much too strong a will for that to ever happen. Draven had shown me what it was to love and to believe in something bigger than yourself. It was the love I had for all those that had aided in my cause. Aided my love for Draven, my search for him. They had followed me like moths to the flame, and I had guided them all to this one moment in time.

This point.

Because they believed in me. And for the love I shared for all of them, I only needed one single thing to rock Hell to its core. Because there was still another level to this place, one they never knew existed until a Mortal did the impossible.

It was called…

Salvation.

A single tear.

That was all it had taken in my vision. And that was all it took now. A single tear shed for damned Gods imprisoned for all of eternity. For it wasn't hatred that defeated them. It was love and humanity that they feared the most and it was what I was giving them. Their biggest fear. To know that they were wrong about us. That we weren't the abomination they thought we were. Because I didn't represent a demonic God, their world had plenty of them to fight.

I represented the one thing they didn't have any longer.

A soul.

The second my tear fell to the ground it soaked in deep and it caused a shock wave, rippling across the land. I looked up knowing what I would see. The mountain was falling and with it the Titan trying to crawl its way out. The ground opened up and it started to fall as it once did, only this time, there would be nothing left of it. It would remain dead and buried, with the Titans imprisoned no more.

Because I had set them free of their eternal chains.

They didn't belong to Cronus.

They were free…*to finally die*.

Salvation.

"NOOO! WHAT HAVE YOU DONE!" He roared and I watched with a smile as the rest of the army fell under unbeatable odds. The mountain continued to fall until it became completely consumed under a level of Hell that didn't even exist. Until now.

"I did what you refused to do. I gave them peace and a taste of humanity…oh and I finally buried that bitch Aurora in there with them!" I told him unable to help myself with this last bit snarled at him.

"That you did, my dear." This came from an incredibly deep voice behind me. I turned and I knew who it was. Every being that belonged here did. Everyone that called Hell home, knew its King.

"Lucifer." I whispered his name like a prayer hushed by all.

"The one and the very same." I turned to face him and bowed my head to show my respect, as what was embedded inside this new side of me. He arched a brow at me in obvious amusement and I had to say I was tempted to do the same.

If anyone had ever told me that Lucifer looked like a sexy pirate, I would never have believed them. But here he was, commander of all, dressed in a long black military style jacket, with black metal buttons framing each side along with stripes of hammered tarnished silver. His long legs were encased in some kind of beast's hide and strapped with strips of cord. Boots that reached his knees were steel capped at the toes into deadly points. A bare large chest on show underneath and skin that looked strangely tanned for a place with no sun.

But it was his face. With his high, sharp features. A long nose, defined cheekbones and long hair pulled back giving him that air of authority he really didn't need. His name was enough. But even so, he had it in just a single look. His pale aqua eyes were intense, as half of me wanted to look away and the other half was too afraid to. It was the first time I had felt fear since coming back to my vessel.

"It seems as though you have been busy," he said nodding to the battle that had long been won.

"And I certainly won't be missing sight of that mountain… *such an eyesore,*" he told me this last part whispered in my ear. I shuddered next to him.

"I had hoped to see you leave me something to occupy my time and I dare say that you have," he said walking to Cronus and placing a hand on top of his head.

"My Lord please, set me free and we could…" He never got to finish as Lucifer gripped his hair and with a simple and sickening twist he snapped his neck. Then he let his body drop to the floor. I gasped in shock. The soulweeds left him and slithered away as if they too feared Lucifer's wrath.

"You don't approve?" He ventured a guess and then tapped his chin once before agreeing,

"You're right, it was far too quick." Then he held out a hand, and dragged his fingers upwards as if the tips were connected to invisible strings attached to Cronus' slumped body. In seconds, he was gasping for air and clearly breathing again.

"Take him," Lucifer ordered sounding bored and out of nowhere creatures with bleeding scales, were crawling on all fours towards him dragging behind them massive chains. They attached them to his body and at first, I had wondered how they were going to manage to get him out of here considering they were no bigger than dogs. But then after the sound of a whip lashed through the air, his body was quickly dragged off into the unknown that Lucifer obviously had planned for him.

"So, you're the one my son gifted my blood to?" he said coming back to me and running a fingertip down under my chin. He was very tall, taller even than Sigurd or Ragnar. I had to tip my head right back just to look up at him and then all I saw was his chin.

"Mmm, good choice. But I must say there is a blood in there that doesn't belong to you and I think now that it has served its purpose, I would do well in taking it back," Lucifer said, before bending slightly and adding,

"After all, we wouldn't want that pure soul of yours getting lost in the dark abyss of this place, that or I would just end up having to build you a palace and make you stay." This was said I know as a choice, one that came with a promised consequence on each side. I could stay here and live life as a God or I could give up great power, power of a God, so that I could claim back my humanity and go back to a life I never thought I could have.

It didn't take me long to decide.

"I choose my humanity," I said firmly just as I heard someone landing behind me.

"Of course, you do." Lucifer said and then turned his attention to Draven.

"Ah the King on Earth gracing my land with his presence,

tell me Son of Asmodeus, do you think this little morsel you own should stay here with me or should I grant her wish for her to return?" I turned to Draven to see him paying Lucifer his respect as he was down on one knee before rising again.

"She is my Queen," he told him firmly, making Lucifer grin.

"Of course, she is, for I only jest. His father is a great friend of mine," Lucifer added speaking directly to me.

"Yes, that is because I am the only dirty bastard that will put up with you!" Asmodeus himself replied after swiftly joining us and getting down on one knee to Lucifer like Draven had. So far, I had been the only one not to have done so and I now knew what that amused look had been about.

"That's true but it might be because I usually just kill the ones that don't," Lucifer replied making Draven's father laugh. I looked back behind me to see that the battle was over and thousands of dead demons were evidence to that as the vast space was littered with them.

"You would miss me and you know it, besides who would bring you your tasty little sins if not for me." Lucifer grinned and said to Draven,

"He always has a good argument, your father."

"Yes, and unfortunately, I have a sister that takes after him," Draven replied dryly making them both laugh. Then he took a step to me making Lucifer tut and hold his hand out to stop him.

"Let me go to my wife." Draven nearly growled the words as you could see he was holding himself back.

"You can have her soon enough, for she has made her choice, and quite quickly I might add, for she wasn't even tempted for a second at the power she harnesses."

"Nor did I think she would be," he said firmly knowing me better than anyone.

"Ah to have such faith. Very well then, I see no reason to prolong things, we are busy Kings after all, are we not?"

Draven nodded in agreement. Then the next thing I knew Lucifer tipped up my chin and said,

"Don't worry beautiful, this will only hurt a bit." And then with only this as my warning, he reached inside my body, making me cry out in utter agony! He had to wrap an arm around me to keep me standing against it all.

"NO! No, let her go!" Draven shouted as I screamed and he was suddenly held back by his father.

"Don't be foolish, boy!" Asmodeus hissed.

"Let me go! I have to stop this! Lucifer please let her go!" Draven begged making him chuckle before telling him,

"That is precisely what I am doing." Then he pulled his hand free that was now coated in blood. I looked down to see that not a mark was on me and when I had expected to see a gaping wound, there was none.

I felt myself go limp in his hold and he hoisted me up into his arms. Then he walked me over to Draven, who until this moment was still restrained by his father. Then he handed me to him, before issuing him with a warning.

"The Infinity War starts with her, King of Kings and it ends…"

He paused and just as I had found that last of my strength, he finished by telling Draven what I hadn't had the courage to tell him, the truth…

"…With your child."

CHAPTER FOURTY-NINE

AFTERLIFE

EIGHT MONTHS LATER

"I swear if this belly gets any bigger I won't fit at this table!" I complained again for what felt the millionth time in the seven days I was overdue. Typical, I thought on a growl. I felt Draven rubbing my belly and like my complaining that too felt like it was for the millionth time, one I liked…*a lot*.

"Is the baby restless again, sweetheart?" he asked me softly whispering in my ear. We were sat in the VIP and the rest of the nightclub was closed. This was because of the monthly council meetings which were certainly a colourful event these days. At first, they had started out as every other month, but the closer to my due date the more and more we saw of the Royal Council. I think they were just worried and it was sweet. But I was also the size of a house, moody and cranky and my ankles resembled overblown balloon animals.

A lot had happened since that battle, also known as 'I can't believe I missed it' day according to Pip…who seriously mentioned it at every opportunity or just because she felt like it. Seriously, even eating cake reminded her of it. But we had won the battle. However, it hadn't been without its losses, something I was painfully reminded of when I finally regained consciousness in the Temple, once Draven had got me back there.

I had woken and the first name from my lips hadn't been Draven for once, but Ranka. I remembered her face, seeing it even now when she landed on her knees after taking Draven's blade through the chest. She had hung on, clinging to life until we returned. I ran over to her where she lay bleeding on the Temple floor and the second I touched her hand she released a deep sigh of relief.

"Now I can go in peace, knowing my part played helped aid the Fates," she told me and then I leaned down and whispered,

"If you want peace my friend, then leave this world showing him the truth, set yourself free," I told her and her wide eyes told me that she knew of which I spoke. So, she nodded and I moved aside allowing Draven to take my place.

"My Lord…I…" she started to say but instead quickly morphed into her true self. Into Ranka the man. He swallowed hard as if waiting for the worst, but I knew my husband, as he knew me. Draven placed a hand on his arm and said,

"I have always known, Ranka." This surprised us all but no one more than that of Ranka.

"And I respected and cared for you all the same…*my loyal friend,*" he told him and Ranka dragged in a shuddered breath before taking hold of his hand and with his dying breath told him,

"It…it has been my… honour to serve you… My…my Lord…*always."* And then he passed away with a small smile on his lips. It was a great loss and one that I cried over along with

Sophia. We may not have had the chance to get to know him in this time, but we did in the past. He will always be the one to save my life and kick start a journey that made winning this war possible.

After this Draven had simply taken my hand in his and walked us both through the rubble of the Temple. The others understood the need for our time together. After all, I had died and come back as a Demonic God, and basically killed all our enemies with little more than a thought…which wasn't exactly part and parcel of my personality. Of course, there was also the matter of Draven now knowing I was pregnant. So yes, everyone knew he needed this. Which was why I heard Sophia enter my mind with only one request.

"Go be together, we will deal with things here…go and take care of each other." And take care of each other we did. Unbelievably the door back to Afterlife was untouched and when I asked Draven how, he simply winked at me as way of an answer. It was only when I noticed something in the rubble that I pulled away from him and said,

"Just give me a second."

"Oh sure, it isn't like we just survived the end of the world or anything," he replied sarcastically. I blew him a quick kiss and then started digging the through the mess at what I thought I saw. Then my grin grew huge and I dragged it up and shouted back at Jared,

"Well, would you look at what I just found!" Then I waved his precious leather jacket at him making the whole room erupt into laughter despite what we had just been through.

But hell, why not…we were family after all.

He took it off me and said,

"I don't think you can class that as survived…*but I sure am glad you did, Doll."* Then he granted me a kiss on the cheek before taking the ruined jacket with him. It was a symbol of us all I think, as we were all certainly looking a little worse for wear. But we had won, the Earth was safe and we had survived… that had been the main thing.

Draven hadn't spoken to me during the walk back to our room, but the second I was through our door he spun me around and just simply held me. My emotions hit their limit and I sobbed in his arms, as I could barely believe it was finally over. Everything the Fates had said had come true just in twisted ways we never believed they would. But all this time I had spent thinking my days were numbered and that immense weight had finally been lifted from my shoulders and it was…

Done.

Well almost.

"Why didn't you tell me?" He had whispered into my hair before pulling back to look at me.

"Because I was afraid. I knew that you believed as I did that me being pregnant was what would have killed me. But now I knew it has to do with the future." And it did. Lucifer's words had confirmed that. Our child would be the end of the Infinity war, one that the next generation would face but we would be ready.

As they would be.

That night Draven made love to me and held me all through the night. It was the first night I didn't dream. It wasn't what I would have planned for our wedding night, but to me, with the war won, it was perfect.

Draven explained that after giving me the choice, Lucifer had taken Pertinax's Blood from me so that I could regain my humanity. Well, most of it anyway as I was still a Vampire, Demon, Venom of God hybrid with a little bit of Angel thrown in there for good measure, thanks to Draven's blood. But Draven knew the truth and he didn't care, just so that we could be immortal together…and now, with a baby on the way. He had only wished that he'd had the courage to grant me a child himself instead of his younger self doing it without his knowledge. I had placed my hand on his cheek and told him that I was sorry and I wished for it too.

To give Draven his credit that, despite this, he warmed to this idea very quickly. So quickly in fact that the second we met back up with our family the next day, he announced it to the world. My mother had burst into tears in seconds, along with Libby but this wasn't the strangest thing to occur. Ari had heard this news and burst into tears for a very different reason.

She had dragged me into the toilets in the hotel we were still all technically staying at in Worcester. Then she had broken down admitting that the night Draven and I had 'conceived' in the past, Ari hadn't been in the next room. She had tried but hadn't realised until it was too late when Vincent had sneaked into her room and stole her away.

She told me that she tried to tell me this before, but she thought she would have had another opportunity to 'help'. And then she wanted to wait until after the wedding, not wanting it to ruin the day to tell me. I couldn't help it, I was in shock. I had held my belly and looked down at myself hating that such an action would only upset her further. But I couldn't help it. I had truly believed.

Sophia had seen the whole scene play out and with Pip in tow, she came into the bathroom to find Ari and I in tears, hugging each other. We told them what had happened and instead of believing it she said,

"Show me." I frowned not understanding at first.

"Drop your shields. Drop everything," she said again and in that moment, I understood. So, I took a deep breath and for the first time since this all began, I started tearing down every wall I had ever built. I was destroying them, no longer caring about preserving my mind, protecting it or anything. I just needed to know right at that second if Ari was right. But in the end, it wasn't Sophia who saw it.

It was Pip.

"Oh my god! I see it! I feel it!" she shouted and my eyes shot up to hers and said,

"Really?!" The hope in both my eyes and voice was testament to how much I wanted it to be true.

"Oh Gods, I can see it too! Oh Keira, you're going to have a baby!" Sophia said.

"I am? I really am?"

"YES!" Both Pip and Sophia shouted together. Then I turned to Ari and grabbed her to me as we cried together.

"You did it! I don't know how but you did it!" I told her and the next thing I knew Draven was barging into the ladies' toilets demanding to know what was wrong. All the girls left to let me explain as the second Draven had felt my mind becoming open, he knew something was wrong.

"I…I thought for a moment that I wasn't…" I didn't need to say the rest as Draven looked down at my belly and then suddenly dropped to his knees. Then he placed a forehead there at my stomach and whispered in awe,

"Our child, I can sense our child." I held his head to my belly and let my tears flow in sheer happiness.

After this, I explained why I had been so worried, telling him of Ari's gift. At first, he had been surprised but understood my concerns, which begged the question of how and when? In the end, the answer hadn't taken us that long as Draven pulled back on my hand. We had been on our way back to meet everyone who was in the dining room waiting for us.

"That night…I felt something, could it be?" he said to himself and when I asked him what he meant, he turned to me with the biggest grin and said the last place I would have ever imagined conceiving a child with Draven,

"In Jared's office…the night before our wedding."

"Oh my god, on his desk!?" Draven's grin got even bigger and said,

"The desk we broke."

After this it was quickly confirmed that it was indeed the night, when in Jared's office, we had heard someone about to walk in to the room, when Draven roared out at them in annoyance. Well, it turned out that someone had been none other than Ari, who had been trying to get away from Vincent. He had been angry and jealous of the part she had played on the stage and they had argued before he had found her and left with her struggling over his shoulder.

But in her emotional state when she had touched that door it had been enough to project her power into that room and stay with us. So, Draven had got his wish after all. He had been the one to create a child with me in this time, as we were always meant to do.

Which brought us back to now and sat back in Afterlife which always felt like home. Of course, since being back here he had also needed to buy a bigger table as his council had grown by considerable numbers. That wasn't the only thing he'd had to buy since I became pregnant, as Draven being Draven had taken possessive behaviour to the next level.

Which meant I couldn't even sit on my own freaking chair without him getting into a caveman style grump. I thought I'd won the fight when my belly started growing so big he couldn't fit me on his lap anymore. But I found out one night that Draven could do smug very well as when I had walked into the VIP that night, I found a new massive chair waiting for me. One more than big enough to fit him with me in between his legs comfortably.

Which was the chair I found myself squirming on now as the baby felt as if it was currently training for a kick boxing championship. Although knowing Draven, I wouldn't be surprised if it didn't pop out and pick up a rattle holding it like a weapon. We didn't know what the sex of the baby was as I wanted it to be a surprise. Of course, to achieve this surprise I also had to build up my shields again, and vowed to do so the very night I had brought them down. As having sex with Draven when he knew your every thought was a little unnerving, and more than a little embarrassing. Especially when he kept saying, 'You want to do what to me now?' and 'You want me to do that to you here?' Oh yes, he'd had loads of fun teasing me and whispering naughty obscenities in my ear.

"I swear if this baby doesn't come out soon I am ordering the spiciest food, drinking raspberry leaf tea, after going for a jog and a quick round of acupuncture and then if all else fails, tying you to the bed and riding you like a cowgirl!" I said not even caring if everyone could hear us. Draven nearly choked on his drink along with a few other council members around the table.

"Jesus woman, why the hell would you do all that shit…last one not counting?" Sigurd asked after banging his beer bottle on the table.

"It's in *the book*, tips on how to bring on labour," Draven told the rest of the table whispering the mention of 'the book' like it was a curse word…that damn book! I swear it had become the next bible in our household. I had shamefully thrown it at him once when he had made the mistake of nagging me to do my pelvic exercises. I hated to admit it but I was an angry pregnant woman…who knew?

Well, Draven certainly did after enduring eight months of 'bitch' Keira quickly followed by tears of sorrow and 'guilt' Keira.

"The book?" Jared asked on a chuckle.

"Oh no, here we go again," Sophia said, obviously having

been party to this conversation quite a few times now, oh and Pip who thought seeing me angry and the size of a cow was the most hilarious thing in the world, her words not mine.

"I will have you all know that I …Oh my god," I said stopping mid flow and then I tensed. Draven tensed also and then the worst and best thing happened.

My water broke.

It also did this all over Draven.

Everyone around the room froze but mainly at our table, one that was full of crazy over protective Alpha Kings, that also didn't have a clue on how to act around a hormonal, over emotional pregnant lady.

"AAH!" I shouted as pain shot through me making me slap the table.

"Keira!" Draven yelled in concern.

"Shit!" Sigurd shouted

"Has her water just broke?" Sophia asked.

"That is a definite yes," Draven replied as he picked me up and set me down. Sophia looked up and down him now it looked like he had pissed his pants and said,

"Yep, she sure did."

"Oh well, would you look at that," Pip said and I bent over the table and shouted,

"Can we try and focus on the lady trying to push a baby out of her please!" I growled before banging the table again as another contraction hit.

"Wait, another one?" Draven asked, obviously knowing everything humanly possible about giving birth as he had read everything there was to know…and I mean everything!

"We need to move her!" Sophia shouted and Draven went to pick me up again but I screamed out and said,

"NO! I can't…oh God…Draven! The baby is coming!"

"What, right now?!" he asked again.

"Oh yeah, like right now!" I shouted back and then the next thing I know, Pip is screaming orders at people.

"Right, Wolf boy, get everyone out of here!"

"Seriously dude, can you ask your wife to stop calling me that!" Jared complained before getting to the job at hand and ushering the rest of Draven's VIP guests out of the doors.

"Just wait for it…" Sigurd said before Pip ordered,

"Shadow Man…"

"Yep, there it is!" he muttered before she shouted,

"…towels, baby blankets, a pillow everything now, it's in their room, go now chop, chop!" she said clapping.

"And while you're at it, add my complaint to Wolf mans' whilst you're adding names to the list." Adam laughed and said,

"You're both dreaming."

"Cupcake sugar pants, you're on gas and air! Go, it's in Dom's office!" Pip said making Adam wince as the other two sniggered before getting back to the job at hand.

"AAHHHH!" Hurry, oh, oh, oh…I want to push…can I push…?!" Sophia helped Draven get me up on to the table and said on a chuckle,

"Not yet, as we won't get far with your jeans still on."

"Zagan, ring Ari and my Brother, they will want to know. Ragnar, stand guard. Takeshi call them." Takeshi nodded as Draven had clearly taken over and I was about to ask who exactly he had wanted him to call, but another contraction hit and I was yelling again.

It was all hands on deck and all those birthing plans Draven had made me sit through, hearing all our options was now out the window. Birthing baths, the best hospitals, the best doctors, music, candles, big round balls to bounce on, well it all meant nothing now. It was just a simple, I am having a baby, now help me get it out and as soon as possible because…

"OWWW! Ow, ow, ow!" I shouted as another wave hit.

"Okay sweetheart, it will be alright…"

"GAS! Get me some GAS NOW!" I screamed just as Adam came running in with the big gas bottle under his arm.

"Here, let me," Sophia said when he started looking confusingly at the tubes and mouthpiece. The second the rest of the group arrived, Draven gave them a look and said a stern,

"Up that end, now!"

"I think that means you sweetie, as you also have a penis," Pip had said to her husband and the men all got the hint pretty quickly. Once Draven was assured all male eyes were very much away from my private girly parts, he started to take my knickers off. Sigurd slipped a pillow under my head and threw Pip the towels, trying not to look. She started placing them under me and Draven gently lifted me.

"Okay, okay, here comes another one! Oh, oh, oh, AAAAHHHH!"

"Gas!" Draven snapped and Sophia said,

"Got it! Here, try this." She passed it to Draven who tested it out first and then handed it to me.

"Here sweetheart, deep breaths." I sucked on it as hard as I could but then when I felt another hit, I started screaming.

"Stupid thing doesn't work!" I said throwing it to one side with a snarl and it went crashing into the wall. My Vamp strength certainly kicked in. But then I felt it coming, that feeling like you had to push.

"Draven! The baby, it's coming! I…I…need to… push!"

"Alright sweetheart, take my hand and push through your next contraction."

"AAAAHHH!" I screamed and heard everyone around me trying to encourage me to push. Hell, it felt like I had my own cheerleading squad with Pip alone, who looked close to spelling my name out with her arms.

"Come on baby, you're doing so good," Draven praised and I shook my head as I felt tears start to fall.

"I can't Draven, Oh, God it hurts!" I said feeling exhausted already.

"You can and will, you're doing so good honey, just get ready to push again," Sophia told me holding my other hand. But that's when Pip started to go strange.

"Do you feel it, King?" she said touching his shoulder and he looked her in the eyes and said,

"Yes…but not now, Pip," he told her and I was just about to ask when the next contraction hit.

"Right come on, one big push now, you can do it!" Draven said gripping my hand tighter as if bracing for my pain.

"No, oh God, okay, okay so it's coming! Draven! AAAAHHHHGGGRRR!" I screamed and gritted my teeth and pushed.

"Oh, Dom, I can see the head, Dom!" Sophia said getting emotional and I saw Draven look up at me and he said,

"Sweetheart, oh my love, we are nearly there, okay…I love you so much," he said kissing me and then I gripped his hand again and he knew…this was the last time.

"Draven!" I shouted his name and he soothed my fears.

"Okay, so one little push now, alright not too much sweetheart and the baby will be here, okay…here it comes, now push!" Draven told me and he let go of my hand so that he could deliver our child. And I did as he told me to, one little push and…

"AAHHH!" our child was born.

Now crying into its father's arms.

"Oh Dom!" Sophia cried.

"By the Gods, she is beautiful!" I heard Draven whisper and my head snapped up and said,

"A girl?! We have a girl?!" I asked on a shout.

"We have a baby girl!" he told me with tears in his eyes and he held up the most perfect little bundle in his arms. I burst into tears as he placed her into my arms and I held her to me as if I never wanted to let her go and would protect her with my life. Sophia handed Draven a blanket and I looked to her to see that she had tears of joy streaming down her face.

Draven wrapped a blanket around our baby and I looked up and saw Pip too was crying, nearly sobbing but she wasn't smiling like everyone else…*she knew something.*

"What is it?" I asked looking panicky and then checking the baby to see that she looked fine. Colour was rising up on her skin, giving her a healthy pink colour. Draven stepped closer to me and kissed my forehead and said,

"Ssshh, the baby is fine. I am so proud of you sweetheart, so, so proud…by the Gods, I love you," he told me tenderly, stroking back my hair and kissing me again, before leaning down to bestow his first kiss on our baby girl's head. But then something started to happen. Sophia was cleaning me up and someone handed Draven something to cut the cord with. Once that was done I started to feel strange.

"Draven, I…something's wrong, my stomach, I feel weird." And I did. Draven reacted straight away.

"Sophia, take the baby," he said, taking her from my hands gently,

"It's alright sweetheart, we are just going to get her cleaned up." I let her go and then quickly after was clutching my stomach in pain.

"AAAHH! What's happening?! Draven, it hurts!" I shouted and Draven was at my side in seconds, holding my hand.

"I know Keira, and we will…I…" Draven didn't know how to finish that sentence as he looked to Pip who was still crying.

"They…they have no…host," she told him and I frowned.

"What is she saying…what does she mean…Draven?!" I shouted his name as I needed him to tell me what was going on.

"Sweetheart I…"

"It's alright son, allow me." A heavenly voice spoke and it was one I recognised…Draven's mother. I frowned, wondering how she could have known unless she was here for another reason.

"Mother I…" Draven was about to speak but she put up a hand to stop him.

"You knew this could happen, as is our way."

"What is she talking about, Draven?" I asked getting so worried now, I was going high pitched.

"My dear, you may have given birth to a beautiful baby girl, but you have also given life to two other souls," she told me softly.

"What?! Ahhha OWW!" I shouted as the pain hit once more.

"Keira!" Draven was holding me close, cradling my head in his chest as I experienced the pain. Once it eased, I looked up at him and asked,

"You knew this?"

"I couldn't be sure, I knew it could be a possibility but… sweetheart I am sorry."

"What? Tell me, what is going on?!" He turned to look at me and held my hand and said,

"Three souls have been created, one is a mortal child, but the other two…well they are souls that need to be protected until the time comes for them to be united with a host," he told me and I frowned, looking down as I tried to process all of this.

"And your mother?"

"She has come for the Angel," he told me and I swallowed hard.

"So, sometime in the future we will have another child, one that will need a Vessel?" Draven nodded and I cried.

"But now, what if…" I couldn't even say it and in the end, I didn't need to as Draven shook his head and told me gently,

"It doesn't work like that, sweetheart."

"And the other soul, who will…"

"I will." A strong voice came from the shadows and I knew it was Draven's father. That was what Draven had meant when he asked Takeshi to call them.

"A demon?" Draven nodded in answer to my question and I sniffed back a sob and said smiling,

"Figures."

"My Lord, its' time," Pip said placing a hand on his arm and giving me sad eyes.

"What the Imp says is true, for we do not have long," his mother agreed.

"Why, what happens now?" I asked and Draven placed a hand on my belly and said,

"It is time to say goodbye and hand their safety over to their grandparents…we will be with them again…*I promise you this my love."* I closed my eyes, let the tears fall and nodded, placing my hand over his at my belly. I knew there was nothing else to be done. Draven kissed me and then nodded to both of his parents to come forward. They stepped up to me and Draven's father couldn't take his eyes off his mother.

"Sarah." He said her name like a purr rolling off the tongue. Like a promise of all he wanted to do to her and some of that probably included worshiping at her feet.

"Asmodeus," she said back and for someone so confident, she suddenly looked anxious as she brushed her beautiful hair behind her ear. She was dressed in a stunning blue gown and she nervously ran her palms down the sides as if she needed to find something to do with her hands. I looked to Draven's father who was watching her actions like a hawk. He looked as though he wanted to devour her whole and then do it all over again.

"AAAhhh!" I shouted in pain again and Draven growled at his parents.

"Can we please get on with this as my wife's pain is not a sight I relish in seeing," he snapped.

"Yes of course. My dear, this may feel strange but please, try to just…let go," she said pausing as if this was difficult for her to say.

"Step back son, we will take care of her, your mother and I." Sarah looked up at him and shot him a look as if it was the first time she had ever heard such a thing from his lips. Draven nodded and said,

"It will be alright." Then he shifted so his parents could take his place. They both placed a hand at my shoulder and the second they made contact I started to feel strange. Like something was being drained from me and the pain I felt started to ease. I didn't see anything to tell me what they had said was true but *I felt it.* And I knew the second that those sweet souls left the comfort and security of my body.

Tears fell and rolled down my cheeks in sadness for them and I wished I had created small tiny bundles for both of them, but then that was obviously not their fate…I just hoped that one day, that fate brought them back to me…

Brought them back home.
To their own Afterlife.

EPILOGUE

FOUR MONTHS LATER

"I swear, just like her mother," Draven grumbled playfully as he joined me on the balcony. He placed a high-tech baby monitor down on the small table and collapsed down in the chair next to me. I had moaned at him about six months ago, when reaching my angry pregnancy peak, that what was the point of having a balcony just off our room if there was no place to sit. This was mainly because I hit a stage very quickly when being pregnant, that I had hated standing of any kind, so moaned whenever I had to.

After this it had taken Draven all of about five seconds of tapping away on his phone to declare, 'Done' and the next day a beautiful outdoor garden lounge set had turned up that was rated highly for one main thing, *comfort.*

Draven knew how to keep his wife happy.

"Did she not want to take a nap again?" I asked also thinking how lucky I was that my supernatural husband didn't need much sleep as he certainly wasn't getting any. But our beautiful little girl was at her happiest when she was up and awake, simply sat in someone's lap watching the world in action around her as if she was taking it all in. She was full of smiles and made everyone around her fall in love with her with a single look and a grab of your hand. I had seen the biggest, baddest, and broodiest supernatural men nearly crumble and become soppy, cooing puppy dogs in her hands.

We had named her Amelia, as I let Draven choose. He told me it was Latin, meaning 'striving' and also 'defender'. I then chose her middle name Faith, as after all, that is what she had represented by coming into our world.

Our little…

Amelia Faith Draven.

It had taken me a while to get my head around what had happened after the birth. I would often cry, finding myself feeling the loss of two souls it wasn't possible to hold in my arms, right alongside my daughter. Draven had understood how I had felt and he too felt it tugging at his soul. But he also knew his world better than I did and he had 'Faith' that one day soon, we would find ourselves reunited as a family. The moment he said this was when I made my choice to give our daughter a middle name.

Shortly after giving birth one by one everyone came to pay their respects and pledge their loyalty and protection to their new Princess. Well, all I could say was I felt sorry for her already for she could get the idea of ever dating anyone right out of her head. Not unless he was someone powerful enough to beat back a small army of badass supernatural kings. I had laughed until tears formed when mentioning the prospect of dating to Draven as his face had said it all…

Murder.

Jesus, but I felt sorry for the day that a kid came knocking to take her to the prom! Especially if Ragnar was the one to open the door and lead the poor soul in to meet her father.

Yep, she was in for a rocky ride with that one.

But she was also the luckiest little girl in the world, for she had the best family you could ever have wished for. Included in this was Aunties, Sophia, Libby, Ari and Pip, as Pip had already had T shirts made, with the words, 'Team Kick Ass Aunty Squid' written on the back. Gifts she had handed out swiftly after the birth.

Everyone there had taken turns holding the baby, but the one who touched me the most was Draven. To see our child in his large hands with the sheer level of love in his eyes as he looked down at her, it was as if she was the most precious gift in the whole world. To me, it was a perfect moment and one I got to relive over and over again, every time I saw him with our daughter.

He was a natural with her. He wasn't scared like I was the first time we bathed her, as she was so tiny. Or when dressing her the first few times, doing it so gently, I was barely getting anywhere, as I was too frightened of hurting her. Draven had merely chuckled, kissed my forehead and taken over, doing so with such ease, you would have thought he'd been doing it every day of his life before that point.

I would hear him at night after feeding her, she would be perched across his naked torso, her little head at his shoulder as he patted her back trying to get a burp out of her. He would be cooing her and whispering in different languages, telling her in Latin how much he loved her. Then this tiny bundle in his arms would let out the biggest of burps in response, which had him chuckling and praising her like she had just won the national spelling bee.

It was the sweetest thing and the first few nights, it made me cry it was so sweet.

"So, just like her mother, eh?" I said giving him a sideways look. Then he placed a hand behind my neck, pulled me to him and said over my lips,

"Yes, both just as stubborn, but both adored all the same." Then he kissed me and it was divine. Then he took my hand in his and started playing with my wedding band as he usually did out of habit. If my hands weren't free his attention then shifted on to my hair, wrapping strands around his thick fingers absentmindedly, as if it was second nature to him.

But I think touching my ring was a comfort to him to know and see that it was there. As if it reminded him that it was all still real and I truly did belong to him. That night, after our wedding and the turbulent events that followed it, we had been in our bed after Draven had just made love to me. It had been slow and sensual and above all intense. Then, lying with one another, he took off my ring and then his ring and showed me the symbol they created when put together. On his ring, he had the part that looked like an 'A' symbol and I had what looked like an 'O' with feet. They interlocked with each other when turned a certain way.

It was my birthmark.

I told him about it, as if it was some secret I blurted out and had been meaning to tell him about for years but strangely never had. He gave me a warm smile and said,

"I know about your birthmark, sweetheart."

"You do?!"

"But of course, I have the same one," he told me and my mouth had dropped.

"What?! All this time and you never told me!" I argued making him laugh again, only harder this time.

"You never told me about yours." Well okay, so this had been true but still, he knew and I didn't.

"Where is it?"

"The same place as yours, hidden away under my hair."

Again, this surprised me and he laughed when I turned his head and tried to look for it.

"But what does it mean? I have seen it around your home, on the back of your chair, as part of your family crest and…" his answer cut me off and it wasn't one I would have ever expected.

"Simply put, it means us."

"Us?" I asked getting high pitched.

"You and I, our union." I frowned in thought and then asked,

"What, you mean like a man and woman coming together, that type of us?"

"No, Keira, what I mean is…" He paused to get closer to my face so that he could whisper,

"Just you and me…together."

"Okay, you are going to have to explain this to me," I complained making him pull me in close and kiss my temple. But after this he did as I asked. He told me that the symbols represent the Alpha, which was him and meant the First. And the Omega, which was me and meant the Last. Then he slipped me beneath him and told me the sweetest thing,

"It means I was the beginning but you were my end…my everything, my only…it is like Vincent said in his speech…*you complete me."* He finished his sentence as he thrust inside me and once seated in the warmth of my body I knew he was only half right. So, I reached up and touched his cheek and whispered back…

"We complete each other."

The ancient symbols that represented our beginning and our end were entwined for a reason and even now, a year to the day, I knew it had been the perfect time to find out and I was glad I hadn't done so any time sooner.

"So, can I give you your anniversary present yet?" I asked

him as it was a year ago today that we had not only become husband and wife for the second time, but also saved the world from the end of days and given it a future for our child. One we knew would grow up to face her own prophecy.

"That depends, is it the baby book in ashes given to me in a little bottle to wear around my neck, like you threatened five months ago?" he joked and it was true, I had threatened that and right after Sigurd had witnessed it had said to my husband,

"Shit Dom, what have you been feeding her for breakfast, rusty nails and broken glass?" Needless to say, I had swiftly taken the book out of Draven's hands and thrown it at the Big Dumb Viking at one of the council meetings. Okay, so he wasn't dumb, but still I had been an angry uncomfortable pregnant lady at the time, so in Draven's eyes there wasn't much I couldn't get away with. Although I had given him hell when he replied,

"No, but I find sex helps with her mood swings, and I benefit greatly from this also." I growled and then banned him from sex for a week, which ended up lasting not even an hour, thanks to him taking it as a challenge. Damn Hot Demon/ Angel King!

The council meeting ended early that day.

"No but if you carry on, it will be your gift for Christmas." I told him making him laugh and say,

"What? No woolly hat this year?"

"Ha, ha." Then I got up and as quietly as I could, so as not to wake the baby, I reached under the bed, no longer in fear of demon sized dust bunnies biting my hand off or Pythia hiding under the bed. Thankfully, all had been forgiven and she was currently living out her life in peace...and in Florida of all places.

I grabbed the gift bag, I had hidden there.

Then I reached for the post, hauled myself up and missed

the step, which meant I went down on one knee, which also meant I had done the unthinkable…I had made a noise.

I turned quickly and saw our baby girl with her eyes wide open staring at me smiling. I think if she could have talked right there and then she would have said one word…

Busted.

"What are you doing awake?" Okay so her answer would have been,

'Because I have a clumsy mummy who doesn't know how to be graceful to save her life and woke me up'.

"Come on then, let's go surprise daddy," I said picking her up and hugging her to me. I snagged her blanket, one her Uncle Ragnar had sweetly bought for her. The thought of him going into a baby shop and buying a pink blanket covered in hearts and flowers had me in near hysterics, after thanking him of course. I told Draven once we were alone, how I would have paid a very large sum of money to have seen the woman's face behind the counter. He agreed with a smirk.

I wrapped the blanket around her and walked outside saying,

"Guess who is awake" I heard Draven groan but the smile on his face said it all. He was happy as this way he would get a cuddle but first, he wanted to watch me for a while holding our daughter. He had admitted to me not long after she was born that watching me nursing her gave him immeasurable amounts of pleasure, of the likes I would never know. Needless to say, that whenever I had hold of her, his eyes would light up and he would watch us with a small, secret smile playing at his lips.

"See, stubborn, just like her mother."

"Well we have to be, don't we kid, when we are surrounded by domineering, alpha males that like to throw their weight around and act like cavemen." I said to Amelia…or my little Emmie as I liked to call her.

"Speaking of which, is my gift a new club, seeing as I need a new one for punishing my naughty little, disobedient wife… that or I could just use the palm of my hand on your behind like last time," he said smirking and I covered my hand over Emmie's little ears and hissed back teasingly,

"Not in front of the baby." He threw his head back and laughed, making Emmie chuckle at the sight.

"Here you go my handsome brute of a husband, happy one-year anniversary." I said shifting the baby to my hip so that I could kiss his cheek and pass him the bag. He pulled out a black box and as was tradition between us, it was tied with a purple ribbon. He smirked and pulled on the end, then after pocketing the ribbon as I knew he would, because he always did, (making me wonder if he had a stash of them hiding in some secret room somewhere) he opened the lid.

"It was my Great, great grandfather's old pocket watch… my dad got it in the will after my grandad died but he gave it to me on my seventeenth birthday as he knew I'd always loved it. I used to sit on my dad's knee as a kid and play with it. See that little dent there, that was when I dropped it when I was five. I cried so hard that day but then my dad told me a story of when he did the same thing when he was my age." Draven reached out and ran a thumb on the apple of my cheek as he must have thought this story sweet. He loved listening to stories of me growing up.

"He said that memories were important to keep with us as they helped shape us into who we were and that they fed the soul. On my birthday, he added a little card saying, 'Time is what we make of it, so make it good and feed your soul with nothing but happiness'." Draven looked down at me and then back at the watch now in his hands as he had dropped the box in surprise. Then I watched as he ran a finger over the dent and smiled to himself.

"Open it," I told him and inside he found a small round picture of me and Emmie, one that I had taken only yesterday.

"Lift up the picture," I added and he sucked in a sharp breath when he did and he read the words I'd had engraved there.

The words…

'You feed my soul, Dominic'.

And his gift to me that day…
He finally told me how old he was.

The End.

ABOUT THE AUTHOR

Stephanie Hudson has dreamed of being a writer ever since her obsession with reading books at an early age. What first became a quest to overcome the boundaries set against her in the form of dyslexia has turned into a life's dream. She first started writing in the form of poetry and soon found a taste for horror and romance. Afterlife is her first book in the series of twelve, with the story of Keira and Draven becoming ever more complicated in a world that sets them miles apart.

When not writing, Stephanie enjoys spending time with her loving family and friends, chatting for hours with her biggest fan, her sister Cathy who is utterly obsessed with one gorgeous Dominic Draven. And of course, spending as much time with her supportive partner and personal muse, Blake who is there for her no matter what.

Author's words.

My love and devotion is to all my wonderful fans that keep me going into the wee hours of the night but foremost to my wonderful daughter Ava...who yes, is named after a cool, kick-ass, Demonic bird and my sons, Jack, who is a little hero and Baby Halen, who yes, keeps me up at night but it's okay because he is named after a Guitar legend!

Keep updated with all new release news & more on my website

www.afterlifesaga.com
Never miss out, sign up to the
mailing list at the website.

Also, please feel free to join myself and other Dravenites on my Facebook group
Afterlife Saga Official Fan
Interact with me and other fans. Can't wait to see you there!

facebook.com/AfterlifeSaga
twitter.com/afterlifesaga
instagram.com/theafterlifesaga

ACKNOWLEDGEMENTS

There are so many wonderful people in my life that I owe thanks to for supporting me in this journey, one I hope will never truly end. I feel like I could have carried writing Keira and Draven's story forever but I know that at some point, everything good must come to an end. And I owed it to them to grant them their Happy Ever After.

But although, their story might have finished it will never truly be over as you will be granted glimpses into their happy world when reading the Afterlife Spin Off series. Also, the Afterlife Chronicles, will give you even greater insight to how their world looks years down the line.

I would like to say a massive thank you to my parents. Especially my fantastic mother who not only has supported me throughout this whole saga but had also watered the seed that she planted all that time ago about publishing Afterlife on Amazon. She edits my words to help make my world as perfect for you as it can be and for that I am forever grateful.

To my own Dominic Draven, Blake my wonderful husband who made me not only believe that dreams come true but also that eternal love isn't just reserved for love stories written in novels.

And I can't leave out my fantastic PA, Claire Boyle, who I am privileged to also call a dear friend. She has been on this journey with me first as a fan and then as a friend and in doing so, has been with me through thick and thin. She is one of the most loyal, hardworking and loving person I have had the honour to know and can't thank her enough for putting up with me. I love you Claire.

Caroline, my dear friend, who is not only the best business partner on the planet, but also one of the greatest people I know and love.

The Afterlife Chronicles is our baby.

There are so many friends I have made along the way since writing this book and like other's books before this one, I have named a few. But this time I will not mention names as I dedicated this book to you all, even those I do not know.

But a special mention must be said for all those of you that spread the Afterlife word to others as I cannot thank you enough. Every kind word you ever said about me or the saga, I thank you. For every letter typed and time taken to write a review, again I thank you. But most of all I thank you for being with me and a part of my colourful world, one made far better with you all in it…

You make it shine.

ALSO BY STEPHANIE HUDSON

Afterlife Saga

A Brooding King, A Girl running from her past. What happens when the two collide?

Book 1 - Afterlife

Book 2 - The Two Kings

Book 3 - The Triple Goddess

Book 4 - The Quarter Moon

Book 5 - The Pentagram Child /Part 1

Book 6 - The Pentagram Child /Part 2

Book 7 - The Cult of the Hexad

Book 8 - Sacrifice of the Septimus /Part 1

Book 9 - Sacrifice of the Septimus /Part 2

Book 10 -Blood of the Infinity War

Book 11 -Happy Ever Afterlife /Part 1

Book 12 -Happy Ever Afterlife / Part 2

Transfusion Saga

What happens when an ordinary human girl comes face to face with the cruel Vampire King who dismissed her seven years ago?

Transfusion - Book 1

Venom of God - Book 2

Blood of Kings - Book 3

Rise of Ashes - Book 4

Map of Sorrows - Book 5

Tree of Souls - Book 6

Kingdoms of Hell – Book 7

Eyes of Crimson - Book 8

Roots of Rage - Book 9

Afterlife Chronicles: (Young Adult Series)

The Glass Dagger – Book 1

The Hells Ring – Book 2

Stephanie Hudson and Blake Hudson

The Devil in Me

OTHER WORKS FROM HUDSON INDIE INK

Paranormal Romance/Urban Fantasy

Sloane Murphy

Xen Randell

C. L. Monaghan

Sci-fi/Fantasy

Brandon Ellis

Devin Hanson

Crime/Action

Blake Hudson

Mike Gomes

Contemporary Romance

Gemma Weir

Elodie Colt

Ann B. Harrison

Lightning Source UK Ltd.
Milton Keynes UK
UKHW041338250221
379328UK00002B/745